PAUL HULJICH was born in Auckland, New Zealand. A university dropout, he co-founded Best Corporation, a pioneering organic foods company of which he was Chairman and Joint-CEO.

In 1998, Huljich was diagnosed by psychiatrists as suffering from Bipolar Disorder, also known as manic depression. That year, he experienced a full mental breakdown, lost his rights as a citizen and was made a ward of the state.

Informed that there was no cure, that he would eventually relapse, and that he would be dependent on medication for the rest of his life, Huljich traveled to the world-renowned Mayo Clinic in Minnesota for treatment and later admitted himself to the Menninger Clinic in Kansas to more fully understand and address his condition. Aided by research and his background in organic foods, Huljich developed a diet, exercise, and wellness plan that would help him end his dependence on medication to cure himself and find true peace of mind.

Since the year 2000, Huljich has not taken any psychotropic or psychiatric medication or any medication related to mental illness. Nor has he suffered any relapse of depression or manic depression, or received further treatment from any psychiatrist, therapist, or doctor regarding mental illness. He has never felt better.

Betrayal of Love and Freedom is inspired by his remarkable true story.

Paul is the father of three sons: Mark, Simon and Richard.

PUBLISHING

www.mwella.com   www.paulhuljich.com

BETRAYAL

of love and freedom

BETRAYAL

of love and freedom

PAUL HULJICH

mwella
PUBLISHING

This book is dedicated to...

ALL PEOPLE WHO suffer from, or know others who have suffered from, any of the following mind conditions:

Anxiety
Attempted or actual suicide
Attention-deficit hyperactivity disorder
Bipolar disorder/manic depression
Compulsive behavior, including addictions to alcohol,
recreational or prescription drugs, and addictions
to sex, gambling or any other behavior
Depression
Eating disorders, including anorexia and bulimia
Panic attacks
Phobias
Post natal depression
Post traumatic stress disorder
Schizophrenia
Any other mind condition

ACKNOWLEDGEMENT

I WOULD LIKE TO thank my son, Simon, for his invaluable contribution to the writing of this novel. From the time when I first shared my story and characters with him, he has joined me on a journey of turning my dream of this book into a reality. I know deep in my heart that this has been one of my life's most treasured experiences.

IT SO HAPPENS that we are both bringing our dreams to reality at the same time. Simon's debut album, ALL or NOTHING, has recently been released. More information can be found at the official Simon Spire website: www.SimonSpire.com

CONTENTS

PROLOGUE

T HERE WAS SOMETHING awkward about the stillness that pervaded the room, as if it were bracing for a predator's strike, the victim now sensing the awful futility of any resistance.

"No one is above the law. No one is above justice." He glances at his prey. "No one."

"Murder," the impact of the word matched by the sharpness of his movement as his gaze now falls on the jury. "Rape." Once again Joseph Hamilton, Assistant District Attorney from the New York District Attorney's Office, lets the word hang, allowing the full weight of these now familiar terms to sink in.

"Murder and Rape!" This time he almost spat the words, as if they were tainting his mouth with a foul taste that he could not rid himself of fast enough.

"What gives him the right to rape her, beat her senseless and then, with his own bare hands, strangle her to death? What gives him the right to end her life?" He pauses, struggling to grasp a side of humanity that was once beyond his comprehension. "We may never know what drives such a person.

"But what we do know," his voice cutting through the room with a renewed sense of conviction, "is that the defendant, Luke Powers", now turning toward the quiet figure seated across the room, "must pay for what he has done.

"There are no exceptions. No excuses. None whatsoever.

"Ladies and gentlemen of the jury, show him that we will not tolerate his acts of barbarism. Hold him accountable for the unthinkable crimes he has committed.

"Look once again at the face of a cold-blooded murderer."

Silence. Satisfied with his work, he delivers his final blow. "The evidence, every shred of evidence, points without any doubt, to the defendant, Luke Powers. Find him guilty."

WITH THE PROSECUTOR'S closing words, the jury forewoman's eyes turned to Mr. Powers. 'They're all the same,' she thought, her career, peaking now in middle-management, affording her this insight into power, its nature and its effects.

'How many times have I seen that same look of innocence on an executive's face? That same denial of any involvement in wrongdoing. And no sooner would they lie through their teeth, than they would casually authorize the misstatement of earnings, skirt environmental laws and strong-arm a state official, all in time to kiss their kids goodnight. And between their stock options and a toothless legal system, the most they'll ever get is an early retirement soaking up the sun with their golf buddies.'

No one could see the clenched hands hidden in her lap. 'But not this time. If there is any chance of this system being the democracy it claims to be, it's here, in the courtroom. No lobbyists; no money; no compromise. Twelve mere mortals, deciding the fate of one of the wealthiest individuals in the country. Your freedom depends on us now.'

The muted voices of the courtroom continued. 'I know his type. Whatever it takes to advance his own interests. I've seen it all before. Sure these people are capable of murder if it serves them – or if it serves their fragile egos, tortured by the smallest suggestion that they are not quite so different from the rest of us.

'Betrayal. Was that it? Did you feel betrayed by her? Is that why you did it, you sick bastard? How I've seen tempers fly when your kind is crossed. The only difference between what I've seen in my time, and murder, is one of degree; it's all the same really – a psychotic mind that can't cope with rejection.'

The expressionless figure at the defendant's table continued his long stare out the window. 'Those blue eyes searching for what you've lost. We all knew you, "Luke Powers: self-made man". They asked us if we were capable of impartiality, of judging innocence or guilt solely on the basis of the evidence presented. What bullshit. I doubt that either the prosecution or the defense believed such nonsense.

'Yet you seem different now, your aura not so palpable. Are you dying a slow death as your freedom drifts out of reach? It's just a concept now – freedom – isn't it? Some vague memory, gone forever.'

"Your honor, members of the jury, Luke Powers is innocent", began the defense, the attorney's eyes appealing to the forewoman for her understanding. The woman in the jury box calmly returned the gaze, a picture of attentiveness.

As RACHEL WALLACE began her confident steps along the front row of the jury, she couldn't help but notice the bleakness of her situation. Convincing a jury of Luke's innocence was no easy task. Even the sharp-minded forewoman was going to have a tough time finding reasonable doubt when the jury deliberated on their final decision. At least she'll approach it with an open mind, Wallace thought.

"Can you, in any way, justify to yourself why a man of integrity, a man of unquestionable character and soundness, would act in such an inexplicable way?" The grim irony of it pulled at her stomach: one of the few clients she actually believed to be innocent could become the first major blemish on her record.

"Furthermore, can you conceive of such an act being followed by an invitation to examine the hotel room in question?", she continued with absolute self-assurance. Sure, the 'Please Service Room' sign was a long shot, but what else could she try? At least there was one person in the room whom she need not convince of Luke's innocence. Throughout the trial, Emerald Steel had sat undeterred behind her fiancé. And yet, what could such a glamorous woman in the prime of her life – a success in her own right – see in Mr. Powers anymore? He had been unfaithful to her, that much was clear. Almost twenty years her senior, and rekindling a flame from his distant past. 'Now look where he finds himself.'

LUKE COULD HEAR Wallace continuing her closing statements, but the voice seemed distant and muted, as if in a tunnel. He was dimly aware of his hands resting on the table in front of him. His own large, long fingers, sat immobile... the very hands that Hamilton had only just finished convincing a jury were murder weapons. Some part of Luke had shut off, retreated to a place of peace and calm, where reality, or the perception of it, was no longer an issue. What was left of him seemed to stand outside of his body, an amused and bemused observer of what was happening to someone he had once known... or had he ever? He was conscious that Hamilton had told the jury about the DNA semen match, about the bruising and abrasions within the vaginal tract, about the crushing of the trachea, the snapping of the windpipe. He knew, without having to look, that some of the jury had been shifting uncomfortably in their seats; others rubbed their foreheads with their fingertips, massaging their minds to acceptance, for the information was so painful that muscles, nerve ends, brain cells needed to be prepared for it. Yet he himself did not react, even though some part of him recognized that this in itself would seem to those who would judge him to be callous and heartless. Every word Hamilton had said was a fact, he knew that. But the facts were disconnected somehow. They had nothing to do with Luke, and even less to do with her... Her? She was dead, she was gone; that too was a fact. And yet, somewhere in the calm warm place to which he had retreated, she existed as though the years between were nothing. She was young, beautiful, passion and fire like a brilliant jewel, and that could not be changed by facts. She existed still perfect as she had always been when he had loved her. Did he still love her?

He wanted Wallace to stop now, to just be quiet. He was tired, and he wanted it to be over. Would they find him guilty? He did not know. Was he guilty? That was a question of far greater importance, and yet Luke did not have the answer to that either. More than anything else the question haunted him, eating into his mind, invading his sleep, consuming all of his energies like some relentless virus. Suffocating under the weight of the unknown, he almost wished the answer to be yes, that way he would know, he could deal with guilt, begin his penance, breathe again – even if every breath reminded him of the breath he had taken from her. And yet, he could conceive of no reason why he would kill her. His anger had been spent years before.

Still, he had believed that his passion had also been extinguished with the passing of time, and he had been wrong. And, above all, there was the evidence, all of it pointing to his guilt. It was the reason why part of him had retreated from reality, for he had no power to argue against it, no weapon to fight with.

With all his money, his influence, channeled into uncovering the truth behind what had happened, it was bewildering that nothing substantial could be found to contradict the prosecution's argument. How could the best forensic experts that money could buy still find nothing to undermine it? Even the ridiculous twenty-five million dollar reward for information proving his innocence had turned out to be more of a hindrance than a help, exhausting him even further with an endless string of dead-end leads. And still, there he sat, awaiting his verdict. There was no escape.

He could not deny that he had been with her. He had made love to her, bittersweet love that rekindled memories wrapped in silk and velvet that were closeted in boxes in the deep recesses of his mind. He had fallen asleep inside her, his hands entwined in her hair. Her long fingers, with the delicate painted nails like sacred drops of blood, had held him close to her. He had thought, at the moment that sleep overtook him, that this was as close to heaven as he could ever hope to be, and yet he was engulfed by sadness even then, for he realized that heaven was not for the living, and his life depended on someone different; on a love that could be sustained in the real world. He had slept deeply, having already said goodbye in his heart, but not realizing that it would be the only goodbye he could ever tell her. He had known nothing from that moment until the police had stormed in, and he was there on the floor next to her battered, lifeless body. If he killed her, then why? Could it have been some warped desire to leave perfection untouched by the world around it, frozen in time forever? If he did not kill her, then who?

Wallace's voice droned on. How long did it take to condemn a man? How long had it been? Hours, days, months — years even? Perhaps it took a lifetime. Perhaps, if he were indeed a killer, he had taken that first step on the journey many years ago. How many was it? More than forty years. Had it started back then, back in 1963? Certainly everything he was, everything he had done, was shaped by that day. Did it shape a murderer? Were the seeds sown on his birthday... his eleventh birthday?

PART ONE

LUKE'S STORY

Forbidden Love

CHAPTER ONE

Summer 1963

THE ROAD FROM NICE was steep and winding, but Joe Powers didn't give a damn. Hell, he was in Europe, with his family, and he would have driven the Volkswagen eight-seater van across a rollercoaster if needs be. This was what he had waited for, what he had promised the family for years. This evening they would celebrate Luke's birthday in Monte Carlo.

Joe Powers was forty-eight years old, yet today he felt like a kid in his teens. It had been a long hard haul to success, but he had never lost sight of the top of the mountain. He had known where he was heading from the age of eighteen, he just hadn't been quite sure how he was going to get there, or how long it would take. When your father drives a city bus, and your mother is a nurse, college is simply a daydream that you dare not even think about. Joe had gone to work in a factory, like any one of thousands of assembly line workers. But then the war came and it had held a tantalizing promise make it through and get a college education, and Joe sure as hell planned to make it through. He was nearly thirty when he entered college on the GI bill – an old man to some of the students, but he didn't give it a second thought. Even his subjects – a chemistry major with business management and accountancy – seemed to everyone but Joe disconnected and pointless. Yet five years later, with breakthroughs in Terylene and new synthetic fibers being researched every day, Joe Powers owned the most streamlined textile mill in the mid north, had paid back the banks their investment, and was on his way to his first million dollars in the bank.

At the time, Penny McMasters was twenty-three years old, a New Zealand girl who had daringly ventured overseas at a time years before all Australasian youth put travel on the top of their list of priorities. She had planned only one week in Chicago on her tour of the United States; then she had met Joe Powers, nearly thirteen years her senior, and like no man she had ever encountered in her quaint and charming homeland.

It was late 1950, food and petrol rationing in post-war New Zealand had ended with the southern winter, and it had taken Penny McMaster three and a half days to fly from Auckland to London via the Pan Am clipper service. After a month touring Europe she spent another day with Pan Am to reach New York. She expected to be back in her tiny home town of Taupo in time for a midsummer New Zealand Christmas. Instead, she stood before the registrar with a man she had known for less than eight weeks, and became Mrs. Joe Powers.

Now, thirteen years later, the entire family was cruising Europe for the summer in a baby-poop yellow van. It had been Penny's idea, for she had seen photographs of young people touring in Kombi-vans and felt a sudden rush of regret for the tour she never finished. Joe had agreed to the suggestion enthusiastically, for he was not a pretentious man. His real wealth had come relatively late in life. Not until he turned forty-five could he really claim to be "stinking rich", with more money than he could realistically spend. By that time there were two daughters to complete the family: Lisa, three years younger than Luke, and baby Jennifer, two years younger than her sister.

It had taken only a moment to get Joe to agree to the trip, but more than two years to drag him away from the business for three whole months. Penny, with her quiet stubbornness, had simply refused to let the idea drop. She had planned and organized behind Joe's back so that she had a solution to every obstacle Joe threw up. She even invited his parents for the summer, for she loved Nan and Pop almost as much as the kids did. She extended the invitation to her own parents, but she knew they would not come. They were quiet, simple people, old before their time, and intimidated by the thought of racing around foreign countries eating food that they could not even pronounce.

And so, seven of the Powers clan, in the sixth week of their trip of a lifetime, bounced happily in the sparse seating as Joe steered the van around the steep bends, to the discordant strains of "Happy Birthday to You." Luke was tired of hearing the stupid birthday song. His younger sisters had been singing it incessantly. Still, it was his birthday, and he had to admit he couldn't complain about spending it in Monte Carlo. He wondered whether he might see Grace Kelly wearing a crown, and whether people like Elvis came to stay with her for their holidays just like regular people went to stay with friends. Lisa and Jenny started on the song again, and Luke groaned. His sisters were not cool. For a start, they were girls, and secondly, they were babies. Luke loved them, he supposed, when he actually thought about it at all, but he figured he could live without them. What scared him more were all the jokes his folks kept making on this trip about maybe enlarging the family. He didn't want any more sisters, thank you! And his parents were too old to be talking that way! What's more, his Nan and Pop, who should have known better, were laughing and encouraging the stupid idea. His Dad had told him many times how lucky he was to have family, and how they were the most important thing in the world. But Luke couldn't help wondering, if they were so important, how come his dad spent almost every working hour at the plant, and why was this the first real holiday they had ever taken together?

He tuned out of the singing, for now his grandparents and his mom had joined in. Luckily his dad had let him sit up front with him, on account of it being his birthday, and that was really cool. Now he wound down the window, with a sideward glance at his father. Joe Powers smiled lovingly at his son. "You okay there son? Nothing bugging you is there?" he asked with his tongue in his cheek, for he knew how much the girls annoyed Luke.

"Oh sure" Luke replied grudgingly. "Like... even if I live to be a million they will already have sung Happy Birthday for the rest of my life."

His father chuckled. "Don't knock it Luke. They're your family, and nothing is as important as your own flesh and blood. You remember that when you grow up." Luke sighed, for he had heard the words before, yet they still bugged him. He leaned a little out of the open window. The air went swooshing past his head, tousling his blond hair, and he could barely hear the singing from the back of the van. He shut his eyes for a moment, losing himself to the sun and the wind.

He heard the screech of the brakes at the exact instant that he felt the van swerve, but it was already too late. He would not be able to recall, for the rest of his life, whether he actually saw the truck that sideswiped them as it passed, or whether he just imagined he did. His eyes snapped open, perhaps there was something... dark, ominous... lurking in his peripheral vision. It could have been a truck, or a bird, or the angel of death. He felt himself flying through the air, and he was certain that he saw the van pass him, disconnected, apart from him. Yet still it didn't register with the boy that anything was actually amiss. He was just flying, that's all, like it was a birthday present from God to get him away from his dumb sisters and their ratty singing. Then he landed on rock, on the shoulder of the road, and he focused for the first time on the yellow van bouncing and somersaulting as it plunged down the cliff below him.

It had been hours, he was certain, since he heard the swooshing of the wind and flew out of the van window. So why was it going down the cliff? And why hadn't they waited for him? Now he realized, with terror, that they were leaving him behind. Was this some shortcut to Monte Carlo? He climbed to his feet and started to scramble down the cliff after them. It did not occur to him that he might be hurt, or in shock, or that there was danger... for he could still hear the singing from the van... only now it sounded more like screaming, that was going on and on and...

Luke would always wonder, in those empty moments in the darkness of night, when he was totally alone, if it would have made a difference if he had reacted more quickly; got to them sooner; not wasted so much time. Even when he reached an age when he could accept that the hours between his flying out of the window and the van hitting bottom of the cliff were, in fact, no more than ten seconds, he couldn't stop himself from wondering what might have been if...

The wheels of the van spun hysterically in the air, as if grappling to get hold of the sky, for the van had landed upside down on its roof, a mangled almost unrecognizable piece of twisted metal that resembled, with its bright yellow paintwork and its black tyres, a crushed sunflower. Luke could see, as he reached the wreck, a small arm, lightly tanned and covered with light golden down, protruding from a smashed window. It belonged to Jennifer – he was certain of that – and he kicked and smashed at the window until there was enough space to drag her body clear. He was vaguely conscious of calling out to them all, telling them he was there, that they were safe, and he thought he heard his mother's voice calming Lisa, but he couldn't be certain he hadn't imagined it. His grandmother was crying, a mixture of pain and terror. He called to her to stay calm, he would get to her next. He pulled Jennifer out of the wreck and laid her on the grass about twenty feet from the Volkswagen. She was unmarked and looked completely at peace, as though she were taking a nap. Luke studied her cherub face, so perfect, so calm. He did not realize that her neck had snapped during the van's first somersault; that she was dead, and at rest, before the van ever found its own resting place. He returned to the van window, conscious now of his Nan's face, upside down, contorted with pain and yet still trying to smile apologetically at a young boy whose birthday had been marred, as though it was somehow her fault. He heard a voice, which he knew must be his own although it sounded far too commanding and in control, telling her to reach out to him, and push off the floor, now the ceiling, with her feet so that he could pull her free. She obeyed without question, but she was pinned by the seat in front which had broken free from its base. He pulled frantically at her shoulders, but she simply screamed with pain. "Leave me... get your mom... Joe..."

Those were the last words she ever said to him as the van burst into flames. He could feel the searing heat from the first blaze of the fire, but he ignored it. He could vaguely see, through the shattered glass, his father writhing and screaming as the flames engulfed him. Still he fought to get the door open, to pull them all free. The flames attacked his arms, pushing him away, yet still he would not give up until the entire van was engulfed in fire, and he could no longer even see the window or the door. He backed away then, in disbelief and shock, and stood by helplessly as his family burned. Only a month ago he had been bemoaning the fact that they were not at home for the fourth of July celebrations, and he had missed out on the bonfire and the firecrackers. Now fate, in a warped display of black humor, had provided him with an even greater spectacle, and had simultaneously taken from him everything he could count on in life.

REUBEN HAYES AND Joe Powers had gone through the war, and then through college, together. Five years younger than Joe, Reuben had studied law and set up practice with the budding Powers Industries as one of his first clients. The two men had stayed friends, as well as business associates, for more than twenty years. Now Reuben had come to France to take his friend's ashes home, along with those of the rest of the family, save for one physically and emotionally scarred little boy who was in the hospital. With Reuben was Wayne Fraser, a twenty-eight year old accountant who was said to be able to juggle figures at such speed that his hands were quicker than the eye of the Internal Revenue Service. Wayne had only recently joined Powers Industries and had not had time to get to know Joe and Penny and the kids well. That, Reuben privately thought, was Wayne's loss rather than Joe's. Reuben had grieved deeply, mourning his lost friend and the family when he heard the news of the tragic accident; Wayne had exclaimed "Shit! All that loot goes to a kid? What a waste!"

It had taken the American consulate the best part of four days to even identify the bodies in the van. Reduced to charcoal, there was nothing left of the Powers family or their belongings except Luke himself. Had it not been for the disturbed mutterings of a burnt boy trying to escape from his nightmare, it might have taken even longer to discover the nationality of the dead. By the time Reuben and Wayne arrived from Chicago, Dan Jeffreys, a career diplomat who espoused the glory of the United States at every opportunity, much to the annoyance of his host country, had already stormed the hospital on several occasions to see Luke, and managed to make enemies of all the medical staff on the case in the process. Now, as the consulate car drove the two men to the hospital, Jeffreys filled them in on Luke's condition, at the same time bemoaning the ignorance of the doctors who expected everyone to speak French because they were too damn idle to learn English. Young Luke Powers would live, that much was certain. The burns to his face and hair were superficial, but his arms were badly damaged, with second and third degree burns that would require skin grafts. The biggest problem, though, was the boy's mental state. He had remained only semi-conscious for the first two days, and that had been a blessing. For when he awoke to a world without his family, he had become catatonic, not moving or speaking, unable to recognize anyone. Reuben gave an involuntary shudder at the mere thought of the pain the boy was retreating from.

The hospital room overlooked the promenade and the beach and the view was spectacular, but Luke did not see it. Luke saw nothing but a grey haze; heard nothing but the trees moving in the wind. It was as if his mind were a clock that someone had forgotten to wind, and incapable of rewinding itself. He did not see, hear or think... and thus he was spared the pain of feeling. He had no awareness of eating, of moving, of even blinking. He simply existed in a vacuum somewhere outside of time and space.

Reuben stood by the boy's bed and wept quietly, but Luke did not respond. The lawyer wanted to take the boy into his arms and hold him, comfort him, but even if Luke had been capable of feeling, it would have been impossible. His face and head were bandaged, and both arms were shielded by steel frames, draped with cotton blankets that reminded Reuben of the prefabricated Nissen huts he and Joe had seen during the war. Luke's body was rigid, his eyes empty; like a dead man's eyes, Reuben couldn't help thinking. He leaned over the boy's body tentatively, careful not to touch him, and searched those eyes for a flicker, a glimmer of recognition.

"Where are you boy? Are you there?" he asked compassionately.

"*Il est la, monsieur,*" a voice said behind him. Reuben turned, and discovered a tall, sanguine doctor in his mid-thirties, his long hair and serene eyes giving him an almost Christ-like appearance. The two men made eye contact, and Reuben knew instinctively that if anyone could bring Luke Powers back, it was this man.

"*Pardonnez moi*. . . er. . . *Je non parle*. . . um. . . I don't speak French I'm afraid. . . *non comprenez*. . . *excusez*. . ." Reuben wracked his brain for basic vocabulary he had not used in thirty years. The doctor smiled at him.

"Please, do not excuse yourself. I speak English enough for you to understand" he said, flashing a warm smile and clearly amused as well as touched by Reuben's attempts to use the language of the country. Reuben looked at him open-mouthed.

"Pardon my rudeness," he stammered, "But I understood that no-one here spoke English." The doctor smiled again.

"We can speak. . . if there is someone we wish to speak to," he said, and the implication was clear that Dan Jeffreys had not made himself popular. "I am Henri Lefevre. Le jeune fils is my patient. What I try to say to you is. . . he is there, inside, lock away. Now it takes much time for us to find the key to unlock, yes?"

Reuben nodded, wondering to himself if a lifetime would be enough time to find the key. Wayne Fraser came to see the boy just once, bringing him a set of baseball cards and some Superman comics, but Luke did not respond and, in truth, it is possible he might not have responded even if he had been whole, for Fraser was neither warm nor empathetic, and he spent the minimum time in the hospital room that courtesy would allow. Yet Reuben came every day for a week. He sat beside the bed and talked to Luke. Sometimes he talked about Joe, and the war, and their friendship. Sometimes he talked about his own family, life in Chicago, music. Once, he tried to talk about the mystery of death, but he found himself faltering at every word. Always he searched the boy's eyes, looking for some response, some clue that his words had been heard and understood. But there was nothing.

The two men stayed until after the inquest. Only then would the French authorities release the pitiful ashes of the family for return to their homeland. Reuben had contacted Penny's parents in New Zealand, simple people whose grief at losing their only child and her family was unimaginable. Reuben did not tell them yet what he already knew; that the wills of both Penny and Joe had designated them as the guardians of the children in the event of the death of the parents. He remembered the day more than two years ago, when he and Joe had drawn up the wills. They had sat quietly in Reuben's office, enjoying a drink.

"You ever been to New Zealand, Reube?", Joe had said. "There's a lake... where Penny's folks live... it's like nothing's touched it for a million years. The trout... I swear they're the biggest on the face of the planet. And I don't know... maybe young Kennedy has the answers but... I get scared for this country. I guess, if anything happened to me... I'd want Penny to take the kids back there. Let them see the beauty – the majesty I guess you could call it... and, basic values of life, you know? I think, maybe, somehow, we lost that here when we figured the value of the dollar was more important."

Reuben decided that the McMasters deserved time to grieve for their daughter before they learned of their duty toward their grandson. They had asked about Luke, been full of concern, but Reuben was aware that they did not know their grandson well, and there was no point in suggesting they come to France to meet a stranger, lost in his own world, who wouldn't recognize them. It was better for them to believe the boy was in safe hands, and would recover, and that they would continue as loving distant grandparents, rather than foster mother and father. They did not ask who Luke's guardian would be, but even that was not surprising. Reuben could only imagine the pain and shock that learning of the death of their only child would bring. To think beyond that loss was inconceivable. There would be time for that, once the first tide of grief had ebbed.

There was one thing more to be considered. Luke Powers was, on paper at least, an extremely rich child. His father's estate, valued at around five million dollars, had been left in trust, with Reuben and Wayne as trustees. Although, Luke would not inherit it in its entirety until he was thirty; Joe had believed that if he had made it big any earlier, he wouldn't have been able to handle it. He would be a millionaire at twenty-one, and he would receive a big enough allowance to allow him to live comfortably in the meantime. Still, Reuben conceded to his accountant colleague, that was of little comfort if the boy stayed hidden in his own private world, safe in the dark shadows where reality could not penetrate. Part of Reuben wanted to stay in Nice to support the only surviving member of his friend's family, yet there was the Powers's business to be run, and his own family to be taken care of, added to by the fact that Luke never once showed any recognition of his presence.

It was to be more than three months before Hayes and Fraser returned to find a Luke that more closely resembled the boy who had left Chicago in the first days of June. Doctor Henri Lefevre had worked tirelessly to drag the boy back from the brink, only to lose him again after each of the skin grafts on his arms. A psychiatrist had been sent for, all the way from the United States of America, which both impressed and annoyed the hospital's medical hierarchy. Yet Lefevre knew that if there were any hope of Luke returning complete and whole, it could only be through the aid of someone who spoke the same language and understood the world the boy had come from.

There was no need for conscious resistance from Luke at first, for he was locked inside a body that did not respond to any stimulus. Within that world were universes of darkness and, beyond those, a sharp line, the brink of time and space. It was drawing him ever closer, yet he resisted that with the certain knowledge that he would fall over its edge and tumble into a bottomless pit from which he could never climb out. Even his subconscious mind did not recognize the name for the pit as insanity itself.

Gradually though, over days or weeks, he couldn't tell which, a tiny speck of light appeared in his mind like a distant star in a clear night sky. Almost imperceptibly it grew larger, the more he became fascinated with it; he wasn't sure if he was moving towards it, or it was moving towards him. Sometimes it would retreat, and unspeakable sorrow would engulf him, but it would always return. He was not aware of the burns as they healed, nor of the operations that replaced the skin on his arms and so he was spared the physical pain and trauma. He focused on the star and, after a long night, it grew bright enough to light everything, and he started to see shapes and shadows. At first he could not define anything, nor did he want to. He would shut his eyes and simply focus on the light.

But now it was growing so bright that he could no longer keep his eyes closed, for fear of being blinded by the star. Soon he began to see things with his eyes open again and the grayness was gradually replaced; the fluttering of a curtain; something red and pink... flowers perhaps; a smile... a woman's smile – was it his mother? Eventually he saw the room, with its sunny yellow walls, the print of the sailboat, the white chest of drawers, the folded counterpane on the bottom of his bed... and two men, one, a doctor in a white coat, thin faced with kind eyes; the other, round faced, tousled sandy hair, and dressed in a sports shirt. They would be his constant companions over the weeks to come. Henri Lefevre, whom Luke learned to call Hank, and Charles Finnemore, a Psychiatrist from Boston specializing in pediatric trauma, who became father, mother and best friend to the boy.

It was not true, he realized much later, that Luke wanted to die. Rather, he did not want to live; not in a world without his family. What he wanted, with the simplicity of a child, was for someone to put everything back the way it was, before the stupid "Happy Birthday" song; before the truck sideswiped them; before he flew out of the window; before the singing became screaming and life, as he knew it, was incinerated. As shock receded it was replaced by anger, an overwhelming fury that almost consumed him. Charlie Finnemore would hold him at arm's length so as not to harm either of them, while Luke screamed and raged and lashed out with bandaged arms, damning every one and everything to hell. Yet the rage could not be sustained, and that was replaced by the guilt. With Finnemore's help he learned to deal with it, to rationalize it in adult terms, for Luke's childhood had perished inside the yellow van. Yet, no matter how much he reasoned that he was not responsible, a small voice at the back of his mind laughed bitterly and said "Liar!"

Finnemore's reports to Reuben Hayes were encouraging. The boy was healing perfectly physically, and there was every reason to suppose that his mind would recover. To make certain, Finnemore recommended long-term therapy for grief and closure once the boy was settled with his grandparents. Reuben agreed immediately. It did not occur to either man that psychiatrists were an unknown species in a small lakeside town in a tiny country on the other side of the world, or that the McMasters would have been horrified at the idea of their grandson seeing such a person even if one had been available.

When Reuben returned, it was once again to plunge Luke into turmoil. The boy did not want to go to New Zealand. He had been there only once, when he was five, and could remember nothing except that there was no-one for him to play with. He knew very little about his grandparents. Apart from that one visit, they had come to Chicago only once, nearly three years ago. He did know that they were not like his Nan and Pop, warm and gregarious. His grandfather had actually shaken hands with him, while his grandmother had kissed his cheek stiffly. These could not possibly be the only people left in the entire world to love him! He sought in vain for alternatives... his great aunt Gussie in Maryland, fast approaching seventy; Reuben himself... there must be someone else. For Luke, Chicago was home and Reuben was the only person left whom he could call family. The lawyer had been Uncle Reube for so long, that it had never occurred to the boy that this was no more than an honorary title. Reuben would gladly have made Luke part of his family, but Joe's and Penny's wills were clear and, besides, the McMasters wanted Luke to live with them. He was all that remained of their daughter, and the only grandchild they would ever have.

IT WAS TO Auckland that Luke Powers flew with Reuben Hayes. The pilot of the plane informed the passengers to adjust their clocks forward to local time, but Luke knew within an hour that he had stepped back in time, not forward, to an era he did not know; or had perhaps not even existed in his own country.

Reuben had read that New Zealand lies roughly fifteen hundred miles, or 2,250 kilometers, to the south east of Australia, its far larger cousin, though most of his colleagues in Chicago had guessed that the country lay somewhere in Europe. He was surprised by the population of only two million; the country was roughly the size of Britain or Japan. Its people were mostly of European descent, and the Scottish made their mark as early immigrants. The native Maori, Polynesians closely linked with the Hawaiians, had lain claim to the islands for a thousand years before the white settlers came, and they refused to give it up lightly. Bloodshed was inevitable, before the two races formed an uneasy truce in the nineteenth century. A relatively new earth mass, formed from volcanic eruptions and rising from the sea, the country was split into two main islands. The North Island, known to the Maori as Te ika a Maui... the fish of Maui, was believed to be a giant fish that Maui caught, after a great struggle while fishing from his canoe, the South Island. Three quarters of New Zealand's population lived on the North Island, more than half of them in the country's main cities, Auckland and Wellington, but most of the country comprised green rich rolling hills, deep volcanic lakes, mountain ranges and fertile valleys. Like a miniature global landscape, Norwegian type fjords jostled for position with Swiss Mountains, Canadian trout streams, Californian beaches and English pastures.

WWII had been over for eighteen years, yet New Zealand, affluent, peaceful, was still clinging to the conservative attitudes and traditions of the past. It was evident in the clothes, the cars, the city, the traditions. Television was a novelty, still only two years old. New cars were difficult to procure and were heavily taxed; Rugby football was a religion rather than simply a sport; The Prime Minister, Keith Holyoake, was an ex-farmer and staunch Anglophile, who spoke the Queen's English as though he had a mouthful of marbles; and the dominion was still staunchly monarchist, with pictures of the young Queen adorning public places. Skirts were long, hair was short, jeans were working clothes only and God, Queen, and country were values that were never questioned. It was not just another country, locked in a different time frame, for Luke. He may as well have landed on another planet, so enormous and overwhelming was the initial culture shock.

They stayed overnight, the lawyer and the boy, in an Auckland hotel, comfortable yet antiquated. Luke spoke very little and although Reuben tried hard to enthuse his young charge by reading the McMasters' most recent letter aloud, he became convinced that the boy's silence was more than a rebuke; it was a silent accusation that Reuben was abandoning him in an alien landscape where he might not survive. It crossed Reuben Hayes's mind, but only fleetingly, to take the boy back to his own family in Chicago and to hell with the consequences, but he argued quite brilliantly with himself that Luke was young enough to adapt; that he needed blood relatives; that Chicago was full of memories that the boy needed to put on hold if he were going to become whole; and lastly, that this was what Joe and Penny had wanted.

The car that Reuben hired was an Australian Holden, new and with leather upholstery, and yet it looked antiquated and uninviting to the eleven year old Luke. It was November, and already there appeared to be preparations for Christmas in the city. Christmas decorations adorned shop windows, and a banner proclaimed the forthcoming Hays' Christmas Parade, yet the weather was warm, and the women wore summer dresses, and flowered hats. Every sight, every sound, was both vaguely familiar and yet confusing and challenging.

The winding, single-lane road to Taupo made for a long and tiresome drive. The countryside, now in the bloom of late spring, was stunningly green and beautiful, but Luke chose not to notice it. Every mile took him closer to a future that held nothing for him. Every hour in the car brought him closer to the last remnants of his past, for Uncle Reube would leave him, he knew that for certain, and he would be alone again.

Lake Taupo was almost in the center of New Zealand's North Island. No-one had been able to measure its depth, but its bed was, only two thousand years earlier, an active volcano that spewed forth red hot pumice and flung it many miles from the crater's heart. There was little left to remind anyone of the angry eruptions of the earth, for the lake is tranquil and beautiful, its banks studded with pine trees and mountain daisies; a haven for fishermen and tourists as well as those lucky enough to live on its shores. Facing south, at the northern end of the lake, stood the tiny township of Taupo. In the eighties it would be developed and new hotels and guest lodges would dot the landscape. But on the day that Luke arrived the small town, with its mixture of white clapboard and brick buildings and old fashioned telegraph poles, sat sleepily contemplating the distant mauve mountains of the Tongariro National Park.

The McMasters' house was not difficult to find, and Reuben drew the car to a halt outside the white timber bungalow with its red tin roof and cottage garden and its picket fence. Reuben honked the car horn, for he saw Luke stiffen in the seat beside him, and wanted at all costs to avoid a scene. Reuben had never met Penny's parents, but he had known her well enough to be convinced that these were decent and honest people. He saw Gwen McMaster first as she hurried from the house, a woman in her mid fifties, pushing a strand of salt and pepper hair up into the bun high on the crown of her head. She was dressed in a paisley cotton frock with a pale blue cardigan over the top, and it seemed to Reuben, as she grew closer, that the blue of the cardigan matched her eyes. She was smiling nervously, tentatively, peering through the car window as she approached. Behind her was Henry, perhaps two years older, reserved if not reluctant. Tall and gangly, with the rich golden red hair that had earned him the nickname "Sandy", he wore his Scottish heritage like a badge. Luke refused to look at them, even when Reuben helped him from the car and gently pushed him towards them, but Reuben could see the tears spring to Gwen's eyes as she hugged the boy to her and then softly pushed him back to arm's length, as though afraid her husband would chide her for such excessive emotion. Sandy contented himself with a squeeze of his grandson's shoulders and spoke first.

"Welcome, lad. This is your home now, and we're proud to have you. We're plain, no nonsense folks, and I expect you'll need some time to get used to us, and us to you, but that's to be expected. Now, mother's got the kettle on, and there's some cold lamb and salad all ready to be eaten, so there's no point us standing out here, is there?" There was an edge of awkwardness in his voice, and Reuben felt sorry for both the McMasters, but Luke simply looked at Hayes with begging eyes, and Reuben had to force himself not to meet the boy's gaze as they entered the house.

Lunch was simple and wholesome, like the couple themselves, and Reuben felt all his doubts retreating. Joe had been right to want something of value for his children, and these people would help Luke face life again gently and quietly, away from the growing frenzy of money-making madness that was fast becoming an inescapable part of the United States. Reuben went with the boy to the corner bedroom, with its two windows and timber walls, that had been Luke's mother's before him. There were still, even after all the years she had been gone, traces of Penny's presence: an old and much loved woolly lamb toy, a swimming certificate, framed and hanging on the wall, some Enid Blyton books on the shelf above the wooden desk in the small alcove. The simple pine bed was covered with a tufted candlewick bedspread, and a small but new battery operated radio stood on the nightstand. It was the McMasters' concession to the life they presumed Luke had led, for there was no television in the house, and very few sets in Taupo itself.

Reuben felt the gut wrenching void of separation even before he reached the car for the drive back to Auckland. He had steeled himself for Luke to cry, to cling to him, to make a scene which would be unbearable for him and embarrassing to the McMasters, but Luke did nothing. Instead he stood, stoically, a little apart from his grandparents, white-faced and dry-eyed, removed emotionally from the world around him, withdrawn once more and determined to feel nothing. It was Reuben who cried as he saw the two waving grandparents and the silent statue of a boy in the rearview mirror.

For Luke, there was no sense of belonging. It might well have been a foster home in a foreign country. His grandmother got out old photograph albums of his mother as a girl, but Luke saw only a grey haze on the page and fought the anger that grew from her seeming lack of sensitivity. He was too young to understand the different ways that grief finds expression. Gwen and Sandy's way of coping with the loss was to remember all that Penny had been; Luke's was to try to block out that his mother had ever existed, for he could never have her back again, and the pain of that realization was too great to bear.

He slept, and ate, and walked down to the edge of the lake, sitting for hours and staring at the water. Sandy had offered to play draughts, the local version of checkers, with him, but he had politely refused. He had no knowledge of Reuben's conversation with his grandparents about the continuing need for counseling, but he would not have been surprised at Sandy's response to his wife that such nonsense might be all right for Americans, but all Luke needed was a good common sense approach and a home routine and environment. For Sandy and Gwen there was an understanding that they loved their grandson and somehow hoped that he would heal them as they were, in turn, healing him. It never occurred to them that Luke's perspective might be different, or that the lack of physical and emotional contact might affect him more than was evident. On Saturday, the third morning, Luke awoke at daylight with a suffocating sense of panic in his chest. He could hear crying, yet he knew it was not him. He climbed out of the bed, with its creaking spring base, and padded barefoot to the kitchen. His grandmother was sitting at the chrome and red laminex kitchen table, her face in her hands. Sandy, looking drawn and shocked, was warming the teapot and boiling the kettle. He looked at Luke as the boy warily entered the kitchen, and Luke was taken aback by the sadness in the man's eyes.

"He's been shot," Sandy said, by way of explanation, but Luke only looked confused and frightened. Sandy opened his mouth to speak, but couldn't. Instead, he shook his head. Luke sat at the table next to his grandparents and drank the milky sweet tea his grandfather put before him. The radio news continued, but the air of gloom that emanated from it was no match for the oppressive state of that Taupo kitchen. Three people, still coming to terms with overwhelming loss, sat apart, unable to comfort each other in this new trial, and an eleven year old boy did not even know what that trial was.

At the end of the seven o'clock news, the announcement came, and Luke heard for the first time who had been shot in Dallas, who had died that November morning New Zealand time. He could not understand why his grandparents were crying. JFK was his President, not theirs. He would not perceive until years later that the slaying of a president, that president, was the murder of hope, the killing of dreams, the slaughter of innocence to much of the free world. All he knew was that something else had been taken from him. He raced from the house and started to run. He had no sense of direction, or of time, and when he finally stopped running, and sank to the ground from sheer exhaustion, he could no longer see the lake, or anything except thick forest. He knew at that moment that he was lost, but he did not care. He hoped that he would never be found, that the forest would just swallow him up, that his dad and mom would come for him, wake him from the nightmare and excite him with plans for the holiday they were all going to take. After all, he was still in his pajamas, so why shouldn't it all be a nightmare? Why shouldn't he wake up in Chicago, safe in familiar surroundings? He curled himself up under a pine tree... and he waited.

It was three days before Sandy McMaster and a search party arranged by the local constabulary found him. For the first twelve hours, Sandy had not been alarmed. The boy needed time to himself, he reasoned, and an eleven year old boy would return once his stomach started growling. It was not until the sun went down and the biting cold of the late spring night crept in, that he felt any sense of urgency. Then, at Gwen's urging, he had gone out to look for the boy. Only a few months earlier an escaped convict, on the run for six months, had been found in an abandoned hut near the lakeside, and the reality of a marred Utopia was rearing its head. Sandy had scoured the lakeside for as long as his flashlight held out, then reluctantly turned back. His sense of practicality told him there was no point in him too getting lost, in the dark, beside a lake that covered nearly four hundred square miles.

On Sunday, after church, Sandy enlisted the help of neighbors and townsfolk, and by Sunday night the police had joined the hunt, after reproaching Sandy for waiting so long. Sandy bridled at the reproach. He had not waited at all, in his mind. He had searched for his grandson from the moment he had realized that the boy was lost, and not simply hiding somewhere in the town. On Monday afternoon a search party found Luke, cold, hungry, suffering from mild exposure. He had found his way back to the shore of the lake and covered himself with an old tarpaulin near a disused boatshed.

There was talk of taking him to a nearby hospital, of pneumonia, of shock, of sending him to Auckland, but Sandy took no notice, and Luke did not even hear the chatter. Later, after he had run the boy a hot bath and Gwen had filled him with mutton stew, potatoes and thick gravy mopped with home made bread, Sandy took his grandson down to the lake and the two sat, side by side, near the water's edge, watching the trout jumping as the sun set between the pines of the forest.

For a long while, neither one of them spoke. Luke had nothing to say to this stranger anyway, and Sandy did not know how to open a conversation with the boy. Slowly though, the tension between them dissolved, and was replaced by a truce-like calm. When Sandy spoke, it was more to himself than to the boy, as though the words were bursting to escape and couldn't be contained any longer.

"She used to love to come here, my Penny." Sandy began softly. "It's a bloody English name, not Scottish... but we never did call her Penelope, only Penny. I reckon it's because she was bright and shiny, just like a new penny." He broke off, almost seeing before him the little girl at Luke's age, an innocent and joyous creature. Luke said nothing. He held his breath, waiting for the next word.

"She loved to fish. She was a natural born fly fisherman... always caught the biggest trout. I had old George Reagan in town make her a special rod, just her size. And she learned to make her own flies... bloody silly colors... pink and blue. I told her they would never fool the trout, but they did. I reckon they'd just come to the surface to get a look at our Penny." He smiled then, but Luke did not see it, for the sun was now blanketed by the trees and long shadows engulfed them. Now the aging man's voice started to falter. "If you like, I could teach you. Her rod's still out in the shed." Luke did not respond. He didn't know what to say, or even what to think. Somehow, despite the fact that the two of them sat feet apart, he felt as though his grandfather was taking his hand for the first time, and he wasn't certain if that was comforting or frightening. He was still considering his response when he heard the choked anguished cry from Sandy's throat, and the whispered words with their tone of finality.

"She's never coming back... not now. God, I miss her so much." Luke was shocked by the admission. And then his grandfather started to cry. And the crying became louder, like that of a child. And, as the man cried like a boy, the boy took his hand and comforted the grand-father he did not know, did not yet love. In that moment, where time was irrelevant and the roles were reversed, some part of Luke knew that his childhood was gone forever.

Y OUR GRAN AND I have been talking," Sandy began and Luke knew, before another word was said, that he was not going to like whatever followed.

It was late January, midsummer, and the days were long and hot, the haze over the mountains deepening from mauve to deep purple in the late evening. Christmas had been bleak and alien to Luke. Where was the snow? Where were the carol singers? Where were all the presents under the huge tree? Most of all, where were his family, and how could Christmas possibly proceed without them?

For the McMasters, Christmas was a time for going to church and remembering Christ's birth, rather than a huge family get together. In the years since Penny had left home, they had ceased to bother about decorating the small pine tree in its tub, and had made only a perfunctory stab at Christmas lunch with a roasted chicken and stuffing. Often the days would be so hot that they would settle for having the chicken cold with some salad. But this past Christmas the couple had put aside their grief and made an all out effort to create Christmas for their grandson. All three of them knew that it was futile, for the absence of family on the occasion only perpetuated the boy's grief, and that in turn led to a reopening of the wound the McMasters felt at the loss of their only child.

Still, they went through the motions, each pretending, for the sake of the others, that they believed the "happy" part of the Christmas greeting.

Remarkably, Luke could identify exactly when things had begun to change. It was the first of January 1964, and with the coming of the new year was an unspoken understanding to start life anew. Luke could not foresee a time when he would ever throw his arms around his grandparents in the same way that he had done with the rest of his family. But he knew, with absolute certainty, that they loved him and wanted only what was best for him. Their love manifested itself in small but telling ways. The way his Gran would put cinnamon in the apple pie, because he liked it that way; the long days that Grandpa spent with him on the lake, teaching him to fish. These were the closest the two came to ever telling Luke they loved him, and yet he knew it, and felt guilty that he could find no way to reach them in return.

The long summer days fishing were what he loved the most. Grandpa would wake him before dawn and they would dress in long rubber waders and canvas hats, drink hot sweet tea and eat toast before heading down to the lake, after taking Gran a cup of tea. There, where the silence was broken only by the trout jumping, Luke could lose himself to the comfort of stillness, a habit that would last all his life. He now accepted, somewhere deep inside of him, that there was a way back — a life ahead. And then Sandy broke the silence.

"Your Gran and I have been talking," he said hesitantly. "It's about your schooling." Luke looked at him questioningly. The small white timber schoolhouse in the town was as far removed from Luke's Chicago school as he could imagine, yet it looked safe and welcoming. It was closed for the school holidays, but Luke rode down there on the bike his grandparents had given him for Christmas and looked through the windows. This, he had decided, could be another safe haven where nothing could threaten him. Now, though, his breath caught in his throat and he felt a growing sense of alarm.

"We decided — that is, we think — it's what your mum and dad would have wanted you should go to one of those fancy schools in Auckland. Taupo's no place for a boy like you Luke." Sandy paused, waiting for a response. Luke wanted to scream, 'Don't send me away... I need to be here. I need YOU.' Instead, he stood silent, implacable, and Sandy mistook the lack of response for tacit agreement.

Only two weeks later Luke's grandparents placed his suitcase in the pre-war model black Ford with its bench seats and drove him to Auckland. The trip was long and hot, and he sweltered in the ugly maroon and navy blazer, the grey shorts, the long socks. He had a sense that he was going to a very fancy prison, and these were his prison duds for the next six years. He sat in the back of the car, aimlessly eating one of the egg sandwiches his Gran had made for the trip, silent, resentful.

He had seen the prospectus for Lloyd's College for Boys, an imposing edifice dating back to the end of the last century situated in Remuera, a short distance to the center of Auckland. He had tried to look suitably impressed when his grandparents had said, in somewhat awed tones, that boys from the very best families went there; but he had been devastated to discover he would be a boarder, seeing Taupo and his only family in the holidays and at half term, for the long drive made weekend trips home an impossibility. Luke had only rebelled once, for some part of him already accepted that there was no point in struggling against what was inevitable. His grandfather had once again excused their seeming dismissal of responsibility for his welfare by telling him that this was exactly the education his parents would want for him. Luke had looked at the elderly man with something akin to contempt and said,

"My folks would never have wanted to make me unhappy… never." Then he had gone to his room and slammed the door, and fought the tears pricking his eyes.

Now, though, as the old Ford drove up the tree-lined driveway and he saw the long red brick building with its portico and its mock Norman turrets, he felt an overwhelming sense of dread. They entered the hall, an oak-paneled affair that featured an enormous double width staircase. In only a few hours, boys from eleven to eighteen, boarders at the college, would be scurrying up and down those stairs, but for now they were deserted. A master came to meet them, young, with a pudding basin type haircut and a freckled face. He wore his black academic gown with as much distaste as Luke wore his own uniform.

"Um… hello there… you must be the McMasters and you, of course, must be Luke." He extended a hand and Luke ignored it, greeting him instead with an informal "Hi." The master looked a little confused by the casual response, but blustered on uncertainly. "I'm Mister French, and I'll be teaching Latin this year," he laughed at the absurdity before the elderly couple had even grasped the joke. "Rather silly isn't it? French, teaching Latin?! Well, you'll be in my class I expect Luke, so we'll have a chance to get to know each other. Perhaps your grandparents would like to complete the rest of the admission papers in the Head's office, and sign you in, and I'll take you upstairs, eh?" There was little time for Luke to respond, for the young teacher had already taken his suitcase and was guiding him by the elbow up the imposing staircase.

The Mezzanine floor was enormous, with large communal bathrooms in each corner, and ten six bedded dormitories. Luke was conscious of French telling him that only junior boys boarded in the main hall, and that after third form, at which time most had turned thirteen, they were assigned a house and a housemaster in the grounds. But he paid little attention. He wouldn't be here that long. Someone would rescue him; or he'd run away; or die if he was lucky!

Mister French showed him to a bed near the window; a cast iron bed with a pale blue cotton counterpane stretched across its surface and tucked in hospital style. A small upright wardrobe and a bedside chest, along with a wooden foot locker, completed what would be Luke's private space for the next two years. At least he had a view from the window. It looked out across a quadrangle; pathways neatly creating a square around a central lawn which carried a statue of the full blown aging King George V, and then, beyond the pathways, the resident houses, the new science block, the trees, the rugby field, the sports oval. It was, Luke realized as his eyes slowly took it all in, like something from a British movie; interesting yet unfamiliar; the novelty of it intriguing and frightening at the same time. What was he doing here? How could he get out? There was no answer to either question.

He put his things away carefully, surprised at his own attitude. In Chicago he had been in the habit of just throwing his clothes everywhere; his Mom had constantly been on his case about it. Even in Taupo, his Gran usually picked up his things even when he had every intention of clearing up for himself. Yet something told him that here, within the hallowed halls of Lloyd's, you played the game according to their rules if you wanted to survive, and it surprised him to realize that he DID want to survive.

He had just finished putting his things away when an elderly, sharp featured, thin-lipped master appeared in the doorway of the dorm.

"Powers?" he asked rhetorically, since there was no-one but Luke in the room. "Your grandparents said to say goodbye. They will telephone you each Friday evening at six p.m., before prep." Luke looked at him in disbelief.

"They're gone? They can't be. They didn't even say goodbye." He heard the catch in his voice, felt the lump in the throat, and the overwhelming sense of abandonment that engulfed him.

"We find it's better to do these things quietly and avoid hysteria," said the master, whom Luke would later know as Mister Hopkins – mathematics. "Well, at least you'll have time to acclimatize before afternoon tea. No doubt you've read the rules. Junior boys may not leave the school grounds for any reason. You'll hear the tea-bell. The dining hall is on the ground floor facing the quadrangle. It'll be a cold tea tonight – many of the boarders don't arrive till late." The master waffled on, avoiding looking at Luke, and Luke only slowly became aware that he was crying. Hopkins cleared his throat.

"This won't do. It won't do at all Powers. Lloyd's boys do not indulge their emotions this way. Pull yourself together man, and try to be worthy of the school." He turned on his heel and walked out then. Luke stood for a moment, trying to control the flow of emotion, but he was helpless against it. He threw himself on the bed and sobbed, allowing self-pity to wrap around him like a warm comforter. He felt so completely alone that he could believe, with very little effort, that the world had ended in the much threatened nuclear war, and he was the last person on earth. One day, he told himself, there would be someone who would not abandon him, someone who would love him completely, some family that was really his. Until then, this would be the last time he would cry!

He must have fallen asleep, for when he opened his eyes, deep shadows from the trees outside fell across the bed. He was conscious of someone standing at the foot of his bed. For a second he thought he was back in Chicago, and it was Rudy, the son of his parents' black maid, Grace. Then he realized it was a boy of about his own age, a Maori boy in the Lloyd's uniform.

"Hey, how you going?" the boy smiled and asked him. "You're Luke Powers, the Yank boy, eh? I'm Hiwi Hanere – everybody calls me Hughie. We're both new boys, eh?" There was a look of uncertainty in the Maori boy's eyes, for an American boy was an unknown quantity, and even in New Zealand they had heard of the rapidly growing Civil Rights movement in the US, suggesting that those of a different color weren't necessarily accepted as equals. Yet beyond the uncertainty, as Luke met the boy's gaze, was something more. It was a plea, or perhaps an invitation, which said, 'We're both out of place here... we need each other. Let's be friends.' Luke looked at the boy again. Hughie appeared to be the same age, stocky, rich black wavy hair, deep coffee-colored skin, a broad face, laughing eyes, and an openness in his smile that refused to be ignored. Tentatively, fighting suspicion, Luke smiled in return. And a friendship was born.

Lloyd's College was a microcosmic world on its own. It could rightly be called "posh" or "La-de-da", but three past New Zealand Prime Ministers, a bishop, and a Nobel Prize winner were amongst its alumni, and the boys who attended were encouraged to think of themselves as being privileged to be pupils. For Hughie, a boarder on a full scholarship, and Luke, openly despised yet secretly admired for being a Yank, it was a strange world of regimen: group showers at six am; lumpy oatmeal and cold toast with marmalade and strongly stewed tea in the dining hall; classes in Latin and Classics battling for supremacy alongside maths and physics; P.E. exercises in the quadrangle; debating and public speaking; an evening meal with some indeterminable form of meat and vegetables, and Prep – the dreaded equivalent of Luke's Chicago homework, which he had often avoided, under the watchful eye of a master. Television was a luxury saved for two hours on Friday and Saturday nights. The TV set in the common room was black and white, and many of his peers did not believe Luke's claims that the set his family had back in Chicago was in full living color. New Zealanders were still in awe of the fact that radio now had pictures, and Luke's stories were simply too fantastic to believe. The most popular shows, such as I Love Lucy, Maverick and Bonanza, were all episodes that Luke had seen, and for a while he made money – sixpence here, a shilling there – by betting his fellow inmates what the ending would be to an episode, until they got wise and threatened to thrash him.

It seemed to Luke that, although Hughie was not castigated for the color of his skin, he was looked down upon for being a scholarship boy whose parents couldn't afford the school. Luke was in much the same boat, for his meager five shillings a week in pocket money was laughed at by the other boys in the dorm, and only Hughie understood how out of place Luke felt.

It took only weeks for the two lonely boys to become inseparable and there was a sense of anticipation for the first break from school of the year. Hughie lived only a few miles from Taupo and Luke would be able to meet his family and thought that perhaps he would feel a new sense of belonging. Both boys were bright academically, and Luke adapted to French and Latin, even though he had never encountered either of them before. Mister French was pleasant, and seemed drawn to Luke in some empathetic way, but Hopkins never missed an opportunity in class to openly deride Luke as a cry baby and a sissy who, like most Americans, was soft and lacking in moral fortitude from years of having life too easy. For most of the time Luke said nothing. He tuned the master out, knowing that it annoyed Hopkins more to see that Luke wasn't listening to him than it would to respond to the provocation. Still, one morning when Luke had been at Lloyd's for perhaps six weeks, Hopkins rode him just a little too hard, suggesting that dollars and cents had been invented because Americans were so lacking in intelligence that they could only add or multiply in tens, and Luke was, after all, an American. Luke retorted that New Zealand was a backwater, a tin pot country that took orders from Britain, and it wouldn't surprise him to learn that Hopkins had to wait for permission from the Queen before he could scratch his ass. The class erupted, some laughing at the obvious putdown, some furious that the interloper had dared to put down their country. Luke was hauled to the Headmaster's office and given his first taste of the cane, smarting more at the indignity of being bent forward over a desk rather than the stinging of the cane cuts. The Headmaster made it clear that any ideas that Luke was somehow too good for Lloyd's had best be shelved for as long as he was a pupil.

Luke found a small crowd waiting for him outside the head's office. Mostly they were victims of Hopkins, who applauded Luke's bravado in standing up to the master's vitriol. There was a grudging sense of admiration for his hot-headedness but within days it had been forgotten, the status quo was restored, Luke was once again an outsider and the sense of isolation continued. There was a mail call every evening before prep, and Luke would attend even though he knew there would be nothing for him. Even Hughie got long letters from his parents, his grandmother, and his eight-year-old sister Kiri, but the McMasters were not letter writers. His Friday evening phone call from them consisted of stilted small talk and they were once again the caring strangers he had encountered on that first day at Taupo. Occasionally there would be a letter from across the Pacific from uncle Reube. Luke would read it out loud, embellishing the mundane by dropping the names of film stars and rock singers; his revelation that Uncle Reube had Elvis over for a barbecue earned him a small but loyal fan club, none of them noticing that the letter had been received during Chicago's winter.

At night he would listen to Hughie, in the bed opposite, giving little sigh-like snores of contentment as he slept. The rest of the dorm was filled with two second form and two third form boys. He could hear the panting and grunting in the darkness of masturbation under the bed-clothes, and felt himself trapped in a well of loneliness. Then he would push the heels of his hands into his eyes to stop any wayward tears that refused to comply with his no-crying edict. Often it would take him hours to fall asleep, the weight of his bedcovers and grief like an anvil on his chest. Sometimes he would awaken hard and straining from an erection. He would take his penis in his hand and rub it, obeying the instincts that had guided life since the dawn of time. Yet the emission gave him no relief, and there was tragedy in the very thought that this was his only outlet.

In late April, two senior boys were expelled for attending an Australian extravaganza, 'Paris by Night', at the St. James theatre, in which naked women adorned the stage with few strategically placed sequins drawing the line between erotica and pornography. New Zealand was not yet ready for nudity. Luke found the whole idea amusing, and a chance comment that all women had the same things led to a rumor that Luke, with his eleven years of experience, knew all about sex. After all, he was a Yank, wasn't he? And Yanks started early — everyone knew that. Luke found himself with a celebrity status he had never expected. His only problem was living up to the undeserved reputation. He found himself sought after in the common room, even by the older boys, and he had to draw on every trashy novel, every magazine and every movie he had ever seen, to invent lurid and often inaccurate sexual scenarios. Hughie would listen, suppressing the urge to giggle. He knew that his friend knew no more about sex than any of them, but he had the advantage of the American gift of the gab that the more staid and introverted Kiwis did not possess.

It soon became clear to Luke that his biggest drawback was poverty. There was a school tuck shop that Luke could not afford to frequent on his limited pocket money. Saturday afternoon outings at the "pictures", usually a cartoon a serial or cowboy movie and then the main film, followed by a tea of steak and chips was a luxury that was barely within Luke's reach.

With so much time on his hands, Luke discovered a lucrative way to supplement his meager allowance, and soon he was doing homework assignments for scholars of all levels for one shilling a time. The money was spent between him and Hughie on Saturday afternoons on the best seats at the Civic Theatre with a box of Jaffas, orange candy covered chocolate balls, and a frozen drink on a stick. For a while, at least, in the darkness of the cinema while Elvis crooned about Blue Hawaii, Luke could lose himself and the pain of separation, and become just another boy out with his best mate. "Powers, you arsehole, I'm going to do you up once and for all." The angry voice belonged to Keith Mulgrave, an overweight fourth-former whose great claims to fame were that he could fart God Save the Queen, and his father was a cabinet minister in the current government. Mulgrave was a bully and a braggart who was only grudgingly accepted because of his father's position in the government and the country's respect for its politicians and democratic process. Mulgrave's marks weren't sufficient to keep him at Lloyd's, but his father's money and stature were. The fourth form boy had paid Luke the princely sum of half a crown, two shillings and sixpence, for a fifteen hundred word essay on the birth of the United States after the war of Independence. Luke had to limit the scope of the essay to remain within the word limit but still managed to quote from the Declaration of Independence and provide background material on the fathers of the revolution. The problem was that Luke had done the same thing for three others in the class, each of whom paid half a crown, and Mulgrave had been the last to hand his in. It hadn't taken long for the senior English master, despite all Luke's efforts to individualize the essays, to see the similarities in writing styles and content in the four essays, nor was there much doubt where the work had originated. Luke had already been given a warning, without being openly accused, by the headmaster who had tapped the cane lightly against his hand for emphasis. Luke had successfully played wide-eyed innocent, all four boys had failed their assignment, and Luke had already paid back half a crown each to the other three complainants. Mulgrave, however, was determined not to be placated.

"Come on, you bloody Yankee bastard," Mulgrave ranted at him. "Put your fists up and defend yourself. I'm gonna whip your hide anyways." Luke looked at the bigger boy in disbelief. As well as being three years older, Mulgrave was some forty to fifty pounds heavier than Luke, and stood at least six inches taller. The inequity of the situation was so absurd that Luke gave an involuntary giggle, which only fuelled the braggart's outrage further. He sprang at Luke, knocking him to the ground. Luke was too shocked to fight back. Instead, he put up his arms and hands to ward off the bigger boy and protect his face as Mulgrave knelt over him, pummeling wherever he could connect with a fist.

It was mild-mannered Mister French who pulled the fourth-former from the eleven year old, breaking up the one-sided fight. "That's enough, Mulgrave," French said with as much anger as his natural timidity would allow. "Get out of here now, and report for detention the next five nights.

I expect two thousand lines... 'I must not use brute force against those smaller than myself'. Now go, before I send you to the Head instead."

Mulgrave looked contemptuously at the young master, who was scarcely any taller or heavier than himself. For a moment French's glare faltered, but he covered by turning to Luke and helping him off the floor. The small crowd quickly dispersed and Mulgrave and his band of cohorts stood apart as French helped Luke to the dormitory. Luke knew that the battle was over, but the war had yet to be fought.

French helped Luke to lie down on his narrow bed, and brought a small bowl of antiseptic and water, along with some cotton wool to gently dab the boy's grazes and bruises. "You know, " he said dreamily, as though talking more to himself than to Luke, "I was the smallest boy in class at school. I think everyone who fancied themselves as a bit of a lad used me as a punching bag. I never fought back. It's so... so primitive, I suppose – physical violence. We ought to learn to love one another." He brushed the soft blond hair out of Luke's eyes and gently stroked his face, letting his fingers linger at the edge of Luke's mouth. "Such a sweet mouth, dear boy. No one should ever hurt such a cherub face." Luke lay very still. His mind was screaming at him that whatever the hell was happening was pretty freaky, yet he could not be afraid of Mister French. He thought he saw tears in the young master's eyes, even as he felt the gentle touch of the long slender fingers, a touch that reminded him of his mother's.

With May's arrival came the first school holidays of the year. It seemed to Luke that Taupo was just a mythical place he had heard about rather than his home. He had already spent more time away from it than he had spent there with his grandparents. This first school break in Taupo held a special excitement, for his grandparents agreed that he could spend three days with Hughie and his family at Tokaanu, a charming village on the opposite shore of the lake to Taupo.

"You Pakeha have to know everything, don't you?" Hughie said laughingly, using the Maori term for non-natives. The two boys were on their way to Marae of the Tu Wharetoa tribe, the tribe of Hughie's family ancestors. "The Marae's not just a meeting place... not a church, or a court... yet it's sorta like all of them rolled into one." Hughie saw Luke's puzzled expression. "It's the place where Maori stand tall... in spirit, in prestige, in custom. I dunno Luke, maybe it sounds corny now but... I guess it's the home of my soul, my dignity... everyone's." Luke looked at him enviously. "The home of my soul," he reiterated in an envious whisper, wondering if he would ever know such a place.

There was a palpable sense of spirituality in the earth itself before Hughie took Luke up the steps to the meeting house. It was as if an electric force was breaking through the soles of Luke's shoes and infusing his body with every step. A few miles out of the belching mud and steam geysers for which Takaanu was known, they now stood at Waihi, on the water's edge. It seemed different here somehow, as though the ghosts of the buried chiefs in the Te Heuheu mausoleum, had given their very energy to the earth.

Inside the great hall Luke gazed in wonder at the huge carvings – the *poupou*, Hughie called them – and the woven *tukutuku* panels representing strength, the path to the stars and to spiritual heaven. *"Haeremai, Haeremai, Haeremai"* Hughie chanted, welcoming his visitor three times in the ancient tradition. For two hours Luke listened to Hughie explain the customs and history of his people to the American boy, who knew nothing about the natives of his own country, except for what he had seen in cowboy movies and comic books.

At night, in the old Victorian timber house that Hughie and Kiri shared with their parents and Grandmother, Granny Moana-Marie would sit with the boys after Kiri had taken her dolls to bed, and speak to the boys in Maori, which Hughie would translate for Luke.

Granny Moana-Marie had welcomed Luke from the moment Hughie had introduced him. *"I manahau a is i mua te mata o te maikiroa,"* she had told her grandson, knowing of Luke's tragic background.

"She likes you." Hughie told his friend. "She says you have been resilient in the face of misfortune."

Luke searched for something witty or smart-assed to say, but instead he mumbled, "Tell her thanks."

Hughie grinned. Tell her yourself," he said. "Just say *Kia Ora*."

"Kia Ora" Luke stumbled over the words, but Granny Moana-Marie nodded appreciatively.

"That's formal," Hughie explained. "Once you get to be part of the family you can just say *"Mihi."* Once again Granny smiled, a rich, brown, gnarled face that exuded a sense of wisdom, against the angelic fairness of the American boy.

"Nga Atua purakau o mua," the old woman began, the candlelight flickering on the kitchen table. Hughie had turned out the light and his parents had gone out for a beer and a game of bingo. "The mythical Gods of old," Hughie whispered, so unobtrusively that over the next two hours Luke was convinced that he understood every word the old woman said in her own language, instead of Hughie's translation.

"Before the world there was nothing, Te Kore, and then Te Poo, the night. The night was forever and in its arms lay Rangi, the Sky Father, wrapped in the embrace of Papa, the Earth Mother. They could not be separated, but their children, the gods, crawled out from between their entwined bodies. Pale and cold, the gods searched for somewhere in the dark night where they could find freedom, light and warmth, and room to stretch and grow to their full might. It was Taane-mahuta, the god of trees, forests, and all living things that search for the light, who stretched himself to his full height, pushing his parents apart. Rangi tried to hold onto Papa, but Taane pushed harder, and the earth and the sky were forced apart, and the darkness and the light were separated. Then Taane and his brothers looked at the soft curves of their mother, the earth, and they saw that she was covered by a silver veil, a mist of grief for her lost husband. And the tears from Rangi's eyes made the rains, and it ran over Papa in pools and streams — rivers and oceans. And Taane loved his parents, even though he had parted them, and he wanted his mother to be beautifully clothed, so he set about dressing her in trees and forests, in leaves and flowers — his own children. But his wisdom had not yet been born, and so he planted his children upside down at first, and for many years Papa endured the trials and errors of her son. Gradually though, Taane learned the ways of nature and his children, and the birds and the insects lived with their brothers and sisters, the trees and the flowers. But Rangi still cried for his wife and Taawhiramaatea, brother of Taane and god of the winds that blow between earth and sky, joined his father. And Taane saw that, while his mother was now beautiful, his father Rangi was empty and

desolate. So he took the sun, Ra, and the moon, Marama, and placed them on Rangi's back and breast, yet still his father languished. "Don't worry, father" Taane told him, "I will find something special to adorn you with." Taane journeyed to the ends of space where the Shining Ones, children of Taane's brother Uru, lived in the great mountain. Taane begged his brother for some of his children and Uru filled a great basket with the Shining Ones. Then Taane took Rangi's deep blue robe and placed five shining ones in the shape of a cross. Then he sprinkled the robe with the Children of light and hung the basket in the heavens. It is the Milky Way, and the children of Uru play and frolic in it, sometimes falling towards the earth to visit their grandmother. Thus did the son serve both his parents, and the heaven and the earth were fulfilled."

THERE WAS SILENCE when the hakui, the old woman, finished her story. Her eyes glistened in the candlelight and Luke glanced sideways at Hughie and saw that he, too, was moved by the story, even though he had heard it many times. Luke could not speak, so overpowered was he by the legend. He drank the sweet hot chocolate that Granny prepared and later, as he and Hughie climbed into their beds, he found the courage to ask, "Hughie… do you believe in God? I mean… not Taane… not gods… no offence, but, like one person, you know, like they say in church?" Hughie leaned on one elbow and looked at him. "Sure I do. I mean, jeez, Luke, nothing would make much sense otherwise, would it?" Luke wished he could have the simplistic faith of his friend. "So, if God exists… why do you think he killed my Mom and Dad… and everyone?" Hughie looked down awkwardly, knowing that there was no answer he could give which would satisfy the empty longing in his friend. "Jeez mate… I dunno. Maybe you should ask God to tell you." Luke did not reply. He lay down in the stillness of the night and thought of what Granny Moana-Marie had said. "Thus did the son serve both his parents." Who was there for him to serve?

At the end of his stay Granny Moana-Marie gave him a book of Maori myths and hugged him. "Goodbye, Golden Boy, and don't be sad. All of the gods in heaven will keep you safe, and your parents will smile on you. I promise," she said in perfect English. Luke was open-mouthed in astonishment. "Gran can speak English when she wants to." Hughie explained. "But mostly I don't want to," the old lady cackled.

Luke spent the rest of the holidays fishing with his grandfather and chopping wood for the fire. He showed his grandmother how to make hamburgers from ground beef, and he helped harvest the vegetables from the large allotment in the back yard, for it was autumn and already the nights were frosty. He thought that he would dread the return to Lloyd's, yet somehow he found himself looking forward to the new term with a sense of anticipation. "You're turning into a right little Kiwi, lad," Grandpa said to him with a sense of pride. Luke did not thank him. He had already discovered that the kiwi was a pretty ugly looking bird with wings so shriveled it couldn't fly. It was hard for him to take the tag as a compliment, even though he knew that the New Zealanders themselves relished the title. Still, although he was American and always would be, he was forced to concede that being a Kiwi was probably not the worst thing in the world to be.

LUKE WAS GLAD for the colder days, and the long sleeved shirts of the winter term; the scars on his arms were a constant reminder of events that needed no reinforcement in his mind. Sometimes, in the showers, he would see the boys looking at him. He had tried to tan his arms so that the burn scars and the skin grafts would no longer show, but the new skin simply colored a bright pink, and the burn scars looked browner, deader than the rest of his skin. No-one ever asked him about his arms, yet he knew that somehow Hughie knew, or had guessed, the truth from the little Luke had told him about his family's accident. Hughie never questioned him about anything, and Luke came to realize that this was the greatest gift a friend could give; the freedom of never having to explain. Still, he sometimes wondered if Hughie had told the others, and there was a tacit agreement not to open the wounds. Once, he thought he actually saw Hopkins wince as he scratched at his scarred arms during a math class. Much of the time though, he was totally unaware of the physical scars, for the emotional scars were deeper, and much harder to carry.

Mister French was no longer teaching at the school, the official story being that he'd accepted a post on the South Island, but Luke suspected something less innocent. School jumpers under the blazers protected the boys from the biting cold and the winds in the City of Sails. For Luke, the southern winter held no great threat. He came from Chicago, the Windy City, where water froze in pipes, the snow could hold a person captive at house, and the central heating suffered a nervous breakdown for several months of the year. Yet when the form one boys turned out for school football, rugby union it was called, Luke was astonished.

"Where's the padding? What about a helmet?" he asked in disbelief as he realized that the shorts and cotton jumper he had been given as sports uniform were not, as he had supposed, just for warming up. He had not thought the question funny, yet he was greeted with howls of laughter. Blenkinsop, the sports master, guffawed the loudest as he shook his head.

"Padding, Powers? You Yanks really are sissies aren't you? No padding here boy. Padding is for poofters. Just sheer guts and skill to get you through." The master challenged him with the words, as if doubting that Luke could make the grade. Luke shrugged resignedly.

"Okay. But it seems pretty dumb to me. Explains a lot, though." Luke replied. Blenkinsop did not pursue the last remark, but Hughie looked at him quizzically.

"Like what?" he asked. Luke grinned as they left the locker room.

"Like Mulgrave having shit for brains. He is a rugger player, isn't he?... just one too many kicks in the head maybe." Now Hughie and Luke laughed together.

"Blenkinsop's full of bullshit" Hughie remarked in passing.

Luke was surprised to find that Blenkinsop had not been bullshitting him about the game. It truly did require skill and guts, and speed. It was a faster game by far than gridiron, and the lack of padding meant a freedom that the American code did not allow.

By that evening, in the dining room, everyone was talking about Luke and his "request" for padding and a helmet. Luke realized there was no point in protesting, or trying to defend himself. His only defense was to play the stupid football game, and play it better than anyone else. He would show Blenkinsop that he didn't need any protection to beat a bunch of Kiwis at their own game, and he'd end up captaining the school's stupid rugger team. At the time, his bravado was simply a defense mechanism against ridicule, and yet Luke ended up fulfilling both his vows, and grew to love the game. Football practice became an obsession with him, and he could often be seen out on the oval, all by himself on the weekends, running for his life, dodging imaginary opponents, or perhaps demons in his mind.

The only time he missed practice was on his birthday. In his team-mates' words, he 'lost it'. Luke kept his vow not to cry, yet the anger welled up like the geysers he had seen in Rotorua and near Hughie's home, threatening to blow him apart from sheer pressure if it did not find an escape route. For Luke the escape was through anger which began to build with the approach of his birthday. His ransacking of the dormitory, while older and bigger boys watched with trepidation in the doorway, became a legend that was to be repeated for years to come; even a cast iron bed was upended and thrown against the wall, and Luke screamed as he trashed the room, as though only his own screams could drown out those of his burning family. When his anger was spent, he curled up on the floor, beside his upturned bed, and refused to speak until his birthday had past, and some semblance of normalcy returned to the world he was forced to inhabit.

And so Luke Powers ended his first year at Lloyd's College. He might have passed for just an average student, son of a farmer, lawyer or businessman. Yet both he and the hierarchy of the school knew that he was not like anyone else. Uncertain what to do with him, the elite schooling system did nothing. He was bright, they knew that much, and he easily met the scholastic requirements. 'Disturbed' was not a word used in a former British dominion in the mid sixties, and although the word delinquent was the new buzz word, it did not apply to boys in private schools with respectable families. Besides, most of the time Luke kept to himself, or with Hughie and one or two admirers, and was no problem in any way. The exceptions were when the boy with-drew completely, seeming to have left the shell of his body, or when he exploded with the frightening fury of a volcano. If he was occasion-ally troublesome, the headmaster and his team decided, it was hardly surprising given the tragedy he had endured. Besides, it was generally conceded that Luke would eventually forget, settle down and assimi-late, and become just another Lloyd's boy.

Sandy and Gwen teased him on the drive back to Taupo for the Christmas holidays; some silly private joke about there being a new arrival in the house, and they'd all have to alter their habits to accommodate their new family member. For a short time Luke thought they had bought a dog, and he greeted the idea with both excitement and trepidation, for he needed to love, yet he was terrified to love something that would die before him and once again leave him alone. He realized with some surprise that this was what kept him from getting truly close to his grandparents; the knowledge that, by their very age, they would one day die and leave him, and he could not survive such a loss for a second time.

But the new family member stood in the corner of the living room on four laminated wooden legs, its one great eye dead and unblinking until it was time for the test pattern to appear. "It's a tele," Sandy said, with little boy pride and a well developed sense of stating the obvious. "Ninety-seven pounds, fifteen and sixpence, and worth every penny they tell me." Gwen smiled at her grandson. "It's sort of your Christmas present dear. I mean, I know you're away and all but, I expect most of the boys have got one, haven't they?" Luke nodded, not sure what to say, or how to thank them. Sandy looked uncomfortable. "Well, actually, we have used it lad. I watched the Olympics from Tokyo. That Peter Snell did us proud with his medals. I never thought I'd see something like that, all the way from Japan. It's a bloody scientific miracle, that's what it is." For Luke, who had never known a life without television, his grandfather's excitement was both amusing and endearing.

The television did bring about changes in their habits. For one thing, all of their fishing was now done in the mornings, for in the evenings the Tele would be on, and Sandy quickly became addicted, watching every moment from the start of transmission until the last strains of God Save the Queen faded after the epilogue and the crackling sounds of static took over the empty screen. Luke spent the summer break swimming and fishing when he wasn't with Hughie and his family. The Hanere family were noisy and outgoing, with everyone talking at once, and argu-ments abounded. Luke was drawn to the sense of familiarity, yet repelled by it at the same time. Music was a huge part of the family's life. The Maori, like all Polynesians, were blessed as a race with remarkable musical prowess, rich and lyrical voices and the ability to sing magnificent natural harmonies. Luke, with a voice just now breaking from boy to manhood, tried to follow the harmony with his frog voice, and delighted in just listening quietly to the five Haneres sing solely for the pleasure of it. Kiri and Hughie shared a record player, and Luke came to love The Beatles, Hughie's favorites who had visited the country in the middle of the year, already superstars before the USA had the chance to discover them. And there were the local artists, girl singers like Sandi Edmonds and Dinah Lee, whose records Luke would play for hours when Granny Moana would let him. The old woman would take Luke for walks with her, and she was so agile that he would have to run to keep up with her. As she walked, she gave Luke Maori language lessons, rapidly barking words at him, daring him to follow her. "Bird... *manu*; Tree... *rakau*; sky... *rangi*" she would chant.

"Rangi..same as the god in the story!" Luke would say excitedly, and she would smile, pleased with him.

"Water... *wai*; Lake... *roto*, ocean... *moana*..."

"Moana? You're called ocean?" Luke asked, chuckling.

"Twice I'm called ocean" Granny replied. "Marie, it's from the French, *mare*. That means ocean, too. Granny Ocean, eh, golden boy?" They laughed together then, and from that moment Luke called her Mrs O.

The new year at Lloyd's saw Luke and Hughie enter the second form. Now, two of their dorm members had left for a resident house in the grounds; and two new first formers, sniveling and pathetic in their first forays away from home, moved in. "Jesus!" Luke exclaimed, his accent just starting to pick up telltale signs of the New Zealand shortened vowel sounds. "Were we really that dumb and drippy?" he asked Hughie. "No way. We were pretty cool, Luke. These blokes are really wet." And the two friends surveyed the new boys, with their hair cut high above their ears, and their shorts big and baggy to allow for growth. It was athletics day time again, and this year Luke represented his school for the first time, bringing home the Inter Dominion School Sprinting trophy for the first time in the school's ninety year history. For Luke, the hardest part of winning was seeing where he was going, for he was growing his hair into a Beatles haircut, a long blond fringe in front and a soft fall into the nape of his neck. He kept his hair plastered back during school hours, so that the teachers would not notice its length, but once he left the starting blocks sprinting at full speed, it flung forward across his forehead and eyes and there was no disguising its length. He awaited with dread the order to "Get a haircut" which the Headmaster would periodically bark at boys during or after morning assembly, yet it never came.

On Luke's thirteenth birthday that August, Reuben Hayes sent him a package from America. It contained comic books, Babe Ruth and Hershey bars, twinkies, and a fabulous bright red new transistor radio, the latest in state-of-the-art technology. Barely bigger than a packet of cigarettes, it boasted a powerful speaker as well as a personal earphone. Luke would simply put the earphone into his ear and hide the radio under his pillow after lights out in the dorm. Then he would listen in the dark, the silence broken only by his occasionally humming out loud to the secret music.

"Mulgrave, you bastard, give it back." Luke spat the words angrily at the fifth-former's smug face and folded arms. The precious "tranny" had disappeared from its shrine in Luke's bedside locker and Mulgrave had not even bothered to conceal his presence as he left the dorm. Now he shrugged and smiled lopsidedly at Luke.

"Jeez, Powers, you're breaking my heart. I don't know what you're talking about. And even if I did, I couldn't give back something I've already sold, could I?" the overweight bully asked with mock naiveté. Luke found himself clenching his fists, yet for every inch he grew, and every pound of weight he gained, Mulgrave seemed to grow and gain two. Luke knew that Mulgrave would welcome an attack. Then he would be able to beat Luke legitimately in self defense. Luke had long ago decided that he would not be a martyr. Surviving at Lloyd's did not include having the crap beaten out of you for no useful purpose. Instead, he investigated further and found that Mulgrave had sold the transistor radio for five pounds, to Capshaw minor in form four, who in turn had sold it for a two pound profit to his brother Capshaw major in sixth form.

"What's the point in creating a stink?" Luke asked Hughie. "Much easier if I just ask Reuben to send another one." "Good idea" Hughie agreed. "Get him to send half a dozen eh? I reckon you could get ten quid a piece for them if you cornered the market." Hughie made the comment half in jest, but the seed was planted, and from it grew Luke Powers's first import business. Soon Reuben was sending parcels every month; "trannies", American comic books and candy bars, as well as the latest records, were all scarce and precious commodities in New Zealand. By the end of the year, Luke's Stateside Auction – the first Friday of every month – was an open secret amongst both pupils and staff, and an eagerly anticipated event on the Lloyd's College engagement calendar. Luke would stand on his tuck box with his hand printed catalogue, every item numbered. He would theatrically build the tension, the anticipation, teasing the bidders with wide-eyed expressions of excitement as he scanned the latest editions of Superman and Spiderman that would not reach New Zealand by normal channels for a year or more, bumping up the price by stoking demand. In a very few months, Luke had real money, more than fifty pounds, that he could spend in any way he pleased. In addition to Hughie, his best friend and accountant, he had a 'staff' of three junior boys who sycophantically followed him everywhere, waiting to do his bidding. At the weekends he would treat all five of them to the pictures – together they saw Elvis in "Kissin' Cousins" three times – and then the group would go to the fish and chip cafe and gorge themselves. And there was Brenda!

She was nearly seventeen, big breasted and broad hipped. She had been to see the Beatles live, and rumor had it she had even crashed the hotel and almost touched George Harrison as he was getting into the lift. She wore tight mini-skirts, in the new fashion, and high-heeled boots, even when she was waiting on tables. Her v-neck jumpers were always low enough for Luke to catch a glimpse of her melon-like breasts as she bent to put the plates of fish and chips before him and his friends. And she would look at Luke from beneath her eyelashes and lick her lips. It was a standing joke that she fancied Luke. Indeed, she had heard of Luke's undeserved reputation as a Yankee sex machine. If she had heard that Luke was still only thirteen and a half, she never said.

"Have you done her yet?" one of his staff members asked mischievously one Saturday evening after Brenda had taken their order. Luke merely smiled enigmatically, trying hard not to betray the dryness in his throat. "You lucky bugger. What's it really like to go all the way?" his friend asked, taking his silence as confirmation. Luke merely shrugged and smiled, and dipped a chip into his tomato sauce before dropping it into his open mouth.

"Stick your tongue in my ear," Brenda demanded, as Luke fumbled to undo the three hook clasp at the back of her bra. He could not imagine what sensation his tongue could produce in an ear, but he dutifully followed orders, sliding his tongue probingly into her ear. She groaned, and reached up and unhooked the bra, freeing her breasts first to his hands, and then to his open grateful mouth. The fact that they were behind a bus shelter, hidden from the road only by a couple of bushes, only added to the adrenalin rush. She parted her legs, even as she reached for the zipper on his fly.

"Put your fingers in me," she demanded urgently into his ear. "Make me come." He didn't hesitate for fear that she would change her mind. He slid his hand clumsily under her skirt, past the top of her stockings and the suspenders, and found the wet crotch of her cotton knickers. His fingers encountered the bristling pubic hair as he found his way around the edge of the leg at the same moment as she undid his zip, reached inside his Y-front underpants and squeezed his already rock hard prick in her fist, taking it out into the chill night air. He slipped one finger inside of her, afraid that he would pass out through a combination of anxiety at being discovered and ecstasy at being in her hand. He was astounded by how warm and wet she was, and he inserted another finger, then started moving them in and out of her, as much as her knickers would allow. He moved faster then, his hand battering against her as his fingers attacked and withdrew, his mouth crushed on hers, teeth clashing, tongues exploring, until he exploded in her hand, crying out into her open mouth, as she started to rub herself against the ball of his hand frenetically. And then, "Have you got a hankie?" she asked pragmatically. "This spunk dries all crusty." The romance died instantly, but not the desire. From that moment until the end of the year he would meet her every Saturday night. He would "feel her up" and finger-fuck her, while she jerked him off. It was safe, she would assure him. Nice girls didn't go all the way. He believed her. He had no reason not to. This wasn't quite what the movies or the novels had promised, but it was sex. And it was the only sex he knew anything about. That is, until he met Michelle Caldicott, and discovered ways of using the human body in ways he had never even dreamt of.

CHAPTER THREE

Y OUR GRAMMAR IS correct, Powers, but your accent is a disaster. You Americans have a way of mutilating vowel sounds which is even more distasteful than that of your Antipodean cousins." The words were spoken in the clipped British tones of Evan Caldicott, the new French master to the junior school.

It was the welcome back assembly for the second term of Luke's third year that introduced Caldicott and his French wife to Lloyd's. The restless mumblings of the boys turned to silent awe as the new master, gangling, long faced and out of proportion, like a Modigliani painting, took the platform with his wife. The woman who accompanied him was slim and long-legged, with warm chestnut hair. Instead of the current backcombed style, the lacquered beehive, she wore her hair loosely so that it swayed and caressed her shoulder blades as she walked. The face, heart shaped with a mouth full and seductive, needed little make-up. Her gaze, through deep blue eyes, was steady and inviting. She was something, and she knew it. What Luke, and four hundred other boys, wanted to know was, what the hell was she doing in a place like Lloyd's?

Caldicott decided, quite early in the term, that several of the boys needed private tuition in French, particularly on their accents. Mrs Caldicott, he told them, had not had a chance yet to make friends, and so the tutoring would give her an interest. Luke was designated Wednesday afternoons, between two o'clock and three, a time that was normally a free period. He did not complain. Spending an hour with a beautiful French woman was no hardship.

Evan Caldicott was a junior housemaster, and he and Michelle occupied a small one bedroom cottage attached to one of the large residential houses in the school's grounds. It was here that Luke duly reported on the second Wednesday of the term.

Michelle, greeted him at the door. He was conscious first, not of how she looked, but of how she smelled. It was a heady, rich and sensual perfume which he later discovered was called "Je Reviens". Luke's translation of that was, "I will come again", and he had no idea how prophetic the name was.

For the first two weeks, Luke truly believed his imagination was racing away with his senses. Every move she made, every word she spoke, seemed loaded with implicit sexuality. He would sit on the upright mahogany chair at the round dining table, willing his straining erection to subside, for he was terrified that she would see and that he would find himself in front of the Headmaster for insulting a master's wife. Yet, could he be imagining the brush of her leg against his, the light tapping of her painted fingernails on the back of his hand, the warm breath from her mouth against his ear when she got up from the table and asked if he would like some cookies and a warm drink? At night he would lie in bed, his "tranny" earphone in his ear, and listen to the broadcasts from Radio Hauraki, a pirate radio station which used a boat outside of New Zealand waters as its transmission station. He would wait expectantly for The Beatles record of Michelle, and fantasized about the Frenchmaster's wife naked while he slowly masturbated, not wanting the sensation to ever end.

In the third week of private tuition, after Mrs Caldicott had tantalized him by demonstrating at close range the correct tongue position for certain consonant sounds, Luke found himself alone at the table, an aching pulsating erection screaming for freedom from its prison. It seemed to him that he spent most of his days now with a permanent hard-on. There were rumors that the school put something into the food to stop the boys from being constantly sexually aroused. Luke didn't believe it but, if it were true, then it certainly wasn't working. Michelle Caldicott returned to the room.

"*Bien, Luke, mon petit chat d'or. Maintenant, une nouvelle leçon. Tournez votre chaise, s'il vous plait.*" Her voice was soft, throaty, but commanding, and he turned his upright chair around to face her, yet he could not look her directly in the eyes, for he knew that she would see instantly his aroused condition. Instead, he concentrated on her mouth, the full lips parted slightly, the edge of her square white teeth just visible, the tip of the tongue, peeping out as if watching him. He saw the edges of her lips curl upwards, the smile betraying satisfaction at having her suspicions confirmed.

"Now Luke," she said in English, "We have a lesson much more interesting. Please, *defaites votre pantalon.* Unzip, yes?" Still he did not look up. He could see his own hand trembling as he followed the command. "Now, take out *votre petit oiseau.* Let me see it." He reached inside his Y fronts and brought out his rock hard penis. This was no different, he told himself, to what he had been doing with Brenda for months, but he knew it was a lie. Shit! This was in school hours, with the French master's wife, and it was all so crazy that he must be dreaming and he'd wake up in the middle of a wet dream any minute now. Only, he prayed silently, if it isn't a dream, please God don't let me come now and look like a stupid kid. Please, I'll never ask you for anything again. Luke saw her smile again, and she ran the pink pointed end of her tongue across her lips.

"*Bon,*" she said quietly. "*Très gros, très ferme.* Now Luke, let us see how well you learn." She slid her skirt up over her creamy thighs to her hips. Luke gasped as he saw she was wearing nothing underneath.

"You will stay very still, and try not to come until I tell you. But if you cannot wait, do not fret. We 'ave plenty of time," she reassured him. Then she put one leg either side of him, straddling the chair, and lowered herself onto him. He felt himself slide into her until he hit what he was convinced must be her heart. She pulled her sweater over her head and her unbridled breasts, small with thimble-like hard nipples, brushed his mouth and he sucked on them gratefully, groaning as he realized he had already come inside her. She reassured him, whispering in his ear, coaxing him with her fingers, her tongue against the roof of his mouth, and soon he was hard for her again. This time she moved on him, riding a horse that was yet to be broken, taming him, slowing him to her stride. Three times in less than an hour she had him, until he felt his brain turn to mush and he was no longer capable of remembering his own name.

On the first lesson following his fourteenth birthday, Michelle took him into the small cottage bedroom and undressed him. "Today, we explore the verbs to eat... *manger, dévorer, sucer, consommer, ronger...*" as she spoke she slid to her knees and took him into her mouth in a way that made him afraid he would lose consciousness.

And so, the education of Luke Powers took a giant step in that year of 1966, and Michelle constantly astounded the eager-to-learn youth with new ways of pleasuring both of them. It was a year when the Maori king, King Koroki, died, two members of the British royal family visited New Zealand, and the country geared itself for the change to decimal currency, yet all of that was somehow forgotten to the boy; for him, it was the year of Michelle Caldicott. Looking back, forty years later, Luke could say that of all the teachers at Lloyd's that had shaped him as a man, Michelle's tutoring was perhaps the most important.

Luke was blind to the reality of the liaison's future. He wanted only to be loved, and so he convinced himself Michelle loved him. Yet the day came, as it inevitably had to, when Evan Caldicott, during a French class, delivered the death knell.

"Excellent, Powers. *Votre accent est maintenant excellent,*" the master said with a pleased smile. *"Les travaux pratiques ne sont pas nécessaires."* Luke wasn't certain he had understood. Was Caldicott saying that he didn't need tutoring any longer? It couldn't be possible. He waited until later in the day, when he knew that Caldicott was on dining hall duty for Michelle rarely ate with the students and staff, and then he went to the cottage. He had expected her to be surprised, to be outraged by her husband's decision, but she merely looked at him. "Luke, you did not think this could go on forever?" she asked with surprise. Luke tried to clear his head, to answer articulately, but he knew the answer would make no sense, for part of him had expected it to go on forever. He begged and pleaded, even though he despised himself for doing so, and she laughed.

It was not a cruel laugh, but rather an amused one, much like a young mother might make at the antics of a child. "Luke, you are so sweet, but such a baby. Look at you now... I want it... give me, give me... it is a tantrum, yes? You are such a child." She put a hand to his cheek, seeing no incongruity in making the remark to a youth who now towered above her with the strong jaw of a man. He snatched the hand away angrily, gripping her wrist tight enough to see her grimace in pain.

"Was I a child when I was inside you with your legs around my neck? Was I a child in the shower when we fucked so hard the tap fell off? Was I a child when I made you come so hard you screamed? You're a bitch Michelle. A bloody bitch and you used me." She looked sad for a moment, then gestured helplessly.

"C'est vrai, mon cheri. C'est la vie." And it was over.

He wanted to cry as he made his way back to the school, but he couldn't. He was angry and wanted to hurt her, but he didn't know how. He thought of Brenda, and how he had stopped going to the fish and chip cafe once he had started his sexual journey with Michelle. He had dumped her, and now he was being dumped. Was this retribution or, as Michelle had dismissed it, just "life"? He would not have believed then that one day he would look back on the whole episode with gratitude and affection. He did not consider then how much she had given him, but only what he had given her and she had ultimately rejected. His family had rejected his love by dying; his grandparents had rejected his love by not being able to express any in return; now Michelle was rejecting his love because he was a child and she was bored.

He found Caldicott, in the half hour recess between lunch and the afternoon classes, in the duty master's study. He did not wait for his hurt and anger to abate. He wasn't even conscious of throwing caution to the wind or what the consequences might be of such a confession. He simply knocked and entered upon the master's command. "Yes Powers, what is it?" Caldicott asked impatiently, as Luke shut the door behind him. "Please sir, if you have a minute, sir, I have something to tell you." Luke drew a breath, conscious of the slight frown on Caldicott's forehead. "The fact is, sir, your wife and I... well, we haven't been having French lessons, not the usual type anyhow. The fact is... " "Stop right there, Powers" the master commanded, but the words were already falling from Luke's mouth. "We've been having sex every Wednesday... sir!" Luke could hear the sound of his own breathing, like a gasping trout landed on the bank of the lake. In the split second of silence that followed, it occurred to Luke that he was hurting Caldicott, and maybe himself more than he was hurting Michelle, but he didn't care. He waited for Caldicott's wrath, but it did not come in the way he expected. The master rose from his chair and slowly and menacingly walked towards the youth. His eyes narrowed and his mouth twisted at one corner.

"You stupid little bastard" he hissed angrily. "You come to me like a sniveling little mouse after what she has given to you! What do you take me for? Do you seriously think I could be cuckolded by someone like you?" His face was pushed against Luke's now and Luke could smell a mixture of tobacco and peppermint on the French master's breath and see the tiny purple vein on the left side of his cheek, the hairs in his nostrils, the slight bloodshot roadmap effect in his right eye. In the moment it took him to assimilate what he was seeing, he also saw clearly, and with shock, that Caldicott knew of his wife's affair with a student. In fact, Luke realized as he remembered Caldicott's original criticism of his accent, there was every chance that the master had set him up for the affair. As if reading his thoughts, Caldicott grabbed him by his school tie, pulling it tight into a chokehold around his throat. "You will tell no-one, do you understand?" Caldicott ordered. "If you do, you will not be believed... but, I promise you, you will be expelled. You had a reputation, Powers... you did not live up to it. Michelle did not get the experienced young ram I promised her, but rather a bleating kid. She had to teach you, and you learned well. But the lesson is over. Move on boy, and be grateful. Make trouble, and you are finished. Am I making myself clear?" They stood like statues for a split second, eyeball to eyeball, the youth's throat still at the mercy of the necktie noose held by the teacher. Luke was both angry and afraid, but he betrayed neither. He looked coolly into the master's face, and did not speak until he was certain his voice would reveal nothing. And then, "Perfectly clear, Sir. Can I go now?" He sounded jaded but confident, as though slightly bored by the whole affair. Caldicott looked at him for a moment in surprise, then released his tie. "Yes, Powers... you can go."

Luke had no memory of leaving the room, of climbing the staircase, of throwing himself on his bed, of the hours he spent silently staring at a pulled thread in the blue damask counterpane. Hughie found him there some hours later, but Luke refused to say what had happened. Later he would wonder why he had never told Hughie about the affair with Michelle, even though he suspected that his friend knew. It was as if there were a tacit agreement between them not to talk about something that was so forbidden.

For months afterwards he endured Caldicott's sideward glare as he passed Luke's desk. He was powerless to move his thoughts away from Michelle. He could close his eyes and feel the soft brush of her inner thighs against his cheeks; the twining of her fingers in his hair; the heavy, rich smell of her, and the bittersweet taste of her on his tongue. Sometimes he would have to excuse himself from the class. He would just make it to the lavatory before throwing up, praying that he could disgorge his emotions along with the school lunch. He got good marks in French, but he was never certain if it was because of his ability, or a concession on Caldicott's part, a bribe for not disclosing the truth. The sudden withdrawal of the overwhelming intensity to which he had become accustomed during those afternoons with Michelle produced a yearning in Luke that was unbearable. He knew that the pain would end eventually, but when?

"For Chrissakes... it's simple!" Luke said with exasperation. "You got two hundred and forty pennies in a pound... a hundred and twenty in ten bob, okay?" The fourth-former surveyed the faces before him, some blank, some grudgingly admiring, some clearly pissed off with him. "Now... a dollar is the same as ten shillings... two bucks the same as an old pound... only one hundred cents — instead of pennies — to the dollar." He looked at them with disbelief. His problem had always been transferring dollars and cents into pounds, shillings and pence. It seemed so much simpler to him to go the other way. What the hell was everyone finding so difficult?

It was July of 1967 and Luke was midway through his fourth year at Lloyd's. Approaching his fifteenth birthday, Luke Powers had made a name for himself around the school. He resisted all orders to cut his hair; he was openly outspoken against the Vietnam war at a time when most of the students had no inkling of what was going on, and he had a thriving business within the hallowed cloisters of Lloyd's College. Every boy at the school knew that, whatever he wanted, he had only to ask Luke. With sufficient money, everything was up for grabs: American records, magazines, cigarettes, candy, genuine Levi jeans and an endless list of other paraphernalia that teenage boys in the highly disciplined boarding school were convinced they could not live without. New Zealand was switching to decimal currency, but to most of the boys, dollars didn't make much sense. Sure, they'd heard dollars talked about in US movies and on television, but it wasn't *real* money, not to them. The *New Zealand Weekly News* included a Rite-Change Computer: two circular pieces of paper that people would glue onto two pieces of cardboard that, by turning one circle over the other and reading what appeared in the little boxes, allowed the user to calculate from one currency to the other, ensuring that he or she got the right change.

For Luke, now sharing a room with Hughie in Pitt House, all of the houses being named after British Prime Ministers, the Stateside Auction took on a new dimension with the advent of decimal currency. Here, he was in his element. He didn't bother trying to figure out the difference between the American dollar and the New Zealand dollar. What the hell, a dollar was a dollar, and Luke would call the bids so fast that the boys would never have a chance to transfer the money back into pounds in their minds. Over the previous two years, the auctions had grown in size and importance. Reuben had questioned the size of the orders in letters to Luke. "What in God's name does any boy want with six copies of a Beach Boys album?" he wrote in one letter, though it seemed to Luke that Reuben already suspected there was something more to the requests. Luke had explained the truth then, and offered to send money for each order, but Reuben had phoned him to tell him not to bother, just to make sure he kept tabs on it all. It seemed to Luke inconceivable that the headmaster, or his housemaster, Mister Forrester, didn't know what was going on, although for all of the year the auctions had been held in the rugby clubhouse, with the goods being stored in sports lockers. Yet

Luke had never been 'sprung' even though he regularly expected it. The closest he came is when he refused Mulgrave credit, and the lumbering youth had threatened to expose him. Mulgrave had never let up on Luke, and Luke was aware that sooner or later there would have to be a moment of reckoning. Still, Luke preferred to pick the time, rather than have it imposed upon him, and he wanted it to be later, rather than sooner. Mulgrave was now in the upper sixth form and due to move on at the end of the year. Hughie was taking book on when the showdown would be, and who would win. Mulgrave was three years older, but Luke was now equally as tall as the bully, and far fitter – the years of athletics and playing rugby for the school had made sure of this. His peers admired him as "a good bloke" and girls would look at him longingly and compare him, giggling behind their palms, to Robert Redford, heartthrob of the moment. Sometimes, when he crossed the quadrangle or was out on the sports field, he would see Michelle Caldicott watching him from a distance. He didn't remember ever speaking to her again after that afternoon in the cottage, but he was surprised to find, after the months since their last encounter, that he no longer felt angry, nor did he yearn for her in the same way. There were other distractions; his business, and the freedom that he and Hughie enjoyed now that they were fourth-formers; a new set of masters to "break in", and a whole school of junior boys who looked up to him in a way that was usually reserved for the upper sixth prefects. Luke was already an entrepreneur in a country, let alone a school, where the word, and its personification, were something of a rarity.

"You're on a power trip, Luke. I don't like it!" Hughie said to him one day, when Luke disclosed the astonishing fact that his bank balance was nearing the one thousand dollar mark.

"Gee, clever pun Hughie. Did it take you three years to come up with that one?" Luke asked sarcastically, baulking at his friend's criticism.

"Took me as long as it took you to become a bullshit artist," Hughie replied, with a frown of consternation. "You've got them eating out of your hand. You're making money out of school chums. What the hell do you call that?" Luke was surprised to see his friend so confrontational.

"I call it business. That's all… business." Luke defended himself.

"Then maybe I'll never be a businessman," Hughie answered philosophically.

"Look Hughie. You know the story. My old folks are great, but five bloody shillings a week. Even you get more than that."

"Even me?" Hughie said, bridling at the perceived putdown.

"I didn't mean anything by that, you know it. I like it that they have to come to me for something. It makes me feel... well, sometimes I kid myself that I belong." Luke turned away, not wanting to confront the truth.

"Shit, man, you do belong. Look at you," Hughie said, but he realized for the first time since their first term together that, despite his best efforts, Luke was still an outsider. He didn't really belong, and he never would, no matter how hard he tried. He had no family – that was different; he spoke with a Yankee accent, even though it now had Kiwi overtones – that was different too; he experienced mood swings – sometimes up and manic and full of life – other times deep and brooding, lost in some private hell none of them could understand. And he had been places, seen things, come from what was arguably the greatest country in the world; he knew what film stars looked like *in the flesh* – all of that was different. Even the fact that he was a great athlete, a bright student and a quick thinker, set him apart in a place where high achievement was something for the other boys to strive for. Almost every boy at Lloyd's College wanted to go un-noticed, wanted to be exactly the same as every other boy, and so Luke, who would never be the same, was destined to stand out. And, for Luke, being different meant never belonging.

It was three weeks before the end of the school year that Luke finally called Mulgrave's debt. He had been taunted for weeks by Hughie that time was running out and Mulgrave would soon be gone. Luke had no intention of allowing the bully to walk away after four years. There were scores to be settled, debts to be paid, not least of which was the hundred and eighty dollars that Mulgrave had run up on a bill to Luke during the auctions.

"Seven days will be just fine." Luke told his adversary as he handed him the bill. "Of course, this has been mounting for months now, and I wouldn't want to have to let it be known round college that you welsh on your debts. Your father wouldn't be impressed." He kept a straight face, but wondered if the amusement showed in his eyes as Mulgrave sputtered with indignation, his face moving through various shades of pink to crimson in the process.

"What the fuck is this Powers? I'm not paying anything." Mulgrave blustered. "You can't prove anything." Luke regarded the bully with disgust. Already the man was evident, a cheat, a bully and a braggart with an appetite for excess and a reluctance to pay his way. Mulgrave would walk over many people in his life, Luke was certain of that, but he refused any longer to be one of them.

"You owe the money Mulgrave, and you're going to pay it, or I'm going to send these to your father, and maybe even show them to the headmaster. I'll go down with you, but it'll be worth it." He held up a small sheaf of papers, bills made out to Mulgrave, all itemized, with Mulgrave's signature acknowledging the amounts. The heavy set youth looked at them in disbelief.

"I never signed those. What sort of bullshit is this?" he asked, fuming.

"Sure looks like your signature to me… what do you think Hughie," Luke asked his friend. Hughie peered closely at the papers.

"Yeah… that's right, I remember him signing those." Hughie said, and John Bowers, a third former who idolized Luke, piped up, "I was there too. You signed the IOUs Mulgrave, now cough up the money." But the smaller boy lost courage almost as soon as he spoke and swiftly moved to a safer position behind Hughie and Luke.

The crowd of boys was growing, until the hallway between the two science laboratories was crowded. There were those who were interested but impartial. They had little time for Mulgrave and his overbearing ways, but at least he was one of them. There was grudging admiration for Luke, but he wasn't their kind… once a Yank always a Yank. Then there were the supporters of both, gathering like flocks of sheep behind their two leaders.

"You forged my bloody signature… you bloody septic tank lying bastard." Mulgrave spluttered in fury.

"Prove it," Luke said, remembering the long hours he and Hughie had spent copying the signature until it was perfect. "Are you denying you owe me this money? What about the records, the penthouse magazines, the Camels? You want everyone to believe I *gave* them to you because we're such good buddies? Bullshit, Mulgrave. Now give me the money or I'll nail you to the wall." Mulgrave tried to snatch the IOUs from Luke's grasp, but he wasn't fast enough. Luke passed the papers to Hughie as Mulgrave launched himself at the American. It had been more than three years since their last fight, and now the scales were more evenly balanced. For Luke, it was a moment he had anticipated every time Mulgrave had shoved him around, or tried to belittle him. He had not been prepared to fight until he knew he could win. It was to be a philosophy he would keep for the rest of his life. If you can't win, walk away with dignity, and wait for the moment. It always comes. This was his moment.

The blow that knocked Mulgrave off his feet and onto his back was a vicious left hook to the jaw. Overweight and under-conditioned, Mulgrave looked at Luke in disbelief. But then he scrambled to his feet and charged, head-butting Luke in the stomach. Caught by the sheer force of the elephant-like Mulgrave, Luke was pushed backwards into the science lab. The crowd followed, and soon the roar of more than fifty students smothered the sounds of smashing test tubes and other paraphernalia as it crashed to the floor. No-one took note of how long the fight lasted, although it seemed interminable. Certainly it was long enough for some enterprising fifth formers to open a book and take bets on the outcome; and it was long enough to cause hundreds of dollars worth of damage within the laboratory. More importantly, it was long enough for Luke to wear the heavier boy down, to split his lip, loosen four teeth, and black both his eyes, as well as receiving two cracked ribs himself. By the time the Deputy Headmaster broke up the fight there was a clear victor, and those who had put both their faith and their pocket money in a Luke Powers victory were cheering loudly.

It was Luke who offered his enemy his hand to help him to his feet. Luke refused to give an explanation to the Deputy Headmaster. His only explanation was that the fight was a "matter of honor." Grudgingly, Mulgrave agreed. Both boys were given a week's detention, and were grounded for the rest of the term, but at the end of the week Mulgrave shoved an envelope in Hughie's hand and said "Give this to the Yank."

Inside was a hundred and eighty dollars. Mulgrave never spoke to Luke, or even acknowledged his existence, again.

The fight was the talk of the school for weeks, until the news that one of the fifth form boys had gotten a St Margaret's girl pregnant took over. Yet, for Luke, the biggest revelation was yet to come.

It came late in the evening, after prep, when Luke went to the bathroom near the prep room. The two seniors smoking in a cubicle did not see him, nor he them, but he overheard the conversation.

"Mulgrave's a pig... always has been. He should have paid up."

"I'm not saying that. I'm just saying Yanks are all the same where money's concerned. They'd sell their grandmothers. Powers doesn't need the money."

"So you say... I don't believe that crap."

"I'm telling you, it's true. Dad's partner's sister is married to a Yank. They live in Chicago."

"So? Chicago's got more people than the whole of New Zealand, twit!"

"He knows this Reuben Hayes bloke that Powers gets all the parcels from. Powers's folks left oodles of money. He's a bloody millionaire or something."

"No way."

"How much do you want to bet?"

Luke closed the door, and made his way to the bathroom on the opposite corner of the landing. He was trying to make sense of what he had heard. It was as if some door had been unlocked in his mind. It was a door he himself had shut in the first place, for the only way of dealing with his pain was to lock away every memory of what he had lost. Yet now, it seemed to him crazy that he had never questioned anything. He had lived a life of luxury; his father had taken them all to Europe; he had always been given everything he wanted in Chicago. How was it possible that he was now so poor? What had happened to his father's business? And, if he was reliant solely on his grandparents and the five shilling a week allowance, which had now been increased to a dollar, what was he doing at what he now knew to be the most expensive boy's school in the country?

He felt angry and confused, not knowing whether his life for the past four years had been a lie. As a fifth former, he could use the telephone with permission, and he immediately asked his housemaster if he could make a call. Yet, as he heard his grandmother's voice on the other end of the phone, full of concern for his wellbeing, wondering why he had made the call, he knew he could not confront them this way. He would have to wait until he could see them face to face.

The Christmas holidays were what kept the students going through the long sunny November days, when the sunlight beckoned from outside the classroom windows. Hughie and Luke packed with a sense of anticipation. For Hughie, it would be a very different Christmas, for his parents and Kiri had moved to Wellington early in the year, where Hughie's father had got a new job working for the railways on the huge roll-on-roll-off car and passenger ferries that linked the North and South Islands across Cook Strait. It would be the first Christmas the two had spent apart since they had met in the dormitory at the start of first form. Luke went to the station with Hughie and saw him onto the train to Wellington, both of them wanting to hug each other, but afraid of such a public display of affection. Hugging amongst fifteen year old boys was confined to the football field. Luke watched the train pull out, and felt a stab of loneliness. Hughie was the brother he had never had, the family he had lost. He turned and left the station, wishing that he could have stopped the train, climbed aboard, pleaded with Hughie to take him along, to keep him safe within the family. He sighed. He just had time to get back to college before Grandpa Sandy and Gran would be there to pick him up.

"WHY DIDN'T YOU tell me? You let me go for years thinking I was the poorest kid in the whole school. Now this!" Luke shouted accusingly at his grandparents, refusing to look at their shocked and hurt expressions.

He had intended to pick the moment when he confronted them... to ease into it slowly, knowing that there must be a logical explanation, even if what he suspected were true. The drive home had been uneventful, and his grandmother had cooked baby lamb chops with mint sauce, his favorite dinner. Luke had hedged, trying to bring up the subject in a roundabout way by talking about the change to decimal currency and the way things seemed to be costing more because of the price hikes to even out the shillings and pence. But it was his grandfather's terse order to "shut off the bathroom light when you're through lad… money doesn't grow on trees you know" that caused Luke to challenge the old man and, before he had a chance to check himself, he had blurted out all his fears and questions regarding his father's estate, acutely aware that it sounded as though he was accusing them somehow of cheating him.

It was Grandpa Sandy who, after initial indignation, sat him down and told him of the trust account and his father's fortune, and Reuben and Wayne's involvement as trustees. It seemed to Luke that his grandfather had the facts and figures too readily at his fingertips, as though he had anticipated the moment at hand for a long time. Luke only half heard what his grandfather was saying, for none of the details did anything to assuage his anger at being deceived. He was rich, and yet he had been made to feel poor.

"It's a lot of money, Luke," Sandy concluded, "and your Dad was a sensible man in thinking you needed maturity in handling it. You'll get a legacy at twenty-one, and that'll give you time to test your mettle till the rest of it comes into your hands. Meanwhile, there's professionals looking after things. Things neither you nor me know the first thing about. And all your bills are paid. But your Grandma and me… we don't profit from you in any way. I'm disappointed that you'd think otherwise." He looked deep into his grandson's eyes, allowing the full import of the words to sink in. Luke felt a sense of shame. He could see his grandmother's distress as she sat wringing her hands at the table, not wanting to look at either of them.

"I didn't think that… honestly. I just… I don't know exactly. Why couldn't you have told me? Why couldn't you have asked Uncle Reuben for a bit more, so I could have had… " He broke off as Sandy gave a cynical laugh.

"'So I could have had' – that's the point, don't you see? We knew it would be hard enough for you as it was, a Yank with a school full of Kiwis. Would you rather we'd set you further apart by making it known you were a rich Yank? You know by now how people think. If you'd started chucking money around, had more to spend than the rest of them, do you think your schooling would have been any easier?" he asked, confronting Luke. Luke thought about his friendship with Hughie, and the way he had fought to gain acceptance despite his apparent lack. Maybe it would have been easier for him to buy acceptance, but at what price? Those who liked him, who had made him part of their circle, had done so in spite of his having no money and little to offer in return.

"No, I guess not," he conceded quietly. "I guess I'm just being selfish. There were things I wanted..."

"We never let you go without anything you needed, boy." Sandy explained. "But that's not the same as wanting. You have to work for what you want in this life." The words sounded trite and old-fashioned, yet Luke knew instinctively that they were true. "The mark of a man is not what he has, but what he is, inside. You'll be a good man, Luke. You'll have money in times to come, but that won't alter you, because you already know what's inside, and that's what counts." Grandpa Sandy took out his handkerchief and blew his nose hard. Luke was certain that the old man was overcome with emotion, even though Sandy gruffly berated the "bloody hayfever" that caused his eyes to water and his nose to run.

Luke fished, sunbathed, swam and watched television for most of the holidays. For the first time he couldn't wait to get back to college. The weeks without Hughie went slowly and even though he wrote two letters to his friend, and rang on Christmas day to say Happy Christmas to the whole family in Wellington, he wanted to be in that room that he and Hughie called home in Pitt House when he told his best friend his secret.

The two boys jumped around with glee behind closed doors when they returned to Lloyd's for the new year. Hughie was several months older than Luke, but now it seemed that he was the younger of the two, full of excitement like a child as he regaled Luke with stories of his holiday in the nation's capital.

"Dad took us on the ferry over to Lyttelton in the South Island. You should have been there. The *Wahine* – that's what she's called – she's a bloody huge steamer with like, massive doors, and the cars just all get loaded on, one behind the other. Then you just go upstairs, and there's a place you can buy tea and food and stuff. It was fantastic. You've gotta come next holidays," Hughie exploded, and Luke grinned.

"Sounds pretty cool," he admitted.

"Cool?" Hughie replied "It's positively icey! What did you do in the holidays?"

"Nothing much," Luke said nonchalantly. "I swam… went to the pictures… found out I'm stinking rich and heir to a fortune… watched the tele… read a couple of books"

"You what?!" Hughie shrieked in amazement, and for the next two hours the two friends lay on their beds and talked about what they would do if they ever had a fortune, not knowing quite how big a fortune was anyway.

For Luke, life was simpler with Mulgrave gone, and the work seemed to get easier for him, rather than harder, which was the general complaint. He could see an end in sight. If he could make the grades for the next two years, he could go straight to university without spending that extra year in the upper sixth form. He knew there were options open to him, depending on his grades for the next two years. He could go into law, like John Bowers's father, a prominent attorney, or maybe become a doctor – he knew his grandparents would like that. Yet over and above everything else was the realization that he was Joe Powers's son. Joe had been a businessman, a manufacturer, a self-made man. And Luke knew in some deep part of himself that he would always be Joe Powers's son: he too would make his own way. Besides, he had already witnessed the laws of supply and demand in action with the Stateside Auctions and had proven he knew how to tap a market. And he now knew there was Powers Industries and Chicago waiting for him. At least now there was a future, and he could see a real reason to push on.

IT WAS DURING what would turn out to be his final year at Lloyd's, on April 10th, that the morning radio news bulletin told of the heavy storms in Wellington. The announcement came that the ferry *Wahine* had hit a reef and was on her side and taking water, no more than four hundred meters away from the shore. There was no sense of apprehension from Hughie. Hell, his dad could swim that easily if needs be, and in any case, the *Wahine* had plenty of lifeboats. It wasn't until lunchtime that the alarm was raised. There were people in the water, and some of the rubber life rafts were blowing onto the opposite coast, rocky and deserted. By the time a senior master whispered to Hughie at three-thirty, after the last class for the day, that the headmaster wanted to see the Maori boy in his study, both Hughie and Luke were nervously expectant.

"It's okay, hoa," Luke reassured him, using the Maori word for pal. "They probably just want you to know that everything's okay." But Hughie looked at him with sad, scared eyes, and they both knew that it wasn't okay. Fifty-one people died that day, drowned in the fierce seas caused by the storm. Howard Hanere, a decent bloke, a good father, was one of them. His name wasn't even mentioned on the news, yet his death left a void in the lives of those who had known him. For Hughie, who shook his head and refused to believe at first what the headmaster was saying, it was only the first of many changes to come. He left the head's office after refusing the offer to see the nurse who would 'Give him something to make him feel better.' What could anyone give him that would compensate for the loss of his father. He knew that he should phone his mother, and Kiri, for their loss was just as great. He knew that Granny Moana-Marie would be mourning the death of her son, and that her pain was probably greater than his, but he felt somehow indifferent to their grief. For a little while at least, he needed someone who could understand, who could take some of his pain. He needed Luke.

He found his best friend in their room, waiting expectantly, knowing the worst without having to be told. Hughie was dry-eyed at first.

"I have to go to Wellington... Mum... there are arrangements, the funeral..." He could not go on. Luke gripped his shoulders.

"I'll get a pass. I'll come with you. I'll take care of things." And both of them knew that Luke was not simply uttering empty platitudes. He would take care of things as he promised. Hughie started to cry then, softly at first, then great howling, gulping sobs. Luke held his friend in his arms, strong arms that would hold Hughie up for as long as was necessary. It was a moment of perfect friendship, when brotherly love overcame all obstacles. It was the moment when both youths realized that friendship could expand into a love that was pure and that there was no shame in exposing weakness to a friend. But, over and above all of that, though neither one of them would see it at the time, it was the day Luke Powers grew up; the day the boy became a man.

CHAPTER FOUR

I T WAS THE end of this final year of his schooling that would witness Luke's first encounter with Rick Dellich. Though the particulars of the race would be long-forgotten by both when came the time their paths next crossed, something inside of each recognized the weight of that meeting, on some level.

Luke was blessed with a natural athletic ability, but had always avoided being drafted to represent the school. But this was his last chance, and he allowed himself to be talked into it. Through each of the heats he was conscious of being watched by the other competitors, and most especially by their coaches, wondering to themselves, Who was he? Why had they never seen him before?

As the first division, champion of champions, one hundred meters hurdles race drew nearer, Luke sensed ultimate victory within his grasp. Already that day, he had proven himself in the one hundred and two hundred meters races, taking first place in both. Were he to win his final race of the day, there would be no doubt as to the winning school at Mt Smart Stadium for the regional athletics championship.

His eyes met those of a boy who must have been his own age, but smaller, thinner. They each held the look; a look that said "something inside me knows you – knows that we are different to the others, that we don't fit in." Yet they never spoke.

Rick had seen the American race and knew what he was capable of. Everything about him spoke of success: his Lloyd's College tracksuit; his coach and other Lloyd's boys gathering around him; the likely months of preparation and training for this event. This racer was ready, thought Rick. He sat down for some final stretching, facing the spectator stands to see if he could spot his family's location.

He noticed the enthusiasm of his competitors' coaches as they began their warm-up routines. "What is this, the Olympics?" he said under his breath as he nervously scanned the crowd, without success, for his own coach. The friend's shoes he had borrowed seemed to be a comfortable fit, but he could detect something different on the soles of the others athletes' shoes – spikes of some sort. Whatever the superficial advantages he was up against, he assured himself, starting at the bottom of the heap had never stopped him before: he would rise to the occasion as he always had when it was something he wanted. And this race meant more to him than the rest of the school year. Though, immediately beneath his confidence lay a sense of defeat from the day's previous events: he had failed to place in any of his earlier races. This was his chance, he reminded himself: the one hundred meters hurdles was his strongest race.

Again, Rick looked around at his giraffe-life competitors, seemingly towering over him with their elongated legs. The American, already with a blue ribbon or two to his name, dug his starting block into the ground in anticipation of his victory.

Luke heard his coach's words, the calming intention of them tempered with the anticipation of a Lloyd's winning streak. Luke was distracted, though, by the boy waving enthusiastically to someone in the crowd. The guy didn't look like a finalist; he looked under-prepared. And he was smiling, but he wasn't waving toward his school's seating area; it was the woman and girl on the other side of the railing that were eliciting the response, as they blew kisses and yelled words of encouragement as the race's start drew nearer. His mother and sister, Luke surmised.

He thought back to his seventeenth birthday, three months ago, and how the rampages that had previously marked the anniversary of his family's death were now a thing of the past. He had control of himself; he could hold it in. Soon he would again see his grandparents in Taupo. For now, he had the support of his entire school.

The sprinters approached the starting line and took their positions. Luke felt the adrenalin energizing his body as he crouched to his starting block and stared down the lane: one hundred meters was such a short distance – there was no room for error. He shut out the activity that was bustling in the stands and brought his mind into focus; he knew that the race required absolute concentration and he did his best to quiet the noise inside his head.

The starting gun shot through Luke's body and he immediately exploded forward. He had tweaked his starting technique until the response had become ingrained in his muscles. He heard a competitor clip the second hurdle and was aware, by the fourth hurdle, that no one was noticeably in front of him, but his eyes were locked onto the remaining hurdle as he pumped his arms and swiftly cleared it. His body was in top condition and he felt as if he were flying, powering ahead until the finish line was crossed. The race was a blur, it was all over so fast.

Luke glanced back down the track at the hurdles he had cleared. He had run well, there was no doubt about it. A crackle over the speaker system drew his attention back to the judges.

"First place, Lloyd's College," came the announcement. The rest of the placings followed promptly, and the other competitors gathered in to congratulate one another before dispersing to their schools' seating areas.

"Mate, you're going to be written into the records!" Luke heard Hughie's excited voice approaching from his side, accompanied by Luke's girlfriend, and then felt a solid slap on the shoulder. It was true. His three wins of the day had included one national record, and the streak would certainly see him written into Lloyd's history books. He had trained long and hard for it, and was pleased. As he looked out into the stands, he caught another glimpse of the shorter competitor. He was fast, Luke had noticed at the race's finish, though he was sure that he didn't place. Before the boy had reached the stands, his family was surrounding him, hugging him, laughing together. Luke sensed a richness that he had never touched.

WHY DID HE suddenly feel so empty, Luke asked himself, making his way through the city streets of central Auckland, not heading anywhere in particular. It was as if the thrill of victory had failed to outlast even the afternoon, ringing hollow even by the time he, Hughie and Laura had finished their first drink at the bar. It was supposed to be a celebratory night: the presumed completion of Luke's schooling years, finishing on a high note. Many of the Lloyd's boys had congratulated him that day, lauding over him not only for his triple-win, but for the consistency with which he had excelled during his time at the school.

But would they still care for him if he didn't excel? What would they all have thought of him had he not won any of his races that day? He shuddered to think, and he was reminded once again of the boy who had lost, but nonetheless shared the day with the family that loved him. But who did Luke have? Hughie? Laura? He wasn't even sure how much he liked her, or which was more important to her: Luke, or the idea of Luke. It didn't matter anymore, he thought. It was most likely over after what happened tonight.

He knew Hughie would get over his outburst, his callous words, his losing it and storming off from the bar, by morning. That was the nature of his dear friend; he understood Luke, he saw the truth of him, not just the image. His heart was big enough to forgive, just as he had many times over the years. Hughie had seen his friend's outbursts. Laura, on the other hand – she was a different story. Surely, she was shocked by his behavior at the bar.

Who cared anyway, he consoled himself. He didn't need her. He didn't need any of them. He could make it on his own – he had proved that much. He didn't require anyone's assistance in making a success of his life. Luke Powers was already a success. And it would remain that way; he would ensure it.

He was tired of people trying to make him happy, anyway, he brooded as he turned off Queen St, Auckland's main drag, and onto a side street. Why couldn't they just leave him alone in his misery? So what if he felt lost, alone, pissed off? What was it to them? If he wanted to be, then so be it! He had earned the right to feel the way he wanted to feel, and if people couldn't accept him the way he was, then alone he would remain.

Uncle's Burgers, read the sign. That'll do, he thought, and stumbled through the doorway, the smell of burgers a welcome relief to the stench of alcohol that had engulfed him back at the bar. He squinted at the menu above the counter, trying to make sense of the words.

"You alright, mate?" came the voice behind the counter.

"I'm fine," Luke slurred back.

"Need some help with the menu? It can get a little blurry at night," joked the manager, well-accustomed to drunk teenagers and university students wandering in.

"What's your best burger?" Luke managed, exhausted, depressed, and starving.

"Well, deciding on the best of the best is no easy task, my friend," the man responded. "But I have something in mind – you'll be pleased with this one, don't you worry."

Luke nodded wearily, waving his hand weakly in appreciation, and slumping his head into his arms. For a moment he drifted off, and was awoken by the manager's nudge on his shoulder.

"Here you go, mate," he said, handing him the burger. "Uncle's house special. Guaranteed to satisfy your appetite for days to come."

"Thanks man," Luke said as he rose from the seat. "I'm gonna eat it on the street – I need some air."

"Go easy, my friend," the manager replied, helping Luke to his feet. "You're not in the best state for walking the city."

"I'll be fine," Luke mumbled, exiting the burger joint and stumbling back onto the street.

Walking to the end of the block, and then leaning against a wall, he started munching on his Uncle's burger. He didn't notice the three young men passing in front of him, until one of them stopped as he saw Luke.

"Hey, look who's here, the pretty-boy from the burger store," he said to the other two. "You a Yank or something?" The man's tone was such that, in a clearer frame of mind, Luke would have immediately raised his guard and answered more wisely.

"Who gives a shit?" Luke responded, not lifting his eyes.

"Well, no one probably," the man approached closer, unphased by

Luke's terse response. "That's why you're eating a fucking burger alone on a street corner, right, pretty boy — isn't that — "

The man's speech was interrupted mid-sentence by Luke's flailing arm connecting with his cheek. It was the only blow that Luke managed to land in the scuffle. Within seconds, three pairs of hands were roughing him up. The next thing he knew, his forehead was rammed into a lamppost, his consciousness dimmed, and he had some vague awareness of raised voices coming his way as he slumped to the ground.

"Come on, let's get him into the truck, we have to get him to the hospital," was the last thing Luke heard before falling into a dream-state.

He came to as a nurse was dressing a split in his lip.

"Here he is," she spoke to whoever else was in the room.

"Just in time." A boy, about Luke's age, came into focus. "I've gotta get the rest of these deliveries done before 5am, or there'll be hell to pay. Luke, we didn't know who to call, so I've been waiting around for you to wake up — how can we phone your family?"

Propping himself up in his hospital bed, Luke's groggy mind eventually came to life, and his last thoughts started to make sense. "I got the shit kicked out of me," he mumbled.

"Yeah, luckily Arthur and I were delivering milk to the store right across the street from you just as those punks were clobbering your head against the lamppost. They ran off as soon as we jumped out of the truck shouting at them."

Luke placed his hand to his head and winced.

"Don't worry," the nurse said. "We think you're going to be okay. The doctors are going to be right in. Probably a concussion — you'll have to stay for a while longer."

"Who should we call, Luke? People will be worried about you," the boy spoke again.

"No, no, my grandparents live in Taupo. I'm supposed to be back at school — I'll have to phone them. I don't care right now. I'm not in any hurry to get back."

"Then I'll come back and pick you up when I've finished my delivery rounds."

Luke looked the boy in the eyes for the first time. "Wait a minute," he said. "I know you – that's how you know my name."

Rick laughed. "I didn't know if you'd recognize me – I didn't even make third place you know," he joked.

"Shit," Luke said, shaking his head. "Strange world." He considered Rick's offer. "Mate, thank you for your offer, but I think I'd probably just be better off on my own for the rest of the weekend. I'll work it out."

"Rubbish mate, you can't go back to school on an empty stomach. If your family's in Taupo, then come meet my family when you get out of here – my mum will be cooking a huge breakfast for when I get home from work. I'll swing by and see how you're doing on my way home. And then maybe you can share with me the secret to winning a championship race," he joked again as he left the room, hurrying off to finish his job for the night. Luke nodded, and smiled weakly.

By the time his erstwhile competitor returned to the hospital, Luke was visibly uncomfortable. After the doctor finished with the ten stitches and his diagnosis of a concussion, Luke's weary mind was having difficulty staying calm: it was the first time he had set foot in a hospital since the death of his family and the months he spent alone in his hospital room. At first, the confusion of the night, his groggy brain and the pain of his body were enough to distract him from the haunting memories. But the more he awoke, the more strongly the panic crept into him breathing, his thoughts, his body.

The nurses were still doing their best to persuade Luke to stay as he exited the room with Rick. They reached the truck, Arthur still in the driving seat, and Luke finally breathed a sigh of relief.

"Thank you for doing this, really," he said. "I would have gone insane if I had to stay in that place any longer."

"Not a problem," replied Rick, noticing Luke's hands fidgeting with his forearms. Much of the skin looked to be scarred, without any hair growth.

"They don't give a shit anyway, the doctors – no one really cares," Luke said, staring out the truck window. "It's Rick, right – the nurse called you Rick?"

"Yeah, that's the one," he said as they turned onto the street and headed toward Rick's home. "Rick Dellich," he said, offering his hand to Luke for the second time in the past twenty-four hours.

"Luke Powers." The two shook.

LUKE AT ONCE felt at home among Rick's family, whose mother immediately started fussing over his desired breakfast.

"Really, Mrs. Dellich, I'm sure whatever you're making will be wonderful."

"Well look around Luke," she motioned to the dining table. "Do you see anything in particular you like?"

Luke was surprised to notice that each of the family members had a different dish for breakfast. "I'm actually a little confused — it's as if there's a full menu on offer here. Each of you is eating something different."

Rick laughed. "Yeah, well, we all have different favorites."

The warmth and affection amongst the family members was palpable from the moment he stepped into the home and watched Rick hug and kiss both his mother and father. And now there seemed to be no end to it. This is it, Luke thought. This is what I want in my life. I want to share my life with my own loving family, one day, he mused.

No sooner had Maria finished in the kitchen, than her motherly ways found a new focus. "Oh, Luke, you poor boy, look at those wounds," she worried, examining his stitches and black eyes.

"Well, at least those giraffe legs are still intact, eh?" Rick piped up. "Help you to win more races?"

Luke laughed. "If you don't mind my saying, I'm surprised that a non-giraffe such as yourself was able to hold his own in the hundred meters hurdles. It's damn impressive."

"Yeah, well I guess I have Arthur to thank for that," he said, referring to the truck driver. "He's always in a hurry — if I'm not back on the truck fast enough each time we make a delivery, he just forgets about me and keeps driving down the street. I sometimes have to run for an entire mile to catch him before he realizes that he left me behind!" They all erupted in laughter; the family knew it to be true.

"Yeah, Rick's just a daydreamer," Rosa offered, hoping to get a rise out of her twin brother.

"What are these funny-looking things here," Luke questioned, point-ing to the pile of crisp pastries in the center of the table, from which Rick was steadily drawing.

"Hrustule," Rick answered, his mouth half full of the sweet Croatian delicacy.

"Hoostra-what?" Luke questioned.

"Here, try one," Maria sprung to her feet and excitedly brought the plate to his side.

"Mmm," Luke responded. "They're delicious!"

"Rick's favorite," Maria said, Rick nodding.

By the end of breakfast, the previous day's gloom had lifted from Luke's shoulders, and though he looked beaten and exhausted, there was a lightness to his spirit. He didn't quite know what he was feeling, but it was almost an unbearable amount of gratitude to this family who seemed to accept him immediately, and without needing him to be anything other than he was. To receive such warmth, and to relax into the family with such ease, was a rare experience. Something similar happened when he spent time with the Henare's, but it was different there: maybe because he had become accustomed to it, and maybe because it was a more gradual process. He didn't know what to make of his feelings while being wel-comed into the Dellich family. It both confused and soothed him.

It was almost midday when Rick finally drove Luke back to Lloyd's College, for his final days at his teenage home. Being a Saturday, there were groups of boarders walking the driveway and the fields, and it was for the most part quiet. Luke stared for a moment out the truck win-dow at Lloyd's, noticing again the isolation that hovered always in the background, but that had receded for a blessed few hours while he was distracted by the ease of the Dellich family.

"Well, I can't thank you enough, Rick," he managed a smile, still wondering if he would ever have something like the sense of family he had just experienced to call his own.

"I only feel grateful that I was there to help, mate," Rick responded.

"And tell your mum thanks again," he gestured, holding the container of hrustule that Maria had insisted he take back to boarding school with him.

"I will, and you can tell her again when we next see you," Rick said.

Maria had written out the Dellich phone number and insisted that he call again. The two boys had decided to be in contact once Luke had returned from his summer in Taupo, and a big part of him wanted to. But somehow, he knew he never would. The reminder of his own life's lack was too painful.

CHAPTER FIVE

I T'S OVER," LUKE said with elation, as he packed for the last time in the room he had shared with Hughie for the past four years. "Now I have to wait till January to find out if I got in, otherwise I'll have to unpack this lot again." Hughie looked at him with a wry smile. The idea that Luke would fail his final exams and not get into Auckland University was just too silly to contemplate. For four years they had shared the small ten foot square room and made it home. Now Luke was leaving, and Hughie tried hard not to show how gut-wrenching the separation would be. Next year some other boy would share the room; sleep in the bed that had been Luke's; put his clothes in the chest that had been Luke's; his books on Luke's shelf; read by Luke's lamp. The room would not be the same, but then neither would Lloyd's College. Luke had come there six years earlier, a broken boy who did not fit in, but somehow the college had changed, had molded itself to fit in with him, and so Luke Powers had left his mark. Now, Christmas was ahead. Hughie didn't have to take the bus; Luke didn't have to wait for his grandparents. Though his birthday was still months away, the two planned a wild premature celebration for Hughie's eighteenth birthday in January, and then they would drive home in Luke's red Mustang. It had taken him all year to acquire the necessary replacement parts from his Uncle Reube in the States after he had picked up the write-off for a nominal sum. It was a great way to launch the car's new life. And, Hughie thought with envy, it was a great way for Luke to begin the rest of his life.

The drive to Taupo, and then on to Tokaanu to drop Hughie home was uneventful. Hughie was severely hung over, and Luke was exhausted from the sexual exploits of a young go-go dancer in high black vinyl boots that they had met at a disco. It was the age of the pill, and free love. True, Auckland wasn't Haight-Ashbury, and Mission Bay wasn't Woodstock, but it didn't matter.

The McMasters greeted both of them with warm smiles and handshakes, and Gwen had baked an apple teacake and insisted on Hughie having two slices with a cup of tea, even though his stomach was screaming out to be rescued. Later, they all watched I Spy together, Luke never dreaming that one day Bill Cosby would be the highest paid television performer in the world and that, in the distant future, his own path would cross the actor's. Then Luke bundled Hughie, half asleep, into the car and drove him home.

Granny Moana Marie was as excited to see Luke as she was to have Hughie home. She hugged him tight and Luke was acutely aware that her head barely reached the middle of his chest, when only three years ago she had been able to look directly into his eyes. He felt a rush of pure affection, of longing to hold onto her after she had gently pushed him to arms length and made appropriate clucking noises of approval over him.

He saw Kiri over the top of the old woman's head. For a moment he didn't know who she was, for it was more than three years since he had seen her. Then she smiled and he thought that his heart had stopped. He had to urge himself to remember to breathe. She had been a girl of only twelve when he had last seen her. He had teased her about her Barbie doll and he and Hughie had been insufferably condescending when she had tried to play with them. Now though, there was a moment of sweet revenge for the girl, for it was Luke who stood and shuffled his feet stupidly like a child, unable to find the words to answer her greeting.

She had grown taller, but that was only a small part of the difference. Her hair, unruly and shoulder length three years before, was now long and silken, and she wore it caught high on the crown of her head in a pony tail, a wisp of a fringe down over her forehead, almost kissing her eyebrows. Her eyebrows themselves, once little more than bushy lines, were gently curved and arched over rich chocolate eyes with golden flecks, and double thickness lashes that kissed her cheeks when she blinked. Her face had been round – podgy almost. Now it was heart shaped, with high cheek bones and a strong straight nose. Most of all it was her mouth that he could not take his eyes off. She wore lipstick, a dusty kind of pink, and the lips were full and soft, with a deep cleft in her bottom lip. He felt mesmerized by her mouth, her teeth, the way her tongue flickered nervously and she would occasionally lick the corner of her mouth. She came to him and he realized that she was quite tall; her forehead brushing his lips. She gave him a sisterly hug and looked up at him. He knew she was saying something, but he didn't hear it. All he could think was that if he bent his head just a little his mouth would meet hers, his tongue would find its way between her lips, and neither one of them would ever need to speak again. Instead he heard a stupid and banal voice, a putrid mixture of Kiwi and Yank accents. It said "Jeez, sis, you went and grew up on me." He wanted to hide in embarrassment.

In the weeks that followed, he spent most of his time at Granny Moana-Marie's house. Hughie would often think up things for them to do, places for them to go, but Luke would make excuses to stay close to the house, close to Kiri. He even suggested that he and Hughie should paint the timber house over the holidays. Dressed in old shorts and tee-shirts the two young men spent long hours up ladders, the transistor radio hanging from the top of the ladder, singing the latest hits as they scraped and painted. Kiri, in short shorts and a bikini top, would bring them cold cokes and potato chips, and Luke would gaze in wonder at the long coltish legs, the perfectly rounded breasts barely contained within the bikini top, the slender shoulders with the clearly defined collarbones, and the *café au lait* skin, darkening in the summer sun. Luke was in love for the first time, and he felt certain that everyone who looked at him could see it, for he was helpless against it. Surely it was obvious to anyone who saw him with Kiri? Yet it did not occur to him that no-one saw it because they saw in Kiri a girl, a child, whilst he saw a woman.

If Hughie had not caught summer flu, and if it had not rained on the day of the picnic, then perhaps it might never have happened. Later, there would be times when they all wished that it had not, but they were few and far between, and Luke was a fatalist; how could he not be after the fatal trip to Europe.

"You guys go ahead" Hughie said, his eyes red, his head pounding. "I'm going back to bed." Already his limbs were aching and he felt as if he was swallowing razorblades. Luke looked at his friend with concern. "No way. We'll stay here. We can have the picnic in your room. Maybe cheer you up." He looked at Hughie expectantly but the older youth only shook his head.

"I don't want to be cheered up. Right now I just want to sleep... or die... I don't much care which." He managed a rueful grin before heading back to his bedroom. Luke appealed to the old woman. "Granny, should we stay and keep him company?" Granny Moana-Marie shook her head. "You planned a picnic, I made the food; now go have the picnic. The boy isn't fit company anyway. You men fold up even with a little cold. God knows what you'd do if you had to have babies. Go on — out, out of here."

Hughie watched his friend and his sister drive away; Luke in shorts and an open neck shirt, Kiri in a button through skirt and a halter top, her hair in braids. "Poor sod" Hughie said to himself with a grin. "He's going to be stuck all day with the kid." Granny brought him a hot lemon drink and he sipped it gratefully. "Luke's the best, don't you think?" he asked his grandmother. "He's better than a brother... I might not like a brother, who knows? But Luke, well, he's the greatest." His grandmother smiled. *"He aha to to tangata i whakakake ai, mehemea kaore ratau e whakakake ana i o taau hoa?"* she said, in the old language, and Hughie nodded. What should people be proud of if not their friends?

Luke and Kiri did not drive far. They picnicked in the foothills of Mt Pihanga, amidst summer grasses and the wildflowers. The rich yellow flowers of the Kowhai trees were dying, and the bees were drinking their fill of the honey nectar even as the golden petals drifted to the ground. Luke spread the blanket while Kiri unpacked the lunch. Granny had packed sandwiches — egg and lettuce, corned beef and pickles — and there was fruit, a slab of Cadbury's milk chocolate, oatmeal cookies and orange juice. After they had stuffed themselves full of food, they lay back on the old grey army blanket. Kiri shielded her eyes from the sun, and Luke turned onto his stomach, afraid that she would see his rigid erection through his shorts and be frightened by it. He kept telling himself that she was only fifteen, that what he was thinking was forbidden by the state and the church, and yet he could see the inside of her thigh as the button through skirt fell partially open, and it took all of his strength not to reach out a hand to touch the tender, inviting skin. Instead, he picked a wildflower and brushed her cheek with it, and she laughed and pushed his hand away. They must have dozed then, for the next thing they remembered was the clap of thunder and then the spitting of summer rain. Hastily they gathered up their things and raced for the car. The rain was growing heavier, and Luke could not get the soft roof of the Mustang up, so they drove in the rain to Waihi, a tiny village on the side of the lake. Luke pulled the car under a huge spreading tree and they raced for cover into the little church of St. Werenfried. Full of native timbers, the church was decorated in Maori fashion, and even the stained glass windows showed Jesus as a Maori, and the virgin Mary as a young *kohine*, holding her *pepi*, the baby Jesus.

They stood silently and looked at the window. The contrast between the tall, muscular, fair-skinned man and the younger, innocent and darker-skinned girl embodied the union of opposites that took place in the coming together of male and female. They were wet, and their clothes clung to them. Even before Luke reached for her hand, they were acutely conscious of the outlines of each other's bodies through their clothes. They turned towards each other and, without a word spoken, they kissed. It was a sweet and innocent kiss to start with, but then Luke pulled her to him, and pressed against her body and their tongues frantically sought each other. He cupped her breasts in his hand, feeling her hard nipples between his fingers. He took her hand and guided it between his legs. She gasped at the touch and pulled her hand away, throwing her arms around Luke's neck to kiss him again.

Later, when the summer rain had passed, they drove along beside the lake until they found a quiet spot, hidden by the pine trees. There they stripped off their clothes and swam. Luke tried to keep his back to her, as he seemed permanently aroused and was aware that his jutting penis would be both frightening and absurd to the girl. Yet, as he pulled on his shorts with his back to her, and she sat with the blanket wrapped around her nakedness she whispered timidly to him. "Luke... I want you to do it to me." He looked at her, not sure he had understood what she said, or what he thought she said. "What do you mean?" he asked foolishly. She bit her lip and looked away. "You know... I want us..." she began hesitantly, "Don't make me say it Luke. I just want you to be the first." She looked away as he crossed and knelt beside her, his arm around her shoulders.

"I... we... it'll hurt you. It always does the first time," he explained lamely, wondering why the hell he was trying to talk her out of something he wanted more than anything in the world.

"I don't care," she replied, "I just want us to... you know... make love." He kissed her and then gently laid her back on the soft scented pine needles and grass. He kissed her breasts, her neck, her shoulders and then returned to her mouth. His hand was wedged between her thighs, which she kept tightly clamped. Gently he eased them apart and raised himself above her. "You tell me if you want me to stop," he said, looking into her eyes for signs of fear or panic. She nodded. He guided himself into her, advancing a little at a time, waiting for her to call a halt and doing everything in his power to restrain himself. He slid his hands under her buttocks, moving her in time to his own rhythm. In less than thirty seconds it was over. He cried out as he ejaculated deep into the well of her, and his body shook. Then he collapsed onto her, and she stroked his head, as though she was much older and wiser than he. He knew that she had felt nothing, had not really even shared the experience, and it saddened him. He withdrew from her and gently found her clitoris with his fingers, slowly bringing her toward orgasm. He realized within moments that this was new to her, that she had never masturbated.

"What are you doing?" she asked anxiously. "All my insides are quivering."

"Shhh," he replied, "I'm showing you how it's supposed to feel." He realized then that without Michelle he would not really have known how to show Kiri the wonders of sex. As she reached orgasm her eyes widened, and she clutched at his arm, whimpering as her body jerked against him.

Over the weeks that followed she became insatiable, looking for new ways for both of them to please each other. She climaxed so hard against his tongue one night that he thought she had died of a heart attack, for she seemed to stop breathing for an interminable time. Luke would drive miles to buy "rubbers" as Kiri was not on the pill, and there was no way she could suggest it to her mother or grandmother without arousing suspicion. Part of the game for them was keeping their passion a secret from the rest of the family. Even Hughie did not suspect, although Luke felt guilty at keeping such a secret from his friend. Kiri took to wearing skirts all the time, but without any panties underneath. Soon Luke began leaving off his underpants, so that he could be ready for her at a moment's notice. The excitement of swiftly stolen sex, sometimes with only two minutes to spare while the family was occupied elsewhere, acted as an aphrodisiac to a passion that threatened to engulf them.

Amid the exhilaration of their powerful attraction, there rapidly grew a more profound connection that at once frightened and awed Luke. It was subtle, at first, as he noticed the comfort with which he could simply be himself with this young woman, possessing a depth and grounding beyond her years. He didn't feel the same need to conceal those parts of his personality of which he was not proud, or to second-guess what he was naturally moved to express in their quiet time together walking the surrounding forests or at the Henare house whenever they were lucky enough to find time alone without attracting attention. There was an acceptance between the two of them borne of an unspoken understanding of each another. Because of its unfamiliarity, it at times felt dangerous. And when the fear of being touched by such tenderness was released, it felt dangerous in an entirely different way: the sense of openness almost seemed overwhelming, as if letting go of himself anymore would result in the world around him simply sliding away as he floated into another world.

On January 22nd Luke read the results for University placings and punched the air in delight. Already he had started growing his hair longer, and the summer sun had bleached almost white streaks into the golden-corn-colored mane. He and Hughie celebrated with a few beers and later, while Kiri was supposedly just walking him to the car, he took her up against the side wall of the house, her legs wrapped around his waist, her head banging against the timber weatherboards.

Luke was torn between wanting to stay in Taupo, so that he was within easy drive of Tokaanu and Kiri, and wanting to get back to Auckland. It seemed to him that he had been reborn with 1970. The decade of tragedy was behind him, and he was out of school and almost a man. Moreover, he was in love, and she loved him in return, and he was not afraid of that; not afraid this time of losing her, and so he let himself be controlled by the emotion, rather than trying to control it. Still, it terrified him, and when he was away from her he tried to find the strength to not go near her again. He did not want to feel possessed by anyone or anything, even love, the thing he craved most. He could not bear to think of going through the same pain again. Then, he would see her, the way her eyes lit up whenever she saw him, and all the doubt was forgotten.

Kiri, who knew in her heart that she was never going to be a great scholar, was to finish her schooling locally, and that meant that she would see Luke during every school break and at every opportunity he had to return home. She could even make the trip to Auckland on the coach sometimes on the pretence of seeing her brother, who was still boarding in his last year at Lloyd's. Still, on the last night before Luke left to start his University career, Kiri clung to him and cried, as if his going foreshadowed the death of their intimacy.

For Luke, University offered a freedom that he had either never known, or could not remember. He had chosen his subjects; he could choose which lectures to cut, which to attend, what to wear, what to think, what to eat and drink. He was aware that he did not always choose wisely, but even that was his choice, and he loved it. He could see the infinite possibilities open to him now that no-one else was making his choices for him.

He knew that his grandparents expected him to study law or medicine, given his high marks. His schoolmasters lobbied heavily for the law, and the McMasters could not understand Luke's reluctance. It was difficult for them to understand his burning passion to go into business, as his father had done. He wasn't sure how yet, but he knew that economics and accounting were going to be of far more use to him. He had spent seven years now in a small Anglicized country in the Pacific. He was not a New Zealander, and never would be; and yet he was no longer an American. He wondered if he needed to define himself as either. The world was opening up. The Vietnam war was beamed into living rooms, as were the demonstrations against it. Luke himself had been part of the Auckland protest the previous year. The local radical student hippie leader, Tim Shadbolt, head of the Progressive Youth Movement, spoke out publicly in the park every Sunday. He talked with the burning fire of a revolutionary and with the restless passion of youth against the war, the Americans, the repressions of the old establishment led by Prime Minister Holyoake. Luke became an avid disciple, dragging Hughie to hear Shadbolt speak when his friend could get leave from Lloyd's in the weekends, then enthusing wildly, waving his fork in the air as the two devoured the T-bone steaks for which the El Matador restaurant was famous.

"Christ, Hughie," Luke would say, "We don't have conscription like the Aussies do, but that doesn't mean we shouldn't try to stop the war. Where does that arsehole Lyndon Johnson get off sending guys to get killed? You think he wouldn't send us if he could get away with it?" Hughie shrugged and put another piece of steak in his mouth. "Shadbolt's okay, I guess," Hughie conceded. "But it's all just bullshit, all this protest stuff. You can't buck the establishment. Ask my people, they'll tell you. Remember Alexander the Great's last words? To the Strongest! Well, that's just the way it is... and there's nothing we can do about it." Luke shook his head in disbelief. "Don't you have any vision, any sense of adventure?" he asked his friend. "Men have walked on the bloody moon, and we sat in front of the tele and watched it. D'you know how far the moon is? A quarter of a million miles! That's about ten return trips to Chicago. And we watched it. Don't tell me there's anything we can't do. Sure we can. We just have to believe it." And he attacked his steak with passion.

He found economics stimulating, even if a little like fortune-telling. The projections were all based on things staying on the same curve, progressing in the same way. Luke knew better than anyone that you could not predict anything by assuming it would follow the same pattern over a given period. I Ie had experienced first hand that everything you expect can be overturned in thirty seconds on a winding road. His lecturer enjoyed Luke's arguments, for they were well outside the normal student questions. One thing became apparent very quickly. While Luke was skeptical about financial trends, he had an innate knack for predicting fads. Once people became a factor in the equation, Luke could see clearly how they would react, which way they would go. He thought in retrospect that the long months he had spent with Lefevre and Finnemore, trying to understand himself, had given him an intimate understanding of other people, though he was just as much of an enigma to himself as he had been since 1963.

Among the many thousands of students at a University at any given time, only a handful are remembered in the years to come. Luke was one of the handful of the years 1970-72. For a start, he looked different. He wore the garb of a hippie... loose, brightly colored shirts, a choker of ebony beads, his hair long and blonde, sometimes with a bandana around his forehead. He was full of confidence, passion, ideas; the perfect successor, it seemed, to the legendary Shadbolt. Never before had a first year student had such an impact on his peers. He organized student rallies, a separate union for first year students rights, protest petitions against the war in Vietnam and the sports tours of the apartheid-afflicted South Africa. When the huge demonstration against the All Blacks Rugby tour of South Africa took to the streets on the eve of the team's departure, Luke and his followers were there in the crowd, throwing paint and flower bombs. It would be many years before he recognized the anger that burst forth in that year at Uni, anger necessary to balance the passion for Kiri. He was in his mid-twenties before he saw that he was not just another student radical looking for something to protest; he was, in part, still a little boy of eleven, furious that his family had been taken from him, that he had been left alone, and striking out at anyone or anything that got in his way. But, in 1970, he was perceived as a powerhouse of energy, impatient to get somewhere, except that he didn't know where. He would hold court at night at the students' favored coffee shop, the Waterloo Quadrant Cafe, where he would order cappuccinos all round for those disciples who saw him as a Christ-like rebel. It was the dawning of the age of Aquarius; the Beatles had sung "Love is all there is." But most of what there was, was sex. Everyone talked about "The Pill" in smug and casual tones. It was a license for promiscuity the likes of which the staid and traditional New Zealand had never dreamt.

"You sleep with other girls, don't you?" Kiri asked him one night, as they lay in each other's arms. He avoided looking at her.

"Why would you say such a dumb thing?" he challenged.

"Because I know you" she replied, with a woman's instinct far beyond her years. "Sometimes I don't see you for weeks. You couldn't go for weeks without doing it with someone." Luke smiled uncomfortably, feeling transparent under her gaze.

"Maybe I jerk off a lot." He said, half-jokingly, but she shook her head.

"You probably do… but that wouldn't be enough for you." There was sadness in her voice, but he recognized resignation too, and he held her tightly, wishing that he could lie and tell her she was wrong.

Instead he whispered, "It's just sex, it doesn't mean anything. It's not like us." He knew that every word was true, and that she knew it too, but it didn't ease her pain.

Yet, from that moment on, what had thitherto been experienced as an underlying, nagging guilt, grew into an undeniable sense of shame and self-loathing. Why did he persist in seeing other girls? What was it that he was seeking in them? Was it the thrill; the distraction; the affirmation that he was wanted? He began to question his habit, and the more he did, the more disgusted he felt.

Luke had seen the hurt in Kiri's eyes, those knowing, wise eyes that were a reflection of her mature soul. And that hurt had drawn his attention to the emptiness he felt within and that he sensed in his flings with various girls. He realized why it hurt not only Kiri, but also himself: he was cheapening something special between the two of them.

He had felt his feelings for her growing. There was a depth to their attraction for one another, and he found himself wanting to spend all of his time with her. He was losing interest in his usual activities, with drinking and partying seeming less appealing than they once had, and Luke noticed that he missed Kiri more with every passing day they were apart. He wanted her, and when he was honest with himself, he knew that he wanted only her. There was a joy and satisfaction in their being together that was unlike anything else he had experienced. He sometimes laughed at himself when he noticed the lengths to which he was going to arrange his schedule around any possible moment that the two could arrange to be together in Takaanu. It was love.

Though he was too young to see with clarity that the hurt and loneliness of his life in New Zealand was part of what was driving his endless seeking, he understood deeply that what he truly wanted was Kiri, and he no longer pursued the passing flings that had become so familiar.

Luke felt himself falling into life's embrace, and he experienced a deep sense of gratitude that was new to him. Kiri's love was so pure, so uninhibited, that it reminded him of the feeling of warmth and acceptance he had felt as a boy from his family. Finally, it seemed, Luke had again found his place in a family. What a gift, he marveled, to fall in love with Kiri, while also feeling so deeply connected to the rest of her family, and to his dear friend, her brother Hiwi. Nothing could be more beautiful.

Even his more practical endeavors were flourishing. His auctions, over the years since he began the monthly sales, had grown into a streamlined business. Reuben had opened a New Zealand bank account to allow Luke to reimburse him for the monthly purchases he was making on Luke's behalf. The amount was calculated at the fixed exchange rate; Luke was then able to make a substantial profit in the resale to Lloyd's students. Since leaving Lloyd's, he searched for a new avenue to continue his trading without direct involvement with the school. One of his younger staff members now purchased the merchandise from Luke, who found himself acting as a middle-man between Reuben's deliveries and the sales at Lloyd's. He was reluctant to sever all ties to his first business and so had created a new role for himself as importer and distributor.

His experience in revitalizing his own Ford Mustang had led him to a new idea for generating profits. The coveted import licenses, granted by the New Zealand government for the highly regulated economy, were ordinarily obtained only through perseverance and contacts. But an easier way to exploit the quasi-monopolies created by the licenses dawned on Luke. He phoned Reuben and requested an expansion of their existing arrangement whereby the US dollars that Luke would purchase from Reuben, reimbursing him in his New Zealand bank account, would now increase substantially. Reuben smiled at his old buddy's son's request. He had taken after his father, and he was happy to accommodate the boy's ambition. The import license was granted to Luke, but it precluded the use of any New Zealand funds for the purchase of overseas goods. The license would have been next to useless for anyone else; only nominal amounts of overseas currency could be exchanged without a serious import license.

In his experience with his own American car, he had found that there was a large, untapped market for American motors. Cars in New Zealand were difficult to come by, and expensive, resulting in each vehicle's life being stretched to the limit. Whereas American cars were often prohibitively expensive, Luke offered the next best thing: American engines – Chevrolets, Fords, V6s and V8s – for self-installation. The engines were salvaged from damaged, second-hand vehicles in America and shipped to New Zealand.

He was making enough money to live the life he wanted to while at university. But he never stopped planning his new life that would begin on his twenty-first birthday. The money that he would inherit was always in the back of his mind and, after attending a seminar by New Zealand's newest business luminary, Ron Wrightson, his dreams of the future were beginning to shine in evermore detail. He made his way up to the front of the Intercontinental Hotel ballroom and managed to introduce himself and briefly express his gratitude to Wrightson for sharing his wisdom. Wrightson's response was succinct. "The concept is simple. Most businesses carry more dead weight than they can afford," he had cautioned the young entrepreneur. "That might be debt, bad business practice, or simply ineffective personnel. Cost effectiveness means cutting out the dead wood to stimulate the new growth. If you haven't got the heart to chop out what's dead, best stay away from the trees." Luke questioned if he was up to such a challenge.

THEY HAD NEVER spoken, the two young lovers, of what discovery would do to them. Luke had kept his relationship with Kiri secret from

Hughie, even though there were times he felt he was betraying their friendship. Better to betray Hughie than place Kiri, or what they had together, in any jeopardy. Kiri told no-one. Yet it was silently acknowledged between them that the day would come when they would have to face their families.

Kiri was still two months away from her sixteenth birthday when she spent the weekend at Luke's new flat in Grafton. He was nervous at having her there, even though he still could not get enough of her. She was a minor, and he was breaking the law and could go to prison, yet that only added to the adrenalin rush every time her legs wrapped around his back and he plunged into her. She had made the excuse to her grandmother and mother that she was coming up to stay with a girlfriend of Hughie's and to shop in Auckland. Hughie was, after all, her big brother, and he would look after her. The trouble was that neither she nor Luke could let Hughie in on the plan without disclosing what they were to each other. It never occurred to her that Hughie, after being told by Luke that he was busy that weekend, would choose to go home to Takaanu.

She arrived home late on the Sunday night, taking the afternoon coach from Auckland, as it wasn't wise for Luke to drive her. She entered smilingly, nursing the secret of her love for Luke, feeling the ache inside her, the soreness of her thigh muscles, the tenderness inside her vagina from forty-eight hours spent mostly in bed, on the floor, in the shower, on the kitchen table, with him inside her. She said hello lightheartedly, not noticing at first the stony glare from her mother and grandmother.

She chatted inanely about Auckland, the shopping, Hughie and his girlfriend. It was only when Granny Moana-Marie said quietly, "Hiwi was here for the weekend. He left this afternoon," that she realized everything was about to fall down around her ears, and she was powerless to stop it.

Luke was woken by the hammering on his flat door. It was after midnight and he was surprised to see Hughie standing there with barely contained fury.

"You've been fucking my sister, you bastard. How could you? She's a kid, Luke... a baby. You filthy bastard." He cried in anguish. He raised his fist to hit his friend, but Luke grabbed it, and pulled him inside the flat.

"She's not a baby. My god, she's a woman. I'm in love with her... and she is with me. You think I set out to fuck her? That's not the way it was. We wanted each other... it happened," he tried to explain. Hughie looked at him contemptuously.

"And it's been happening ever since?" he asked.

"Yes... God help us, it has. She's the most important thing in my life. It isn't our fault that she's so young." Luke said softly.

Hughie looked at his friend. The anger was abating now. This was Luke, and Luke was special. Luke loved his sister, he believed that. And he was just as certain that Kiri hadn't been raped, or seduced, or anything else. She was too much her own person for that, so she must love Luke in return. He could accept it, but it didn't change anything, and he felt the anger rising again. "Try telling that to my Mum, and Granny, you stupid bastard," he said angrily.

Luke did try to explain it, but Granny Moana-Marie was in no mood for explanations. *"E aroha ana ahau ki a ia,a, e hiahia ana ahau ki to marena ki a ia,"* he offered, but she snorted contemptuously. "Do not use our language. You are not one of us. You say you love her and want to marry her? Yet you betray a child, you betray our traditions, you betray our friendship. You are not *mokopuna*, grandchild, to me. She is. Now, you will leave this house, and you will not return, you *poriro!*" the old woman hissed with outrage. Luke did not need to look up the word to realize she had called him a bastard. He started to protest, but Kiri came running from her room.

"Please Luke," she entreated. "Just go. They don't understand. Give me a chance to really talk to them. I'll change their minds. You'll see." But she never did.

CHAPTER SIX

POW! SKATEBOARDS WAS beginning to take off and Luke was pleased that the exploding trend in the US showed no signs of letting up. He had managed to bring the company into the black with three months at the helm after purchasing it from the receivers. After changing the name, he wondered what it was he had actually paid for – only the equipment and the continued employment of the designer, churning out forty boards a week. But, then, he had paid next to nothing for the operation. He was hoping to emulate Wrightson's approach on a smaller scale but was frustrated by his limited capital. He had noticed, however, through his experience in importing, that he had the ability to add value. The only way he could expand his business interests with his limited resources was to scour the accounting firms – Price Waterhouse, Deloitte, Coopers and Lybrand, Ernst and Young – for businesses, in receivership, that all others had given up on. The difficulty was in getting the receivers to take him seriously, and so he ended up having his lawyer, Michael Portman, who had done the paperwork for his importing operation, front for him.

He saw that, by buying at such a low price, his risk was minimal, and he relished the challenge of breathing new life into a failed business. The first of his salvage attempts, an auction house, was already generating reasonable profits. He was initially attracted to it because of his earlier involvement in auctioneering at Lloyd's and, he could see, the margins in the industry were staggering. What held the business back was its owner who squandered the profits at the local horse races. Luke kept him in the business to share his experience in the industry and the two became friendly; Luke could see that this man, who downed nearly a bottle of gin each day, was a lost soul, and he found comfort in the connection. His sudden death from heart attack while making love to a woman served as a wake-up call for Luke.

A week or two after his jovial friend's death Luke collapsed, exhausted, after another wild night of sex with Elaine. The two had been seeing one another for three weeks, and their connection went little further than the meaningless sex they had enjoyed multiple times each night since meeting. The last time he had taken her from behind over the edge of the bed, with her face down on the mattress. It became almost painful for him as he pounded his engorged member into the willing girl, and her long-nailed fingers reached behind and grabbed his buttocks. When he started to come he suddenly became afraid. It seemed that he could not stop ejaculating. He could feel the blood pounding in his head, and his heart seemed to be breaking through his chest wall. He could not breathe and he collapsed on her back.

"Wow, that was something else," Elaine said, with more exhaustion than enthusiasm. "Hey, Luke… get off me will you? You're squashing me. Luke?"

Jeff was asleep when he heard the girl scream. Luke's flatmate raced from his bedroom and down the short hall to Luke's room. Somehow Elaine had extricated herself from Luke's weight, and stood with the bedsheet wrapped around her, watching in panic as Luke fought for breath.

"Holy shit," Jeff muttered under his breath as he helped Luke off the floor and onto the bed. By the time he had found the doctor's number and was ready to dial for help, Luke was breathing more normally and protesting that he didn't want any help. Jeff made the shaken Elaine a cup of coffee and said goodnight to her when she left. Then he returned to Luke's bedside and waited for his dozing friend to open his eyes.

"Jesus Christ Luke. You're only twenty years old and you're fucking yourself to death! You think you're immortal or something? What the hell are you trying to prove?" The two had become close friends during their time at university and living together. Jeff was angrier than he had ever been with his friend, but there was fear mingled with the anger. Luke did not answer him, he just turned away. Yet, as the night gave way to the dawn and he lay there sleepless Luke thought long and hard about what Jeff had said. What was he trying to prove? He thought perhaps Jeff was at least partly right. He wasn't trying to prove he was immortal, he knew that. But maybe he was trying to prove that he was alive... or that he had a right to be alive; had a right to have survived that day nine years earlier. He didn't know for certain, and even if he had known, he wouldn't have had the solution. All he did know was, whatever he was trying to prove, he needed more of everything to prove it; more challenge, more success, more money, more sex. He wondered then what it would take to move from "more" to "enough." For several weeks afterward he stayed celibate, pouring all of his energy into his business ventures, hungry for more challenges, looking for ways to push the market in his own small way.

He had just turned twenty and the last two years of his life had been successful by any external measure. He was surprised at the ease with which he was able to understand different industries and businesses. He felt as if he were a business surgeon: arriving in a crisis, evaluating the situation and then responding with precision. He took two sick businesses and turned them around. But a phrase frequently sprung to his mind; Physician, treat thyself. If he was so adept at remedying such situations, why couldn't he, after all this time, fix what had really mattered to him; Kiri?

In the first few months after their discovery, the two young lovers wrote to each other every day. Kiri had been packed off to Christchurch in the South Island, where she had older cousins who were asked to look after her until she finished her schooling. Luke had begged her family for forgiveness, for understanding of his love for both Kiri and for her family and the place they held in his life, but it was useless. His words meant nothing to Granny Moana-Marie, the woman who had become a grandmother to Luke, himself, and who now seemingly did not even acknowledge his existence.

Her letters to Luke welled with her loneliness, her emptiness without him. He would read them repeatedly until he had committed them to memory. Then, wherever he was, he could conjure up her voice as though she were speaking to him, letting the sounds of her love fill his head, until, one day, he was unsure whether he really knew what her voice sounded like anymore. His frequent phone calls to Christchurch had not once been received, every one of them ending abruptly as soon as Luke was identified, despite his attempts to mask his voice. And not once had he been allowed to see Kiri, even given his two desperate flights to Christchurch when he never made it past her burly cousin at the front door. His persistence, which continued with failed attempts to meet Kiri while out of the house and out of the reach of her family, had reached such a level as to warrant police involvement, Kiri's cousin had threatened. It did not appear to be an empty threat, and a friend of Luke's studying law confirmed its validity, especially given Kiri's status as a minor. That was the final nail in the coffin; so long as Kiri's family wanted Luke out of her life, any possible success on his part to reunite with Kiri would likely be met by the threat of legal action. Kiri had been under the age of sixteen during their relationship, and Luke had been eighteen. It constituted a crime. No matter how hard he pushed, he knew her stubborn family always carried the ultimate weapon of the threat of imprisonment.

Defeated, Luke could not bring himself to sustain the painful efforts any longer. The futility of it was made all the more acrid by Kiri's apparent lack of determination or commitment. Where was she? Why had *she* not devised a way to be in contact with *him* other than their love letters? Why hadn't she convinced her family of the truth of their love? It seemed her family was more important to her than he was, he surmised with a deep bitterness.

He could not write to her in the same way. Instead, his letters were full of news, detailing what he was doing rather than what he was feeling. There seemed to be a block between his heart and his mind, and his brain refused to commit to paper the myriad of emotions that welled inside him for her. There was an empty space inside him that she had filled. Now, he was hollow again. He knew he was a lesser person without her, and if that was not love, then he couldn't imagine what was.

But the weeks stretched into months, and the daily letters became weekly letters. There were girls after Kiri, some whose names he could barely remember. They gave him momentary pleasure, but no release from the loneliness. Initially, he had refused to take a girl to the Grafton flat. Kiri was the only one who had shared his bed there and, in a strange sense, he felt that he would be betraying what they had had together. Besides, one part of him lived in hope that they could survive the separation with their love intact, and so he excused his sexual rampages as mere physical interludes that had nothing to do with him and Kiri. Sometimes he had taken girls to friends' rooms, or to One Tree Hill park, where they would make out in the back of the car. But the local police were starting to patrol, and a student whom Luke knew vaguely from school, had been caught with his girlfriend in the police flashlight. In a frenzied effort to put his clothes straight, he had caught his penis in the zipper of his fly. His yells and hopping around alerted other parked couples, and the police were forced to excuse themselves for what was mistaken for police brutality. Luke was determined that he was not going to travel the same road, and so he began using the flat.

After a while, there was no trace of guilt left, nor any trace of Kiri's memory in the bed. There had been too many others in the year or more that passed. Yet still, inside of him, he thought of her as the one woman in his life. She sent him photographs, and he felt the ache of realizing that she was changing, growing up, and he was not part of it. One last time, he took some money from the bank and traveled down to Christchurch to see her. He had not planned to fight over her, but the violence was inevitable. He was punched and hit, Kiri's cousin electing to teach Luke a lesson himself, rather than waiting for it to be delivered in court. He thought he caught a glimpse of her behind the curtains in the front room of the little house, but he couldn't be sure. He returned to Auckland sick to his stomach, the sense of failure overwhelming him. He had failed to rescue his family, failed to keep them close to him; now he had failed to rescue the girl he loved. Some part of him knew then that she was lost, dead to him as his family was. It took him several years to admit this to himself, but that was the moment he gave up fighting for her.

Luke did not see Hughie for months after Granny Moana ordered him from the house. He wanted to call his friend many times, but something told him that Hughie would come to him when he was ready to pick up the friendship, and it would be unwise to push him earlier. It was November, and both college and university were breaking for the long summer recess. Hughie turned up quite suddenly one Friday afternoon. He and Luke looked at each other; Hughie in the long grey slacks and maroon blazer; broad shouldered and medium height, the curly hair cropped short; and the tall blonde haired hippie in the jeans and flowing shirt, hair to his shoulders, the wide blue eyes filled with a pain and knowing beyond his years.

"You really loved her eh?" Hughie asked bluntly and Luke nodded.

"I still do," he replied. Hughie looked at him for a long time, as if waiting for his friend to somehow betray himself. Finally he gave a grunt of satisfaction, and turned and walked away without another word.

Luke spent his first Christmas without his friend. His card to the family was not acknowledged. His gift to Kiri was returned un-opened. Later, he received a letter from her explaining that she had not been allowed to keep it. He walked alongside the lake where they had first made love, and felt the gnawing emptiness inside of him. He was aware that his grandparents somehow knew of his disgrace with Hughie's family, even though the subject was never broached. He had grown as close to them as they would allow. He was so tall now that he could see his grandfather Sandy's thinning hair, and his grandmother, when he hugged her, would barely reach to his armpits.

He had noticed in his earlier visits to Taupo that his grandmother was having some difficulty with her oven. The dishes that she had always prided herself on were not coming up the way they should, as the old wood-fired oven was nearing the end of its life. He knew, however, that the McMasters would continue to make do with what they had until they were forced to drink cold tea. He purchased the new Champion oven in Auckland – a sturdy, no-frills appliance with simple controls that he hoped would not intimidate his grandmother – and made the trip to Taupo that summer with the roof down to make room for the appliance in the back seat, wrapped in Christmas paper. On Christmas day, his grandparents were astounded to discover the truth behind the mysterious, large present that had been sitting in their living room, and they were humbled that their twenty year old grandson would do such a thing.

"Don't you understand?" Luke said. "I wanted to give you something, just for being here. If I hadn't had you…" He let the rest of the sentence hang, for the reality was that if he had not had his grandparents, he would have been totally alone. Gwen McMasters took his hand and squeezed it, then patted his cheek.

"Luke, my dear. You have given us something, surely you can see that? You gave us yourself, and that gave us back your mother. That's something you can't measure in money." He felt foolish then, and still a child, despite all of his success. Yet, in spite of his grandparents' protestations, he could not shake the feeling that he had not done enough for them, that he had not earned their love and respect, even though common sense told him that it was given freely and did not need to be earned.

That Christmas, he observed his grandparents and was struck by the ease with which they lived. Somehow, despite Grandpa Sandy's constant talk about the value of money, it seemed to have very little value for the McMasters. They had everything they needed, except for their daughter and her family. They were the most contented people he had ever seen. He wanted to know how they got that way, how they found that peace, but he knew he could never ask them. His grandfather would have snorted, and berated him for talking rubbish; his Grandma would simply be embarrassed. He had never seen them hug, never seen them kiss, rarely seen them even touch, except perhaps for a hand on a shoulder, or a slight brushing of shoulders, and yet he knew in his heart that they loved each other deeply. Was that the answer, he wondered? Was love so overpowering that it made money insignificant?

They were all that was left to him now, and yet he knew that it wasn't enough. He was glad when the holidays ended and he returned to university. Auckland was now more familiar to him than Taupo and, if he had a home at all, it was the flat that he shared with Jeff, costing him twenty dollars a week.

FOR HUGHIE, IT was difficult being at university knowing that, though Luke was close at hand, there was still a gulf between them. Hughie was studying law, the first in his family to aim that high. The young man was well aware that he would need to work doubly hard to get where he was going, for despite the popular myth that the Maori were treated as equals and racism didn't exist in New Zealand, Hughie felt instinctively that he was being measured at every step to see if he was making the grade. Often he feared he wasn't, that he was aiming too high. Those were the days when he longed for Luke's reassurance. Luke, he knew, did not judge him in the same way that he had judged his friend. It occurred to him that he had never seen Luke judge anyone, and that only made him miss his friend more. He did not know if it was pride that stopped him going to Luke, saying, "Let's forget it. You're my friend", or if he was simply too embarrassed. He was well aware, though, that Luke would not come to him. He would have to make the move. There was never any doubt in his mind that Luke would just smile enigmatically, slap his shoulders, and they would get on with their friendship as though nothing had interrupted it. Still, he hesitated, and he did not know why. Perhaps some part of him knew that he needed to find his own feet. Luke had supported him all through college when they had been two misfits thrown together.

But now Luke was one year ahead, and already making a name for himself. Hughie discovered within his first term that there was barely anyone on campus who did not know the name, Luke Powers. It seemed he was dividing the student movement into two camps; those who were avid followers and those who still considered him a loudmouthed Yank with money. Already Luke's import operation was generating a sizable profit. Yet, at the same time he was being hailed as a natural successor to Shadbolt in the Progressive Youth. He was both businessman and radical; establishment and anti; a mover and shaker in an Indian shirt and love beads. He refused to conform to anyone's image of him, including the nonconformists'.

Hughie would go to hear his friend speak out against the war still raging in Vietnam. Australians just across the water had been conscripted; young men of twenty had their names drawn out of a lottery. Their prize was a tour of duty alongside their American cousins in the war zone. Luke was conscious that if he had still been in Chicago he would likely have been drafted into a war he did not support. New Zealand had no draft, and Luke debated passionately that it should stay that way. Those career servicemen had no choice in where they were sent, but it was unconscionable that young men should be sent to kill other human beings involuntarily. Hughie would cheer loudly with the other followers. Sometimes he would know that Luke had seen him in the crowd, could feel his friend's eyes upon him. Even then he would avoid the moment and look away.

It was during his second year of study that Hughie began working at the Auckland docks between semesters as a 'seagull' – a wharfie. He had searched far and wide for a job that wouldn't require a constant commitment that would interfere with the heavy workload he was dealing with at university, and when his older cousin, Whai, was able to put in a good word for Hughie with the unions he knew it was the perfect fit. Even with a ticket to work on the docks, finding work wasn't easy: it meant turning up at six a.m. every morning and vying for a spot on a crew for the day. If he wasn't picked, Hughie would hang around for the rest of the morning in case more work opened up. But the money he earned on the good days more than made up for any idle hours and he was raking in more than he would be in any other job.

But within weeks, Hughie's enthusiasm had changed to cynicism.

"It's just like a supermarket down there," he complained to his cousin. "Everyone helps themselves but there's no checkout counter. I tell you, Whai, I've seen containers opened unofficially and pilfered. I've seen guys sitting on their fat bums doing no work all day and drawing big money to do it. I've seen them complain to the union that they're working too hard, and then the union organizes a go slow. Go slow! How the hell can you go any slower than doing nothing?" he asked, but Whai didn't reply. "I walk away when I see a crate being opened, or an import assignment being wrongly inventoried, but I can't convince myself that the problem no longer exists simply because I refuse to see it."

"It's no different to how it's always been, Hiwi," Whai told him. "Some blokes are honest, some aren't. Stuff goes missing, the insurance pays. Work goes slow, the employer pays. At least the worker doesn't lose... that's something to be grateful for." The older man's apathy shocked Hughie. "Grateful? We're supposed to be a noble people."

"It's a job, a good job. I don't slack off, and I never stole nothing in twenty years, 'cept a radio once so's I could hear the coronation broadcast from London. It all balances out in the end," Whai offered.

"It's full of freeloaders... no, that's not true... they're crooks!" Hughie huffed. "The whole system needs a good clean-out. If someone were to report all this shit to the government, there'd be action." "Bullshit" the older man replied. "You think the government doesn't know about the crooks? The union's too strong for them to do anything about it, so they just close their eyes. That's all. You close yours too, and you'll get on real well."

But Hughie could not just close his eyes. Even though he did the job, he started taking notes every time he saw a crate opened, or cargo sitting untouched for days on end on the dock. Once he saw a new car, a Holden Premier straight out of the hold of a cargo ship from Sydney, being driven by one of the older seagulls on a joyride along the quay. When the front indicator was smashed as the car grazed the warehouse, the foreman marked on the inventory that the car had been damaged in transit. Hughie made notes, unaware that other eyes were already taking note of him making notes.

Whai liked to go to the pub for a drink after his roster was over. Sometimes one drink would become three or four, sometimes nine or ten. It was on one of the latter nights that Gerry Dalgleish, foreman on North Quay, bought Whai drink number eleven, and started to ask him a few innocent questions about his cousin, Hiwi Hanere, smartarse and potential troublemaker. Whai spent the next two hours and six pints of Lion Red, telling Dalgleish how Hughie was going to be a great lawyer, savior of his people, and reform the waterside at the same time. Hughie was an honest man, a man of integrity, Whai insisted, and Dalgleish believed him. That was what made Hanere a threat.

It was soon after Christmas. The Seagulls had a backlog of cargo that should have been cleared in late November. Hughie had not been picked for the crews the last few times he had turned up for the morning calls. He assumed it was because his discontent with the rotting of the system was known, but now the workload was such that he could not be overlooked, and he found himself rostered for a double shift clearing the holds of a cargo ship which had been sifting at the dock all through the Christmas break with its holds full. The days of container shipping were just beginning, and there would be enormous modifications to the wharves over the next few years. For now, cargo was still lifted from the ships' holds to the quayside via cranes and huge nets. Dalgleish assigned Hughie to the dockside, where he would guide the giant cranes to lower their nets full of cargo down to the ground. The foreman was pleasant, if not overly friendly. Hughie was a good worker, he conceded to the student, even if he was a little overzealous. Still, Dalgleish explained, it wasn't policy to have discontent amongst the workers and, he assured the young man, he did not personally sanction the abuse of the system.

"By all means keep your eyes and ears open lad, and you tell me if there's something you think I ought to know. Not silly bugger stuff, like the blokes taking an extra fifteen minutes for a smoko, but serious stuff, thieving and all, and I'll deal with it. No need for any of it to ever reach outside ears," he explained, and Hughie believed him, because there was no alternative if he wanted to keep the job.

Hughie was glad to be safe on the dock. Some of the crew worked down in the holds loading the nets, or bringing the crates to the deck. Once the nets were secured, one man rode down on top of the net, holding onto the thick rope, a foothold through the holes in the net. Hughie had ridden the net only once, and had felt horribly sick. He knew it was job that many craved, for it brought an unequalled adrenalin rush to the day, yet he never volunteered for it, and was always happy to change places if he was assigned.

Once the net was emptied on the dockside, Hughie and one other, a Hungarian man called Alex, who spoke bad English, would stack the crates on the palettes for removal to storage in the bondhouses, awaiting customs inspection. Hughie saw the net swing out over the side of the ship in his direction. "Ripper" a large Australian wharfie, rode the net. It was his favorite position, and sometimes he would swing round on the giant ropes as though performing in the circus. Hughie had long considered Ripper to be a little crazy, always looking for a new rush. This day, he turned his eyes away, not wanting to watch the antics of the mad Aussie.

He did not see Ripper, in exchange for the two hundred dollars Dalgleish had given him, release the ripcord which held the net together at the bottom. He did not know that the "accident " about to engulf him was actually a carefully calculated warning that he should keep his mouth shut. He didn't have time to react, or jump clear. Even when Ripper, realizing that he had miscalculated and the entire cargo could engulf and kill the two men below, called out to him to move, there was insufficient time to do anything but stumble backwards. Crates of farm machinery, bales of cotton, tea chests of household goods, all freed from the imprisonment of the net, raced towards the dock at frantic speed. Alex cried out in terror, but Hughie only stared in wide-eyed surprise as the cargo crashed down and brought with it darkness and silence.

CHAPTER SEVEN

H E WAS AWARE of the searing pain, even though he could see nothing except a myriad of shapes and colors racing towards him as though he was somehow floating in outer space, in the midst of a meteor shower. He could hear voices, muffled and distorted as if from the end of a long tunnel. It seemed to him that he must still be on the dock, for where else could he be, and yet he could see no daylight, and he appeared to be moving. Then, Hughie would remember much later, he was lifted or he floated, and he was traveling quite fast towards a light. He could see two people in the light. One, a Maori chieftain, strong and tall, dressed as a warrior. Hiwi knew instinctively that this was Rangi, whom his grandmother had spoken of so often. The other was neither male nor female... it was a being of light, arms outstretched, welcoming. Hiwi could see no face, and yet he knew that the being was smiling at him. He flailed his arms, trying to increase his speed, to reach the light sooner, where he knew he would be safe. Then Rangi stepped forwards.

"Hiwi, you bring us your soul, your *wairua*, but your *mahi*, your work on *whetu ao*, planet earth, is barely begun. Go back, *whakahokia he pai mo to kino.*" Hiwi found himself retreating from the light, yet taking with him an overwhelming sense of love. And the Maori chieftain, the god Rangi's word followed him. "Go back. Return good for evil."

Hughie opened his eyes for only a moment. The face bending over him was not that of an angel, but of a nurse, young and compassionate.

"My legs?" he whispered. Even though he could barely focus, he could see the concern, the pity in her eyes.

"Please lie very still Mister Hanere. We're here to help you. I'm going to give you a shot now. Just relax." She slid the hypodermic into his arm and before he could form the next question he had slipped into a warm and restful dark space where he was safe.

LUKE ARRIVED AT the hospital the day after the accident. He had rushed to the hospital the first he had heard of Hughie's accident and had not yet given any thought to what it might be like to see Kiri once again. He felt the breath sucked out of him as he entered the room and came face to face with Kiri – so tall, beautiful, smiling at him with tear-filled eyes. He couldn't discern whether it was joy or pain that was shooting through his body, but certainly it was a feeling of such potency that he couldn't recall when he last experienced such a moment.

The former lovers' fleeting reunion was cut short as Luke's mind abruptly returned to Hughie and he scanned the room for his friend. But he saw only Granny Moana-Marie, Hughie's mother and Kiri. They were anxiously awaiting the doctor's return from the operating theatre; Hughie had gone into surgery for a second time. Luke didn't need to be told that he had not been forgiven, for the encounter with the women was strained beyond that of normal concern for a loved one. He wanted to put his arms around these three generations of women and hold them close to him. He was prepared for them all, himself included, to weep for the man they knew and loved. He could have handled that. Instead, there was cool hostility. More than two years had not altered the fact that he had betrayed the family.

The doctor entered the room. He was experienced at breaking bad news, but there was no easy way for him to approach the family. He looked at the faces before him; three of them dark-skinned, eyes full of the pain of defeat coupled with nobility; the fourth fair and gentle, yet with a stubborn chin beneath the sensitive mouth, and blue-eyes filled with anxiety.

"There's no easy way to say this, I'm afraid." The doctor began, and Mary Hanere gave a short intake of breath, as if she had been stabbed.

"The fact is, the young man has suffered horrific injuries. Five of his ribs were cracked, two punctured a lung. His spleen was ruptured and we had to remove it. We're still hoping to save his left kidney. But " He was forced to look away from the tragic expressions before him.

"Please doctor... tell us the whole thing." Luke pleaded. The doctor swallowed hard. No matter how many years he spent breaking this kind of news, it never got any easier. "He... his spinal column was severed," he said without emphasis, and the old grandmother cried out in pain. Her daughter was incredulous. "What's that mean? He'll walk again though, won't he doctor?" she asked, begging for reassurance. The doctor licked his lips, knowing the blow he was about to deliver.

"I'm afraid not. It wouldn't have made any difference but... I mean, it's the spinal damage which ultimately is irreparable but..." somehow he could not say the words. Luke was growing impatient.

"But what? He's going to die, is that it? For Christ's sake tell us," he cried out and grabbed the man's arm. The doctor winced at the pressure and gently released Luke's grip with an understanding hand.

"I'm afraid we've had to amputate. He's lost both his legs. I'm truly sorry," he concluded. Mary Hanere collapsed then, her sobs like a cry of anguish. She had lost a husband to the sea, and now she may as well have lost a son. The three family members, shattered emotionally, clung together for support, and once again Luke realized he was the outsider. There was no-one for him to hold, to comfort or have them comfort him. He was conscious of the tears quietly welling in his eyes, and the pain of loss crushing his chest. He had prayed so often for his family to have lived, yet they did not. Now, Hughie was alive, and Luke felt like praying for him to die.

The doctor excused himself, but Luke followed him down the hall, away from the grieving family, and gently restrained the medic.

"Doctor, isn't there anything? I mean... I can pay for private specialists or whatever it takes…" Luke's voice broke and he started to sob quietly.

"Son, " the doctor said gently "We don't take off legs if there's any other choice. We were already completely satisfied that the young man's spinal column was beyond repair. If we hadn't taken the legs he would have died from loss of blood or complications later.

"I know this is hard for them – for you – to accept. But he's alive. That's what counts now."

He walked away then and Luke watched him go. There were a million questions that Luke wanted to ask, but he could only think of one, and he called after the doctor. "Does he know?" The doctor turned and shook his head.

"No. And I think it's better that we wait until he starts to recover. We need him to want to live," the doctor said as he reached the end of the corridor. Luke turned and faced the family. What were they thinking, he wondered? They simply ignored him, and he felt their implicit statement that he did not belong there; as though he had no right to grieve for Hughie. Kiri avoided his eyes, and he did the same, the circumstances complicating their potential meeting to such an extent that it was better for both of them to avoid any kind of contact altogether. Hughie weighed on their hearts too heavily, and the family's presence was too ominous, for anything else to find space to surface at that moment.

He waited there for the rest of the day until Hughie was ready to be wheeled back into his own room. Hughie slept peacefully, awaking only occasionally into a state of semi-consciousness at which time the medical staff monitoring his condition would activate his morphine drip. Luke wanted to go to his friend's side, to take his hand and somehow give him strength, yet he could not even do that, not without the family's permission, for he was not family. Once again he felt alone and apart, and the black dog of depression bounded up to greet him once more.

Luke could see that it would be some time before his friend would be ready to talk. The two had barely spoken in over two years and

Luke desperately regretted their failure to make amends before such a catastrophe.

For Hughie, there were weeks of grayness, worlds of shadows. He was conscious of a variety of faces whenever he surfaced, but he could not put names to them, even those he knew and loved. Worst of all was the pain in his legs, a pain that even the drugs could not dull. He never saw the Maori God or the light being again, and somehow he knew inherently that he was not meant to die, but he was afraid to come back to life; afraid to discover what had happened and how his world had changed; and so he clung to the shadows like the life support system which he didn't even know existed, or kept him connected to the real world.

Luke came to visit early in the morning or quite late at night, when he knew there would be less risk of bumping into the family. He got to know the nurses well and one would admit him after visiting hours. Sally Rogers would often sit beside Hughie's bed, willing him to fight, to live.

"You know they haven't told him yet?" she asked Luke in the third week of Hughie's recovery, as she and Luke shared a cup of tea in the cafeteria. Luke looked at her in amazement. "He's awake most of the time now, even if he's not exactly talkative," Sally continued, "And he's constantly complaining about the pain in his legs. Oh, I know what you're thinking, but it's pretty common. Amputees almost always think they can feel something in the limb that's gone. Itchy toes, that sort of thing."

"Oh Jesus," Luke groaned, almost unable to bear the thought of the misery that Hughie still had ahead of him. "What do you tell him?" Sally gave a wry smile and looked quizzically at Luke. "Us? We don't tell him anything. The family has forbidden us to. I heard his mother though. She told him that his legs were healing, that the pain would go away. What's he going to do when he finds out?" she asked. Luke looked worried. "What are you suggesting? I should tell him? Is that it?" he challenged her. "I don't know" the young nurse replied. "You're his friend, but there's obviously something heavy duty between you and his family. If you could just get them to give the medical staff permission, a doctor could do it. Pretty soon he's going to be sitting up, then he's going to be asking to get out of bed. Are we going to wait until he tries to put his feet on the floor to tell him he no longer has any feet?" She was conscious that she was growing angry and frustrated, but she made no attempt to hide it. Luke shook his head, not wanting to hear.

"Don't... please, don't say that. I'll... I'll talk to the family... or try to anyway," he said without much confidence.

Later that night he sat beside his oldest friend's bed. Hughie would surface and smile at him, and Luke would talk about the old days, the first term at boarding school, as if it were another life and they were two old men looking back across the chasm of time. When Hughie asked Luke to scratch his right foot, Luke opened his mouth, determined to tell his friend the truth and to hell with the family. But he looked into Hughie's eyes; dark, hurt, trusting, and he could not bring himself to deliver the ultimate blow. He was a coward, and he knew he had no right to judge the family for their cowardice, for they each loved Hughie even more than he did. Instead, Luke reached down, and mimed scratching the foot that was no longer there on the end of the leg which was also not there, until his friend sighed with satisfaction and claimed the itch had gone, thanks to Luke.

Only a few days later, Luke was leaving just as Kiri arrived for a visit. She looked fresh and beautiful in the button-through summer dress with a white cardigan around her shoulders; half child, half woman. Luke felt himself growing more awkward even as she walked towards him. He waited to see if her mother or Grandmother was with her, but there was no-one, just the two of them in the corridor.

Even the nurses had disappeared, as if these two young people were finally being granted time alone. They walked towards each other, stopping with a no-man's land between them. Luke knew not what to do with the cauldron of emotions that was overloading his body and sending his heart racing, so he stood there, silent, until Kiri spoke.

"How is he?" Kiri asked in the soft, innocent voice he remembered.

"How would he be?" Luke replied, suddenly angry with her for standing there, close to him, and angry with himself for not handling it. "When are you going to tell him the truth? You can't go on lying like this." Kiri looked shocked.

"Lying?" she said. "That's not what we're doing. What difference is it going to make. Will it change anything? We want him to live Luke."

"You think I don't?" Luke answered angrily.

"I know you do," she said gently, "So try to understand. He's getting stronger every day. The doctors say he's past the worst – he'll live. Even if he doesn't want to, he'll live."

"Then tell him for God's sake. If you don't, I swear I will." Luke confronted her. "We will... just ten more days, that's all," she said, as if asking for his sanction.

"Ten days?" he queried. "What difference will that make?" Kiri looked at him with surprise.

"You've forgotten, haven't you?" There was an edge of sadness as she spoke. "It's his twenty-first birthday next week." Her eyes filled with tears and Luke groaned. He had forgotten. It seemed inconceivable that Hughie would turn twenty-one – he had been the oldest in the form at Lloyd's, and it reminded Luke of his own impending coming-of-age. He put out his hand and gently brushed a single tear from her cheek.

"Don't cry," he tried to comfort her, though his voice was bereft of emotion, as he tried to suppress his own distress at the uncertainty of Hughie's state. Other than his grandparents, Hughie was all Luke had left of his family, now, and he feared for his dear friend. "It's okay," he continued. But she shook her head.

"No it's not." she replied. "It won't ever be okay again. Oh Luke!" She looked at him with the deepest sadness. She never for a second doubted Luke's love for her brother, nor for her. It broke her heart to see him again and be reminded of not only what had been lost between them, but of what Luke seemed to have lost in himself. Without his saying a word, she could sense the emptiness and hurt that had resurfaced with renewed vigor after the death of their relationship.

"What's happened to you?" she whispered as she gazed intently at the man before her, placing her hand softly against his face. "Oh my love, how it hurts me to see you like this," her eyes, full of concern, settled on his. The love emanating from her hand, pouring from her

teary eyes into his, took hold of Luke before he knew what was happening, and he abruptly began to cry with panicked, uncontrollable,
breaths. She took his head in her hands and the two cried together in
the deserted hallway of the hospital.

It seemed to last forever. And then, as his breathing slowed, Luke
spoke. "I love you, Kiri. I need you."

"I know. But it's too late. It's *whakakoretia, rahuitia*... forbidden."
She sounded strangely calm with a strength of will he remembered,
the same strength that had first asked him to take her on the banks
of the lake. But instead of easing the pain, her deep knowing and
understanding of life only made him miss her more. Her love for him
enveloped his being, and he held her tight, remembering the magic in
her embrace, wanting more than anything to experience the perfection
of it, one more time. "Please, you know you can make me do anything.
Don't make this more painful and complicated than it already is, for
both our sakes." He found himself nodding in agreement, without even
consciously making the decision. Then, she was gone, moving away so
smoothly that he had no recollection of removing his hand from her
warm skin. She was past him, and he caught only the fragrance of her
hair as she passed and disappeared into Hughie's room. He felt weak,
and a little nauseated.

Luke walked purposelessly through the hospital corridor, stalked by
an awful dullness in his stomach, reminded of the interminable time he
spent in hospital as an eleven-year-old. Now, once more, he was losing
his family, but in a new way: rejection. And the pain of such a rejection,
of being ostracized from one's family, was unlike any other he had
experienced. Why did love hurt so much? Why had he brought so much
pain to himself, and to this family, in the name of love?

He knew though that from that moment on, whenever he saw her, he
would be seeing not his lover, but his best friend's sister.

THE ROOM WAS decorated with balloons and streamers, and old-fashioned paper chains. There were perhaps twenty people there to celebrate Hughie's coming of age, including the nurses who had cared for
him in the past weeks, friends from the university and college days, the

Hancre family and Luke, apart from the rest, wanting to be close to his friend, yet knowing that Granny would prefer him to be elsewhere. Hughie sat propped up in the bed, smiling. He could see the outline of the steel cage that covered his legs under the bedclothes, but he was not concerned. At least most of the drips and drainage tubes were out of him now, and he was starting to feel like his old self.

"Up until yesterday I still looked like one of Dr Frankenstein's creations," he joked.

"You're looking pretty fit considering," one of his tort law classmates remarked and Hughie waved his arm triumphantly in the air.

"Yep, won't be long before I'm running round the hospital. You nurses better watch out," he quipped happily, looking at Sally in particular. His mother put her hand to her mouth and turned away, even as the other partiers laughed and pulled streamers. A bottle of champagne was opened and poured into tiny medicine cups while a young nurse kept an eye on the corridor.

"A toast," Hughie's cousin, Whai, said raising the tiny paper cup. Somehow Whai blamed himself for what had happened. He wanted to believe that this was all a tragic accident, but he could not. He had been on the wharves long enough to sense an air of conspiracy about the incident. Ripper had been white with shock as Hughie lay crushed and others rushed to move the heavy crates from him, yet had not hung around for the police to come. Dalgleish talked about Hughie being careless and not really conversant with procedure, and yet Whai knew the opposite was true. He couldn't shake the guilt, but did his best to raise his cousin's spirits. "To our boy, who today becomes a man." The others joined in with their own congratulations.

"This is ridiculous," Hughie said. "It's my birthday and I'm going to make a speech." There were cheers of encouragement from all sides.

"And I'm gonna stand up while I do it." Hughie grinned, and threw off the bedclothes in the split second that it took for everyone to register what he had said.

It seemed to Luke that he had trodden this path before, and still could not fathom the nature of time that it was capable of slowing almost to a halt. He saw the bedclothes thrown back in slow motion.

He saw Hughie move his torso, preparing to swing his legs over the bed. He registered Hughie's frown of consternation and disbelief, and then the shock of realization that hit his friend with a force that caused his head to recoil.

He even took in Sally's look of compassion as she moved at snail's pace towards the bed, and the way Granny Moana-Marie's hands flew to her mouth. He saw the guests look away, knowing what was to come. All of this was like a carefully choreographed ballet, slow and graceful and performed in total silence in an interminable two seconds. And then the silence was shattered. Hughie screamed, and he kept on screaming until everyone bar Luke had left the room, unable to deal with their own pain, let alone his. He screamed until Sally injected him with the tranquilizer, and for several minutes afterwards until the screams became sobs. Then, with Luke beside the bed holding him, he looked accusingly at his friend and, hoarse from the screaming, hissed accusingly, "You should have told me man... you should have fucking told me." Mercifully Luke did not have to explain or excuse himself, for he knew that Hughie was right. Hughie, overpowered by the drugs, fell into a deep sleep. Luke was left alone beside his bed, to apologize softly over and over again, and hope that somehow his friend could hear him.

IT WAS NOT just the realization that he had lost his legs that caused Hughie to slide into a dark abyss of self loathing and self pity. In time he might have learned to walk with prostheses, but the additional news that his spine had been severed was like a death sentence to him. Along with the physical loss was the loss of all he might have been. He was bitter and resentful, not just towards the docks, his cousin, even Luke, but towards the entire world.

"They set me up... the whole world did. They told me I could be something, someone. A lawyer. They promised me if I worked hard enough... and I did, I swear I did. Then they took it all away..." he ranted bitterly to Luke days after his discovery.

"You will be something. You are something" Luke reassured him with a sense of urgency. "You're still you, you still have everything to give." The look that Hughie gave him was one of pure rage.

"Don't fucking patronize me, Luke," he spat at his friend. "I'm a cripple who'll end up on welfare. Tell it how it is."

"It doesn't have to be that way," Luke protested, but Hughie would not let him finish.

"How would you know? Look at you... what the fuck have you ever had to fight for? I'm a Maori. That means I start the race two strokes behind. And now I've got no fucking legs to run with. You know any-one who wants a native with no legs and half a law degree?"

Luke couldn't argue with Hughie's anger, and there were no words he could say that were more than platitudes. Within days he was aware that Hughie was withdrawing from all of them. Luke no longer cared if the family wanted him there or not, he spent as much time as the hos-pital would allow by Hughie's bedside. But Hughie refused to eat and had stopped talking to anyone. Luke tried to make conversation, give reassurances, but it was hopeless. Eventually Hughie would not even look at his friend. Some weeks passed, and Luke finally lost patience.

"You can lie in that bed forever feeling sorry for yourself. I can't stop you, but how bloody pathetic is that?" Luke rebuked his friend. "You have a brain, a mind, a heart. Okay, you won't ever walk again – face it and deal with it. But Franklin Roosevelt governed America from a wheelchair." Hughie looked at him with disgust and spoke for the first time in days.

"Was he Maori?" he asked accusingly. Luke sighed.

"No, but he had one thing you don't. He had courage." Hughie snorted with contempt and looked away.

"Why don't you piss off and leave me alone, Luke. You don't belong here," he said with quiet determination. "You belong to the past, and I don't want to keep being reminded of it. I have no future." Luke walked from the room. He knew that Hughie would fight back, but he didn't know when or how, and that scared him. It seemed to Luke that he was cursed, and that maybe that curse was transmitted through him to those he loved. His family had all died. He had become close to Hughie, and Hughie's father had been drowned tragically. It was true that fifty-one others had died with him, but hundreds had survived. Then there was his love for Kiri. It should have been perfect and pure, and yet it split the family apart and caused her untold pain. Now, Hughie's legs were gone and he would spend the rest of his life in a wheelchair. Would it all have happened if Luke had not come into their lives? Did he somehow carry this fate with him and inflict it on others? He had made a life for himself in this tiny country, and yet he felt it tolerated him rather than accepted him. He was making money faster than he would ever have believed; yet where was the sense of purpose, of belonging? In a few weeks he would attend his graduation ceremony. In months he would turn twenty-one. But New Zealand was no longer his home, if such a thing would ever exist for him.

CHAPTER EIGHT

"H APPY BIRTHDAY TO you..." As the strains of the birthday song died away, Luke saw, for the first time in the ten years this had been his family, tears in the eyes of his grandparents. They were getting older and eventually he would have to face losing them, and then there would be no-one. He pushed the thought away. Today he felt particularly low, in a way that he hadn't felt for five years or more. Reaching maturity was supposedly a big thing in any young man's life. It was a moment to be anticipated through the preceding years, and then shared with those who had given a man life and now set him free on whatever path he chose to follow. It was a moment when a man was faced with being alone, his own person in every sense, for the first time. It was a moment which did not, could not, exist for Luke Powers. He had experienced years of being his own person, of looking for a life path without help, and now that his twenty-first birthday had arrived it seemed strangely anti-climactic.

The party at Taupo was small, for he had celebrated in Auckland with his friends and the serious drinking had lasted for several days. Now there was just Luke and his grandparents. The neighbors, and the local vicar, had popped in to wish him well and share a glass of beer or sparkling wine, and one of his Gran's home-made sausage rolls, but the person whom Luke wanted more than anyone else to see did not arrive, or call, although there was a birthday card in the postbox that day. Hughie was home, Luke knew that much, but Luke had not seen him since that day in the hospital. He knew that he would have to make the move, and go to Hughie, and he would have to do it soon, or the opportunity would be gone forever. But first he had to spend this day with his grandparents. He owed them that much at least.

Sandy McMasters held out the small package to him. "Go on lad, take it, I've been waiting ten years for this moment," he said and smiled proudly. Luke had received an engraved Parker fountain pen and a leather writing case from his grandparents, and so this additional present was a complete surprise. He swiftly tore off the flowered wrapping paper and opened the worn velvet box. Inside was a gold pocket watch, Sandy's gold pocket watch. Luke had seen it only a few times over the ten years he had lived with them, and he knew that it was Sandy's most precious possession.

"I can't take it, Grandad. It's the most touching present ever, but I couldn't." Luke protested, finding it difficult to put the words together.

"You can and you will lad, for it's yours by birthright, and who else am I going to give it to. My Grandfather gave it to me on the day we left Aberdeen. He told me to remember that, even on the other side of the world, family was pure gold, like that watch. I never saw him again, but I always remembered. My dad kept it for me until I was twenty-one, and now it's yours, just as it should be. Grandfather to grandson, and one day, God willing, you'll give it to your grandson. Now you be sure to pack it when you're leaving."

Luke looked at the old man in surprise, for he had dreaded breaking the news. "How…? What…? How did you know I was going anywhere?" he asked, and even his grandmother laughed.

"Heaven's above, Luke. We're your family," she offered by way of explanation. "We've always known you wouldn't settle here, at least not until you tried your wings in America. You're Joe Powers's son. None of us has forgotten that. We spoke to Reuben last week and told him to expect you." He could see the brightness glistening in her eyes and knew that she was fighting back tears. He put his arms around her, including his grandfather in the hug. He could sense the inner battle they waged between warm affection and natural reserve, yet he chose to ignore it. "I owe you both so much," he said with heartfelt emotion. "I don't know how I can ever repay you." His grandmother stroked his cheek. "Just be happy, Luke, that's all the repayment we will ever need," she said. He nodded, but he wondered if she realized that the payment she asked for was the one thing he couldn't guarantee.

Tokaanu in late winter seemed bleak to Luke as he drove there two days after his birthday celebration. Maybe it was the rain, or the biting cold. More probably it was because he knew he would be confronting Hughie for the first time since he had left the hospital. Luke stopped the car outside the weatherboard house. This was the house where he had found family again, had listened to Granny Moana Marie's stories in the Maori language, had teased a little sister mercilessly, and then later fallen in love with her and been banished from the inner sanctum for that forbidden love.

Now, as he tried to summon the courage to walk the few yards from the car to the door, he could scarcely remember the way the house had once welcomed him. All he felt was a sense of foreboding. He had telephoned from Taupo; the old woman's voice was bereft of any welcome, but she had conceded that Hughie wanted to see Luke and that he could come to the house. The strain and tiredness that were evident even through the telephone line had left no doubt in Luke's mind that Hughie's rehabilitation was taking its toll on everyone. Hughie was in the garden; strange on such a cold day. But the thought occurred to Luke that perhaps this was a concession to the fact that Granny did not want Luke in the house. At first the two looked at each other, men who had grown apart without realizing it . Then, the boys who had known and loved each other through the trials and tribulations of boarding school and adolescence, surfaced, driving away manhood and replacing it with friendship. Hughie's eyes filled with tears, and he grasped both of Luke's hands as his friend stood before him.

"Jesus man! It is so good to see you," Hughie exclaimed in a voice loaded with emotion. Luke could smell the scotch even from there, and hear the slight slurring of speech. Hughie had been drinking – he was probably drinking constantly from the look of him... and only then did Luke look at him, for it was less painful to think of his friend as a hopeless drunk than a hopeless cripple. What he saw was a young man, with tortured eyes, sifting in a wheelchair. Hughie's face was thinner than he remembered, and yet unhealthily bloated at the same time. His eyes were bloodshot, ravaged by pain and booze. His stocky frame showed signs of losing weight, and yet his shoulders and arms were broader and more developed from pushing the wheelchair. And his legs were... gone. It was difficult for Luke not to look at the empty space at the front of the chair, where once there would have been calves, ankles, feet. Now Luke concentrated on looking his friend fully in the eyes as he crouched beside him.

"Silly question but, how are you? I mean... you look really great." Luke stammered, and realized that Hughie knew he was lying. Hughie laughed, and the full stench of alcohol hit Luke in the face.

"I look like shit, and you've always been a lousy liar, but thanks. I'm okay. They tell me I'll live to a ripe old age. What a fucking terrible thing to tell me, huh?" The bitterness inherent in the question left Luke with no reply. "I'm really sorry about your birthday, pal. I'd make some lame excuse, but really, I wouldn't have a leg to stand on." Hughie laughed without humor, and Luke winced with pain. He did not want to be here, did not want to experience this, but he knew he had to. For Hughie didn't want to be there or experience it either, and fate had given him no choice. Whatever Luke's pain was, he couldn't even begin to imagine Hughie's torment. And so he ignored the sick jokes, he ignored Hughie's drinking several beers and his explanation that he only got onto the "hard stuff" after lunch, and the two men talked for hours. They talked about New Zealand and where it was heading; they talked of Vietnam and the possibility's of the war ending, now that Nixon was in the White House; they talked of boarding school and their friendship, and reminisced about schoolmates. They didn't talk about the future at all, until Hughie pointed out how careful both of them were being to avoid it.

"It's logical, I suppose," Hughie said with resignation. "After all, I don't have a future." "That's only true if you let it be true Hughie, you know that," Luke said. Hughie baulked. "Hey man, don't pull that bullshit on me. I won't be patronized okay. You stand there on two good legs and tell me I have a future? How? Where? I'm a bloody crippled Maori with half a law degree. Have you looked through the classifieds lately? Seen how many jobs there are for cripples, even qualified ones? None. Zero." Hughie stared at his friend, not willing to let the question drop. "You think I should enter a sheltered workshop? Take up making plastic placemats or weaving baskets? You sanctimonious bastard, Luke!" He looked away from his friend, trying to control the rage that engulfed him. Luke fought his own rising anger and frustration.

"I think you should finish your degree. You could if you wanted to, you know that," he said. Hughie laughed cynically.

"Even if I could... what for?" he challenged.

"For yourself... because not to is a waste. Because..." And suddenly Luke felt himself choking on emotions he had forgotten, and the words were stuck behind the dam in his throat. Hughie saw Luke's expression change, and looked at him in hostile alarm.

"Don't you pity me," he almost spat the words at his friend. "Don't you dare pity me." And Luke felt his throat relax, and the words he had not wanted to say spilled forth.

"Then stop pitying yourself. Stop getting drunk and, most likely from the look of your eyes, stoned too. What's the point? Your legs are gone. They're gone. But your brain, your heart, your spirit. Do you want to kill them too?" he challenged. Hughie looked at him defiantly

"Maybe I do." he answered. Luke turned away, frustrated and angry.

"Fine. Then put a bloody gun to your head and blow your brains out. Do it quickly and spare all of us the dubious pleasure of watching you dying by degrees. If that's what you want." Luke saw, even by the shocked expression in his friend's eyes, that this was not what Hughie wanted. There was still a glimmer, a spark that signposted that Hughie wanted to live, if he could only discover how. His friend's voice was softer, more conciliatory when he spoke.

"I don't know what I want, so let's drop it. Let's talk about you. What do you want?" Luke shrugged and managed a wry smile.

"I feel just as hopeless as you do. I don't know what I want either," he conceded. Hughie nodded. It was as if he could read Luke's mind, and the closeness that had grown over ten years between them was restored.

"But you're not going to find it here. You're going away aren't you?" It was more of a statement than a question, and Luke registered no surprise that Hughie had known. "I'm going back to the States… to Chicago, where I was born," he replied, and Hughie nodded.

"That figures. You made a place for yourself here, but only because you forced us to change shape so you would fit. You're not a Kiwi, never have been," he proffered.

"I'm not so certain I'm a Yank either. Maybe I'm a Kank?" he joked lightly.

"More likely a kink," Hughie retorted, and the two laughed together for the first time that day. Luke felt again the warmth and affection for the man who was not quite, yet much more than, a brother to him.

"I have to go back to sort out my trust fund anyway. I think there's some money coming to me from my dad's business. That doesn't necessarily mean I'll stay," he said, verbalizing for himself as well as Hughie his intention to keep his options open.

"It doesn't matter whether you do or don't. You won't come back here. It's too small for you," Hughie replied, and Luke felt a sudden sadness that what Hughie said was true, and that meant that he would be leaving things behind that he would have wished to take with him, including Hughie's friendship.

IT WAS NOT a huge change seasonally to go from an Auckland's late winter to a Chicago's early fall. The windy city was already living up to its name before he left the airport. As the cab drove him along the freeway and, at his request, through the city, Luke felt as though he had landed on another planet. He recognized nothing; had no sense of homecoming; felt no connection to the city of his birth. He was loathe to admit that he found it overpowering and intimidating, and tried to convince himself that this would pass. After all, he belonged here. But even that wasn't true. He had belonged in a quiet suburb with tree-lined streets. He had belonged in a family that lived in a house full of love and laughter. But that had not made Chicago his home. A trip to the city itself had been an adventure even in his childhood, so why should it be different now? His dad had taken him every season to see the Chicago Bears play, but a stadium was a little world of its own, and had nothing to do with the towering skyscrapers and the traffic din that now assailed him.

He arrived at Reuben Hayes's office in mid-afternoon. The man who had loved his father gave him a handshake first, and then threw decorum to the wind and bear-hugged him. It was the first, and only, time that Luke felt he was home in Chicago. The lawyer had intended to meet Luke at the airport, but had not received the telex telling him what flight Luke was on. Luke dismissed his apologies. The cab ride had been important, but he was glad that he had Uncle Reube to himself, without the presence of Wayne Fraser. Luke sat on the leather couch and Reuben took the seat to his right next to the coffee table. For over an hour Reuben talked to him about his father and the company and how it had continued to grow in spite of Joe's death. Then came the business end of the afternoon. "Well, son," Reuben said, and the use of the word son made Luke start, for he had not heard it in so long. "Let's get this blasted will thing out of the way shall we? After all, that's why you came all this way." Luke did not try to explain that the will had been the least priority in his coming. It was something that needed to be addressed, and it might as well be now. Still, he was not prepared for either the generosity, or the intricacy of his father's provision. Reuben broke it down simply for him.

"What it means is that you get a million dollars straight away. It's yours, free and clear, has been since your birthday," the old lawyer said, and Luke choked on his coffee.

"I hadn't expected anything like that." Luke told him. "Does that mean the plant is being sold?" Reuben chuckled. "Gracious me, no. The company is worth maybe fifteen to twenty million dollars, and it's increasing all the time." Luke looked at his trustee in disbelief. Even for Luke, who knew more than most men of his age how business worked, the figure was astronomical. There were a few millionaires in New Zealand. Wrightson, his idol, was one of them, but Luke had not expected to be joining the ranks at such an early age. Reuben smiled at his shocked expression and continued.

"Everything becomes yours when you turn thirty, Luke. Now that may seem a long time to wait, but we're talking an awful lot of money here. And, you know, you're dad never made it big till he was much older than that. Not that a million bucks at twenty-one makes you exactly poor." He laughed raucously and Luke found himself laughing even louder, breaking the tension, and the sense of alienation that had been building since his plane landed.

"Of course, even though it's in trust, it's your company." Reuben reassured him. "I expect you'll want a seat on the board, and some hands on involvement. Tomorrow I think it would be a good idea if we took you to the plant and you can see how it works. Then you'll be able to form some opinion as to how you'd like to ease in. Of course, apart from your directorship, we'd expect that you'd have a salaried position with the company. My God, it's good to have you home Luke. You look more like your Mom, God rest her, but there's your dad's jaw, and the way you hold your head." Luke smiled at the excited lawyer, but the truth was that he remembered very little now about the small idiosyncrasies that had made his parents individuals. In photographs they were two-dimensional smiling people. He could remember how they smelled, the sound of their voices and their laughter, but he could not see, in his mind's eye, anything. Every time he tried, he was overpowered by the vision of flames and the black smoke of death.

"There's the house too, of course." Reuben continued. "That's yours, free and clear of all encumbrances." Luke was surprised. He had never asked about his old home, but had always assumed it had been sold. "It's empty?" he asked in surprise. Reuben smiled wistfully.

"For ten years. That's too long for any house to be empty, Luke. Oh, my trustee powers allowed me to sell it, or rent it out, but I just couldn't do it. Part of me knew that you'd be coming back one day and… it's your home. It's been cleaned every week. I mean, you could move in, right now, tonight if you want to. I have the keys." Even before Luke could answer, the old man crossed to his desk and produced the keys that he already had waiting for Luke. Luke stared at them in astonishment. It was the same brass and leather key ring that he had given to his father the Christmas before they had gone to Europe, and he knew every one of the keys on the ring. There was the front door, the back door, the inside porch, the garage, the greenhouse, the games room. And suddenly he could see the house as it was on the morning they had left it; bright and shining in the early watery sunlight. He would go back, he knew that in an instant. But not now, not in the dark. There might be ghosts, locked in memories that would haunt him, leap at him from the shadows, and he had no wish to encounter them at night.

"I think I'll take a hotel tonight. See the plant and the house in the morning," Luke said, lost in his thoughts.

"You'll do no such thing, Luke Powers," Reuben told him. " Ethel and I sort of suspected that you might not want to stay at the house. You'll come stay with us. The spare room is all made for you and there's no way I'm taking no for an answer so you may as well save your breath." Luke chucked to see the lawyer so adamantly laying down the law. "I wasn't planning on arguing," he replied, and Reuben nodded with satisfaction. "Good, then it's settled. Now, we could go to some fancy restaurant for dinner, but Ethel's making pot-roast. You wouldn't remember of course, but Ethel's pot-roast is to die for." And suddenly Luke could recall the smell, the rich aroma of the meat and the juices, the gravy, the hot biscuits; the string beans and baby carrots, and he smiled. "I do remember," was all he needed to say, and no more discussion was necessary.

The spare bedroom was decorated in early American colonial, an Amish patchwork quilt adorning the bed. The pot-roast had been all he remembered; Ethel fawned over him more effusively than his grandmother, and he was regaled with stories of the Hayes children, including Reuben junior, who had just completed law at Harvard and joined a prominent firm in New York. The evening had been homey and welcoming. He snuggled down under the blankets as the night was cool, and told himself that this epitomized everything that he had missed or tried to block out of his head through the years between. And yet, before he fell asleep, he was aware of the emptiness inside, a yearning not for place but for past; and an uneasiness that he could not lightly dismiss.

The following morning he traveled with Reuben in the Lincoln Continental. They met Wayne Fraser for breakfast, Luke plowing into a stack of hotcakes and syrup and Canadian bacon with all the enthusiasm of a ten year old boy. Then they journeyed together to the plant. It was smaller than Luke remembered from his childhood. But then, almost everything was, he told himself. Beyond that, though, it was foreign to him. He could remember coming with his father to the office which overlooked the factory floor. He had always been fascinated with the giant machines that created the fiber like something, to his child's mind, from a science fiction comic. Now though, he was faced with an adult's perspective. He quickly realized that his interest in textiles was limited to the novelty of the non-stick fry-pan, and whether he needed to iron a shirt. He met those workers who had been close to Joe, and grappled with his memory to find their names. More often than not he was unsuccessful; his boyhood visits to the plant had been an interesting time-passer, and a chance to be with his dad more than anything else. He had been told the names of the stalwarts of course, but his ten-year old mind had not been interested enough to store them away. Now, as he talked to Monty Dwyer, the foreman, or Margaret Teasedale, who had been his father's secretary, he found that the only thing they had in common was a mutual love and respect for Joe. That should have been enough, but it wasn't. Time and time again, in the three hours he spent at his father's plant, the rhetorical question was raised, "So, you've come to take over where your dad left off?" It was a natural assumption. People on all sides were telling him that he belonged there. It was a ready-made niche where he would be instantly accepted with respect, simply because he was Joe's son. Why then, was he fighting it?

"They must think I'm some kind of freak," he told his trustees as they sat drinking coffee in the workers dining hall. Reuben looked at him quizzically.

"Why's that?" he asked.

"Well, I'm Joe's son, but I don't know what Joe knew. I'm not even interested in learning what Joe knew. I have this funny accent which makes me sound like a muted duck, and I'm quite certain that they have me pegged as some kind of hippie who doesn't own a decent suit. If I were working here, and had been for half my life, I sure as hell wouldn't want me in charge of the company, or anywhere near the place. No way." Wayne laughed and shook his head.

"I think you may be right... about some of them anyway. They've been here since your dad started and they're pretty set in their ways. Guess you're not that interested in business huh?" Luke shrugged.

"I'm not that interested in textiles" he replied, "but I think the move to buy the new equipment is a good one. It'll save us about one and a half million dollars a year in the long term and we can amortize costs, maximize depreciation and recoup maybe ten percent by on-selling the old machinery for scrap. That should allow us, if the world market stabilizes and we expand into researching new synthetics, to increase our overall profit percentages by about seven to nine percent over and above what we're now achieving." He took delight in seeing Wayne's open-mouthed expression. He didn't like the accountant much, and he disliked even more the suggestion that he was some kind of hick from a tin pot country who was playing out of his league. Hell, he could run this company with his eyes closed; streamline it and push its growth through the roof if he wanted to, but he didn't want to. He heard a guffaw of laughter from Uncle Reube.

"Serves you right Wayne. You know what the boy's been up to in New Zealand. Serves you right for thinking he couldn't cut the major league. I think we may just have us a general manager here," the lawyer said with smug satisfaction, but the alarm bells started ringing immediately for Luke.

"I think I have to tell you now, that I've got no intention of moving into the company. It's obviously being competently, if conservatively, run in exactly the way my dad wanted it to be. Now, if I were really turned on by terylene, polyester, ban-Ion and all that other stuff, maybe there would be a point. But I'm not, and there isn't. Let the company stay the way it is. I think maybe I'll move into something completely different." Luke finished his speech in a hurry, allowing no room for argument or discussion. He saw Reuben and Wayne exchange looks. What could he read there? Disappointment from the lawyer? Satisfaction from the accountant? It was irrelevant, for his mind was made up.

"But your place as heir, your profits, your directorship…" Reuben asked. Luke tried to reassure him.

"I'll be here, as required, for meetings," he promised. I'm very proud of what my father built and I'm very pleased with how the company has been run. Of course, I'll be following the performance of the company." Luke was the only shareholder and wanted to extract as much money from the cash cow as he could without jeopardizing its growth. "I would like to discuss with you, at some time in the future, a dividend that would be acceptable to you without sacrificing the growth of the company. If I'm needed, of course I'll involve myself. But we all know I won't be needed. I haven't been for the past ten years. Why should things be different now? I don't think there's any point in my spending anymore time here. And I have something else important to do," he concluded.

"Where are you going?" Fraser asked as Luke got up from the table and shook their hands. He needed only one word to reply.

"Home."

THE HOUSE ON Rushmore Crescent seemed so unchanged that he momentarily lost awareness of his adult self as he drove up to it in the rental car. He had been driving around in circles for the best part of an hour, unable to find his way there through the labyrinth of freeways and streets that seemed completely unfamiliar to him. Or maybe, he thought, part of him had been afraid to actually get there, to confront the past. He slammed the car door and walked up the front path to the imposing entrance. It was not a huge house, but it was prestigious without being pretentious, and that had summed up his parents in his eyes. He put the key in the lock, almost expecting that it would not fit; that the lock would have rusted in the intervening years. It turned instantly, and the door opened before he even expected it, and he found himself standing in the hallway. There were fresh flowers on the hallstand; Reuben must have told the cleaning lady he was coming. Autumn flowers – chrysanthemums – he thought, though he wasn't great at recognizing anything other than roses or wild flowers. The carpet in the hallway had been laid only a year before the holiday that ended his life. It had been really "cool" at the time. A new nylon carpet with a strong geometric pattern. His parents had allowed him and his sisters to view the available options and Luke could remember complaining that his folks were old-fashioned. The three children had yelled with excitement that the house was now the hippest in the street. Now it simply seemed old-fashioned and outdated. The living room had not changed. The large scrunchy couches looked exactly as they had done when he and the girls had bounced on them. The kitchen, with its walnut cupboards and yellow trim – his mom had loved yellow, it was for sunshine and daffodils she said – stood waiting for him. Even the electric kettle stood on sentry duty. The percolator was in its place on the stove. Nothing had changed, and yet nothing was the same.

He climbed the stairs slowly to that most intimate part of the house, the bedrooms where his parents had made love, where the girls had fought, where he had put model airplanes together and shot baskets through the hoop on the back of his closet door. He felt faint as he wandered through the girls' bedroom. The white frilly bedspreads with the pink rosebuds still adorned the white Queen Ann beds. The ornate white wicker shelves held the Barbie doll collection. The Spirograph and the bead making sets, the half finished pictures from the painting by number kits... all looked as though they had just been put away, maybe for a short time till the girls returned from summer camp. He moved with feet of lead to his own room, needing to see it, and yet dreading it at the same time. He could see his hand trembling as he reached for the doorknob, and he hoped for a voice to ring out and stop him – "Stay right there mister. What the hell do you think you're doing? Desecrating the memory of the dead?" But of course, there was no voice. Yet it would have been correct, for the boy who had lived in the room he was about to enter was dead, as dead as if he had died in the blazing van. He entered the room and caught his breath. He had tried to imagine this room many times over the past ten years, and yet its image had always been hazy or distorted. Now, though, it was so dazzlingly clear that it shocked him. The plaid bedspread. His desk with the bright red upholstered chair. His school pennants, the football posters, the basketball hoop. His model airplanes hanging on strings from the ceiling like a mobile. The old teddy that he had been given at his christening, old and threadbare even when he had left it ten years ago, sat on the bookshelf looking at him lopsidedly as if to say, "What took you so long." He picked it up to study it, but the moment he felt it in his hands he felt the pain in his chest, and he could not breathe. For a second he was afraid that he was having a heart attack: dead at twenty-one, after ten years of borrowed time. How ironic that would be! Then he realized that there were emotions inside him screaming to get out. He did not, could not, cry, but sobs of pain without tears racked his body and he writhed on his childhood bed with the agony of despair and loneliness. When it passed, he lay there quietly, looking at the posters, remembering the games where he had seen his superstars play. Then he left the house, locked the doors and drove away in the rental car. He did not say goodbye, even though he knew he would never return, and he took nothing with him except a threadbare teddy bear. It was all he needed to remind him of what was lost and could never be found, no matter how hard he looked.

REUBEN HAYES LOOKED at him in disbelief, yet he could see that Luke was serious. "But, you are an American Luke. You've said yourself that you never really belonged in New Zealand. Where then?" The disappointment was obvious in his voice. Luke smiled apologetically.

"I don't know. I wish I did. Maybe America is just too much for me in one hit. Maybe I'll try Australia. You know, like a stepping stone. But whatever happens, I want you to sell the house. It's lonely, it needs company... a family who will love it the way we all did. It's been alone too long." Luke was wistful as he replied.

"And you haven't?" Reuben challenged. "Adjustments aren't easy Luke, you know that better than I. But you're not giving this a shot, son. The company will be yours one day. You have to remember who you are." The lawyer had meant the words to be supportive, but he saw Luke tense at them.

"Who am I Uncle Reube? That's the problem. I don't have any idea. Sure, I'm Joe Powers's son, but who is that? Joe Powers has been dead for ten years. Dead. I can't define myself that way for the rest of my life," Luke said.

"You don't have to. Once you start running the company you'll establish your own identity with everyone. It's what you were born to," Reuben replied softly.

Luke sighed. "Someone else's expectations huh? I can't do that either, Uncle Reube. I wish for your sake, and dad's, that I could. But he couldn't be the same as his father, any more than I can be the same as mine. I have to live *my* life according to *my* needs. I don't even know what they are, but I sure as hell have to find out."

CHAPTER NINE

"Y OUNG, AMBITIOUS ENTREPRENEUR with one million US dollars to invest seeks highly capitalized partner to invest with in dreams and visions and bring them to reality. The South Pacific is hurtling towards the future and I'm going with it. Who's coming with me?" Hughie finished reading the advertisement aloud and gave a low whistle as he turned to look at Luke. "You laid it on with a trowel, didn't you pal?" he asked with a grin. Luke gave an abashed smile and shrugged. "Hey, it's the American way." The two men sat on the small back porch of Hughie's old wooden house, bought with a worker's compensation payout. It was early winter, and cold, and Luke could feel the spear-like steel of the chill grey air thrusting through his flesh to his core. Hughie, relaxed in the wheelchair which was now so much a part of him it was difficult for Luke to remember how strong his friend's legs had been, fortified himself with endless nips from a rapidly diminishing bottle of scotch. Luke had tried to take the bottle away and, when that had proved futile, had attempted to joke Hughie out of the drinking binge. It was useless. Hughie had joked that he never drank scotch before midday, but he would often consume several beers for breakfast. Now, he handed the advertisement from the *New Zealand Herald* back to Luke, and turned his attention to the scotch bottle.

"So, do you think anyone will reply?" he asked before putting the bottle to his lips. Luke thought about his reply. He had also taken a prominent advertisement in the business section of the *Singapore Times,* the *Sydney Morning Herald* and the *Hong Kong Daily.*

"No doubt I'll get people by the busload hoping to take my money," he answered. "But what I'm looking for is a mentor. I could continue to make money, but that's not enough. I want something more." He was surprised by the derisive snort that Hughie offered in reply.

"Easy to say when you're rolling in it ." His friend could not keep the anger from his voice, but Luke didn't bite. He had learned in the past few hours that almost anything could make Hughie angry, and it would do no good to point out all the times he had offered his friend money and been knocked back.

"How many replies did you get?"

Luke laughed. "The advertisement was only in yesterday. Give me a chance. It's a box number, so it'll be a few days before they start coming in. There's no mad hurry. That's why I thought I'd take a few days down here."

"Come slumming in the past while you wait for your future, huh?" Hughie asked with an edge of resentment. "Well, why not? You've got it all, haven't you Luke? Anything you want just lift your hand and snap your fingers, isn't that right?"

Luke could feel his own anger rising, but it would do no good to decry Hughie as a self-pitying drunk, or remind him of the loss of Luke's family and past. Instead he looked deep into his friends eyes, and answered softly.

"I wish it were true, mate. Then I'd be able to snap my fingers and you'd get out of that chair and walk again."

Hughie held his gaze for a long time, until his eyes filled with tears, but Luke could not be certain if they were caused by emotion or the sheer physicality of staring him down without blinking. Then Hughie almost spat the words at him bitterly.

"With what? I've got no legs, remember?" and he span the wheelchair round and went back into the house. It was the only time he could remember, apart from the aftermath of losing his family, that he felt totally helpless. He could see that there was every chance of Hughie descending further into the pit of despair in which he found himself entrenched for the remainder of his life. He would always be cared for: though Hughie's family was struggling, New Zealand provided free health and a sickness benefit. University was still offered to all at a negligible fee and Luke desperately hoped that he could bring Hughie around to recognize the opportunities that were available to him.

Later that night, Kiri came to visit. Now married to a mechanic in Rotorua, she brought her twin baby boys, not yet able to walk. It was the first time he saw Hughie laugh, as if the crippled man with no legs empathized with the babies, kicking and wriggling on their backs, who had not yet learned to use theirs.

Luke watched his first love tend to her babies. Though still in her teens, the agelessness of motherhood had softened her cheeks, rounded her body. A myriad of emotions overwhelmed him, seeing her for the first time in two years. Most potent of these was not so much sexual desire as an uncontrollable yearning to melt into her and become part of her. Yet that was coupled with a sense of melancholy he had never known before, not even when he had first learned of his parents' and sisters' deaths. He would never hold her again; never make love to her; never declare his love. Once it had been forbidden to him, but he had taken it anyway.

She raised her head from changing one of the boy's nappies. Her hair brushed against her face and her eyes seemed to look straight into his soul. He was aware, in that moment, that she had read his mind, knew every thought. She gave a gentle nod of her head, a sad smile playing at her lips, as if to acknowledge their shared regret.

He had to turn away then, for fear he would cry in front of her, and he was engulfed in loneliness. He tried to understand his feelings for her and determine if he still loved her or not. After all this time, he still could not answer the question, nor grasp the nature of his feelings for her. But he was still in love with the memory of being in love with her, and it terrified him that he might always be that way, emotionally trapped by what was past. He knew that whatever replies came from the challenge he had placed in the paper, he needed to go somewhere that was so vastly different from all that he cherished, there would be no room for memories to haunt him.

After a makeshift dinner of fish and chips, Luke found himself alone with Kiri while Hughie went to make coffee and crack open a full bottle of scotch. Luke did not have to be told that Kiri felt the same pain for her brother as Luke did himself. "It's been nearly two years, Kiri. Has he done any work at all?" he asked, with grave concern. She shook her head.

"He talked about finishing the degree, but then, when he heard the news about his spine, he just... I don't know, gave up I suppose. It's like he's accepted that his lot in life is to be a cripple on welfare, and he doesn't have the strength or the will to fight it."

Luke was confused. "What news about his spine? Is there something wrong, something worse?" He was almost afraid to hear the answer, but Kiri looked at him in surprise.

"He didn't tell you? You didn't notice?" Luke shook his head, unsure that he wanted to hear what she had to say, and wishing he had never asked the question. She sighed. "Something worse? Yes, I suppose it is for him," she said in compassion without pity. "He's not paralyzed, Luke. The damage to the spinal cord is far less than they diagnosed and it's repaired itself rapidly. He has ninety percent movement and flexibility to the hips and legs. He could walk now, except..." she couldn't continue, and Luke, almost disbelieving at the cruelty of it all, whispered the words for her.

"Except he has no legs."

The following morning he told his friend that he knew the truth, and Hughie laughed bitterly. "What a joke huh? It's hard enough in this world when you're born the wrong color, race, whatever. You try to make your way and half the time you don't have a leg to stand on. Well, here I am, *all* the time, without *two* legs to stand on."

"You could walk Hughie, you know that," Luke replied.

"Artificial legs? Fibreglass or plastic.... that sickly pale beige color they paint them to pass for skin? Not me mate! They took my legs. They didn't even try to save them. Don't tell me they wouldn't have made the effort if it had been you. But what's one lousy Maori more or less? Sickness benefit's roughly the same as the dole, so he won't cost the country any more in handouts if we chop his legs off."

Luke angrily span the wheelchair round to face him.

"Cut it out. You think those doctors were racists, that they did this deliberately? You're not that bloody stupid Hughie. You want to blame the whites; you want to blame the world. You don't want to accept the reality of the situation. But I don't believe you're a racist, or a loser, or a no-hoper who has to spend the rest of his life defined by that chair." He hoped to spark some fight in the man, but Hughie just shrugged resignedly.

"That's the difference between us, then," he replied. "I do."

Luke left later that day for the drive down to Taupo. He had managed to at least get Hughie to consider getting back to his degree before his brain became so pickled in alcohol that it was no longer of any use. For a moment, but only that, Luke had considered coming back to New Zealand and putting the time into rebuilding Hughie. Yet he knew instinctively that he could not take control of another man's destiny. Hughie himself was the only one who could reclaim his life.

Taupo was changing, slowly and subtly and almost imperceptibly to those who had never left. But Luke could see the signs. It would take ten years, he figured, for the tourist boom to be realized, but those who now flew across the ocean and around the world for the trout fishing and the lake, and the luscious mountain surrounds, now outnumbered the Kiwis who came for their two weeks annual holidays. One thing that had not changed was the house where he had first been welcomed eleven years before. His grandparents had not changed either. They were still an uneasy mix of deep affection and physical reservation, stiffening when he embraced them both. His grandfather made the grilled baby lamb chops and minted peas that he loved so much, and they talked until well after midnight. It was a sign to Luke of their love for him, for he had never known them to stay up past the witching hour, except once a year on New Year's Eve.

He told his grandfather of the newspaper advertisement, and his anticipation of replies.

"All kinds of countries are moving into manufacturing. Look at the Japanese, ten years ago their cars were a joke, now they're into prestige vehicles, televisions, refrigerators, you name it. Korea will be next, maybe Thailand, somewhere like that. They want to work, and wages are low. Australia can't compete, neither can we. Wages are too high, work ethics too low. All I have to do is find the challenge... the right country, the right product." He was aware of the mounting excitement in his voice, the need now to get back to Auckland. The anticipation of the replies that awaited was overwhelming him. But Sandy merely looked at him whimsically.

"And then what?" he asked his grandson. Luke was taken aback by the question.

"Well, I guess I make a lot of money," he joked offhandedly. But Sandy was not amused. "You've already got a lot of money. You sold the house in Chicago and you've been purchasing more businesses – both here and in Australia – than I can keep up with. You could live off the interest of the million in the bank or wherever and never need to work again. That's not what you're after. We both know that."

"Then what am I after?" Luke asked defensively. The old man smiled.

"You won't find it gallivanting around the world Luke. What happens when you run out of countries?" And Luke felt suddenly uncertain and vulnerable. It was a question he had never dared to ask himself. Sandy got up from his chair and crossed to Luke, prodding his grandson's chest with his finger.

"Here lad. That's the place where the heart dwells, and you have to make room for the spirit alongside it, or your poor soul will wear itself out with gallivanting. It's not out there somewhere, lad," and he gestured wildly towards everything beyond the walls. "It's in here, that's where you'll find it. But it's a much longer journey than you're ready for just now." Luke could find no argument, for he knew the old man was right. But he knew, just as certainly, that he would make that chase, futile though it may be, across the world, never certain whether he was running to, or running from, that unspoken need.

BOWEN TERRACE SAT halfway up the mountain on the Island of Hong Kong. The skyscrapers and Victoria Harbour could be seen from it, and then Kowloon and the New Territories of China beyond. The Chinese believed it was beneficial to live on a mountain overlooking water, for there lives The Dragon, and both dragon and water mean wealth. Those who built their luxury mansions overlooking the water were not so much interested in the view, as the dragon's path, for it is a fact, born before time, that the dragon comes down to the water every morning to swim. Like many other ancient mansions, with their glazed green tiles and shiny red bricks, The house of Miss Anna Chen boasted a hole, a perfect circle, through the center of the single wall that linked the two wings of the mansion. Her late father, the industrialist Chen Lee Xiao, had made and lost several fortunes in China.

Then he had fled, at the start of the war, years before the communists took over in 1949, taking with him his wife and two children, a small chest full of priceless jade, and as much cash as he could carry. They had lived in a small flat on the Kowloon side of Hong Kong for two years, in a poverty stricken block that allowed one window per family. There had been temptations to sell the jade and make his family comfortable, but he had resisted them. He knew that the dragon had visited them in the past, and would again, if he found the right place. Did not Kowloon itself, taken from its original name of Kau-Lung, mean nine dragons? Nine peaks surrounded the peninsula, indicating great wealth in the hands of the dragons. Was that not the reason why the British, the yellow-hairs, prospered and became rich?

For nearly two years the once wealthy businessman worked in the markets and cared for his family. The money he had brought with him was worthless now that the Communists had seized the banks. But the jade was growing in value every day. And so he worked, and every moment when he was not working, he looked for a place that would become a sanctuary for him and his family. Only then would he exchange the jade. It was thirty-six years earlier, in the year of the Tiger, that he ran up the steep hill, climbed the hundreds of steps, and found himself at the far end of Bowen Terrace, away from the traditional verandah of Victoria Peak, where hawkers sold on weekends, and lovers visited the goddess's shrine. There he saw it, the place that he knew was destined to turn his fortunes around.

The house was old, and in need of repairs. Most of the traditional houses had been replaced by stucco Hollywood-style bungalows or Georgian and Victorian copies as the British hierarchy had moved aside for the American influx of wealth. Very little was owned by the Chinese as there was no need, in those years before the revolution, for them to leave the sophistication of Shanghai, or the culture of Peking, to settle in the British colony. The British had, as they always did, made themselves benevolent dictators of Hong Kong, and now claimed it as a British outpost. Mostly the Chinese worked for them, and the new breed of Anglophile Chinese businessman capitalizing on the growth of Hong Kong wanted a new house with all the luxuries that money could buy, but Xiao was not one of them and never would be.

He stood at the gates, guarded by the green glazed lion statues and saw beyond the traditional roof and the green and red of the house. Green represented wealth, and red happiness, and the house was halfway up the mountain; high enough to be impressive, yet not so high as to be ostentatious. But it was the hole in the wall that sold Xiao. He knew that the dragon would take the most direct route to the water in the morning, straight through the hole rather than around the houses or over the roofs. And he knew that the dragon would return, wet from its swim, and shake itself to shed the excess water as it passed through the hole on its way home to the peak; and that water, along with scales from the dragon's back, would shower the house with wealth. This was the house he had waited for, and he had to have it if he were to know a future like the past that had been stripped from him by the revolution. The house was then owned by a Dutch stockbroker whose wife knew nothing of the tradition or legends of her adopted home, and abhorred the green and red monstrosity. She was ready to leave Hong Kong, with its overcrowded harbor, its humidity and pollution, its low-minded high society from the English middle class. Xiao was able to purchase the house, including some exquisite hand carved Chinese antique furniture that the mistress of the house had stored away – she so despised the house – for half the value of the jade. The other half of the money from the antique jade set Xiao up again in business, and never again did the family have to live in one room. The dragon came each day and shed his wealth on his way back to his lair, and the family prospered. Each morning, just after dawn, Xiao and his wife and children would assemble on the terrace and symbolically greet the dragon on his way to swim with "Tso Shan," a formal good morning.

Each evening they would reassemble to say "Toh tse," 'thank you for your gift,' as the dragon returned to the peak.

It was on this same terrace, in 1974, also the year of the Tiger, that Miss Anna Chen, forty-six years old and arguably the wealthiest woman in Hong Kong if not the entire East, completed the morning ritual of greeting the symbolic dragon when her personal assistant and chief advisor, Thomas Ho, joined her. Thomas had been with Miss Anna, and her father before her, since he graduated from the University of Shanghai in 1955, after years of boarding school at Eton. A remarkably refined and educated man, part butler, part confidant, he carried with him a collection of international newspapers, for he and Miss Anna had spoken at length of the need for her to diversify and extend her business empire further into the South Pacific area.

He accepted, as he always did, her invitation to join her for breakfast in the small parlor that offered the finest view of the harbor. The first of the day's Star ferries was making its run from Kowloon to Hong Kong Island, and Miss Anna watched it with a smile, remembering the many times she had traveled the ferry as a child. Now her forays were made in a Mercedes with Dennis Yip, her "wild young man of business," at the wheel, as Thomas, though a man of impeccable taste and manners, was an over-cautious driver who tried Miss Anna's patience. The breakfast table was set with a curious culinary marriage of east and west: plain boiled rice and dim sum seeming quite at home with toast and marmalade; lightly brewed Orange Pekoe rubbing elbows with Brazilian coffee, and a jug of boiled milk. The two ate delicately and silently, for it would have been impolite to discuss business at a time when the digestive system requires one's full attention. Finally Miss Anna put down the tiny porcelain cup, and the day's business commenced. Not until two hours later, when all matters of importance were settled, did Thomas broach the subject of the somewhat audacious advertisement in the *Sydney Morning Herald*.

Miss Anna read it with some amusement. "They are forthright to the point of barbarism, these Australians, are they not Thomas?" she asked in a surprisingly girlish and lilting voice. He allowed himself a polite smile that did not betray the depth of his feelings for her, even though he was certain that she already suspected them. There was a tacit unspoken agreement that her position made her unattainable as a wife. Despite Thomas's education, largely at the expense of an English benefactor, he was not an acceptable mate for a woman in her position, and so he used his natural reserve as a way of keeping his distance from her.

"I agree in theory, Miss Anna. However, the young man who placed the advertisement is not an Australian but, apparently, an American." he informed her. She laughed delightedly.

"Ah, that explains so much. America, the home of the Barbarians. And yet he writes from Sydney?"

"He has business interests there, and he was raised in New Zealand, a marginally more civilized country I believe." Thomas allowed himself another smile as he gently teased her. She looked at him approvingly. He was so thorough in every piece of information he conveyed. "And, what's more interesting is that the same advertisement is scheduled to run in your own newspaper tomorrow morning." Miss Anna pursed her lips without taking her eyes off the newspaper.

"Since you have looked into it so extensively, I must assume that you believe he is someone who might be of interest to us. Otherwise you would not have brought the newspaper to my attention," she surmised, and he nodded in return.

"He is, for his age, quite remarkable. I think perhaps he may have the eye of a visionary, and yet he is a capitalist at heart."

"More profit than prophet, eh Thomas?" She teased, and he allowed himself a discreet chuckle. She continued. "Does this visionary have a name?"

Thomas nodded. "He does. His name is Luke Powers." She raised an eyebrow. "Really? He sounds more like an actor, or cowboy star. But if you are satisfied...? Let us meet this Luke Powers."

LUKE RETURNED TO Auckland to find sixty-three replies awaiting him. Some were little more than begging letters, but several warranted serious consideration. Two were from Fiji, one from the Cocos Islands, four from Papua New Guinea, and the rest from local businessmen, some of whom he had brushed shoulders with, although they had no way of knowing that when they replied to the box number. Some of the schemes proposed were ill conceived, or hare-brained, and Luke knew that he might as well give his one million dollars away in hand-outs. Of those that seemed to have a sound financial base, two were with men he had sworn never to deal with again, and the others were safe and uninspiring. He was beginning to think that the whole idea had been a waste of time when the letter arrived from Hong Kong. It was polite and brief, written by a Thomas Ho. It outlined succinctly the business activities of the holding company Eastern Star, and asked him to come to Hong Kong for meetings "which might, hopefully, prove mutually beneficial." Enclosed with the letter was a first class ticket, and instructions as to how he would be met, if he chose to make the trip. Luke was impressed and delighted. Whoever this guy was, he had balls. He had even booked a flight for the day after Luke had arranged settlement on a business he was selling, as if somehow he had known that Luke would be free then.

It took Luke only a moment to make his decision. Thomas Ho had added in his letter that a room would be reserved for him at the Peninsula Hotel, at Eastern Star's expense. A room, not a suite, Luke noted. This suggested a company that treated its colleagues well but without pretension. That alone was enough to intrigue Luke, and besides, he had never been to Hong Kong. What did he have to lose?

The flight was shorter than he expected, and he watched from his window seat as the plane circled Hong Kong and came in to land. He was convinced that they would either crash into the mountain or topple off the runway that extended out into the water, and be lost forever at the bottom of the harbour. In the four days since he had received the ticket, he had done as much checking on Eastern Star as he had time for. He knew little except that it was the fourth highest listed company of the Hang Sen, the Hong Kong stock exchange, and that alone was enough to interest him. He found himself excited, with a knot of anticipation in his stomach as he made his way from the plane to the flight lounge.

He knew instantly that the young man who met him was not Thomas Ho, who had written to him. Dennis Yip was in his late twenties, perhaps thirty, Luke decided. Open and friendly, dressed expensively yet casual, Dennis had the easy manner and the American accent one might expect from a graduate of the Harvard business school. He talked incessantly as he collected Luke's case from the baggage carousel, yet Luke could see Yip appraising everything about him, from his shoes to the quality of his baggage.

The trip from the airport, on the island, to Kowloon and the hotel was made easier by the tunnel beneath the harbour, which had opened only two years earlier. Over half a mile long, set nearly a hundred feet below the bottom of the harbour, it cut the journey by as much as twenty minutes in the peak hour traffic. Luke asked questions during the journey, for he had been surprised to learn that Eastern Star was headed by a woman, and Thomas Ho's name did not even appear on the Board of Directors list. "I thought women were pretty much second class citizens in the East," he ventured, and Dennis laughed without reserve.

"Well, they're not ball-breakers like the Americans, and they're not as loud or, shall we say, uninhibited as the Australians, but there's a growing number of powerful business women in Hong Kong, and even more in the Philippines and Taiwan. Miss Anna is tiny, but she packs a helluva corporate wallop in those dainty hands." the Chinese man explained.

"Miss Anna?" Luke queried. "It kind of conjures up an image of a little old lady in a Kimono." Dennis gave him a disapproving sideways glance.

"Get your countries right, Luke. The Kimono is Japanese, not Chinese, and we may look the same to you, but we're not exactly blood brothers. Long before Pearl Harbor, the Japanese wanted China. As for Miss Anna, don't expect a little old lady. She may be old enough to be your mother, but not mine, and she shops twice a year in Paris. She also happens to be the most respected business woman in Asia, and you're privileged to have her interested in you." Luke did not reply. He realized he had made a faux pas and, if Dennis was testing his suitability as a candidate for her approval, he had failed miserably. He tried to stammer an apology for his crassness, and was relieved when he felt the iciness dispel and Dennis once again talked to him as an equal.

"Chen Lee Xiao had the empire earmarked for his son," Dennis explained. "He groomed the boy from childhood, and made him a director at twenty-one. He even chose the right wife, the right house, and the right name for their only child. Miss Anna didn't mind. She traveled, studied, had more freedom than she might have otherwise. She was an artist then. A painter, you know. She had no interest in the business or empire building. But then the old man — and his son — they were both killed in a plane crash. Must be sixteen, seventeen years ago now. And that was it. Miss Anna inherited Eastern Star, and there were those who said she'd bring the empire down." He chuckled to himself.

"But she didn't?" Luke asked rhetorically. Dennis gave a grunt of admiration.

"She tripled the holdings in the first ten years, and the company has returned fifteen to twenty percent dividends over the past five years when things were slowing. She's a walking miracle. I did a thesis on her at Stanford, sent it to her for her approval. That's when she offered me a job."

"And does she still paint?" Luke asked with interest, wondering how this dynamo balanced business with her creative spirit. Dennis looked at him in surprise. "You know, nobody's ever asked me that. I honestly don't know," he replied.

The car drew up the driveway to the entrance of The Peninsula, past the fountain around which the three wings of the hotel formed a U shape. Along with Raffles of Singapore, it was arguably the east's most famous hotel. But while Raffles had fallen into disrepair, and lamented the departure of the British Raj and tigers under the billiard tables, the Peninsula had retained its class and elegance and had only a few years earlier been renovated. The door to the car was opened for Luke, and a uniformed valet took his case. He walked through the magnificent glass doors, held by a white uniformed doorman. The short squat figures of the door gods, known as Huffer and Puffer, magnificently etched and painted with gold leaf and bronze powder, kept evil spirits from the guests. On either side, majestic arches signaled the unobtrusive opulence of the hotel foyer with its dark wood and royal blue upholstery. It was early evening and, as Dennis lead Luke to the reception desk, the newcomer could see an orchestra playing on the mezzanine balcony, reached by the stairs on either side of reception. Dennis signed him in and then turned and offered a hand to shake. "I'll be in touch. Just relax, charge whatever you want, see the sights. Just be careful if you go across the harbor to Wan Chai."

Luke did not understand. "Wan Chai? What's that?"

"Well, with the Vietnam war and all, I guess the Americans on R&R would call it pussy heaven. It's the red light district and, believe me, it isn't as quaint as they made it out to be in that 'Suzie Wong' movie," Dennis warned half jokingly.

"How long before I see Miss Anna?" Luke inquired. Dennis shrugged and smiled apologetically. It was clear that any answer would only be a guess.

"Not long," he offered, and was gone with a wave of his hand, leaving Luke to pondering the answer's similarity to the 'how long is a piece of string?' conundrum.

He followed the bellboy to the room, spacious and elegant. From his small balcony he could see the famous clock tower and the lights of Hong Kong Island. He knew he should be jetlagged, but he was too excited to sleep. He walked a few blocks and found a most unlikely spaghetti house where he ate pasta and drank Chinese beer and the whole bill came to little more than two Australian dollars. It was dark when he left the restaurant, and he wandered up Nathan Road, marveling not so much at the shops as the likely electricity bill. He had never seen so many neon lights in his life. The brightness was almost painful to his eyes. Later, he watched a TV show in what he presumed was Mandarin, and fell asleep on top of the bed.

Miss Anna could see the Peninsula hotel from the terrace of her house if she had chosen to use binoculars, but she was not voyeuristic by nature. Of greater interest was Dennis Yip's impression of the young man she had brought to her territory. "Bright, pleasant, polite. Pretty low key for an American. Mostly he asked the right questions. Nothing too crass. Something though..." Dennis searched for the right word. "He's not depressed – or inhibited. But there's something there. A sense of..."

"Melancholy?" she suggested, and Dennis realized that was exactly what emanated from Luke, yet he would never have picked the word. He did not, however, have Miss Anna's advantage. She already knew everything there was to know about Luke Powers's past.

"In your estimation, Dennis, how long should we leave our young friend to adjust before we meet?" she asked. Dennis thought for a moment.

"Three days… maybe four if you push it. He's young, and a little bit green, but he's not starry-eyed and he's no pushover. I get the feeling he's not even that interested in money," he replied. Miss Anna looked incredulous.

"He did not ask how much I am worth?" she asked doubtfully, for she knew that every time she met a proposed colleague, that was the burning question.

"No," Dennis assured her. "But he did ask something strange." Miss Anna was curious. "And what was that?" she asked. Dennis looked uncomfortable, wondering if he had said too much to Luke.

"He… er, he wanted to know if you still paint."

She smiled, and try as he might Dennis could not determine whether she was amused or simply satisfied. But long after he left she stood on the terrace, wondering about Luke Powers, and pondering how her instincts never let her down.

CHAPTER TEN

Hong Kong's autumn was marginally cooler than its summer, and slightly more humid than Auckland would have been. For nearly two days Luke stayed close to the hotel, watching from his window the Star Ferry wind its way backward and forward, and the Chinese junks maneuver their way between the tankers and cargo ships from all over the world. At night he went to Jimmy's, a steakhouse frequented mostly by British and Australian ex-pats, hungry for a slab of meat and a familiar accent. He never stayed away from the hotel for too long, in case Dennis or Thomas Ho should call: he knew little of the etiquette of the East, but Miss Anna was paying his bill, and he didn't want to appear disrespectful, even though he had never met the lady. On the third day, he ventured out in business hours, checking out the Hang Sen, the Hong Kong stock exchange, watching the fortunes of Eastern Star and the modest yet stable turnover and yield of its shares. He moved further, talking to bankers and stockbrokers, who perceived him as a potential player in the market. He was surprised to find that Eastern Star owned everything from newspapers to Supermarkets, and manufactured such diverse products as bicycles and Chinese herbal remedies. Everything he learned about the company, and the mysterious woman who ran it, convinced him that here was a place where he might fit in and find the challenge he so desperately wanted. All that was holding him back was the enigmatic silence from his benefactress.

He telephoned Dennis Yip and invited him to the hotel for lunch, careful to pay for it with his own credit card, so that the invitation would not seem hollow. He was aware that Dennis was amused by his attempts to find out more about Miss Anna and why she was keeping him waiting, but he could not help questioning the man.

"Can you play Mah-Jong, Luke?" Dennis asked him, as Luke struggled with his chopsticks to raise the delicious fresh steamed shrimp dumplings to his mouth.

"I can't even play Chopsticks," he replied with a grin. "Why? Were you figuring on asking me for a game?" Dennis laughed.

"You know, I never learned to play when I was a kid, though my mother used to have her friends over at least once a week. It always seemed to me like fancy dominoes, even though Confucius invented it. But later, when I knew business management was what I wanted to do, I had to learn to play. Hell, up till then I figured it was just a game." "And it isn't?" Luke asked innocently. Dennis shook his head.

"It's a psychological test. You can tell everything you need to know about a man by the way he plays. Mahjong games in business are as important as contracts." Luke looked surprised.

"Really? What? You mean, you lose a game and bang goes the deal?" he asked.

"No. It isn't so much whether you win or lose, but how. Kind of like chess, in a way." Dennis responded, and he noticed Luke's expression of understanding at the comparison to chess. " If you don't take it seriously, or if you make stupid moves, or you're too tentative, you're a bad business risk. But if you're mature, prepared to give up some ground, have a game plan, and are determined to stick to it, then you're someone to be reckoned with." He looked deep into Luke's eyes, while Luke grappled with the information.

"So, I guess the point you're making is not to rush things, but be prepared for when they happen," he asked. Dennis smiled.

"More than that. Whizz kids are the buzz, Young Turks of industry, all that bullshit Time Magazine feeds us. You've got to have those qualities, sure, but someone like Miss Anna doesn't take chances on some young hotshot pissing away a fortune. So you need patience too. Hong Kong is still China, no matter how much we all protest otherwise. Twenty-three years from now they're supposed to claim us back, though I can't see it happening myself. In China, natural energy, Chi, determines how long something will take. And you've just got to go with the flow. You fight it, and it's bad Feng Shui all round." He placed a reassuring hand on Luke's shoulder.

"Don't worry" Luke told him. "I'm here now, and I'll stick around as long as it takes for her to check me out." Dennis chuckled.

"Luke. She had you checked out before you even landed at Kai Tak. Now the game is on, and she's learning what kind of a player you are."

IT WAS ON the evening of the fourth day that Luke Powers's life changed irrevocably. He had spoken to Thomas Ho that morning. Ho had called and, with a mixture of British charm and Chinese formality, had offered Miss Anna's apologies. Some problems with international money exchange for a new business acquisition were keeping her from greeting Luke in the manner she would have hoped. Thomas conveyed her deep regrets and suggested that he might send a car to perhaps take Luke sightseeing. Luke had thanked Ho, but preferred to make his own way around the tourist attractions. He had taken the ferry across the harbor, then hopped the bus to Repulse Bay. The tourist book told him that the favorite bathing spot had once been called Shallow Water Bay, until the British had built armaments to repulse pirates. There he had walked on the sand, watched by the five meter statues that looked constantly out to sea, protectors of the fishermen. He had eaten a burger in McDonald's and laughed at seeing Ronald McDonald with Chinese eyes above the all-American smile. The South China Sea lapped lazily against the beach as a junk, under sail, made its way across the bay. It was idyllic, and different from anything he had ever known, but he was alone and longed for Hughie's company to share the adventure.

Later he had stopped off at the little fishing village of Stanley, where the markets in the narrow street were just beginning to earn more for the residents than fishing ever could. He bought a collection of souvenirs, more as a reaction to the overwhelming selection on offer than out of necessity, and noticed the cheap pocket radios that took him back to his days boarding at Lloyd's. He did not bother to haggle about the price. He was killing time, and the cost was negligible.

It was still daylight when he returned to the Peninsula, though dusk was closing in fast. He smiled a hello to the doorman and gave a nod to Huffer and Puffer, who seemed to look at him disapprovingly. Then he was in the foyer, grateful for its tall ceilings and cool grandeur. He made his way toward the staircase as his room was on the first floor. He had his hand on the banister, his foot on the bottom step, when it happened. She appeared from out of nowhere, and he froze with awe. She was younger than his twenty-three years, by how much he could not tell; and yet she was ageless, timeless in the way that great beauty always is. She was tiny by comparison, perhaps five foot two inches... certainly no more, her skin delicate like aged porcelain, or young ivory. She was Chinese, that was obvious, and yet not quite of this country, or even this world. Her hair was jet black, with such a sheen that it seemed almost metallic. It was long and wavy, and caught at the nape of her neck with an exquisite jade clip. Her face was heart-shaped, the mouth full as though drawn by some Victorian artist with a vision of cupid. Her cheek bones were high, accentuating the upward turn of her cat-like eyes; the lashes long and thick, brushing her cheek as she modestly kept her eyes lowered. Her body was almost that of a doll. He thought her waist was small enough for him to place his two hands around, and yet she was soft and round, not thin and angular, and he could see the fullness of her breasts through the perfectly tailored linen shirt. Her suit was pure Paris, Chanel perhaps, or Yves St Laurent; Luke did not know enough about women's fashion to pinpoint the designer, but he noticed that her shoes and bag were hand-stitched Italian leather. Everything about her was classically elegant, timelessly beautiful, and he was struck dumb in her presence. She passed him without so much as a sideways glance, creating a breeze of "L'Air du Temps' in her wake. He felt the stirring in his groin, the growing sexual arousal she created with her passing.

"God, how I want this woman," he thought as she moved across the foyer toward the doors. But, more than a sense of possessing her, was the overpowering desire to become one with her, part of her, even if that meant allowing her to possess him.

He tried to speak, to call after her, but his throat was constricted and no sound came out. He could see the doorman open the door. He glimpsed the soft black wave of hair against her back, the curve of her ankle as she disappeared through the door. He knew he had to make a move now or it would be too late, and yet his feet refused to budge. By the time he forced himself to move to the door, she was gone, and the doorman could only explain haltingly that the young lady had left in a taxi. Luke raced back inside, to the reception desk. He was aware of the urgency in his voice, and how odd he must appear to the cool and refined duty manager, but he could not help himself. He wasn't certain whether it was true when he was told that no-one had seen the young woman and that she did not match the description of anyone staying in the house, or whether the management was simply protecting her privacy. What he did know for certain was that he could not leave Hong Kong until he found her.

He walked the streets until late in the night, hoping that he might see her, although common sense told him that she was probably dining with an ambassador, or playing hostess to an industrial mogul rather than shopping in Temple Street. He stopped various taxis and asked the drivers if they had seen her, but he was surprised to find, in a country where English was the official language, how few could understand what he was trying to say.

It was after two a.m. when he finally gave up the search and returned to the Peninsula. He fell asleep fully clothed on the bed and dreamed of her loosening the black, metallic silk that was her hair, feeling it brush against his chest as she lowered her body toward his… the phone rang. The fantasy ended. He half expected it to be her and was more surprised when Thomas Ho politely invited him to breakfast with Miss Anna.

He showered hurriedly, and chose his clothes with care, conscious that he had never before been so concerned with making the right impression. He had declined the offer of a car and driver and instead took a taxi, marveling at the view behind him as the cab climbed halfway to Victoria Peak before depositing him at the huge gates where the glazed lions stood guard. This is it, he thought; this is make or break time. He wasn't certain why his mouth felt so dry, his palms so sweaty. He had his capital and his business interests and he was on an all-expenses-paid trip to a fabulous and exotic port. If nothing came of this meeting, so what? It wasn't really going to matter. Except that something told him that this was more important than he realized, and that if he ever wanted to see the girl again, he must first gain the approval of Hong Kong's most powerful woman.

"HAVE YOU BEEN yet to the top of the peak, Mr. Powers?" Anna Chen asked as they stood on the terrace, still in the exploratory stage of their meeting, although the formalities had been hastily dispensed with.

"No, not yet. Of course, I hope to do so, but I'm sure you understand that sightseeing was not my primary reason for coming to Hong Kong." Luke explained politely, and thought he saw the glimmer of a smile on his hostess's lips.

"It affords a remarkable view from Taiping Sham... the lion view pavilion" Miss Anna explained in her faultless English, "And the trip to the top in the tram, what the Italians call the fernicula railway, is most exciting. You must put it on your list of things to do before you leave Hong Kong." His heart sank. Was she dismissing him already, or merely making polite small talk?

He had been there less than an hour, and was starting to relax. The one hundred Hong Kong dollars he had paid to his maid at The Peninsula had given him a scant knowledge of some basic Cantonese phrases, enough to surpise Miss Anna with "Tso Shan. Nei ho ma?" She laughed, and for a moment he thought perhaps he had mistakenly said something self deprecating or outwardly funny, rather than the "Good morning, how are you?" that he had practised in the cab. He had looked helplessly at Thomas Ho, whose expression was truly inscrutable, but Miss Anna let him off the hook by clapping her hands and saying delightedly. "Well done, and I am well, thank you for asking. I am impressed that you would risk embarrassment to embrace the language of your host country, but I think perhaps our conversation will be more cordial if we proceed in English, don't you?" Luke smiled. "It will certainly be longer. I'm afraid that was the extent of my Chinese, except for Kei Toh... which I hope means how much, and that's not something you say to a lady." he was horrified by his own words. "Idiot" he berated himself silently, for he could see she was taken aback by the feeble attempt at humour. How could he have waited so long and blown everything in just a few moments. Then she started to chuckle, and the chuckle became a laugh, and the laughter grew.

"Forgive me" she said, wiping tears of mirth from her eyes, "But if you could only see your face!" and Luke decided it was easier to join her in laughter than die of embarrassment.

A short time later they sat down to breakfast, and Luke was grateful that he had practiced his chopsticks technique as he maneuvered sweet sticky rice to his mouth.

"You hold your chopsticks near the end" Miss Anna remarked. "That is a good sign." "Oh?" Luke looked at her with curiosity and waited for her to continue.

"It means you are independent, and will always make a good living. But then, I think we both already knew that," she said teasingly. Luke studied the plain bamboo.

"I had heard that the chopsticks of great people, such as yourself, are made of silver" he said, playing along with the small talk and hoping to impress her with his knowledge of her culture."

"It is not so much the wealth, as the power, of your enemies," she explained. "You see, silver chopsticks are useful if someone is trying to kill you. They turn black if there is any poison in your food. On the other hand, they are of very little use if a speeding car runs you down." Luke looked up in surprise. She was quite straight-faced, but the twinkle in her eyes gave her away and he laughed with her at the joke.

For more than an hour they talked of Hong Kong, of Chinese story of creation and Pan Gu, the sleeping giant in an egg, whose shell formed the heavens and earth, and Nu Wa, the goddess who was so lonely she created people out of mud after seeing her own reflection in the pond. Luke realized, as his hostess compared the creation myths with the basic beliefs of Christianity, that Miss Anna was intelligent and well read, charming and witty, but there was no sense of the business mogul he had expected. Until, less than a minute after the table had been cleared of the breakfast things, she turned to him inquiringly, with a voice that was all business and said.

"We have a manufacturing plant, bicycle parts, in the New Territories. Overages are running at more than twenty percent instead of the eight percent contingency built in to the original five-year budget. This has cut returns drastically. The question is, do we downsize? Restructure the budget and accept higher production costs? Do we expand to create economies of scale? Or investigate middle management error and have a general clean-out?" She looked at him challengingly, but clearly inviting him to match her. He was caught off-guard by her directness for a second. This is it, he thought, the game is on now and she's a serious player. He cleared his throat, took a split second to calm his mind, and allowed his instincts to kick in and take over. Then he talked for more than twenty minutes of the pros and cons of each of the options she had outlined, asking relevant questions about other possibilities, including increasing productivity through profit sharing. She spoke only when he asked her a direct question, but she nodded often. When Luke finally stopped talking, he wasn't even certain of what he had said, but he knew he had impressed her and passed the test, and he felt strangely elated, as though his first grade teacher had given him a gold star. A Chinese manservant brought fresh tea and a bowl of fortune cookies. At her bidding he broke one open.

"Please read it aloud for me," she asked. "It's really quite amazing how accurate some of these things can be." Luke unwrapped the small roll of paper, surprised to see the prophecy printed in English, and read to her.

"You are embarking on a great journey. Do not underestimate the power of the driver." She clapped her hands delightedly.

"You see," she said. "Quite remarkable really. But I think we would both have to look at this as a good omen, don't you think?" Luke nodded, surprised by the insight shown by the small roll of paper. Thomas Ho appeared at the doorway. Luke did not see anything more than the slightest gesture of his head, and yet Miss Anna turned to him and smiled.

"Would you excuse me for a moment, Luke?" He realized that this was the first time she had used his first name, and the familiarity surprised him. "Some pressing business on the phone. It shouldn't take more than a few minutes. Please, enjoy your tea." He stood as she left the table. It was not something he would normally have done, though his father had insisted on it when he was very young, yet somehow he wanted to show her that she had already earned his respect, and the gesture seemed quite natural to him.

He gazed around the empty room as he sipped the delicate Jasmine tea. Casually, his glance fell on the bowl of fortune cookies. Idly he picked one up and broke it open, unraveling the tiny slip of paper. His eyes widened with surprise at the words. "You are embarking on a great journey. Do not underestimate the power of the driver." He broke another cookie, and then another and another. All held the same prophecy. He wasn't sure whether to laugh or be annoyed, but he had to face the fact that he had been scammed by a tiny middle-aged Asian woman. Thomas Ho appeared at the door, and Luke suddenly felt guilty, like a kid again. He hastily shoved the broken cookie pieces into the bowl, but he was aware of the raised eyebrow, the quizzical look.

"Miss Anna sends her apologies Mister Powers. She has been called away. She asks if you would do her the honor of inspecting some of Eastern Star's holdings with her on the day after tomorrow?"

Luke stammered a reply, conscious that he had somehow breached etiquette by destroying all the fortune cookies. He got up from the table awkwardly.

"I... er, I couldn't resist. I had to open them. And... er, " Luke tried in vain to read the expression behind Ho's implacable mask.

"You discovered they all held the same fortune?" Ho prompted him.

"Yes! I, um, I certainly hope it won't cause Miss Anna any embarrassment, my opening up the others." Luke shifted awkwardly. Thomas Ho smiled then.

"On the contrary Luke. She filled the fortune cookies that way because she was certain you *would* open the others," he said, and Luke was dumbfounded. Scammed twice in one morning.

"She's really something, isn't she?" he commented admiringly, and he could see from Ho's expression that the comment had earned the Chinese man's approval.

"As the fortune cookie says, my friend, do not underestimate the power of the driver. I'll arrange to take you back to Kowloon."

THE TAILOR, WHO spoke as much English as Luke spoke Chinese, raised Luke's arms and measured swiftly but methodically. The shop was small, in Hankow Street just off the main bustle of Kowloon's Nathan Road. It was late afternoon and Luke was being measured for shirts and suits which would, he was assured, be ready in twenty-four hours. Dennis watched the procedure with some amusement, for he still preferred American style and Italian tailoring.

"It's not like I'm applying for a job," Luke said, with some impatience, as the tailor lowered one arm and raised the other. "I'm looking to make an investment. A million dollars for Chrissakes. My money's as good as anyone else's." The remark was prompted by Dennis's observation that anyone who got a second interview with Miss Anna was clearly in with a shot, since she did not suffer fools gladly. Dennis laughed at his new friend's frustration.

"Exactly. You're money is precisely the same as everyone else's. It isn't special, and that's why she's not interested in it. But *you*, buddy, that's a different horse altogether. You might be special, and that interests her. If I told you some of the corporate names that have tried to form partnerships with her, and she's turned them down cold, you'd be amazed. We all figure she's checking you out as a future Taipan."

"Taipan? In Australia that's a deadly snake. I'm not sure it's a compliment." Luke said smilingly.

"Take my word for it, it's a compliment." Dennis explained. "The Taipan is the number one man, the big boss. For a traditional Chinese company, having a Gweilo as taipan would be a huge step."

"A gweilo?" Luke asked.

"It means a foreign devil… pale, like a ghost. Don't worry, it's a term of affection. It means we like you… or, more importantly, she does." Dennis replied.

"Miss Anna?" Luke said with some surprise.

"Sure," Dennis assured him. "She called you 'our gweilo friend', and that's a good sign. So hang loose, buddy. When success is inevitable, lay back and enjoy it. Oh, and I like you too."

Dennis declined Luke's invitation for drinks and dinner, and Luke found himself on Nathan Road, making his way back toward the Peninsula, uncertain what to do with his evening. He must have been daydreaming, for he did not see the girl until after he had collided with her. He was conscious of the impact, and looked down to see shopping bags and packages scattered at his feet, and then his eyes moved slightly to the left and he saw the red shoes. They were not platform shoes, as current fashion dictated, nor the classic hand-stitched Italian styles of the wealthy, though they were clearly expensive. They were stiletto-heeled court shoes, with a low vamp, on tiny feet above which stretched slender legs in dark panti-hose. The short, black dress hugged rounded hips, and the smart tailored red wool jacket barely covered the breasts which were fighting the dress for freedom. Above them, the shoulders and neck were slender, the face was round and perfectly made up, the lips the exact shade of red as the shoes and the jacket, the eyes rounder than he would have expected, the black hair short and slightly teased. All of this he took in less than a second as he stammered an apology and crouched, with her, to help retrieve the parcels. They were outside Nathan Road's Chinese Emporium, and she had clearly just left the shop. He knew the perfume, "Arpege," for it had been worn by one of his Auckland girlfriends. He was swamped by sexual desire, as he had not been laid in some time. His gaze became fixated on her tongue. Sticking out between her slightly parted lips as she concentrated on collecting her packages, it seemed almost pointed, turned up at the end. He straightened and looked into her black eyes, which glinted with interest.

"Forgive me for being a clumsy idiot. And please allow me, that is, if you have no one waiting for you, to buy you a drink and perhaps some dinner to make amends." She smiled with closed lips, and he knew instinctively that he would be inside her before the night was over.

He learned little about her over dinner except that her name was Nancy Kwong, she was twenty-two years old, and she was a partner in a small business; she didn't elaborate on what. She encouraged Luke instead to talk about himself, and he found himself telling her things that he had told no-one, not even Hughie, for here was a girl he would probably never see again, and there was both comfort and safety in the kindness of a stranger. Later, when he picked up a peeled lychee to put into his mouth, she directed his fingers to her own mouth, took the lychee from them, and then sucked on his juice-wetted fingers in a clear signal that it was time for them to seek some private pleasure place.

He lay naked under the sheet; she had teased him with an order not to touch, just to watch. He lightly kept his hand across his erect shaft, so that it would not absurdly spring to attention beneath the white sheet, waving maniacally like some tiny ghost in a haunting. She undressed slowly and tantalizingly, leaving on only the red high heels. Then she sat on the foot of the bed, her legs apart, and he stared, dry mouthed, at the black curls fringing her rich, coffee-colored folds. She stroked her fingers between her legs, murmuring incessantly to herself, bringing herself to a climax with a strangled cry. She stayed like that until the shaking of her body subsided, and Luke was afraid to move in case he came and she mocked him. Then, she withdrew her hand, slid up the length of his body, and placed her dripping fingers into his mouth. His first taste of her was from her own hand, but he sucked hungrily on her, her nails grazing the inside of his cheek. He reached for her, but she slid out of his grasp. She returned to the bed with a bottle of oil, and the pungent smell of orange blossom and sandalwood invaded his nostrils and made him giddy and nauseated with desire. She oiled her breasts and body, then stripped the sheet from him, sliding up and down against him, his penis, close to bursting, caught in a canyon between her breasts.

"Now we fuck, yes Lukey?" she asked, and he needed no further invitation.

She left before dawn, refusing his offers to take her home, but shyly asking for money for a taxi. Part of him was glad to see her go, as he was tired and satiated and most of all was afraid that somehow she would know that through the long night of love-making his mind had wandered to thoughts, not of her, but of the exquisite girl with the jade hair clip. Still, within minutes of her going he wanted her again, and was glad that she had accepted his offer of dinner that evening. He killed the day by visiting the bird market, sitting at a little cafe table and listening to the songs of thousands of canaries; the Chinese men brought their birds in ornate carved wooden cages, and hung them on hooks for all to see and admire. Large amounts of money changed hands as the birds were sold, and traded, or simply shown off. Later, he saw a wedding at a temple, the bride dressed in traditional red for happiness. White was the color of mourning and reserved for funerals. Luke reflected cynically that some weddings might also be funerals, burials of the spirit of individuality, so the western custom of wearing white might kill two birds with one stone.

That night, he and Nancy went to Jimmy's for T-bone steaks and beer, and then she took him to a new nightspot off Wong Chuck Hong road. It featured topless dancers on the bar and psychedelic lights, and it was noisy and smoky. Yet, on the overcrowded dance floor, Nancy was able to dance with her body against his, and even unzip his fly and put her hand inside his underpants to play with his cock, without anyone noticing. They drank boilermakers, drowning the shot glasses in pint pots of beer and downing the lot in one hit, and he was amazed that she could handle alcohol far better than he could. Through the dim lighting he could see a constant stream of Chinese men in business suits and heavy gold jewelry making their way through a small door at the back of the club. Some were accompanied by exquisitely beautiful girls dressed in the traditional high-necked, slit-skirted cheong-sam. Nancy followed his gaze and patted his cheek.

"You not want to get involved through there Lukey. Gambling… Fan Tan, that illegal, also opium den. Opium very bad… smoke first, later become hook and then heroin, both from poppy, big business from Golden Triangle… Cambodia." He started to laugh, thinking that she was creating local color to impress him. But then he saw by her eyes that she was serious, even afraid, and he felt an adrenalin tingle in the pit of his stomach. In Auckland it had been hard enough to score a joint when he was at university. He had thought Sydney quite wild, for there seemed no shortage of pot up around the King's Cross area, though it held only the mildest of attractions for him. But this was a different world, a world of books and Hollywood movies.

"You're serious, aren't you?" he asked, putting a hand to the nape of her neck and comfortingly pulling her face towards his.

"Chinese gangster very bad, very cruel. I am respectable girl, you are businessman. We stay together, okay?" She smiled as she lightly kissed him, flicking her snake tongue into his mouth, and it was a signal to both of them that there was more enjoyment to be had from each other's bodies than from the noisy nightclub. He pulled her chair out for her and she rose with a delighted giggle. As he turned, he did not see how close the table behind was to the one they occupied. He bumped against a young Chinese man in an expensive suit. The man held a glass of Scotch and Coke which spilled over his shirt and jacket, and sprayed one of his companions. Luke was quick to apologize for his clumsiness, but he saw the fury in the Chinese man's eyes as he stood and used the flimsy paper cocktail napkin to wipe the drink from his shirt and clean the Patek-Phillippe watch that adorned his wrist.

"You are a clumsy, barbaric oaf," the Chinese man spoke in measured tones, and with the accent of someone who had learned his English formally. Luke shrugged helplessly. "It was an accident, and I have apologized. I'll be happy to pay for the cleaning bill," he reached inside his suit jacket, but the Chinese man grabbed his wrist.

"You will not insult me by imagining you can placate me with money. You westerners think that you can buy anything," he turned then and muttered something in Chinese to his friends, who laughed awkwardly. Luke did not need an interpreter to know that the man had insulted him. He pulled his wrist free.

"I don't think there's any point in continuing this, " Luke said angrily and turned to offer his hand to Nancy, who had backed away against a pillar. But his antagonist grabbed his shoulder and turned him around.

"Apologize to my companions," he ordered. Luke bridled angrily.

"Like hell I will," Luke replied, shrugging free from the shorter man's grip. He saw the man's fist as it pulled back to hit him, and grabbed his arm before he could make contact, twisting it up the Chinese man's back until he yelled out in pain. Luke thrust the man down into his seat before releasing him.

"I'll assume that you're drunk rather than having the manners of a pig," Luke derided. He pulled a hundred dollars from his wallet and threw it on the table before turning to the other man and the two young woman at the table.

"I apologize to you," he said in a conciliatory tone, "But the apology is for the embarrassment your friend here has caused. If I were you, I'd choose my company more carefully. Come on Nancy." He held out his hand to her and noticed that she was trembling as he led her from the club. He did not have to look around to feel the man's eyes boring into the back of him, but he was surprised by the nervousness in Nancy's voice.

"You make him lose face. Him going to be very bad enemy for you. You not go that club anymore Luke."

"You know this guy, Nancy ?" Luke asked, but she shook her head.

"Not need to know, have eyes to see. Please Luke, we go to bed now, make fucky fucky and forget all about him. Please...?" he laughed with delight to see the little girl inside the woman, and knew that he could not refuse her.

LUKE SAT IN the air-conditioned luxury of the Mercedes, watching the hills and paddies of the New Territories pass as Thomas Ho explained the intricacies of the Eastern Star corporate structure. He had shaken off the fatigue of a night of wild love-making, but could not entirely shake the boredom of the bicycle factory tour. That had been the nadir of a day driving from one Eastern Star holding to another, trying desperately to assimilate all the figures that Thomas Ho quoted so easily off the top of his head. Luke was still struggling to get a fix on Ho's position within the hierarchy. He was certainly more than secretary, yet less than managing director. The one thing Luke garnered for certain was that Ho was Miss Anna's most loyal supporter and protector. As the car sped back towards Hong Kong, Luke mulled over in his brain all that had occurred in the past week. He had left Auckland looking for excitement, a new challenge to shake him out of the apathy of having too much money too soon. He felt quite at home in Hong Kong. It was British enough to be familiar, and Asian enough to be exotic, but it was hard to imagine himself getting excited over the profit margins of a bicycle factory, no matter how hard he tried. He liked Miss Anna; he even admired the way she did business, but it was not his way, and it did not excite him. He knew as soon as Thomas extended her invitation to join her at the house for dinner that she would make some kind of offer, but he felt no sense of elation, only unease. It was certainly not his intention to invest his money in something safe and secure that would afford him stability without any adrenalin rush. He thought that it would be easy to thank her graciously, decline, and fly back to Auckland or maybe Sydney to explore the other possibilities which were still open to him, except for one thing. Somewhere in Hong Kong was the girl with the jade hair clasp, and he knew that he would feel no peace until he saw her again and found out whether she was attainable. That was the adventure Hong Kong offered, not the chance of buying into Eastern Star.

But just as Miss Anna had surprised him in the past, she once again proved how unwise it was for him to trust preconceived ideas. Dinner at the house was gracious and British in both food and setting. Conversation centered around the water shortage and the price of bottled drinking water, and the anti-inflation riots in Kowloon that had seen demonstrators clash with the police. Miss Anna jokingly suggested that the demonstrators might have benefited from Luke's student expertise, and he was flattered that she was openly acknowledging the extent to which she had investigated him.

After dinner they sat on the terrace, drinking coffee, watching the lights on both sides of the harbor, a veritable fairyland in the dark where all traces of poverty and pollution were hidden. She asked politely his opinion of his tour that day. He answered in equally polite terms, praising the overall efficiency of each of the holdings, suggesting with all modesty some minor improvements.

"Eastern Star is as extraordinary corporate empire, Miss Anna" Luke said with all honesty .

"But it isn't your cup of tea?" she countered, and he shrugged agreement. "Good" she countered, and he was surprised with the vehemence in the word.

"Eastern Star is a middle-aged corporation run by middle-aged people. It offers little in surprises and excitement, and if you had been enthralled by it, then you would not be the man I take you for, Luke Powers. If I were you I would be on the next plane out of here." Once again there was a sense in her voice that she was teasing him affectionately. Luke was confused.

"I don't understand. You brought me all this way... why?" he asked bluntly. She put down her coffee cup and turned to face him.

"Thomas thinks you are perhaps a corporate visionary, a man of ideas, a man for the future," she challenged him. Luke looked deep into her eyes.

"And you? What do you think?" he asked.

"I think I pay Thomas large amounts of money not to be wrong. But what he thinks only confirms what I feel, have felt, from the moment I saw your slightly ridiculous advertisement. You must have known that such adventurous idealism would bring forth all kinds of, how would you call them, "nutters"? And yet your instinct told you to take the plane ticket and come to Hong Kong. You want adventure, something to challenge, new markets to conquer? So do I." And Luke was suddenly interested once more. "You placed an advertisement in the newspaper. What did you have in mind?"

Luke gathered his thoughts. He hadn't expected such an invitation but now jumped at the opportunity to discuss his ambitions. "After reflecting on and researching your operations and interests," he began, "and after having the opportunity to view your operations, a number of ideas have sprung to mind. I'm confident in the synergies that I can see between two of my businesses in Australasia and your manufacturing operations. Southeast Asia offers the lowest-cost manufacturing available and, using your existing distribution and manufacturing infrastructures, I believe that we can take skateboards and kit-set cars global. And I have big ideas for a new direction in travel in response to the energy crisis." Miss Anna listened silently. Luke continued. "The products that I have in mind are at the forefront of fledgling industries, and I've proven their viability in little old New Zealand. I know that we can take these products global, and I'm willing to invest my million dollars in their expansion, with minimal risk to you, to exist side-by-side with your operations."

"I'm interested," Miss Anna responded. "But will a global push not require more than a million dollars?"

"To demonstrate my faith in your integrity, I'm prepared for these entities to be developed under the Eastern Star umbrella. I'll put everything I have into them if you'll be willing to support their growth with Eastern Star's horsepower." He looked her directly in the eye. "A partnership." He watched Miss Anna process the information and sensed that he had caught her attention.

"And there's one more thing," he said. "I don't want to appear disrespectful in any way, but there is one part of your existing business that intrigues me. The pen business." She looked at him quizzically. "I've seen that the pen is mightier than the sword, and if you would grant me the opportunity, I would very much like to learn more of your publishing and broadcasting operations. I know that if we were to become involved in business together, I would merely be a junior partner, but this is an area that I would be honored to explore – to evaluate – to review. I sense that the upheaval in the media industry is coming to a head and that a new business model will emerge. I think we can make a play for something big here."

Miss Anna said nothing but turned to face the harbor. She thought that she could almost feel the dragon sweep by as her eyes fell on the hole in the wall in front of her.

"I will match any investment that you make in Eastern Star's new ventures. You will have access to my worldwide infrastructure and the freedom to develop the new operations as you see fit." Luke struggled to keep the smile that he felt forming from taking hold of his lips. "Show me what you are capable of."

CHAPTER ELEVEN

"Miss Anna, I trust you, and I want to prove it." The connection that Luke felt from Miss Anna was more motherly than any other relationship he could remember since he was eleven. In the nine months since working for Eastern Star, he had grown closer to the woman. It was a connection that, as far as he could see, no other enjoyed with her, for she had taken him in and he knew that she saw in him great potential – the potential that he himself could feel.

He had passed the test laid down before him. POW! Skateboards had leapt ahead in production and sales and made inroads into new markets. His idea to parlay his engine-importing operations into an inexpensive kit-set product that was exported in parts and assembled in the country of sale was now poised for launch and considered by Eastern Star Motors to be a brilliant idea for capturing an as-yet unexploited market for cheap vehicles. He had stepped up to the challenge presented to him and knew that he had won his mentor's approval.

"I want to share with you an idea that I have been working on ever since OPEC exerted its influence on the markets." The two sat across from one another on the balcony overlooking the harbor, while Thomas Ho listened from a distance. "I want to build the cheapest, most fuel-efficient car the world has ever seen, and one that will be practical for everyday use." Miss Anna listened without a word to the young man sitting across from her. "The US car manufacturers are going to lose market share to the Japanese – their cars are too large for these gas prices. We have car-less days in Europe, people queuing up at gas stations in the US, and all the while the energy crisis shows no sign of abating." Luke continued, not waiting for any response from Miss Anna until he had conveyed to her the thrust of his idea. "The mini came close, but it didn't move with the times. And, people felt small on the road in such a low-to-the-ground car. This car will be small in length – two seats only, with the rear of the car no more than a foot behind the back of the driver's seat – but still tall enough to give the feel of a regular car. We'll use your existing operations in Malaysia to produce it cheaply. I've got more – a lot more – on how this can work. And I want us to make this thing big. A fifty-fifty partnership. You and me."

"I assume," she began, "that your half of the ownership is attributable to your research only?"

"All of my money is tied up in our existing projects," he replied.

Miss Anna considered the proposal. It was an ambitious plan, one that carried with it risk, but her faith in the man had never been stronger. "We will make preparations for beginning work on the product imme-diately, beginning with a presentation by you of your full vision for the direction. I will speak to my lawyers today to draw up the contract before you disclose your full research." She turned her head to Thomas.

"That's not necessary, Miss Anna. I trust you, and I want to prove it. A verbal agreement from you is as good as any contract."

Thomas looked tense. Miss Anna smiled. "You trust me that much, Luke?"

"Yes."

"This is highly unusual," she continued, her eyes warm. "I am hon-ored by your faith in my integrity, and I accept your offer."

Luke was pleased to find that his sense of Miss Anna's sincerity had been correct. He felt at home amongst the Chinese; they valued fam-ily and he was beginning to feel that he was being welcomed into Miss Anna's circle not just as a business partner, but as a family member.

Luke worked hard, sometimes fifteen hours a day, seven days a week, but he loved it. This was the international scale business he had hoped for, and he learned to survive on perpetual jet-lag. For a while he stayed at a serviced apartment in one of Miss Anna's properties, uncertain in the first few months of just which way his future would develop. But within three months sales were such that he realized he would need not one home base but several.

"A hotel room is not a home, Luke" Miss Anna mildly reproached him, a concerned pat of the hand on his arm. He liked the attention, liked the rapport that had grown between them. Yet there was an edge to the relationship. It operated on two levels, the business and the personal. On a personal level Luke was certain that Miss Anna liked him, and had a real concern for his well-being. It was not quite motherly, more the affection of a aunt, or perhaps an older woman with whom one has had a brief, burnt-out love affair. He looked down at her hand, almost miniscule on his arm. He was constantly surprised that within this tiny woman was the steel-edged energy to run a business empire. Yet that surprise constantly reminded him of the other, and more predominant edge to their relationship. He was, first and foremost, a junior business partner, and he had no doubt whatsoever that if she was ever forced to make a choice between business and any personal affection for him, she would cut him loose without so much as a second thought. It was this sense of uncertainty that added excitement and awareness to all their dealings, for he knew full well that he could never take her for granted. "It's a serviced apartment – it's convenient for me right now," he answered.

"You need to get out of that hotel and find an apartment. Dennis will help you," Miss Anna continued, and Luke laughed.

"That has the ring of an order rather than a suggestion," he told her. She looked mildly surprised.

"You think I would try to control your private life?" she asked innocently, and he shook his head.

"No. You know that I wouldn't buy that, and besides, you're far too busy. But you're right about finding a home base, and I've already been looking. If you want to waste Dennis's time that's fine, but in the long run he isn't going to influence where I live," he spoke smilingly, but with sufficient conviction that she would understand that he had no intention of allowing her to intrude into his private life unless he invited her.

It took some weeks for him to find the apartment, as rents were horrendously high, sometimes ten times more than he would have expected to pay in Auckland. Finally he found it, a two bedroom executive apartment with a study and a dining room, and a view of the harbor from the lounge. He insisted on finding the place himself and, when he phoned Dennis to for his opinion on the rent before he negotiated the final amount, he was told that, at five thousand Hong Kong dollars a month, he had a bargain. It was not until he invited Nancy around, once the place was furnished, that he discovered why the luxury apartment was so reasonably priced.

"Very bad Feng Shui, Luke. I don't come inside," the girl said, hanging back in the hallway. Luke was both exasperated and curious.

"Okay, so tell me what this is all about," he asked, conscious, from the months he had now lived in Hong Kong, that Feng Shui was not to be laughed at or discounted even by Westerners. She backed away toward the elevator, looking around her.

"See how front door is placed at end of this passageway, with more passage either side?" she asked. Luke nodded. The front door faced a T-junction, but it seemed of little importance to him.

"Bad spirits, demons, come down passageway and not know which way to go. So, they wait, and every time you open door, demons rush inside. Very, very bad," she ended vehemently. Luke controlled his desire to laugh, for it was clear the Chinese girl was deathly serious. Nor did he laugh when she told him that if he would not move, then he must place a mirror strategically on the front door frame, so that demons racing down the passageway would see their reflection, think it was another demon coming towards them, turn tail and run away, thus saving Luke from the bad energy. Even as he carefully hung the mirror according to Nancy's instructions, he learned that the words meant wind and water and that the balance between them, the Chi, made the difference between prosperity and misfortune. Sha, or evil forces, traveled in straight lines, mostly along man-made routes, and certainly along the corridors of his apartment building. Nancy had recognized that immediately. The Chinese girl had numerous stories of people who had buried their ancestors in a place with bad Feng Shui, and had lived to pay the penalty, and Luke was conscious that, although there was little difference in the sexual relationship he enjoyed with her, her traditions and philosophy were totally alien to him. Only when the mirror was hung, and the demons repelled, would she consent to come into the apartment, and even then she insisted that Luke move some of the furniture.

He christened his new king size bed, an American import, with wild love-making. He plunged into her, kneeling above her with her legs stretched full length under his armpits, her smooth buttocks lifted from the bed as she buffeted against him while rubbing her own nipples in a frenzy. She came first, shuddering and bucking beneath him like a wild animal, but he was distracted by the memory of the girl on the stairs and for a moment he lost concentration and his erection started to subside inside her. He saw the questioning look in her eyes as she realized what was happening. Then she hoisted herself to a sitting position, forcing him back and rode him frantically until he felt himself start pumping and spasming into the dark well of her.

Later, when he returned from the bathroom, she was standing naked on the bed. He walked to her, her small round breasts at mouth level. He took one into his mouth, sucking gently, then biting softly as she moaned. She did not have to look to see his erection grow once more. Still wet from him and for him, she stepped off the bed and onto him, wrapping her legs around his waist, and impaling herself on him.

"Fuck me so hard you break me in two, Luke," she murmured into his ear, and it would have been bad manners for him to refuse.

FOR SIX MORE months he kept her as a mistress. He never said he loved her, and he made no pretence that she was even remotely as important as his work. But she was there when he needed her, and she was undemanding except for the odd occasion when she would awkwardly ask for money to cover a shortfall in rent. It crossed his mind occasionally that it was strange that she always called him and she never answered her phone. Nor did she ever talk about her own business or her family. He should have asked questions, but he didn't, mostly because he didn't want to waste any energy on the answers. He was in Hong Kong less than half of the time, yet he never bothered to look for sex while he was in Singapore, or Kuala Lumpur, or Sydney, or the rare occasions when he made it to New Zealand, usually not even in Auckland long enough to make the trip to see his grandparents. He supposed that part of him had prioritized the business as being of greater importance. Where the business trips were short and energy-consuming, he would simply fall into bed at the end of the day and sex would not even be an issue. But there was another, more disturbing element to his perverse fidelity. He felt that to have sex with a stranger in a transit city would be to defile his commitment to what he had at home in Hong Kong. But that did not mean his relationship to Nancy. It meant the intangible connection between himself and a porcelain goddess he had only seen once and had not even met.

The kit-set cars had begun export to the US: the shell was manufactured in Malaysia, broken down to a compact size and then reassembled in the US with engines salvaged from unwanted second-hand vehicles. Tariffs were largely skirted, the cars were inexpensive and, although no mileage guarantee could be offered by the company, consumers were willing to take a chance on the powerful cars for at such a price. The ZipCar had moved into the first round of manufacturing, and Luke was pleased with the progress his ventures had shown. Miss Anna showed her appreciation by inviting Luke to accompany her to a cocktail party with the British High Commissioner.

Luke waited in the small drawing room of Miss Anna's house, sitting uncomfortably in the rosewood chair and admiring the lacquer screen with its delicate carving and inlaid pearl.

"The five panels represent the seasons, and the Wu Hsing, the five agencies of the Universe," Thomas told him as he handed him the Scotch and soda on the rocks that Luke had requested. "See... here?" he traced the pattern with his fingers, lightly, reverently. "The green dragon symbolizes spring, which comes from the east, and its element is wood. And here the scarlet bird of the south, for summer and fire... here the autumn, metal and the winter from the north. Its element is water."

"That's four seasons. What about the big yellow dragon in the center panel?" Luke asked with idle curiosity. Thomas nodded sagely.

"That is the center... it is earth," he replied. "The screen, it is hundreds of years old, a present to Miss Anna on her coming of age from her father." Luke took a deep swig of the drink and, without looking at the older man, said, almost casually, "Does she know how you feel?" Thomas was silent. Luke looked at him and smiled knowingly. "You're not denying anything, I see." Thomas bowed his head a little.

"I think perhaps you see through me because neither one of us quite fits in, Luke. To pretend that I don't know what you're referring to would be an insult to your intelligence. To presume that she has given me a single thought other than as a trusted employee would be to insult her station. I am silent because either choice would be unworthy of us all." He looked deep into Luke's eyes, asking for understanding and Luke was suddenly embarrassed by his own gaucheness. He nodded and turned away. In Thomas's eyes he had seen also a declaration of love for the woman they were both waiting for, except that Luke had only a few minutes to wait, and Thomas, they both knew, would wait a lifetime.

Miss Anna looked stunning in a long silk cheongsam-styled dress that married the Chinese tradition with Parisian cut and style. She insisted that Luke drive them in the Mercedes and he noticed how Thomas's hand brushed his employer's shoulders as he carefully arranged her wrap around her shoulders. 'Poor bastard,' Luke thought as he opened the door of the car and saw Thomas watching them from the entrance. 'He's in love with her and she'll never know.' But then he saw the wistful look that Miss Anna gave towards the doorway, hidden in the gloom of the inside of the car, and realized that she felt more than she revealed, or at least had some awareness of Ho's true feelings. What would compel a culture or a people, he wondered, to ignore their own feelings simply because it would break with custom, tradition? It occurred to him then, as he drove to the British High Commission, that he may never truly understand the Chinese, no matter how long he might spend with them.

THE BALLROOM OF the embassy was huge and lavish, and filled with guests in dinner suits. "Tonight you will meet the elite of 'Honkers' Miss Anna told him. "See that man there?" she said, nodding towards a figure in an expensive tuxedo, "Chairman of Jardine Matheson. And there, the managing director of Hutchison Whampoa." She had named two of the crown colony's largest British commercial firms, or Hongs as they were known. Luke looked at the men with interest, and then at the rest of the company in the room.

"Not many Chinese," he observed matter-of-factly. Miss Anna chuckled.

"Oh, it is hard enough for us to become taipans in our own board-rooms. But for a Chinese to take over a major Hong and wrest it from the British? That would take more courage than most of us have." Luke looked quizzical.

"It's hard to believe that you don't have the courage" he said to her without a trace of false flattery. "Neither myself, nor Eastern Star has the will," she replied. "I am still Chinese, and in a little more than twenty years the British will be here as foreigners only. But I will always be Chinese. I have nothing to prove." And with that she swept into the ballroom on Luke's arm, and proceeded to captivate the very men whom she claimed were unconquerable.

Two hours later, as the guests dispersed to go their separate ways for dinner engagements, Luke was battling stultifying boredom with the aid of his fourth drink for the night. It was then that he noticed the girl making her way towards him. He had seen the attractive blonde several times during the evening, watching him over the rim of her glass, or with a sideways glance as she held animated conversations with various guests. She was attractive in a very British way; honey-blonde hair pulled back into a chignon, a black and silver mini-skirted brocade cocktail dress stretched taut against pointed breasts; her shoes a little too sensible for the dress, her eyes sporting extraneous amounts of eye shadow. She looked as though she might be more at home with horses and hounds, he thought; a kind of sexual Princess Anne, well bred but dull. Except that there was nothing dull about the way she looked at him from under her heavily mascara'd lashes, or the way she ran her tongue along the rim of her glass. Now, as she came towards him, he could see that she moved, not like a horse, but with the litheness of a cat. She extended a hand and he shook it, conscious of her nails tickling his outstretched palm in an invitation too vague for him to instantly accept.

"Hello," she said in the clipped tones of one who was either to the manor born or had spent thousands on elocution lessons. "I'm Celia Hackforth-Smythe." He knew the name, for her father was a senior diplomat at the embassy, and widely tipped to be the next Governor of the crown colony.

"I'm Luke Powers," he responded, finally rescuing his hand from hers. She smiled and gave him the look from beneath her lashes again.

"I know. Would I have been flirting with you so outrageously through this crashing yawn of a party if I had not known who you were?" This time there was no room for doubt about the invitation in her voice.

"Is that what you were doing?" he played along with her.

"Don't tell me you didn't even notice," she cried in a mock wail.

"I noticed," he replied, wondering, against his will, whether British girls were as frigid as mythology painted them. As if reading his thoughts she shifted her position so that her back was to those left in the stately room and, un-noticed, she grasped his crotch through his elegant dinner suit pants.

"In the good old days the lady of the manor fucked the gardeners... you've read Lady Chatterley I presume? But now, good staff are so hard to get, we fuck Yanks instead." Luke was so surprised he did not reply. She moved her mouth close to his ear. "Follow me, but do try to be nonchalant. Let's not advertise, even though you chaps do it so well." And she walked away without a backward glance, as though she had dismissed him after a perfunctory conversation. He kept her in sight, but he was certain that no-one would imagine for a moment that he had followed her. He lost sight of her after she left the ballroom, and he wandered out into a deserted hallway. He had no idea where it would lead, or, indeed, where she had gone. He was halfway along the hall, passing door after closed door, when one opened, a hand grabbed him and pulled him inside. As the door closed behind him he saw that he was in a downstairs powder room. The glistening white toilet pedestal was offset by a porcelain sink with brass taps, and an ornate gold mirror filling the wall directly behind it. He had no time to speak, for her tongue filled his mouth, and then she spoke breathily into it.

"My poor Lady Jane is wet and weak just thinking about your John

Thomas. Is he thick and hard? Will he come ever so fiercely? Hurry, hurry up and stick him in me." She fumbled at his belt and his zipper, reaching in and grasping his semi-hard penis, which sprang to life in her hands. He quickly freed himself and she pulled the mini-skirt up over her hips. He saw instantly that she had already discarded her panties, and he reached to pull her to him but she held him off.

"No, no. From behind... I want to see," she murmured, and turned her back on him. Leaning over the sink, her legs parted, she watched in the mirror as he guided his cock into her and started to move inside her. She moaned but then commanded, "Harder... hurt me. Do it. Shake the mirror off the wall." He withdrew, but only for a moment, then he slammed into her so hard that her forehead hit the mirror and she muffled a scream of delight.

"Yes, yes... make it last. Fuck me till I pass out," she commanded as he used all his strength to ramrod his organ as far into her as it would go. Again and again he slammed her against the sink, her white buttocks slapping against his stomach until she came with a scream and collapsed back against him, and he emptied himself into her. He collapsed then against her back, exhausted, but she seemed no longer interested in, or even aware of, his presence. For perhaps a minute she stayed stock still, murmuring under her breath. Then, matter-of-factly, she moved, causing him to slip out of her and wonder with some embarrassment whether he should speak. She turned on the taps and gave herself a whore's wash before drying herself on the hand towel. Luke, meanwhile, re-zippered and arranged his clothing, trying to think of an appropriate exit line. Only when she was fully restored to her former state did she smile at him.

"That was nice," she said as she patted his cheek almost condescendingly.

"Nice?" he asked with some surprise. It was not a word he was accustomed to hearing in connection with his lovemaking. She looked amused.

"It was super, really. And I'm sure it will keep getting better... if we get lots of practice."

Luke began several months of balancing two sex lives along with a business life that was all-consuming. He had bought a vintage MG roadster in British racing green. In a colony where taking taxis or ferries was the preferred method of transport, the open top car turned heads wherever he went. Celia would wrap a long chiffon scarf around her head and wear sunglasses, for the summer was approaching, as they drove to Repulse Bay for Sunday brunch. Nancy loved to stand up and wave to people as they fought the traffic on the highway to the New Territories. The two women knew of each other's existence, but both chose to ignore it.

It was on Nancy's birthday, after drinks at Bottoms Up, the favored go-go bar of the moment, that Luke encountered his adversary again. He had promised Nancy he would take her dancing, and the disco was new and trendy, and expensive. He was tired, having only arrived home from Sydney the previous day, and for once he did not feel like sex with the beautiful Chinese girl. He had bought her a stuffed toy Koala, and an opal bracelet which she immediately assumed were birthday presents, and he didn't have the heart to tell her the truth; that he had completely forgotten her birthday. The night out was by way of compensation, but he knew the second he met the Chinese man's eyes, that it had been a mistake. He saw there irrational hatred, and cruel vindictiveness. The man nodded his head, acknowledging their mutual recognition, and then he was gone, in the crowd, and Nancy was demanding in her most coquettish manner that he dance with her.

It was perhaps two in the morning when they left the club and made their way back to the car. Nancy was singing an ABBA song that had been playing as they danced, and she did not notice the damage to the car as they approached. But Luke's steps faltered, and he looked at the MG in disbelief. The soft roof had been slashed, as had the bucket seats inside. The windscreen was shattered, and the paintwork blistered from what appeared to be hot oil. He had wanted the car since childhood, and even if it could be restored, it would never mean the same to him. He knew, irrefutably, who was responsible, but he could not understand why. Surely a chance accident, a spilled drink months before, did not warrant this kind of retribution? Nancy was in shock, but that turned to fear when Luke told her of seeing the Chinese man in the club. His first instinct was to call the police, but Nancy was close to hysteria as she begged him to say nothing of the man or the earlier incident.

"This very bad, Lukey... very, very bad. He know who you are. How else to find your car like this? You must understand about gangster. It like Mafia in America." Luke was incredulous.

"You're telling me this is an organized crime vendetta? Come on, Nancy. I've read about this Triad thing, but it's not happening here, not to me." Even as he spoke some chilling instinct told him he was wrong Nancy gripped his arm and looked at him with beseeching eyes.

"Please, Luke. Just say car was vandalized. Maybe this is end of it. Please, don't make them come after us." He found himself promising her, against his better judgment, and the police report stated simply that the car had been vandalized by a person or persons unknown.

Luke's insurance paid for the repairs to the car, but he could never convince himself that it was the same. He sold it and bought an E-type Jaguar. He sensed a change in Nancy from that night. She asked for money more often and sometimes, after giving it to her, he would not see her for a week or more when he was at home. He knew the relationship was waning, even though she constantly professed her love for him, but he was unprepared for Thomas Ho and Dennis's visit with an edict from Miss Anna.

"You know that it is not Miss Anna's intention to interfere with your personal life, Luke" Ho began, and Luke suppressed a cynical smile.

"Why do I get the feeling that's precisely what you're here for?" he asked, fully expecting that he would be cautioned about his indiscretions with Celia, for he had already heard on the grapevine that her father did not consider him to have a suitable background for dating his daughter. But it was Dennis, not Thomas, who openly broached the problem. "Who you screw is your own affair, buddy," Dennis began in an almost casual fashion, "But, Jesus, don't flaunt it in public when the girl is a whore." Luke was confused. Obviously Dennis could not mean Celia, and that left only one other possibility, yet Luke wanted to believe there was some kind of mistake.

"What are you saying?" he asked. "I don't know what you're talking about."

Dennis sighed. "I'm talking about little Miss Round Eyes Kwong. I can see why you'd pay for it. You get good sex without wasting time doing the date bit, but Jesus, you tell her any of Eastern Star's business and she tells it to another client of hers and that's heavy duty shit my friend." Luke looked from Dennis to Thomas. He had to ask the question, even though he already knew what the answer was.

"Nancy is a call-girl? That's what you're telling me?" Without their confirming it he understood instantly the increasing demands for money, the reason she never spoke about her work, how little he knew of her life when she was not with him. His pride was hurt; his male ego was such that he wanted to believe he was irresistible to the girl without financial inducement. Yet part of him was relieved, for he felt now that he owed her nothing, especially love, and he could not love her. They had had a business contract, even though Luke had not been aware of it, and she had been well paid for her time.

It was easier for him to promise Miss Anna that he would break off the relationship, than it was to actually end it with Nancy. He could see quite rationally his partner's concerns about pillow talk, and there was no point in explaining that he never discussed business with Nancy. Now that he had time to think about it, he never really discussed anything with her. He simply responded to her chatter, or her babytalk, with only the most superficial interest. She was there for sex, and he had not allowed himself to consider any other need in his life, let alone think of her as the one who might fill that need. Somewhere in his mind he knew that the girl from the Peninsula was the only one who could touch him, hurt him, make him face his own vulnerability. Yet he was angry and resentful that his mentor clearly saw him as a stupid adolescent ruled by his dick, incapable of keeping sex and business in separate compartments. He phoned Miss Anna himself and told her that he would break off the relationship, but he politely made it clear that he would not have his private life monitored, and that what he did in his own time was his own business. He prided himself on being his own person, and he had not traveled thousands of miles to let someone else rule his life.

Nancy looked at him in disbelief as he gently explained that what they had was over. Tears stung her eyes as her voice faltered, and she sounded impossibly young and wounded, like a vulnerable child.

"What did I do wrong? I bore you, right. Maybe we try poppers, make you come extra hard. You want to fuck me in ass? That okay. What you want, Lukey? You tell me and I do it for you. Please." She started to cry then and wiped the back of her hand across her runny nose. He realized with a start that she was much younger than he had allowed himself to be convinced of; probably no more than eighteen, and that saddened him further.

"I want to help you," he said in an attempt to salve the gnawing concerns growing in his conscience. "You should have told me you were a whore, Nancy." She looked at him, defensive and angry.

"Not whore! Not work on street in Wan Chai. Respectable call girl, only do business man. But not love them, Luke. Not till you." There was such conviction in her voice that he believed at that moment that she did love him, and that only made him feel worse.

"Why don't you go into business, legitimate business? I'll help you, maybe a little shop, or a market stall." He realized how inane this sounded even as he said it. She looked at him cynically.

"Market stall? That what you think of me. I have talent for fucking. THAT my business. You not want to buy, okay, but don't insult me. I a person, Luke, not a machine." There was a certain dignity to the way she recovered her self-respect and quietly packed the things that she kept permanently at the apartment. He hesitated about offering her money but, in the end, he gave her five thousand Hong Kong dollars. She looked at it quietly before pocketing it.

"That a lot of fucking, " she said, "But don't expect me buy market stall with it."

As he saw her out of the apartment for the last time, she glanced up at the mirror he had placed above the front door months before.

"You not take that down, Luke. Keep Sha away from home, promise me," she pleaded.

He felt foolish even as he made the promise, and he stood at the door until she vanished into the elevator. Then he returned to the apartment, and a peculiar moroseness overtook him; peculiar because it was not triggered by her loss, but by his realization that he felt no loss at all.

He was away for several weeks, keeping an eye on the marketing strategy for each of the potential territories in preparation for the launch of the ZipCar. They had reluctantly decided to hold off from the US market: people would not feel comfortable traveling such distances in the ZipCar on freeways. Much of Europe, however, with its car-less days and crowded streets, was a perfect fit for the compact and fuel-efficient car, as was Asia.

When he returned, he allowed Celia to move into his life. He accepted an invitation to the Hackforth-Smythes; for Sunday dinner, and enjoyed the succulent traditional roast Angus beef imported directly from Scotland. He found Celia's parents to be pleasant bores belonging to a class he had never encountered before. Nor, despite the help that Miss Anna employed in her own home, had he ever been in a situation where one race, considering itself superior, ruled over another. The Hackforth-Smythes kept a houseful of servants, all Chinese, and mostly refugees from mainland China. Sir Godfrey Hackforth-Smythe addressed them in the manner of a benign dictator talking to simple minded aliens; Gillian, his wife, adopted a more haughty and contemptuous attitude toward them.

"They really are quite impossible. Not a brain in their heads as a race," she said over the fish course. Luke couldn't help but notice the irony of her speaking in generalities of a race that had perfected porcelain, printing, explosives and a variety of other world changing innovations at least a thousand years before their western counterparts, and whose civilization dated back to a time when the British were still painting themselves with woad! Sir Godfrey laughed.

"Now my dear. They're not totally cretinous. For the most part they're willing enough to learn, they simply haven't got a clue. And one does have to overlook some rather nasty habits. But then, they're quite capable of assimilating once they set their minds to it, and they'll work like ruddy coolies, twenty-four hours a day if you tell them." He laughed at his own pathetic joke. "And we're doing them a service, Luke. They have regular employment, satisfactory wages and conditions, and they're a damn sight better off with us than they would be on the streets, or four families crammed into one room. Quite ghastly, and they breed like rabbits, you know."

Luke could only smile wanly, and sip his iced water. He saw, for the first time in his life, what it must have been like for the black Americans in slavery at the hands of their masters. It astounded him that basically decent people could show such utter disregard for another race. At least in his country, although it was not an excuse, the African Americans were not indigenous; yet here were British aristocracy, in a country to which they had only a tenuous claim, treating the indigenous people as though they came from another planet.

Later that night, after Celia had insisted that he orally bring her to a climax for the third time in less than an hour, he broached the subject of her parents insular and antiquated prejudice. Celia was shocked.

"Prejudiced? Mummy and the dad? Oh Luke, wherever did you get such an idea" she asked with genuine surprise, catching him on the back foot.

"Gee, I don't know" he answered facetiously. "Maybe it was the fact that they said the Chinese were cretinous, dirty, and had the sexual habits of animals." She laughed affectionately and kissed him on the nose.

"You silly old thing," she replied. "That's all true. You can't be a racist if you're telling the truth, now can you?" he was amazed by her flippant self-delusion.

"Sure you can," he answered, not prepared to let her get away with the sweeping statement. He saw her mouth harden, the coolness in her eyes.

"Well, darling, we all know about the little 'chink' in your armor, don't we?" He felt himself bridle at the snide remark about Nancy.

"Don't worry bunny," she continued. "I don't blame you for getting a little chow on the side. I'm sure that yellow is very attractive in certain light. Most of the British men here have fucked their way through all the chink girls that don't need paper bags over their heads. I understand. After all, they have to be good for something. But you and I, we're good Anglo-Saxon stock Luke, and when we fuck, it's a fucking of like kind, and there won't be any little yellow mutant bastards resulting from it either." He was angry with her, and shocked by a racism that was so entrenched she was unable to recognize it. He wanted her out of his bed, but she had already moved down his body and taken his penis into her mouth, sucking at it hungrily. He withdrew from her mouth when he realized he was about to come, and ejaculated over her. She squealed with faint disgust, but his anger towards her had not abated. Before she had a chance to reach for a tissue he threw her over onto her back, and went down on her, pinning her arms to her sides with his hands. He licked and sucked her clitoris until she came once more with a shudder, but he did not stop. He bit her vulva with enough pressure to hurt but not damage her, rubbed her hard with his face, then returned to her clitoris with his tongue and his teeth. He did not count her orgasms, but he knew that they were becoming increasingly uncomfortable and wearing for her. He worked on her for what seemed like hours, exhausting himself, but knowing that her exhaustion and discomfort were greater. Still he felt angry, and his penis was engorged once more. Finally, when he knew that he had wrung all the juices from her body, he plunged his cock into her up to the hilt, forcing her knees back hard against her stomach. He could feel her dryness, his member grazing against the walls of her deep tunnel, and he knew that he was hurting her. He didn't care, and she never asked him to stop, even though her face contorted with pain. Long after he came, he kept her pinned under him with his full weight. Then finally, more disgusted with himself than with her, he rolled off her.

"The fucking of like kind, eh, Darling?" he said, quietly mocking her. She did not answer, but when she rose from the bed he noted with some satisfaction that she had difficulty in walking. The satisfaction was short-lived. Dressed, and ready to return home, she kissed him lightly on the mouth and said

"You were absolutely marvelous tonight. Next time, I want you to tie me up."

She let herself out, and Luke lay there in the darkness and sighed. Here was what every man was supposed to want, a lady in the drawing room, an insatiable whore in the bedroom. She was perfectly bred material for a corporate wife, and yet he felt more empty than ever.

H<small>E WAS ASTONISHED</small> when Miss Anna told him she was giving a birthday dinner for his twenty-fourth birthday. It did not seem possible that he had been in Hong Kong for that long a time, and yet in some ways he could not remember living anywhere else. He was still sporadically seeing Celia as the sex was tantalizing, yet he was feeling increasingly trapped, knowing that both she and her parents had given him the seal of approval as husband material, and he was terrified he would wake up one day to find Mrs Celia Powers lying in the bed beside him. He noticed Miss Anna's raised eyebrow and quizzical expression when he explained that he would come to the dinner alone. Everyone, including his partner, assumed that he and Celia were now a couple, but he gave no explanation, and Miss Anna did not press him for one.

It was a hot and humid mid-summer night. The drought of the previous year had broken, although the typhoons had come late that year. He thought of Taupo now, cold in mid-winter. A hand-knitted sweater from his grandmother had arrived in time for his birthday and he felt a twinge of homesickness. Despite the number of trips he had made to New Zealand, he had seen his grandparents only once, and was shocked to see them aging faster than he had expected. Now he was on his way to a surrogate family; Miss Anna, Thomas and Dennis. He was conscious of the affection inherent in Miss Anna's throwing him a birthday dinner. There were greetings upon his arrival and small gifts. Miss Anna had painted for him the view from the terrace, explaining girlishly that she was rusty and had little time to paint these days. It was not a delicate watercolor in the Chinese tradition, as Luke might have expected, but a bold and original oil painting full of energy and passion with which he was genuinely delighted. But the real surprise came when a figure, a stranger, stepped out of the shadows of the hallway and came toward him. "Luke," he heard Miss Anna's voice as if in a tunnel. "This is my niece. She's just returned from Switzerland." His mouth was so dry that his throat closed up and he could not speak. He could barely hear and it seemed to him that his vital organs were shutting down, even though he felt more alive than at any time in his life.

"Hello. I'm Jade Chen," she said in a voice that resembled the tinkling of wind-chimes in a light breeze. He took her extended hand and held it.

Here she was, the girl from the stairway of the Peninsula; the girl he had stayed in Hong Kong for. He looked into her eyes and he saw himself reflected there. But he also saw recognition, and something more. He saw that she knew, as he did in that split second that their eyes met, that they belonged irrefutably to each other, and from that night on their lives would never be the same again.

CHAPTER TWELVE

I HAVE TO SEE you." Luke said the words without looking at Jade, in what amounted to a whisper. All through dinner he had been conscious of her presence, even though she barely raised her eyes to look at him, and never once spoke directly to him. He did not know what he had eaten, or if he had eaten at all, although he supposed he must have or Miss Anna would have commented. Somehow he held up his end of the conversation, even making Miss Anna and Thomas Ho laugh occasionally, but he was acutely aware that any one at the dinner table would have had to be blind not to notice how being close to Jade Chen affected him. As if to reinforce his fears, when they left the dinner table Dennis muttered to him as he passed. "Don't even think about it!" and Luke could only wonder if his feelings were as transparent to the others.

Even when they went to the terrace for coffee, the heady scent of "L'Air Du Temps" searched him out in the night air. He sensed she was avoiding him, and wondered if perhaps he had mistaken her interest. That was why he spoke, when he finally found himself momentarily beside her. She gave an almost imperceptible nod of her head and, as he started to ask how, she whispered, "Be patient. I will find you," and moved away to talk to Dennis.

He did not speak to her again that night, and yet he felt a sense of

pure joy, elation, just knowing she existed, and that she was everything
that he remembered and more. That she was so tantalizingly close, and
yet untouchable, only added to the euphoria. Miss Anna, rather than
Thomas, showed him to the door at the end of the evening. Jade had
already excused herself and gone to her room and Luke had found himself
talking shop with Dennis and Thomas, a heated discussion about profit
margins and exchange rates. Normally Miss Anna would have been the
most knowledgeable and most vocal in such a discussion, but this night
she sat quietly, deep in thought, before finally smiling apologetically.

"Gentlemen, if you don't mind, we're all working people, and my
capacity for hospitality is waning. Rather than be a bad hostess, may I
suggest that we once again wish Luke a very happy birthday and say our
goodnights?" The suggestion was clearly a directive that could not be
ignored, and Luke barely had time to gather up his painting, his book on
Confucius from Thomas, and the expensive but garish wide tie that was
Dennis's gift. At the heavily carved front doors, near the still pond full of
water lilies and golden carp, Miss Anna seemed to relax, and smiled for
the first time in hours.

"Happy Birthday Luke. I hope it was the first of many we will share,
and that it was everything you expected," she said with genuine affection.
He was overcome with an impulse to hug her, but settled instead for kissing her cheek. She seemed startled and he hastened to apologize.

"I'm sorry. I know that's probably not the done thing, but I couldn't
think of any other way to thank you. You've given me so much." She nodded, yet beneath the warmth in her voice was a strong sense of warning,
of laying down boundaries for the future. "I would gladly give you most
of what I have, for you are a truly remarkable young man," she told him.
"But it would be wise for you to realize that there are some things which
are not mine to give, and that may not be taken. I hope you understand."
She looked at him questioningly, and he found himself answering, "Yes,
I understand," before they said their goodnights and she opened the door
for him.

In truth, he did understand, or he certainly thought that he had. He
was being told to stay away from Jade, pleasantly warned off. Yet he was
conscious that he had told her only that he understood what she said, he

had not promised to abide by it. Nor was there any way his mentor could enforce his acquiescence, for he knew that if Jade wanted him, what Miss Anna wanted would become irrelevant, no matter how much he respected her.

From her window, Jade watched Luke leave. She felt giddy, almost faint with longing for him. In Switzerland she had heard a Charles Aznavour song, "To die of Love," and finally she understood what it meant. She opened her diary and wrote, ' Today I met Luke Powers, the man I will love for as long as I live. There must be a way I can marry him.' It was not written as a fanciful daydream one never expects to be fulfilled, but with the romantic practicality of someone who has grown up believing that all things are possible.

Jade knew only too well the story of her grandfather's flight from China, and the treasure of Jade he had brought with him. She had heard, from the age when she was able to understand, of how he found the red and green lion house, and traded half the jade for it, using the other half to build an empire and become a great Taipan. She had honored her grandfather, for it was tradition, and she still visited his shrine with her Aunt Anna, and burnt money so that he could have whatever was necessary in the world of the dead. Still, she had not loved him, although she had never confessed that to anyone. In truth, she was afraid of him until the day he died, as she knew her mother and father had been. She believed, perhaps because she needed to believe, that her parents loved each other, despite the fact that they met only twice before their wedding day. Her mother had been a gentle creature, daughter of a once wealthy and noble Mandarin family who had lost all their possessions when the Communists came to power. Unlike Chen Lee Xiao, they had not escaped. Jade's maternal grandparents never reached Hong Kong, although their daughter arrived as a refugee to the crown colony in the same year that Britain crowned its new queen, the year Luke Powers was born. It was Jade's maternal great uncle, who had worked in the markets with Xiao in the days when he had first made Hong Kong his home, who had told his old friend of the arrival of his niece, a veritable pearl of breeding and gentility, and it was decided over a glass of rice wine that a marriage contract should be drawn between the girl and Xiao's son. The children were never consulted and, in any case, would not have argued. It was Xiao who had chosen the name Jade for his only grandchild, and who had mapped out the future for his son and his son's offspring. No-one disobeyed; except Anna, who was the first in the family to anglicize her name, and who refused to be bound by outdated traditions. Yet, when Xiao and his son and heir died tragically in a plane crash, and Jade's mother succumbed to cancer less than a year later, it was Aunt Anna who stepped into every role that was needed; corporate head and heir, Taipan of a great business conglomerate, and mother to Jade, who was barely nine years old at the time.

For a little girl, almost crippled with grief, to be left in the charge of an aunt whose own personal battles had yet to be fought, was frightening and overwhelming. And yet it seemed to Jade, looking back, that although she had known her aunt to be spoken of as wild and rebellious, a woman who had turned her back on traditional Chinese values, Anna Chen swiftly fulfilled all expectations of Chen Lee Xiao's heir.

Jade remembered how, on her thirteenth birthday, Aunt Anna had said to her, "Never be afraid. Never say 'I cannot' or 'they won't let me.' It isn't tradition for a woman to head a company like Eastern Star, and it shocks many people. But that is their problem. One day, you will inherit the company. How far you go with it is up to you. Only you can defeat you. But remember that, to succeed, you must never forget those who paved the way for you. It isn't simply pointless tradition that we venerate the ancestors, living and dead. We sacrifice for them, as they sacrificed for us. To do anything less would be unacceptable in any culture." Jade saw no reason to question the wisdom. It seemed to her that her aunt had everything a woman could want except perhaps a man to love her, and she was certain that Thomas was willing. It wasn't until she was older, and leaving for a trip to Paris before the new term at her Swiss school started, that she saw the longing in her Aunt's eyes as she talked of Montmartre and the Sorbonne where she had spent one year. Then she realized what Miss Anna had given up, and wondered if she had, indeed, defeated herself. She knew the plans her aunt had for her future and for Eastern Star, and she understood the principal of respect for the elders, but they both seemed impossibly distant to a girl who was still only nineteen years old. She didn't need to bother with such things, and it would be years, she told herself, before she needed to make any decisions. But all of that was before she saw Luke Powers, and knew that the future was there, at that moment, standing in front of her.

LUKE HAD STEPPED out of the elevator and was halfway down the corridor before he noticed that there was a girl sitting outside his front door, hunched over her knees. For a moment he thought, or perhaps hoped, that it was Jade. Then she raised her head, the face tearstained and bruised, and he saw that it was Nancy. She got to her feet and tried to speak, but began to cry silently instead. He wanted to ask her what she was doing there but he knew, with the wisdom of a man celebrating his twenty-fourth birthday, that now was not the time to ask. She was in trouble, that much was obvious. He took her into the apartment, sat her down and poured her a stiff Scotch, which she gagged on. He noticed a bruise on her arm, as well as the one on her face, but he still did not ask the questions forming in his head. Finally, when she had stopped crying, wiped her nose, and sat cross-legged on the floor like an appealing child, she looked at him quizzically and said.

"Why you don't ask me what happened? Don't you know I'm in big trouble?" He smiled at the frankness that was even more attractive than the raw sexuality she had exuded the day he had met her.

"I figured you would tell me when you're ready," he explained. She nodded, as though the response made perfect sense to her.

"Okay, I'm ready," she replied. And as she started to speak, the words came tumbling out over each other. She told Luke of her pimp, and how he had been her first lover when she was only fourteen; of how her father had been killed, crushed between two sanpans, and how her mother had taken over the fishing business. Luke learned for the first time of the seven brothers and sisters, five of them still living on the sanpan, on the harbor at Aberdeen. He heard how her pimp had set her up with any number of visiting businessmen, "Some of them old, Lukey. Very wrinkly, drink too much, but they come fast and give good tip so I make more money for family."

"So how come I never met this guy," Luke asked. "Why didn't he set it up between us?" She blushed and looked uncomfortable.

"Meeting you was very good fortune, but accident. I try to keep it from him. I not wanting to think I'm just a good-time girl. I like you so much, maybe even love, and I don't need too much for myself — just see one or two old client when you busy or away, and give him money from that, like always." She said it so matter-of-factly that Luke couldn't help smiling, even though he knew his ego should be bruised from the knowledge that others were sharing her body at a time he thought she was exclusively his. Now her eyes clouded, and there was a heavy emotional tremor in her voice as she continued. "Then, he finds out about you, and was very angry. You went overseas, and I think, I will tell Luke when he comes back. But I didn't. Remember when I started asking for more money?" she asked innocently.

"I remember," he told her gently.

"That was for him," she explained superfluously. "Then, when you said we could not see each other any more, he was so angry with me. He hit me very bad, said he would put me on streets or pick-up bars like a common whore. I'm not a common whore, Luke, am I?" She came to him, searching his eyes, her arms around his neck, and his body remembered everything they had ever done together and wanted more of it. He gently extricated her arms.

"No sweetheart, you're not a common whore," he told her.

"Business is bad Luke. He wants me to get back with you. He knows who you are, and says he will get money, if not from you to me, then he will blackmail you. You getting very well known in business. He says you could be ruined. We had very big fight and he hit me again, very, very bad this time." She trailed off, and turned away, the voice becoming little more than a whisper. "I don't know what to do, so I tell him I will go to police, and he will go to jail. He so angry I run away. I could not think of any other man who would help me." She did not look at him, for fear of seeing rejection in his eyes.

Part of him wished he could love her, wished it didn't matter that she was not Jade. He didn't want to hurt her, but he knew there was no other choice.

"Listen to me," he told her gently, taking both her hands into his own. "It can't be that way again Nancy. I'm in love with someone else." He saw the pain the words produced and knew in that moment that he had not been simply a client or a meal ticket to Nancy, she had loved him in her own way.

"She same girl you think of when you make fuck with me?" she asked with resignation. He was surprised that what he thought were deeply hidden feelings were actually so transparent, but he nodded.

"Yes, even though I didn't actually meet her until tonight." He realized he sounded foolish, and he saw the glimmer of hope in her eyes.

"Maybe she not want you at all. Then you come back to me," she suggested, brightening considerably at the prospect, and he couldn't help smiling.

"Nancy, we had some wonderful times, but it's over," he told her. "Just the same, I'm not going to see you hurt. I want you to think very seriously about whether you want to go to the police. If you get this bastard charged, maybe you have a chance to start life afresh. I could help you get a job."

"What job? You want me to earn shopgirl's money?" she asked in disbelief, and he knew that it was hopeless. Short of marrying and raising her own family, there was no way Nancy was going to turn her back on a way of life that was now a part of her.

It was after three in the morning when Luke drove Nancy to Aberdeen, the fishing village just a short drive from Kowloon. It was more a suburb than a village, with half the population crammed into tiny Housing Commission flats, the other half living on sanpans and junks in the harbor. This floating community ran electrical cables from the quayside to the boats, and Luke had been amused, the first time he had visited Aberdeen, to see entire families on the little boats, which did not have toilets or running water, crowded around a television set. He could never shake himself of the smell of Aberdeen, for the Chinese would strip the fish meant for their own consumption, and hang the strips up to dry. It seemed to Luke, as the Jaguar sped towards Nancy's home, the most incongruous place for her to live, and he couldn't reconcile dried fish and sanpans with the beautiful creature he had bumped into on Nathan

Road. Nancy slept in the passenger seat, and the trip was faster than usual as there was little traffic on the roads. He was loathe to wake her, even after he pulled up the car close to the waterfront. She was stretching like a cat, and he was about to ask which one was her home, when he saw the flames, tiny at first, like the flickering of a candle. It was the light that caught his eye first, but then the silhouette of a man, seen in his line of peripheral vision, that caused Luke to turn his head. The figure jumped from boat to boat until it reached the dock, and then ran off into the night. By the time Luke turned his gaze back to the flickering flame, the entire sanpan was in flames, people were screaming, and Nancy, hysterical, was yelling something in Chinese that he didn't understand; all of this in no more than three seconds, and yet time seemed to have slowed almost to a stop for Luke.

He wasn't conscious of getting out of the car, of moving to the edge of the dock, of feeling Nancy tugging at his sleeve, urging him forward; of her wildly quavering voice as she screamed at him that it was her mother's boat, her home, and he must do something. He could see that the boat was engulfed in flames now, and people were pushing past him, knocking hard against him. Some were on their way from the boats to the safety of the dock, shaken with fear that their own boats would succumb to the blaze. Some ran from around him, in the direction of the fire, hoping to save the people, Nancy's people, whose screams cut through the night air. Yet still he did not move. He would figure later that perhaps thirty seconds passed, thirty seconds in which he might have saved Nancy's mother, or one of her three young brothers, or little sister. He would also figure later that it was the first birthday since his eleventh that he had felt truly happy, and had forgotten what birthdays signified. Now, the past came back to torment him once more, and the thirty seconds that passed in reality were for him thirteen years. He traveled back in time, and the burning boat was not a boat at all, but a Kombi-van; and the screams were not those of Nancy and her family, but the screams of his own sisters.

He was helpless, rooted in place. He knew in his heart, when he confronted himself later, that he could have done nothing, yet he despised himself for not even trying.

"Bastard… you filthy bastard" It was Nancy's voice that brought him back to reality, but the words were choked by sobs, and almost drowned out by the sound of the fire engine as it raced for the dock. And in that moment, where past and present blurred and seemed to merge and hold each other briefly, he thought he saw his father walking towards him through the flames, burnt almost beyond recognition, charred skin and raw flesh, blackened lips drawn back over large teeth in a macabre grin. He thought he heard his father's voice saying, "Happy Birthday son. You'll remember this one, huh?" Then he realized that the figure was real, but it was not heading towards him, but to Nancy, and he could see, though only just, that it was the figure of a woman, Nancy's mother, and the lips were pulled back over her teeth not in some ghoulish grin, but as part of her screams of agony. He could smell, amongst the acrid fumes of the fire and the putrid stench of the fish, the familiar sweet smell of barbecued flesh; and he turned and vomited on the dock.

HE STAYED WITH Nancy at the hospital. The girl who had once given her body so readily and with such joy was now remote and distant, shrouded in a veil of her own grief. He knew that the part of her that blamed him for not acting was not thinking rationally, for he could see the unspoken apology in her face. He knew that she blamed herself far more than him, yet that was irrational too; if she had returned to the boat instead of coming to his apartment, she could have perished like her siblings. Her mother's life now hung in the balance and Nancy, fighting her way back through shock, managed to whisper to him;

"Please, not tell police about pimp. It get in paper that I am good-time girl, and shame the memory of my family." Luke could only nod numbly, trying hard to grapple with her belief that sparing the honor of the family was of greater importance than bringing a killer to justice. The police, for their part, didn't seem surprised by the fire or the death toll. There were a few raised eyebrows as to what Luke was doing there, but the questions were discreet. It was Luke himself who felt the need to excuse his behavior in taking no action. The worst part of the night was when Nancy, tears in her eyes, accepted the cash which was all he had to offer her and he knew, without either one of them saying it, that he would not see her again, despite his offers to help her and her promises that she would call.

It was daylight when he drove home, but already the harbor was a hive of activity. He slept fitfully for a few hours and then went to his office in the Eastern Star building. He noticed that the South China Post had a story on the fire, its interest lying largely in the fact that he, wrongly identified as an Australian businessman, had somehow been involved in the tragedy. Luke felt an empty hole open in his stomach when he saw Nancy described as his companion. He wanted to call Jade immediately, to ask her not to jump to any conclusions, but what could he say? 'It isn't what you think...' But it was. He knew she would see the report, or someone would show it to her. In some ways it was a blessing. He had promised her that he would wait for her to contact him. If she did not, he would understand that the report had given her the excuse to close the door on a relationship before it began. If she did, it meant that she was so interested, or perhaps already so emotionally involved, that nothing he did could make any difference.

For two days he waited, with the growing fear that she had cut him dead, and then, just before he was leaving his office on a Friday afternoon, his direct line rang. "Luke Powers," was all he said before the voice, which he recognized immediately, spoke without first identifying itself.

"The Lantau Island ferry, Sunday morning, ten o'clock. Please do not approach me. Wait for me to speak to you." Then the click of the phone being hung up, before he even had time to respond. Yet the hairs on his arm were standing up, his skin tingling as if from a minor electrical shock, and a wave of anticipation broke over him with the force of a Tsunami. He wasn't sure how he would live until Sunday, or even if he would live at all until he could see her again. There was a sense of mild self-contempt for his idiotic schoolboy reaction. This was worse... and better... than what he had felt for Kiri. More importantly, he knew instinctively that this was real love; the love of two souls who were made to be together, and the implications were frightening. He did not really know this girl; had never touched her; was unaware of what went on inside of her; and yet he was willing to accept that she was that part of him that had been missing all his life. What if she did not recognize this? What if he was just a man, a date, a passing interest, to her? He told himself it couldn't be that way. Everything that had happened to him – accepting the offer to come to Hong Kong against all common sense; passing her on the stairs at the Peninsula; staying in the colony and working with her aunt; being at Miss Anna's house when Jade arrived back from Switzerland – it all seemed pre-destined, and there could be no other reason than that they were meant to be together. Despite his reassurances to himself, he barely slept on Saturday night.

THE ISLAND OF Lantau was only a short ferry ride from Hong Kong. Larger than its neighbor, but with only a small population, many of them British colonials with holiday homes, its main attractions were the quiet beaches by the fishing villages, and the Po Lin Buddhist monastery high in the middle of the island. On weekends it was a place for families to picnic, for young lovers to walk, and for would-be lovers, like Luke and Jade, to meet.

He saw her board the ferry. How could he not notice her luminescence even with the pale chiffon scarf tied around her head and neck, and the large sunglasses that concealed most of her face? She wore a white shirt, he noticed, and a simple Swiss peasant style skirt. Her legs were bare, and the natural leather Italian sandals had thongs which wound their way around her legs high above the ankles. Luke thought they were the most provocative shoes he had ever seen, but then, everything about her was provocative; even her innocence and simplicity. She passed him without so much as a sideways glance, and sat some eight or ten rows in front of him. He could see a tendril of her hair desperately trying to escape from the scarf, and it only served to arouse him. A Chinese couple with five young children sat beside and opposite him; and he had learned enough of the language in the months he had been in Hong Kong to know that he was the major topic of conversation; everything from his 'straw-colored hair' to his 'long legs, like a cricket.' He could not help but smile, for he knew the Chinese believed crickets brought good luck, and it seemed to him an omen that he had been compared to the insect. He passed the trip listening to their idle banter, trying to understand and interpret as many new words as possible, yet never letting them know, by even the bat of an eyelid, that he knew what they were saying.

Almost everyone on the ferry was on their feet and thronging toward the gangway before the boat even docked at the wharf at Mui Wo, just as the crowd had pushed forward, crushing those ahead of it, when the ferry had been boarded. Almost without realizing it, Luke found himself next to Jade. He turned and looked at her exquisite profile and was about to speak to her when she whispered for his ears alone, "Someone may be following me. Do not lose me." She never once turned her head, or made eye contact and, almost instantly, she was caught up in the flow of the crowd as the gangplank was put in place and the passengers swarmed onto dry land. Some went into the small town around the wharf, others headed for the various bus-stops. Luke kept Jade always in his line of vision. He saw her board a bus and he followed, noting that she sat in a front seat and watched, peripherally, every person who boarded the bus. Only after the bus was underway did she seem to relax, but it was not until they made a stop in the fishing village of Tai Fuk that she made her way back to find a seat beside Luke.

He waited for her to speak, for he was afraid that he would break one of the rules of this game she appeared to be playing, a game that he clearly wasn't sure how to play at all. For a few minutes they rode in silence, her leg against his. The nearness of her was making him lightheaded, and he wished he knew more of how to court an Asian woman, or even how to behave. But it was the girl who had been to Paris, and to school in Europe, not a Chinese peasant, who finally spoke.

"You're very quiet," she said with uncertainty. "Does that mean you're not pleased to see me?" He smiled at the transparency of her flirtatious approach, and looked at her for the first time since he had boarded the bus.

"I wouldn't be here if I didn't want to be with you. Of course I'm pleased. God, I'm ecstatic." He smiled then and Jade felt the warmth and depth of his feeling for her.

"Me too" she replied. "I know I'm not supposed to say things like this, not in Chinese custom anyway, but I haven't been able to think about anything else but you for days." She returned the smile, and he felt as though he was melting under its intensity. He reached out and took her hand, holding it tightly in his own. He noted the delicacy of her fingers, the overall smallness of the hand, and the soft contrast of its color against his own. More important than what he saw, though, was what he felt. It seemed to him that a circuit somehow wired them together, and he could feel the charge running through his body, directly from her heart to her fingertips, and through them to his fingertips, carried swiftly through his arteries. For a long while they said nothing. The bus labored to climb the mountain to Ngong Ping, where the monastery was situated, and below them, through the dirty windows, Luke surveyed the astonishing beauty of the landscape. He gave her every chance to tell him the reason for the subterfuge and intrigue of the trip, yet she said nothing. Finally he couldn't bear it any longer.

"So, what was that all about then?" he asked as nonchalantly as he could. She shrugged, clearly not wanting to deal with any questions.

"It was nothing, I guess," she said with a sheepish smile. "Maybe I'm just a little paranoid." Luke was astounded that she now seemed so dismissive.

"Jade! You make secretive phone calls; you're practically disguised; we have to act like strangers. What the hell is going on here?" He was firm but gentle, and there was no way she could avoid giving him an answer, even though she hesitated.

"Okay, I'll tell you," she said reluctantly. "I... it's Aunt Anna. She's overly protective, you know, and she has this thing about how I behave; the honor of the Chen family name bit. So she wants to know every place I go, what I do, who I go with. You know, all that sort of stuff." Luke raised an eyebrow. It seemed unlike the Miss Anna he dealt with to be so old-fashioned, especially with someone like Jade, who didn't seem either irresponsible or disrespectful.

"At your age?" he asked with surprise.

"She also thinks I'm still a kid." Jade giggled. "Maybe I am. You don't even know how old I am."

"Sure I do." Luke replied. "You'll turn twenty on the sixteenth of next month. You like Fleetwood Mac, the Eagles, and Mozart, and your favorite books are Germaine Greer's *The Female Eunuch* and just about anything by Rod McKuen, which is a pretty weird combination." She laughed delightedly.

"You've been researching me! That's outrageous," she said with mock indignation.

"Sure. How else would I know if we're compatible? You might have some shocking habits I couldn't live with, like eating Sara Lee Blueberry danish in the middle of the night with a glass of cold milk." He was teasing, and she gave a mock squeal.

"But I love doing that." She protested and he shrugged.

"Okay... guess I can live with it," he responded, and she took off the dark glasses and he looked into her eyes, knowing as he did so, that he could lose himself in them forever.

"So, you think Aunt Anna wouldn't approve of me as a date?" He asked the question innocently, but he saw the flicker of concern and doubt in her eyes.

"It's not that simple," she answered, and let the statement hang. A small warning bell went off in his head, but he willed it to stop, and ignored it from that point on.

"Sure it is," he reassured her. "We just go to her and tell her about us." It sounded so easy when he said it that he wasn't prepared for the vehemence with which she answered.

"What us? This is only the second time we have met. I don't even know you. Who says there is an 'us'?" And, even though he knew she didn't believe what she was saying, he felt angry that she was choosing to deny what he was so ready to concede.

"It's the third time, counting the hotel. And you know damn well there's an us," he countered. "What's more, there's always going to be an us. Now that scares the shit out of me, and probably you too. But it doesn't have anything to do with how long we've known each other."

"Maybe it does," she answered softly, contritely. "Maybe we've known each other since the beginning of time." And, without saying the words, he knew that this was the first declaration of love between them.

They left the bus, along with the other travelers, at the monastery and passed through the grey stone archway that led to the courtyards and temples of Po Lin. The air was heavy with the smell of incense, and Luke watched as Jade joined other worshippers lighting bundles of incense, holding them as if in prayer and shaking them. He wanted to ask her what she was doing, but he was so hypnotized by the sheer presence of her that he forgot. Almost an hour went by before she volunteered to him; "I asked Buddha to one day give us a son." She spoke shyly and without pressuring him at all, but he turned her to face him, her breasts lightly touching his stomach, for her face was barely up to his chest, and he felt himself harden against her and saw her eyes, heavy with desire, widen with both fear and anticipation.

"Or sons," he whispered to her, his desire overtaking him. "I want you Jade. I'm in love with you... I want..." He broke off as he saw her lips part, her tongue flicker nervously. He bent his head to hers, wanting her mouth as much as the rest of her. He wanted to swallow her, drink her in so that he somehow could become her, or she could become him – it didn't matter which. She pulled back first.

"No, Luke. This is not right. This is a holy place," she stammered.

"What I feel for you is holy," he answered. She took his hand then and they ran back to the bus-stop, but the bus had gone. They hailed a taxi which had just dropped off some German tourists and had the driver take them to Tai Fuk, which was the closest place where they could find a hotel of sorts. For a few extra dollars, the bored Chinese innkeeper asked no questions, but showed them to his best room. They didn't speak, and the second the door was closed he gathered her into his arms, terrified that the anticipation of wanting her so badly, and the length he had had an erection, would make him orgasm before either one of them could get their clothes off. Still, in spite of the agony, he did not want to rush. He picked her up and put her on the bed, and slowly undressed her. She was so exquisite it took his breath away, and he wanted to envelope himself in her. He spent what seemed like hours, although it was probably no more than half of one hour, touching her with his hands and his mouth, examining every inch of her. Then, without warning, he saw tears start to well in her eyes and he sat on the bed and stroked her face.

"Jade, if you don't want to, I'm not going to force you," he reassured her.

"I do want to," she answered miserably. "But I'm afraid you'll hurt me.

I've never done this before." His eyes widened. It had never occurred to him and yet he knew it should have. "You're a virgin?" he asked, knowing that the question was redundant before she nodded her head. He thought then how strange it was that the only two women he had ever truly loved in his life had both known no other man before him. It should have aroused him more, that sense of being the first, and yet he felt the excitement starting to subside, and he became aware of the shabbiness and tackiness of the room. He reached for her clothes and quietly started to dress her. Jade began to cry.

"You're angry with me, aren't you?" she asked, and he took her face in his hands, feeling overwhelming love for her.

"I'm not angry sweetheart, but this is not a place where a girl makes love for the first time. I want it to be perfect for you. I'm taking you home, to my place. When we're old, married fifty years, the grandkids are grown and we think back to the first time... I don't want it to be this place that we remember."

She threw her arms around his neck then and they both knew, that although it would not be the place where she lost her virginity, this cheap, rundown room would always be the place where Luke first asked her to marry him.

CHAPTER THIRTEEN

T HEY DID NOT speak that night after Luke closed the door to his apartment. They moved to his bed like one person, and he felt his senses heightened, as though he could see through his own skin, and through hers, to the blood coursing in their veins, the nerve endings in their fingers. He had taken LSD once with some graduating students at university and experienced similar sensations, but without the joy, the ecstasy that came with loving Jade. Even the black silk hair spread on his pillow seemed to writhe of its own accord and he could feel its ebb and flow, as though it were an extension of himself. It was as if each of them gave up their identity to become part of one being, as though they had somehow melted together, despite her initial pain as he eased into her for the first time. The sensation was so overwhelming that Jade cried silent tears of happiness for both of them.

By the morning, the strange sensation of having somehow left the earth and melded completely in some other ethereal dimension had passed, to be locked in a secret compartment of each one's memory. Neither Jade nor Luke would ever examine it, for fear of debasing it or, even worse, having it disintegrate under their appraisal. In its place came the giddy euphoria of love with a healthy mix of sexual lust. They made love in the kitchen, on the couch, the floor, even the dining table.

They filled the bath tub almost to the brim, and sat facing each other as they gently soaped each other's bodies. The sex was long and languid, the water slapping against the side of the tub as they moved in a gentle circular motion, the soap making their skin slip against each other. He felt that they could stay like this forever. Her hair was damp from the water and the steam, but he could smell too the sweet perspiration that the heat and the sex evoked from her, and when he finally came inside her, gently and with a long sigh, the water was already turning cold and he could see tiny goose-bumps on her ivory skin.

It was the beginning of a new world in which no-one existed except the two of them. He learned more about his adopted home, its ways, its people, than he had ever expected to. For Jade, Luke was the hero of every book she had ever read, every movie she had ever seen, a "yellow-hair" in a land where yellow was the color of the gods. For Luke, the years of burying his grief and loneliness were over, and he let the ghosts of his parents, his sisters, his grandparents, escape from the prison of his mind, and drift away from him in dreams.

"I haven't thought about them at all," he told Jade, as they sat on the floor of his living room, watching the lights from the other side of the harbor through the window, "Except on my birthday... and when I went back to Chicago to sell the house. But now, I dream of them every night, when I should be dreaming of you."

She laughed, the warm ringing sound of bells, and sipped the wine he had poured for her.

"You don't need to dream of me, my love, for I'm always part of you. They have been buried for too long. It is not our way, she said quietly, realizing even as she looked at him, that he didn't really understand. "Even after Chinese die, the family does not act as though they are gone forever. They travel to some place we can't see or touch, but still we keep a shrine, and pictures of them, and bring food, and money in case they need anything. So they are always part of us, and must be respected for their position in the family." Luke felt an overwhelming rush of emotion, love for her, sadness for what had been lost.

"What if you can't believe that? What if you try, but you still end up knowing that they're just a pile of ashes scattered on a foreign countryside? There is no afterlife, no other world where they're just living like the invisible man and his friends?" He turned away, fearful that she would see the anguish in his face and think him weak. She moved to the window, watching the lights reflected in the water, and when she spoke it was to quote poetry that Luke had never heard before.

> "Bright shines the moonlight on the water,
> Perhaps reflected from frost on the ground,
> Lifting my head I gaze at the bright room
> Bowing my head, I think of my family home."

She turned then to find him watching her with astonishment.

"Did you write that?" he asked in awe. She smiled and crossed to him, entwining her arms around his neck.

"Only if I am a very old man, twelve hundred years or so," she teased. "Li-Po was a great poet from the Tang Dynasty, but I think he understood you, as you understand him."

"I have no home, Jade, and I don't need one," Luke answered defensively, aware of his own vulnerability.

"But you love me," she countered simply.

"I love you," he answered. "Completely, hopelessly, endlessly... so sue me!" he joked. She did not laugh, and her eyes looked through his own and deep into his mind, his heart.

"Well then... I am your home," she said, and he knew that this simple statement held more truth than anything he had ever heard before.

LOVING JADE CHEN meant, for Luke, entering a world full of past and future, the old and the new, but it was also a world full of secrets.

"Let me tell her," Luke pleaded incessantly every time Jade insisted that they keep their meetings private and hidden from her aunt. "She loves you, and I know she likes me. Why wouldn't she be happy for us?" Jade would become defensive, even anxious, at the prospect.

"You don't understand," she would argue. "She thinks of me as a child, and you're a business colleague. She would never agree to our seeing each other, not until I'm older." "You don't know that," Luke countered.

"She might consider it a great match, especially once she understands that I want to marry you."

"Oh, so now you want to approach her as if this is a business deal? How do you think I would feel knowing that?" Jade asked petulantly. She looked so child-like that he laughed and gathered her into his arms.

"Okay, okay," he capitulated. "We'll keep it secret... for now. But some day..."

"Some day had better not be until I turn twenty-one," she replied, softening. "If she finds out you have deflowered her closest relative, she's liable to cut off your balls and sell them to the Chinese Apothecary, and then you'll be right next to the Rhinoceros horn and Tiger Claw!" They fell together on the bed, laughing, and she tore hungrily at his shirt and his trousers, making her way down from light kisses on his chest, and he gave in to her, as he knew he always would.

There was a certain edge of excitement for both of them that keeping the affair secret brought to the relationship. They could not be seen publicly, and so it was impossible for them to visit any nightspots, or even dine out in the better restaurants. Instead, they would meet on the tiny island of Cheung Chau, where not even a car was allowed, and eat fresh crab, steamed with ginger, from the seafood stalls. They rode bicycles, and Jade gave Luke Chinese lessons.

"Xie Xie," instead of thank you, became second nature to him, as did "shi" for yes, "bushi" for no, and a host of other phrases. But it was Jade who clapped her hands in delight when, one night after a minor disagreement, Luke solemnly declared "I kno pa-chang P'ai-pu-hsiang."

"Do you know what it means?" she asked him, stifling her giggles. He looked bashful. "I guess I'm in real trouble if it means your face has all the appeal of a stunned mullet!" he replied, remembering an Australian expression that had always appealed to him. "I hope it means it takes two to make a quarrel... so I'm not going to fight with you."

"IT MEANS," SHE said, moving towards him, her eyes now hooded with wanting him, "You cannot clap with one hand... but you also, my darling, cannot make love with one body," and she pressed against him, the force of her tiny figure surprising him with its insistence, and her arms around his neck pulled his mouth to hers and her tongue invaded his mouth.

"YOU CANNOT HIDE the truth from me, my friend," Miss Anna told him after a meeting at which Luke had put forward new ideas for an entire range of new ZipCars. The vehicle had made inroads in Asia and the larger European cities were beginning to respond. "I know your secret." Luke felt his nerve ends shred, tingling under his skin, his throat constricting even as he tried to avoid her look.

"Secret? What secret." He managed to sound genuinely surprised as he asked the question. Miss Anna smiled and nodded.

"You know very well," she accused. "You are bored with Hong Kong and missing your family."

Luke hoped that the relief he felt was not apparent in his expression.

"Oh," he said as nonchalantly as he could, and smiled at the suggestion that Hong Kong, Jade's home, could ever be boring. "I'm not bored. Maybe just a little restless... pre-occupied." He hoped this would be enough to allay any further discussion, but Miss Anna had secrets of her own.

"But you need to see your family, and so you shall. I've cleared your workload here and booked the flights. You can check the Singapore, Indonesian and Australian markets on your way to New Zealand, and then you must take two extra weeks and just relax. We can manage without you for a month." She smiled affectionately.

"A month?" Luke asked in alarm, realizing how interminable it would seem without Jade, but Miss Anna only read his reluctance as part of his commitment to the company.

"Luke, you cannot just work yourself to death," she said with genuine concern. " Do you think I haven't noticed how tired you look? Seen the dark shadows under your eyes, watched the weight dropping off you?" He suppressed a smile, tempted for a moment to tell her that the reason for his physical deterioration was his love of her niece, and the long nights spent doing anything but sleeping and eating.

"I'm fine, really," he countered. "I don't think it's a good idea for me to go away for such a long time, not when we're still establishing the new lines and territories."

"You have been here for over two years next week," Miss Anna said, and he was astonished to realize that it had been so long. "You will hear the figures before you go, but I can tell you un-officially that the new company is thriving and you have tripled your investment." He was surprised. In the past few months he had forgotten about money completely, except for the few dollars spent on baubles for Jade. It was not a shock to hear that his ideas had generated big profits, but the thought that he was now worth three million dollars was daunting at twenty-four years of age. He tried in vain to reason that he should not make a long trip, but a number of short trips to the various markets, but he stopped when he realized that Miss Anna was growing both impatient and suspicious. With as much grace as he could muster, he accepted that he was going "home" for a well-earned holiday. There was no way of telling her, without betraying the promise he had made to Jade, that 'home' was here in Hong Kong.

"I DON'T WANT you to go," Jade told him quietly, her voice catching in her throat. "A month is too long. Not now, not yet. I'm not sure enough of myself. What if you met someone else, a blue-eyed blonde perhaps?" He stifled a laugh, for he could see how serious she was, but he couldn't keep the twinkle out of his eyes.

"Someone like Celia Hackforth-Smythe?" he asked, and she relaxed and laughed, for he had told her of the affair and his horror at the English girl's prejudice, and Jade knew that if there ever was a threat to their love, it would not come from Celia. She smiled, but he saw the sadness in her eyes, and knew that he could not leave her for that long.

"Come with me," he said, and saw at once the doubt disappear from her face.

"You want me to?" she asked.

"Of course I do," he replied.

"Then I don't need to. I'm just being silly. I know that you love me, or you wouldn't ask me to go with you," she replied, satisfied with the decision. But now, for Luke, there was a sense of urgency he had not expected.

"Please, I'm being selfish, but I can't spend four whole weeks away from you. I want you with me. I want you to meet my grandparents, Hughie, see Taupo, Auckland... and I want them to meet you. After all, you're going to be my wife. Please Jade, there has to be a way." He knew that the final words would sway her, for they were words she had said to him only hours before. They had spent the day with Jade showing him the new refugee camps that harbored the lost souls from Vietnam and Cambodia who did not receive the status which greeted the Chinese refugees from the mainland who arrived by boat or across the mountains into the New Territories. They had traveled to Ping Shan, and Jade had introduced him to the nuns who ran the Catholic orphanage. A dedicated group of women – Dutch, Chinese, even Scottish – they had welcomed Jade with almost as much joy as the children themselves as she distributed sweet dumplings, kites, wind socks and small papier mache dragons. The trinkets cost little, but the bright colors and the love with which they were offered enthralled the children. Luke had stood back, watching her surrounded by waifs, hungry for love, who clamored to embrace her. He could not help thinking of the children they would have together, and how they would cling to their mother. He imagined them a motley hybrid collection of his fairness, her darkness, his blue eyes, her brown, his side-eyed, raw-boned westerness, her delicate, eastern charm. Still, though the combination was hard to imagine, he knew they would be perfect, for they would be her children as well as his.

She had been silent for much of the trip home and, when he had questioned her, she had cried for the children who depended on the love of strangers, because there was no family for them to turn to.

"You can't break your heart over this, sweetheart," he had told her, but she had refused to listen.

"They are little children. They need to be in homes with a mother, a father who will love them. There are people all over the world who have no children and want them. Why can't these children give love to those people and be loved in return."

"You can't fix something like this, it just isn't possible," he had gently tried to warn her, but she looked at him with the pain of the children she had left.

"There has to be a way," she said simply and determinedly.

Throwing the words back at her was a challenge Jade was more than willing to meet. Within two days she had laid a plan before Luke with all the practicality of a business partner rather than a woman in love.

"While you're in Singapore, Malaysia and Indonesia I'll stay here, that way I won't be in the way while you do the business routine," she said, and he was charmed by her approach. "Then I'll tell Auntie A that I'm going to Switzerland for three weeks, leaving a few days after you leave. I promised Elsa, she's a friend from school last year, that I would go. I also want to spend a little time in Geneva, talking to the UNICEF people. Then I can fly to New Zealand and meet you for perhaps ten days, and arrive back in Hong Kong before you do. " He was delighted, but could not suppress his laughter.

"You're setting up an alibi!" he accused, and she smiled enigmatically.

"I shall go to Switzerland, see Elsa, visit Geneva... so I won't be lying. I just won't mention exactly how long I'll be there, or the fact that I'm taking a long way home," she explained innocently, and he picked her up, hugging her against him, his hands in the long ebony hair as he whispered 'thank you' to her.

On the evening before he left for Singapore, Jade left the house and walked along Bowen Terrace right next door. It was a favorite place for people to walk their dogs and jog — the new fitness fad. But it was not either of those that Jade was pursuing. Instead she met Luke by the rock known as Lover's rock, and the shrine to the Goddess of Love, where lovers, and those who loved in vain, or not at all, lit firecrackers and incense and burnt letters of request for the goddess to touch the heart of someone and let them be loved. Luke watched, speechless, as Jade lit her own incense sticks and spoke quietly in Cantonese to the brightly painted, slightly garish statue. Then, as the shadows deepened, they watched the lights come on in Wan Chai below them and across the harbor.

It was Dennis who took him to the airport, trying to make idle conversation, but Luke did not feel like talking, and they traveled much of the way in silence until Dennis took a moment in the heavy traffic to turn and look at Luke.

"Maybe it's none of my business," he said candidly. "But frankly, I wouldn't be moping around because you're leaving her if I were you. I don't think she's worth it." Luke reacted in surprise. Did Dennis know what Luke thought they had successfully kept hidden.

"What? What are you talking about?" Luke asked, confused. Dennis grinned. "Celia. You had a fight, right?" the man asked.

"I... no, we didn't. I've just had other things..." Luke stammered an explanation, but Dennis shook his head disbelievingly

"Come on Luke, the whole town is talking about it. You and Celia were hot stuff. Now it's iceberg time. I saw her at a party last weekend. She walked away when I even mentioned your name. What did you two fight about? Or is it something *that* personal?" Dennis prompted. A million thoughts crowded Luke's head. He had completely ignored Celia from the moment he met Jade. He had not returned her calls, even though he had not meant to be rude, and he knew that their last night together had done nothing to make her understand the growing contempt for her he was feeling. He had been invited to the embassy the previous month, and he knew he should have gone, but it had clashed with the only chance he and Jade had to celebrate her twentieth birthday alone, and there was no way he would miss that. He made a mental note to write to Celia while he was away, explaining that he had met someone else, and wishing her well, but some part of him knew he would not write. It was better to leave things as they were through his neglect. He turned to Dennis, and shrugged ruefully.

"As a matter of fact, it wasn't personal at all," he explained enigmatically. "She seemed like a good idea at the time. But good ideas have a shelf life."

"You bastard you!" Dennis said jokingly, with grudging admiration. Yet Luke could not help but feel that he had been a bastard to Celia, and no-one had deserved it more.

THE TWO WEEKS passed faster than he had expected. The sheer anticipation of having Jade meet the only other people who mattered in his life caused the days to fly. And then he was home again and his grandmother was making him baby lamb chops with minted peas; and his grandfather was putting new hooks and lures onto the fishing lines.

It was spring, and Taupo was more beautiful than he remembered, yet the calm and serenity were un-nerving after the frenetic pace of Hong Kong.

He had wasted no time telling the McMasters about Jade and her impending visit, part of him afraid that, although they were good people, their old-fashioned and provincial attitudes would somehow see them reject the idea of his marrying an Asian girl. He steeled himself for an argument that never came. Instead, there was a look between Sandy and Gwen that he could not read; disappointment perhaps, or fear for him? In a matter of seconds it had passed and his grandmother patted his hand.

"You seem happy, Luke, and that's something we've waited a long time for. If you're happy, your granddad and I are too," she said lovingly, and Luke hugged her.

He drove his Mustang up to Auckland to meet her and was amazed at how fast his adopted homeland was hurtling itself into the last quarter of the twentieth century. True, the sky scrapers would seem like stunted off-spring of the great towering buildings of Hong Kong Island, or Chicago, yet they were altering the skyline of the city in such a way that it seemed to be changing more with every visit he made. He arrived to find that the plane was running three hours late, and so nervous was he that had he stayed at the airport he would have been quite nauseous by the time Jade arrived. Instead he went to Hughie's place with dreaded anticipation of seeing his friend again.

For Hughie, the transitions of the past year had been as difficult as they had been easy for Luke, yet there was a sense that finally the man was taking command of his life again.

He noticed that Hughie wasn't drinking, his hair was cut and he had shaved. The house, too, had lost its air of despair and hopelessness, yet Luke hardly dared mention the future, for fear of sparking the old fires of resentment and self-pity. He contented himself with a platitude.

"You look well" he said offhandedly, and Hughie searched his face for the meaning behind the remark.

"Well, well? Or just well for a man with no legs?" he quipped and Luke felt the sinking sensation in his stomach, but Hughie surprised him by continuing, without a trace of self-pity.

"I'm probably going to be the first legless lawyer in New Zealand, Maori or otherwise. Just like that show on the tele… the new one with the Perry Mason bloke… Ironside. Can't you see me at a trial? Your honor, this witness doesn't have a leg to stand on!" and he laughed openly at Luke's astonished expression, realizing that his old friend was still trying to assimilate what he was saying. "Don't look so surprised mate" Hughie said gently. "It was you that was pushing for it, remember?"

"You're really going to do it? You're going to finish your degree?" Luke asked with growing excitement.

"Well," Hughie grinned from his wheelchair, "it's either that or top myself. I can't sit in this chair weeping buckets of tears for ever. They just run down between your legs and collect in the seat and it's like sitting in pee!" They both laughed at the joke, more comfortable with the humor than the gut wrenching emotion that had brought Hughie to this moment in his life. They shared a coffee and Hughie busied himself preparing the spare room for Luke and Jade, for it would be too late for them to drive to Taupo that night. Luke protested that they could go to a hotel, but Hughie would not hear of it.

"Look here, it's not the first time I've stayed under the same roof as you and listened to you performing on the other side of the wall. Make the most of it. From what I know of your Nana and Pop, you'll be relegated to separate bedrooms, and any hanky panky will be severely dealt with! Besides, I want to meet her. She's got to be special if you want to marry her." Their eyes met, the unspoken memory of Kiri between them, yet Luke knew there were no recriminations in his friend's mind, just a genuine desire to put the friendship back on the level it deserved.

Later, after calling his grandparents to prevent them from worrying, he waited at the airport. Jade, impatient to get through customs and immigration, had had her passport and papers ready, and then had left them on the plane, causing a frantic search by the ground staff. Suddenly, she was through the doors and into the waiting area, and there was Luke, beaming. She ran toward him, and he picked her up and kissed her deeply, both realizing at the same moment that they had simply marked time for two weeks until they could be together.

"Don't ever leave me for that long again," she whispered, and he answered instinctively, "Never."

Luke sat quietly watching as Hughie and Jade talked and laughed, his old friend regaling his new love with stories of Luke as a boy, the time at Lloyd's, the entrepreneurial period when Luke's auctions were raking it in. Jade listened, eyes shining, clapping her hands with delight and laughing at each new anecdote.

"What about girls? He must have had girlfriends?" Jade asked, with a teasing glance at Luke. For a moment Luke and Hughie looked at each other, each reading pain in the other's eyes, but Luke need not have worried.

"Well sure he did," Hughie said flippantly. "I mean, have a look at him, he's sort of cute in an overgrown blond teddy bear way." Both of them looked at Luke, who smiled bashfully. "But I can promise you one thing," Hughie continued. "Not one of them was as beautiful, or as perfectly right for him as you are." Jade kissed Hughie's cheek impulsively and Luke felt overwhelming love for both of them.

Later that night he and Jade made love in the single bed they shared in Hughie's spare room. They could not sleep even afterward, but lay exhausted in each others arms, the sheer exhilaration of being together causing a stubborn rush of adrenalin.

The following morning they drove to Taupo, where Jade received a more formal but just as genuine a welcome from Sandy and Gwen. Luke suppressed a smile when he saw that Hughie had rightly predicted separate bedrooms and a proposed roster for using the bathroom to ensure Jade's privacy. Nothing was said about them sleeping together, and Luke realized that it was simply not a possibility as far as his grandparents were concerned. He would respect their wishes, even though the thought of her sleeping in the narrow bed down the hall tantalized him to a point beyond sleep.

The holiday passed in an accelerated time frame, each day seeming shorter than the one before. They drove for miles, walked in the forest, picked out a site on the Northern edge of the lake where they would one day build a house, daydreaming about the future, for it had taken Jade only a day to fall in love with the area that reminded her of Switzerland.

They made love wherever they could find a place and time, and it occurred to him as she lay dozing in his arms under a travel rug on the bank of the lake, that this might be the exact same place where he had first made love to Kiri six, or was it seven, years or lifetimes ago.

In the evenings Jade helped prepare the dinner, and Luke even got his grandfather to set the table and shell peas, things that the old man considered largely "woman's work." He was conscious of the old man growing forgetful, even senile, although Luke knew he was only seventy. The two men went fishing while Jade and Gwen busied themselves in the garden. He sensed no awkwardness from his grandparents toward the beautiful Asian girl. This was the one he had chosen, and everything else was irrelevant. Yet sometimes he would see, when he and Jade were out together, the sideward glances, the raised eyebrows of people they passed. He knew the interest could be sparked by her incredible beauty, but he also knew that mixed relationships were still something of a novelty and he wondered if he was being judged, and then despised himself for wondering. In Hong Kong, there was nothing unusual in the middle classes in seeing white men with Asian women, and he had felt comfortable under any scrutiny. Now, though, he felt defensive with an irrational need to explain himself to strangers, and he wondered if there were perhaps a streak of racism in him that he had never seen before.

It seemed impossible that, less than two weeks later, he was driving her back to Auckland and putting her on the plane home. Taupo suddenly seemed empty and cold, and he withdrew into himself. His grandfather joined him on the porch that evening, handing him a cold beer which he did not want, but did not have the heart to refuse.

"Your Jade is a lovely, lovely young woman Luke," the old man said. "But... I have to say this..." Luke tensed, waiting for warning, the prejudice, the pep talk. The old man hesitated only for a moment, cleared his throat and continued. "I can't think what you're pussyfooting around for. If you don't marry her quick smart, I'll divorce your grandma and marry her meself." It was a blessing in the only way the old man knew how to give it. Luke laughed and hoped that in the misty grayness of the twilight, old Sandy would not see the mist of loneliness already clouding his grandson's eyes.

IF MISS ANNA ever suspected anything, she gave no indication, and Luke had stopped questioning Jade about the need for secrecy and simply accepted that this was the way the relationship would work until Jade turned twenty-one and could openly announce their plans to marry. They ventured further afield for their meetings, often traveling separately to Macau where Luke was amused by a Chinese population who spoke Portuguese and whose greatest source of income was the local casino where Jade won a small fortune on the roulette wheel. Even that was too risky for them, for many of the Hong Kong businessmen came there to relax and gamble, and she was recognized on more than one occasion. Christmas came swiftly and they exchanged their presents in secret. Jade gave Luke a small jade dragon and an English translation of Li-Po's poetry. He gave to her the title deeds, in her name, to ten acres of woodland on the banks of Lake Taupo, and a heart shaped diamond-studded jade pendant which she reluctantly put away. In public, at the Eastern Star and affiliates Christmas party, they were polite and friendly acquaintances, careful to arouse no suspicions. They even sat opposite each other at a Christmas lunch in Miss Anna's home, where they pulled Christmas crackers across the table, but Jade spent most of the lunch in conversation with Thomas, leaving Miss Anna free to talk to Luke.

"You are perhaps wondering why I have not given you a Christmas present?" she asked, and he was surprised, for no such thought had entered his head.

"You gave me a present," he said, recalling the expensive Alfred Dunhill toiletries she had presented him with at the Christmas party. She smiled.

"If you were really that easily satisfied, you would not be the man I take you for," she said. "This is my present, Luke. Zip and POW! have become important parts of the Eastern Star family of companies, as you have become an important part. The changes you've recommended for the *Hong Kong Daily* will take us on a new adventure and I'm hoping that you will continue to explore our media interests." Luke smiled, excited by the prospect. "At the next board meeting, in March, I will formally announce your appointment to the board of Eastern Star as a director of the holding company."

Luke looked at her in astonishment. He could not lie and say that he had never thought about it, but he envisaged at least five years of hard work, if he chose to stay that long, before he would be accepted onto the board of one of Asia's largest companies, and he had never been certain that he would stay that long. But now it was being offered to him already, and he felt overwhelmed.

"I don't know what to say," he stammered.

"Yes would be a good word to start with," his benefactress and partner teased. "If I'd had a son, I would have been happy for him to turn out like you... except perhaps for the Aryan looks, but you can't have everything. You've never disappointed me, Luke." There was nothing in her tone to suggest it, but Luke could not help feeling she was referring to his heeding her implicit warning that Jade was out of bounds, and he felt a twinge of guilt.

On New Year's Eve he found a moment to whisk Jade into the shadows and kiss her deeply.

"Happy 1977, darling," he whispered. "This is the year you become Jade Powers." Jade clung to him, thankful that he couldn't see the tears pricking her eyes.

The Chinese New Year, weeks later,, signified the coming of spring and a new beginning. Tradition held that everything be cleansed and Luke watched and listened to Jade explain the custom as she gave his apartment what his grandmother would have called 'an old-fashioned spring cleaning.'

"Zao Wang is the god of the stove," she told him, adorable in a designer apron over track suit pants and an old polo shirt of his. "Now, just before New Year, he takes a holiday and goes back to the heavens to visit all the other Gods." He looked at the funny, round-bellied, merry statue that Nancy had given him when he had first moved in.

"Do you think we should pack something warm for him?" Luke joked "The weather could be lousy up there". Jade collapsed in fits of giggles. Later he helped her fill the god's open, smiling mouth with honey, so that he would say only sweet things about them when he joined his family of deities. They spent the weekend before New Year cutting out shapes from shiny red paper to decorate the windows.

"I love our New Year," Jade said with a sense of warm reminiscence. "For the West it all happens in one night, and mostly it's an excuse to party all night and get drunk. For us, it is so much more. I remember my mother in her red dress, red ribbons in her hair – Auntie Anna too. Even the oldest spinsters dress in red as a sign of hope and future happiness, for the spring means birth and love. And so we celebrate for two whole weeks and a day, and the firecrackers and the lanterns drive away the demon who devoured the sun. He's afraid of red, you know, because it is a positive color ." Luke found her childlike simplicity endearing.

"Is he?" he asked simply. "Then we'll need to paint the whole apartment red, to keep the demons away from you."

"You fool," she laughed. "You don't really understand, do you?"

"It doesn't matter. I believe in you, and you believe in all this, so I sort of get involved by proxy, right?"

Still, he joined her in attending the temple, watching the dragon dances and making the food for the party the two of them held to welcome the hearth god home. It was unspoken, but understood between them, that next year the party would be bigger, and they would no longer be without friends and confidants.

The March annual general meeting of the board came swiftly, and Luke felt nervous at the prospect of joining the directors at the forty foot long mahogany table in the board room. He felt all eyes upon him as he entered the room. Most of the directors he knew at least by sight, for they represented the major players in Hong Kong business. Some of the faces were unknown to him and one, that of a young, good-looking but arrogant Chinese man in flashy expensive clothes, was disturbingly familiar, yet he could not place the face into any locale or time frame.

Miss Anna welcomed the directors, officially opened the meeting, asked that the minutes be waived and tabled, as the first order of business, new appointments. She met no opposition, and so she continued.

"It is my happy duty to announce the appointment to the board of Luke Powers," she stated with obvious pride. "Those of you who do not know Luke will certainly know of him, and if there is anyone who has not yet heard of him, then shame on you, for his ventures over the past two years now constitute almost four percent of total company revenue.

He has earned his place on this board and I know that you, like me, will want to welcome him and give him every consideration."

Luke found himself acknowledging the warm but restrained applause and mumbling his gratitude with unaccustomed awkwardness.

"And secondly I would like the board to welcome Wong Li Peng, whom some of you may know as Peter Wong. " Miss Anna gestured to the young man Luke had seen earlier and, as the Chinese man stood, the doors started opening within Luke's head and he entered a memory, a nightclub with Nancy on his arm, and saw the same face that he now saw, react with anger over a spilt drink.

"Wong Li Peng," Miss Anna continued, "is joining Eastern Star as joint managing director."

Luke barely heard the words, for the image in his mind's eye had been replaced by the racing green MG, trashed and forlorn in the street, and Nancy's frightened face as she warned of organized crime and repercussions. Yet the final words could not be ignored, for they hit him in the guts like a Mac truck, assaulting him with frightening brutality, despite Miss Anna's soft tones.

"And many of you will know, of course, that this honorable young man will soon be part of my family after a long betrothal, when he marries my niece, Jade."

CHAPTER FOURTEEN

S TOP LYING TO me!" Luke almost spat the words at Jade, refusing to be moved by the tears that sprang to her eyes. "You told me you love me, that we'd be together. Dammit, what kind of an idiot have you played me for?"

She put her hands on his arm but he pulled free. He did not want her touch, for it only made him feel the depth of his love for her, and that would undermine the anger. Right now he wanted to be angry. He was entitled to it and he was not prepared to surrender it even to Jade.

"You won't even try to understand. I have told my Aunt I will not marry Wong Peng." He could hear the desperation in her voice, but he looked at her archly.

"Really? Well maybe it lost something in the translation, because she seems to have other ideas."

"Why won't you at least listen to me?" Jade pleaded. "You've been here long enough to know that the ways of the Chinese are different. Marriages are still arranged here. Wong Li Peng was seven years old when I was born. My grandfather and his father arranged the marriage, and my father and mother never disagreed with Grandpa. Auntie Anna may have, except that he made her swear that she would always carry out his wishes. If he hadn't died, maybe this would all be forgotten, but now I have to wait until I am twenty-one and I'm free to make my own choices. That's why I've been stalling. That's why I was so happy when he went away last year. That's why I never told you about him. I'm *not* going to marry him. I'm *not*. I'm *not!*"

She broke down and then started to cry, and his anger melted, washed away by her tears. He realized how difficult it must have been for her, betrothed to one man, loving another, having to keep each a secret. Now he understood why she had never let him speak to anyone about their relationship; why they had steered clear of anywhere public. It was not simply because her aunt would not approve, but because she was already promised to another man and had fallen in love with Luke. He didn't for one moment doubt the latter. Yet some speck of doubt gnawed at him, eating away and he hated himself for voicing the thought, but he could not stop himself.

"What about you and him? Have you ever...?" He knew it was a mistake as soon as he saw the shock and horror on her face.

"What are you saying? You know that I haven't? You were the first." Her voice trailed off, ashamed not for herself, but for him, and suddenly he was ashamed for himself, yet felt the pressing need to save face.

"That's eight months ago, and you are engaged to the guy," he countered. She looked at him for a moment and then, silently, picked up her bag and the silk jacket she had been wearing and silently left the apartment. Some part of him knew that if he let her go he would never see her again, yet his feet seemed rooted in place. He forced himself to move and run after her, calling her name. She was about to enter the elevator when he caught the doors, holding them open. She looked at him, her face streaked with tears. "If there's one person in this world I was sure believed in me, it's you," she said reproachfully yet with resignation. "How can you doubt me?" He gathered her to him, whispering abject apologies into her hair as he held her. But he could not drive away the question that was overpowering him. What the hell did they do now?

Neither Jade nor Luke had ever envisaged that a relationship that was already a secret could possibly become even more furtive, yet they had no other choice. Luke had to deal with two separate issues: protecting Jade and what they had together; and dealing with Wong Peng, who had clearly targeted Luke as a trouble-making adversary from the moment of their first encounter. Luke was not fooled by the young Chinese man's apparent attempts to smooth the waters between them, even when Wong Peng came into his office uninvited and seated himself in the black leather and chrome chair close to the window overlooking Happy Valley.

"I think we should get to know each other better," Wong Peng said, smiling without any warmth. "After all, we're going to working together closely, and I don't want you to think of me as your boss." Luke gave an equally cool smile and eyeballed the man.

"That's good" Luke replied, "Because it hadn't occurred to me, quite frankly. I think of Miss Anna as my partner. I don't think of anyone as my boss." Wong Peng laughed.

"I like that. You have balls. I think what happened in the past should stay there. Maybe I was a little over-reactionary." Luke nodded.

"You are obviously far more than the thug you appeared to be at our earlier meetings," Luke countered, and saw the man's eyes narrow further. "And I guess you're right. We need to establish a working relationship, and brooding about my trashed MG isn't exactly going to help that, is it?" There was a moment of recognition between the two men, and it only confirmed what Luke had always known; that this man was capable of almost anything. Wong Peng laughed.

"No, it isn't. What do you say we go out for some drinks, maybe some gambling? I know some girls with very special skills. I could introduce you to delights of the Orient you will not even have imagined?" Again, the empty smile accompanied the words. Luke feigned confusion.

"I'm sorry, I must have misunderstood. Aren't you engaged to Miss Anna's niece or something?" he asked ingenuously. Wong Peng gave him an arch look. "I am neither married, nor dead, Luke. The latter might curtail my personal life. The former certainly will not, even though she is an exquisite creature, don't you think?"

Luke felt a moment of rising panic, a shortness of breath. He knows! A little voice in his mind was screaming the words, and Luke's fear was not for himself, but for Jade. In a millisecond he had recovered his composure and returned to his cool gaze. "I really don't know the lady, Mister Wong, but she certainly is what we 'Yanks' call a looker," he said, playing up the coarseness that the Chinese associated with his race. Wong Peng nodded, seemingly pleased.

"Thank you" he replied, with the first trace of warmth in his voice. "I like to have beautiful, precious things around me. And it is a bonus when they are actually functional." For a moment, an image implanted itself on the screen of Luke's mind; Jade, naked, held down on the bed, while this leering creature, her husband, fucked her without love. Nausea rose in Luke's throat, but he forced a smile.

"And please," Wong Peng continued. "Call me Wong Peng... or Peter if you prefer it. Most of my friends do."

"I'll try to remember that, Mister Wong," Luke responded, and the veil was drawn across Wong Peng's eyes as he nodded and left the office.

"I'M TELLING YOU, he knows," Luke held Jade to him and whispered the words with dread. "No," she replied, pulling away and looking at him. "He could not know. It isn't possible. But we cannot meet in Hong Kong anymore."

"What are you saying? You don't want to see me?" Luke asked in disbelief.

She ran her fingers through his hair. "My foolish Golden one," she told him. "I want to see you every day of my life. But, until I am twenty-one, which is only a few months, we must meet somewhere else. I will tell my Aunt that I plan to make weekend retreats with the nuns in the New Territories, to prepare me for my marriage."

"Every weekend?" he asked, with a sense of relief, for he dreaded the idea of long periods without her."

"Yes. It is only for a few months," she reassured him. "And even when you're away you can easily fly to meet me and we'll have two whole days every week together."

"Okay," he agreed readily. "But where? We need somewhere safe, but civilized... Somewhere..." She put her fingers to his lips, already way ahead of him, and spoke only one word.

"Singapore."

IT WAS A little over ten years since Singapore had separated from
Malaysia and become an independent republic. In that time it had
grown from the war-shattered island still trying to find itself into a
thriving port with an exciting city that was constantly in a state of
development and change. But even with the forward thrust of 1970s,
it was hard to imagine that twenty years later this would be the model
for Asia, a thriving city welcoming the twenty-first century with an
unsurpassed trading future.

Luke had always liked Singapore in the fleeting visits he had made.
Each time he had stayed at The Goodward Park on Scott's Road with
its imposing driveway and green gardens. Raffles, despite all its colonial
charm, had seen better days and service, and was now visited largely by
American tourists who had heard the stories of Elizabeth Taylor's suite
and were far more interested in the celebrity status of the past, and the
famous Singapore Sling cocktail, or tea in the Tiffin room, than in
The Salkie Brothers who had built the hotel, or the legends of the tiger
under the billiard table when the British Raj were in residence.

Now though, Singapore was to become a second home and the first
place where he and Jade could live together openly. They decided to
forego living in hotels, and took an apartment.

The apartment was unspectacular, but in a new block out towards
Buena Vista. The rent was reasonable by Hong Kong standards and
Luke bought a car and paid three months' rental for the apartment. He
would fly to Singapore on Friday evening, and Jade would generally meet
him at the airport. The five days separation would seem interminable
to both of them, but for two days they became Mr and Mrs Hayes,
Luke using the name of his trustee. They would make love to the point
of exhaustion in the tiny bedroom. On Saturday mornings they would
greet their neighbors and hit the markets, buying exotic fruits they
had never seen or heard of before, like the durian, which Jade thought
tasted like velvety custard, while Luke was disgusted by both its smell
and texture. But Rambutans and starfruit, and the sweet and musky
brownskinned Chiku, were delicious. They would sometimes go to the

Arab market in Bugis street, or to the People's Shopping Complex in Chinatown, or lunch at one of the curry houses off Serangoon Road in Little India, and Jade would buy fine Kashmiri silk. Sometimes they would hire a boat from Jardine Steps and go to Pulau Seking, one of three small islands, barely inhabited, where they could strip off their clothes, lie in the sun, and make love with little fear of being discovered. At night they would often dine simply from the hawkers at the Satay Club or Newton's Circus, where the endless sticks of chicken satay, accompanied by gado gaddo, or nasi lemak, were so delicious that they would stuff themselves until they couldn't move. Sometimes they would eat seafood, fresh cracked crabs in chili sauce, or eat Hokkien food in Food alley. The choices were endless. Jade liked to visit the Fuk Tak Ch'i temple in Telok Ayer Street, for its Shen philosophy encompassed Buddhism and Confucianism as well as Tao beliefs that Jade also embraced. Sometimes they would go to Tanjong Pagar Road and buy Chinese herbs, have their fortune told, and take a Rickshaw ride. Life was good, and they marveled at how easily they could slip into the role of newlyweds from Friday night to Monday morning, and just as easily resume the lives expected from them in Hong Kong.

They lived the fantasy for several months, until the time of the Dragon Boat festival. Jade had explained to Luke the legend of Qu Yuan, a poet and state minister who had killed himself because he was so ashamed of the corruption in government. When the noble man had thrown himself into the river, weighted down with a rock, the villagers gathered and beat drums, and thrashed oars on the water to frighten the fish and water dragons so that they would not eat the body. Luke thought the story was quaint and charming, as most of Chinese folklore was, but nothing prepared him for the huge twelve metre boats with their ornate and garish dragon heads, or the cacophony of the drums and the oarsmen. This was pageantry that both locals and tourists loved, and Luke and Jade were caught up in the excitement of it, as teams from all over the East competed, and the spectators stuffed themselves with steamed dumplings freshly cooked by the food hawkers. It was, Jade said only moments before it fell apart, a perfect time for them.

Celia saw Luke long before he was aware of her presence. At first she was not certain it was him, for he was clad only in jeans and a tee-shirt, his hair tousled, his nose slightly sunburned, contrasting with the dark sunglasses. She tapped him on the shoulder and he whirled around and grabbed her, thinking it was Jade, whom he had left momentarily to buy them both a cold drink.

"Well, that's quite a welcome," Celia purred in her clipped English tones, "And here was I thinking that the entire day was a dead loss." Luke extricated himself gently from her. "You're not enjoying the races?" he asked rhetorically, his eyes darting left and right of her, looking for Jade. Celia gave a low throaty laugh, like a sexual call to an animal. "No, Poppit. I can think of much more exciting ways of banging and thrashing about." In spite of himself, Luke laughed, still finding it difficult to equate this rather proper looking and sounding English rose with the sexually predatory creature he knew.

"Well," he replied, trying to move away as the crowd constantly jolted them into body contact, "Have fun." Her hand moved swiftly, unseen by the milling throng, and grabbed him by the balls through his jeans.

"What about John Thomas? Is he doing much banging and thrashing about, or is he just a spectator these days?" She murmured the words with a sensual smile and he cursed his dick for even stirring with interest when he wanted no part of this woman. "He, er... he's not very interested in the festivities," he replied, trying to back away from her.

"Liar," she mocked him. "Let's go back to my hotel and fuck all over the suite, including the top of the wardrobe if you like." He felt a sense of alarm that she could be so blatant in a crowd of people, as though her sex drive was oblivious to social graces. "Celia," he said hesitantly, "You know it's over." She shook her head.

"No darling. You want me. *He* wants me," She tickled at his fly with one finger, as she eased her grip on him. "I'll let you come all over me if that's what you want." And even with his great love for Jade, he was tempted for a moment to say yes, knowing he could use her in any way he had ever fantasized and she would love it.

"Well, you're very lovely and tempting," he forced himself to be gallant, "And I'll probably regret this later, but I made a new year resolution to give up the baser things in life. And you, my darling, definitively fit into that category." He kissed her lightly on the cheek, a kiss devoid of any sexual connotation, and pushed his way through the crowd before she had a chance to react and follow him. There was an overwhelming rush of relief as he saw Jade's tiny heart-shaped face, the lips parting in a smile as she saw him; her eyes filled with a deep and abiding love that he still could not believe he deserved.

"You were a long time," she said gently as she took the bottle of Coke from him. "I bumped into someone I knew" he said with an off-handed shrug.

"Oh...? Who?" she asked, more out of idle curiosity than any real desire to know. He put his arm around her, noting the happiness that even the slightest body contact with her produced.

"No-one who matters," he reassured her and added, as if to reassure himself. "Don't worry, we're quite safe."

"My rook to Queen's Bishop's four and check in three moves my dear Godfrey," Wong Xu Lim said with quiet satisfaction, and Godfrey Hackforth-Smythe raised an incredulous eyebrow.

"Good heavens Wong, I do believe you've done it again," he said with a joviality that belied his natural antipathy toward the Chinese. And it was true that his opponent was one of the wealthiest men in Hong Kong and, like Anna Chen, very much the taipan of his own Hong, a business empire that equaled Eastern Star; those elements dictated a certain degree of respect from the British diplomat.

The two men sat on the comfortable verandah of the country club, overlooking Repulse Bay, playing chess, an indulgence they allowed themselves once a month as an act of marrying diplomacy and business with mind games and sheer enjoyment. On the arm of Godfrey's chair, in a white chiffon cocktail dress, hair hanging to her shoulders like strands of honeyed wheat, sat Celia.

"Oh, well done, Mister Wong," she said with obvious relish as she clapped her hands. "Daddy rather fancies himself as a chess player, too. He'll probably sulk for days." Her father shot her a disdainful warning look, but Wong Xu Lim suppressed a smile. "I am blessed with a natural ability in this matter Miss Celia, and I'm sure affairs of state take a much greater toll on your father's time than my humble business interests do on mine," he said.

"Oh I don't know," Celia said, and the brittle edge to her voice wasn't lost on her father. " I imagine you have your hands quite full right now. Your son's wedding is only a few months away isn't it?" The old man nodded.

"Yes, indeed. Two of the biggest company's in this Crown territory will be joined together but, even more importantly, I shall welcome a new daughter of exquisite beauty and grace." Wong made no attempt to conceal the obvious pleasure in his voice. Celia smiled casually.

"Yes, she is lovely isn't she, young Jade. I saw her in Singapore. She and Luke seemed to be having a super time. I hadn't realized they were such good friends." Though the words were innocent, the connotation behind them was obvious, and Celia felt her father tense in the chair. Her eyes stayed on Wong, who betrayed no emotion, but blinked slowly like an inscrutable tortoise.

"Singapore?" Godfrey Hackforth-Smythe asked with a snort. "With Powers? What in God's name were they doing there together?"

"I can't possibly imagine," Celia said with sufficient smirking innuendo to provoke a guarded explanation from the venerable Chinese man.

"Ah, yes, Singapore!" Wong began hesitantly, as if buying himself time to fabricate an explanation. "I believe the bride is choosing some things for... what is the word... her trousseau? It would seem natural that Miss Anna would entrust her niece to someone who could look after her in a foreign country. After all, such travel is not appropriate for a young woman of Jade's standing on her own. Quite natural that chaperone should be a man whom Miss Anna trusts and, since Powers is like a son to her, who better to take care of the precious flower who is like a daughter." He halted and looked challengingly at Celia. She responded politely but with a voice heavily loaded with sarcasm.

"Oh, of course! Sort of, the brother looking after the sister? Silly me! Why ever didn't I think of that?" And her tone clearly indicated that the idea had never occurred to her because it was preposterous. Wong Xu Lim merely smiled and nodded.

When Wong Xu Lim called two days later and subtly and politely inveigled an invitation to afternoon tea on the terrace, Miss Anna did not suspect the bombshell that was about to explode around her. It was not as if she did not have meetings with Wong from time to time over business matters, and now there was the wedding to consider, as well as his son's progress and assimilation into Eastern Star. It would have been customary for the two associates and soon to be in-laws to have observed etiquette and tradition whilst tea was being served and consumed, yet Wong dispensed with the banalities, at the same time observing the social graces expected towards one's hostess.

"I would ask a favor, Chen Qing Nan" The old man played his opening gambit.

Miss Anna nodded. "If I may request one in return, that you use my western name, Anna." He gave a smile of acquiescence.

"I know that you honor the wishes of your late father, and the betrothal pact we made when his grand-daughter was born."

"Of course," Miss Anna replied. "Is that not why I have appointed Wong Peng to my board, and my side? Soon he will become as a son to me, as Jade will become a daughter to you." The old man pursed his lips, his brow furrowed in a frown.

"That day cannot come soon enough, dear lady. And for that reason, I would ask that it come sooner." He held Miss Anna's quizzical look, and she knew from his eyes that there was some dark territory that he wished not to cross into; dark enough to warrant him pressing for an early wedding. She felt her own lips tighten with nervous anticipation.

"Sooner is better than later, I agree," she said politely. "But the wedding needs many months of preparation. Jade will not turn twenty-one until late August, and we have always agreed..." He interrupted, to her surprise.

"What we have always agreed may be of no consequence, Anna. I ask this favor to avert a potential catastrophe." She felt her pulse quicken and was conscious of her own heartbeat.

"What catastrophe? Please. You must tell me what is troubling you."

Wong Xu Lim told her of the English girl's seemingly chance remark which was clearly intended to promote anguish, if not trouble. He told her of what his investigation had disclosed in the thirty-six hours since; that Luke had taken an apartment in Singapore; that Jade had, on at least six occasions he had been able to determine, visited Singapore and met with Luke; and that he believed the two were having what he termed, "a tryst, a relationship contrary to the natural behavior of one betrothed."

Miss Anna listened stony-faced, fighting to remain implacable. Then she managed a watery smile as she placed her hands around the delicate porcelain teapot which smelled sweetly of jasmine.

"Tea?" she asked, with all the equilibrium she could muster.

For Anna Chen, the realization that Jade was in love with Luke and he with her, was simply a matter of acknowledging what she had already known in some part of her, and had dreaded. In a perfect world, she would bless these two, the golden giant, and the porcelain fairy and rejoice for them that they had found that rarest of commodities, real love. But she knew that Hong Kong was not, of itself, perfect, and neither was the world that surrounded it. Even further afield the heavens were also impaired, for her father should have been resting in peace, and yet she felt his spirit everywhere. She had not given up her own fight for individuality, and the breaking of tradition, without a great struggle. She and her father had argued long and bitterly, and she suspected to this day that he had paid off the young Italian painter she had lived with in Tuscany that summer and had hoped to marry. She doubted that Luke could be paid off that easily, yet she knew Jade was not strong enough on her own to defy her relatives, living or dead. What she did not know was the X factor; how much strength did Luke bring to Jade?

There was no question in her mind of dissolving the betrothal. It would mean a massive loss of face on both sides, and a disastrous business decision. But, even more importantly, such defiance of laws laid down by one's ancestors, particularly a father, would have meant being haunted by ghosts, not only his, but those of others who had befriended him in the other world. Chinese tradition even had a festival of the Hungry Ghosts, when those spirits ignored or defiled by their ancestors returned, en masse, to haunt the living and wreak havoc. Anna Chen believed, with her Western sophistication, that it was a quaint but rather silly and mindless tradition, but she was still Chinese enough not to put it to the test. She had inherited her father's empire, and her father's wishes. Both needed her full commitment, and there could be no turning back.

She half-expected Jade to lie to her and deny everything, but she was wrong.

"I love Luke. I don't love Wong Peng." the girl said. "Try to understand my feelings. There is a man I want to marry, yet you say I cannot. Then you offer a man you want me to marry, and I say, I cannot." For Anna Chen, the words were an echo of what she had said herself nearly twenty years earlier.

"You mean, 'will not'," she said gently, but Jade shook her head.

"No, I mean cannot. I did not make this stupid arrangement, but I cannot marry that man and sleep in his bed and bear his children. I can't. Please don't make me." Jade started to cry and Anna steeled herself not to give way to the girl.

"Hush," she told her niece. "You're talking romantic nonsense. Luke Powers is an attractive young man, but he is not one of us. Has it ever occurred to you that he might be as interested in your fortune as he is in you?" Jade laughed wryly.

"He didn't even know who I was when he first fell in love with me. Why do you want to cheapen this?"

"What is there to cheapen?" Anna Chen asked with dread. "Have you been sleeping with this man? Have you?" And despite all Jade's faith in herself as an emancipated woman, she heard herself denying her own physical needs.

"Of course not. You know me better than that," she lied, conscious that it was the first lie she had ever knowingly told her aunt. The two women held each other's gaze for a moment. Anna Chen did not want to believe that Jade would lie to her, so she accepted the improbability of the lie, and Jade knew that, with that acceptance, something had gone from their relationship which could never be restored. The most important thing for Anna Chen was that Jade had not been sexually defiled before the marriage, and that was what she chose to believe.

"Listen to me Jade. There are choices we can make for ourselves, and choices that are made for us. There is little to say that one is better than the other, though perhaps there is some satisfaction in making one's own mistakes. I don't know. What I do know is that you have known what your place is to be since the day of your birth. It is not as if this has suddenly been sprung on you without warning. This alliance is important to the Wong family and to us. We have only twenty years or so before China takes over. Then it will be Chinese who hold the balance of power, and the Hongs will change hands. Your children, Jade — they will be the first generation of Chinese Hong Kong industrialists and manufacturers. They will be the new Taipans, the elite. But only because of this alliance." She spoke with fervent passion that quieted but chilled Jade.

"And what about passion, and love?" the girl asked. "Don't they count at all?" Her aunt nodded, choosing her words carefully.

"Yes, they do, and I would pray that you will have both. But they do NOT count as much as loyalty and duty and family. Imagine the royal family of England if they suddenly decided they would not fulfill their duty and marry who was chosen. The monarchy could fall. You may not think of yourself as royalty my dear child, but there is truly very little difference. You are a princess, Wong Peng is a prince. In time you will love each other, feel that passion that you feel now. Together you will found a dynasty. Only in romantic novels does the princess run away with the traveling salesman." She saw that the words stung Jade, and the girl raced from the room. Miss Anna had no doubt that she was racing to the arms of the man she loved, a man that Anna might have chosen for her niece if they had lived in New Zealand, but they did not. She did not try to stop the girl, for she had seen something in Jade's eyes, behind the veil of tears. It was resignation.

Whatever Jade told herself, or even told Luke, Anna knew that Jade was first and foremost Chinese, and she would honor her elders.

Luke greeted the revelation that their affair was no longer a secret with a mixture of despair and relief. He knew the implications of Jade's Chinese heritage and the conditioning of centuries of tradition, but at least now he could deal with the situation up front. His anger was directed not towards Anna Chen, but Celia Hackforth-Smythe, who clearly had malevolence in mind when she exposed them. Luke was able to comfort Jade and dry her tears, but he took the first opportunity to confront Celia, waiting for her outside the elegant and expensive apartment block that the British government paid for. She seemed surprised and delighted to see him, but it lasted for only a moment. There was not a single doubt from his expression that he was in a dangerous mood, and her pleasant hello was greeted with a silent grabbing of her arm, slamming her against the wall.

"You bitch, you screwed up, nympho neurotic bitch," he hissed at her, frustrated by the fact that the abuse only made her smile.

"Sweetheart, I didn't know. It was just one of those stupid off-handed remarks that backfire," she explained lamely. "Believe me, it was an accident." He studied the face with cold appraisal.

"You are an accident, Celia. Stay away from me, and from Jade. Do you understand?" The threat was overt and she shuddered, but whether from fear or arousal he couldn't tell.

"Luke, sweetie, think carefully. If anyone is going to have to stay away from Jade, it's you." She spoke gently, rationally, as if feeling genuine compassion for his plight. "It's a terrible thing darling, but it's simply the way it is here. In your heart, you know that."

He felt sick, for part of him knew that she was right. It was the way it was in Chinese custom, and he could see how he might be seen as a usurper, a destroyer of what was important. Yet none of this could be right if it meant he and Jade had to be apart. "Things change, Celia," he told her, unable to sustain his anger towards her. "Customs are made obsolete every day, as this one will be."

"Perhaps," she answered. "But not in time to stop her marrying Peter Wong." And once again Luke experienced the terror of worrying that she was right. She saw his doubt, and pressed her advantage.

"I'm sure you loved her... love her. I can live with that. But you have to understand how futile it is darling, and what a super life we could have together. Think of it Luke. Imagine you were president of a multi-national company… or some powerful senator in your own country, who is the wife you would need on your arm?" He looked at her in disbelief. My God, he thought, in the midst of all this she's proposing to me!

"You?" he asked rhetorically, but she seemed to take it as a confirmation.

"Exactly darling. We have great sex, and we haven't even begun to scratch the surface of our darkest fantasies. I have breeding and class, and you have charm and money. There is absolutely no limit to how far we can go together." She moved against him then, her body pressing against his, her tongue running over the rim of her mouth in the same way he had watched it run over the rim of his swollen cock, and for the first time he realized how snake-like it was, and was surprised that it hadn't occurred to him before. She was a deadly and toxic serpent. He pulled away without any sense of arousal and looked at her in disgust.

"You're a great fuck, but a lousy rationalist, Celia," he told her. "Whatever the outcome, you won't have the satisfaction of succeeding. I love Jade, I always will."

"But darling," reasoning with British aplomb. "You'll never marry her."

"Perhaps not." Luke countered. "But I can promise you this; I'll never marry YOU!" and he walked away and left her smarting from the rejection.

Luke's meeting with Miss Anna was formal and reserved, yet with no more joy than the encounter with Celia. Miss Anna was the cool-est he had known her in the years since they had met. She told him simply and coldly, as if talking to a child who has disobeyed, that he had placed her business empire at great risk, and that he was to desist immediately any relationship with Jade. He might have tried to see her point of view, if she had not commanded him but rather voiced her concerns. But she left him no room to maneuver with his back to the wall, and so he had to attack.

"Let me make this very, very clear," he said, trying not to lose his temper. "You did not buy me, and you do not own me. I invested in a business. I am your business partner. Nothing more, nothing less. If I screw up a business deal, then I'll answer to you. But don't you ever dare to presume that you control my personal life or that you can tell me what to do or who to see, because you lose if you do... and you may lose Jade for keeps." He glared at her, realizing that she had physically backed a step away from him as he confronted her. He knew from the dead expression in her eyes that he had already killed their friendship, and part of him grieved for that. But her friendship was nothing compared to his future with Jade, and he had no choice but to make her see that she risked losing her only family completely. Miss Anna, though, had retreated only to regroup and reconsider. The very fact that Luke was so angry told her that he was not thinking rationally, and she used this to her advantage.

"I think you have not thought through that a business deal, no matter how well done, can be undone. It is true you are a young man of wealth and considerable skills, but it is also true that on this island, in this territory, my power is greater than yours. If you and I were to part ways, you would find it difficult to invest in any other business in Hong Kong." She did not even have to raise her voice for Luke to know that he had been threatened. "Meaning you would make it difficult," he stated.

"Correction," she told him coldly. "I would make it impossible. There is nothing you can do to change what is already twenty year old history between the two great hong families. However, there is a great deal you can do to change your own business status... for the worse."

He knew that to tip his hand any further would be counter-productive. In the end, it only mattered that he could change Jade's mind and have her marry him instead. He believed that once he and Jade were a fait accompli, Anna Chen would see the advantages of having him and his fortune, small though it was, as part of the family in place of Wong Peng. He nodded, as though capitulating.

"I get the message, loud and clear," he answered her. She gave a sad smile, yet there was still no warmth in her eyes.

"Good," she told him. "Wong Xu Lim and I have discussed the

situation. The wedding will be moved forward and will take place in six weeks' time. I hope that you will be back in time to attend." His head reeled from the onslaught of the sentence.

"Six weeks? Back... what are you talking about?"

"I have arranged for you to go to Shanghai and Beijing. We need a market study on the potential for opening up into mainland China, and no-one knows the market like you Luke." He was so stunned that he could not manage a reply.

CHAPTER FIFTEEN

J ADE THREW HER head back, and the black hair thrashed around her face like the beatings of a raven's wings. She fought for her breath as her body seemed to be tossed skyward, rhythmically, creating poetry with its arc. Her voice, soft cries against Luke's deeper growls of passion and desperation, rose to a crescendo as she arched her back, poised over him. He could see the creaminess of her breasts, the warm nutmeg of her nipples, but he could not reach them with his mouth, and he was content to let her set the pace, the rhythm, for he had never seen her so wild. And when at last she cried out in her orgasm, like a dying bird, and fluttered down to rest against his stomach, he held her to him, afraid to ever let her go. He knew within seconds that she was crying, for melancholy overpowered him, and he found it hard to swallow. Tomorrow he would leave for Shanghai, and some part of them was behaving as though this was all there was, despite the fact that they had plotted and planned, and knew differently.

Weeks had passed since Miss Anna's ultimatum. Jade had managed to postpone the wedding by insisting on changing the design of her traditional red Chinese wedding dress. Miss Anna, in turn, had postponed the trip to China for Luke, leaving little doubt that she planned for him to be away at the time of the wedding. If Luke had worked hard throughout his life, it was nothing compared to the grueling schedule his benefactress now put him through. He rarely worked less than fifteen hours, and he would crawl home to his apartment and collapse on the bed for what little sleep he could manage. Sometimes Jade would leave the house and join him for an hour or two, and their lovemaking took on an urgency that was both exciting and disappointing. No more the long languid nights and mornings where they had time to explore each other. Now, clothes were swiftly discarded and time-consuming foreplay was both unwanted and unnecessary, for the anticipation of stolen interludes was enough to have them constantly aroused.

Several times Luke had asked Jade to leave with him, but she clung to the hope that her aunt would change her mind and give her blessing. Luke would argue, but it was pointless. Jade was adamant that she could stall the wedding at least until her twenty-first birthday and then call it off altogether. Luke was just as certain that it would never happen that way.

"Just be patient. Everything will change when I am twenty-one," she told him, but he shook his head in disbelief.

"Why will it? Why should it. All that will change is you will be a few months older, that's all." he replied. "If you can't face her now, if you can't defy your ancestors, then you never will."

Eventually she had agreed that when the wedding could no longer be postponed, she and Luke would elope a day or so before, leaving no time for either family to postpone or make excuses. In the meantime, Luke was left with no doubt that Wong Peng was aware of his secret meetings with Jade, though he seemed content to believe that the honor of deflowering his bride was his alone.

At the special board meeting convened to change the status of Chen motors within the holding company, Luke found himself railroaded by Wong Li Peng on a point of order. It was not so much that he was beaten, as made to feel stupid in front of the board, which had only a few short months earlier made him so welcome. He cornered Wong later when the meeting dispersed.

"You son of a bitch. You did that deliberately to get back at me," he accused the man. Wong gave him a withering look.

"You? You are nothing to me. You think I don't know of your little games with her? I don't care, as long as she comes to my bed whole and is a dutiful wife, she can harbor romantic delusions of you for the rest of her life." Luke was appalled.

"You'd let her be that unhappy? She doesn't want to marry you," he said.

"That's of no consequence." Wong replied. "Grow up Powers. I don't love Jade Chen, and it isn't necessary for me to do so. It's a business arrangement. But, just as I would fight to stop a hostile takeover of this company, I will fight for her. She is my property, and no yellow-hair takes my property and gets away with it." He walked away, perhaps sensing that Luke was about to hit him, seeing the fist close tight with rage and frustration.

Luke tried once more to see Miss Anna but she politely refused through Thomas. "She truly is busy, Luke," Thomas explained with a hint of shame in his expression.

"That's bullshit and you know it. For God's sake man, you of all people must know what I'm going through," Luke pleaded, remembering how he had first recognized Thomas Ho's love for his employer. Thomas smiled sadly.

"It is because I know what you are going through that I say to you, let go. It will pass, as it must," Thomas cautioned, but something in his face gave him away.

"It hasn't passed for you Thomas... and it won't for us," Luke told him quietly.

Wong Xu Lim was surprised by Luke's spur of the moment visit, but too polite to turn a business associate away. His mistake was in asking rhetorically and out of politeness only, "How may I be of service to you, Mister Powers?"

If Luke had been Chinese, or cared more about the rules, he might have played the etiquette game. As it was, he responded bluntly. "Call off the wedding. Don't make two people miserable for the rest of their lives."

"I am not at all convinced that my son will be miserable with his new bride," the old man countered.

"I wasn't talking about your son. I'm talking about Jade and me. I'm begging you, don't do this!" Luke pleaded.

"It is inhospitable, I know, to refuse a guest when one has asked for the request, but I cannot help you," Wong Xu Lim said with regret.

"But. . . " Luke managed only a word before the old man held up a hand to silence him. "Please. There are no buts. In time they will grow to love each other in their fashion. Sometimes a marriage can survive far longer without the complications of passion. My son needs to marry. I need to see him marry. The Chen and Wong business empires need amalgamation to become the most powerful conglomerate in the east. Jade needs a husband who understands her ways; OUR ways. Chen Qing Nan needs a son and heir, and what other means does she have of obtaining one? Hong Kong needs this family dynasty to survive the new rule of China in ninety-seven. And you talk to me of your needs, and of the girl's? Forgive me, but they are of no consequence." He turned his back, and Luke knew that from that moment, no matter what he said, he ceased to exist as far as the old man was concerned. He stormed from the house, knocking over a painted screen in his anger.

For a long time Wong Xu Lim did not move. He knew in his heart that Luke Powers was a better and more worthy man than his son, and yet he had to believe that Jade would be Peng's salvation. The boy had been trouble for most of his twenty-seven years, and yet the old one could not turn his back on his own flesh and blood. Part of him wanted to tell the little Chen girl run. . . go with your golden hair, be happy; but it would not have been the Chinese thing to do.

Wong Li Peng had no second thoughts about marrying Jade. She was beautiful and rich, and he would own her. She was untouched, too, both his father and her aunt had assured him of that, and thinking about her body, the tiny mouse's hole of her that would feel his cock before anyone else's, made him salivate with anticipation. He would be gentle with her as long as she was willing, but if she gave him so much as a single word of dissent, he would shove his cock so far down her throat that she would choke on it. He wondered what skills, if any, she might have in bed. He knew she had been to boarding school and hoped she had dabbled in sex with other girls. He liked to watch two girls licking each other, playing with strapped-on dildos while they simulated sex. Sometimes he would simply watch and masturbate. Other times he would wait for one girl to be on top of the other and would then leap on her back, fucking her deep in the ass and forcing her dildo rhythm to match his own. He never told any of his peers, for they belonged to a nouveau riche Chinese elite that bored him. Even in childhood he had been bored by the money, the ease with which everything came. He had taken to shop lifting by the time he was in his early teens; mere trinkets at first, then jewelry from the shop that his mother frequented before her death. The adrenalin rush of walking out of a store where armed guards stood sentry, with a diamond concealed in his palm, tantalizingly close to being in full view, was usually enough to give him a hard on. He would go then to the nearest men's room and jerk off while he sucked on the diamond. Later, he developed a trick of picking up girls and taking them to the nearest toilet or even sometimes a storeroom in a hotel. The deal would be simple. He would put the diamond in their mouths and force them to their knees. If they could suck him off and swallow all of his juice without swallowing the diamond, it was theirs. By the time he was seventeen, he was renowned for his little tricks. Sometimes he sold the stolen goods to Chinese Mafia, or exchanged them for a few lines of cocaine. He was fascinated by the idea of organized crime and read avidly about the strong powerbases of the Triads in America. To him it was amusing that, while the lowlifes he met who had clawed their way from the slums to become gangsters dreamed of being filthy rich, he was the rich boy who flirted with being a gangster. He was aware that were expectations which had to be met, and he paid lip-service to them. He would be a good managing director for Eastern Star, for his business instincts were sharp and well-honed, and he knew how to screw the last dollar out of his opponents. But he would need to indulge even more in the darker areas of his life if the stultifyingly boring corporate side of his life were to be at all bearable.

IT SEEMED TO Luke that they had been asleep for hours when he awoke to the sound of knocking at the door. At first he thought he and been dreaming, but the knocking persisted, and so he slipped out of bed and wrapped a towel around himself, pausing to gaze with a sense of wonder at the body of Jade, hair across her face, her lips slightly parted as if in prayer, asleep and at peace. He crossed the living room swiftly, up the narrow hallway to the front door. He had the security chain across and so the door opened only a few inches, yet Luke was taken aback to see Thomas Ho standing there, eyes lowered with embarrassment. Luke swiftly released the chain and opened the door. "Thomas? What the hell are you doing out here?" he asked, knowing the answer before it came. Thomas gave a smile tinged with regret.

"I'm sorry," he said. "I realize how late it is, but, I have to take her home." Luke blinked, realizing how foolish his words sounded even as he spoke them.

"Her? What makes you think she's...?" He broke off, for the older man's expression clearly begged him not to treat either of them like fools.

"I followed her Luke, at Miss Anna's instructions," he said simply, and Luke became both defensive and angry.

"If you followed her you've been here for hours. Why the hell did you wait till now?" Thomas Ho looked at him in surprise, as though the answer was self evident.

"I wanted you to have some time together. It was the only thing I could do for you. But now, I have to take her home." Luke sighed, conscious of the man's empathy. He held the door open and Thomas Ho entered, taking pains not to glance towards the bedroom even though Luke did so.

"Can't you just go back and say she wasn't here?" Luke asked plaintively. Thomas shook his head sadly.

"She didn't send me to find out if Miss Jade was here. She *knows* she is. I've been sent to bring her home, that's all." Luke sank down onto the royal blue couch and ran his fingers through his hair.

"Please Thomas," he said. "Let me bring her home. Don't make me wake her and let her see you here. She'd be mortified. Please. I swear I'll have her home within the hour if you just give me a break." He thought for a moment that Thomas would refuse, but his friend simply nodded and moved to the door.

"One hour Luke, for all our sakes," were the last words that he spoke before letting himself out.

Luke quickly but gently woke Jade from a deep and dreamless sleep. Not until she was showered and dressed did he sit her down gently and tell her about Thomas's visit.

"It's crunch time now, sweetheart" Luke faced her as he said the words. "We can't pretend we're not sleeping together. She knows that we are. We have to face her now, tonight, and lay it on the line." He saw Jade's face pale even as she heard the words.

"I can't. What will she say?" Jade replied, and he felt impatient with her and grabbed her arms.

"It doesn't matter what she says. No more games. We do what we should have done in the first place."

"But where will we go? How will we live?" she asked.

"Anywhere you like. And we're not exactly paupers. If I cash in now there should be at least five million or more, and you get your inheritance on your birthday regardless of whom you marry. But none of that matters. We'll be together."

"But we won't be able to come back to Hong Kong?" she asked plaintively.

"Probably not," he told her honestly. "But I thought we decided long ago that we were home to each other?" She nodded silently, tears filling her eyes.

"I know," she said, with an emotional break in her voice. "But it is so hard. Could we go to America? Start afresh there?" He wrapped his arms around her, already decided that this was exactly what they would do.

"We can go to the moon if that's what you want. But I don't ever want to lose you," he murmured and she put her head on his chest.

It was after three in the morning when they drove to the house on the hillside, but Miss Anna was there waiting for them. There was no reproach or recrimination, and Luke was caught off guard, for he had been prepared to defend Jade first and himself second. There was silence so heavy that it would have taken both hands to carry it, as Luke explained their plans for the future, lamely concluding;

"We want you in our lives, but we know it can't be here, and we're sorry for the hurt. But in America I'm still willing to be part of what we started. Maybe I can continue our operations there. It's the largest market on earth." He had hoped for some enthusiasm or at least acknowledgement, but it was not forthcoming. Instead she looked long and hard at Jade who, at first, avoided her gaze, then met it squarely.

"You are absolutely determined to do this terrible thing to me, to your ancestors?" she challenged. Jade nodded.

"I cannot marry Wong Li Peng. My heart, my home, is wherever Luke is," she said simply. Miss Anna nodded and turned to Luke.

"It will take two days to complete the paperwork. Then a bank cheque will be drawn for you and I would ask that you both leave Hong Kong immediately. Goodbye, Luke Powers. I shall not see you again." Those were her last words before leaving the room, but Jade caught her breath in shock.

"Luke? What does she mean? What about when we're married, our children? I couldn't bear it if she… " The rising panic overwhelmed her and she started to shake like an accident victim in shock. Luke stroked her hair.

"It's okay. She's hurt and she feels we let her down. She needs time, that's all. This'll pass, and we'll name the first girl after her. She won't be able to stay away. I promise." The following forty-eight hours were spent in getting Jade a visa for the United States, and making plans to go first to Auckland to finalize Luke's business holdings. He called his grandparents in Taupo to tell them that he would probably be having a Las Vegas wedding, and to invite them, even though he knew they would decline. Next he had to pack up the flat, dispose of his furniture by giving most of it to Dennis, and reassign the lease. He saw Jade only once, and it was a strange euphoric meeting for them both, reminiscent of the mystical time she had passed him on the stairs at the Peninsula, for it was the first time they had met without any secrets between them, certain that their future was assured.

He felt a greater tinge of regret when he packed up his office and said goodbye to the staff he had become close to since his arrival in Hong Kong. He was nearly twenty-five years old, and yet he felt in many ways that he had never grown up, for his childhood had been taken from him on his eleventh birthday. Now, when everything had come easy for him, he was facing a new life, with a wife, in a country that embraced talent but gave no quarter to those who failed. Strangely, he did not feel daunted. With Jade beside him he believed he could do anything.

Wong Peng's office was a corner suite in the tower with windows on two sides. It was a suite befitting a managing director and heir to a dynasty. He stood behind the desk in a perfectly tailored Italian suit, his hands manicured, the gold and diamond ring on his little finger heavy enough to take a man's eye out if he chose to attack. He did not ask Luke to sit, and Luke, who would normally have confronted him, felt no need to push the limit. After all, he was leaving with millions and with the Chinese man's intended wife. He had nothing to prove, and there was no point in wounding Wong Peng further. "Miss Anna has requested that I settle your account with the company," Wong said icily. "I have subsequently drawn a bank cheque for all of your entitlements, and this will henceforth sever your connections with us. Do you agree?" Luke could have argued that he had profit entitlements for years to come from the products he had actively created, the markets he had opened, but all he wanted was to leave with his dignity intact. Besides, five million dollars was a sizeable nest-egg, and more than enough to get him started in America.

"I agree," he said. "And I want you to know, and pass it on to Miss Anna since she won't speak to me, I'm not sorry for falling in love with Jade, but I am sorry that it has to end this way... for all our sakes."

Wong Peng seemed faintly amused and smiled archly. "Well, what is the saying you have in prizefighting? May the best man win?"

Luke grinned wryly. "Except for this time, prizefighting's never given me much pleasure," he responded.

"Nor will it," his adversary stated enigmatically. There was a moment of awkward silence, then Luke's eyes fell to the cheque he could see sitting on the blotter pad. Wong Peng followed his eye line and picked up the cheque.

"Well then, this is for you. Goodbye," and he handed the cheque to Luke. Luke nodded and turned toward the door. He had not meant to look at the amount on the cheque, for that would be demeaning to both of them, yet something made him read it just as he was about to put his hand on the door handle. He looked at it in disbelief, certain he was somehow reading it wrong.

"Wait a minute," he said haltingly. "There's a problem here. This cheque is for a million dollars." He looked at Wong Li Peng and saw the Chinese man's icy stare, the faint trace of a smug and condescending smile at the corners of his mouth.

"Those are my instructions; to return to you your original investment," he said matter-of-factly. Luke shook his head and moved a step towards the desk.

"Uh-uh! No way" Luke parried. "What about profits? Even last year my share was up to four million."

"What about set-up costs? And losses caused by your desertion of the company? What about your breach of your original five-year contract? I think this is a generous settlement." Wong Peng countered.

"Contract?" Luke asked. "We had no formal contract."

"You gave her your word. In China, that is binding." Wong Peng now made no attempt to hide the contempt in his voice. "If I were Miss Anna, I should sue you. If she were me, she would probably kill you. Either way, you would do better to leave with the money you came with. You have betrayed her and made her lose face. That is untenable in our world."

Luke was staggered. He had known how far Miss Anna had withdrawn from him, but he had not yet accepted how much he had hurt her. Nor had he realized how capable she was of retaliation, although it should certainly have occurred to him that she would deal with him in whatever way she could. He had neither the will nor the time to stand and fight. Nor was he convinced he would win. There was no choice but to cut his losses and move on. What had he lost anyway? He had his original stake, and he had Jade, who was beyond price. He nodded at Wong Peng, accepting the verdict, then turned and walked out of the office. He did not look back. He didn't even stop to close the door.

Wong Li Peng sat in the deep leather chair behind his desk. He allowed himself the luxury of a smile. The smile became a chuckle, and the chuckle a full-throated laugh. Luke Powers was gone, and it had not cost the ten million dollars Anna Chen had told him to pay. True, the full amount had come out of Eastern Star's account, but only ten percent had gone to Powers. Wong Peng had pocketed the other ninety percent himself, confident that neither Powers nor Miss Anna would ever compare notes. If things did not pan out his way, it was a barely adequate compensation for losing his bride. If they did, it was pocket money with which to indulge himself. Either way, he was joint managing director of Eastern Star, and his only possible business rival was now history. The taste of success, seasoned with revenge, was very sweet.

Luke picked up the airline tickets for the following day's flight, bought some last minute souvenirs, and returned to the apartment to finish packing his personal belongings. He was astounded that everything he needed for the future could fit into two suitcases, and things that he had thought were important to surround himself with now seemed of no consequence. He spoke to Jade, but only briefly, for she was also in the middle of packing, and then grabbed a snack from the fridge. He sat on the couch that Nancy had re-arranged so long ago that it now seemed in a different lifetime. He picked up one of the skateboarding magazines from the coffee table and admired the POW! logo, barely visible on the board in the photograph — one of their endorsing professionals had made the front cover. He flipped through the magazine and noticed an advertisement for POW! skateboards, but the wording lacked punch — it was something they could work on. He was about to make a note to himself when it hit him that 'they' no longer included him, and for the first time there was a genuine sense of loss. He had loved the challenge of creation, and the faith Miss Anna had shown in him. He wanted it back, but the price was too high, for he could not give up Jade. Overall, he had to believe he was still on a winning streak, no matter what he had lost in the process. And then Jade called again.

"Luke? Please, please don't say anything. Just listen to me." Her voice was barely more than a whisper, and he felt a gigantic knot in his stomach, as if some huge hand had taken his guts and twisted them. He knew what she would say even before she said it, but he had to hear the words.

"I'm listening," he told her in a curiously distant voice as if he was outside of his own body, watching and listening in slow motion.

"I cannot explain it. You always have an argument, a sound reason for me to change my mind. And I let you because I need your strength to make me change my mind. But now, I have to tell you, please don't hate me darling. I can't. I can't leave Hong Kong and my family. I can't go with you." The words grew in speed and intensity and he could feel her pain even as she said them.

"You're going to marry him?" he asked, once again knowing the answer.

"You don't know how it is with us. It is my duty, I can't change that," she said with resignation.

"Bullshit," he replied. "Jade, you can change it. All you have to do is say no and mean it. Come away with me, have the life we planned and I won't let them touch you. You're letting these people manipulate you. " He heard a strangled choking sob, and knew how much it was costing her not to break down.

"And you?" she asked. "I love you, but aren't you trying to manipulate me?" "I'm trying to save you, Godammit!" he yelled down the mouthpiece.

"At what cost Luke? How many people do we hurt in the process? Maybe you can live with that, but I can't." She was crying quite openly on the phone now and with every sob he could feel her resolve getting stronger, feel her slipping away from him, and he wasn't sure how to fight it. She was distant and, over the phone, he felt a growing sense of powerlessness. He wanted to reach out and make her listen to him.

"Just don't marry him. Don't marry me if you need more time. We'll go away, see how your new life will be, give your Aunt time to get over this. Or I'll stay in Hong Kong. There's no reason for me to leave without you anyway. Just don't rush in, don't marry him." He was aware of the frantic fear in his voice, but he could not control it.

"Rush?" she gave a sad little laugh. "Oh, Luke, don't you understand even now? I have been preparing for this marriage for twenty-one years. You're trying to halt time, and for a little while I thought you could. But you can't Luke, nobody can. It's finished, and I will make Wong Li Peng a good wife. But I will always love you, my dearest."

"No" he shouted, terrified that she would hang up the phone. "Don't go. We have to talk this through..."

"We have," she interjected sadly. "And it's finished. Goodbye darling. Forgive me some day." He heard the click of the phone even as the next protest was forming in his throat. She could not mean this, not after all they had been through to come so close to being free. He hastily dialed her number, but there was only a busy tone. He threw himself down on the couch and sank his face into his hands. He didn't know whether to cry or smash something. He only knew that he couldn't let it end like this. Not until she had told him to his face.

Miss Anna held Jade in her arms while the girl sobbed. She stroked her hair and murmured to her. "Never doubt that you have done the right thing child. Love passes, no matter how special or permanent it may seem, but family is forever. He was an interlude, a special gift to teach you how to love. He came, perhaps as a master, a lamplighter for the path ahead of you. But he is not of you, of us, and you will know in time that it could never have been. Now you will fulfill your destiny, and let your ancestors sleep in peace. I know it seems stupid and antiquated, but neither you nor I has the right to change tradition. We are what we are." And Miss Anna wept too, knowing that she had hurt the two people she loved most in the world. She wept also for the certainty of the inevitable, and her own sense of loss.

Luke wasn't sure how many times he tried to phone that night without success, but he was determined not to give in. He would take a cab to the house and hammer on the door until Jade spoke to him. He was aware that Miss Anna's hostility might lead to her calling the police or having him evicted, but it was a chance he had to take. He had two tickets on the early morning flight and one of those was for Jade. He refused to acknowledge the possibility that he might have to leave her behind. He reached for his jacket and headed for the door. He stopped dead in his tracks at the sight of two heftily built Asian men, the size of wrestlers, waiting in the corridor. He could see, with his peripheral vision, a third waiting down the hall near the elevators. For a second he felt like laughing. There was a moment, when time hung frozen in space. He looked at the two goons. The goons looked back.

"Sorry guys," he quipped without betraying his nervousness "If you're the Avon Ladies you picked a lousy time to call." They did not laugh, but mumbled something between them in Chinese. Then the taller of the two gave a polite nod and spoke in fractured English.

"Compliments Miss Anna and Miss Jade Chen. They want make sure you don't miss your plane. We will take to airport." The accent was thick enough to slice and serve on sandwiches, but Luke resisted the temptation to laugh and tried to move past them. "That's very kind of both of them, but I have someplace I have to go first." He explained. He was totally unprepared for the force of the hand that grabbed him and hurled him back into his apartment's doorway.

"I don't think so," the Asian gorilla told him. Luke tried once more to pass, but this time he was greeted by a punch to his lower abdomen that caused him to double up in pain, and before he had a chance to defend himself, both the goons were upon him, kicking and punching, and there was no chance for him to do anything but shield himself with his arms and hope that he did not pass out. He could not measure how long the beating lasted, but he knew it would pass faster if he did not resist. He told himself that Jade could not know of this, and he was right. He speculated that Wong Li Peng was somehow behind it, and again he was right. But then, he dismissed the thought and reasoned that Miss Anna was so powerful no-one would dare use her name unless she were the initiator. In that, he was wrong, but he would never discover the truth. He fought to remain conscious even as they dragged him down the corridor to the lift. He seemed to drift away momentarily to a calm place where he could hear water, but then he realized, as reality slapped him across the face, that it was raining, and the three goons were pushing him into the back seat of a car, an old American limo. For a second he was resigned to the fact that they were going to kill him and dump his body, like some bizarre re-enactment of a gangster movie. Then he heard the words Kai Tak, and knew he was being taken to the airport. They hustled him from the car at the airport and half dragged him through the entrance. He could see the airline check-in desk ahead of him. My bags, my passport, the tickets, he thought, but could not formulate the questions. As if reading his mind, his attackers placed the suitcases at the end of the check-in queue, and shoved the ticket and passport in his hand. The biggest of the goons brushed him down and straightened his jacket.

"Please not to miss this flight. It will be the only chance you leave Hong Kong. You not take it, you die here." He spoke the words with difficulty, yet with the monotone quality of someone who has been taught

exactly what to say. Luke nodded and joined the queue. He willed himself
to be outraged, indignant, anything to overcome the cloud of self-pity
and despair that was raining in his private world.

"Traveling alone, Mister Powers?" the ticket agent said, looking at
the spare ticket with some confusion. Luke nodded. He looked back for
a moment, wondering if he could still make a break for it, stay and find
Jade, but he didn't have the strength to fight both physically and mentally. He found himself herded through customs and swiftly and then
he was in the departure lounge and there was no turning back. He went
to the men's room, marveling at the professionalism of his assailants.
Not a mark showed on his face, even though he was conscious of two
of his teeth being lose. To look at him, no-one would ever suspect there
was anything wrong, except for the pain in his eyes. Like a zombie, he
handed over his boarding pass and was ushered to his window seat.
He sat there, numb, even allowing the stewardess to do up his seat belt
for him. He had tried various ways to exonerate Jade over the past few
hours, but now he no longer had the patience even for that. Whether
intentional or simply through her own lack of courage, she had sold
out both him and what they felt for each other. He watched the lights
of Hong Kong beneath him as the plane banked steeply and turned,
and he made a promise to himself that he would never love with that
intensity again.

FOR LUKE, THE only way to survive was to do what he had done thirteen
years earlier. He withdrew into his own Twilight Zone, where emotions
ceased to exist. He went home to Taupo, and did not need to give explanations; for his very presence and his pain ravaged face were sufficient
testament to what he had been through. He surmised that his grandparents must have called Hughie, who in turn phoned him. But Luke was
incapable of conversation except in monosyllabic form. Even later, when
Hughie drove down in the special car adapted for him, Luke could not
speak to him. Instead, he gripped his old friend's hand and held tight,
trying to convey that some small part of him understood now the pain of
amputation, for Jade had truly been a part of him.

He went trout fishing with his grandfather, conscious of the old man's efforts to reach him, but withdrawing even further at the realization of his closest relative's impending mortality. He's going to desert you soon, a small pin-prick voice insisted, and Luke would fight back the panic of being left again.

It was Gwen McMaster who discovered him sitting at the kitchen table in the dark just before dawn one night. She made hot chocolate for them both, for it was winter in New Zealand and bitterly cold, and she sat at the table with him.

"It's time for you to go. You know that." She uttered the simple statement as though picking the words from his own mind. He looked at her blankly.

"Go? Where?" he asked, unwilling to answer for himself.

"America," she replied simply. "Maybe not Chicago if it's too painful. But somewhere there. It's where you belong Luke. If it weren't, you would not have planned to take her there. Now you have to go alone."

"I don't want to," he murmured, but was conscious that the words were not entirely true.

"I know," she answered wisely. "But it isn't a case of want, is it? You have to." And he knew she was right.

He spent a few weeks by himself, visiting the places of his childhood, saying goodbye to the past. He stood on the land he had bought for Jade and wished that one day she would stand there too and know what she had lost through her weakness. He visited the tiny church of St Werenfried, where he and Kiri had sheltered from the rain and first kissed. Then he went to Auckland and walked through the University grounds, caught in a time warp with its red brick walls, its Norman turrets. He was surprised to find most of the masters still there. How was it possible that in those years so little had changed for the school, when everything had changed for him? He stayed at the Intercontinental, where he had first been inspired by Ron Wrightson. He was divesting himself of everything holding him to New Zealand and Australia, for he knew that when he came back it would be as a visitor, a tourist, and not as an expatriate. For Luke, that was the only way he could move on.

He went drinking with Hughie to celebrate his twenty-fifth birthday. He had two reasons now to both love and dread the day, for it not only commemorated the death of the family, but it was also the day when he had finally met Jade. Was it really only a year ago? He got blind drunk while Hughie, whose future now seemed more assured than his own, stayed sober. On the way home, they passed the fish and chip shop where the melon-breasted Brenda had introduced him to sex. All of the memories came flooding back, and he said goodbye to each individually.

ON THE DAY that Luke finally boarded the plane for Sydney, then onwards to Los Angeles, Jade, her long hair caught up with red silk tassels, the red lace dress draped over her tiny frame, became the wife of Wong Li Peng.

She said only what was necessary to complete her vows, the Tao priest smiling reassuringly at her. She did not look at her groom, and she took no food or drink at the wedding feast. She looked only at her aunt, expecting to see at least happiness for her sacrifice, but Miss Anna was fighting back her own tears. Both families had joined together to present the wedding gift, a beautiful house overlooking Repulse Bay. It was white, the Chinese color of mourning, and Jade thought it an appropriate color, for she felt as though she were dead.

She stood rigidly as her husband tried to kiss her, and sensed his tension when she opened her mouth but did not respond to his thrusting tongue. He pulled the red lace dress from her and she withdrew slightly to take off her own underwear, buying time; anything to avoid his hands upon her. She let him look at her for a few moments, before covering herself with her hands. He pushed her roughly on the bed, pulling off his own trousers. He tried to part her legs, slapping at her thighs when she resisted. There was no attempt to arouse her, for he wanted the frightened virgin, the adrenalin rush of sexual power. Later she could learn to please him.

He pushed her legs apart and roughly thrust a finger into her, grunting to discover, as he had expected, that she was dry and not ready for him. It only aroused him more and his short thick penis became engorged. He wet his fingers in his mouth and rubbed the head of his cock with saliva to moisten it. Then he poised himself on his knees above her, grasped her legs and lifted them, and thrust into her. He expected her to scream; he expected resistance and the tearing of her hymen. Instead the dry walls of her tunnel stretched around him and he knew this was no virgin. He withdrew, knowing without asking who had been there before him.

He slapped her hard, and she cried out and scrambled from the bed. He grabbed her, hitting the other side of her face. She tried to bite him and he closed his hand in a fist and punched her in the stomach. She fell to the bed, doubled in pain, knees drawn up to her stomach. He pushed her, still in that position, over onto her stomach and held her hips as he fucked her like a dog, screaming at her that this was how all bitches and whores should be treated. Later he held her down by kneeling on her shoulders and raped her mouth, coming deep in her throat and almost choking her.

She waited for him to fall asleep and then she crawled away to the bathroom, sat on the floor, and cried. She cried for herself, for her Aunt whom she could never tell of the humiliation, for Luke whom she had lost but would always love, and for the children she would inevitably bear this monster. With Luke, this night would have been one of tenderness and passion as they gave to each other. Instead, her first night as a married woman was one of violence and rape.

It was a pattern that would last all of her married life.

END OF PART ONE

PART TWO

RICK'S STORY

Beyond the Edge
and Back

BASED ON A TRUE STORY

CHAPTER ONE

W HAT WAS *THAT? What woke me? I'm so very cold. Where am I?*
Oh... hell... I remember; this can't be happening. Even my
shivering bones feel cold — is that what woke me — the cold?

How does a man who supposedly has everything suddenly wake up with
nothing? Lying here, wide awake — what the hell am I doing here? How
could this happen to me? What did I do to deserve this?

Damn it, I'm weak — I've never been weak! Never have my challenges
overwhelmed me — and now life is a bottomless pit — sliding deeper and
deeper by the day. Dragging me down and down. And they have a name for
it. They call it Bipolar Disorder. Manic Depression. Never would I have
imagined something as unbearable as this.

What is this place? A prison in all but name. 'The Jennings Clinic'
— you've gotta love those euphemisms, they make life a whole lot more
palatable. The same way we feed children their greens — 'Open wide for the
airplane!' But this is not just greens; who knows what drugs they're going to
make me swallow. I'll find out soon enough.

I've seen movies where they talk about the first night in prison. This can't
be much different. Except that I've already spent the past two years imprisoned
by my mind. As if it weren't enough to be paralyzed by this inescapable gloom,
even the government finds it necessary to revoke my status as a citizen. 'A ward

of the state', the letter told me. And then I voluntarily waive my rights of free-dom for the privilege of being treated by the Jennings Clinic, Topeka, Kansas — I must be mad. If only I, too, could escape to somewhere over the rainbow.

'One Flew Over The Cuckoo's Nest'. That's what it reminds me of. Electric shock treatment; brain surgery; forced medication. That was a scary movie. But a movie, nonetheless — Jack Nicholson went right on to his next character. This is real! This is happening! When will I be leaving? Certainly, I have no say in the matter.

How can I ever call myself normal again? The doctors tell me, if I con-tinue with the medication, I may be able to call myself normal again, some day. But I'm only a shadow of my former self. Who am I now? Am I the real Rick, or has he vanished forever? Either way, the people back home will never see me in the same way — I'm branded for life. Almost an outcast in some respects — a potential part of the human experience that people would much prefer not to acknowledge exists. It's too scary. Taboo.

It shames me. I don't know anyone else who has had this problem. They all seem to be capable of dealing with life — but not me. I've always risen to every challenge! I've shattered every obstacle! Not anymore. I no longer even qualify as a normal human being.

This separation from my family makes it even worse. Kate and the two boys. The center of my universe. 'Life isn't fair. Life is what you make it.' My own words to my two sons, Michael and James. 'At the very end of your life, only two things will truly matter to you. One, if you are lucky, you will have filled your life with many wonderful experiences. And two, if you are very, very lucky you will be surrounded by a few people who love you. Nothing else will matter.' I doubt very much that this experience will fall into the first category.

I can barely force myself out of bed to the bathroom. The small sink, shower and toilet crammed into the corner of the room. Maybe another layer of clothes will help alleviate the cold. I should have asked for a sleeping tablet. Tucking in the sheet and well-worn blanket on my bed — I can't help but notice that a tall man would have trouble sleeping on it — my feet extend right to the end. Can't they at least give me more than one blanket? I would give anything to feel warm, safe and loved.

There goes another tear — rolling down my cheek, to my ear lobe, to the small, hard pillow. I thought I could hold it in, but no — I can't stop them anymore. If only I could find a dry place to rest my head now — the damp evidence of a man's true emotions, seeping into the pillow, meeting my face wherever I place it. Maybe if I turn it over I can escape the dampness for a time. So many tears. There's no use in holding it back now; no one can see me. Even if they could, what more is there to hide?

Trying to think of the people I love. Trying to focus on my achievements and the dreams still to make a reality. Any thought that could be deemed beautiful is treasured but fails to distract me from the pain, that pain that persists relentlessly like a skipping CD — questions repeating in my mind over and over. . .

What was that? The nurses checking on me. Every damn half hour — that's what woke me. That's why there are no locks on the doors. How long do I have to put up with this? Did I really waive my rights? Did I really leave my fate in the hands of four strangers?

Their ultimatum left me speechless. Sign away my freedom? Agree, on paper, that neither I nor my family will have any power in determining when I leave the clinic? My eventual question was the obvious one, 'How long do you think I'll be here?' Silence. No reply. Finally, from Dr. Burke, head doctor of the committee of four, 'That will depend on your progress'.

I pushed for more. 'One month? Two? Three? Dr. Burke?' Again, silence. Then, 'We don't know, Rick. We can't give you any indication regarding when you would be ready to leave.'

What a bombshell. The second time in, what, nine weeks that I've lost my freedom — that indispensable human birthright. What could matter more? The first, taken from me; and this time it would be surrendered voluntarily. Only yesterday afternoon. They knew — Kate, Mum, Rosa and my best friend, Steve, all knew that the unequivocal ceding of authority to the doctors was a requirement for my treatment. They knew before we arrived in Kansas. I asked them and they each nodded, with tears in their eyes.

I searched those eyes for answers, feeling so alone, so vulnerable, so helpless. I searched Kate's eyes trying to read her thoughts, possibly obscured from me in our strained relationship. Strained to near breaking point — bereft of warmth and intimacy, and our love veiled under the awful weight of the past two years. She told my mother that she no longer had any feelings for

*me. And I had seen her reluctance to nurture the boys' fragile respect for me;
'You need to earn their respect'.*

'*Mum, Rosa, Steve, would you please leave Kate and me to be alone.*'
*There wasn't a cloud in the sky. The air fresh and clear as it stretched into
eternity. We walked silently to a park bench in this unfamiliar part of the
world. A small lake lay amongst a background of freshly cut green lawn,
the smell of which engendered a passing sense of comfort as it took me back
to the simplicity of childhood.*

*There wasn't a lot to discuss as we sat on that park bench. I felt so tired
of it all, traveling all this way from New Zealand with such high hopes,
such determination and willingness to do whatever was necessary to improve
as a human being. I merely rested my head in Kate's lap. I told her I felt
cornered. It wasn't long before our eyes had welled with tears.*

*They had all known about the conditions of the ultimatum. Did that
mean that they thought I was unstable? Did they approve of such measures? I could quite easily return to New Zealand to seek further help
without compromising my freedom. Why didn't they tell me before we
arrived? Shit! They no longer have any faith in me. Our twenty-two
years of marriage could not even convince Kate to share such pivotal
information with me. Her only response is to say that the decision is mine
to make. Not exactly a vote of confidence. I never wanted to become a
burden on my family. They must feel like hell — no power whatsoever to
help me. All they can do is cry tears of desperation.*

*All I want is to fall asleep in Kate's lap, her slender hand gently stroking
my hair and forehead. I want to fall asleep in the knowledge that I am loved
and respected, comforted and protected like a child. I want to feel that I'm
loved, unconditionally. But the reality could not be more different. 'Darling,
Kate, I've decided to meet their request and sign away my freedom for you,
for the boys and my family, and for myself. I need to return from the edge
that I've been treading. I need to learn from the edge and return stronger. I
need to rediscover myself.'*

*Rosa said herself that, though I seem to be okay, I'm still not well. My
mother, my poor mother — how I must have burdened her. First she had the
slow death of my father to deal with, and now her son like this. . . I can
see the pain on her face. She's lost respect for me. I almost sense that she's*

disappointed in me for not living up to who I used to be — that tirelessly upbeat man, Rick. Where did he go?

Is he still here, in this room? At 5:49 a.m.? Dad, I miss you so much. I hate to imagine what you would think of me now. Dad, what would you think of me now?

I miss you.

Do I believe in myself? Do I feel I am a good man? Am I still a man? Am I capable of fighting for the life I want and the way I want to live my life, with love and freedom? And can I surrender my freedom in the knowledge that I will win it back, fight for it, a second time?

Can I enter the lion's den — have I the faith, strength and belief in myself to conquer my own demons? Can I survive such a challenge and keep my battered spirit intact? I committed myself a second time; I gave up my freedom, knowing that if I can conquer fear — the fear of no love, the fear of no freedom — then fear will have no power. I will truly be free.

Maybe this is my chance to prove to myself that I can. I will not allow my spirit to be broken, as tempting as it may be to capitulate. I will accept the challenge and, no matter what happens, maintain my sense of self, and improve as a human being. Get a hold of yourself, Rick! Think of all the people, from all over the world, who have experienced much more frightening challenges than you. Yes, even worse than this!

CHAPTER TWO

R ICK WAS AWOKEN by noise in the hallway just as the sun began creeping over the hills on a peaceful, early-spring morning. As he lay in bed he felt drained of vitality, but remembering his instructions from the previous day, rose and proceeded to get ready.

The shower offered only a light stream of water. If he had been in a hotel he would have lodged a complaint and he almost smiled weakly to himself at the thought of complaining to the doctors about the unsatisfactory water pressure in his shower.

As he stared in the mirror, bewildered by the person he had become, he reached for his shaving razor only to find it wasn't there. The image of the nurse examining his personal belongings – each and every item he had brought with him into the clinic – flashed through his mind. Unless he wanted to arrive at his first meetings in the clinic looking worse than he already did, he would have to request his shaving razor, a process the nurse had assured him would be required every time he wished to shave.

It was strange; Rick had been pleased on first meeting the nurse to find that she was friendly and welcoming. She had escorted him and Kate to a small room in the professional ward – it was the only time Kate would be allowed to visit the personal quarters – and made the comment that Rick was very fortunate to receive his own room. Most patients shared a space.

On seeing his new, supposedly superior dwelling, he shuddered at the thought of having to economize any more; it was tiny, sparsely furnished and the single, reinforced window appeared to be bulletproof.

Well, I know that I'm not bulletproof, that's for sure.

"Now, I'll need to inspect your belongings, Rick," she had said. What surprised him was not the request, but the sudden change in her demeanor: she was pleasant enough but had adopted a mechanical approach to the whole encounter and inspected, in minute detail, every item. Nothing could be hidden from this medical professional: all would be revealed and he felt a sudden sense of vulnerability that was totally unfamiliar. It was as if every facet of his very soul were being examined, generating an apprehension for the moment when something is found that shouldn't be there.

Without a hint of sympathy, the nurse had confiscated his razor. Then his Rogaine. He still had a reasonable head of hair and, though it had begun to gray, he did his best to conceal it, doing all he could to hang on to his existing hair. "Shit, I need that more than ever now, don't you think?" She smiled. She was hardly mean-spirited, just practiced. It was obvious she had conducted many such inspections before and maybe, Rick thought, the whole facade of tending to each patient's every whim and insecurity needed to be debunked as early as possible, as if to say, 'Get over it, there are more important things to concern yourself with now.'

Returning to his current predicament, he found the nurse on duty – not the same one now – and asked to use his shaving razor. It was promptly provided.

"Have you completed your crisis plan yet, Rick?" she said.

He had glanced at the assignment but resented the idea of having to complete homework at someone else's request. "Not yet."

"Well, when you get a chance be sure to hand it to us," she smiled.

He doubted he would ever feel comfortable in the clinic – a prison that seemed to mirror the confinement he felt within his own being, restrained in a chemical straightjacket.

The first activity for the day would be a one-on-one session with a psychiatrist, one of the four who sat on the panel which, the day before, had interviewed him and told him he would not be free to leave the clinic until the doctors had decided the time had arrived.

He thought back to his last session with a psychiatrist, in New Zealand. The last time he saw that psychiatrist, Bradshaw, could hardly be deemed a real session... dammit, he didn't even want to think of her. He wanted her out of his mind. He wanted to forget her.

"Dr. Friedman will be with you shortly," the nurse said as she passed by Rick, seated by himself in the small room.

How did he ever come to meet Dr. Bradshaw? It seemed like a different world now as he thought back to it: life was rolling along at a relentless pace, business, the new house, Kate and the boys. But he couldn't deny that there was something deeper gnawing away at him, something that refused to grant him respite. He couldn't quite put his finger on it but what stood out at the time more than anything else was his father's death. That slow, agonizing death. The sight of his father fading right before his eyes tore him apart. He couldn't let it go. His sleep was troubled, at best, and the grief seemed to stalk him at every turn.

Grief. That's what it was. That's why he went to a psychiatrist. And Dr. Claire Bradshaw came more highly recommended than any other, her TV appearances earning her the reputation as one of New Zealand's top three mental health professionals. And she was a woman; that was perfect. Rick wanted a woman's understanding, a woman's empathy. He knew what kind of a man he was — he was patently aware of the potency of his feelings, the weight they held in his life, and his need to be connected to that. They required someone who could understand the sensitivity that defined this man's experience.

The clock hit nine a.m. Within a few minutes he would be meeting with a psychiatrist. But how could he trust someone in that position again, someone who held the key to his well-being — the key to what he so desperately yearned for above anything else — and who could decide whether or not to reveal that key? Bradshaw had decided not to. She had handed him something, telling him it was a key, until he discovered otherwise. He was drinking his own death, but it was not a poison that could be recognized until it was too late.

'Where is the evil in you?' she had said to him one day with a quizzical expression on her face. 'Everyone has evil in them. But I can't seem to be able to find it in you.'

Was that her rationale? Did her sadistic curiosity get the better of her, motivating her to drive him to the edge, just to see what was there? Was it the thrill of playing God?

He would eventually discover that she had her own issues, but by that stage, it would be too late. Even if it had been brought to his attention early on, he wondered if it would have made any difference. The details of the situation didn't bother him in the slightest on their own; though, in light of her manipulation, it was possible that they played a part in her dynamic with Rick. Her marriage had recently dissolved, with her husband re-settling with his long-time mistress. Rick was aware, from the early stages, that Claire Bradshaw was separated, but knew nothing of the particulars surrounding the marriage. Though the idea that she may feel some degree of resentment toward her husband, which could complicate Rick's own treatment given his own problems with Kate, had surfaced in his mind, he had quickly dismissed it: he was in her office to deal with his own problems, not hers.

But on reflection, and on discovery of the circumstances of the separation, he could see that he had been too quick to dismiss her own issues as potentially playing a part in his treatment. 'You're a very unusual man, Rick. You have considerable power, but you choose not to use it.' Again, she said it with that look in her eye, searching his expression for a sign of the evil that she was so certain resided somewhere beneath his innocent exterior. There was something sinister about her approach to Rick.

Had he been too forthcoming in his sessions with her? Surely, that was the point of any kind of therapy. He told her of his excitement in building his business, of his love of his family, and that nothing brought as much joy to his heart as did spending time with his family. Rick opened up about his enjoyment of sex and what he thought was a healthy sexual relationship with his wife.

He was successful, that much was clear. Did she resent it, or feel threatened in some way? If she did, did she even know that she resented it, or was it subconscious? It was ironic: here he was, a new arrival at a psychiatric clinic, himself playing the role of psychoanalyst to his past doctor. *Why didn't I get a second opinion earlier, instead of at the last minute?* he would occasionally find himself asking. *Could I have stopped the train that soon became a runaway, if I had just seen a different psychiatrist?*

Regardless of her motives, the facts told a story that couldn't be denied. Her diagnosis of Rick's situation was anxiety. He was on Tryptanol for a number of months to aid with his sleeping difficulties, but with little benefit. The dosage increases seemed to have little effect and this was the second drug that she had prescribed; the first affected his libido so adversely that he had requested a different approach.

His attempt to move countries ended with his return from Australia to New Zealand three months later. It had been a momentous move, Kate and his two sons uprooted and attempting to establish a life in a new country, a three-hour flight from the city they had always called home. It was supposed to be an exciting new adventure, and it was, until Rick made the decision that he would later discover had confirmed Kate's worst fears: they would return to New Zealand, and Kate would abandon her hope that her husband might one day be true to his own desires, rather than the wishes of those surrounding him.

Not long after their return, he woke one morning to find himself unable to get out of bed.

He had grown accustomed to getting out of bed and thinking over his current business situations until the day began, but he found himself unable to muster the strength to rise. Instead, he lay there and was surprised to feel overcome with fatigue. *Maybe the higher dosage of Tryptanol is finally kicking in.* He woke again at seven-thirty. He couldn't remember the last time he had slept like that. He knew his first meeting of the day was at nine a.m., so immediately went to sit up in bed. But even this was too much to ask of his body. He felt as if he hadn't slept all night; he felt as if he hadn't slept in days.

His body was shivering. The room was heated and he had never felt cold in there before, but now he pulled the bedding close as he tried to generate warmth. It was no use. He lay there shivering. Kate was getting ready for the day when she heard Rick's movement in the bedroom. She came out to see him.

'I didn't want to disturb you, you looked like you were sleeping,' she said.

'I can't get up,' was all Rick could manage. Even talking seemed strenuous.

'What do you mean?', Kate said, moving closer. 'You have things you need to do, don't you?'

'Can you cancel them, darling... I need to stay here for a while.' Rick kept his eyes closed for the conversation.

I just can't bare to think of it. Why can't I face the world today?

He drifted off to sleep again, waking with the ringing of the phone. Kate came into the room once again and gestured to Rick to take the call. He couldn't do it. He could barely move. She made some excuse to the caller and knelt by Rick's side asking what was wrong with him. But he couldn't manage an explanation. Everything was wrong. He felt afraid to talk on the phone. He felt afraid to leave bed. Each small problem in his life kept repeating in his mind, and each seemed overwhelming in its own right.

Rick expected to feel some improvement as the day progressed, but the cold and fatigue persisted. He still felt as if he hadn't woken up. He couldn't escape the biting cold that seemed to infest his body. Kate ran a hot bath for him and helped him out of bed. He lay in the water a while and felt some relief from the cold, but the world still seemed too much to face. The day wore on without change: he lay in bed, struggling to stay warm and hoping to escape from the world. The darkness of the room offered a sense of security; a hiding-place which he clung to.

The next morning came, and he awoke with a more pronounced feeling of dread. The cold still pervaded his body and he felt more afraid than the day before. Kate fielded his calls throughout the day as a sense of urgency grew among the callers. Rick knew people were waiting for him, that business was calling. But he couldn't bring himself to meet with anyone or talk on the phone. It was all too much. Everything scared him. He remained in bed.

For yet a third day, Rick failed to show any signs of improvement. He still could not bear to face the world. The burden was too much; his body felt as if it were ready to shut down. The simplest of tasks seemed overwhelming. He remained in bed, motionless, and unwilling to confront the world awaiting him.

Kate phoned Dr. Bradshaw and was told to bring Rick in immediately. He sat in his usual seat, this time with Kate next to him. Kate described the situation and Rick did his best to articulate the despair that seemed to have enveloped him.

Dr. Bradshaw spoke directly to Rick. 'This is serious. You have acute depression. This is bad.' Thoughts of what that meant rushed through Rick's mind. He had come across people who had dealt with depression; he had read about it and heard people mention it as if it were a state of pronounced unhappiness. But what he was feeling was more than mere unhappiness. It was overwhelming. *Is this what it feels like to be depressed? How do people cope?*

'You have to be very, very careful, Rick. I'm going to prescribe something for this and you have to ensure that you take a break from everything that's going on in your life. As much as you can, take a break from it. I'm giving you Lithium. Keep taking the Tryptanol. It should work relatively quickly.'

'Doctor, I've already tried a number of drugs. I don't know if I want anymore,' Rick said, unable to find the energy to convey his disappointment in the drugs' performance.

'Would you rather feel like this?' Rick didn't answer the doctor. 'Lithium is going to help you, definitely. We have to monitor you with blood tests but you shouldn't have problems if you drink a lot of water.' She handed the prescription to Kate. 'Don't worry, there's nothing wrong with taking Lithium – even Ted Turner takes it.'

Rick took the medication. When he woke the next day, he was relieved to feel somewhat closer to his normal self again. On the second morning after he began the Lithium, he rose from bed and noticed that energy had returned to his body. He returned the missed calls from the previous days and rescheduled the meetings that Kate had canceled on his behalf. Life appeared to return to normal.

"RICK," THE NURSE called as she reentered the waiting room at the Jennings Clinic. "Dr. Friedman will see you now."

He didn't move immediately.

Alright, Rick, you've gotten yourself into this one. You know you're going to have to trust these people now if you ever want to get your life back. Yes, you have to trust the same profession that got you into this mess in the first place because you've tried yourself and no one else can help you.

Come to think of it, who am I kidding? I wish that it were only Bradshaw who is responsible for this — wouldn't that be convenient? The perfect enemy: a stranger who came into my life and destroyed it because of her own sick mind. Wouldn't that be a tidy explanation? Just a freak occurrence with no apparent cause — like a car accident.

"Rick?"

"Yes, thank you," He stood and approached the psychiatrist's door.

CHAPTER THREE

S O, RICK, HOW are you settling into the Jennings Clinic so far?"
The office was plain and homely. Dr. Friedman's glasses were large,
drooping deep below his kind eyes. The window to the right offered a
glimpse of the clinic's peaceful surroundings. Maybe Rick would take a
walk later in the day if he could get permission from the staff.

"Well... I'm coping," Rick tried, with a slight smile.

"I know, it takes some getting used to," the doctor replied with a
laugh. "There's a lot going on for you here — I'm sure there are many
areas that we'll be discussing together and also much that you'll be talking about within other groups. But today, I think it's best if we begin by
understanding, together, exactly why it is you're here at the clinic."

*Should I tell him about Bradshaw? What she did was as evil as murder-
ing a human being... No, I can't. Doctors stick together, they don't turn one
another in. No, why am I even thinking about it? I've already decided to sign
myself over to these new doctors. Bradshaw is in the past now.*

"Well, doctor, it's quite simple really: I have no choice."

"And what do you mean by that?"

"No one else can help me. I've tried to beat my condition with the help
of my family, my friends, eliminating all the external factors of stress in
my life... I've asked my own personal doctor to explain the situation to

me, and I've come to one conclusion: no one understands it. No one can explain to me what bipolar disorder is or how I can get my life back. Sure, they can give me clinical facts, but they're just words. I want solutions. I went to the Mayo Clinic – I pinned all my hopes on that place, knowing how many heads of state and others go there – the King of Jordan was even staying on the level above me. But even they couldn't help me – they told me I'm in good physical condition and that, with the drugs, I'm normal." Rick looked directly at the doctor. "But I'm still not myself; I'm not normal. And, even if I were, what would that mean when I'm taking this psychiatric drug – Epilim – influencing my mind? I'd be living under the control of drugs for the rest of my days. Doctor, I want my life back. I want to beat this condition. That's why I'm here."

Dr. Friedman nodded. "Well, Rick, that's quite a clear explanation, and I am impressed by your commitment to your health. You've certainly traveled a great distance to come to the Jennings Clinic."

"I'll do whatever I can to understand this condition, so that I can be a better human being and stop taking any drugs."

The man behind the desk leaned forward in his chair, his eyes searching for the right words before they came back to meet Rick's.

"Rick, your treatment here will proceed one step at a time," he said casually. "There are a couple of things that you might do well to understand about your condition. The first is something that you'll hear again and again during your stay here: the first step in dealing with your condition is to accept it." He let the words sink in. "That means that you should view your condition as no different from that of a diabetic's. Bipolar disorder is a condition that should be viewed just as you would look upon what may appear to be a more purely physical condition such as diabetes."

Rick had heard it before, but equating a physical disorder with one related to mental and emotional stress seemed flawed to him. Yes, he knew there was a physical component to bipolar: he had heard the functioning of the synaptic nerve endings likened to the shorting of a fuse on a circuit board. But if the short circuit was caused by something as intangible as mental health, how could he think of it as being physical? Still, he had promised himself to keep an open mind, despite his suspicions, and give the doctors the benefit of the doubt. He was at the clinic to learn all he could, to absorb whatever information was available.

"The second point about bipolar disorder that I want to share with you from the outset, Rick, is that medication will be necessary for the rest of your life. There are no two ways about it: those very few who try to live without it crash, almost without exception. It's not long before they have a relapse." The doctor did his best to inform his patient without discouraging him and it was not a part of his job that he enjoyed. However, to allow a patient to become fixated on such a dangerous course of action would be irresponsible. Patients needed to understand that drugs had become a part of life, even if it was initially a shock. Some patients preferred to live with mood swings rather than be medicated, but ultimately the result was always the same: they would always be at the mercy of the condition.

Again, Rick had heard it before: cover-up the flaw with medication. Cover rather than cure. *Of course you want me to wear my chemical straightjacket for the rest of my life; that's the safe option. But it's also a prison sentence — better to be drugged up and docile than to take a chance on being real again.* "I understand," he nodded to the doctor, not for a second abandoning his hope for life without dependence on drugs.

"Well, Rick, I hope it doesn't come as too much of a shock — I can see it's something you feel strongly about. Let's move on." Both men were relieved by the suggestion. "I wonder if you could tell me about the day of your breakdown — tell me about what actually happened, if you can recall."

Rick went to speak but found himself unable to begin. Did he really have to tell this doctor about that awful day? How could he bring himself to share such things with anyone? And where could he possibly begin the story — there was so much to tell.

"Maybe I could start by asking a few standard questions," the doctor added, sensing the hesitation. "Were you suicidal on the day?"

The doctor's voice was so nonchalant and amiable he might as well have been asking, 'What's your favorite color?' There seemed to be something about the doctor that invited a degree of trust.

"No, I wasn't."

"Have you ever been suicidal?"

He thought for a moment. "No."

"Is there any history of mental illness in the family?"

"No," he answered, though he had already provided that information when checking in the previous day.

"On the day of the breakdown, did you ever become convinced that you were someone other than yourself?" There was no answer. "Sometimes it's someone you know personally, but often not, for example, Jesus, or some other figure."

Shit! That's a standard question? "Yes."

"Okay. And can you remember what happened on that day?"

Rick sighed and looked out the window. It was not something he cared to remember, but he knew it was the next step and he searched his memory. "You know, I can remember pretty clearly what happened up until the breakdown, but not much of the actual episode itself. I know that the people who were present know what I said and what I did, and they've shared that with the Crisis Team and the Mayo Clinic, but no one's ever really told me what happened."

"That's fine, let's just go into what you do remember about the day."

"How far back do you want me to go? I mean, I haven't talked about this before – and I don't know if I'll be able to get it straight in my head without starting a few days before – that's when I remember things start-ing to go very wrong."

"Wherever you want to begin."

Again, Rick expelled a full breath of air and rubbed his eyes. Then he took another deep breath and let it out, shaking his head slowly from side to side as he delved into the dormant memories.

He began, "I couldn't sleep for days. I think it was three days, three nights, with absolutely no sleep leading up to the actual day. And leading up to that I had been doing all sorts of crazy things – phoning people, saying things, not remembering any of it... "

'WHO ARE YOU talking to?' Kate asked as she entered the room, concerned by the frantic speech she caught from down the hall. She was used to hearing him talk nonsense to his family over the past weeks: he spoke about his school days, his life and a number of unrelated issues from the past that had upset him. It was as if he was for the first time acknowledging pain that he had always carried, but it made no sense to whoever listened. Still, listen they did, for fear of being rebuked. But this was the first time Kate had witnessed her husband doing such a thing on the phone, and she worried about who might become aware of just how bad his condition had become.

'No one,' Rick replied as he hung up the phone. His paranoia was becoming so pronounced that he no longer trusted his wife or mother.

'Rick, you were talking to someone. You weren't making any sense.' Something in him realized that what Kate was saying was true, but he couldn't remember whom he was talking to, nor what was said.

'I don't know. I don't know… I can't remember,' he said.

It was soon brought to Kate's attention that such calls were frequent, though Rick could never recall the conversations. Steve, his best friend from childhood, flew over from Sydney and began living in the house, and Rick's mother, Maria, now spent days there, too. Kate, Steve and Maria started sharing the responsibilities of tending to their beloved Rick as they watched him drift further and further from anything resembling the man they knew.

Rick told his family that he wanted to visit the Mayo Clinic. He had heard stories of miraculous recoveries at the world-renowned health center, of Presidents and celebrities whose health was restored. He wanted a full medical evaluation, and he was certain that the Mayo Clinic would have the answers he was looking for. Kate, Maria, Steve and Rosa all volunteered to accompany him. They booked their arrival in Rochester, Minnesota, for March 19th. They would first fly to Los Angeles, then to St Paul, and then drive to Rochester. The family were relieved to have some help on the horizon; no one was equipped to handle a person in Rick's condition. Already, they had asked for a friend's medical assistance. The doctor visited Rick's home and strongly advised psychiatric attention, but Rick refused unequivocally. His mistrust of the psychiatric establishment was entrenched: Dr. Bradshaw had manipulated him, the drugs didn't work, and he didn't want to give anyone that much power over his mind ever again.

The doctor prescribed sleeping tablets and valium. Neither worked. To the family, the visit to the Mayo Clinic couldn't arrive fast enough.

"SO YOUR WIFE was having trouble caring for you at this stage," Dr. Friedman noted.

"Yeah, they all were – even my elder son. I wanted to keep it out of sight from my boys, but I couldn't do it forever. Michael wanted to take me out for lunch – this is still two or three days before the break-down – but he could tell that I wasn't right. People in the restaurant, too, noticed. My eyes were glazed, lit up, as if there were an excess of alertness. Maybe I looked like a young child who had over-indulged on sugar or something... anyway, I remember, I couldn't pay attention to anything for more than a few seconds and I was even having trouble understanding Michael's questions."

Rick had shifted his chair so that his body was now angled toward the window. He stared out the window as he spoke, the doctor sitting back in his own chair. "But I really knew something was wrong when I couldn't speak. Michael asked me a question, which I vaguely heard. I opened my mouth to speak, but nothing came out. Unbelievable, right? Scared the shit out of me. I literally couldn't speak. I had been a slave of my own dysfunctional mind for months, but this was something new –," now Rick even allowed a laugh to escape, " – now I couldn't even will my body to perform a task as simple as saying a word. Scared Michael, too – a nineteen-year-old having to see his father in such a state. He took me home right away and I lay on the couch while Mum massaged my hands. I was simply exhausted – really – but at the same time, I seemed incapable of resting.

"I guess," he paused. He was speaking slowly, stopping often, as the memories drifted back into his awareness. "I guess I was crying out for help in my own way. I was always wanting to talk to my mother, my wife, anyone, and talk and talk about my life. But the doctors and my family – none of them knew what to do. No one could help me. I would have liked to think that, if I ever got myself into a crisis situation, those who loved me would rescue me, or that the doctors would whip out the right pill just in the nick of time," he paused as Dr. Bradshaw's face shot through his mind. "But the truth is, they were powerless. My family may have wanted to save me, but they couldn't.

"So... I don't know... all I can say about those days leading up to the breakdown is that everything seemed to snowball into my feeling lost, overwhelmed, unloved, and unable to function as a normal human being. I could feel myself slipping into a dark hole but I just couldn't stop. And there was no one who could help me."

The room was silent for a moment before the doctor spoke. "And what happened on the day?"

Rick shifted uneasily in his seat. There was so much going on in his head it was like a DVD on fast forward. He wanted to slow it down, put the pieces in the right order. Or maybe he wanted to put the player on pause; freeze the memories on some visual he could live with. He suddenly felt overwhelmed and put his hand to his forehead. The doctor was an expert at reading such a gesture.

"I think perhaps that's enough for a first session. Unless of course you want to...?"

"No... no. I'm having trouble putting it all together right now. This isn't easy for me." Rick explained.

"If it were, you probably wouldn't need to be here," Friedman reassured. The doctor smiled. Rick returned to his room, disoriented, exhausted, and relieved to have been spared, for the time being, having to relive that terrifying day.

CHAPTER FOUR

THE SEVEN PATIENTS and the psychiatrist were seated in a circle in the center of the room. Rick recognized some of the faces from his short time in the ward, and though it was evident that some knew each other, he had never spoken with any himself. His second night had been marginally more restful than the first. All of the issues from the previous night were competing for attention in his mind as he tried his best to sleep, with the addition of a new cause for concern: the looming group therapy session.

The scattered exchanges died down and the room's attention settled on the psychiatrist. "Welcome," he said. "My name is Dr. McMahon and I will be facilitating this group therapy session." He was relaxed when he spoke, in no particular hurry, and wore an eager smile as he looked around the room at the seven men and women seated in the circle. "It's always exciting to begin a new group. Some of you may have met, but I suspect that we each know very little about one another. If you've never participated in a group such as this, then I would invite you to stay open to what may arise during our time together and examine your everyday boundaries, and then ask yourself if you may be willing to reveal a little more of yourself than you might usually be prepared to do.

"There's no pressure here – nothing we'll be requiring of you. It's simply an environment in which you can be yourself, share a little of who you are, and in your sharing and partaking of what your fellow group members have to offer, take something away from these sessions that you may otherwise have been unaware of."

Rick didn't know what to make of the doctor's opening. Such a group was certainly new to him.

"And I want to assure you that everything that is said in this room is strictly confidential. By participating in this group, we each agree to keep what is said by whom only within this group, and to never divulge details or identity to anyone outside of the group." There were nods of consent.

"Now, I'm going to begin by introducing myself and giving a little background on how I came to work at the Jennings Clinic and then we'll go around the room and each of you can introduce yourselves."

He began with a self-introduction and then the introductions moved around the circle. One of the men, Scott, was already known to Rick as he shared the room across the hall. A friendly man, he seemed perpetually busy on his laptop computer, and it being the professional ward, Rick surmised he must still be in contact with whatever enterprise it was he was involved with. Of the other two men, one introduced himself as a lawyer, and the other didn't mention his occupation but noted that it wasn't his first time in the clinic. One woman was instantly recognizable to Rick, but he was unable to place her until she spoke; she was an actress, no longer at the peak of her career, but there was no question that she was a familiar face to every person in the room. Another woman introduced herself as a pediatrician from Chicago, and then there was one patient whose eyes barely left the ground in front of her. She spoke only two words: "I'm Julia."

"It's a pleasure to meet you all," Dr. McMahon said at the end of the round. "And now I'll invite you, one at a time – and we may well have time for only one person today – to tell a little more about why you're here at the clinic. What are the challenges that have brought you here in the first place? What are the challenges that you're dealing with now?

What do you hope to get out of your time here? So, whenever you're ready." He motioned to the center of the circle with an open hand.

The room went dead. Everyone's eyes were trained either on an empty piece of space in the distance or on the floor in the center of the circle, waiting for someone else to make the first move. Rick was exceedingly nervous at the prospect of speaking first. There was no way he was going to speak today — surely one of the others who had done it before would lead the way.

The silence persisted and Rick began to feel awkward. But looking around the room, he noticed that some people appeared perfectly content just sitting, collecting their thoughts, and enjoying the calm. It occurred to him that maybe there were those in the group that weren't nervous about speaking but who were simply preparing themselves. After all, what was the hurry? No one had anywhere pressing to be, that was for sure.

Rick, too, began to relax. The silence seemed interminable, but it was somehow comforting. He noticed that one of the men, sitting on the opposite side of the circle, had his eyes closed. And then they opened.

"Well," he began slowly and almost inaudibly, stopping to clear his throat. "I think I'll go first." No one else spoke; the room remained quiet.

Joel had built his life through commitment and hard work, rising to the top echelon of academia in America and then founding his own specialized law practice. Rick saw parts of himself in the man's attitude toward his work and wondered if such an unerring determination had been the cause of the lawyer's downfall. The repercussions of Joel's discovery that his wife was having an affair sent a shudder through Rick's body.

"I couldn't believe that she would do that. What more could she want than everything I had provided — I had tried to do everything for her, for my daughters — but I couldn't be everywhere at once. I had to make sacrifices for the lifestyle we enjoyed... well, whatever it was, the marriage ended. She left. And I was devastated. I really found it too much to cope with." He sighed and sat back in his chair. "I don't know what happened — I was exhausted, depressed, and one day I just broke down." He didn't display any anger as he said the words, but the pain at what he had to say next was obvious. "And then she took the kids. She took my daughters. Ironic, really, that an attorney couldn't win custody of his own children, but they claimed that I wasn't of sound mind, and she won full custody."

The loss of his entire family played on his mind unceasingly and consumed him, eventually leading to a diagnosis of bipolar disorder.

It shocked Rick to hear that it was his third stay at the Jennings Clinic, but it was Joel's explanation as to why that got him worried.

"I was okay for a few years – after my first stay here – but then, all of a sudden, the drugs stopped working. I was taking the medication that had kept me together for about five years, but then I had another breakdown and I was back to square one. So I came back here, pulled myself together again, and changed medication. And I was okay again – I didn't have a wife, I saw my daughters only occasionally, but I was okay.

"And then something happened that..." his voice began to waver but he continued, "My father, my own dad, betrayed me. It's still difficult to say it, I guess I'm having real trouble accepting that that is what's happened, but there's no denying it – he hasn't denied it himself, but he can't give me an explanation as to why he would do such a thing.

"He divulged to my partners in my legal practice that I had bipolar disorder." The room, still silent, emitted a collective shudder. Rick felt the hair on his arms stand on end. "And now... they've forced me to sell my stake to them for next to nothing. They threatened to throw me out on grounds of mental instability if I didn't cooperate – I had no choice. The law firm that I founded – taken from me. Can you believe that?" He looked up briefly then returned his gaze to some vague point on the floor. "And I've gone through a lot – I could handle losing my business. I could handle seeing my kids once a goddamn month and watching them drive off with their step-dad after a weekend with me. But when I found out that it was my own father behind this? That he told them about my illness?" He shook his head, lost for words.

"I've confronted him about it. I've looked him in the eye and asked 'why?', but he refuses to discuss it. He flat out refuses – that's all – won't even acknowledge what I'm going through. Acts as though nothing has happened. Why can't he at least tell me that he thought I deserved it? Or that he thinks I'm sick and I shouldn't practice law? Or that it was some bizarre, inexplicable mistake of his?

"He won't say a word to me about it. And then, this time when I broke down, it was as if something took control of me and I was evicted right out of my own body. In plain daylight, I walked into a department store – it was a Best Buy – picked up a TV and walked right out the front door. Past security, the alarm beeping and all, and I took a few steps before they stopped me. But I was out of control – they had to subdue me, the cops came, everything. I was convicted but didn't have to serve any time – instead I'm here to recover, regain some sense of composure. Well, at least the courts' view on the illness is a two-way street, right? Damned me the first time over my children, but saved me the second.

"So, that's why I'm here. All those things that were important to me have gone – none of them remain. My family – any way you look at it – and my work. So maybe I'm here for a fresh start."

No one spoke, no one moved. Rick wanted to say something – anything – but what could he say? He was dumbstruck. He had heard the 'golden rule' mentioned in the clinic already: 'Never, ever, tell anyone about your illness.' Though his time so far in the clinic had been brief, the strength of the doctors' conviction on this point, and on the patient's acceptance of his condition and need for medication, made the two tenets stand out in his mind and generated much reflection on whether or not Rick would be able to withhold such a defining episode in his life from those he met.

The reasoning was clear: such information grants a person frightening power over an individual. Blackmail was simple and, it was said, rampant; court cases could be decided by such a diagnosis; without a high degree of difficulty, a person suffering from such an illness could be wrongly stripped of his rights and committed to a mental institution or, worse yet, manipulated with such efficacy that he would drive himself into such a position.

The golden rule was one point on which the psychiatrists were unequivocal. Parents were not usually included in the caution, but Joel's experience highlighted, in a perverse way, the rule's merit.

They all sat very still, absorbing the immensity of the man's pain and allowing him space to deal with what he had just revealed. Not a word was said. There were slight nods of the head, there was eye contact, there were tears. It was as if by sharing Joel's story, each one in the room had walked with him a little through those years. There was pain, but there was also release.

Dr. McMahon broke the silence gently, thanking Joel for his willingness to open up to the group. "Does anyone else have anything to share?" He happened to look at Rick, and it was as if McMahon had unlocked a compartment in his mind that he had forgotten existed, and the image was so sharp it took his breath away.

Why has it taken me so long to remember this? I must have blocked it out. But it still doesn't make sense. Nobody has ever mentioned it. It's as if it never happened... a conspiracy to make things appear normal — to make me appear normal. Why? Was it because the business needed me? Or maybe they were embarrassed, or scared for me — or of me.

It was a board meeting like any other board meeting — except I hadn't slept. I rarely slept then, only days before I lost it. I had tried to fill myself up with work and the family in the years before, and there I was, tired, not just through lack of sleep. Tired of the business, the endless decisions, the multiple phones that never stopped ringing, the getting on and off planes — the blank faces waiting for me to say yes, or no, when I didn't want to say either. They were all there, all the usual suspects. Those who believed in me, those who wanted to be made rich, and those who just wanted to get the hell out of the board room and onto the golf course. I didn't want to look at any of them — not that day.

It started with my tie. I suppose my ties were my signature, part of my identity. I loved the patterns, works of art; what they could stand for and communicate without words. But that day, I don't remember the exact day, I took off my tie at the board meeting. I took it off and looked at it. It was as if I was seeing the pattern for the first time; the intensity of the colors, the texture of the silk. It was something I had never done before. The room was very silent. Even without looking up I knew that every board member was focused on me. I could feel their eyes, questioning, judging. I knew I should have folded the tie, put it on the boardroom table neatly and made some excuse about the room being warm. I must have been sane because I knew what I should have done... but I didn't do it. Instead I threw the tie. I threw it at Rosa, sitting there looking smug. I threw it wishing it was something heavier — not heavy enough to hurt her, but at least heavy enough to scare her. She barely blinked, but I heard the sharp intake of breath around the table.

Then, suddenly, I started undoing my shirt, tearing off my jacket. I wanted them all to see I could do what I wanted — I didn't have to make their decisions — I was free to make my own. I kicked off my shoes and undid my pants, wriggling free; throwing each piece to a different board member or across the room. Here I am... Here's what I've become — a fancy suit and a $300 tie... you all want a piece of me, so take it, take it. I never said it. I'm not sure I even thought it, not then, not during the bizarre striptease. I heard gasps and murmurs and saw, just for a split second, the shock and mortification in my sister's eyes. Then I stood there, naked except for the black briefs I always wore — a whole drawer of them identical in every respect. I didn't want one more day that was identical to the day before; one more board meeting full of the same routine, one more designer suit I could hide inside.

If someone had stopped me; shaken me; held me; hit me even and forced me to look in the mirror, would I be here now? But no-one protested, no-one spoke, no-one even looked at me. Could they even have done anything for me at that stage? Did they know any more than me about my condition? No. It was too late. I was out of control. It was as scary for them as it was for me. Someone, I think it was my personal assistant, put my jacket around my shoulders and led me outside. Kate came to get me and I remember she was white and tears kept pricking her eyes.

Rick became conscious of eyes looking at him. Not just Dr. McMahon, but the others in the group. What had he said or done? Had he spoken out loud without meaning to?

"Rick, is there something you want to say?" Dr. McMahon asked gently.

Do it... tell them... get it out there and over with... share it, that's what this is for. They won't judge you. For God's sake do it. But once again his mouth would not obey the orders.

"No. Nothing."

CHAPTER FIVE

IT WOULD BE his fourth day in the Jennings Clinic, he thought as he lay in the narrow bed, readying himself for his next session with Dr. Friedman. He knew he wanted to share the events of 'that day' with the doctor, and tried to make some kind of sense of the memories that led to his breakdown.

Three nights in the place already seemed an eternity. It was still dark outside, but it wouldn't be long before he was reminded of everything he had signed away. Rick knew that he would soon eat a breakfast of granola with apple juice and talk to near-strangers, a stark departure from the warmth he had become accustomed to at home where the dining room would be alive with his children hastily passing through on their way out into the day, Kate's voice talking to his two sons like music to his ears. Or was the separation modifying his memories now...?

Certainly, none of the people he would be eating with this morning would be on their way out into the world, going about their lives with all the excitement and drama that came with it. He knew, on admitting himself to the clinic, what he was giving up. They were the two most precious gifts that life could offer; the joy of being with the family he loved and who loved him, and the independence of being his own man, making his own choices, living his own life. But, he reflected, it was only now in the presence of these two gifts' exact opposites – this loneliness and confinement – that he could fully appreciate just what he had relinquished.

Joel's account, the previous day, took him back to his own first experiences with bipolar disorder, the previous year. It crept up on him without his knowing what it was; and without his realizing just how bad things were about to become...

⌐⌐

IT WAS STILL months before the day of his actual breakdown, and his four days of bed-ridden acute depression came to a welcome end with Dr. Bradshaw's Lithium prescription. For some time Rick was overjoyed to feel in control of himself once more. He even sensed a new optimism growing within, despite the problems in his relationships with Kate, his sister, Rosa, and her husband, Andrew. But after three weeks on the prescribed Lithium, he noticed something closing in on him. It began as a shift in his perception of life from that which he loved and enjoyed to something that had lost its glow. And then it became a burden. The underlying feeling of dread in his abdomen that had stalked him for years returned with a vengeance. He had first noticed it as a longing to spend more time with his dying father. And from there it had grown, never absent for long. Now it was overpowering and within days he slipped back into the state of despair that he had experienced three weeks earlier. He felt powerless to escape it.

Dr. Bradshaw's response was to increase the dosage of Lithium, and it worked. For three more weeks, Rick felt himself again. And then he crashed, sliding uncontrollably into the gloom that he feared more than anything. His psychiatrist once again increased the dosage.

'Rick, you have to realize that you've subjected yourself to excessive stress for a prolonged period of time. You've taken on a lot and, let's be honest, it may have been too much. The relationships we've talked about – your father, your friends dying, your problems with Kate and your sister – they all affect you more than you realize.' She had seen depression many times and recognized it as a person's refusal to confront his own pain. Whether that person's vitality was exhausted in avoiding the pain, in suppressing it or in being controlled by it, made no difference in the end. 'I think your energy has been drained without your being aware of it. Most people deal with these things by expressing their anger, by saying goodbye to things that don't work for them. You haven't done that.' Rick was having trouble understanding the situation. *Why can't I just be happy again? It used to be so easy.*

The pattern continued. Each month, Rick would experience a state of elation, of absolute euphoria. He would make reckless business decisions based on an irrational sense of optimism: he felt as if he could conquer the world. It would be followed by a steady decline in his mood until it reached utter depression – a near total absence of energy coupled with a world that seemed to reflect a profound sense of isolation and dread – at which time he would voice his frustration to Dr. Bradshaw. Her response would be the same each time; a higher dosage of Lithium, while holding the Tryptanol dosage steady.

Eventually, the doctor told Rick that there would soon be little she could do for him; he was nearing the maximum dosage of Lithium. Her advice was to eliminate stress from his life, but he had already done all he could toward that end. In desperation, he took a vacation with Kate to the south of France.

His hopes for Provence gave way to further dismay once he hit rock-bottom after their first week. Maybe it was the gloomy weather, he wondered, desperate for a solution. So they flew to another of his favorite places on earth: Hawaii.

Still, he felt the dread growing within, relentlessly surrounding him. It was no use: no matter where he went, or how much money he spent, and no matter how luxurious or pristinely pure his surroundings – nothing worked. It seemed there was no escaping his uncontrollable bouts of euphoria and depression, these moods that took absolute control of him and overwhelmed any hopes of avoiding their full force.

In his frustration, he sought the opinion of one of Hawaii's top psychiatrists. What he was told shocked him.

The doctor welcomed Rick and Kate into her office and Rick felt comfortable in her presence. The couple described the cycle of the past few months and their attempts to overcome it. The doctor listened carefully, nodding her head, but saying little.

'And you say your medication has been changed several times?' she asked. Rick nodded. 'Well, show me what you're taking now.' Rick presented the two drugs. The Lithium was in a small plastic bottle and the Tryptanol tablets in a small box. 'And which are you taking now?' the doctor asked.

'Both of them,' Rick replied.

The doctor examined the instructions for each carefully and looked confused. 'That can't be right,' she responded.

'My psychiatrist prescribed both – this is what she's told me to take.'

'Mr. Dellich, are you sure that you've been instructed to take both of these medications concurrently?'

'Yes, absolutely.'

The doctor sat for a moment in silence. 'I don't know what to tell you. The two medications, at such high dosages, are incompatible for someone displaying your symptoms. I wouldn't recommend such a treatment.' Rick couldn't believe what he was hearing. 'As far as your condition goes, you're displaying symptoms of bipolar disorder – that's very serious – but if your symptoms have persisted, even worsened, the way you've described to me, this prescription should be modified immediately. It concerns me that your psychiatrist has not already done so.'

The vacation came to an abrupt end. He was bewildered by what he had been told and tried to find an explanation for Dr. Bradshaw's behavior. His condition was getting more difficult to understand by the day.

By the time he arrived at Dr. Bradshaw's office, he was in no mood for friendly conversation. He had touched down in Auckland early in the morning and, at 8 a.m., left his house with his cell phone, informing the receptionist that he would be making an impromptu visit. The confusion had grown into exasperation over the eight-hour flight. He was desperate to hear his psychiatrist's explanation.

'Rick, is there a problem?' Dr. Bradshaw asked as Rick entered the office.

'Why have you been prescribing me a dangerous combination of drugs?' Rick demanded, the frustration evident in his voice.

'Excuse me?' Dr. Bradshaw was taken aback. 'Are you making some wild accusation? Because I have to caution you — ' Rick's anger was greater than hers and he interrupted her, tossing both medications onto her desk.

'These two drugs aren't supposed to be used together the way you've been using them. I trusted you. I told you about my marriage, my child-hood, my sex life, my hopes, my fears. Why did you do it?' Her look was that of a thieving child suddenly realizing she has been caught red-handed. The doctor didn't answer immediately and Rick continued. 'I saw a psychiatrist when I was away and she told me — '

'What?' she shot back. 'You saw someone else?'

'Is there something wrong with that?' Rick queried.

'I am your psychiatrist, Rick!' her voice exploded. 'You are not to go sneaking around behind my back checking on my methods!'

'I had to! I've been up and down for months and you can't do anything about it!' Rick said, his arms waving in exasperation.

'Are you trying to tell me I haven't been doing my job?' she said, her eyes penetrating Rick as the anger overcame her voice.

'That's exactly what I'm saying! You never even mentioned that I could have bipolar disorder. Your prescriptions are dangerous! Why? Is it your way of finding the evil in me?'

'Well then, why don't we see how you do without the medication!' she replied, her voice now loud enough to force Rick to take a step back from her desk.

'Fine! Let's do that!' He stormed out of the room. It would be the last time he ever set foot in her office. It was the last he saw of the doctor for three months, until the day of his breakdown, when she and three others appeared out of nowhere and made their way down his driveway.

CHAPTER SIX

"M Y STOMACH STILL turns every time I dare to think of anything to do with that day," Rick, again in Dr. Friedman's office, told the psychiatrist. It was only their second meeting, but already Rick felt more at ease with the doctor, sensing the man's sincerity. He wrestled with his memories of Bradshaw, his fears of the misuse of the great power granted to healers of the mind always hovering on the periphery of his consciousness.

Rick had left Dr. Bradshaw's office for the last time with a gut-wrenching sense of hopelessness, not knowing what would become of him, or where to turn. His anger at Dr. Bradshaw provided a distraction from the feeling that he was lost in unfamiliar and frightening territory, and he soon convinced himself that he would soon be his old, happy self once again, now free of Bradshaw's influence.

He hadn't known, at the time of storming out of Dr. Claire Bradshaw's office three months before his breakdown, that her greatest wrongdoing had just been committed. Her treatment had been questionable throughout: the potentially dangerously-high concurrent dosages of the two drugs; her inability to gauge Rick's response to the drugs and adjust her treatment appropriately; her failure to raise bipolar disorder as an explanation for the extreme mood swings, all would eventually come together to paint a picture of a psychiatrist whose treatment was, at best, careless.

But it was her willingness to allow Rick's powerful doses of medication to be ceased with such abruptness, without warning him or his wife of the grave danger involved, that would forever haunt him, leaving him to ponder her sinister intentions. Rick would later discover that such a course of action could trigger suicide attempts and psychotic episodes.

"Those days leading up to the breakdown," Rick's gaze again found focus somewhere on the other side of the room's window, "I just wasn't myself. More of it came to mind since we spoke last time: a business meeting where I stripped all my clothes off; my elder son threatening to leave his school hockey team if I didn't stop ranting at him like a madman about Henry the Fifth from the sidelines of one of his matches. Kate would sometimes find me tending to my bloodied and bruised feet – I had taken to jumping off walls around the house, daring myself to go higher and higher. I don't know if I thought I was invincible, or if I relished the danger... I honestly can't understand it now. But I must have been going mad. Who does such a thing?"

"It's probably more common than you think," came the calm voice of Dr. Friedman, who had been listening silently.

"Even something as bizarre as that?"

"I've seen countless manifestations of mental imbalance, Rick," the doctor answered. "I don't say it to discount the uniqueness or legitimacy of your experience in any way – I don't mean that. I just want you to know that you don't have to see your behavior as being shameful or inexplicable."

Rick paused, letting the words sink in, seeing if he could sense what it would be like to begin to let go of some of that shame. It was too heavy though, too raw and unprocessed. And he knew there was more of it to come, more that he had not yet acknowledged in himself; it was going to get worse before it got better, starting with the day his life finally collapsed.

"It all just snowballed into those final days, those sleepless nights, leading up to the day I broke down. My family was powerless; terrified.

I was on a runaway train. We all sensed it, but were at a loss for help. Nothing worked."

Rick was quiet for a moment. The doctor waited, then encouraged him gently, "Can you remember the day?"

He sighed, and then nodded. "I remember how it began," he said. "What a day that was... I had a meeting in the morning. But I was in no mood for meetings, so I wanted to keep it short. We were sitting at a table outside at my home — it was reasonably close to the swimming pool. I began the meeting and, a few minutes in, a cell phone rang and one of the guys answered the call, saying that he would phone the caller back. I told them that I wanted the cell phones off — I wanted the meeting to be a brief one. So I resumed the business and, after a couple of minutes, the same phone rang. It's hard to believe now — I've always been so courteous, so polite — but I snatched that phone right out of the executive's hand and tossed it straight into the pool." Rick giggled to himself. "I still can't believe it — you should have seen the guy's face. He was shocked! And so was I. But I continued with the meeting and concluded it. Then I went back into the house to find my mother — I was really not feeling well at all.

"Steve was spending a lot of time with me, doing his best to cheer me up. And, that morning, I wanted to get out of the house — I wanted to go for a drive somewhere. So we decided to go buy some things from the supermarket. Just a short drive down the road. Steve has since told me that I looked okay — my eyes looked reasonably normal — people weren't staring at me like they sometimes had been.

"We got the groceries and on the way home I asked him to stop and get gas. He said he would do it on his own later, but I persisted and he stopped. It was the gas station I always went to on my own. He started filling the car and I wandered inside... all of a sudden, something came over me. I was convinced that I, ah..." he was clearly having trouble sharing the story, "I thought that I knew the truth about the Kennedy family. And I was telling people I needed to speak with the Kennedys urgently. I started writing something on a newspaper and told the attendant to see that it was delivered to the Kennedys, then I took out my wallet and started handing the other customers in the shop and forecourt hundred dollar bills. And no one wanted them! They thought I was mad, they wondered what the hell I was doing – but I insisted. I wouldn't take 'no' for an answer and, eventually, some people accepted them."

"Does that behavior – trying to rid yourself of money – mean anything to you now?" the doctor enquired.

Rick thought for a moment. "Maybe it does. Maybe I was tired of its importance… of its power…" he drifted off into silence, his eyes pondering the possibility.

"And your friend, Steve, how did he react?" the doctor continued when it was clear that Rick was ready to move on.

Rick felt a wave of empathy for his friend. He had put him through hell just as he had the rest of the family. "Steve saw what was going on. He tried to get me to leave, but I wouldn't. He tried to guide me into the car but I was out of control – there was no way he could get me back into the car. So he called for backup – two of the men who were still at my house from the meeting earlier, the one with the phone and another guy – and within a couple minutes they arrived and got me into the car."

"Did you go willingly?" Doctor Friedman asked.

"No, I put up a big fight. I lashed out and struggled. I hit one of them, far bigger than me, and I bloodied his nose. What a scene that must have been – three men in suits subduing this guy who's ranting about conspiracies, throwing away money, and forcing him into a black Mercedes…

"And then came the worst of it… "

⌐

'FORM A CIRCLE around me.' Rick was in the foyer of his home. Maria; his best friend, Steve; Kate; his twin sister, Rosa; her husband – Andrew; and Rick's two business partners were all there, as were a handful of close family friends. Two of them had witnessed the end of the commotion at the gas station and had followed the car back to Rick's home. All had converged on the home as they received word of Rick's state. He ordered them to form a circle and no one dared disobey.

Rick approached each person in the circle. One by one, he told them of personal grievances he had with each. He spoke of things they had done in the past, both to him and to others. He revealed some of their most personal secrets and rebuked each person there for the trouble they had caused him. No one spoke. They all listened silently to his assessment, knowing they had no option but to endure the unbearable episode until Rick was good and ready to move on to something else.

After half an hour of berating them, of accusations and tirades toward those dearest to him, he walked out the front door to the fountain where the water shot up into the air and then flowed from one level down to a lower platform. At that moment he felt transformed. He slowly walked around the lower platform, making the sign of a cross with his hands. 'I am Christ.' His family and friends watched in horror. 'I am Jesus Christ,' he said as he continued to make the sign of the cross.

And then a noise from the long driveway caught his attention. People were walking toward him.

Who are these people? I don't know them. This is my house!

He walked back into the foyer. 'Who let those people in?' He turned and saw the four people walking up the steps to his front door. There was a tall, slender man in a suit. Next to him walked a nurse. A firmly-built, stocky man with a serious look walked behind them.

I had better be careful. I bet he has a straight jacket.

As the fourth person came into view, Rick was stunned with alarm. It was Dr. Bradshaw. Rick stopped his ranting and did his best to assume a calm posture. He smelt trouble.

'Rick, we've come to talk to you. We are the crisis team,' the man in the suit began. His accent was clearly American. 'We've been called here to see you. I'm Doctor Bob Stanley.'

Rick looked more placated now. 'I'm okay now.' He realized as he said the words that he had no recollection of the past half hour. He was sure there was something about the fountain and people standing in a circle, but the rest eluded his memory.

'Rick, you're not okay. You need medical help,' the doctor said as he regarded Rick's troubled face.

'I'm going to the Mayo Clinic tomorrow – I'll be okay,' Rick replied.

'You're in no condition to travel.'

'Look, you can handcuff me to the airplane seat,' Rick offered.

'No, that's not possible.'

There was a pause. Then Rick asked the question that had been on his mind since their arrival. 'Who called you, anyway?' No one answered, because no one knew. Except Kate. She had called the team after consulting with her father. She saw no other option. Rick would one day come to understand it was her only option; without that decision, would the others have let his madness continue?

All were silent.

Maria came forward to the crisis team. 'Rick can stay at my home – with nurses, too. That might be easier for everyone.'

'That's out of the question. But, in any case, Mr. Dellich's wife is the only person with any say in Rick's treatment.'

'What do you mean?' questioned Maria.

'Under the Health Act, all authority in deciding on matters of mental soundness fall to a person's spouse. Only in the event of Rick being unmarried would you have any influence in the decision.'

Maria could not believe what she was hearing. 'But I'm his mother! Here's his sister, all his closest family and friends – what do you mean – we're powerless?'

'All decisions rest with Mrs. Dellich,' Doctor Stanley answered.

'But she's not in any condition to make decisions right now,' interrupted Steve. 'She's been through a lot and she may not have a balanced perspective.'

'I'm sorry, it's the law.'

Steve threw up his arms in frustration. 'This is bullshit!'

Dr. Stanley suggested that Kate meet with the crisis team. The rest of the family, in a state of desperation, asked Kate to include another person in the meeting. She chose Steve, gripping his hand tightly as though she would fall if he let her go. They joined the four members of the team in the formal dining room, adjacent to the foyer. The doors were closed and the family waited nervously together on the black and white marble floor, while Rick sat by himself on the front door steps, watching the fountain.

What the hell did I just do? Did I say I was Jesus?

The thought of someone in the house betraying him and calling the team angered him immensely. He couldn't get it out of his head.

What are they talking about in there? Are they going to lock me away?

Those six people, talking, controlling my destiny. My fate's in their hands now.

He looked around at the house he had so meticulously designed. It was perfect. Though it felt as if it were under invasion.

Will my family fight hard enough for me — or are they ready to let me go? Are they going to make me take drugs again?

He sat some more. Waiting nervously. Nothing to do but wait for the verdict.

'Rick, come inside with us.' It was Steve. They had finished their meeting. Rick's top priority was to stay calm. He knew that another outburst could seal his fate. They all sat around one of the ends of the table – the four members of the crisis team on one side and Rick, Steve and Kate on the other. Doctor Stanley did all the talking.

'Rick, how do you feel?'

Rick sighed and looked at the doctor. 'I know I'm not myself, but I feel I'm not a danger to myself – I'm not suicidal – I don't know what my family has said.'

'Yes, they've confirmed that you're not suicidal. Can you remember everything you've done in the past hour?'

'No. I remember saying I was Jesus. I remember telling my executives I was upset with them, and maybe my friends, too… but nothing else.'

The doctor spoke again. 'First of all, Rick, you are not well. You are definitely not well.'

'If I could just get to the Mayo Clinic – '

'I know the Mayo Clinic,' the doctor interrupted. Rick's heart was set on a miraculous recovery. 'It's a fine institution, but you're not going anywhere.' Rick listened. 'My colleagues and I feel that you should have to go to a mental institution immediately.' Rick felt a shudder pass through his body. 'But your family feels differently. It's a very unusual situation, but your family has requested to pay for twenty-four hour nursing staff to stay with you at your home.'

My family has still fought for me. Even Kate.

'Furthermore, your family has said that if you were to go to a mental hospital, people may become aware of your condition were you not in solitary confinement. From what we know, you are respected in the business world and this could be very damaging to your business career and your standing in the community. Have you understood everything I've said so far, Rick?'

'Yes, doctor.'

'If we were to grant this special request for you to remain at your house under twenty-four hour supervision, the opportunity would cease immediately if for any reason your wife, Mrs. Dellich, is finding your behavior unacceptable in any way. Similarly, if any member of our professional team, by which I mean the nurses who will be monitoring you, feels that you have failed to fully obey any of their requests, the arrangement will be terminated immediately.' Rick suspected that the team was taking a risk themselves by failing to institutionalize him from the outset; if anything were to go wrong, the team would be responsible for the decision they made.

Dr. Stanley continued. 'If you do not follow every request made of you, despite this being your own home, the deal will cease immediately and you will be taken to a mental hospital. Do you understand this, Rick?'

'Yes, Doctor.'

'Because you are not well, and by your own admission, you agree with that assessment – ,' Rick nodded, 'You will have to take medication.'

'What if I don't want to take any drugs because I've lost faith in the doctor here,' Rick said, pointing at Doctor Bradshaw. 'I took everything she asked me to but none of it worked.' Dr. Bradshaw didn't react.

'Rick, maybe you would be more comfortable if she were not in the room right now?' Rick nodded. Dr. Bradshaw left the room. Dr. Stanley continued. 'I will reiterate, Rick, that if you do not do what we feel is necessary for you right now, we will take you away immediately. Do you understand?'

He felt like a cornered animal. There was no escape. He could see the predator approaching, but there was nowhere to turn; it would be an agonizing death. His only option was complete surrender to what awaited him.

'Yes, Doctor, I understand. Have I a choice of medication?'

'We understand through Dr. Bradshaw that you were taking Lithium. There are only two options – Lithium or Epilim.'

'Why do I have to take it?'

Dr. Stanley sat forward with his hands resting on the table. 'It's like a transistor that's not in balance. The drugs will help the loose wires that are out of alignment to heal.'

Rick considered the explanation. 'What's the difference between the two drugs?'

'Lithium works through the kidneys – it's a salt. Epilim works through the liver. It's your choice. They both do basically the same thing. But you have to take one of them now.'

Rick thought to himself for a moment. He didn't want to experiment with a new drug when he was in such a vulnerable state. But Lithium had already failed. 'I'll take the Epilim.'

'Okay,' the doctor replied, turning to the nurse and the other man in the team to discuss the dosage. They came to an agreement. 'Rick, you'll be taking this medication regularly – three times a day. It will be supervised by the nurses and I will also be visiting you every day. It will take some time for your body to adjust to the Epilim. Do you understand what I've said – do you agree with what we're doing here?'

'Yes, doctor.'

'Good. Furthermore, as of today, you have lost all of your rights as a citizen of New Zealand because you are mentally unfit. This is important – it means that all contracts you enter into are null and void.' Rick listened in disbelief. 'You are now a ward of the state as outlined in the Health Act. We will take your passport, your identification and your credit cards. You cannot sign checks. You cannot sign contracts. You will receive a letter from the government confirming this officially, but it is effective as of today. Do you understand?'

Rick couldn't speak. He nodded. He felt a tear begin to form in his eye. The humiliation in front of his own family was too much.

Even if my family still loves me, how can they ever respect me again?

Michael was upstairs recovering from surgery on a sports injury – surely he had heard much of what had taken place.

Why is this happening to me?

The doctor opened his briefcase and handed the Epilim to the nurse.

'How long could I lose my rights for?' Rick asked.

'We don't know, Rick.'

'How long could I be a ward of the state for?'

'Again, we don't know.'

He grasped for a lifeline. 'Well, will it be days, or weeks?'

The doctor paused before answering. 'We really can't say.'

'Well, when do you think I will be able to book for the Mayo Clinic?'

The doctor gave a look of finality. 'Rick, we cannot tell you. For now, you have no choice. You are a ward of the state. Do you understand what I'm saying?'

Rick looked out the window at the gardens, the palm trees, the pool. It all looked so peaceful, but he realized that he was now a prisoner in his own home. 'Yes, I understand,' he said quietly. 'I've lost everything. I've lost everything I've worked for.'

'I've lost my freedom.'

"So can you remember what you said to the people in the circle?"

"No, not at all. That scares me – who knows what the hell I said? Maybe it's better that I never know."

"And do you remember what you did or said when you thought you were Jesus?" Dr. Friedman asked.

"No, I don't really. It's gone." There was a pause. "But what I do remember is what I wrote in my diary that night – after the crisis team had given me the medication and I was in my bedroom. I have a small appointment book that I carry with me in my pocket – I seldom write anything personal in it, it's just a calendar with my meetings and that sort of thing. But that night, I sat on my bed and I wrote three lines.

"I only remembered this when I happened to reopen my diary at the same page last week. And now it's so clear, plain as day: the only two things I care about in this life, and the two things that I felt were now utterly absent from my life. The same phrase, written three times:

"Love and Freedom."

CHAPTER SEVEN

R ICK HAD HEARD mention of the clinic's IQ test before, and that
night, as he sat in the common room with his new friends, he
was again encouraged about the test, which he had reluctantly agreed
to take when speaking with one of the nurses earlier in the day. He
was struck by the common bond between patients at meal times in
the dining hall, or in the common room, and was beginning to feel
a strong rapport with some of the other patients, despite their short
history together. He was welcomed with open smiles that immediately
warmed him inside. He loved to be with people and it was a reassuring sign for him to sense the other patients' implicit understanding of
his discomfort, as it was obvious to them that he was a newbie. Their
interactions were more akin to close, lifelong friends than to people
who had, perhaps days, weeks or months earlier, been complete strangers. He could sense the comfort that each person felt within the group;
there was no acting, no projection of a false image, and all were simply
content to be themselves.

Still, he wondered if he could ever manage the same degree of ease in
such a place. He wasn't sure he was ready to place his faith in a community that was fostered by an institution that he still regarded with deep
suspicion, and he still felt like an outsider in the place.

Rick again considered the prospect of the IQ test. Everyone else had taken the test, and it was usually an encouraging experience; most found the result reassuring and a way to reinforce a sense of self-confidence. It had been suggested to him more than once by the staff and he found himself in the uncomfortable position of making excuses as to why he didn't feel in the mood for it. But he couldn't dodge it forever: he woke the next morning in the knowledge that his appointment was at 10 a.m.

Why was he the only one resisting the IQ test? Was it because of Rosa — because he had grown up with a twin sister who outshone him at school, whose constant taunting almost convinced him that he was stupid?

I'm tired of passing tests. All my life I've had to prove myself, rise above others' doubts. And now, reliant upon this medication, they want me to prove myself once again. But who are they to say what I can and can't do? How can a single test measure a person's abilities? I've already proved myself on enough occasions for this lifetime. . .

⟵⟶

RICK SPOKE IN hushed tones to his friend, Steve, seated on the desk to his right. They were doing their best to hatch a plan for an after-school activity, which was proving more exciting at the high school as the two pushed the boundaries of acceptable behavior. St Peter's College, although somewhat sterile compared to the carefree convent, offered new potential for the eleven-year-olds eager to grow into independent young men like the seniors at their school. Gone were the days of sneaking home for lunch: the journey to the all-boys school would take him from the Eastern Suburbs into the central city. He found it easy to avoid any class participation from the back row of the crowded classrooms, Rick's entry-level year alone having 120 eleven-year-old boys split into three classes. He was aware that his first place win in the under twelve-year-olds' division of the annual long-distance running race had earned him a degree of respect from his peers. Though, as he sat in the back row of the room eager to avoid Brother Donovan's gaze, he felt a growing sense of nervousness: the lesson was taking the form of a class reading of the text under study. The order was alphabetical and William Carson appeared to have finished the final paragraph of Chapter Three of *The Adventures of Huckleberry Finn*.

'Okay, moving onto chapter four now... Rick, your turn,' directed Brother Donovan.

'Uh, Brother Donovan, Chapter Four's missing from my book,' replied Rick hesitantly. The teacher approached Rick's desk and leafed through his novel.

'Rubbish, Rick, here it is – predictably placed between Chapters Three and Five.' The class let out an audible laugh. 'Come on, stand up and do Mr. Twain's masterpiece justice. Just the first paragraph, then followed by Mr. Donald.' Rick stood timidly and stared at the clusters of letters in front of him.

'Chapter Four.' He cleared his throat. 'Well, three or four,' he began slowly and then paused. 'M... mon...,' again he paused. He skipped it and tried the next word. 'Run,' he managed. 'Al... alo... '

'Along!' boomed Brother Donovan. 'Three or four months run along!'

'Three or four months run along,' repeated Rick, 'and it was well,' he stammered, 'into the w... wine... '

'Dellich,' interrupted Brother Donovan, 'how old are you?'

'Eleven-and-a-half, sir,' he mumbled.

'Indeed. And you cannot read.' Rick felt his cheeks burn as the pulse in his neck began throbbing. 'From now on you will spend every woodwork lesson with our remedial reading teacher, Mrs. Duxton. We have to sort you out.' Rick hid his eyes in his book for the rest of the class as he listened to the words of freedom that flowed so easily from Huck Finn.

RICK ROSE OUT of bed. Before taking a shower he asked the nurse on duty for his razor so that he had it ready. She brought it to him, adding a friendly reminder for the crisis plan that all patients were required to complete on their first day. "Sorry, I haven't finished it yet," Rick responded.

"Well, we're waiting," she replied and continued down the hallway.

I feel like I'm back at school. What's the point in filling out a crisis plan when I haven't even learned anything from the clinic yet? Shouldn't I be doing it at the end of my stay? God, I wonder when that will be.

Why did I hate school anyway? People telling me what to do, when to do it, how to do it. Or what I'm capable of, what I'll become. . . not so different from this place. I'll prove them wrong. I've done it before. . .

⌐

'DELLICH! WHAT NUMBER is under my hand?' Rick's drooping head immediately shot up and looked straight ahead. The sleepless nights he had spent delivering milk to clients with his father were beginning to catch up with him. The number on the blackboard was concealed by Brother Cooper's hand, who could see that Rick had not the slightest awareness of the class discussion. He had already suffered one punishment that day so he decided not to push the teacher any further. The searing pain of the strap had become a daily occurrence – a ritual, even – since the discovery of his failure to complete homework and the subsequent routine checks. Rick's school day would probably feel incomplete without a visit to the Headmaster's office.

'Rick, you will amount to nothing. You will be sweeping the streets!' Brother Cooper, his suspicion now confirmed by Rick's silence, approached the back row of the classroom. The number under his hand was eight – damn it, the same number he chose yesterday! Maybe he should have ventured a guess, but then he suspected that a correct answer would only infuriate the teacher even more when the next opportunity for punishment arose. 'Hands out!'

Rick's arms were outstretched, his palms upward-facing. Cooper's left hand gripped Rick's wrist to ensure that the full impact of the tightly-stitched leather strap, a half inch thick, would be absorbed by Rick's palm. In one swift movement the strap shot out from the sleeve of Cooper's monastic robe and into his free hand, a maneuver that had earned him the name 'Quickdraw Cooper.' The 'switch', to which he had become accustomed at home, paled in comparison to the sting of the heavy strap. But then, Brother Cooper's handling of the instrument was exceptional in itself: for his first two years Rick had endured the wrath of Brother Donovan, but he wondered how much longer he could withstand the passion that Quickdraw Cooper was capable of channeling through the leather strap. After three licks on each hand, Brother Cooper returned to the blackboard and resumed the introduction to algebra. Rick's mind had already drifted to his ambitions for the future; he would certainly not be sweeping the streets, but he didn't expect the Brother to understand that.

It was a verbal test and Dr. Friedman had volunteered to take Rick's appointment. By the time he sat in the seat opposite the doctor, Rick had already made up his mind. He would not allow the clinic to pigeonhole him. He would not be defined by someone else's standards of intelligence.

His thoughts returned to Forrest Gump, a character who had immediately captured Rick's heart when he had watched the movie with his family in Hawaii, and who was all the more pertinent in the Jennings Clinic. He was a true hero; refusing to be defined by anyone else's standards and living his own life unhindered by what others saw as severe limitations. He was his own man and lived freely.

Rick once again noticed the reinforced, bullet-proof glass separating him from the clinic's gardens. *His mother was right. Life is like a box of chocolates.*

The doctor handed Rick three cards, each featuring abstract patterns in black ink, with the instruction, "Tell me what you see here, Rick."

He gazed at them in turn, trying to decipher the patterns, wondering why it was that he was unable to make anything meaningful from the designs. All he could see was strange, otherworldly spiders. Was he supposed to see something else?

"I really don't see anything here, doctor. I don't know what to say."

"Rick, how many states in the USA: forty-nine, fifty or fifty-one?" The first question was clearly designed to ease the patient into the test.

"Forty-nine." The doctor glanced at Rick, who stared straight back.

"Okay, where might you find the book of Genesis?"

Rick pondered his response. At least he may be able to get some cynical pleasure out of this. "I hear there's a new place on the internet – Amazon or something – they would probably have it."

The doctor made no comment. "Rick, can you tell me what a 'brook' is?"

It's a stream. "Sorry, I don't know."

"How many miles is the flight from New York City to Paris?"

Rick hesitated. At least this time he didn't have to pretend he didn't know the answer. "I don't know."

"What's sixty-four minus seventeen?"

Shit, maybe I had better give them one right answer, or else they may lock me up forever. "Forty-seven."

The doctor nodded, and then noticed a tear escaping Rick's eye. The doctor knew how Rick felt; he had seen it before and took no personal offence from Rick's reaction to the hospital's procedures. In time, the patient would come to life. He knew that much. "Rick, we don't have to complete the test."

Rick felt a sense of relief and comfort in the doctor's understanding. He wiped a tear from his face. "Thank you." He returned to his room and lay on his bed, staring at a photo of himself, Kate, and their two sons; four people who were nowhere to be found in the isolation of the Jennings Clinic.

CHAPTER EIGHT

THE LAWYER'S STORY continued to play on Rick's mind. He couldn't take his attention off the betrayal that Joel had experienced. It sickened him. And what worried him even more was Joel's return to the clinic. The disease was apparently a life sentence, even with the drugs that he had been taking.

Over the next two days, he was touched by the openness of his fellow patients and shocked by what he heard.

Scott was the second in the group to speak. Dr. McMahon appeared somewhat surprised by Scott's decision to open the second day in the group and it soon became clear why. It was not his first stay at the clinic. His private jet allowed him to check himself into the clinic when needed with relative ease, always maintaining his residence and business interests in South Africa. Yet, in all his stays with the clinic, and all the group therapy sessions that he had been a part of, he had never found the courage to step forward and reveal his own pain to a group.

It was perfectly acceptable to participate in the groups without saying a word. Patients were encouraged to do so until such time as they felt ready — for some it was the first day, and for others the time never came. Scott had resolved to step into the unknown and explore parts of himself that he preferred not to look at.

It was clear to Rick that this man was a success in the worldly sense. He was good-looking, athletic, confident, if a little guarded. In their brief conversation one night the two foreigners had discussed travel, Scott mentioning his love for the Mediterranean where he maintained a 120 foot yacht with a permanent crew.

Rick had been itching to ask what a man from South Africa was doing traveling half-way around the world to the Jennings Clinic, but the time hadn't seemed appropriate. On reflection, he realized that others may well be wondering the same about himself. As Scott began his story, Rick could see the man's anguish written all over his face, and his own breathing became more restricted.

"They shot her right in front of me – I saw her die." Scott soon revealed that he had witnessed his wife's murder. There was a sharp intake of breath around the circle. Rick could feel his head swimming. *I don't think I can bear this. I don't want someone else's pain on top of my own. It's too much.* Part of Rick wanted to get up and leave right then, without having to hear the details. His eyes met Scott's but he realized the South African was unaware of him or any of the others at that moment. It was as if he were still there, his wife's blood covering his hands, her murder taking place right then as he spoke.

"I held her as she died. And the blood – the blood sprayed out of her neck. I tried to stop the bleeding with my hands – but it was no use." His voice was exasperated, choking up. "I wash my hands constantly – whenever I can – I just can't get rid of that feeling. That feeling of the warm blood covering my hands – every time I look at them, I see it," he said, holding his palms in front of his face, his teary eyes glaring at the imaginary woman in front of him. "I see her. I see her blood."

To listen to the story was a harrowing experience. Suddenly, they were thrown into a world of violence and agony; they were grieving for someone they had never known. Rick could see that Scott was reliving the nightmare as he spoke; perhaps it was the first time he had talked about it to anyone other than a therapist, and each of them in the room had become part of it. There was no question in Rick's mind that Scott had loved his wife dearly; she had meant the world to him. On its own, his wealth and personal freedom rang empty. He was unable to escape his torment.

He had found some short-lived relief in cocaine, but ultimately it only worked to drag him further into the whirlpool of despair. It was a tragedy too horrific for him to confront.

How could I ever deal with watching Kate being murdered? How could I ever cope with such a thing?

Scott had revealed the tragedy in graphic detail, but had only spoken for a few minutes. There was so much left unsaid. Who murdered his wife? What of his treatment, his condition, or his life in South Africa? He hadn't even mentioned his diagnosis – was it acute depression? Bipolar? Something else?

Scott said nothing more. He shut down. Rick looked to Dr. McMahon. His face, though marked with a concern and empathy at what Scott had shared, was beaming. It was apparently a huge step for Scott, and it was not hard to understand the enormous challenge he faced. A couple of people in the group voiced their gratitude to him, but there was little that could be said in words.

The next patient to speak had immediately caught Rick's attention the day of the first session. He had commented on Rick's watch; it was a Rolex and he said he used to have the exact same model, and then began reciting the specifications and model number, all of which was new information to Rick. He wore a boyish smile that, though somewhat inconsistent with the surroundings, was nonetheless endearing.

A long, deep silence had followed Scott's story, and where Rick was traumatized by the last man, he was intrigued by the next.

He, too, was no stranger to the Jennings Clinic. From a well-to-do New England family, he had felt a calling to the ministry and voiced his utmost commitment to his church and his parish. He appeared genuine and sincere, and Rick imagined him being a very effective vehicle for his religion. His voice betrayed a strength that was nonetheless disarming.

But as he began pouring his heart out, the story took a bizarre turn. The root causes of his condition, bipolar disorder, were not singled out, but he talked in detail, his frustration evident in every word, of its disturbing manifestations. He had exhausted his share of the family fortune on countless luxuries: the finest watches, the fastest cars, gam-bling, over-committing himself on houses. Whenever he felt overcome by the highs and lows of manic depression, reckless spending became his crutch.

As he recounted the next stage of his downfall, the man's shame was palpable. His emotion was so unencumbered, so free-flowing, that Rick imagined he had told the story many times before. He had stolen money from his own congregation. The very people who trusted him, who sought his guidance, and who no doubt looked to him as a representative of the ideals toward which they strived, had been betrayed.

He struggled to understand his transgressions. "I don't know how I could be capable of such a thing. Do I have the devil in me? How can I ever forgive myself for such a thing?"

His family had tried to help, but had since abandoned him. He had been through the family fortune, through his congregation's assets, and in and out of psychiatric care. His family was out of solutions.

Rick's heart went out to the minister. He was struggling. Here was a man who aspired to the highest standards of morality and who had failed miserably. It was a shame that one of the relatively few positions of trust in the world should be occupied by someone who was unable to fulfill the expectations of the position. What did it mean that one who had tried so hard to embody those principles had failed more than those who had not tried hard at all? Were the virtues he was striving for unattainable? And what did it mean to those who looked to him for direction? Possibly they would be disillusioned, maybe they would forgive, or perhaps some would surmise that the answers to one's deepest questions could not be found by searching anywhere other than within one's own heart.

Yet Rick couldn't help but suspect that the minister was not being totally honest with himself. Was he really ready to change? Was he really prepared to give up his addictions, to resist them, and work through his pain? Or was he just dancing around the pain, acting out the drama of what he had done without ever really confronting it? His tears, his shame, had all been real, but they were well-entrenched now. There didn't seem to be any commitment to resolution, any commitment to letting go of it.

It was strange; this man was in the clinic to get help, but Rick worried that he was only fooling himself. The minister reminded him of a politician who, after many years of convincing others of his story, finally begins to swallow it whole himself. It saddened Rick, but it was his honest assessment. As long as he refused to admit to himself what he really wanted, he seemed destined to make the Jennings Clinic his second home.

He'll be back.

Rick arrived at the third group session apprehensive as to how the day may proceed. He didn't want to speak. But he knew that the time would soon arrive when he would have the choice of either stepping up to the challenge or postponing it, possibly making it even more difficult the second time. He wondered what he would say, how much he would reveal, how people might view him in light of his story. Would he learn something from revealing himself, and would it go some way to healing what he felt?

The whole issue of why he was in the clinic was still a mess in his own mind. Yes, Dr. Bradshaw had contributed to his going over the edge. But, he had to admit, she was a catalyst, not the cause. *So what was the cause? Why am I here?*

He observed that the South African and the minister were both reluctant to look their pain directly in the eye. To them, it was too horrible to face. What did that mean to Rick? He hadn't been through those terrible tragedies, and wondered if that meant that he hadn't earned the right to go crazy, traumatized by life. It was difficult for Rick to accept that, for him, it was not one terrible experience, but a thousand tiny cuts that led him to the same place in his head as a man who had seen his wife killed.

The next patient to speak carried an air of distinction and credibility. She was a pleasant lady, and when she introduced herself as a doctor, Rick could see it immediately. Indeed, she was the quintessential doctor, a picture of professionalism and, evidently, one of Chicago's foremost pediatricians.

What gave her away, as Rick peered deep into her eyes, was the fear. He could sense it. And as her story unfolded, he began to understand it: this was her last chance. She feared losing her daughters. It was her third offence and, in desperation, her legal team had advised offering to institutionalize herself to avoid a conviction. The judge relented, but the stakes had never been higher.

She was a wonderful lady with a deep, caring love for her children, and still in love with the husband who had left her. The behavior that she exhibited whenever she was unable to cope with her acute depression, was what some would diagnose as a form of obsessive compulsive disorder, though she herself made no reference to the disorder, instead viewing it as a kind of addiction. It was an addiction she had dealt with since her early twenties and that had escalated to the point where she now made a habit of stealing designer purses.

She was petrified of a conviction and the loss of any involvement in her daughters' lives. But it didn't seem to Rick that the addiction could be attributed solely to the stress of her work or a broken marriage; there was an imbalance that lay at a deeper level, the nature of which was anybody's guess. Rick's curiosity almost got the better of him, but he felt that he couldn't disturb the calm, poignant atmosphere that she had created in the sincerity of her sharing.

Joel, however, clearly felt differently. He asked, in his soft-spoken voice, if the doctor was aware of the original cause of her addiction and her depression. Was it something she could identify?

Within seconds, the tension on her face converged into a pained expression and tears streamed from her eyes. It was something too unbearable for her to come to terms with. The flow of tears was the ultimate way out; no one could be expected to talk in the midst of such visible anguish, and she said no more.

Suddenly, Rick felt an awful nervousness overcome him. There were only three people left in the room who hadn't shared, and one of them, Julia, seemed wholly absorbed in her own world, the only words ever to have escaped her mouth being her introduction, 'I'm Julia'.

Was it now his turn to speak? If he didn't, was he missing an opportunity to beat this condition? That was what he was here for – that's why he signed his rights away to the psychiatrists – to understand his condition and to be free of it. If he didn't step up to the challenge now, how could he ever expect to get through this? He would be lucky to be in the lawyer's or the South African's shoes: at least they get out of the clinic before they come back – Rick would be lucky if those damn psychiatrists ever decided to give him the key. And then what about Kate and...

"I would like to speak."

Rick let out an audible breath. It was the actress. He would be spared today.

"This is not my first time in a clinic," she said.

Oh God, does anyone make it out? I'm doomed. I am doomed.

"But it is my first time here, at the Jennings Clinic." There was no question about it; she was beautiful. Most people arrived at the clinic looking half-dead and Rick had observed one woman, arriving at the clinic the same time as he, as she gradually began to take an interest in her appearance after almost a whole week. It made sense that people who were grappling to hang onto their right minds became totally unaware of their physical appearance.

But not this lady. Even after turning fifty, she was glamorous, and Rick could scarcely imagine a man who would not be attracted to her.

Her eyes drew the attention of the room as had her perfume on that first day, the day that she had given a name that each person in the room knew not to be her real name. Why had she not used her real name? Surely there was no hiding the fact of who she was; certainly, Rick was not under any illusions as to her identity and he considered himself one of the lesser-informed celebrity-spotters currently in America. Was it the pressure that the name implied? Did she somehow feel that the person she was revealing in the clinic did not stand up to the image that the name evoked in people's minds?

She projected an air of confidence, happiness and serenity and maintained a sparkle in her eye. No one would suspect that she would have any cause to check herself into a psychiatric clinic. But, Rick wondered, would her story be an act? She was good at it – it was her profession. Is she simply playing the part of the victim, overcome with pain and depression, a repeat of the minister's performance? Or would they see the real person in all her vulnerability.

She began to tell her story in her easy, melodious voice. Rick couldn't help but be absorbed by her eyes and captivated by her movements – so effortless and self-assured. But beneath it all, he detected an ocean of regret.

Hers was a familiar story: she arrived in Hollywood with nothing but a dream and clawed her way up the ladder, believing that reaching the top would satisfy her every desire. She reached the top; the world was hers. For a time it excited her but eventually left her feeling empty. She said that she could feel herself gravitating toward the dark side but decided that she was strong enough to flirt with the highs on offer without being consumed by them. By the time that she was able to truly understand the path that she was choosing, it was already too late. Her acting career had taken her into a life that was too much for her to handle. The flattery, the attention, the excess had all taken their toll without her even realizing it. At first she had only flirted with the temptations on offer, convincing herself that she could savor the sweetness of excess and still maintain her perspective. With time she became powerless to resist the potent lifestyle that slowly consumed her, but it was only with the arrival of the autumn of her career, as her glamour faded, that she could see how far she had drifted from anything real.

Her addictions to drugs, alcohol and sex had already taken hold strongly enough to follow her from clinic to clinic. Rick could see her passing in and out of the most fashionable clinics on the West Coast, a victim of the psychiatric revolving door, and his heart dropped. As her story progressed, her voice changed, and into it crept an unmistakable sense of resignation. There was no doubt that, if she could have her life over again, she would choose very differently.

She revealed that she suffered from acute depression. She longed for substance in her life, to be with people who knew who she really was, who accepted her for who she was. She was tired of living characters and never living herself. And what broke her heart more than any of it was her missed opportunity to have what she yearned for above all: a child. Twice she had fallen pregnant, and twice she had aborted, postponing the life that she sought in the interests of keeping alive the career that she had come to depend on for more than just money.

In a twist of fate, she was no longer able to bear children. She felt she had missed out on one of life's most precious gifts. But more importantly, Rick could see that, to her, it was an experience, though not her own, that she treasured above all else and that was now out of reach. In a weak, quivering voice, she smiled as she spoke of the life she imagined, filled with tenderness, sharing and love. It was the life that was once within reach, but which she denied.

Each person in the room was touched. Rick, who had so successfully contained a huge portion of his emotions for the duration of the group therapy sessions, felt the current rising within him. He was moved to tears. The dam had held up under Joel, Scott, the minister and the doctor, but the cracks that had appeared with each story now gave way to a river of tears that he was powerless to stop.

The other members of the group tried to reassure her that it was never too late to be true to oneself; her life was still in her own hands. She was a beautiful human being. Her choice to expose herself revealed it clearly to Rick. It had been no act; she had spoken from the heart in all her need and weakness. Rick was humbled. Could he do the same? Would he reveal his own demons?

It was no longer a choice: he owed it to himself.

CHAPTER NINE

R ICK LOVED TURKEY. Specifically, he loved turkey wings, and Steve was proud of himself for finding four large turkey wings for his dear friend. Since his second day, when Rick decided that his taste was too particular to be accommodated by the clinic, Steve had delivered restaurant-prepared meals for both his lunch and dinner. The other patients in the common room had even taken to guessing his choice for the evening.

The wings were roasted and lightly seasoned with salt and pepper, the restaurant substituting plain mashed potato and coleslaw, with no dressing, for the usual accompaniments before neatly packaging the meal for pick-up.

Rick couldn't have asked for anything more.

But his mind was elsewhere. Steve was the sole friend of Rick's staying in Topeka – the rest had returned to New Zealand, the plan being for them to take over from Steve soon. While he felt sorry for Steve, who was having trouble entertaining himself in sleepy Topeka and looked forward to their twice-daily meals together as much as Rick did, he found himself unable to give his friend his full attention. His mind kept drifting back to the group and the people that he was so suddenly bonding with. It was almost as if the pain they shared was melding them into a single being.

"Something on your mind?" Steve ventured before his next mouthful of the lamb cutlets sitting on his plate.

Rick sighed. "Yeah, I'm sorry, Steve. There's just so much going on in this place — I'm having real trouble getting it all straight in my head."

"Can I do anything... is there anything you want to tell me about?" he asked hesitantly, unsure of what he would be able to do if the answer were 'yes'.

"No, Steve, thanks. But it looks like I may be doing enough talking tomorrow without going into it tonight — that's what I'm preoccupied with now. If you don't mind, it may be best if I just take some time to think things over."

"Sure, Rick." He was concerned. Rick had arrived in the clinic thin and weak, but after only six days he looked more gaunt than ever. More worryingly, his whole demeanor had deteriorated, not improved, in his time there. He looked defeated. Steve hoped that, beneath it all, the resolve that he had seen so many times in his friend was awaiting its opportunity; that is was only buried, and not lost. "Hey, mate, you know where I am. Call me if there's anything you need."

"Thanks Steve."

"I'll be expecting the lunch order tomorrow morning," Steve said as he stood to leave. Rick managed a strained smile.

Rick took a walk on his own through the ward. He would have liked to have gone outside, but that required a buddy, and he needed time on his own. The rules of the clinic became more irritating by the day. Inexplicable, too: of the patients he had spoken to in the clinic, he seemed to be the only one who had been required to sign away his right to leave at his own choosing. It didn't make any sense. The others came and went of their own volition. Was it because he was a foreigner? But Scott was from South Africa. Had his own family insisted on such a measure? Such a request would be just as puzzling. Maybe it was because he was a first-timer — most of the others had been in an institution before. *There's something to look forward to: membership benefits.*

But it was no time to speculate on the motives of the doctors running the place. Tomorrow, the group would look to him to tell his story. Sure, Julia hadn't spoken yet either, but Rick guessed that each one in the group shared his skepticism that she ever would. These people had honored him with their vulnerability. He still couldn't come to grips with the agony and torment that possessed their minds. It was a rare privilege to be invited in to such hidden layers, and he now felt a strong sense of duty in honoring these people's trust with his own sharing.

If he didn't step up to the plate on this occasion, he knew he would be severely disappointed in himself. It was an opportunity to move forward and it was obvious to him that this was the next step. And he would carry an awful sense of guilt knowing that others had opened up to him so bravely while he had failed to do the same.

To honor them would mean exposing the depths of his soul. Was it too soon? He could relate to what each of them had said and wondered what the common denominator was. He still felt that each person had withheld some part of themselves that was just on the brink of their own awareness, as if some pain were still too great for them to accept. It felt like each person, despite his or her openness, was nonetheless avoiding something.

Rick had to admit, there was most likely a lot that he was avoiding himself. There existed in his mind a swirling mess of ideas and emotions in which he was immersed, unable to make sense of it all.

Walking the limited corridors of the ward soon got old and as he entered his room he caught a glimpse of his gaunt face in the mirror. *Wouldn't it be nice to walk in there and tell them about Dr. Bradshaw. I bet that would scare the shit out of them. 'The whole thing's a fraud! The medical institution wants to control us!'* But he knew it would do no good. As much as he resented it, he needed the doctors; no one else was equipped to help him. He couldn't deny that he was depending on the psychiatrists to show him a way out of the mess in which he had become entangled. And that was it: somehow, he had awoken in this nightmare. How?

As he prepared himself for bed, he went back to the beginning. There was his father; grief; guilt. He felt robbed of time with his father, cheated out of the relationship that meant so much to him, despite his commitment to visiting his dad, Ned, every day.

Kate and the boys floated into his mind, and again he experienced more of that nagging guilt. He had let them all down. Despite his best efforts, he could never fulfill his responsibilities as Chairman and joint-CEO to the newly-public company without it encroaching on the precious time with his wife, his sons and his dying father. He had made time to visit his father every day; he always thought of Kate as his top priority. But no matter what he did, there was never enough time.

What went wrong? Nothing was more important to me than my family. I loved my work — I had a dream: to feed the body and, one day, to feed the soul. What happened?

⁓

EVERYONE SAID IT couldn't be done. The bacon, ham and small goods — frankfurters, salamis, sausages and the like — industry was said to be a dying one. It showed lack of growth, over-capacity, low margins and, to top it off, it was considered an unhealthy product in an increasingly health-conscious society. And that's what made Rick want to fight for a product worthy of the consumer's loyalty. He recalled the day that he resolved to bring a superior product to the market.

Rick stared at the food in front of him. The egg yolks, destined to be discarded, sat at the side of his plate — he had salvaged the whites, as was his habit, and now looked to the rest of his meal.

'Auckland must be suffering from some kind of bacon shortage, my darling?' he commented to Kate, sitting next to him in the small dining room of their two-bedroom apartment.

'That's two whole packets sitting there in front of you,' she said as she held a spoonful of fruit to Michael's mouth as he sat in a high chair. 'I removed all the fat before I cooked it, because I knew you wouldn't like it,' she added.

Rick examined once more the breakfast laid before him. 'But there's nothing left,' he replied in disbelief.

'I'm telling you, two packets. I removed the fat, and what you see is all that was left,' she said, still feeding her younger son. She no longer taught at the local primary school, but on occasion gave piano lessons at the couple's apartment. The instrument had been a wedding gift from her parents.

'I have to see it to believe it,' Rick continued. 'Do you have another packet to show me?' Kate retrieved a packet of the bacon from the refrigerator, handing it to Rick.

'Ah,' Rick exclaimed, 'I see now.' He held the packet in his hand and peered closely. Only a narrow space in the package's printing revealed a glimpse of the product; the rest was obstructed. 'They hide it from you, so you can't see what you're buying.' He looked again at the plate in front of him. 'Why didn't you go with a better brand?'

'That's the best,' answered Kate.

'No...' started Rick.

'It's the best. You wouldn't touch the other brands with a fifty-foot pole,' she said, eyebrows raised.

Rick began reading the ingredients list and winced. Kate could see that her husband was unlikely to be eating a large breakfast that morning. He stood and took the packet to the kitchen where he opened it. 'It's all water! This bacon is swimming in water!'

'Now do you see, honey?' said Kate. 'That's two packets' worth, right there in front of you. You won't find a better breakfast in Auckland.'

As he studied the industry, the rise of General Motors sprung to mind. Ford had been the established market leader and Alfred Sloan, as CEO of GM, attempted to overtake his competitor through the acquisition of existing brands. But Ford's sizable lead in market share persisted. Rick saw that Sloan's move to offer superior quality at the same price was what eventually gave him the edge: Sloan had studied his competitor's product, added extra features to his own, but charged no more for the upgraded product. Rick was sure that he could see a similar opening. After months of research, he was ready to share his idea.

He kissed his father's cheek, as he always did, as Ned entered the room. They sat together at the dining room table, enjoying a plate of Maria's *hrstule*, a Croatian delicacy. This is the way food should taste, Rick thought. Ned was onto his second cigarette by the time Rick raised the subject that had been on his mind for months.

'Dad, I'm going to start a new business.'

Ned pondered the statement. 'A new property?'

'No, a new industry,' Rick revealed. 'I have a plan.'

'Son, you are too ambitious.' Ned crushed the cigarette in the ashtray. 'You have a stable, lucrative business – three, even – the delivery businesses are still bringing in a good earning. No one could ask for more. You're lucky, and you should learn to be content.' Rick still felt uncomfortable with stability. There was something more that he wanted.

'That won't be the case for long, Dad. I'm selling the property business, I'm selling Dellich Products, and I won't have time to run the milk vending business. I'm putting it all into my new venture.' Ned was lost for words and took a sip from his teacup. Rick had spent his as yet short life building businesses through determination and vision. The audacity of throwing it all away on a dream bemused the older man; would his son never be satisfied?

'Bacon, ham, small goods. That's what I'm going to make.' Unable to contain the excitement he had concealed for months, he stood and began pacing the room. 'And better than anything else out there. There are too many players in the market, it's over-supplied...'

'Are you kidding me?' asked Ned. 'Pork products – a dying industry? And you already know that there's excess capacity – none of them make any money.'

'And that's why it will work! Because these companies are dinosaurs. They're outdated – their processing plants are outdated – they haven't upgraded their factories for a decade. Their product is shit! The food they make is not fit for the pigs they cut it from!' Ned looked perplexed. 'We'll invest in a cutting edge facility and that's how we'll combat their economies of scale. We'll be a lean, mean machine and twice as efficient as any of them. And our product will be the best!'

'Rick, I'm sorry, but the odds are heavily stacked against you. Your last new venture was the most difficult business I've ever seen, and you made it work. But this is by far the riskiest!' Ned urged, in reference to an earlier venture of Rick's.

'Of course this is a gamble. I could lose it all. But I can see an angle here. And, this time, I won't have any fallback plan. I'm going to use every cent I can find of my own, and then I'm going to take whatever the banks will give me. It's all or nothing!' He abruptly dashed out of the room, leaving Ned still scratching his head.

Food should be enjoyable, and it should be good for the body. It should enhance our lives, not limit them.

He intended to introduce organic foods to the market, but knew that it wouldn't be a viable product from a newcomer. He had to establish a respected premium brand first, one whose natural products were of superior quality, then he could expand the business to accommodate his vision.

Good, Better, Best
Never shall I rest
Until my good is better
And my better best

The words repeated in his mind as he walked Tamaki Drive, winding its way along Auckland's waterfront. *Naturally Best,* he thought. *That's what it will be called. That says it all.* The culture would be firmly embedded in the name: the best people, coming together to make the best product, and having a flow-on effect to being the best performers.

He shared his vision for the new venture with Andrew and Rosa, and they were immediately eager to be involved. Rick couldn't have been happier: it would be a family affair, and to bring such a dream to reality as a family unit was, for him, the ultimate.

Most thought Naturally Best would never make it off the ground. Many months were spent researching equipment, factory layouts and headhunting employees, both internationally and domestically. Secrecy was paramount; the established industry players would surely do everything in their power to curtail a potential entrant before it could even get started. The Best team avoided the standard industry architects and put out word that the large site that had been purchased was a planned expansion for their existing business.

The most cutting edge machinery had been sourced and brought together from Denmark, Japan and Germany, forfeiting any bulk-order discounts in the interests of quality. It was to be a relatively small factory, but streamlined, and with extra floor capacity to allow for expansion. Naturally Best had become a family affair: Ned supervised the construction, Kate and Rosa took turns in bringing lunch for the team and even Rick's grandfather, an expert mason from Croatia, supervised the laying of the drains.

Even once the factory had been built, progress felt painfully slow. The staff payroll was growing and overheads were mounting, but a product launch was nowhere in site. After six months of manufacturing trials, Rick and Andrew were still unsatisfied with the quality and refused to set a launch date. Each day, Rick and Andrew would meet with the production manager, George Holden and Chris T, the marketing manager, and other division heads. The board room, in which they met, housed an expansive, oval table, reminiscent of the round table at which all opinions were valued.

Rick had sensed his team's growing apprehension. As the underlying tension came to a head, they implored him to be realistic about the standards he was demanding of the new factory.

'Rick, your standards are too high. What you ask is not achievable,' Chris T ventured.

'My standards are not too high. Yours are too low!' he responded.

'No,' responded George. 'Ours are rational. This product is already as good as anything on the market, and things will continue to improve.'

Andrew and Rick insisted that more fat could be removed from the product and less brine added. They had included custom-designed smokehouses for the bacon and ham in the factory. Manuka wood, the Maori-named species of tea tree, was used to smoke the product to achieve flavor and quality superior to the standard smoke essence-injected product on the market. But the two men refused to accept the product before them as worthy of Naturally Best's name.

'From now on, this is no longer a board room,' Rick began. 'This is the war room.' The men seated at the round table looked tense. Parallel to the board table, three imposing bronze sculptures rested upon a console. Rick had chosen each for its symbolic value and had explained their meaning to his team. The elephant – the gentle giant, the one who uses its strength responsibly and whose stamina can see it through the longest of journeys. He told the team that they were plodders, not high-flyers, and that they would go the distance together. At the other end of the console stood the cannon, always aimed at the board-room table, representing decisiveness, strength and action. And finally, resting between the other two, the bronze scales, weighing up the wisdom of each decision.

'From this room we will wage our war,' he announced. 'We will fight for new standards!' Rick's comment elicited a reluctant smile or two from around the room. 'I'm Captain Kirk, this is the Starship Enterprise, and we are going where no man has gone before!' The exasperated faces in the room couldn't resist giving way to laughter. The development stage of the business was more labored than any had expected. Their trial and error experimentation had taken many months, not weeks. 'We don't want our product to be only as good as what's on the market. We want to become leaders, not followers.'

From that day on, activity at the factory was constant. The machinery worked twenty-four hours a day, except for the required downtime for machinery maintenance. The management set their alarms at various times throughout the night, driving to the factory and back home again to monitor the progress and issue new instructions. Rick continued to preach the virtues of perseverance as exemplified by Edison's invention of the light bulb, all the while feeling the pressure growing. Ned had taken to voicing his concerns out loud as more and more money was poured into the product development phase – he worried that they had over-invested and were going to lose everything. His concerns about the direction of the business were unsettling the team to such a degree that Rick sent his father home until such time as his attitude had improved.

But, in time, Captain Kirk could see that even the company's most loyal supporters' enthusiasm was waning. George Holden was unable to hide the discouragement written on his face; Chris T worried that Naturally Best would be paralyzed in the research and development phase forever. Rick and Andrew acquiesced. The launch date, which had time and again been tentatively set and then postponed, was cemented. Naturally Best bacon and ham would be in supermarkets on the first Monday of May, 1985. Rick pressed the factory even harder to reach the desired level of quality in the limited amount of time they had. He reiterated to the team that the product was good, that it had become better, but that it was still not the best that it could be.

Trial product continued to be dumped on the market without Naturally Best branding until the last week of April. Finally, Rick and Andrew were satisfied. Millions of dollars had been spent, and a good deal of it was not their own. The manuka-smoked bacon and ham was of a quality they had never experienced elsewhere. They had crossed into the final frontier; a new world opened up before them. Rick commended his team as they pressed on frantically with the preparations for the launch. As April ended Rick sent as many team members home for the weekend as was feasible.

He left the factory on Sunday evening and arrived home to Kate's cooking and his sons. After seven years in their apartment, the family had moved into a house that Kate adored. She could see that her husband was exhausted as he walked through the door and collapsed at the kitchen table.

'You don't look well, honey,' she said as she took Rick's hand.

'You know what's riding on this, don't you?' Rick told her as he stared blankly at the table in front of him. Kate nodded. Rick put his hand on Michael's head and the boy smiled up at him.

'I know how much you love this house, sweetheart,' Rick was looking at his wife now. 'But if tomorrow doesn't work, we'll be lucky to be living in a trailer-park.'

HE HAD SLEPT only fleetingly during his time in the clinic. Lying on his single bed he pulled the thin blanket over his body and reflected on his situation: here he was, a champion of natural foods, never budging in his belief that food could both taste good and be good for the body, putting sleeping tablets and psychiatric, mind-bending drugs into his body. At first, he had refused. But the amount of emotion and hurt to process, both his own and others', was making it almost impossible for him to get the rest he needed in his depleted state. *Hell, they've already got me on a drug cocktail. What's the harm in throwing a sleeping tablet into the mix?*

His mind returned to Naturally Best, the culture, the soul of the place that enabled them to exceed all expectations.

⌐⌐

AS RICK HAD known, the consumer was still king and the higher standards were recognized, the Best team scrambling to expand capacity by opening new factories and releasing new products. Everything about the company was different. Rick had devised an innovative scheme for providing lucrative incentives to their contracted delivery team. It was worth it: 'You're our shop window,' he would tell the truck drivers. He insisted on monthly accounts, prepared by an independent accounting firm to ensure their objectivity, as one method of monitoring performance. At the same time, Rick always had an eye on the movement of the labor, sales and capitalization ratios, often working them out weekly on the back of an envelope to ensure the most efficient utilization of their resources. He was aware of the potential for growing businesses to drop in efficiency and was quick to rectify any bottlenecks he could see developing: overheads had to be minimized.

He and Andrew met with each department manager every morning before commencing the day, always taking time during the meeting to review the Mistake Book, containing all of the reported inefficiencies from the previous day. Rick made a thorough sweep of the factory floor at least once a day, his over-sized stopwatch in hand as he timed new employees at their tasks to ensure they were improving toward the more experienced team members' capabilities. It wasn't unusual to see him operating a forklift or sweeping the floor to demonstrate the correct technique if a worker was not giving the task his full attention. He referred to himself as 'the office boy'.

Naturally Best earned a reputation for paying its team members the most in the industry and expecting excellence. If ever a worker became dissatisfied with his or her job, he was encouraged to request retraining for another role. The steady stream of applications removed any need for advertising vacancies and resulted in a non-existent human resources department, all hiring and firing, at whatever level, coming through Rick's office, including headhunting for key positions. Important roles in the company often went to women, a rarity in the industry. Many capable potentials were turned down, and often those with no experience whatsoever were invited into the Best family: the most important criteria were enthusiasm, loyalty and faith in the Naturally Best dream.

He dubbed the team the 'United Nations' in reference to its ethnic diversity: there were Vietnamese, Laotians, Middle Easterners, Europeans, Polynesians and more. Rick enjoyed the wealth of different cultures and beliefs and the way the people came together, reminding them at times that united they stood, and divided they would fall. 'All for one and one for all,' he told each new team member.

A committee of company staff was set up to aid employees in crisis. Team members were encouraged to come to the committee with difficulties meeting rent payments or escaping a situation of family abuse. Rick and Andrew personally funded efforts that the committee approved to rectify the situation and ensure the well-being of the employee, who would in turn repay the loan, in time, from his or her pay check without interest.

The industry players tried to cut them down at every turn, but Best outmaneuvered the opposition on every occasion. Rick recalled the invitation to join and lead the industry's trade group, which he declined, sensing that those who had done their best to tear them down on entering the industry would surely not make the best partners. 'The Cartel,' he dubbed them, and categorically refused to fail the consumer by joining with the established powers who wanted nothing more than to emasculate the competitor unnerving their shareholders.

Rick's proposed response shocked the team. 'We have to put word out that we're going broke; that we've overextended ourselves and are failing to make any money.' Andrew, Chris T and George looked at each other wondering if they had heard right. Rick continued. 'The opposition will think our success is unsustainable. We can use that as cover to strike. Their false confidence will grant us an opportunity to grab more market share, and all the while they'll be waiting for us to keel over and die at any moment.'

The three men sat in silence as they considered the proposition. Chris T spoke first. 'But Rick, we're proud of what we've done. What about our faith and belief in the company? How can we bring ourselves to tell people we've failed, when we've succeeded where people told us we couldn't?'

'We have to swallow our pride for the good of the company, for the good of the Naturally Best family,' Rick answered. 'It's a delicate matter.

We have to seed the rumor to key people only, and ensure that our suppliers are paid immediately. We'll do it in such a way that the rumor reaches the opposition — they'll think we're expanding too fast and unable to maintain our success — without unnerving our own team.

'We can't join the cartel — they won't be comfortable with us until our standards drop to their level. And if we don't take action, they're going to fight us with a united front that will be tougher than anything we've experienced so far. One by one, I hope to see the major players either merge, or close down. This is a time of aggressive expansion for us.' His kiwi accent changed ever so slightly as he invoked Churchill's battle cry, 'We shall fight on the beaches, we shall fight on the landing grounds, we shall fight... '

The high points in Best's rise flashed through Rick's mind. They expanded into Australia despite heavy resistance from the established players who were assumed to be behind the anonymous threats, sabotage and theft. Healthy eating options to meet the consumers' increasing demand for convenience foods were brought to the market: natural meat, fish, poultry, dairy and vegetable products. Organic foods, an integral part of Rick's dream, soon came into focus. Farmers were paid premiums to convert to organic methods.

But New Zealand and Australia were too small; they wanted another mountain to climb. Rick wanted to know that Naturally Best had risen to the highest standards demanded by any market in the world. He wanted to succeed in the toughest, most discerning market in the world, and one that, if they were successful, would provide opportunities for expansion they had never dreamed of. It was 1988 and there was one market that stood out from the rest as being willing to pay a premium for exceptional quality: Japan.

The experts told him to forget it: outsiders had little chance of entering the Japanese food market. And, if it ever could be done, it would without doubt require ten years of persistence. Rick had targeted the company, Roku, on the basis of its founder and president's pioneering vision for organic foods. He, Andrew and Chris T flew to Japan to meet with representatives of the company, but it would be difficult to convince Roku that a four-year-old manufacturer from New Zealand could be of any value to the conglomerate – a distributor whose presence was felt throughout Japan.

The relationship began with Rick's words: 'We are not as large as many of the fine companies that produce for you. We do not have a long history.' The five men facing the New Zealanders listened as the translator spoke. 'But we channel an enormous amount of resources into research and development; into new products; into new standards. We make products that we believe in. And we are heavily involved in developing organic foods. We have been told that you are also very interested in this area.' Rick, Andrew and Chris T found it impossible to discern any indications of approval or otherwise from their hosts. 'We feel that we have a responsibility to the consumer: to produce foods that are not only of excellent quality, but that are also as free of artificial additives as possible.' Rick continued to look straight ahead at the group before him as he made his offer. 'I mean no disrespect to anyone, but is there a product that your exceptional manufacturers have been unable to supply due to restraints of volume, cost or product viability?'

The Roku team returned later in the week to the New Zealanders with an item. The well-oiled Naturally Best machine shifted into a higher gear; the Roku project became the top priority and a huge portion of finances was diverted to fund the research.

Within a year, Naturally Best's organic products were being exported to one of Japan's largest food distributors.

Rick recalled his first encounter with Mr. Sekikawa, Roku's founder and president. He had flown to New Zealand to inspect Best's facilities himself before forging the partnership.

Rick felt an instant connection with the man. During their time together, they discussed their organizations' cultures and beliefs, and the Japanese man smiled as he told Rick he looked too young to be the chairman of a company. The older man carried himself with an unshakable composure, but Rick also sensed a warmth and an openness. At one of the tasting sessions arranged for the visitors, Mr. Sekikawa praised the quality of the wine he had been served and asked Rick for his opinion.

'I'm sorry, I don't know much about wine,' Rick replied.

'I'm surprised you don't enjoy wine, it is one of life's simple pleasures.'

The Japanese man appeared to be pondering something before he continued, 'Mr. Dellich, what is it that you do for enjoyment?'

'I love Naturally Best. And I love my family,' Rick gave a smile, and for all its innocence, Mr. Sekikawa seemed to notice that something was missing.

'To love is wonderful. But what is love without freedom?' Rick listened, unsure that he was following his colleague's line of thought. 'So long as you keep it caged, the spirit cannot fly.' The men both sipped their cabernet sauvignon. Rick could see that Mr. Sekikawa had almost finished his glass, while the red liquid he held in his own hand had barely been touched.

The deal was cemented on a handshake; no contracts were signed. As the meeting came to a close, the two kindred souls spontaneously hugged one another. Mr. Sekikawa's staff were shocked, having never witnessed such a gesture from their president.

Looking back, Rick could see that Sekikawa was giving him a warning. Did he somehow have a sense of the danger that Rick would one day face, even all those years before Rick himself was confronted by it? Was there something even back then which, had he been aware of it, he could have changed?

Ultimately, there was only one challenge remaining: the stock exchange.

Rick, Andrew and Rosa listed their debt-free company, retaining eighty percent of the shares. Naturally Best continued to expand into organic foods and the Japanese and Australian markets. The following year, Rick was approached by one of the world's largest food conglomerates that was impressed by Best's performance. Rick and Andrew liked the management and sensed their sincerity and capability. Continental Food Group made an offer to go into partnership with Naturally Best and, after long discussions and reflection on the issue, Rick and Andrew decided that it had the potential to be a particularly fruitful relationship, reassured by Continental's understanding of what made Naturally Best a success: the culture. The buyers were excited by the unique culture of Best and were adamant they would not interfere with it, often remarking on their love for the attention to detail they experienced in their dealings with Naturally Best, right down to their founding country's flag being flown right alongside Naturally Best's and that of the host country whenever they visited a Best-owned factory.

Rick saw it as a new direction to bring Naturally Best to the rest of the world. Best had grown to comprise over five hundred team members, Rick knowing most on a first-name basis. Continental Food Group, with a worldwide staff of seventy thousand, could open the company to a new realm of opportunities.

The global conglomerate offered to purchase Rick, Andrew and Rosa's shares, being the majority holders, for a premium and to pay four dollars per share to every other shareholder. The three declined the premium on the grounds of their belief that all shareholders be treated equally, persuading Continental to instead assume the brokerage fee for all share-holders, which customarily was deducted from the seller of the shares. The three majority shareholders also required contractual assurances from Continental that key Best management would not be replaced and that Andrew would remain a Director on the new board, while Rick would remain Chairman and Director. Continental agreed and, on May 5th, Naturally Best was de-listed from the New Zealand stock exchange. After two years of life in the share market, the share price had risen from a dollar forty to four dollars. Taking into account the dividend payments and bonus issues, it amounted to a return of three hundred percent.

Rick was humbled by the letters he received over the following weeks from investors expressing their sadness that the ride was over, but expressing gratitude for a job well done. He was overcome with emotion as he read of families who told him of their plans for the money — to buy a boat or their own home; pay off their mortgage; make additions to their house; purchase a business or make a pilgrimage to the Himalayas. He felt a sense of pride at his fulfillment of his respon-sibilities to those that had entrusted him with their savings. After two and a half years, the company's market capitalization had grown from 36 million dollars to 158 million dollars.

BUT AS HE lay in bed in the Jennings Clinic, the sleeping tablets failing to overcome his active mind, a sadness seeped through the nostalgia. It had been a sublime journey; his dreams had been fulfilled and exceeded. But it wasn't to last.

He remembered his father's face, glowing with pride, as he attended Naturally Best's first Annual General Meeting after listing on the stock exchange. But it was to be the only such meeting he would attend; within a month of the meeting, he had finally succumbed to the prostate cancer he had fought for years.

Watching his father fade away tore him apart, and all the while he was plagued by guilt over his responsibilities as Chairman and joint-CEO of a newly-public company. He felt that work had robbed him of precious time with his dying father, despite always managing to visit him every day. It was never enough. It always felt rushed; inadequate.

And there was so much he wanted to complete before his dad left the world. He had promised his father that the dream house he was building, the house that Ned initially refused to believe that Rick was serious about, would be completed within Ned's lifetime. It was not.

On two occasions, Ned had bought his son a set of golf clubs – the first a Ping set, the second Callaway – and accompanied the gifts with instructions to his son to take time in his life for himself. But Rick had touched neither; any day not spent at the office was spent with his family. Over the years, Rick had watched some of his closest friends pass away. It was an eerie feeling to witness people so young fading so quickly. Each of them urged Rick to let loose a little, to enjoy life because it could end without warning. It was ironic: all his life Rick had worked with the aim of attaining freedom. In a sense, he had succeeded. Yet he didn't feel free. Chris T's words to Rick in revealing his melanoma, which would eventually take his life, came back to him:

'All those years of fishing on Lake Taupo, ha?' The hole in the ozone layer, affecting the southernmost parts of the globe, was thought to be the cause of New Zealand's alarmingly high incidence of skin cancer. 'Hey, at least if I die, it'll be from having too much fun,' he laughed. 'But not you, my friend. You've gotta take some time to relax.'

The head of the psychiatric department at the Mayo Clinic had suggested that Rick was a workaholic. And then there was Kate. He vividly recalled telling her, under the Eiffel Tower, that he had sold Naturally

Best. Her complaint had always been that she was third in the pecking order: first came Rick's parents, sister and extended family; second was work; and third was Kate. It was an assessment he never accepted, but after selling the company, he was sure that there would be no doubt in Kate's mind who came first.

What happened to me? Was it already too late? His mind was foggy; scattered. It was exhausted and could offer no more insight. *Am I going to bore them to death tomorrow with my Naturally Best dream? I know there must be more to it than just work. If I want to get out of here, I have to keep peeling back the layers until I reach my core. I have to know my core. I hate this place.*

Sleep overtook him. He spent the remainder of the night in a state somewhere between waking and sleeping. But never at rest.

CHAPTER TEN

T HE EIGHT MEMBERS of the group filtered into the room that had become the sanctuary for their wounded spirits, a stepping stone that held the promise of transformation. If embraced, it could become the gateway to the beginning of a new era in each one's life.

Rick knew it. And he knew that what he took away from this first major opportunity for understanding his predicament would be directly related to how far he was prepared to peer into his soul. But what exactly did that mean? He couldn't get his mind around it. There was work, Bradshaw, Kate, his father – grief and...

"All right, then," began Dr. McMahon, before thanking the group and talking in a way that seemed encouraging, though Rick was only vaguely aware of the words as he did his best to get a handle on what he was about to say. Throughout his life, he had only done the most basic planning for any occasion that called for speaking before a group, preferring to allow the talk to develop organically. Yet, this talk presented a new challenge: he really didn't understand the subject matter all that well. He would be exploring a mystery, and in some ways would be every bit as much a passenger on the ride as would be the other seven people in the room.

Dr. McMahon had finished speaking and a silence settled in. It continued undisturbed for some time. Julia sat in her usual withdrawn position. Rick would be the next to speak, and everyone knew it. It was almost funny: each person waiting for Rick to begin; Rick knowing that they were waiting for him; and each person aware that Rick knew they were waiting, but adopting an air of aloofness so as not to pressure him.

"I think I'm going to speak now," Rick said, breaking the silence. He started to talk, slowly, recounting his dream that became a reality in Naturally Best. His ambitions had driven him since childhood when most of his out-of-school hours were spent supplementing his pocket money. The fruit-juice delivery business began in his first year of university, growing until the business, on top of his efforts in developing small houses, no longer allowed for lectures.

He had been working for as long as he could remember and hadn't stopped until he hit the wall. His father was always present in his story as the unheeded warning. How many times had he told Rick to slow down, to enjoy what he had? Rick recalled some of his favorite moments with his father: enjoying Maria's cooking together; the family holidays with Kate and the boys as well as Andrew, Rosa and their children; Ned's part in the house that Rick built for his family until the cancer left him too weak to be involved.

The group laughed softly with Rick as he related his father's colorful personality through Naturally Best's time of confusion when the management was certain they had fallen victim to industrial espionage. The opposition seemed to anticipate Best's every move and Rick had the offices swept for bugs, but found nothing. They were left scratching their heads until Chris T happened to pay a visit to Ned's favorite drinking spot one evening. He was startled to see the CEO of one of their competitors sitting at the table with an unwitting Ned and his friends, drinks in hand. Ned's fatherly pride had gotten the better of him and he found himself unable to keep as tight-lipped about Naturally Best as the secretive company would have liked. It hadn't taken long for the leak to be noticed by other members of the industry.

He remembered the day his father had told him of his cancer and then the long, drawn-out battle. Rick often accompanied his father to his constant visits with doctors, though the ensuing night would always be a sleepless one as the experience and his father's situation played on his

mind. He wore a smile on his face when he saw Ned and Maria for dinner, though he found himself unable to eat the lovingly prepared food as
the sight of his fading dad tore at him inside. As time went on, he noticed
the pain on Ned's face; he had refused to take painkillers in the hope that
it would prolong his life. Rick's sleep became increasingly fleeting and his
energy began to falter. But business pressed on.

Rick could scarcely believe his eyes as Ned sat with his grandchildren
for a photo one summer's day. It was the first time he had seen him in
shorts for months. His legs resembled toothpicks. His whole body was
emaciated. Rick had begun to notice the number of shaving nicks on
his father's face as the skin sunk deeper into his cheeks and seemed to
thin out. He found it almost unbearable to watch his father's life fade
right before his eyes. He knew Ned was proud of him and Rosa, but he
wanted to share more of his life's adventure with his dad. He endeavored
to complete his dream-house, his novel and the next stage of Naturally
Best with his father witnessing every triumph.

Always the voice of moderation, Ned was at odds with Rick's ambitions to see Naturally Best complete the full cycle of business development by floating it on the stock exchange, asking if they would ever be
satisfied with their success. But, to Rick, it wasn't about attaining a level
of success; it was about expanding the Naturally Best family, a unique
brand of excellence, and bringing it to the people.

The sixty-five-year-old was equally critical of the family home that
Rick envisioned. He shook his head in disbelief, incredulous at the archi-
tectural plans presented to him by his son, until Rick explained how he
felt about this part of his dream.

'Dad, what's wrong with enjoying the success that we've been blessed
with? I know it's not a normal house, but what if we experience this
together as a family — even if it's only for a short time? What if we build
our dream and get to live it? Isn't that what life's all about? Isn't that what
I've been trying to do for the past forty years?'

Ned sighed. He paused for a while and then let out a laugh of resignation. 'OK. I see. Why not, ha?' He smiled at his son. 'You know, you
could use one of those lawns as a putting green — put those golf clubs to
use. You were a caddy for so many years, at least you could give the real

thing a shot.' Rick smiled at his dad's joking. Ned took a sip from the energy drink that he routinely used. 'Rick, I'm very proud of you. But you'll never get away with this.'

Rick pondered the statement. 'What do you mean?'

'You've done well at keeping a low profile. But I don't think you can get away with this one. People will notice. The green-eyed monsters will get you.'

Rick still found it hard to understand what his father was saying, so he asked the question that he had been waiting to ask. 'Dad, will you help me build this home?'

Ned laughed again. 'I'll do what I can.'

With the public listing of the company, Rick felt a new sense of responsibility toward his duties as Chairman and joint-CEO of the company. He was now the custodian of people's hard-earned money and he could not bring himself to give the company anything less than his best. He was touched to see his older son, aged nine, checking Best's share price in the newspaper as he came home from work one day. Kate informed him that it was a daily occurrence, and he felt his heart sink as he noticed the yearning to spend more time with his family.

As his sleep patterns continued to deteriorate with the thought of his father's limited time, he found his energy levels sinking lower by the day. Kate's concern that Rick seemed unable to hear her when the two talked at night led him to see an audiologist to test for hearing loss. 'Selective hearing' was the diagnosis. Rick's ears were fine, but the pace that he was attempting to maintain was beginning to take its toll.

He saw more and more of his father. He would bring Ned movies to watch as the older man lay on the couch doing his best to feel comfortable. Rick made him popcorn – popped with a thin layer of olive oil on the stove top and sprinkled with sea salt – and the two sat together and talked. As time drew on and the new year came, Ned's weight had plummeted to such a level that all Rick could see was skin and bone.

Rick was still traveling constantly to Australia and Japan to push Best's expansion in the large markets. He felt a constant heaviness around his chest and he noticed that even breathing had become an effort. For the first time, he began to gain some insight into a feeling that had been lurking somewhere inside his abdomen and chest, but had up until that point evaded his understanding. The understanding surprised him: he was becoming resentful of his work and his responsibilities to the company.

As the feeling grew stronger he became overwhelmed with a sadness at the way he had to scrounge for scraps of time to spend with his father. Rick had already lost Chris T, George Holden and his long-time friend David in the past year, all to cancer. Life seemed so fleeting. So many wonderful people had vanished, and before he knew it, so would his father.

Every spare moment he could find was now devoted to seeing his father. Rick did his best to wear a cheerful face for his father through to his last days. He told Ned again and again how lucky he was to have had him as a dad, and how much he loved him. Ned tried to find the words to express his sorrow for whatever he felt had gone wrong, but Rick cut him short, telling him there was nothing to apologize for. Ned told his son how proud he was of him. The two talked and talked.

Rick noticed the toll it was taking on his mother. She tried in earnest to make her husband comfortable. She gently massaged his frail body and attempted to find food that he could enjoy, as the drugs affected his taste more and more. Rick noticed his father's temperament changing as the discomfort became unbearable. Minor details became major irritations. He became paranoid about a sun spot on his hand that would possibly pose a potential threat in another decade. It was something that Rick would find difficult to understand until he was confronted by his own challenges.

One calm, March morning as he got ready to leave his home for Best, he received a phone call on his home line while the sun was still creeping over the city. He feared the call would bring news of his father's condition deteriorating further. The blood transfusions that had afforded him temporary energy boosts were now almost completely ineffective, and his mother had told him that the morphine dosages were being raised every two days. Ned had been in the hospital for two weeks, but was now back at his home. Maria told Rick of his father's request: 'Not here. Let me die at home.'

'Honey, it's for you. Someone from the *Sunday Star*,' Kate handed the phone to Rick.

'Mr. Dellich, I'm Sandra Nelson from the Sunday Star — I've been trying to reach you at your office for some time now,' she said as she cut quickly to the chase. 'I'm writing a piece on the house you're building and would very much like an opportunity to interview you.'

Rick's head ached from another sleepless night. 'Ms. Nelson, I'm sorry, I would really prefer if we could do this some other time. I have a lot happening right now,' Rick answered.

'So do we all, Mr. Dellich. But I think it would be in your interests to grant me an interview,' she insisted.

Rick explained it as simply as he could. 'My father's very ill. He doesn't have long, and I'm doing my best to spend time with him before he passes away.'

She was undeterred. 'I'm writing this article with or without your opinion, and if you want to give me the green light to write without your comment, go right ahead.'

Rick thought for a moment and sighed heavily, 'OK. How about I p.m. at my home?'

'Thank you, I'll see you this afternoon.'

Rick arrived home to find the journalist and a photographer waiting for him at his driveway.

'Mr. Dellich, would you mind if we take your photograph?' she asked as they approached the front door.

'I'm sorry, please, no photographs.'

'Yes, I've noticed you're camera-shy,' she said as they went to take their seats around the coffee table. 'You don't grant interviews. In fact, no one seems to know anything about you.' Rick listened passively, unable to stop thinking about his father, confined to his bed, awaiting death. 'You seem to be a man who's hiding behind a pillar. What is it that you have to hide, Mr. Dellich?'

He was taken aback by the question. 'I don't have anything to hide — I just want to quietly get on with my life.'

'Well, you must have squashed a lot of people to get where you are,' she said bluntly.

'We're not all like that,' he responded. 'I like to think that I've been a reasonable human being and I've worked extremely hard.'

'It seems that you're building an enormous house,' she continued. 'I would appreciate it if you could tell me as much as possible about the house.'

Rick paused. 'We're building a dream home. I get a lot of enjoyment from being with the people I love. What we do in our private lives is our business, no one else's.'

'Well, tell me a bit about it. For instance, we've been told it has extensive garaging – can you elaborate on that?'

'Look, I don't really want to get into this. My father is very ill – he's dying. Can we at least leave this until sometime after Easter? I'll guarantee you a real interview for that time.'

She was unreceptive to the offer. 'I'm sorry, but I need this now. I need this piece to get printed soon – it's my work.'

'Well,' Rick answered, 'If it's a question of your being paid for your professional services, I would be happy to compensate you for the delay in payment from submitting the piece in a couple of weeks. It's just because of everything that's going on right now: I'm trying to fulfill my obligations of being an officer of this public company and then reserving every piece of spare time for my father. This interview is robbing me of time to spend with him.'

'I don't want money, I want this article to be printed.'

Rick sat back in his seat and examined the woman's expression for some time. 'It sounds to me like there's something else motivating you. What is it?' The woman made no reply. 'Well, I was hoping to convince you to exercise some restraint in our hour of need, but I can see that your mind is already made up. This interview is over.'

Rick drove to his father's house. There was a nurse standing beside the bed. The morphine drip in Ned's chest was now releasing a constant stream and his consciousness was fading. Rick took his father's hand and looked down upon his sunken face.

'Dad, it's me, Rick.' His father's hand was limp. 'I love you so much, Dad. I'm so proud of you.' Rick's voice was barely louder than a whisper. The nurse had told him that Ned was aware of what he was saying. 'I'm so lucky that you inspired us to live life. Thank you, Dad. I'll always try to live up to what you taught us.'

Rick closed his eyes and held his father's hand to his face. 'I love you, Dad.' He knew that his father had heard him.

Rick left the bedroom and found Maria waiting for him outside. Her eyes held Rick's and he could feel the love emanating from his mother as she smiled. The two sat together on the couch, but not a word was spoken.

The phone rang. Maria answered and gestured to Rick for him to take it.

'Rick, I'm sorry to track you down like this, but I thought you would want to know right away.' It was the project manager from the house building site.

'Go ahead,' Rick said.

'People have been turning up all afternoon trying to take photos – they just walked right past the 'No Trespassing' signs. We threw them off the property right away.' Rick just listened. 'But, I'm sorry to say, I think they took photos from the neighbors' property. They had consent so we couldn't stop them. And later, it seemed like a helicopter flew over.'

'Thanks for letting me know.'

'I'm sorry, Rick.'

Rosa and Andrew arrived shortly after. They, Rick and Maria stayed together well into the night, spending time at Ned's side and sitting together in the living room. Others would stop by at various times bringing food and flowers and checking in on Ned.

The following day, Easter Sunday, Rick continued to talk to Ned as he held his hand closely. He told him of the wonderful experiences they had shared together. And he told him how much he was going to miss him.

Early on Monday morning, Rick sat by the bed with all of the close family. Ned's breathing had become labored and heavy. Rick could see his father was slipping away.

Then his face took on a sense of peace, and he died.

The following week, Rick found himself stripped of the comforting cloak of anonymity he had always enjoyed. The front page of New

Zealand's largest circulating Sunday publication was devoted to a photo of the partially completed house he was building and an article speculating on its intricacies. Next to it was a photo of Rick and an article describing an attempt by him to bribe the author of the piece.

What surprised Rick most was the speed with which the news traveled. By the end of the day he had received calls from friends in Singapore commenting on the house and his apparent success with Best.

He drove to his father's grave. The engraving on the tombstone had not been finished, and a mound of dirt still covered the site.

'Dad, you're right,' he said as he watched the sun setting behind Auckland city. The early autumn air was still warm on his skin. 'I didn't get away with it.' It wouldn't be the last time he would visit his father.

The Board of Directors implored Rick and Andrew to disclose their earnings publicly in order to clear up any confusion: the law did not require public companies' officers to disclose their earnings, and it was likely that the market was assuming the worst.

But Andrew and Rick refused to reveal their earnings from Best on other people's terms, even though the truth could not have been any more beneficial to their credibility: they were rewarded on the same basis as all shareholders – no severance packages, no golden parachutes, no personal expense accounts and a salary of only a dollar a day.

They preferred to hold off revealing any of their personal details until, two years later, they had sold the company. Once again, Rick saw himself, this time pictured with Andrew, on the front page of the newspaper, shown in a decidedly different light from his last appearance. The heading read, 'Joint-CEOs only received raise in leap year.' It was true that the two always felt they had earned their weekly pay check.

"IT WAS SUPPOSED to be the end of my working life," Rick said to the group, who had listened intently to his recollection, as he mentioned his and Andrew's decision to sell Naturally Best after two years on the stock exchange. "I felt so guilty for not spending more time with my dad. And for not having enough time for Kate, too. I couldn't sleep. My doctor prescribed me sleeping tablets, but they made no difference. So I started seeing a psychiatrist. We talked about my dad, about work, about

Kate... the psychiatrist gave me medication to help with anxiety... and later depression. To tell you the truth, I think she did a pretty shitty job, but I won't get into that.

"The thing is, it wasn't the end of my working life. Andrew and I stayed involved with Best's new owners until it turned sour and they managed to degrade the company into mediocrity. It's all but disappeared now. It was sad to watch the soul of the company vanish before our eyes as the culture that helped it thrive gradually faded.

"So it was supposed to be a time for family. Andrew, Rosa and I invested in property and other businesses, but there was always someone asking for advice or assistance. The phone never stopped ringing and it seemed that nothing had changed. My psychiatrist told me that the habit of working compulsively had become too ingrained for it to just melt away with a change in my circumstances. It was true that my workload was nowhere near as demanding as it had been for many years, but she said that I was still in the mode of trying to fix everything – of seeking solutions for every situation. I had acquired so much momentum that it was difficult to stop; my mind always busy and never at rest. No matter what I did, no matter how relaxing an environment I tried to create, I never felt rested. She told me that the years of neglecting myself and my personal life were catching up with me, and it was time for me to change. I tried, I really did." He wanted to blame Dr. Bradshaw for her part in it, but he knew it was not the right setting. And as the words left his mouth he realized the simple truth in her advice. If he had been able to change earlier, would he had to have taken her careless prescription in the first place? He no longer knew anything for certain.

"We relocated to Australia for a short time – it was part of wanting to start a new life with my family. But it didn't work out. I was already too far gone. My energy was low and... no matter what I did, I felt an ache inside my body, like a broken heart. Wherever I went, I seemed to carry an emptiness with me."

The group remained silent, some of them nodding very slowly as if coming to terms with what Rick was feeling, all of their eyes resting softly on Rick. His face was drained and he paused for a while. He had been talking for an hour. Rick could feel the rest of the group right there with him, their hearts reaching out to him. He knew what it was to give this feeling of compassion and it was something that revealed itself palpably amid the integrity of each person's story.

But to be on the receiving end of such a powerful energy was almost overwhelming; it was easier to shrink away from the love that emanated from those around him, despite his deep longing for such an all-accepting love. Accepting that gift from the others in the room was a challenge in itself. He felt as if he were being held by caring hands, reassuring him that it was safe to travel deeper into the pain so frightening in its appearance. He felt comforted.

"I wasn't in a good state. But Kate —," his voice caught, "she didn't give me the love I needed. I don't know, maybe she couldn't anymore, I don't really blame her," he said shaking his head, the room beginning to blur in his moistening eyes. "And then... I know it wasn't just work, there's no way it was just work... there was more, I just can't see it." Something was rising up inside of him, and all he could feel was the power of it that seemed to be amplified by the force of the group's nurturing presence. "And I feel like the ones I love the most have been trying to destroy me."

He immediately stopped as he realized what he had said. Rick was shocked. How could he say such a thing — it made no sense. *Oh my god, are the drugs talking now? What are they making me say?*

Rick sat there, bemused, running the sentence over in his mind. The whole feeling of the room seemed to revert to something more normal. The people were still right there with him, looking with calm eyes, listening intently, but he somehow felt different. His own words seemed to have shocked him out of whatever it was he had felt so strongly. Something had happened, but he couldn't say what. Regardless of the sudden change he felt, he had still told all of his story. He had said it all as best he could, to the best of his understanding, despite still not being able to grasp it himself.

"Thank you," he said with a nod as he glanced upward at his friends. Some had glistening eyes, and all of them seemed to emit a kind of gratitude and a hint of a smile that extended from the depths of their being. Again, he knew the sensation, just not from the receiving end: to watch a person open so innocently, without reserve, was an uplifting experience. It was one of those rare moments, unsurpassed in beauty, in which life revealed itself in its purity.

Before anyone could begin to wonder what would happen next, an unfamiliar voice made itself heard. "I want to speak." It was barely a whisper, but nothing more was needed in the absolute stillness of the room. Julia didn't move her head or her eyes, still trained on the ground in front of her, but a determination shone through.

Rick could feel his pulse, still recovering from his own time in the spotlight, pounding away in anticipation of what the next minutes would hold. The breathing of the group members was all he could hear as everyone awaited Julia's next words.

Her face was impossible to read. Surely, she was swimming in a cocktail of psychiatric drugs – that much was clear from her eyes. It was difficult to infer her age: anywhere from her twenties to forties would be a viable guess, as whatever she had experienced in her life had taken a toll on her physically as well as psychologically, each movement she made appearing to wrestle against the strain that had accumulated over the years.

"I'm tired of it all," she began in a whisper. "I'm tired of carrying all this crap around my whole life." The tension in her face was painful to look at. "I've tried to escape it, but I can't. I've tried to take my own life, but here I am, and nothing's changed. I'm still in this place, taking medication, trying to find a way out, but it never works.

"No matter what I do, or where I go, I can't get the image out of my head. It haunts me. I can't escape it – I can't escape him, dammit," she said, her hands jerking in exasperation. "My – my *father*," she said the word with such disdain that Rick's body jolted, "forced himself on me as a child. As a child and a teenager – he came into my room, drunk, and he had sex with me. I can still smell his goddamn drunken breath." Anger crept into her voice as it took on a frightening tone. "How could he do that! How could he do that to his daughter! That was me! That was me that he destroyed and cursed for the rest of my life."

Her anger demanded to be heard as it took command of the situation. Her voice took on a new strength and identity. "I cried out for help but they didn't believe me. And then, one day, my mother found out. And he blamed the alcohol – he hid behind the alcohol. He didn't stop. He crept into my room for his short-lived pleasure while I lost myself. They didn't even stop him!" The raw pain that had sat dormant for so many years suddenly erupted.

"But he knew what he was doing – believe me, even though they don't want to see it – he knew what he was doing alright. That's why he drank – it was his excuse to come into my room and have his way with me. His alibi. And they never even stopped him! How could he do that!" She spoke it with such rage that the sound cut through Rick's body and sent shivers through his spine. It was an abrasive sound, the sound of pure, free-flowing pain.

Then the words turned to noise. Tears streamed from her eyes as she pressed her hands tightly against her face. The sound of her cries filled the room and rang in their ears. There was nothing left to hinder the torrent of energy that flowed from her in noises that sounded more animal than what was usually understood as human; yet Rick felt as if what he was witnessing was more fundamentally human than he, or anyone else, would choose to experience. His own restraints gave way and he felt his heart open, his cheeks wet with tears. What Julia was experiencing was felt, in some part, by every person in the room.

It continued for minutes until the intensity of her cries died down to a whimper. Her body heaved and everyone in the room felt the impulse to reach out, to hug her, to offer whatever they could. They longed to hold her and show her that she was not alone; that who she was was more beautiful than she could imagine. But they knew that it was something that Julia was unable to accept. She had cut herself off from all those pieces that were too agonizing to bear until there was nothing left.

"I've been here three years. I feel like I'll never be free." Her voice had returned to a barely audible whisper. Rick yearned to tell her that she would be okay; she would make it.

And then something began to take hold of him inside. A panic made itself known and grew with incredible speed until all Rick could feel was an awful sense of alarm. What was it? She had said something, but the words had floated through his mind, his full attention absorbed in Julia's experience.

'Three years.' He heard her words again in his head. *Three years? I've only been here a week. Three years!* The room, still focused on Julia, was deathly still, but Rick was now itching to leave. They sat for a few more minutes, no one saying a word, until it was clear that Julia had settled and had no more to say. Then movement began and there were soft-spoken words as each person expressed, as honestly and tenderly as they could, their heartfelt feelings for Julia. They wanted to reach out to her, but knew that too open an expression would not be received in the spirit in which it was intended. She barely said a word. Neither did Dr. McMahon, who was apparently stunned by the experience.

Now outside, Rick headed straight for the head psychiatrist's office, the fragility of the group session replaced with terror. His time at the Jennings Clinic was over; he would tell the doctors he was ready to leave. He would not fall into the trap of staying in the ward forever. He only had so much time left before he was institutionalized. He would save himself before it went any further.

CHAPTER ELEVEN

D OCTOR BURKE WAS seated at his desk as Rick was welcomed into the room.

"Rick, a pleasure to see you. Are you here to deliver your assignment?"

Rick struggled to calm himself, knowing that he would have to make a good impression if he were to succeed in his request. "Actually, Doctor, I was hoping to make an appointment to talk with you at some stage if it's not too much trouble."

"Anything that we can talk about now? I'm not due at the next class for another twenty minutes."

"Well, sure – why not," Rick answered.

"Take a seat. What's on your mind?"

"I wanted to let you know that, during my stay here at the Jennings Clinic, I have learned a great deal about myself, my condition and my treatment."

"Well, I'm happy to hear that you're finding your time here to be of value," the doctor smiled.

"Yes, it's been an invaluable experience for me and I feel strongly that I'm ready to return to my life now," Rick said with confidence, certain that the doctor would understand his position.

The doctor didn't speak immediately. "Rick, you've only completed your first week here." Rick shifted uneasily in his seat. "You've just begun to settle in. Don't you think a little more time could be of benefit to you?"

"How much time?"

Dr. Burke hesitated.

"How much longer do you think, Doctor. A month? More?" Rick attempted to mask his concern, but he was in no state to be able to deceive a psychiatrist.

The doctor looked at the man sitting opposite him, his face a picture of anxiety, and did his best to brush aside the question. "Why don't we just see how it goes, Rick."

See how it goes! So I can make this place my second home like every other goddamn victim of the psychiatric institution in this place? So I can stay here for three years!

Rick sat motionless, brooding over his lack of autonomy. What could he do to escape? The situation was hopeless, he concluded, as he stared out of the reinforced glass window. Regardless of how much he pleaded with the staff, he knew they would only release him on their terms, not his, and that the more desperate he appeared, the longer they would make him stay. He had truly become a prisoner.

Rick could feel the anger building but he managed to control himself. He was left with no choice; arguing would only worsen his position. It was a no-win predicament. He made it known to the doctor that he was unhappy with the situation and that he wished to leave immediately, then left the office for his room.

He found himself in the unbearable but not uncommon position of having to conceal what it was that he yearned for most in the interest of increasing his likelihood of receiving it. He had been at the Jennings Clinic for seven days, eight hours and fifteen minutes, and he was convinced that he had served his time. He looked around the tiny room, little more than a cell. How long would it be a substitute for home? He couldn't bear to think about it.

There was a knock on his door, and before he could reply the head nurse had walked in. She smiled at Rick but saw that the patient was visibly disturbed. Rick was fuming inside but did his best to hide it.

"So, Rick, how's everything going? Are you settling in alright?" she asked innocently. The absurdity of Mrs. Morse's entering his room immediately after a confrontation with Dr. Burke purely out of coincidence was not lost on Rick, but he played along.

"Actually, I'm not," he replied. "I just had words with Dr. Burke. I want to leave. I'm ready to leave this place."

"Well," she began in a conciliatory voice, "I can see why you might feel that way, being away from your family, in a different environment. I can understand it." Her tone irritated him: it seemed to soothe Rick's aggravation to some degree, but he wished it weren't so. He had every right to be angry. "But Rick, what's the harm in taking some time out for yourself? Taking some time to really get to know what's going on inside, understanding what led you to this place to begin with."

"I know," he replied, "I've gotten a lot out of this experience. But I feel that I'm ready to leave now." Rick could feel his nerve ends shrieking and he worried that he was shaking all over.

"Rick, possibly you've worked very hard for most of your life, never taking time out for yourself – always on the go." He couldn't disagree with her. "And now, when you finally have the opportunity to do something constructive and worthwhile for yourself, you want to leave."

He thought about what she was saying, his whole body steeled against accepting her logic.

She continued. "You've traveled all this way from little old New Zealand. So what if it takes one month, or two or three – don't you deserve to sort your life out? What's that amount of time in the whole scheme of things?" He didn't answer. "It's not much, Rick. It's a shame you can't see it – the benefit of doing this for yourself. Who knows? Maybe you don't want to see it. You just might want to be self-destructive and repeat the old patterns of what led you here in the first place. I think you should think hard about what you're saying."

Much to his irritation, Rick found himself unable to fault her reasoning.

"And by the way, you still haven't completed your crisis plan," she said over her shoulder with a smile as she left his room.

Alone in his room, Rick wrestled with the ideas that the nurse had planted in his mind. He could feel the adrenaline coursing through his body, the frustration that he was determined to hide from the staff growing ever stronger. Short of confronting a staff member, there was no choice but to sit in his room until the pent-up energy subsided. The situation was hopeless: he had signed away his rights to doctors who were politely refusing to restore them. But what if he were to demand to leave? Would they still be so polite? Had he literally, in fact, become a prisoner? At least it was a prison that allowed turkey wing deliveries, he consoled himself.

What drove him to make such a reckless decision in the first place? His predicament was entirely his own doing, and he had only himself to blame. He picked up the photograph sitting next to his bed. There he saw himself, smiling, next to Kate and their two sons. Immediately his throat tightened. It seemed like an eternity since the four of them had last been together, and with each passing day the promise of when they might be reunited seemed to drift further and further out of reach.

The room was oppressive; he could feel the walls closing in on him, the sense of being trapped suffocating him. He sought permission from the staff to go for a walk around the clinic's grounds before the sun set. Breathing in deeply the fresh, early-spring air, Rick watched the sun sink behind a cloud and felt a sense of awe at the vastness of the sky. It was still cold and crisp, and he thought of how the summer would be dying in Auckland just as the winter was fading here, on the other side of the world. He turned back toward the unassuming buildings of the Jennings Clinic.

I chose this. This is what I wanted. Because it's my only chance. I can find no other way.

Memories of his two sons flooded his awareness. *What use am I to them in this state? I can't give them my best until I've conquered this condition. Kate, too — how can she ever cope with me like this?*

The nurse's words returned to him. As irritating as it was, he began to see the sense in what she was saying. He had to give it to her, she had handled him expertly. Clearly, he was not the first to demand a premature exit from the clinic. The nurse was absolutely right, but he was loath to admit it: he still had much work ahead of him here, at the

Jennings Clinic. Maybe he was scared of what he might uncover if the exploration continued. But it was true: what was the harm in taking this time for himself, this time to rebuild himself?

Rick didn't know whether to laugh or cry. He had taken on the challenge of committing himself to the clinic of his own free will. It was his decision to walk into the lion's den; a decision that was rooted in a determination to rebuild himself.

I can fight to become a better man. I can rebuild myself. The choice is mine alone. It's up to me.

CHAPTER TWELVE

R ICK AWOKE WITH renewed determination. It had been his first reasonable sleep for weeks. The room felt warmer. His granola even
tasted better. And he enjoyed the company of his fellow patients as never
before. He had no idea when he would be free of the clinic, but he knew
there was purpose in his being there.

His first class for the day was on addiction. The doctor's face adopted
a quizzical look as he noticed Rick entering the room. He had encountered the patient in a different class and was surprised to see him taking
a seat in the class.

"What are you doing here, Rick?" he asked quietly as the other
patients trickled into the room. "You know this is a class on serious
addictions – drinking, drugs, gaming... I don't remember seeing anything about addiction in your file – is there something else you want
to share with me?"

Rick's expression was new to the doctor. Throughout the previous
week Rick had exuded a sense of resistance to his circumstances, but it
had now been replaced with a hint of enthusiasm. "That's correct, doctor, I don't have a serious addiction problem, although the odds are I'm a
workaholic, as the doctors at the Mayo Clinic told me. But I have family
and friends at home and two sons – who knows who might need my help

in the future? I want to learn all there is to know about mental illness. I believe it will be the most urgent problem of the new century."

The doctor nodded. "Well, it's good to have you here, Rick," he said as he returned to the front of the room.

Many of those suffering from acute or manic depression took refuge in some kind of addiction, often recreational drugs or alcohol. Alcohol often started out innocently: a glass a day to calm the nerves at night. But regularity gave rise to dependence, especially given that alcohol was, in itself, a depression mechanism that offered only temporary relief and held the potential to disrupt restful sleep. But it wasn't the only outlet available: sex, work, gambling also provided escapes from an uncomfortable existence.

Rick began attending every class he could fit into his schedule. He was surprised that mental illness could strike people from all walks of life, from over-achievers such as Churchill, Mozart and other icons, to the many everyday people he met in the clinic. He questioned them all about their lives, each of their stories a testament to the human spirit. And in those moments of shared vulnerability, connections were instantly formed. He jogged in the mornings with some of his new friends and took pleasure in his body's gradual recuperation. He noticed that, with Steve's daily restaurant deliveries, he was beginning to regain some of the weight he had lost in the previous months. He chuckled to himself at the irony of it: his sons often used to tease him about his noticeable pot-belly – evidence of his love of good food – but now he was struggling to combat the sudden loss of weight that had left him gaunt.

As his eagerness for understanding grew, he approached the return to wellness for the mind with seriousness and objectivity, hoping that perhaps he could become one who could help prevent others from traveling the same painful path that he had. He had been to the edge and now had an opportunity to share his understanding with those who may be heading in the same direction. He sometimes wondered if his enthusiasm for learning and potentially sharing his experience was a distraction from his own emotional pain. Regardless, he was grateful to the Jennings Clinic for creating an environment where such an exchange between patients could occur, and seized the opportunity.

There was one thing of which he was certain when it came to mental illness: prevention was the key. Once a person had gone so far as to suffer a full breakdown, recovery became so much more difficult. Prevention required facing the pain without the impulse to run from it. It meant staring it square in the eyes without succumbing to its control.

The golden rule had been hammered into the patients, but Rick knew deep down that he couldn't keep his experience a secret from those he wished to help. If others were to benefit from his ordeal, he would need to share his experience when necessary and, if he fell victim to blackmail or rejection, it was an acceptable price to pay for the possibility of helping someone avert such misery.

There was no doubt in Rick's mind that the issues confronting society in the upcoming decades would be ultimately inseparable from mental illness and its countless manifestations. It was a tendency of the human mind that often lay dormant, but the pressure of modern life had the power to trigger these tendencies as never before. And it existed in degrees. At the Jennings Clinic, Rick witnessed some of the most crippling cases. But the less noticeable forms of mental illness pervaded society with a stealth and momentum aided by a preoccupation with symptom relief.

Drugs were prescribed with alarming nonchalance. They were often the first response to complaints of mild depression, anxiety or phobias. Just as worrying was their appeal to parents. Attention-deficit/hyperactivity disorder and a number of other childhood difficulties were being treated with drugs. It seemed that the more research that was conducted, the easier it was becoming for medical professionals to pigeon-hole patients and prescribe what had now become standard medication. Even family doctors were all too ready to casually hand out free Prozac samples, with the advice, 'See how you do on this.'

It scared Rick. Were people becoming so unwilling to move through life's challenges that they were making their lives and those of their children dependent on pills? How could society become so scared of the natural cycles of life – the very cycles that offered people the growth and expansion in their horizons that was their birthright. *We don't exist for the purpose of stagnation*, he thought. But that was exactly what people were choosing.

He saw that mental illness was being treated as any other ailment. Symptom relief was the approach of choice, and popping pills to escape discomfort had become second nature to a large segment of society, sleeping pills being a perfect example of the treatment of psychological disorders by medication becoming an acceptable practice in contemporary society.

But the approach was distracting people from the most obvious questions: why can't you sleep? Why are you perpetually unhappy? Why can't you concentrate? To answer such questions with a pill was to invite their presence into one's life indefinitely, Rick concluded. The unexamined issues were bound to resurface in a more malevolent form at some stage, usually precipitated by a particularly challenging set of circumstances in one's life. Just as numbing out the pain of a broken leg would not ensure its healing, so it was with psychological pain and the underlying issue.

As his investigations into the nature of mental illness continued, he was struck by its prevalence. It affected people from all walks of life. And, once ignored, it took people to such depths of despair that they no longer had a choice but to seek medication. At that stage, the choice could no longer take into account the road to recovery: the only goal became to make it through the next day.

He felt they had all shared a similar path, if not at first obvious from the outside. The bulk of his research was conducted in the dining room where each of the wards came together and it was done at a level that was unattainable for most health professionals. Rick shared the shame and vulnerability of each person he spoke to and in this he was non-threatening. The degree of openness it engendered allowed Rick a glimpse into each person's pain, as he tried to absorb every scrap of information he could about the mysteries of mental illness.

There was the baker who, determined to make a better life for his wife and children, worked extreme hours until exhaustion, at which time his wife left him for another man. She had enjoyed the lifestyle he provided, but sought elsewhere the excitement that his commitment to work left unfulfilled, taking their children along with her. With the loss of his family, his despair overflowed into his business, which promptly collapsed with his nervous breakdown.

It wasn't unusual to find those who dedicated themselves to work, often in the hope of providing well for their family, devastated by the appearance of a slick Jim or slick Jane ready to take advantage of the situation. The baker was but one example, and the busy executive, putting in up to eighty hours a week, another. Her husband was the homemaker, and many times she would spend her evenings sitting in bed on her laptop, struggling to meet report deadlines, while her husband awaited her attention. In the end, she would fall asleep, exhausted, to repeat the same cycle the following day. The discovery of her husband's involvement with a slick Jane, in this case a friend of the family, pushed her to breaking point. Having been institutionalized, she didn't know if she would ever be able to return to such a career again.

Rick met a shop assistant whose initial stress was due to her struggle to meet the rent and support her children. She longed for a husband or boyfriend to shoulder the responsibility for her loved ones and did her best to stave off the depression that she felt building inside. But she saw no other option than to continue her two jobs, not knowing what would become of her children if she were unable to support them. She pushed on until her body would take no more. Finally succumbing to acute depression, and forced to swallow her long-defended pride in her ability to care for her family on her own, she found herself in the clinic and, having accepted defeat, she placed her children in the care of her parents.

A number of his fellow patients' problems found their root in a failed marriage, like the wife of a successful insurance broker who had always suspected that he had played up behind her back, but was reluctant to confront the disloyalty. She told Rick how she had been too afraid to hire a private detective and, instead, was more comfortable avoiding the reality of her situation. She made the bottle her friend. It started with only one drink a day, and she was at a loss to explain how she had slipped into alcoholism without even noticing, until it was too late. It was a pattern that Rick saw again and again amongst those with drinking problems, a domino effect whereby deep disappointment and hurt drove what began as an innocent distraction into a crippling addiction as the despair became overwhelming.

The insurance broker's wife even suspected her husband's full knowledge of where he was driving her. He had pushed her and picked on her in every way possible and, once she had become a heavy drinker, threatened to leave her, taking their children with him. He knew that the children meant everything to her. It was a plan that fitted his aims perfectly. He pushed her into a mental institution, saved the cost of alimony and a divorce settlement, maintained custody of his children, and was still able to have girlfriends with an ironclad excuse for never marrying them: his mentally ill wife would be unable to handle the shock of divorce.

It was the perfect solution for any unwanted spouse, and one that seemed to happen more than Rick cared to believe. To top it all off, forced medication could ensure an indefinite stay in an institution. The drug companies would have a secure customer for life, the insurance companies shouldered the burden of the costs, opting for drug-treatment rather than more costly therapy, and the plotting husband or wife walked away free of any responsibility.

The youngest of life's wounded warriors, as Rick came to think of them, was the twenty-one-year-old sprinter with Olympic aspirations. Even twenty-one seemed a push for the youthful, innocent-looking black girl whose determination had proven fatal. The long hours of training, on top of her studies, had taken her to breaking point. She relinquished her dreams and, confined to the clinic, focused on a new goal; a return to life, whatever that may hold for her.

Whatever the story, Rick felt that they were all in the same boat, each person struggling to move forward and reclaim the freedom that had hitherto been taken for granted.

In his new sense of purpose at the Jennings Clinic, he found that the days moved quicker, no longer weighted down by the resistance he had once felt for the place. He was sometimes accumulating more information than he could make sense of at the time. But the first-hand knowledge that he gleaned from his time with other patients was proving invaluable in his own recovery as he endeavored to apply everything he was learning from the experience of others, as well as the doctors' advice in the classes and therapy sessions.

The doctors often had clear advice, and it was useful. But Rick suspected that what they had to offer was not the whole picture, but only a big piece of it, not least because only precious few of them had ever experienced a nervous breakdown themselves. He still questioned their insistence on a lifetime of medication after an initial breakdown. He did the same of the excuses they offered people for justifying their conditions, often attributing mental illness to genetics. Though he acknowledged the possibility of genetic dispositions for conditions of the mind, from a practical standpoint Rick saw it as an excuse, and a dangerous one. It was not difficult to find statistics to support a theory, whatever that theory may be, and in this case Rick suspected that, as far as hereditary mental illness was concerned, learned behavior from parents was often more to blame than genetics. It was not to discount that genetics could play a role, but he watched how a simple statistical tendency could become the excuse a person needed to justify their behavior. Much like an alcoholic rationalizing his crutch by blaming his father's alcoholism, mental illness was something that needed to be moved through; it was not a pattern that should be allowed to remain in place, regardless of an inherited tendency.

His search for understanding continued. He saw how others were able to progress as each person found the courage to face their pain, to admit to their own role in their downfall, and to change their ways. He was certain that, the more he could learn about his condition, the sooner he would find the secrets to rebuilding himself. He had become the clinic's star pupil. Dr. Burke congratulated him on his crisis plan and mentioned that it was one of the best he had ever seen. Rick had adjusted well to his new way of life, and no longer felt the full force of his initial resentment for the clinic and its curtailing of his freedom.

One evening, awaiting sleep to take him, he felt something that he hadn't experienced for some time. Contentment. He felt peaceful. For a moment it was enjoyable, until a thought shot through his mind and abruptly brought him back to the waking world: *I feel comfortable here.*

It had been a month since he arrived at the Jennings Clinic. Without his noticing, it had tamed him. In an instant, he understood the veiled threat that had almost slipped through undetected: how long would it be before he was more at home in Topeka than in Auckland? His greatest fear was to lose his freedom; never did he suspect that he would be at risk of handing it over so willingly. The time to move to the next level had arrived, and the impetus for change would come from no one but Rick himself.

CHAPTER THIRTEEN

O NCE MORE HE found himself in Dr. Burke's office. But this time, his request was one for which he could not accept refusal. The possibility of developing an unconscious dependency on the clinic frightened him. In his musings, he often likened the clinic to a jail, and he reflected on the likely difficulties of leaving such a secure system to reenter a world that demanded an entirely different set of skills.

Much of the usual decision-making and responsibility of everyday life had been removed from patients to allow them to focus on the work at hand, and in doing so, the patients were insulated from the pressures of outside life: there were no arguments, no bills to pay, no external conflict. The clinic was a place where each person felt loved and respected, and bonded with the people around them, not least because they were all in the same boat together. The clinic was safe; that was its appeal. But Rick didn't want to become so comfortable in the warmth of the new family that had taken him in that he was unable to resume the adventure of life. It was a perfect place to rebuild oneself, but Rick knew that he must, with haste, return to the world he had left.

But even more than his fear of becoming institutionalized, it was Kate that drove him to approach Dr. Burke a second time. It seemed an eternity since Rick and Kate had last been together. She had spent the past weeks in New Zealand and Rick was having difficulty containing his excitement at her impending return to Topeka. At the same time, he was unable to delude himself into thinking that it would be easy to rekindle their relationship. He sensed that he would have to win back his wife, but it was something that couldn't be done from the confines of the Jennings Clinic. He had become a star pupil and it was something that he intended to capitalize on.

"Dr. Burke, I want to thank you for refusing my request last time we met. I am very pleased that I have finally embraced my new home and learned a great deal – many skills to deal with rebuilding my life and coping with life in the outside world. And I would like to make a suggestion: that I move to a halfway house." The doctor raised an eyebrow slightly. "What I mean is," Rick continued, "the idea of having a transition phase from one environment to the next is something that I imagine is very effective – like the prisoner on parole, the reformed drug-user in a halfway house. I know that the Jennings Clinic has some day patients and, due to my wife's arrival, I would like to make the request that I become a day patient." He knew that his request was not a simple one, and he also knew that it would only be granted if the doctor was convinced of Rick's speedy recovery. Rick had to put the full weight of his conviction behind what he was saying. "I want to ensure that my marriage is one of the twenty percent that remains intact. I would be very grateful, Dr. Burke, if you were to entrust me with this amount of conditional freedom, and I can assure you that it is not something that I will abuse." Rick's voice exuded a calm confidence. The doctor sat back and considered the proposal. "I'm ready for this, and I want to get a feel for these new tools – to ease into it – before I make the full transition to life outside the clinic."

The doctor looked at Rick and smiled. "Rick, I'm pleased with your progress. We all are. And I know how difficult it was for you to get used to the way we do things around here." He paused for a moment. "I'm going to grant your request, on the condition that you report to the clinic for the full day's classes every day."

This time, it seemed so easy. Rick grinned. "Thank you, Doctor."

The next day, Kate would arrive. He was nervous. Tonight was his final evening with Steve. They wasted no time in taking advantage of Rick's newfound freedom. Jackie, Steve's girlfriend, had arrived the previous day to meet up with Steve before the two headed to Europe on vacation, and the three headed into Topeka like there was no tomorrow. For the first time in four weeks, Rick would venture beyond the boundaries of the clinic.

He was elated. The restaurant was a welcome change to their setting in the common room, with the NBA blaring in the background. Rick had done some serious investigation into the best restaurant in town, the doctors unanimously suggesting the one he now found himself in. The nurses had been more candid, quoting the residents' joke about the sleepy town: 'the best thing about Topeka is the I-70'. Rick longed for the day that he could drive down the I-70, away from Topeka and away from his imprisonment. But, for now, dinner with Steve and Jackie at a restaurant was all the excitement he could handle.

As they were seated at their table Rick felt a strange mix of relief at the refreshing sense of freedom, and apprehension: what if people there could tell, somehow, that he was from the Jennings Clinic? His eyes scanned the tables but, it seemed to him, he was not attracting an undue amount of attention. He recalled the lunch with his son those months ago in Auckland where he could feel himself standing out from the crowd, but this time it was different, evidence that he had improved. Still, he hadn't mixed in the real world for a number of months, and one of those had been spent in a psychiatric clinic. He had become accustomed to people who understood mental illness. He decided to act with caution, lest he unknowingly give himself away.

"It's okay, everything will work out — you'll see." It was Jackie. Rick was embarrassed that she knew. He felt her searching his eyes, wondering if he's crazy, maybe a little worried that he was going to erupt at any moment: was he now a complete nutter? Was he going to flip out? Demolish the table?

He put his interpretations aside and responded, in a calm voice, though not sure if it was him talking or the Epilim, "What do you mean, Jackie, 'everything will work out'? I'm different from you and Steve — you haven't been where I am. I'm branded. People think of us as weak." They had already placed their orders and Rick paused while his bottled water arrived. "I imagine there's a strong stigma attached to people like me."

Steve interrupted, "Oh, come on, mate, you're exaggerating a bit there." Jackie was nodding in agreement.

"No I'm not," Rick replied.

"Rick," Steve responded, waving a hand in dismissal, "you're just the same as everyone else."

"Yeah, yeah, of course you are Rick," Jackie assured him enthusiastically.

Rick felt a degree of annoyance at Jackie's insistence that he was normal; he could sense her analyzing him since her arrival. But he said nothing of the inconsistency, deciding instead to allow an objective experiment to speak for him. "Okay, I'll prove it to you." Steve and Jackie shifted nervously in their seats, Steve glancing around the room in anticipation of Rick's next move. "People view us differently," Rick repeated as he caught sight of the waitress returning to pour Steve and Jackie's wine.

Rick struck up conversation with the waitress. She was in her early thirties and smiled eagerly at his questions, clearly pleased to be talking with the affable man with the accent. The two made friendly conversation for a short time before she took up the line of questioning that Rick had been waiting for.

"So, where are you from?"

"New Zealand."

"Oh, I love your accent," she said with just enough enthusiasm to suggest to Rick, and the other two people seated at the table, that she was perhaps more interested in the man than the accent. "I hear it's a beautiful country."

"It sure is," Rick answered.

"So then, are you enjoying Topeka? Where are you staying?"

Checkmate, Rick thought. He had to work to suppress his glee. "I'm staying at the place up on the hill," he said, pointing in the direction of the clinic. Her reaction was immediate. Her facial expression changed to one of unease and, try as she might, she was unable to hide the tension. Rick said nothing, letting his answer hang without any elaboration. The waitress told him she would be back with their appetizers.

"I rest my case," Rick said to the table with a smug grin. Steve and Jackie didn't reply, but instead fidgeted with their wine glasses.

"Rick, she would react differently once she got to know you," Jackie ventured.

"Well thank you, Jackie. You're both very supportive, but I'm only being realistic here," Rick said. "Did you know that eighty percent of all relationships fail when something like this affects one of the parties?" He thought of Kate, who would be arriving the following day. Would he be among the eighty percent? "I think this problem is only going to get bigger during the coming years — the stress of our world, the drive to succeed and improve, trying to fix everything, trying to control everything, working to the clock," he was rattling off his list with conviction, "striving to match other people's abilities, striving to be like other people — no one comfortable with who they are and everyone knocked around by a complicated world." Rick continued uninterrupted. "There's no use in sweeping this under the mat, it's not going away. And, from what I've seen, if the dangers of living like this aren't made public, the problem's going to compound into an epidemic. It's happening to people of all kinds — even children are being told it could be in their genes. It's fast becoming a drug-dependent world, and then how do you know who you really are? Maybe this is what people want on some level — a controllable, docile community. People don't want to admit that this taboo subject is sitting right in front of them, staring them in the face. I know that, if I ever see someone on their way to where I've been, I'm going to do everything I can to prevent them from going there." Satisfied with his speech, he turned his attention to his appetizer.

CHAPTER FOURTEEN

THE FOLLOWING AFTERNOON found him alone in the Jennings Clinic grounds, awaiting Kate's arrival. He sat on the very same park bench that had witnessed his decision, his head cradled in Kate's tender hands, to sign into the clinic. It was a beautiful day, the air crisp and invigorating.

He was anxious to hear news of his wife and sons. The two had spoken on the phone every day, but there was only so much that could be conveyed over the telephone lines. Rick had been longing to once again set eyes on the love of his life, and his stomach fluttered as her face flashed across his mind.

She didn't yet know that he would be free to stay in a hotel room; he wanted it to be a surprise. He wondered how easy it would be for the two to slip back into the way they used to be now that the extremes in Rick's mood seemed to have subsided. He yearned to feel the nurturing love that flowed so freely from Kate in their earlier years. There had once been an innocence between them; an openness that existed without effort.

But it had faded. Why, he could not say, but he had watched her patience with him diminish over the years. The warmth that had once lifted him into a fuller experience of life had evaporated, replaced by a resentment that overshadowed the love that he knew she still felt for him. His experience of Kate was now of someone who mechanically went through the motions of being in love.

She had never found it easy to open up with her truest feelings. It was something that became clearer as their marriage progressed. Whatever she was holding back accumulated, constricting the ease with which her love had previously flowed. When it did surface, it either carried a heavy dose of tension or it was voiced with an emotional distance. He knew that there were matters with which she was unhappy, most of which could be summed up in her own words: 'I come third in your life. First is your family; second is your work.'

It was true, he thought, that he made huge sacrifices for the freedom of lifestyle that he wanted to attain for his wife and children. And, he had to admit, the times that he had stood up to Rosa and Andrew's and his parents' wishes for harmony within the family were precious few; he had made a habit of caving in to their every demand, regardless of its absurdity. But, in Rick's mind, Kate had always come first.

He remembered telling her, under the Eiffel Tower, that Naturally Best had been sold. Now, with his condition motivating him to hand control of the family firm over to Andrew and Rosa, he was sure that any doubts of where Kate stood in the pecking order would be laid to rest. Rick was confident that her anger toward him would dissipate. She would be number one in his life, and if she were unable to see it, he would endeavor to prove it to her.

Realistically, he knew that even that would not be the end to their troubles. From a position of not spending enough time with his wife, he felt that in the lead-up to his breakdown he had approached the other extreme in his wife's eyes: spending too much time with Kate. Many of his previously tolerable habits became intolerable and she was constantly reminding him to change his ways. She wanted excitement from life, but Rick had reached his limit. He recalled the many times that their plans to socialize at night were canceled at the last minute when Rick was unable to summon enough energy. Kate saw no reason why he couldn't sleep in the afternoon to save his energy for the evening. As Rick had discovered, no one understood the severity of his condition, especially before the breakdown. It should have been a time for him to slow down and spend quality time with those he loved. Maybe disaster could have been averted if only...

She didn't know any better — no one did.

It was difficult to blame her for any part she may have inadvertently played in his downfall. She had tolerated much. Why had she become distant? Who knew — maybe it was the pressure of a changing society and jealous friends telling her that she did too much for her high-maintenance husband; maybe it was as simple as her feeling that she came third in the pecking order. Rick knew that the six years of watching his father die had taken a toll on their relationship as every spare moment away from work was spent with Ned, which only depressed him further. Business called; the construction of the new house called; friends phoned well into the night seeking business advice. By the time he and Kate settled in for the night, his energy was spent. And then she had borne the stress of watching her husband react to a chemical cocktail for the best part of a year, followed by a nervous breakdown that would have scared a stranger senseless, let alone a life partner who had never known Rick as anything other than invincible.

He remembered the awful pangs of guilt a month earlier when he had entered the clinic. *I've let Kate down. I've failed her.* Even with 'guilt' featuring as one of the major topics of the clinic's sessions, he felt as if the emotion had a firm hold over him. He couldn't shake the feeling that he had failed Kate, as well as his sons. It was an impression that any one of Rick's friends within the clinic was well aware of, owing to his frequent mention of it and his insistence on dwelling on such a failure.

But it was an emotion that he felt less strongly now, having reached the end of his time as a live-in patient. The guilt was there, but he found himself unable to accept full responsibility any longer. It was something that he would keep to himself, though. His focus now was on winning back the love of Kate and doing whatever it took. He was determined to be in the twenty percent of couples that stayed together following a nervous breakdown.

To think of everything that she's been through, he thought.

To think that I almost got us killed in France. That I placed the life of the person I love most in jeopardy by letting things get so bad.

The awful memory of Kate's grip on the steering wheel, her knuckles white with tension, returned to his mind.

⌐⌐

THEY HAD LEFT New Zealand for a vacation, on Dr. Bradshaw's recommendation, still several months before the day of his breakdown. She had advised Rick that there was little more she could do for him; it was up to him to eliminate stress in his life. With the Lithium dosages increasing, Rick doing everything in his power to avoid stress in his regular life in Auckland, and not yet being aware of the danger he was in under Bradshaw's prescription, the only solution they could muster was an extended holiday.

They chose Provence. The last time they had stayed in the South of France, the two had led a carefree existence: jumping fences to pick fresh cherries together and enjoying lazy picnics under a secluded tree with local wine. It was a favorite destination of Monet and others who found it a perfect place to appreciate nature's serenity. Van Gogh, a victim of mental illness himself, had honed his art in the region when he spent time in Arles. Painters often commented on the unique light that was found in Provence and that added a new dimension to visual art. The rolling countryside inspired them and lifted their spirits to create some of the most revered works of art the world had seen, and Rick hoped it would have a similar effect on his own sense of wellbeing.

But, this time, it was not to be. They arrived just as Rick's mood was reaching a low point in the almost-monthly cycle of elation and despair that he was unable to escape. Instead of arriving to the full glory of spring or summer, they had instead arrived at the end of October, and the sky was a perpetual gray.

He wished that the two of them could play like children again. He wished Kate would take him on a picnic, despite the weather, just so that he would know she still felt for him. He longed to feel her loving hands on his skin, massaging him with the local lavender oil they had once bought.

Though he hadn't quite grasped just how far Kate had been pushed, the day that he was certain would be their last obliterated any doubt surrounding Kate's state.

That morning, knowing how much Kate had already tolerated, Rick had phoned his mother, hoping to talk with someone close without burdening his wife further. It only angered Kate more to watch her once-strong husband seeking refuge in his mother, not his wife.

In a state of desperation, unable to shake his gloom, Rick asked his wife to take him for a drive through the countryside, hoping it would boost his mood. The frustration, even anger, at the situation was written all over Kate's face: it was supposed to be a time of recuperation for Rick, but all that their isolation had done was to highlight Rick's worsening state. There was no respite for Kate: not in New Zealand, and certainly not in France, witnessing her husband's inexplicable decline twenty-four hours a day.

They made their way to the car they had rented, the car that Rick had envisaged taking them to a different picnic destination each day in this precious part of the world where his worries would miraculously vanish. As soon as the car lurched forward with Kate behind the wheel, Rick could sense that something was not right.

Even as they traveled along the chalet's graveled driveway toward the open road, her aggression was evident, the wheels struggling for traction. Rick was thrown against his door as she turned sharply onto the road and floored the accelerator.

'Kate, calm down,' he tried, but his body was weak. He could barely summon the energy to speak the words.

She was visibly shaking, her jaw clenched, and soon the tears began to stream down her face. Before he knew it, they were flying along the rural road, far in excess of the speed limit.

'Kate, what are you doing!'

She didn't respond. Every corner she turned was a brush with death; all that would have been required for it to be their last was a vehicle driving in the other direction at the right time, as Kate swerved in and out of the opposing lane. She passed every vehicle they approached; her foot on the accelerator was unrelenting.

Rick felt the adrenaline rush through his body. 'Through sickness and health, till death do us part' – the words echoed in his mind as he stared at the wedding ring on her finger, the diamond seemingly having lost its sparkle; her white knuckles gripping the steering wheel; her face a picture of absolute despair. Those long, slender fingers – many times he had watched them grace the piano keys, and now they trembled in a mighty crescendo, building to the climax of this long-simmering drama.

That's when it struck him: *This has gone too far.*

Something caught his eye and he glanced ahead to see an oncoming truck rounding the approaching corner, its horn blaring. They were in the wrong lane, but Kate appeared to be frozen in place, unable to move. Rick reached over and put his hand over Kate's – it was stiff, lifeless. As best he could, he frantically jerked the wheel to the right, sending them back into their own lane, and then inadvertently straight over the road and onto the grass verge.

'Brake!' he yelled.

The car's momentum was abruptly disturbed, the wheels locked and they slid along the damp grass until the impact of the gutter and then the sturdy fence post brought them to a halt.

Neither one was injured. They sat there, panicked, at the end of their wits. Kate was beside herself. She sobbed hysterically. Rick was at a loss to know how to calm her down. He paced back in forth in his mind.

What's wrong with me? What am I pushing my wife to do?

Rick lay awake through the night.

She can't handle it anymore. I almost got us killed. What if we had died? What a waste of a life that would have been. Who would be there to hug our kids? To guide them? It's not just me who's getting to the end of it now – she is too. Dr. Bradshaw said she's doing everything she can. What am I doing wrong? Something has to change.

The following morning, Rick told Kate they were leaving Provence. It wasn't working. They would go to Monaco. Surely, if the peace of Provence couldn't satisfy Rick, then the sophistication of Monaco could. They stayed in their favorite hotel: the Hotel de Paris.

If it was elegance Rick was after, he couldn't have asked for more: the dining room's ceiling was opened up on their first night to reveal a clear, starlit sky, under which they tasted the most delicate, exquisitely presented flavors. The following morning, to compensate for his frustrated dreams of cherry-picking in Provence, firm, sweet cherries, resting of a bed of ice, were brought to him in a crystal bowl. After breakfast, the couple received spa treatments, overlooking the port and the Mediterranean. All Rick could think about through his massage was how he wished that it was someone who loved him who was touching his body, rather than a complete stranger.

Monaco was breathtaking, and the atmosphere invigorating. But it had lost its luster. The food, the setting – everything that Rick once enjoyed – felt lifeless. He waited for it to inspire him. He had been sure that, with the freedom to purchase whatever was missing, he would find something that worked. The discomforting realization that it might not work was beginning to dawn. They were running out of options.

Giving the simpler things in life one more shot before he threw in the towel for Monaco, he and Kate attempted a picnic, only to be told by the police that it was forbidden.

Rick had to admit it: it wasn't working. He guessed that Kate had almost reached boiling point when she heard his next request, though her willingness to try whatever offered a chance of success being what it was, it wasn't evident in her response: 'Let's go.'

They left for Hawaii, hoping that its serene purity would hold the answer. When even this failed, Rick's absolute absence of power to change the situation became undeniable. That was when he discovered the truth about Bradshaw. That was when everything changed. That was the beginning of the end for the life that Rick new.

RICK TOOK A deep breath of the mid-afternoon, Kansas air and opened his eyes to the peaceful green surroundings. From the parking lot a figure appeared, only faint, but there was a familiarity about the movement that left Rick in no doubt of the figure's identity. His heart leapt. As Kate's features became barely visible, Rick couldn't suppress the grin that rose to his face. He was like a child on Christmas morning. As she walked closer, Rick could see that he was not the only one having trouble containing his excitement.

Their eyes met and Rick felt like he could leap into the sky and touch the stars. They embraced without words. Rick wanted to say something, but the words didn't come. Kate broke the silence.

"I've missed you, I can't believe how much I've missed you," she said, her makeup smudging on Rick's shoulder. "How are you feeling?" she said, pulling back to meet her husband's eyes.

"Well, not bad at all. In fact," he said, picking up a concealed overnight-bag from beside the bench, "so good that I think you and I should ditch this place and paint the town red."

"Rick, what are you talking about!" Kate responded, the panic written all over her face. "You can't just leave!"

"Whoa, whoa – I've got permission. I'm a day-patient now."

Kate was dumbstruck.

"You think they would let me walk out here with my bag if I weren't allowed to go? Watch – the security guy's going to let me waltz right through the front gate."

He approached the entrance, Kate struggling to keep up behind with her hand planted firmly in Rick's.

"Enjoy your evening, Mr. Dellich," the security guard nodded.

While Kate struggled to get her head around what had transpired in the last two minutes, Rick jumped behind the wheel of the car that Kate had arrived in and headed straight into the city.

They ate dinner and spent hours talking about Auckland and their two boys. It was a relief for both of them to be back to some notion of normalcy. On arriving at Kate's hotel after dinner, Rick could sense that she wanted to be close to him. She had held his hand all the way from their departure from the clinic to reaching the restaurant. But the honeymoon bliss was not to last. Their first night together in a month convinced Rick that his marriage would need work.

They both wanted to make love; they both wanted to feel loved. But Rick felt a distance in his wife's embrace, and couldn't help but notice that a barrier had grown between them. He wondered to himself if her warmth was possibly motivated by pity for him, or out of fear of losing him.

They talked well into the night and Rick made the request of her that had been on his mind for weeks. "Kate, when we return to New Zealand,

I want you to help me win back the respect of our sons. Please, for all our sakes, do not criticize me in front of our children." The two were lying in bed, the only light in the room generated by Topeka's lights filtering through the blinds. One of Rick's deepest fears was that he had lost the respect of his sons.

"You have to earn their respect," Kate replied.

Rick looked at his wife's silhouetted face. They were tired and the conversation for the night came to a close. Rick sensed that, despite his goal to rebuild himself and his life, there existed a more immediate concern: winning back his wife.

It was the same as it had been for years; Rick felt a chasm between them and an absence of physical and emotional love. To go through the motions of physical love only worsened the situation – the resentment he sensed from her was almost tangible at such times. The two seemed unable to meet at one another's level, never able to satisfy each other. Rick needed love, but it wasn't there; Kate wanted the old Rick, but he wasn't there. Both of them were stuck in the past.

Rick was reminded of the special occasions when he made every effort to choose the perfect gift, often having a one-of-a-kind piece of jewelry designed especially for Kate. But it meant nothing to her; it even angered her. Her words echoed in his mind as he fell asleep, finding a measure of comfort in the warmth of her body: 'I don't want a new ring! I want the real Rick back!'

Oh Kate, my Kate, my love, my life. What have I done to you? I can feel your heart leeching its essence, as if there's a gaping hole in there that we're powerless to heal. How can a love that was so breathtaking become this? I know how much you want to forgive me; to let go of your hurt; to let go of your anger. I see how you try. But, with all our efforts, why are we failing already?

You arrived today with such high hopes. I saw it in your eyes – your desire for me, your excitement to see me again. My spirit flew, my heart soared. But tonight, beneath the calm waters of your exterior – submerged, lurking – your iceberg of hurt revealed its ominous presence, and now all I feel is its heavy shadow.

I was hesitant to make love tonight. I promised myself, at the beginning of the day, that despite my longing for you, my longing for union with you, I would resist. . . I knew it would be too hurtful for both of us to do so while pain and confusion lingered, I knew I couldn't handle being close to you physically if I couldn't feel your love. But I saw the hurt in your eyes: why would I not want to make love to you? What was wrong with me? Why had I rejected you? Of course I wanted to, more than anything. And so we did. . . or we tried. . . but was it an expression of love, or was it just sex? I felt your resentment as soon as we began, but by then it was too late; when we embraced to kiss, to hold, to become one, I felt it. I sensed your hardness and your coldness throughout, and it broke my heart. The magic that was once there had evaporated. I hoped that the pain we once had would dissolve enough after this month away. I had hoped that it would be a beautiful reunion of two becoming one.

What have I done to you?

It pains me to see you needing sleeping tablets — you never needed them before I started losing it. How long has my failure kept you awake at night? The first time I wrapped my arms around you today, I was scared for your health — I've never felt you so thin and weak: your body has lost its life. Is that what I've reduced you to? And now, I ask why I awoke after we fell asleep in sadness, and I know the answer: it was the pain. The pain of letting you down. The pain of loving you so much, but not being able to reach you. The pain of the gulf that separates us, emotionally and physically. How can we make love, both of us wanting only each other, and neither of us feel fulfilled, but only more alone? Is that what we've become? Is that how bad it is?

This is why I entered the lion's den. This is why I signed myself into the Jennings Clinic. I could have stopped after the Mayo Clinic — I could have gone back to my life like everyone else would have, knowing that they had advised me to do so, knowing that they had said I'm fine. But that wasn't enough for me. I knew I had to find myself once more, for you Kate, and for the boys. That's why I'm here in this lonely place. Because I love you. Because I'm sorry. And now, just as I thought things were looking hopeful, I discover the full magnitude of the task that awaits me. Without you, Kate, I'm a goner.

I wish I could hold your heart in my hands; maybe my hands could warm it, bring it back to life. If you weren't lying on your side with your back turned to me, I would gently press my ear to your chest, and listen, hoping to comfort myself with its beat. But would I hear anything? Or has the leak, now having slowed to a trickle, left only emptiness? How can I ever refill it?

CHAPTER FIFTEEN

T HE STRAIN HOVERED somewhere in the background for the rest of the week. By day, Rick spent time at the clinic attending therapy sessions, classes and enjoying the company of the kindred souls he had come to love. Kate, too, had her own counseling sessions to deal with the impact of Rick's ordeal. At night, Rick reveled in his newfound freedom: he could now take a walk outside whenever he chose, eat dinner out with Kate, and shave without needing to ask a nurse for his razor. He had been somewhat concerned that the change in environment might present some kind of challenge, but was relieved at the ease with which he could handle the new setting.

The two did their best to resume a normal relationship, but the strain that made itself felt that first night hovered somewhere in the background for the rest of the week. The pace of progress left Rick disheartened. It was clear that resurrecting the flame of love between him and his wife would take work, and frustration with his situation began to build. How could he ever convince Kate of his strength, his ability to be everything she hoped for him to be, while he was still stuck in a mental institution? And what of the question that lurked persistently in the back of his mind with its insidious taunting: *how can I ever be myself in this chemical straightjacket?*

He could not, however, escape the reality of his situation. He had not cleared through everything that obstructed his full expression of the real Rick — he knew that much. Demons that he dared not search for just yet awaited his attention, and he sensed that he would never be truly free until he was prepared to look deep inside without flinching.

But Rick questioned whether the clinic had anything further to offer. He felt that he had made every effort to take what he could from the clinic, but now it was time to apply that newfound wisdom in the arena of daily life. That was where he would break free from whatever was holding him back, in the intensity and challenges of everyday life.

Even if he remained in the clinic for another six months, he doubted whether he would make any more progress. He was beginning to wonder how much ground he had, in actuality, made on his road to recovery: he sensed that the work in the clinic was the easy part, and maybe the most challenging stretch of it all would be trying to rebuild his life.

And then, what if he *were* able to reclaim his normal life: would he forever be wondering to what degree he was the real Rick, condemned to an artificial, drug-induced sense of normalcy? Was he ten percent Rick, eighty percent Rick? How could such a thing be defined? The new tools were certainly of value, but it was time to put them into practice. Any further progress would be won in the arena of everyday life.

He could live in a bubble no longer. At the end of the week, he made an appointment to see Dr. Burke, hoping that it would be the last such meeting of his life. The doctor listened carefully to Rick's case. He questioned the patient; asking about everything from his current sleep patterns to his plans on returning to New Zealand, if it were decided he was ready.

He made a request: if Rick were to be released from the clinic, that he return again, after six months, for a checkup.

Time after time, Rick had listened to the doctors' words of encouragement regarding psychiatric medication: 'Oh, it's nothing — just a chemical imbalance in your brain.' Yes, he recalled the day, shortly before his breakdown, when he could sense the imbalance beginning. It was the most frightening feeling he had experienced, and he had been powerless to stop it. But there was more to it. There were deeper layers waiting to be exposed. He couldn't help but think of the revolving doors, the patients returning again and again.

I don't want to use Band-Aids. I don't want to keep coming back. What was the trigger that sent me to the edge? I still don't know. But I want to find out. I want to fight on.

"I will seriously consider it, Dr. Burke. I've gotten a lot out of my stay here."

"I hope you do, Rick," he replied. "I'm going to recommend to the committee that you be allowed to leave the clinic."

The doctor's decision to allow Rick to return to New Zealand was almost too good to be true. After so much struggle and drama within the clinic, Rick now found his freedom returned to him with little effort at all. The months of dealing with mood swings, depression, drugs and losing his rights as a citizen, had culminated in these two weeks in which he casually reclaimed the right to sleep in a hotel room, and then to return to his life. The moment was surprisingly ordinary, and could have felt anticlimactic to one who had so arduously fought to reclaim what had been lost if Rick had not had his friends to share in the victory.

Rick's final day at the clinic was one of the most difficult of his stay. So suddenly had his freedom been returned that he and those many with whom he shared a deep connection were unprepared for the farewell.

Not all were still present at the clinic. The minister had left abruptly and almost undetected. Rick had caught wind that he had been drinking which, on top of his numerous other transgressions during his years of involvement with the clinic, convinced the staff that he was not taking his treatment seriously. Apparently he had been asked to leave. Joel had already ended his current visit a week earlier. Julia, too, was absent from Rick's impromptu farewell gathering: she was confined to a secure ward after a recent suicide attempt. How he wanted to hug them both and tell them he would never forget what they had given in their honesty and their courage. Rick paused in front of Scott, and was surprised to see the other man's eyes glistening with tears. He hadn't told Scott what an inspiration his courage had been, but somehow he sensed there was no need.

Those remaining said their goodbyes with bittersweet smiles for what had been shared, and for what had been won. There were many people that Rick spent time with that day, and as he left he wondered what would become of them. Would they leap forward and move back into their lives with confidence and purpose? For how much longer would the Jennings Clinic be their home?

At least Rick had somebody ready to take him home, which was more than could be said for most of the patients. When the time came for them to reenter the world, it would likely be on their own, their family long since having abandoned them. And could anyone truly blame them? It got to a point where it was too scary, too painful, to witness a loved one leading such an agonizing existence.

Rick embraced his friends for the last time, wondering if they would ever see each other again, and Dr. Burke's request for a checkup in six months returning to his mind. There were many issues on which Rick had found it necessary to compromise: he had accepted his condition, all the while resenting such an approach; he knew he would have to continue his Epilim medication for some time – the doctors told him for the rest of his life – as much as he detested it. But while he told Dr. Burke that he would consider his request, he knew deep down that he could never bring himself to go near Topeka again. He had been to the edge, and it was an experience he was not prepared to repeat.

CHAPTER SIXTEEN

THE SUMMER TEMPERATURES had persisted past autumn's arrival in Auckland. The air was warm compared with the freshness of Topeka, and Rick enjoyed the hint of humidity in the breeze brushing against his face through the taxi window. The floral scents, the feel of the air, spoke unmistakably of the city that had always been his home. He smiled as it warmed him inside.

Such relief did he feel at his return that the past two months almost seemed like a dream, or a nightmare, from which he was just awaking. It was like a different world now – that tiny room, that prison of a clinic, wondering if he would ever again be free... and now, he thought, he was free. Just like that. It was as if he had to keep pinching his arm to remind himself that he was now allowed to take a walk whenever he chose. He could now eat whatever he wanted. And he was no longer answerable to a committee of doctors in whose hands rested his fate and his future.

What made him ever choose to visit such a place – that clinic, he wondered. Why didn't he just check himself into one of those rehab clinics that all the celebrities used? Good food, beautiful surroundings, leave whenever you want. Had it really been necessary to put himself through such drama?

He knew he could have gone to a fashionable clinic – a place more akin to a hotel than a prison. He could have escaped the pain for some time — distracted himself with a vacation of sorts. But he knew it was the easy option. If the Jennings Clinic's revolving door had shocked him, how much worse would it be at a more leisurely institute? He hadn't wanted to be comforted; he wanted confrontation. Confrontation with whatever it was that drove him to the edge — that same shadow that was the root of all pain, all addiction, and that would only release its grip when a person refused to avoid it any longer.

I'm pleased I did it the hard way. So far, it's working — I'm still sitting next to Kate. I'm on my way home.

I won.

As the taxi moved closer to the city, his brief encounter with victory, too, began to take on the appearance of a dream. It was as if the thirty-minute drive from the airport to the home provided an agonizingly short respite from the reality of his situation. He felt like a mountaineer who, thinking he had reached the summit, smiled as he hauled himself up over the final ledge, only to find the full grandeur of the mountain revealed before his eyes and the true summit far beyond his vision's reach.

Shit, he thought. *I'm glad I did it the hard way! I'd never stand a chance now if I had taken the easy option from the start.*

The home was close now. Rick shuddered as they passed the gas station where he had ranted about JFK and dished out hundred dollar bills. He smiled wryly to himself, shaking his head. It was still difficult to believe it had gotten quite that bad. *I'll have to find a new gas station now*, he thought.

They turned off the road and onto the quiet street that Rick had driven down so many times. They took a right at the fork, just before the street would take a sharp drop to become level with the beach, still a three-minute drive away, and there, as they rounded the final corner, were the gates to the house of his dreams: Waterford. The driver stopped abruptly as Kate searched her handbag for the gate-opener.

But Rick didn't move. So much had changed in the previous months. These tall, elegant gates had been transformed from the guardians of his beloved sanctuary into the boundary of a prison during his time as a ward of the state. They had betrayed their purpose on that day that they opened themselves to four strangers who had come to take Rick away.

He heard a beeping noise from Kate's hand and they gracefully opened, welcoming Rick back to the life he had temporarily left.

The home had been part of his great dream for his family. It exemplified the ideals that had always been so close to his heart – family; unconditional love; experiencing all the beauty and wonder that life had to offer.

The car crossed the threshold of the open gates and at once Rick could sense the life that the gardens exuded. It was all so richly green, so vibrant, the foliage lining the driveway on both sides. The fronds arched ever so slightly toward the center of the driveway, as if wrapping those entering or exiting the home in a nurturing embrace.

The taxi came to a halt beneath the arching porte-cochere, and though vaguely aware that the driver was unloading the luggage and awaiting payment, Rick was unable to take his eyes off his surroundings as he attempted to drink in the familiar setting. In one of the upper corners of the porte-cochere, he sighted the birds that had nested there for years.

The colors were more alive today than they had ever been. But it was what the house represented that touched his heart. This home was created out of love, a love that asks nothing in return, but wishes higher and higher expressions of itself, seeking only the exaltation of its own, powerful, gift. It was built out of a man's love for his own family.

How lucky he was, he thought, to still be surrounded by those who loved him. It was more than he could say for many of his friends back in Topeka.

From behind him, he heard the sound of water lightly dancing from the fountain – the same fountain upon which Rick had proclaimed himself Jesus, he thought. It had been designed to resonate through the porte-cochere that extended out from the steps leading up to the front door, and also to be heard distantly from the master bedroom.

The years of planning that went into the house flooded back to Rick: the three sets of architects he went through to find a team who could understand his vision of perfection – a work of art that would stand the test of time; the bemused expression on his father's face that day he had showed him the plans for the house; the planning, re-planning, re-drawing of plans and the exploration of hundreds of scenarios to ensure that the size of the house did not impede a natural flow and an ease of living. Years went into the design and Rick had pored over every detail.

He wondered, what use was any of it without the good health to enjoy it?

The architects told him it would take three years to build, but Rick found a contractor who promised completion within a year: he was desperate to finish the masterpiece in time for his father to be able to admire the creation. But Ned slipped away before he could witness the realization of Rick's dream. Rick had longed to share the experience with his father, to stand side by side with him as they looked in awe at the abundance of life's gifts and were humbled by the good fortune that had smiled on them. But it wasn't to be.

"Rick, the man looks about ready to leave – " Kate began.

"Sorry," he said, fumbling for his wallet and paying the patiently waiting driver. The car looped around the circular end of the driveway and continued back down toward the front gate.

The black and white marble chessboard floor opened before him as Rick walked through the front door. To his right was the formal lounge that opened onto the deck surrounding the room, from which steps descended to the gardens, the summer colors of the lounge creating an airy and open feel. And then adjacent to it he saw the entrance to the richly-decorated billiards room that housed the full-sized oak billiards and snooker table.

In front of him, a staircase ascended to the outlook at the back of the foyer and then split into two as it doubled back to the third floor, one side leading to the master bedroom, and the other leading to the hallway that gave access to the upstairs lounge, the boys' bedrooms and the guest bedrooms. The landing above him, connecting the two staircases, framed the foyer to create an entrance that was every bit as impressive as Rick had envisioned.

He remembered the dinner parties: the formal lounge and billiards room alive with laughter, dinner in the formal dining room, the music of the string quartet perched on the landing resonating through the foyer

— just as it would when Kate would occasionally grace the grand piano with her playing — the guests dancing on the chess-board floor.

Wow, do I really live here? Is this real?

The contrast with the Jennings Clinic could not have been more pronounced. He climbed the stairs, slowly and ponderously as if trying to take in all that he could, to the master bedroom. He walked around the spacious surroundings, opening the French doors onto the sandstone deck to survey the view of Rangitoto sitting in the Waitemata Harbour. He breathed in the floral-scented air. It was intoxicating. He felt giddy; elated. The native birds, nestled amongst the rich greenery of the home's gardens and trees, sang loudly, as if to no one in particular, as if they were simply overflowing with joy. Even they found sanctuary in the home.

He browsed through his walk-in closet and noticed designer suits that he had never once worn. He couldn't quite grasp that everything he was looking at was his to enjoy — it all seemed so foreign after his long absence. His room at the Jennings Clinic would easily have fitted into the closet — the bedroom itself was two thousand square feet. Why would he ever want to waste his time being stressed out? With all this to enjoy, and the family he loved so dearly to share it with, why did he never allow himself to relax into the life that he had devoted himself to building? He was like a master chef who had never tasted his own delights.

Rick wandered down the hallway to his sons' rooms. Though they were at school and college and wouldn't be home until the afternoon, Rick couldn't help himself; he could hardly wait another moment to see them. Each bedroom he walked into sent shivers down his spine. They were still; quiet except for the birds outside, but it was as if each of his sons were there in the room with him. The sense of innocence was inescapable; just standing there seemed to make life seem a whole lot simpler. He wondered if they had questioned the explanation of a combined business trip and vacation offered for his long absence. With what Michael had seen during the days leading up to his father's breakdown, he would surely suspect something out-of-the-ordinary. But neither of the boys had spoken a word about it.

He continued through the home, getting lost in the magnificence of every detail. The casual observer would never have noticed the care that had gone into designing a home that wasn't intimidating, or soulless, as a house of its size was often liable to become. It felt like a home. It was easy to live in. Each room had its own mood and its own design features and color scheme, even each of the fourteen bathrooms, from the different marble floors and ornamental mirrors to the individuated towel designs. Many of the rooms had been designed to accommodate candle-lit dinners for two if desired, to allow a variety of experiences within the one living environment.

He liked knowing that, if a person so desired, he could cover all three stories without treading a single stair, facilitated by the eight-person, automatic elevator, and ramps that allowed for easy use of the carts for luggage and groceries all the way from the ten-car garage to the main kitchen or bedrooms.

He found himself strolling leisurely through the gardens. They were vibrant, full of life, just like the house should be, he thought. It had always been the intention to create a home that, while only a fifteen-minute drive from downtown in New Zealand's largest city, was a sanctuary of peace and happiness that could have been miles from anything resembling a city. He remembered designing the main lawn with his sons and himself in mind: a place where they could play touch rugby or cricket. An extensive drainage system had to be built to compensate for the wet Auckland weather so that the grass could be used any time of year. The lawn, lined with six towering, hundred-year-old Phoenix palm trees, acted as a buffer between the home and the tennis court.

The outdoor swimming pool, its two sun-bathing islands at either end surrounded by shallow moats of water, sat adjacent to both the home and the north end of the lawn.

At the south end began a path that led up to the pavilion. It made its way to the foot of the stairs, surrounded by gardens, that led up the mild incline to the croquet lawn and then to the serenity of the pavilion which also housed the barely-used squash court. A second driveway had been built there to ensure that the service personnel for the house could enter and exit without disturbing the peace of the family home.

Rick chuckled to himself as his father's words from those years ago came back to him. 'But Rick, you don't play squash,' Ned had pointed out, reviewing the plans for the house.

'I played once when I was nineteen. I want to play again,' Rick had shrugged. *I guess you were right about that one, Dad.* He still didn't play squash.

At least Rick had been right about the indoor pool. It was the part of the house his heart had been set on from the beginning. He gazed up to the arching, nearly-three-storey ceiling. Shafts of light shone through the roof, designed in cedar wood to create a honeycomb effect at the same time as allowing for ventilation. Turning slowly on the spot, he admired the French doors that surrounded the entire wing. Double-glazed to maintain a comfortable temperature in and out of the water, they allowed for the swimmer to enjoy tranquil views: on the east side, of the lawn and the tennis court; the west side, lush gardens and more lawn, and, for backstroke, the cedar ceiling, high above.

Off to the side of the wing lay the movie theatre, strategically placed at the end of the house to provide refuge from any activity. And, above it, a walkway lining the upper wall, overlooking the indoor pool, and leading to a gazebo that enjoyed the morning sun and a perfect view of the tennis court.

He gazed back at the twenty-five meter pool in front of him. *I wonder if I can do a length underwater?* He had never done it before, but after what he had overcome in the past months, he felt more confident than ever now.

Rick went to make a move back up to his room for his swimming shorts, but then remembered that he was now back in his own home. He could do whatever he wanted. What was stopping him from jumping in right now in his clothes? Or, better still, removing every single item of clothing and *then* jumping in?

What the hell, I'm going in now. He threw off everything except his underwear and made for the other end of the pool. He pushed and pushed with all his strength but came up only halfway down the pool, gasping for air.

"Dad!!!" A voice, echoing through the expanse, and muffled by the water dripping off his face, caught Rick's attention from behind.

It was James. He was the first to arrive home for the day. But how had the hours slipped by? Had Rick been walking around the house in a daze ever since stepping out of that taxi?

"Jamie," he said, more to himself than to his son, who was beaming at him from ear to ear. The nine-year-old dashed toward his father and leapt, clothes and all, into the pool, landing right next to the overjoyed Rick. He held his son under the arms and lifted him out of the water, looking deep into his eyes. All at once, a wave of emotion shot through him. This was everything to him. This was his family. This was what he had fought for in that damn prison of a clinic.

"What's wrong, Dad, aren't you happy after your long holiday?" the boy asked innocently, noticing the emotion that had overtaken Rick's face.

Rick paused, not knowing how to convey what he was feeling to his younger son. Words would never come close. He hoped that, one day, James would know the full force of the love that could exist between father and child.

"I *am* happy," he said softly to James. He stared at his son, not moving, trying to come to terms with what he was feeling. "I'm just so happy to be home again."

CHAPTER SEVENTEEN

"S O, MR. DELLICH, I see you visited the Mayo Clinic not too long ago. Did you find it beneficial?" The older man, certainly in his seventies, looked up with eager eyes.

"Yes, I was impressed."

"I would expect so. I happen to have worked there — a fine institution, one of the best."

Rick was beginning to like his new psychiatrist already. He was semi-retired, so Rick had been pleased to be taken on as a weekly client. The visits were a requirement of his ongoing care, especially given the Epilim he was still taking. He couldn't help but feel like a released criminal wearing an ankle bracelet to monitor his every move: keeping an eye on all the loonies who were liable to flip out at any moment, despite having convinced the authorities of their sanity. But could he blame them? Just remember the revolving door at the Jennings Clinic, he thought. Maybe *he* would be the next one to flip out.

"I've always held the clinic in the highest regard, Doctor. Though, even the head of the psychiatric department at the Mayo referred me to another institution in the end... it's strange, such a renowned health clinic not being equipped for the care I needed. It's as if there aren't a lot of people who fully understand mental health."

"That's quite true, Rick. It's by no means a fully developed branch of medicine – plenty of divergence in opinion here, research still pointing us in a number of different directions, and the number of different conditions that we treat seems to grow by the week. And that's coming from someone who's been in it since the forties." Bradshaw's face flashed through Rick's mind: *there's a person with a pretty damn divergent opinion on prescribing drugs.*

"In New Zealand all that time?" Rick wondered.

"No," Dr. Korovin leaned back in his chair, a nostalgic smile forming. "I was born in the USSR – thankfully though it nö longer goes by that name – near the Aral Sea. But my family fled from Stalin's persecution when I was still a boy, arriving in London, where I was fortunate enough to attend medical school. That's where I practiced until my wife and I moved across the globe to NZ in the seventies."

Rick listened, wide-eyed. What a powerful experience, he thought, to be forced from one's country to a totally foreign land, narrowly escaping the butcher who murdered millions. It reminded him of his own father's fleeing Croatia with his parents. To leave the home of one's forebears for a new life in a tiny country on the other side of the globe, without knowing a word of English, was a challenge to say the least. Such drastic changes could only be undertaken in desperation. When there was no other option. Caution was thrown to the wind and all the eggs were placed in one basket. That's what such a monumental shift required.

He had only met the doctor fifteen minutes ago, but already Rick could sense the man's integrity. Maybe this man could help him reclaim his strength. Although the monitoring was a requirement, and despite his resentment at being under supervision, Rick knew that if he were to have a chance at fully rebuilding his health he would need all the help he could get. And if he were to have a chance at rebuilding his life, his marriage, and his family, he would need to do everything in his power to leap forward in his health, whenever an opportunity presented itself.

The two chatted some more before Rick heard an echo from his second day at the Jennings Clinic, a day he would rather not be reminded of.

"So, Rick, why don't you tell me about what happened on the day you had your breakdown."

Hell, not again. . .

CHAPTER EIGHTEEN

IT HAD BEEN over two months since Rick had met with Andrew and Rosa to discuss the family firm. *It's good to be home,* he thought to himself as he anticipated the arrival of his brother-in-law and sister – it seemed like so long since he had last seen them in Topeka. He looked out onto Kohimarama Beach. The office suite was a far cry from the incessant activity of their former base at Naturally Best adjoining the factories, the delivery trucks circulating and a whole office floor alive with people, discussions, phones. Here it was simply the boardroom and three offices, each overlooking the beach, and Rangitoto staring back at them across the ruffled water. The only sounds were the passing of light traffic between the sand and the building, and the blend of conversation and silverware on plates that occasionally drifted through an open window from the café below.

He thought back to the last time he had been in the room and the argument that broke out between him and his sister, not long before his breakdown. He winced at the mere thought of it; the culmination of all the tension that had existed between them since the sale of Best. Or had it always been there and simply become more obvious as time went on? On the surface, it had been a difference in opinion on business strategy. But the personal conflicts had added fuel to the spark until Rick knew he no longer had the energy to deal with the business. His final words at the meeting once again sounded in his head: 'Let's see how the family firm does under your control, then.'

"Rick." His awareness snapped back to the room. It was Rosa, approaching him with open arms. He smiled and embraced his sister. And then Andrew.

They talked firstly about Rick's later weeks in the Jennings Clinic; about Kate and the difficulties that lay ahead in resuscitating the relationship. They spoke of Maria – Rick had seen her the night he arrived home – and also of Andrew and Rosa's children. It was odd to witness life's speedy progression: already Rick's nephew had completed college and left New Zealand, and the older of his own children would be done with college in a year.

"Well, I suppose we should get down to business," Rick said. "Where are we with our investments?"

Rosa brought Rick up to speed with their existing investments – the property developments and financing of various startup companies, as well as an extensive global securities portfolio, and several intellectual property-driven projects with the potential to make a difference in people's lives.

It was their vision for the future that put Rick on edge. As Rosa and Andrew outlined their strategy, he became nervous at the apparent lack of cohesiveness. The direction was unclear and he questioned their next step, a substantial shopping center, office tower and apartment complex in Melbourne, Australia.

The three discussed it back and forth, but it was obvious that they weren't seeing eye-to-eye. Rick voiced his hesitations: there was no vision for the firm's future. He had always considered his own leadership of the firm to be marked by a strong vision, as well a pragmatism for bringing that vision to reality. But what he was now hearing lacked what he felt would be needed to continue the firm's progress, and he voiced his concerns to Rosa and Andrew.

As the discussion heated up, Rick could sense a growing resentment at his attempt to steer the firm. After all, he had relinquished the final decision-making to Andrew and his sister shortly before his breakdown.

And he was aware that he, himself, had always held the reins throughout their business partnership, since the inception of the fruit juice business, through his chairmanship of Naturally Best, and into the running of the family firm. He had given them control of the firm, but that didn't mean he was about to stand by and watch what could be mistakes happen. As it had always been, the firm did not act until all three agreed on a decision. The firm operated by consensus, and it always had, from the days of Best through to the present. It was an arrangement that honored the importance of family, the sanctity of that uniquely incorruptible relationship. Nothing mattered more to Rick.

"Rick," Rosa began when the conversation had apparently reached a stalemate. "I can see that you're not going to agree to this investment. But if you won't allow the firm to invest in it, we're prepared to do so personally."

The words shocked Rick. "Personally? You mean we would withdraw capital from the firm for our own, personal investments? You mean stepping down our operations?" He struggled to grasp the proposal. "If you want to make your own investments, then that's your choice, but the idea seems to have come out of nowhere – after twenty years of acting as a single unit." He shook his head, bemused. "I just think of everything I've done for this firm – I've never sought to take my investments for myself. Every time, I've placed them in the care of the family. And you're saying that you suddenly want to change the way we do business? I don't get it."

"Rick, let's be realistic here," Rosa replied, her eyes glaring into Rick's. "You can't expect to run this firm the way you used to. You've had a nervous breakdown. You're not well. You can no longer expect to handle the kind of pressure and decisions that you once did. I know it's not what you want to hear, but your doctors are under no illusions about it: they've said, more than once, that you'll never be the same."

Rick didn't know how to respond. He sat there, dumbstruck.

"Rick, we have no desire to step down the firm's investments. But you can't expect to be in control anymore. You have enough to take care of in your own life – let us run the business."

He sat for a few moments in silence, gazing out the window at

Rangitoto. An image of the old lions in the pride making way for the new flashed in his mind. He had lived a full life in the business world. His dreams had become reality; indeed, the reality had even exceeded his dreams. There were no grounds for dissatisfaction in his business life. His personal life, however, was a different story, the challenges that awaited weighing heavily on his heart, his marriage and his own mental health both seriously in question.

Maybe Rosa was right. He had more pressing issues to tend to. But their earlier willingness, or threat, to part ways at the drop of a hat dug deep into his abdomen. It hurt to think that they could be so casual with what Rick had always considered so precious. He remembered promising his father, shortly before he had passed away, that he would look after the family. Ned sought assurance that the family would continue as a unit and that Rick would take care of his sister. It was a promise that Rick had made without a second thought. It was an ideal that he had placed in front of his own happiness or that of his wife, to the possible detriment of his own marriage.

But what Rosa had said seemed to make no sense. It was as if the unity of the family meant nothing to her. What of the motto by which they had always conducted business, *All for one and one for all?* Did they no longer have any need for him now that he had, by their estimation, outlived his usefulness? He still couldn't quite believe what he had heard earlier in the conversation. He could argue till he was blue in the face, but in any case, he could see that as far as the two other people in the room were concerned, his tenure at the helm was up. It was time to make way for the new. And he had a bigger problem to deal with: getting his life back.

"Well," he said, turning back to his sister and brother-in-law, "I just hope that you're right about this new strategy."

CHAPTER NINETEEN

Rick's NEW PSYCHIATRIST had highly recommended a two-person team, one male and one female. Rick was pleased with the advice but Kate had not taken to it with such enthusiasm. She had been seeing her own therapist who had made a recommendation, and given that Rick was determined to prove to his wife just how important she was, he decided not to question her preference.

"Kate, let's start with you," the counselor after the initial introductions and an outline of how she worked. "Tell me about the situation between you and Rick. Tell me about what's working, things that aren't working, perhaps areas in which you would like to see some change."

Kate prepared to speak, and it was clear that she was nervous about the setting. "I love Rick, but I'm not happy with the way things are. I feel that," she began hesitantly, "I feel that I'm not heard, that Rick doesn't listen to me. He's already taken a hearing test and was told that his hearing is fine – he just doesn't listen. And it's not always easy for me to express to him how I feel – he has an easier time with that. So, with him not listening and my not always being able to articulate to him exactly how I feel, it seems to me that he doesn't understand me – I just feel like I'm not being heard." There was a pause before she continued.

"And I also feel that I'm not appreciated in what I do. He doesn't know how to turn a dishwasher on; he never does any shopping, or laundry – he just leaves his clothes lying around for me to pick up; he can't cook a thing; I'm always preparing his clothes for the day and packing his suitcases; and I just feel as though he doesn't appreciate what I do." Rick's mind questioned the criticism, his thoughts turning immediately to their live-in housekeeper and Kate's freedom in not having to work, but he was determined to not allow even a word of protest to leave his mouth.

"And then there's his family. His family has always come first," she said with exasperation. "His sister, his brother-in-law, his grandparents, his mother – he's forever trying to please them. We moved to Australia to live our lives but returned to New Zealand almost immediately because of his family. I've always felt that I've come third in his life: first was his family, second was his business, and then there's me."

The room grew quiet and it seemed that Kate was satisfied that she had voiced her grievances. The counselor turned to her husband.

"Rick, I would like to invite you to share your feelings on what has been said and to add your thoughts on the situation between you and Kate."

Part of Rick wished to voice his disagreement with what had been said by Kate. He wanted to tell her that he felt she always had come first and how he vividly recalled promising her, under the Eiffel Tower, to sell Best and spend more time with her. *Yes, I was ambitious. Yes I worked hard for us. Yes I wanted to share with all of my family. But I still feel that you came first.* He wanted to explain that he couldn't bring himself to continue living in Australia those two years ago, regardless of his family circumstances; it had all gotten to be too much and he could feel himself fading. But he thought better of defending his position. Kate had been through a lot, and though it wasn't readily apparent, he could sense that she was deeply angry with him.

"I have only two things to say," Rick began. "The first is that I would like Kate to bring to my attention all of her grievances here, today. I want to know everything that's bothering her: if she's unhappy with my performance in the bedroom, if there's anything else that she's unhappy with, I would like it to be brought up now." He turned to Kate, who indicated that she had said all that she had to say. "Well, I want to prove to you, Kate, that you do come first in my life. And I am going to do everything I can to become the best listener I can be. And I'll do everything I can to help with the housework in whatever way would please you."

He spoke to both the counselor and Kate. "I don't have any grievances to discuss. I want to make the changes that my wife would like to see. But there is one request I have of her. Kate, please do not criticize me in front of our sons. This is the only thing I ask of you."

CHAPTER TWENTY

S HIT, I FEEL like a circus clown, he thought as he reflected on the number of projects he was juggling. It was as if the people around him expected Rick to be able to immediately resume his life after his return from America. They were almost oblivious to the mountain he still had to climb. He had resolved to change his habits, his health, his approach to dealing with stress; reevaluate his involvement with business; forge a new relationship with his children; and repair his stalled marriage. All this, while simultaneously coping with bipolar disorder and ensuring, at all costs, that he did not suffer another breakdown.

The irony of his complaining thoughts was not lost on Rick. On the one hand, he resented the weekly meetings with his psychiatrist. Although he struck up a friendship with the older man, there was no doubt in Rick's mind that he had been branded: he was a manic depressive and this meant constant monitoring. He was required to visit with the psychiatrist every week. And, every month, a blood sample would be taken and tested to ensure that Rick was still taking his Epilim. He was under surveillance; he was different; and there was no denying it. It was a tough pill to swallow; he was 'different' now.

On the other hand, Rick wanted his family to appreciate the immensity of the task that lay before him. He wanted them to understand just how much he was being asked to change, but he hated being seen as 'different'. *I guess I can't have it both ways,* he concluded. If offered a choice between being branded as a manic depressive or being accepted as the old Rick, with all the expectations that it entailed, he would choose the latter in a heartbeat.

Each day demanded of Rick nothing less than his best. He sensed that the marriage counselor was balancing a dual responsibility and it placed Rick under an uncomfortable degree of scrutiny: her usual marriage counseling was complicated by the fact that, in the back of her mind, she was unsure of just how stable Rick was. Was he capable of being a good husband? Would he reach breaking point and physically harm his wife? Rick was aware that he was no longer a standard case with anyone: he was a wild card. An unknown quantity.

The marriage counselor was beginning to frustrate him: little progress had been made and he also grew to privately resent the scrutiny. *I know I have faults,* he pondered. *But I'm not going to let the medical profession snuff out all of my peculiarities. I don't like egg yolks: big deal. I'm not going to eat them. I don't care if people think I'm quirky: I'm still going to eat six egg whites whenever I want. And I know I can't spell. I never could. I'm not going to bother changing that one, either,* he thought as the counselor took note of some of his idiosyncrasies.

In his efforts to live up to Kate's expectations, Rick became an avid student of homemaking. Over the weeks, he learned the skills of grocery shopping, laundering, and dish-washing. Though there was much for him to absorb in a short period of time, he found great satisfaction in doing work for those he loved. He was pleasantly surprised by the nature of the profession and reflected to himself that, for those who did not have to juggle the demands of a full-time career, homemaking must be a wonderful way of life.

He enjoyed preparing his sons' school lunches and took great pride in the quality of his work. He carved roasted chicken along the grain to achieve the most desirable texture and then layered it with carefully measured ratios of avocado, lettuce and cucumber. His sons seemed to somewhat appreciate the care that had been taken, but were unable to match their father's excitement at the quality of the lunches.

No sooner had Rick begun to separate the whites from the colors than Kate announced her intention to take a trip for a week with a friend, and as a test of Rick's progress, asked him to tend to the running of the household. Anticipating his first thought even before he could give voice to it, she stipulated that asking his mother for any help would be cheating.

Rick was desperately trying to win back her respect. He had been disappointed in the counselor's approach and began to privately question her abilities, but he had never mentioned this to Kate and continued with the weekly, and sometimes twice-weekly, sessions to prove to his wife that he was serious about changing. The week on his own was a further opportunity to surprise her.

Every day, he made his own bed, prepared his sons' school lunches, and visited the supermarket. He was relieved to discover that his training had placed him in good stead for his test: he had mastered the dishwasher and washing machine. By far, the biggest challenge was in the kitchen. Kate was an excellent cook and Rick knew he couldn't compete. But he fumbled through a few simple dinners, and though it was not up to the usual standard of food presented in the Dellich household, it was adequate.

Kate returned expecting to hear complaints from Rick that he found it difficult to cope. To her surprise, he was able to tell her that he found the week extremely rewarding and, in fact, noticed that he had a lot of free time, to which Kate's response was, "Try doing it for twenty-two years."

Despite his efforts to rectify his shortcomings in Kate's eyes, Rick felt frustrated with the counselor and with the lack of progress in his marriage. He had done everything she had asked without reservation but the two had grown no closer over the months, nor had Kate stopped criticizing him in the presence of their children. He began to feel that his wife's accumulated anger toward him would inevitably magnify any minor annoyance into a major issue.

His personal psychiatrist's revelation to Rick that bipolar disorder moves in cycles and was liable to return within the next year or two, also played in the back of his mind. The psychiatrist had confirmed to Rick that, even with the drugs he was taking, the condition would return within seven years, if not much sooner. Rick was told that another breakdown could occur within a month; six months; a year; at the very maximum, seven years, but that it would probably strike sometime soon, and that it always did, without fail.

He had been prepared to rebuild his life, but to learn that he could be hit once again with the severity of manic depression was a huge blow to Rick's confidence, and a catastrophe that he was determined to avert. On more than one occasion, psychiatrists had disclosed to Rick their opinions that schizophrenia and acute depression were more easily treated by drugs than bipolar disorder. Schizophrenia could be managed readily with drugs in most cases, but controlling the opposing poles of euphoria and severe depression, as was the case with bipolar disorder, was a challenge when it came to drug treatment.

A dysfunctional marriage, in which he sensed an undercurrent of anger and a dearth of affection, would only contribute to the likelihood of suffering another bout of manic depression. Life was moving at full steam ahead and he could see that his stress levels were going nowhere but skyward. Both his marriage and his health were proving more complicated than he had expected and it was clear that, to have even a chance of making it through the challenges he was navigating, he would have to be at the top of his game.

Rick began to research optimum health. He hired a personal trainer and tried to wind down his business affairs to a minimum. He read widely on diet and exercise in the hope of enhancing his overall health and increasing his chances of making it to the top of the mountain on which his eyes were firmly set. His priorities were clear: he would rebuild his relationships with his wife and his sons, and rebuild himself to beat the condition that stalked him.

CHAPTER TWENTY-ONE

R ICK'S FEELINGS FOR Helen had grown rapidly and he was frequently going without sleep to ensure he could spend time with her. Barely twenty years of age and doing his best to build his business interests after withdrawing from university, while juggling his commitments to his father's milk delivery operation, he sometimes pulled up to her second-floor apartment in the wee hours of the morning, and to avoid waking her roommate climbed the drain pipe to her bedroom window. Their love flowed unimpeded from open hearts, innocently expecting nothing more from each other than the tenderness they shared in their time together.

But as the sleep deprivation began to catch up with him, he found himself unable to sustain his energy, occasionally falling asleep at the dinner table as Helen laughed to herself, staring at the man she had fallen for. The wake-up call came on one of Rick's late night delivery shifts to the ships at the Auckland Ports. The truck's heater was blasting on full to combat the mid-winter chill. Rick could feel his body relaxing uncontrollably as his mind began to wander. Jack's panicked voice from the passenger seat woke him with a start. Through his fogged-up glasses, Jack could see the approaching obstacle: Rick, dozing at the wheel, had veered off the road and onto the wharf. A shipment of New Zealand's finest timber awaiting export smashed through the front of the truck, blocking their path into the sea below and stopping between Rick's knees, just short of the driver's seat.

He had escaped disaster once, and did not wish to tempt fate further. Rick decided to take time off for vacation for the first time in years. The week spent away with Steve in Queensland, situated in the sub-tropical waters to New Zealand's north, allowed Rick to reflect on the direction of Dellich Products. It had been a year since he had withdrawn from university to focus on business, but things were not moving fast enough for him. He needed something bigger – something more than the steady progress of property development or an industry of limited scope such as delivering drinks to Auckland's central city. He needed something with real growth potential.

He resolved to find such an opportunity when he returned to Auckland. But his most burning desire was to see Helen again – a week apart was too long.

Rick arrived in Auckland late on a Sunday afternoon and rushed straight to Helen's flat in the city for the dinner they had arranged a week earlier, before his departure. He wore a permanent smile throughout the meal, so elated was he to be reunited with the girl he felt he was falling in love with. He was almost oblivious to Helen's tension, but became vaguely aware of a certain unease surrounding her. He could read a degree of hesitation and confusion in her facial expressions, and her eye movements betrayed a nervousness he had never seen in her before.

'What is it? You don't seem yourself,' he questioned as he retrieved his credit card from the waiter and the two stood to leave. She was silent for a moment until they exited the restaurant. Rick opened the passenger side door for her.

'I'm going to walk home, Rick.'

'Why? Let's go for a drive, there's so much I want to talk to you about. I haven't seen you for a week!' he said, unable to contain his excitement.

'I can't see you anymore.' Helen couldn't bring herself to look him in the eye as she said the words. Her throat caught as she continued, 'Here, this is for you,' she said, handing Rick an envelope. 'Please don't call me. Don't come to see me. I just want to be left alone.' She kissed Rick on the cheek and turned in the direction of her apartment. Rick felt the coolness of her tear on the side of his face, and stood motionless as if waiting to awaken from a dream.

The letter was written in the flowing handwriting that he had grown used to from the letters she occasionally mailed to Rick to brighten his day. But the tone was alien. 'I think you're a lovely guy and I thought we had something special. I wish you nothing but happiness, but it's best for me if I don't see you anymore. Please don't contact me. I'll miss you.' Rick felt his stomach turning and the awful sensation of loss burning in his chest. He dashed up the street to Helen's house and beat on the door incessantly until Helen's roommate answered the door.

'She doesn't want to see you, just stay away, please. She's upset enough as it is.'

'What's all this about?' begged Rick, but the door closed before he could finish his sentence.

He caught sight of the drainpipe that had so faithfully provided him access to his beloved when all other points of entry were blocked. He scaled the wall and, on reaching the top, could see Helen sitting on the edge of the bed, her makeup running with tears.

'Helen, I love you!' yelled Rick through the window.

She turned to him, her face a mixture of distress and relief. 'I love you, too,' she managed as she opened the window a crack. 'But it's not going to work. Don't make this any harder on me than it already is.' She closed the window, drew the curtains, and Rick knew that now was not the time to reason with her. He headed home, determined to discover the motivation behind Helen's inexplicable behavior.

For three months Rick tried in vain to contact Helen. Every phone call ended the moment he spoke. Her co-workers at the health spa had warned him, as had her roommate. He could only guess that his letters were discarded without being read.

Rick's only choice was to let it go. He did his best to forget the warmth of their affection for each other and the simplicity of their love. He almost succeeded. But the unresolved hurt, the abrupt withdrawal of the one who had stolen his heart, nagged at him insistently.

In Kate's arms, he did forget what had passed before. His memories of past relationships faded until they were all just a fondly-remembered period of his earlier life: the drama of young love; the mystery of a woman's heart. *They're right*, he thought. *People can do the strangest things*, he lightly mused one day at a friend's mention of Helen's name.

The drives home after Kate's Friday night shift soon grew into hour-long drives out of Auckland to reach the lesser-known beaches for Sunday picnics. Rick always ensured that he had secured the champagne and nibbles on the Saturday, before the shops closed for the rest of the weekend, and Kate never failed to bake a batch of Rick's favorite cookies in preparation for the outing. Rick began to think that Kate's cooking rivaled even that of his mother's.

His favorite dish of Kate's was her breakfast crepes. He had never known someone to achieve such delicacy in the texture. Kate would smile to herself as she watched Rick work steadily through a tall pile of the nearly paper-thin crepes. His appetite was seemingly insatiable. The two had been seeing each other for five months before Rick received the phone call that shook him.

He had agreed to meet in the Domain, Auckland's inner city nature reserve. The autumn chill was tempered by the midday sun as Rick and Helen walked together over the green hills overlooking the harbor. Rick knew Helen would have no problem finding another man after him; the striking blonde had continuously turned down approaches from men during the time the two had been together. But he could see that she had been unable to replace what they had.

'I made an enormous mistake, Rick,' she began after a long silence. 'I haven't found anyone that I feel strongly about,' she said, turning her head to Rick as they continued their stroll. 'It's taken me this long to realize that what we had together was special.'

Rick gazed at her incredulously before his eyes fixed on the distant clouds as he struggled for a response. 'What the hell are you talking about? You left without any explanation.'

She looked down in front of herself, still walking slowly. 'I know. I made a terrible mistake. It's my fault.' Rick, lost for words, walked on next to Helen. 'I know how much you value your family, Rick. I know how much they mean to you. And I thought I could trust them, too.' Her words were punctuated by abrupt pauses, and Rick could hear that she was having difficulty verbalizing her explanation. 'Rosa told me things about you.'

Rick let the words sink in for a moment. 'What? When?'

'When you were in Queensland for a week – just before it ended between us. She phoned me – invited me out to lunch. Of course I went. I thought she was trying to make me feel welcome in your family. I always enjoyed seeing your family.' Rick listened, unable to bring himself to speak. 'She told me that you're not what you seem. That it's all just an act.' The words stung Rick. 'She said that you're selfish, demanding, that you could never be faithful to any woman. That she knew you had already seen other girls during the time we were together.'

'And you believed her?' Rick asked in disbelief.

'She's your sister! She said that if anyone knew you, it was her. That she was telling me this to save me from getting more hurt than I was already going to be... that's why I left as soon as she told me – because it broke my heart as it was – I didn't want to get any closer to you.'

Neither one spoke for a time, the only audible sound the birds in the nearby trees and the hum of the occasional passing car.

'Rick, I want to confront Rosa with you, in front of your parents. I want to get this out in the open. They should know what she did.'

'No.' Rick spoke quietly. Ned had so often emphasized the importance of family to his children, and Rick knew such a rift in the family would break his mother's and father's hearts. Besides, Rosa had since gotten married to Andrew and had become a mother. Rick was confident that his sister had changed, or that she one day would.

'I want you back, Rick. I should have come to you, I should have told you. I see that now... but she's your sister – why would she do something like this?'

'I don't know why!' he blurted. 'I can't believe it.' They stopped walking and stood overlooking Auckland's Harbour Bridge. 'I'm shocked. But I wish I could say I'm more surprised.'

'Are you seeing anyone?'

'Yeah,' he replied.

'Is it serious?'

'Yes.' Another long pause. 'You wouldn't even talk to me. I was in agony for months.' Helen cringed as she listened. They continued walking until they reached their cars. She sat with Rick for a long while, asking for another chance. She pleaded with him to allow her to bring the incident before his parents, but it was out of the question as far as he was concerned.

'Please call me,' she said as they parted. 'I miss you.' And Rick couldn't deny that a long-forgotten part of himself still missed her.

Maybe I should have confronted her. Rick eased the car out of the driveway, the Waterford gates closing behind him, the distant drama surrounding Helen replaying in his mind. The day, so far, was ordinary. But that would soon change.

In the end, it didn't matter, he reflected. He had found Kate. Besides, it wouldn't have done any good.

Rosa would have screamed her head off, balled her eyes out and slammed the door. The first words to break our silence would have been my apology. In the end, I would have given in.

His thoughts drifted back to the vacation in Spain, a year before his breakdown. The tension in his body became at once noticeable, as if he were actually back there on the Costa del Sol, waiting for the sun to elevate his mood, doing his best to relax, wondering why the anxiety medication and sleeping tablets weren't working. It spooked him to recall that feeling; that awful sense that something wasn't right and the inability to understand just what that thing was. Seen from his present situation, it was a dark picture: it was the beginning of a downward spiral that would only be halted by his arrival at the bottom. The memory of the night that he refused to let it slide any longer still sent a pain through his belly like a wound that wouldn't heal.

They had chosen to begin their time in Spain by visiting Andalusia. The region was renowned for its food and wine, and Rick eagerly anticipated the famed cuisine as he sat in the formal dining room with Kate, Rosa and Andrew. The conversation centered around the charitable trust that Rick and Andrew had formed after Ned's death to support the dreams of underprivileged, terminally ill children. The foundation had been running smoothly, granting requests for specialized study, experiences of a lifetime and family vacations and they were happy with the progress. Rick had received a phone call earlier in the day that he was excited to share with the others.

His appetizer of pinchitos arrived, and he decided to share the good news with the table. 'Andrew, you've known that for some months I've been talking with Penny Lucas about becoming involved in the foundation.' Rosa's eyes turned to her husband, who looked only at the plate in front of him. 'She is the most successful fundraiser for charitable trusts in the country,' Rick said. 'And, out of all the people who approach her every year — the many charities that seek her help and which she turns down — she has agreed to be a part of our foundation,' Rick announced with an excited smile. His announcement was met with silence. Then Rosa spoke.

'Rick, I'm not happy about that.'

Rick pondered her response for a moment before replying. 'Why?'

'I'm just not comfortable with it,' said Rosa.

'But surely there must be a reason?', Rick said, confused. 'Do you know her?'

'No. I just don't want her to be a trustee.'

'Rosa, right now there are two trustees, both men, and neither one with any fundraising skills. We've put over a million dollars of our personal savings in there, but it's not going to last forever. Don't you think we need to raise funds for the future?' His question was met with silence, so he continued. 'Don't you realize what a privilege this is? Penny gets approached every year to become involved with charities, and she still only works exclusively with one: her own. This is the first trusteeship she's ever accepted. She can ensure that this charity really does something special,' Rick pleaded with his sister. 'There's no one better for this organization. She's a wonderful person. Andrew's met her. You were happy with her, Andrew?'

'Well, not really, Rick,' Andrew responded.

Rick was shocked to see that Andrew's view of the situation had changed without warning, but continued with his line of thought. 'Look at this sensibly. We want maximum value in helping people — the purpose of this charity is to help children, and we can't do that without money. We need to raise funds. We need exposure to garner contributions.'

'Well, that's up to the trustees,' Rosa replied.

'The trustees?', Rick asked incredulously. 'The trustees will be over the moon about this! Andrew and I have already spoken to both of them. You appointed Daniel – even he thought it was a great idea.'

'It's not going to happen, Rick,' Rosa said. She continued eating with all the composure of a practiced diplomat. Nothing disturbed her poise. Even her words, as curt and icy as they had been, emanated from a presentation that was difficult to reconcile with the intent that was being projected: her generous rings of golden hair, unusual for her Croatian lineage, rested on slight shoulders graced, on one side, by a tastefully revealing black dress. Her perpetually wide eyes gazed out innocently at the world, while also betraying a force of personality that was unmistakable, and her prominent cheek bones drew one's attention to an intriguingly delicate mouth, one that wove effortless conversation with a seemingly inimitable self-assurance. Everything about her spoke of beauty, glamour and grace.

Rick was now fuming inside. The realization that Andrew and Rosa wanted to control the trust for their own purposes was staring him right in the face. Many times he had relented to their requests but this time it was different. This was not a personal matter, this was about something bigger than any individual. As their plates were cleared, he started up again.

'This trust is not about us – it's about the children and families we're helping – and I'm not going to let you sabotage this charity unless you give me a good reason why Penny should not be involved,' Rick directed to his sister.

'I'll give you a good reason,' she said. 'Daniel will resign if you make Penny a trustee.'

'What?' Rick questioned. 'That's ridiculous. Andrew and I spoke to him two months ago – he agreed it's a good idea. Have you heard differently since then?'

'Yes, I have. We've spoken to him.'

'Oh, why does that not surprise me?' Rick replied. 'This is unbelievable. You want me to go back to Penny and tell her, after months of discussions, months of paving the way for her involvement, that the offer she finally accepted has now been revoked? And all because you're uncomfortable with the competition. You don't want her overshadowing you.' No one spoke. 'I spent months with lawyers setting up this charity. You were happy to join when all the work had been done and now, when you no longer need me, you're telling me I have no say whatsoever so you can use the charity for your own purposes?' Rick continued.

'This charity was always ours,' Rosa shot back.

'That's simply not true,' Rick answered. 'Furthermore, it's not about you or me. It's about something bigger. And you're holding it down because you don't want to share the glory with Penny. You're threatened by her. Just like you're threatened by anyone you can't control. Just like you've always been threatened by any success that might come to me, or even by anyone I might become friends with.' Rosa's eyes narrowed. 'That's right, Rosa, I know you've sabotaged my friendships. But this charity is not about you and me, it's bigger than both of us.'

'Rick, if anyone's got it in for you, you brought it on yourself,' she said. The anger was growing in both their voices. Kate and Andrew had noticed that they were drawing some attention from the nearby tables, but the siblings were now overcome with passion and the argument showed no sign of subsiding.

'I even know what you did with Helen.' Rick was looking Rosa directly in the eye.

'Helen who?'

'Helen who I dated before Kate and who you took out for lunch,' Rick answered.

Rosa gave an expression of unfamiliarity. 'I don't know what you're talking about.'

'I left Auckland for a week. I came back and she didn't want to see me because of the things you told her.'

Rosa's face grew red with anger as she stood to her feet. 'That's a lie!' she yelled.

Rick stood to meet her and continued at the top of his voice. 'She sat in the passenger seat of my car and pleaded with me to take her to see Mum and Dad so that she could expose you!'

Rosa's eyes widened in rage, 'You're lying!' she shouted.

Rick kept going. 'She wanted to expose you but I couldn't do it out of respect for our mother and father. I wanted to let it go because I thought you would change. But you haven't changed! You're worse! You keep destroying everything that I try to build! Why do you hate me so much!'

Rosa didn't answer Rick's question. All activity in the room had ceased. It was silent. The restaurant was full – the men in their jackets and ties, the women in their evening-wear – all staring at the table. Rosa burst into tears and hurried to the ladies' room. Rick sat down. Nobody at the table spoke.

Rick spent the rest of the trip in an ever-deepening state of unhappiness. He fell sick and spent days in bed. The night of the argument, he had begged Kate to leave Spain with him the following day. He found her unable to understand the magnitude of the situation. To him, it was confirmation of the suspicion that had been growing in him for years: that his sister would stop at nothing to seize control of whatever she could once Rick had outlived his usefulness. To Kate, it was another of the many arguments that she had witnessed since meeting Rick. And she knew this one would end in the same way they always did: with Rick's surrender. She pressed Rick to prove to her that this one was different from the rest. If he would stand up to his sister and press for what he knew to be the best move for the charity, then Kate would leave with Rick immediately. But Rick's response was the same as it always had been: 'I have to do what's best for the family.'

RICK NOTICED HIS pulse quickening as he recollected the confrontation. *I was a fool to give in to her.*

The charity was now, years later, all but inactive and slowly fading into nothingness. He was angry. Angry at Rosa, his sister; Andrew, the friend who was not what he used to be; but most of all, he was angry at himself. For years he had appeased his sister. The disagreements had become predictable, every one of them escalating until such time as Rick threw in the towel, whether that required Rosa's tears or a Rick racked with guilt over the possibility of a family rift.

Her force of will knew no bounds, even when her own mother was involved. Rick had watched his mother yield to Rosa time and again over the years. When a disagreement would arise in the earlier years, Rosa's young children, who at any other time would call their grandmother without fail every morning, ceased their calls and visits at their mother's request, whether it be for days or weeks, until Maria capitulated to Rosa's demands.

As he pulled up to the Kohimarama office, he wondered: was he being petty? He had certainly considered the innumerable squabbles to be somewhat trivial relative to the amount of turmoil they created within the family. It had only added to his reluctance to allow the tension to damage the unity of the family over any of the individual issues that had caused so much conflict. They *were* such petty issues. The arguments *were* so childishly handled, regardless of how conciliatory, or not, was Rick's approach.

But there was something not right. Something deeper. Rick had begun to sense that something was very wrong with his and his sister's relationship, but he still couldn't seem to grasp it with his mind. A pattern was emerging, but only a sliver of it was as yet visible. Its imagined presence, alone, was enough to send a shiver through Rick's body. It was as if he had been blind to something innately sinister for a very long time. But he could not yet bring himself to fully understand what he sensed was forming before him.

Irrespective of the suspicions inching their way out of his subconscious, what Rick now had to say to his sister could not wait. He thought of Joel, his lawyer friend from the Jennings Clinic, and the sickening betrayal he had fallen victim to at the hands of his own father. It had shaken Rick to the core. But never had he imagined that such an unthinkable set of circumstances could befall his own life. He opened the door to find Rosa, with Andrew by her side, ready to begin what they thought would be the weekly business meeting.

CHAPTER TWENTY-TWO

R ICK DID HIS best to contain his anger as he entered the room, his sister and brother-in-law seated at the board-room table. He stared into Rosa's eyes, trying to see the person behind them. But all he could see was his sister, his own blood.

"I need to ask you both something, and I want you to be honest with me. I deserve to hear the truth."

"Of course," Rosa replied.

"Someone has been telling people around town about my condition. Someone has been spreading the word that I had a nervous breakdown, that I'm a manic depressive."

For a moment, no one spoke a word.

Then, "Dammit." It was Rosa, shaking her head. "We all agreed that it would remain quiet – each person privy to this information understood the measures we were taking to cover for your absence. How would it get out? I can't believe anyone in the circle that day would just let it slip – none of them is stupid enough to do that."

"That's what I thought," Rick responded.

Another pause. And then Rosa: "We can't have this getting out. It's bad for the family name."

"I have a feeling that that's part of why you rushed to my side at the time of my breakdown."

"Rick, are you kidding me? You're my brother. What other reason would I need?"

"I don't know, Rosa, I wouldn't expect you to need another reason, especially given that I've accommodated your every request for as long as I can remember." Rick was now looking directly across the table at Rosa. "But whatever it was that placed you by my side through much of the ordeal, it appears that your reasoning has changed."

"What do you mean?"

"I mean that, whereas once you kept the whole thing quiet to save yourself from embarrassment, you're now doing the opposite. I think you're the one who's been disclosing my condition."

Rosa began to shake her head slowly as her face flushed ever so slightly. "Rick, you're still not well. That crazy brain of yours – forever spouting a hundred wild new ideas a minute, always with something to say – it's finally failing you. It's making you crazy. You're not well."

"I can see it in your friends' eyes," he retorted. "I can see it in the way they look at me, and the way they talk to me. They know. You're making me out to be some kind of loony – some has-been confined to a damn rocking chair for the rest of my life."

"What the hell are you talking about, Rick? This is crazy talk – you've lost it. If anyone does think you're a loony, they saw it for themselves." The excitement in Rosa's voice was growing ever so slightly, but it was nowhere near the unabashed anger in Rick's. "You think people don't notice that you're different? Have you ever listened to yourself? Once you get talking, with every one in the room swallowing it whole, thinking what an innocent little angel you are, you don't stop – the number of times I've heard you go on and on about all the terrible things going on in the world, how people should treat one another, what's *really* important in life and all that crap you won't shut up about. Even I start to wonder what's going on for you upstairs."

"So that's why you find it necessary to destroy my credibility – because you're tired of me talking and people listening? Or do you want me out of the way for good now that you and Andrew are running the business and I apparently have outlived my usefulness?"

"You know what, Rick, next time you're having your head checked, maybe you should have them take a look at your eyes, too."

"What the hell does that mean?"

"Here you are attacking your own sister for something that I haven't even done, while you're totally blind to the colossal failings of your wife."

"Kate?"

"Unless there's a second wife you're not telling us about – "

"Kate has not had an easy time. And the two of you have not helped."

"Rick," Andrew interrupted, "She wasn't there for you when you needed her."

"She was there for me as much as she was capable at the time," answered Rick. "How could I expect any more after what I had put her through?"

"That's it," said Rosa. "Leading up to your breakdown, during the breakdown, after the breakdown, all we heard from you, time after time, was your guilt at having failed your wife and sons. Did you ever stop to think about that? Ask Mum – she'll tell you. You couldn't stop talking about how you had let them down, how guilty you felt, how you hadn't lived up to their expectations."

Rick thought back to his sessions with Dr. Bradshaw, the months leading up to the breakdown, and his time in the clinic. It was true – he had been racked with guilt all along, carrying a heavy burden that he was only now beginning to recognize as such.

But I did fail them, didn't I? Could it have been guilt that drove me to the edge? That terrible guilt of failing my wife, my sons?

"Rick, we've never had a problem with you," Rosa spoke calmly. "Any problem that's ever come between us has been Kate's doing, not yours. You're my brother."

Well, there's sure as hell been no shortage of drama between the two of you. His memory triggered a glimpse of the numerous disputes and arguments that had plagued the family from the beginning. The standoffs between Rosa and Kate; Kate's disappointment in Rick's capitulation to his sister's wishes every time; the endless competition. It reached the point where the two women agreed to leave an inventory of their purchases at each designer store to ensure that one would never purchase the same garment as the other, which led to each of them phoning Escada or Versace in Sydney and Beverly Hills regularly to ensure first pick of any new arrivals. And then there was Rosa's competitive approach to handling and dominating the social scene.

It was petty. Childish. Rick wanted no part of it, but it was having an affect on him. On the few occasions that he did seek to intercede in the Rosa and Kate disputes, Rosa's tantrum would be all the more animated for it.

"Oh, believe me," Rick eventually responded. "I'm well aware of the number of problems you've had with Kate."

"After all you've done for her, all your constant concern for her wellbeing and that of your sons, she should have been there for you, Rick." Rosa's voice quieted. "She abandoned you. She drove you to your breakdown."

For a second he stared at her in disbelief. Where did this viciousness come from? He looked at her and held her eyes. His voice was quiet as he tried to control the choking emotion rising in his throat.

"Don't you dare say a word against her. Do you have any idea what I've done to her? What I've put her through?" Rosa was aware of his rising anger.

"I only meant," Rosa began, but Rick didn't want to hear it.

"I know what you meant Rosa. You don't stick the knife deep in someone's back — you just keep pricking it until your prey bleeds to death. Kate has been to hell because of me, and you want to keep hurting her? I don't know what's wrong with you, but I can tell you one thing. Say one more word against my wife, and you will no longer be welcome in my home."

CHAPTER TWENTY-THREE

W HAT THE *HELL* *is going on with Rosa? She can't be right, can she? There's no way.*

Rick turned it over in his mind; his sister's extreme accusations. He couldn't stand to hear her talking like that, but her insistence and her repeated criticisms of Kate were beginning to linger.

Am I completely blind to what's going on in my life? I don't understand it anymore.

Six months had passed. Rick felt he was losing ground on all fronts. He felt no closer to his wife than he had been before beginning counseling. The rift seemed to be spilling over into his relationship with his children, too, and the family looked to be drifting apart. Where his younger son used to say goodbye to him each morning with a kiss on the cheek, he was now subconsciously taking his cues from Kate and barely uttered a word.

Six months, he thought. *Six months. . . and no progress. How can I ever rebuild myself in this situation — in this hostile environment? My wife, my sister, my children — where are they when I need them?*

Am I here, in this life, to support others and get nothing back when I need it? Am I some kind of money machine?

Despite his efforts to rectify his shortcomings in Kate's eyes, Rick felt frustrated with the counselor and with the lack of progress in his marriage. They decided to try a new counselor.

The first session with Christina affirmed to Rick that the problems between him and his wife were deep-seated and may not be easily resolved. The counselor had begun by asking Kate if Rick had ever physically harmed her. She replied that he hadn't. The counselor followed by asking if Rick had sworn at her or made her feel worthless. She again replied, after some thought, with a "No". The question then came as to whether he had ever abused her in any way. She hesitated for a moment, then replied with a "No."

"Well, then he has to have done this – no one ever passes this one," Christina said with surprise in her voice. "Has your husband ever lost his temper with you?" She shifted back in her seat slightly, confident in the answer that she would receive from Kate.

Kate took a long time to respond. It was clear that she was racking her brain for a memory of the kind Christina was asking for. Both her and Rick knew that the counselor was expecting to hear a "Yes" from her. But she found herself eventually replying, "No."

"No?" the woman behind the desk said with widened eyes. "He's never really lost his temper with you?" The only sounds in the room were breathing and the ticking of a clock. Kate said nothing. "Well," the counselor said. "He apparently has lost his temper now, because he says he's considering leaving you."

Rick was taken aback upon hearing his own words repeated. It sounded so serious, so shocking. But it was true – he had opened the session by explaining his impatience and frustration with the situation to both the new counselor and his wife, concluding by saying that he was at a loss for more ideas of how to restore the relationship. He had done everything he could but still felt he wasn't receiving the affection or support that he needed from his wife. He had begun to realize that there was no quick fix for years of accumulated disharmony, especially when the tension had always existed beneath the surface. It was as if he was only just becoming aware of the dissatisfaction his wife had long experienced, but seldom voiced.

"Why do you think he is considering leaving his marriage?" the counselor directed to Kate.

She was quiet for some time. She wanted to dissolve the barrier that had been erected over the years, especially in those turbulent months leading up to and following Rick's breakdown. But, try as she might, she couldn't let go of her own frustration, her own need for validation in the relationship. "I think I've pushed him too far and too hard," she replied. Kate's face was contorted, a cauldron of despair, frustration and sadness.

"Well, maybe that's true," Christina replied. "But we're not looking for anyone to blame here. That won't help us. Kate, maybe it's true that you've pushed Rick, but maybe you, yourself, have also felt as if you've been pushed. Tell me what's been difficult for you?"

"I can't quite put my finger on it," she replied. "There's too much involved for me to really understand what's happened to us — I've tried, but I can't see it clearly. Yes, for some time there's been something not right between us. I've felt that I haven't been seen. And yes, of course it worsened when Rick had his breakdown. That was the hardest part for me. So much was lost. Rick had always been strong, but almost overnight he became fragile, unstable, not himself." She bit her lip. "I found it so hard. I had to keep it all together on my own. I felt as if I was going to lose it myself, but how could I? Where would the children be? If I didn't hold it together, what would happen to our sons?" The room returned to silence.

"I've tried my best in being a good soulmate, mother, partner, I really have. And I know Rick has, too," she said softly, glancing toward her husband. "I've said it before, and I still believe it: if there's any one factor that's damaged our marriage, it's Rick's family."

If only I could give Kate what she wanted. If only I had the strength to turn my life around enough to prove to her that she's the most important part of it. I thought I could, but I'm finding the challenges too huge. I can't bring myself to cause more friction with Rosa and Andrew; I love them too. It's all just too much for me. I need her support to recover. Then I will have the strength to prove it to her. If only she would believe that.

The rest of the session proceeded as expected. The three explored the past, how Rick had prioritized his work and family over his wife, and the toll the breakdown took on the relationship. Kate could not let go of the resentment she had experienced ever since their move back to New Zealand from Australia. She had never been heard, and at the time had no choice but to go along with the decision to succumb to the pressure from Rick's family and swallow her own feelings on the matter. She accepted that she had lost Rick, that he could never give her what she wanted. From that day on, she stopped expecting anything from her husband, and a gulf grew between them, without Rick's ever noticing until it was too late.

Christina was busy, but Rick and Kate dropped everything else in their lives to work in with her schedule; both were committed to repairing the marriage. There was a big part of Rick that regretted not having met Christina earlier. The six months they spent with their first counselor seemed to go nowhere, but it was clear that Christina had a better understanding of how to facilitate the sessions. It occurred to Rick how much the fate of a relationship could depend on the wisdom and communication skills of the counselor. Had they begun in the right vein, perhaps the marriage could have been salvaged, but now he was unsure that they had the energy to continue.

As the weeks passed, Rick's hopes for the relationship faded. He yearned for sincere emotional and physical love from Kate; he wanted to play hooky and go to the movies during the day; he wanted to enjoy picnics together. At times, he was overwhelmed with guilt and couldn't shake the feeling that it was all his fault, but he still believed that, as a human being, he deserved affection from his wife. It was something that he needed. But his efforts had come to naught. He could only surmise that Kate was too angry with him to leap to the place where he was waiting for her.

Maybe they were both reaching a stage of exhaustion where neither one could continue any longer, he pondered. But, then, he knew that wasn't the case. He was sure that his wife could continue with things as though there were no problem. *Maybe she doesn't need the affection from me; maybe she doesn't need to be close to me.* She could quite easily fall into the pattern of so many other couples that Rick had witnessed when love and affection slowly withered, leaving an uninspiring friendship in its wake, a bizarre familiarity underlying a mutual resignation.

Rick couldn't help but take a glum view of relationships. He was sure that, if people were to follow their hearts, the divorce rate would be close to ninety percent as opposed to fifty percent. But most people were held back from a fear of not finding a replacement relationship. 'What if I'm alone? Is he, or she, as good as I can get?' So many couples were held together by their children, or maybe their financial situation, reluctant to accept the drop in living standards that came from separating a dual-income home into two households. He couldn't help but think that most people found the stifling predictability of a stale marriage preferable to the unknown.

But it was not something that he could buy into. He knew of men and women who would remain in a relationship and seek love, physically and emotionally, through extra-marital affairs. It was something that he couldn't do.

As the counseling sessions continued, without any noticeable improvement, Rick found himself considering the option of leaving home. He wasn't sure that it was something he was capable of. After all, he had only recently recovered from a nervous breakdown. Could he handle such a move?

He thought of his dreams for him and Kate – the girl he had always pictured spending the rest of his life with, the two growing old together and spending many years watching their grandchildren grow up. Kate knew Rick well. She knew that he could never bring himself to break up the family that meant everything to him; he loved his sons too much, and felt too great a responsibility toward them, to do that. She knew that he would stay at any cost, and Rick couldn't disagree.

CHAPTER TWENTY-FOUR

I F I DON'T *listen to myself this time, I'm gonna die.*
  I don't know how I know, but I do.
  No more breakdowns, no more close calls. This is my last chance. If I'm not true to myself now, I won't be around to fix my mistakes. For too long I've ignored my heart; this time, I must listen.
  This is my last chance.

He didn't know what was happening to him. He only knew that it was real.

Something was changing inside of him. It was a change he had felt only intermittently during the previous six months, but that had now crept into his everyday awareness. It was a warning, something deep inside crying out to be heard.

It was a knowing that, were he to continue in his marriage without regard for his true feelings, he would be forsaking the very life that flowed through him. Would it manifest itself in the form of a heart attack? A stroke? Cancer? He didn't know. But it was more than a hunch; it was an imperative from the truest place within, signaling without ambiguity, that he could not live in contradiction to his heart's longing to love and be loved, and also expect to live much longer.

Had the breakdown itself not been warning enough of the extent to which he had neglected the call of his innermost self? It was a call that Rick heard loud enough, but for whatever reason he gave himself – duty to family, a refusal to accept that people or circumstances were not living up to his ideals – he ignored.

He had already refused to heed the warnings of his friends' premature deaths – Chris T and the others who passed long before anyone thought their time was up – as well as the constant ache that had preceded his own breakdown. And he had been lucky to emerge relatively unscathed. But he knew that he couldn't push his luck a second time; he had to be true to himself.

Shit.

He stared into the mirror, searching deeper and deeper, but for what, exactly, he didn't know.

What's happening to me?

There was no mistaking what he felt he had to do. But was it real? Was he really going to do this? He didn't know that he had the strength.

CHAPTER TWENTY-FIVE

THE EMPTINESS THAT Rick felt within was echoed by the soulless hotel room. He was alone, and the room bereft of the warmth that he associated with his home. Checking in at the front desk, he had felt ashamed, as if he were being caught in the act of doing something horribly wrong. He struggled to convince himself that what he had done was not a cruel act, but something that he knew was right.

He hoped that one day his sons would understand his predicament; that the family he loved had to change somehow, either with his voluntary departure, or with his death. He understood that much, and nothing had been so clear to him in his life.

But what an awful morning it had been. Kate had pleaded with Rick not to leave. She looked so vulnerable, so helpless. Like a child. An abandoned child.

He shook his head, hoping to rid himself of the haunting image of his abandoned wife — the wife that he had abandoned.

Yes, you. You abandoned her. You abandoned your family. There's no denying it.

He almost had not found the strength to go through with it. *I'm the one breaking up this family*, he had cried to himself as he saw the pain written on their faces. James, his younger son, and Kate, were emotionally beside themselves. His older son was more understanding, though all were bewildered. The move was totally unexpected. Even in Rick's mind, the reality of it seemed difficult to grasp.

But he found himself doing the unimaginable: leaving the home he had built for his family — a home that he had always pictured as a place of love and joy — not knowing if he would ever see the place again.

Kate even placed herself in front of the car as he drove toward the gate. Both had tears streaming down their faces. She did everything in her power to prevent his departure, but such acts could only delay the inevitable. Rick drove out of those tall, iron gates, and into the open, not knowing where he would go, what he would do, or when he would awake from the nightmare into which he had fallen.

Until he found himself in the hotel room. The cold, empty, lifeless hotel room. So small... but still much larger than his room at the Jennings Clinic.

His mind jumped back to his hopes during his stay there. 'I'm fighting for my family,' he had told himself so many times. 'I'm fighting this condition to win back my family, to be there for the ones that I love.'

He couldn't help but look back at that man, those months ago, and see a fool. A fool who had deluded himself, who had believed in a family that was, in fact, doomed. A fool who, on arriving back home ten months ago, had resolved to climb Everest. And failed.

He sat on the edge of the bed and stared out of the window at the grey, Auckland weather. The office towers, with their bustling crowds and activity, only made him lonelier. No one could know what he felt at this moment. He was utterly alone.

Rick picked up the phone by the bed and phoned Kate. She had made him promise to phone her. He had agreed.

"Come home. Please, *please* come home."

Kate begged. Rick only listened at a distance, not wanting to be swayed, knowing what was the right decision. Kate promised they would work things out together — she would do anything. "Please, just come home."

Despite Rick's agony that was only exacerbated by the heartless hotel room, despite the yearning he felt for his family, he held his ground and remained firm.

Until he heard James's voice through the phone. His younger son cried. He told his father how much he loved him, and asked him to come home. He was beside himself. He missed his dad desperately as he lay on his parents' bed, trying to sleep, but finding it impossible.

Rick was unable to stop his eyes from watering.

He left the hotel room and returned to Waterford.

Total time spent at the hotel: two hours and nineteen minutes.

CHAPTER TWENTY-SIX

K ATE WAS VISIBLY nervous following Rick's return to the house. She anxiously tried to read his mood and discern his true feelings. Was he giving up on her? Would he leave again?

As difficult as it was for her to form the words, she requested that, were Rick to leave a second time, he give her prior warning. She knew that forewarning was a luxury she could not rely on, but the prospect of her world collapsing around her once more was too much to bear; she would do everything in her power to keep it intact.

Rick did his best to reassure his wife that he was committed to bridging the gap between them. But he felt himself wince with every promise, as if the very thought of spending the rest of his life within the confines of a conflict-ridden marriage echoed through his body with grating disharmony.

Both had tried everything to make it work. There was no individual flaw that could be singled out by any outside observer; both had been completely faithful throughout the marriage; there were no external circumstances that were placing pressure on the relationship. Yet it was fast becoming a marriage of convenience, one where Rick would persist only for the sake of his children. But what use would he be to his children if he died an early death? Surely he was of far more use to everyone alive.

He knew that he could no longer sleep in the same bed as someone whom he sensed harbored deep resentment toward him. He felt the negativity pervading each and every exchange between him and his wife. Though she constantly sought reassurance that Rick was committed to the marriage, it was a request motivated by fear, not love.

It had been a week since his brief encounter with the hotel. That was an impulse decision, lacking the power that planning and forethought can add to such a momentous move. Without those foundations, the attempt had failed and only postponed the inevitable.

His heart was weighted down by grief and guilt as he went about executing his final departure. The boys were at school, Kate had planned to be out for some of the day and had accepted at face value Rick's assurance that he would meet her at the afternoon counseling session.

He felt like a thief in the night, moving through his bedroom with two suitcases, selecting those clothes that he thought would be of most use to him. He did his best; clothing selection was an area that had always fallen into Kate's domain, save for the hundreds of ties that he chose from each day.

What a bizarre situation. I'm nervous about someone seeing me in my own home.

There were suits he had never worn, dozens of pairs of shoes he couldn't remember buying. He was surprised to see the full extent to which he and Kate had become shopaholics, and he was reminded of his irrational shopping behavior in the lead-up to his breakdown. Until then, he had been bemused by the stories of celebrities and their shopping binges.

In the end, he transported some of his wardrobe to his mother's house and took only one suitcase, along with his toiletries, with him to the hotel. He had already planned to stay in a different hotel from the previous week, and had determined to remain there for longer than two hours.

He left the house that he had so carefully designed for the family of four, overwhelmed by a concoction of regret, hurt, sadness and guilt, the currency of a failing marriage.

HE WATCHED THE cell phone ring, and ring, and stop. And then ring, and ring, and stop. The caller wasn't leaving messages.

It was a call he knew he had to take; his had been a far from dignified exit, and one done in the full knowledge that a resolution of sorts would be necessary. He was out of the house now and knew he would not return; he was now sure he possessed the strength to face Kate or whatever else may eventuate, while still holding his ground.

"Kate, I'm sorry," he said as he opened the phone.

The ensuing pain and anger that flowed from the other end of the line tore at Rick.

"How can you leave like this! You coward! How could you do this to me!"

The voice continued and Rick knew that there was nothing he could say. He could only listen, each word tightening around his chest.

She demanded that he face her. It was a request he had to meet, despite the chaos that he knew such a meeting would involve: he could only imagine the despair that she must have been experiencing, given that he had already had days to prepare himself for the move that had abruptly been thrust upon Kate.

He parked on the street and walked nervously down the driveway, the gates automatically closing behind him. The driveway was lined on either side by lush greenery, and as he rounded the slight bend before the fountain he saw Kate, at the front door, awaiting him. Scowling. Her face contorted with tension.

It was the same fountain that he had photographed James in front of on his first day of school, that Rick had often passed as he walked amongst the gardens and palm trees shortly before sunset, and in which he had only a year ago claimed that he was Jesus.

The ensuing argument between the couple on the steps leading up to the front door took a heavy toll on both of them. It was the most emotionally dramatic encounter of Rick's life, an exchange of pain that erupted inside each of them. For Kate, it was as if her body was being torn apart as the man of her life abandoned her. Rick did his best to remain calm. His mouth felt bone-dry.

Are the drugs helping me keep it together? Is this gonna push me over the edge? Am I going to have another breakdown — at this fountain, just like last time?

It lasted for twenty minutes, but it felt like a whole day. It was agonizing. And then Rick could take no more. He turned and headed to the gate, hastily making his way down the driveway.

If it weren't so tragic, it could have been funny: never in his life had he imagined that he would be escaping from his own home, his wife in hot pursuit screaming at him, as he scaled the wrought-iron gates and leaped to the ground on the other side. A neighbor who, on occasion, had dined at Waterford, witnessed the heart-wrenching prison break with horror in her eyes.

Kate's need for her husband, in all its fury and desperation, poured forth as Rick wiped the tears from his eyes and wearily made his way to his car across the street.

CHAPTER TWENTY-SEVEN

M ARIA WAS UNSURE of how to respond to Rick's request for her spaghetti and meatballs recipe. "Are you crazy? Make something simple if you're having the boys around."

"No, Mum, I want to make something special for them."

"But you don't even know how to cook. I'll make it for you and bring it to the hotel."

"Mum, I'm serious, I have to do this all by myself. Tell me how to do it."

It would be their first meal together in Rick's hotel suite after a nightmarish week of loneliness and desperate explanations. Kate was still in a state of shock, and Rick felt much the same way, still wondering when the reality of his family's collapse would finally sink in. He had phoned his sons on the day that they returned to a broken home, saying that though they may no longer be sharing a house, they were still a family. He was determined to make his new home as warm and welcoming as the one-bedroom dwelling would permit.

It was fortunate that he phoned Maria early in the morning, as the gathering of cooking utensils, the correct dishes and the ingredients, along with the preparation of the food, would consume the rest of his day. Rick ensured that the meatballs would be of the highest quality by selecting filet mignon cuts and personally witnessing the grinding of the many pieces of meat. The butcher looked at Rick as if he were mad; he wouldn't know how right he was in some people's eyes.

Rick finely diced the onion and parsley, rolled them into delicate balls with the ground beef, and then lightly spiced them. With a touch of olive oil in the frying pan – one of the new additions to the kitchen – he pan-fried the small morsels of meat and placed them on an oven tray, ready for the final process to finish them off. The sauce was infused with fresh ingredients – garlic, tomatoes, onion, mushrooms – and, on his sons' arrival, the dinner was well on its way to readiness.

Given the hours of work the meal had required, he was stunned to see it vanish before his eyes after only twenty minutes on the table. He had sliced some fresh pineapple and watermelon for after dinner and inter-spersed the platter with fresh berries, kiwifruit and passionfruit. The entire meal was over within forty minutes. How could something requir-ing so much effort be over so quickly? He gained a new appreciation for the standard of dining to which he had become accustomed courtesy of Maria and Kate, but that he had always taken for granted.

Father and sons spoke for some time, and though the evening could almost have passed for a normal family dinner, it was obvious that the situation was new for those seated around the table. An air of sad-ness lingered behind the everyday talk of the boys' days at school and university.

Like all things, the night eventually came to a close. Rick wouldn't accept any help with the dishes. He hugged his sons tightly and kissed them, the door closed and then there he was, alone in his room, just him and the remnants of his first family meal as a single father. The suite had a small lounge and kitchen, with an expansive view of Auckland's harbor and the transiting ferries. He watched the comings and goings of the city, wondering how many shared his fate. How many, amongst those crowds, had been bitterly disappointed by a failed marriage? How many had come from broken homes themselves?

So many. So much disappointment... heartache... sadness.

How many had found true happiness in a relationship? He chose not to depress himself further by musing on the answer.

And how many realized how quickly, and how dramatically, life could pull the ground out from underneath one's feet?

How it can all sneak up on a person, and being so absorbed in wherever it is we think we're going, one never notices that everything that's held dear, everything that brings meaning to one's life, is not all that it appears. That it can vanish in a heartbeat.

He thought back to the counselor's frightening statistic at the Jennings Clinic: eighty percent. Eighty percent of marriages that had been affected by a nervous breakdown failed within two years.

He thought back to his high hopes, only months ago: *'I'll beat the odds! I can do it! The others failed because they didn't try hard enough — they just weren't prepared to work at it. But I am. Nothing is more important to me than my marriage. I'm going to make this marriage stronger than it's ever been!'* Even now, he found it impossible to accept that it was outside of his control, certain that he should have altered his life earlier, before it was too late.

Rick looked toward his bedroom. That empty, lonely bed. The first night had been achingly solitary. Rick hadn't slept at all that night. He missed knowing that she was next to him — he used to love placing his feet on hers to stay warm. The second night was just the same. And a week later, little had changed.

Maybe tonight he would sleep peacefully. Maybe tonight he would dream only of good things. Maybe tonight, after cleaning up after his sons — who would soon be asleep in the home that once housed four, now three — maybe then he would find peace at the end of the day, in the world of dreams.

CHAPTER TWENTY-EIGHT

J APAN, INDO-CHINA, RUSSIA, the former Yugoslavia. Rick's thoughts kept returning to the places she had appeared. There were more, certainly, but his mind always locked onto one: Medjugorje, in Bosnia-Herzegovina, the Former Yugoslavia. It bordered Croatia. He had never been there, to his father's birthplace, and the thought of it saddened him: it had always been a dream of his to visit Croatia with his father, but it would never be.

The documentary he had happened upon a number of years earlier while on holiday in Hawaii, detailing sightings of the Virgin Mary, had resurfaced in his memory. Why? He didn't consider himself a religious person. Was it because he was down on his luck, alone and desperate? Was he searching for something to hold onto? Was it his Catholic upbringing subconsciously directing his search for meaning and answers? He couldn't say.

He was grateful for his belief in a divine presence, in something deeper underlying his ephemeral existence. He felt that he had a healthy respect for the diversity of religious beliefs that covered the globe. But out of that foundation, he couldn't see exactly why it was that he was so drawn to Medjugorje.

Rick was doing everything possible to be there for his children, especially his younger. The tension between him and Kate made it a challenge and the two saw each other often when their sons' lives required so. He spent with James as much time as their lives permitted, regularly picking him up after school to buy a smoothie, Rick opting instead for a green tea. The boys had dinner at their dad's hotel suite, which was soon replaced by a house, every week. On one occasion when he was short of time to prepare a home-cooked meal, instead taking them to one of the city's best restaurants, he was pleased to hear that they preferred his cooking to the restaurant meal.

As much as he would have liked to take it as a stellar review of his culinary skills, it was the atmosphere of sharing the night together at home, and the appreciation of Rick's efforts in doing something special, that his sons had grown attached to. Nonetheless, Rick accepted it as confirmation that he had graduated from, in his own estimation, a 'non-performing' cook, to an 'apprentice'.

But he felt that life had settled enough for him to make the trip that had been on his mind all week. He would go to the place where the Virgin appeared and ask for a new life, for a second chance.

His impatience for Medjugorje contended with his desire to make the journey a profound one. He decided to visit, for the first time in his life, his father's birthplace. He flew from Frankfurt to Split, Croatia. As the plane touched down in the country of his forebears, he had difficulty containing his emotion. With the first step he took on Croatian land, he knelt and kissed the ground. There was a deep sadness that welled up within him; he had spoken many times with his father of visiting Croatia together, as a family. Now he found himself making his first visit to the country alone, without even his own children. It was an eerie sensation.

At the same time, he felt a profound sense of gratitude for his heritage. Walking the streets of Split on his first night, the many voices speaking the language of his grandparents evoked fond memories, as did the sound of voices singing to piano-accordions, just as his grandfather had when Rick was a child.

The following day, he caught a ferry to the island of Hvar, and made his way inland to the village of Bogomolje, his father's birthplace. Wherever Rick ventured, he was delighted by what he found: fresh grapes, fresh figs and the scent of lavender. It had always seemed strange that Ned had been so keen a boater and fisherman, but had never learned to swim. Now, on the small island of Hvar with its largely undisturbed coastline, the inconsistency was even more striking.

Rick even located the very house in which Ned had been born. If only he could have seen it with his father at his side, he lamented. Regardless of his absence, Ned's presence echoed through Bogomolje as Rick took in the quiet, idyllic town, donkeys and all, where nothing much seemed to happen.

His next stop on his Croatian tour was the island of his mother's parents. He took a ferry from Hvar to the jewel of the Adriatic, Korcula, and then to the town of Blato. It was every bit as picturesque as he had been told, something he was struck by the moment he approached the town and was welcomed by the endless towering oak trees that lined the first mile of the town's quiet main street. So at home did Rick feel on the island, amongst the people and the simple yet delightful cuisine, that he returned to the town center, Korcula, on the coast, and stayed two more days.

Medjugorje awaited. Just as his father had done those many years ago when he left a stumbling Croatia for the unknown, on nothing but hope, Rick would now embark on a new life, full of promise. He stayed a night in Dubrovnik, and at 5 a.m. the following morning crossed the border into Bosnia in a taxi, happy to have found an obliging driver on his arrival.

Tonci drove the long road to Medjugorje, all the time wondering what it was that had motivated Rick to travel from the far side of the world to visit the place. Not that it was unusual, but when someone asked him to drive to the sacred site, he couldn't help but wonder if the pilgrimage was motivated by a special purpose — a sickness, a death, finances, or simply a desire to feel a deeper connection to life itself. He was unable to discern his passenger's exact intentions but guessed, judging by his willingness to hire a taxi driver for the entire day, it probably wasn't money, and he was traveling alone, so no doubt it was something serious, not just a sightseeing detour. He was tempted to guess that it was a mid-life crisis; another Westerner getting exactly what he wished for only to find that it wasn't quite what he wanted after all. Whatever it was, he hoped the New Zealander would find what he was looking for; he liked him.

The roadside buildings looked decrepit. The toll of the war that had ravaged the country for years following the fall of communism was still clearly visible, as if Rick was simply passing through during a ceasefire. It hadn't been quite as noticeable in Croatia, though some of the buildings still bore shell marks, and numerous hotels had never reopened after housing the hordes of refugees in the aftermath of the war.

But here, in Bosnia, the price of war was on full display. The desolation of the area was undeniable, many of the houses they passed on the way now reduced to mere skeletons, many without roofs, or torn wide open to reveal a mere shell of a building. They stopped for lunch, and in the eyes of those he saw, he thought he could read the pain and horror of war. It seemed that the children were healing more quickly, the loss being heavier for the older generations. Still, the people had nowhere to go, no other place to escape to, and life had to go on.

As they continued their drive, the closer he looked, the more surprised he was. Indeed, life had not ground to a halt; it continued in spite of the darkness that had gripped the region for so long. He saw farmers tending their meager crops; children playing innocently with one another; mothers walking by the roadside as they transported their simple supplies from the villages back to their homes. Some of them wore effortless smiles. They were living life with full abandon. Perhaps they had accepted the life they had come to know, no longer waiting impatiently for things to improve. Maybe they had discovered, in the stark simplicity of their trying circumstances, that all those things that are strived for, all those things that one hopes will add meaning to one's life, in fact added nothing.

Rick couldn't say for sure what it was, but he could see peace in the eyes of those he passed. It was a quality absent in his own life. But he was trying.

How can these people's spirits not be broken after all they've endured? They're stronger than me. The war didn't break them. But life broke me.

He noticed a road sign reading 'Medjugorje, 30' and felt his stomach begin to churn. Everything that this personal pilgrimage meant rose up inside him. He wanted a new life. He wanted a second chance. And he couldn't deny that, at that moment, this meant the world to him. Deep down, he held a desperate need to be inspired, to know that he had a second chance in life. He needed to *know* that he had a second chance.

He wanted to understand what this life was for. To be shown the way to love. To feel alive once more. In his thoughts, he earnestly begged whatever it was that he hoped he might encounter at this site, to show him the way to what it was he longed for.

The words were repeating in his head in all different varieties. He didn't know whom he was directing them at, but he felt an urgent need to be heard. He wanted to know that life had not abandoned him. He wanted to know that he wasn't alone.

He was getting nervous; what if the second chance he yearned for never arrived? What if he were stuck in this state of limbo for the rest of his life? Alone, at the mercy of bipolar disorder, hurting.

What if it never changes? What if I'm always like this?

As they entered the town he was surprised by the commercial element: tourists by the busload and stores selling what appeared to be every imaginable keepsake. Though, he had to admit, it only made sense in light of such an influx of visitors. It was unavoidable. He wondered why he had expected any differently.

Tonci pulled the car over to the side of the road.

"This is it," he said, turning to the passenger in the back. "I'll be waiting for as long as you take — don't hurry yourself. This may be the only time in your life that you set foot in this area."

"Thanks, Tonci," Rick replied, surveying the area from the taxi. He felt unsettled. Was this it? Would he simply walk to the altar and stand there for two minutes amongst the crowd — was that what he traveled all this way for? He grew nervous at its simplicity. Would his life really change in those two minutes?

"I'm a bit confused, Tonci. Where exactly do I go... "

"Right over there," he pointed. "The altar. That's where people pray. And take a walk around the village. There's plenty to see."

A line of people moved slowly around an altar. Some knelt in prayer while others fixed their eyes on the biblical illustrations behind the altar.

"Is that really where she appeared? At the altar?"

"Oh no," he said quickly, "Up there." He was pointing to the top of the hill. It was steep and rocky. It looked as if no one was up there.

"Up there?" he said incredulously, the excitement creeping back into his voice. "Then what's everyone waiting for?"

Tonci stared at the earnestness of the expression on his passenger's face, then suddenly burst into laughter. "You don't see that?" he said between his chuckling. "It's a bloody hill without a trail – just rocks. You think people want to climb that thing?" He continued to giggle to himself, but Rick just gazed up at the slope. "But not everyone traveled all the way from New Zealand," he continued in a quieter voice. "For many people, seeing this place is important, sacred. And most come here with requests of great urgency." He looked Rick directly in the eyes, the smile that had earlier shone from his face now totally absent. "But I can see that what you're searching for means everything to you."

Rick felt his body tremble with conviction.

Yes, this does mean everything to me. This is it.

The driver had read him like a book.

"I bet you're not going to be satisfied with the village," Tonci said.

"Damn right." Rick exited the taxi and made his way to the foot of the slope. He was struck by the sincerity of those he saw. Each had probably traveled far to Medjugorje. He watched them pray with fervor, with the utmost faith, it appeared, certain of their Virgin's power to heal. She was so real to so many people.

He felt strange. Almost as if he were in the wrong place. They probably had much bigger problems than he did, he reflected. The hardship that the country's inhabitants had faced for years again came to mind. How had they endured such challenges? How had their spirits not been broken?

Am I weak? How did I fail? How did I fall. . . I must be weak.

He began his ascent up the slope. He hoped that his journey to Europe, to visit this very spot, would not be in vain.

I want another chance. I want to live again.

As he climbed higher he turned to look back down at the village and the crowds. It was a tiring climb, but it made the event all the more momentous. Each step he took was filled with purpose and determination. Each step reminded him of everything he had lost. It reminded him of everything he had come here to claim. It was a rite of passage; an initiation. It was a day he would never forget.

He reached the top, feeling light-headed as he caught his breath: the ascent had been one powered by his conviction of beginning a new life, and he had clamored ahead without regard for pacing himself.

His breath returned and he took in his surroundings. It was an unassuming place, but there, in front of him, was a marker denoting the site of the apparition in 1981.

Rick was moved. He crouched in front of the marker.

A deep sense of failure and regret gripped him, something that had been building inside of him ever since he left his family, yet only now did he allow it to make itself felt in his awareness. It was overwhelming.

Rick let out a breath, shuddering from the emotion that was stirring.

He had failed in his life. He had failed to be strong; failed to keep his family together; failed to appreciate the joy and richness of life. He had forsaken the precious life he had been gifted.

I've failed.

His body began to tremor with the weight of the past pouring out.

I have failed.

But here I am, ready to start a new life.

He looked up, to the clear skies overhead and took a deep breath.

This is it. This is where it begins. I choose a new life — a life that I won't waste. A life that I will live to its full potential.

The breeze brushed against his face and he felt the power of his words resonating through his body.

I will rebuild. I will find love. I will live life. I vow to use this life for only the highest purpose.

Yes, he had failed. How he wished he could have kept his family together. He had fallen into the doctor's dreaded eighty percent statistic. But he was still alive. He hadn't flipped out yet. His world had been turned upside down, and he was still Rick.

To be sure, he had failed at his most cherished goal: his marriage, his family. But he was beginning to think that it was the price he had to pay to avoid the greatest failure of all: betraying one's own heart.

A small rock by his foot caught his attention. He bent down and picked it up, gripping it with both hands. He would take it with him wherever he went in the world, to remind him of the life that he would embrace. To remind him of the life that he would not waste, but would live with all his heart.

Please, God, let me know that I have a new life. Let me know that I'm okay — that I'm heading in the right direction. Please, let me know.

Suddenly, an impulse came over him to grip the rock in both hands and consummate his new life with a display of divine strength. He squeezed the rock with all his might, with every ounce of strength he could muster. A sense came over him that he could crush the rock with his bare hands. Energy coursed through his body and he channeled it into his hands and into the rock.

Nothing happened.

He relaxed his grip, exhausted, and felt a pinch of disappointment. Rick turned around in a circle and saw nothing but an everyday scene: a hilltop, some rocks, a village of tourists and pilgrims below. He wondered if it had all been a waste of time.

Rick started back toward the edge of the hill. He placed the rock in his pocket, discouraged that he never received a sign that his prayer had been heard. All this travel, all this expectation, and nothing but a long taxi ride, an empty hilltop and a damn rock. The view from the hilltop wasn't even anything special.

He went to make his way down to the foot of the hill, his body still tired from the climb up. As he stepped off the lip of the hill and set his foot down on the loose, gravelly ground below, he slipped and his legs shot out from under him. He landed, buttocks first, on the rough, unforgiving rock below him.

"Shit!" he roared.

Pain shot up through his tail bone and for a moment he writhed and winced. It hurt.

It hurt so much that he couldn't help but erupt in laughter at the absurdity of the situation. He lay back on the hard ground and chuckled uncontrollably.

There he was, climbing down a hill in the middle of nowhere, so uptight over the lack of drama at the site where an apparition once appeared that he had forgotten to look where he was walking.

It was ridiculous, and he knew it. What had he been expecting, anyway? That the Virgin Mary would appear to him, saying, "Yes, I now give you permission to live your life"?

He laughed uproariously from the hilltop. Why did he insist on taking life so seriously? He was laughing so hard that his chest was beginning to hurt as much as his tailbone. Rick lifted himself off the ground, brushed the dirt off his backside, and continued down the hill, perhaps a little too light-headed for an entirely safe descent, but too caught up in the comedy of the moment to worry about such things.

Yes, I have a new life. Of course I have a new life. What the hell was I waiting for?

As he neared the taxi, Tonci, too, began to smile. He didn't know what had happened up there on the hilltop; maybe he should try it himself some day, though he hadn't yet felt the need. But whatever happened, he could see that the man returning to his car was not the man he had picked up from the hotel in Dubrovnik. This man was different. This man had peace in his heart.

CHAPTER TWENTY-NINE

S ITTING IN THE doctor's waiting room, it occurred to Rick that many of his most awkward moments took place in such a setting. His usual physician was on vacation and in his stead a female doctor was taking patients. *Why did I leave this till the last minute? I should have thought of it weeks ago!*

The doctor popped her head into the waiting room and called Rick's name. *Dammit, why does she have to be attractive! This can't get much worse.*

Sitting opposite the doctor, whom he had never met before, he wondered if there were any way around the topic he wished to discuss. It was clear, though, that he had no option.

"I'm leaving for the United States tomorrow, on a trip with my friends." He stopped, not knowing how to continue.

"That's great," she responded. "A vacation?"

"Well, yes and no. They go every year to raise funds for an international charity they're involved with and, because I'm recently separated, they've asked me to join them this year — it should be a lot of fun." He said it without great enthusiasm, knowing in his heart that he wished things had turned out differently and he were instead going on a trip with his wife and boys.

"I'm glad to hear it. And what was it that you wished to see me about?"

"It's about – " he paused. "Wow, this is harder than I thought." He smiled to himself at the inadvertent irony of the wording he had used. "Well, to tell you the truth, I was hoping to speak to my own doctor about this."

"Mr. Dellich, believe me, I've heard it all before." Rick was beginning to think that maybe he would be comfortable revealing his concern to her.

"Okay, well, what can you tell me about Viagra?"

The two shared a moment of laughter before the doctor launched into a summary of the drug: varying dosages were available, from 40 milligrams to 100 milligrams, she had prescribed it to people from the age of eighteen up to eighty, and her recommended dosage for a first-time user would be 40 milligrams to 60 milligrams.

More embarrassing for Rick than enquiring into Viagra was the background to his concern: he was on Epilim, and his entire self-perception was tainted with self-doubt because of it. Furthermore, he had had only one sexual partner for over twenty years and didn't know what to expect, but he was certain that it was time for him to begin dating, and he felt that the time away with his friends would provide a perfect opportunity.

Their discussion continued past the allotted time for the appointment but the doctor didn't mind; she was enjoying the debate as Rick weighed the pros and cons of taking the drug. He eventually decided to ask for a prescription. But as she was writing it, he found himself speaking out abruptly.

"Wait." She looked up. "No, I don't want the prescription." He paused for a moment. "When I think about it, Doctor, if I were to take Viagra, I could in a way be forced to always take it, because if everything turns out okay, I would never know if it's me or the drug. I'm already on Epilim – I accept it, though I don't like it, and now I'm faced with a choice over how I think of myself as a lover. I want to be the real Rick as much as possible – I want her to accept me for the man I am. I don't know if I'll meet anyone, but I've gotten a lot out of this conversation. I had a choice and I've made one. Thank you."

The doctor was still smiling. "Well I had a good time talking to you about Viagra, too."

A week into the fundraising trip, Rick met a woman with whom he instantly bonded. She had lost her husband to cancer and the two spent some evenings together, as friends, sharing the hurt and loneliness each one had experienced. And then, on the last night before each was due to leave the Midwestern town where they had met, it happened. They made love, though it was unexpected by both. Rick felt that it was a wonderful experience and, when he went to leave his hotel room in the morning, he noticed that two envelopes had been slipped under his door. The first was the hotel's express check-out service, but underneath was a beautiful letter from the first lover of his post-married life.

Meanwhile, he was experiencing a mixture of emotions at the knowledge that his marriage was formally over, as had been confirmed soon after he and Kate separated. So sure had he been that it was over, he had informed his attorney that he wanted settlement on the terms of divorce within four months. Attorneys on both sides said that such a timeframe was unrealistic, given the property involved. But Rick wanted closure; to drag out such a process would only tear away at him and his wife even further, and he knew that neither wanted any more pain than was necessary.

He declined to seek representation from any of the aggressive matrimonial lawyers that were recommended to him, instead opting to remain with the husband and wife legal team that had handled his business affairs in the past. He instructed his own attorneys that any correspondence and any files pertaining to the settlement be copied and retained in a file so that, if at any time in the future his sons wished to examine whether or not Rick had been fair to their mother, they could see it for themselves.

Kate's lawyer was surprised by the settlement offer they received from Rick and they promptly accepted. The process had taken less than four months, with little disagreement expressed by either side. Rick could not bear to see his former wife, the mother of his children, struggling or financially worse off than she had been. Though he still experienced the full brunt of her anger toward him in the exchanges they had, usually in the mutual involvement they had with their children, he knew that he could choose to not react in kind to the pain that she felt; to do so would simply be fueling the fire. He had heard so many nightmares about people who had shared their lives, loved one another, slept in the same bed and had beautiful children together, suddenly being dragged into a vicious circle of pain and attack, sharing a new depth of hurt that their children also became party to. Rick vowed to never say a bad word about Kate in front of their children. He tried to allow what she said to flow past him.

"It's worse than a death," Kate had said at one stage.

"I agree," Rick had responded. At least if a loved one died, the fond memories were able to sustain those who had lost. But for the memories to become tainted with the hurt of rejection and separation overshadowed what was once beautiful. It was, at times, excruciating.

The relative ease of their divorce begged the question, why was there usually so much animosity over divorce settlements? The lawyers' response: money. It was clear that, in many cases, this was a flame that was fanned by the matrimonial attorneys. Though Rick had met many in the legal profession who served their clients with the noblest of intentions, it seemed that some did not want a quick and easy settlement for their clients; they would much prefer to prolong the legal battle, sink their teeth into a good fight, and keep the meter running until the two parties could no longer bear the crippling legal fees. But how could such a process not take a toll on the whole family, the children included? Rick felt strongly that, more important than what was said to children, was the example set.

Although the settlement had been reached within four months of Rick's departure from home, it would not be executed, in accordance with New Zealand law, until the separation had been official for two years.

Two years, he thought longingly, eager to begin a new journey of love. *Whoever you are, wherever you are, I swear I won't let love die the next time.*

CHAPTER THIRTY

W AIT, WAIT. WHAT do you mean – right now?" Rick questioned. "That's unreasonable."

"Yes, now please," came the voice on the other end of the phone.

"But you only saw me a few days ago, and I appeared normal to you then, or you would have said so," Rick continued, bemused by the sudden request. "I'm in a meeting at the moment, and busy all day with meetings. Can't it wait until tomorrow? I can come in then."

"Rick, please, you must come and see me right away."

"This is absurd – I get out of my meeting to find five urgent messages from you and your clinic requesting that I ring you immediately. I only just turned on my cell phone for an expected phone call to do with the meeting I'm in at the moment. And now you want me to cancel everything and drive to the clinic – what, now? I don't understand – what for?"

"A complaint has been lodged that you are acting abnormally and that you have stopped taking your medication," replied Dr. Korovin.

Rick tried to wrap his mind around the answer. "I can assure you I haven't been acting abnormally, and I haven't stopped the medication."

"Rick, I insist that you meet with me immediately. This cannot wait."

"So what are you saying – that I have no choice? That if I don't cancel my meetings to comply with your wishes, some drastic measure could be taken against me to force me to comply?"

"Yes, Rick, you must come to my office immediately."

Rick was finding that even within the bounds of his own family, there was no escaping the difficulties involved with the perception that he was a ticking time-bomb. As the first Christmas since his leaving home approached, Rick and James made plans to take a trip together on Valencia, Rick's boat. He loved spending time on the boat and he often took it out for day trips, sometimes on his own and sometimes with friends, enjoying the peace of the sea and the freshness of the air as the waves gently lapped against the vessel.

The Bay of Islands was where he would take James – they would spend ten days up there on the sleek, fifty-five footer. Michael and his girlfriend would later join the two. It was six days before Christmas that Rick received the urgent phone call from his psychiatrist.

He made his way to his car on hanging up the phone, and drove directly to the doctor's office, doing his best to rearrange the rest of his day's schedule during the drive.

On arriving, he discovered that Dr. Korovin was still en route to the office: it was the doctor's day off, and he was driving from Auckland's North Shore all the way to work for the express purpose of examining Rick. The nurse told him that the doctor would be arriving shortly.

Rick was agitated but was doing his best to suppress it. He was unsure of how to voice his views respectfully. Dr. Korovin was a man he respected, and with whom he felt a degree of sincere friendship. He had never told the doctor of his experience with Bradshaw, and of the consequent wariness with which he regarded the profession. Every psychiatrist was well aware that patients were not to be taken off a high dosage of psychiatric drugs abruptly; doing so could drive them to suicide. Bradshaw had done just that. And if it didn't drive him to suicide, then, he surmised, she still hoped to confine him to a chemical straightjacket for the rest of his life – if she didn't succeed in physically killing him, she almost did psychologically. She had witnessed his swings between euphoria and depression, and had responded by increasing his dosage of a drug combination that she knew could be dangerous. It had left its scar, and he considered it a sadistic crime. In his time with Dr. Korovin, and with those at the Jennings Clinic, Rick's suspicions of the profession at large had eased. And though he still questioned the amount of power that rested with psychiatrists – as he had seen, they had the potential to wield the power of life and death, and often, he could only assume, without their patients' knowledge – he gladly cooperated with the doctor's requests. But it was moments like these that his frustrations triggered a painful memory of Bradshaw's megalomaniacal control over his life.

He knew the nurse well from his weekly visits and, with some care, voiced his frustration.

"Susan, this is ridiculous. How would Dr. Korovin like it if he were the one being summoned at a moment's notice – ordered to comply, and you dare not disobey them, because they'll lock you away?"

"Well, I'm sure nobody likes that," Susan responded. "But, you must realize, you're condition is being monitored – we would hate for something to go wrong."

"But I told the doctor on the phone that I'm still taking my medication. That should be enough; instead, I'm at the mercy of a doctor and whoever it was that told him whatever it was they said." His speech was calm, belying the aggravation pent up inside him. "And, what's worse, I'm not even permitted the basic rights to react as any reasonable person would. How would you, or anyone else, feel in this situation?" He didn't wait for a reply. "Some form of irritation or anger is the normal response. But am I allowed to express those basic human emotions? No, I'm not. If I did, they would say there's something wrong with me – they'd keep me under surveillance, tell me not to take my sons away for Christmas, maybe increase my dosage of Epilim. If I act normally, people interpret it as abnormal. So, I just have to sit here and pretend that I'm happy to be treated like a prisoner." Anyone hearing the voice from a distance without paying attention to the words would have mistaken it for pleasant, everyday conversation, such was Rick's care in controlling his composure.

"I'm sorry Rick, I know it's not easy." She understood everything he had said, but there was nothing she could do.

Dr. Korovin entered the room, and they made their way to his office. He apologized to Rick for doing as his duty as a psychiatrist dictated.

Rick expressed his disapproval of having to prove to the doctor that he had not neglected his medication; could he not be trusted?

"Rick, Kate's therapist phoned me to lodge a complaint. Kate had expressed concern to her that your friends were worried that you're not yourself lately, and that you've stopped taking the Epilim."

Rick sighed. "'Not myself'? What does that mean? That I'm express-ing emotions within the normal range of human experience? Am I not allowed to deviate from the state of placidity prescribed by those around me? Do I have to remain unresponsive and withdrawn from everything that happens around me? Does any normal person act like that?" Dr. Korovin's face had a conciliatory expression. "Can't you see for yourself that I'm stable? Do I look like I've lost it?"

"No, you don't. But it's the way things are for now. People are con-cerned for you – for your wellbeing. It's my responsibility to confirm that you are still taking your medication."

Rick stayed on the premises for the next two hours while his blood test was run. On leaving, he phoned Kate, telling her how shocked he was that she could believe he would endanger James's life by taking him on a boat in an unstable condition. She wouldn't reveal which friends had expressed concern, but Rick already knew. It was someone who, himself, had been to the edge, and to whom Rick had confided his own condition. To know that this trust had been breached by his friend's speculation, behind Rick's back, was a further demoralizing letdown.

Later that night, Rick received a phone call from Dr. Korovin. The doctor made some excuse about forgetting to wish him a Merry Christmas, but it was clear that he was checking on his patient's condition. Rick had reclaimed his full rights as a New Zealand citizen; he was able to stay on top of things and hold it all together despite the momentous changes he had made in his life; he was optimistic about the future and eager for the adventures that awaited him; but the reality was that he was branded for life by those that knew what he had experienced. It was as if he had a gun held to his head; one wrong move and he was gone.

CHAPTER THIRTY-ONE

H IS SEARCH NOW intensified. Rick could not grasp precisely what it was that he was searching for, but he was driven by a strong feeling that there were certain flaws in his approach to life that he could do without. Falling short of entertaining any delusions that he might one day eliminate all flaws and reach a state of near-perfection, he nevertheless sought to improve his mental and physical wellbeing to the best of his ability. And, underlying all of his efforts, was the search for the elusive simplicity, the inner peace, that Rick hoped for above all else.

He approached his health with renewed vigor. Optimum health was his goal: he would bring his body into alignment with its natural state, its optimal state. Ever since his return to New Zealand, he had maintained his focus on improving his health, knowing that he had to use every tool at his disposal to rebuild a new person; a new Rick; a new life.

The experts all had their own ideas of what worked and what didn't, but most appeared heavily biased toward a single approach. The further he explored the topic, the more convinced he became that perfect health was like the earth itself and, indeed, all life; well-being was to be found in the establishment of a natural balance.

His goal was not to achieve such a state at the expense of the lifestyle to which he had become accustomed; he loved a variety of foods, and he also wanted to be able to enjoy his life without his health regime impinging on the freedoms he had come to love. His approach to living in optimum health would rest on a balance between lifestyle and commitment, a balance that was sustainable and enjoyable.

Rick had already enlisted the help of a personal trainer with whom he trained three times a week. The former New Zealand bodybuilding champion prided himself on his views of attaining physical well-being and, in general, Rick liked his approach. But no matter how often he worked with the trainer, he still felt that there were areas of his health that were substandard; his appearance and energy levels were not where he wanted them to be and his pot belly and cellulite, unusual for a man, remained stubborn in the face of the fitness regimen he was following.

His research was thorough. He explored all aspects of health with the aim of tailoring a program to his own needs and achieving harmony between spirit, mind and body. Cellulite became a top priority, and as with every topic, the experts differed on how to deal with it, some advocating ointments with intensive massage treatment, many conceding that it was there to stay. Rick started to understand that the most effective way to approach losing weight was to do it gradually, as attempts to shed pounds abruptly usually resulted in the same weight being regained at some later stage. But a slow shedding of excess weight allowed the body time to recalibrate to a new mode of functioning so that the change in body weight could be a lasting one.

As his research continued, he spoke to specialists, he spoke to friends, and he read extensively. As far as weight loss was concerned, it seemed that most people were engaged in a battle in which they would succeed in losing weight through sheer determination, only to regain it through force of habit.

He moved on from his personal trainer and took charge of his own fitness routine, deciding to put what he was learning into practice. He made swimming a habit, and in his travels acquired an appreciation for the bodies of water around the world, the Adriatic becoming his favorite. With Waterford no longer his residence, he joined a gym but soon came to the realization that the chlorinated water was not good for his skin. At the gym, he noticed that it was sometimes obvious who the most dedicated swimmers were: their eyes sagged from the day-after-day pressure of goggles. Furthermore, he met girls who had begun swimming at an early age and regretted the changes to their body that it caused. After several months of regular swimming to kick-start his body's recovery, he gave it up, satisfied that it had served its purpose.

Steve, who had been a successful cyclist earlier in his life, recommended cycling. Rick tried it out but was unable to cope with the traffic, exhaust fumes and the vigilance required to stay safe on the busy streets. Mountain biking sounded appealing, but it was impractical. Running, too, was a mode of exercise to which he had a strong aversion. He dated a number of women who had taken up running in their teens or early twenties and who, by their mid-thirties, attributed constant knee and ankle problems to their years of pounding the pavements. It concerned Rick that orthopedics had become a growth industry and he was certain that a hip replacement was something he would rather avoid.

Daily jogging had the potential to overwork various parts of the body, and Rick had certainly experienced firsthand, as a sprinting and steeple-chase champion in his teenage years, the toll that such activity could take on the body. Though it succeeded in raising the heart rate and releasing stress, he felt it was not natural enough to be sustainable; to Rick, the ability to run developed in the human body, as in all land mammals, as an outlet for the fight or flight response, not for prolonged, repetitive use.

There was no doubt in his mind that the best exercise for long-term wellbeing and health was walking. His research and personal experience confirmed to him that it was the most natural way to exercise the body, though it did require a greater time commitment than many other forms of exercise: one hour and twenty minutes was needed, every day, to lose weight through walking. If possible, the waterline, hills or anywhere covered in grass or a soft surface was ideal; pavements had a tendency to place undue pressure on the joints.

Juicing became a daily ritual. He spent the first part of the morning juicing fresh, raw and, where possible, organic vegetables. He was reluctant to alter his diet too much as food had always been one of his greatest pleasures. He refused to surrender his freedom to enjoy steaks and desserts, but it was clear to him that it was necessary to re-examine the issue of diet. As always, he found his solution in balance, with juicing becoming an important means of supporting his overall health.

He refined his meditation technique and developed his own stretching routine, drawing on what he had learned from his experience with yoga. The routine was one that could be practiced easily in a hotel room as he was adamant that, for his health regimen to be practicable, he would have to make it as convenient as possible by cutting out the need for gyms. With perseverance, the pot belly and cellulite left him for good. He was beginning to feel better than he could ever recall.

His forays into dating continued in Auckland. Rick held high hopes of finding his soulmate, but was uncertain of how to go about it. The information he gleaned from the Cosmopolitan's and other women's magazines gave him a feel for the dating scene, but he soon discovered that experience could be the only true teacher of the turn-of-the-century dating game.

A pattern soon emerged. He went out with a number of women whose company he enjoyed, always confident that his feelings toward them would grow. But, in every case, he found himself feeling guilty as his potential girlfriend's feelings grew faster than his; indeed, he wondered what was wrong with him for not feeling more strongly about the wonderful girls he had been out with. Each time, before the relationship took off, he would go through the hurtful ordeal of ending it, explaining that he couldn't continue to create an expectation of a relationship when he didn't share the same feelings.

So desperately did he want to fall in love that he frequently blinded himself to any shortcomings that he encountered, only to be rudely awakened to their presence further down the line. The more Rick became involved in the dating scene, the more he was surprised by the world of intrigue he had entered. Rumor and gossip lurked at every turn, one of his first dates revealing that Rick's activities never went unnoticed. "Everyone talks in this town," she had said. "Now that you're separated, people consider you an eligible bachelor. You can't do anything in this town without word of it getting back to me." Rick was horrified.

It had been one year since he had left Kate. Not only had he rebuilt his body, but he had changed his way of life. The challenges kept coming, and he kept meeting them head-on. He was learning, slowly, to say 'no' to those things that no longer served him or for which he could not spare time and energy; he did his best to make following his heart a way of life, only becoming involved in activities that felt right for him. The answer had been simple: tend to the spirit, the mind and the body, and then establish a balance between the three. In that state of wellbeing, life was beautiful regardless of the challenges that life may present. He knew that the time had come to take the final step on his journey to wholeness.

At his next session with the psychiatrist, he raised the prospect of planning his withdrawal from the medication that had served as a necessary bridge between his state of crisis and wellbeing. Dr. Korovin thought for some time before speaking.

"Rick, you do know what you're asking for, right? You do know what the odds of making it without medication are, don't you?" Rick didn't answer. "A tiny percentage of those who try actually succeed in living without symptoms. Most find themselves living with constant pain. Some end up committing suicide. I'm not saying that it's completely outside the realm of possibility — you're a strong man, and you've surprised me — but I want you to consider it carefully before we go ahead with what you're proposing."

In spite of his impatience, Rick let the issue sit for the rest of the session. He had already given the idea a great deal of thought, but wanted to assure the doctor that it was a sound decision, and not an impulsive one. He waited for the following week to explain his position.

"Doctor, I feel that I've faced my demons and prevailed; I've studied and implemented a plan for optimum health; and with your ongoing counseling and supervision, I'm confident that I can live fully without the drugs. I want you to monitor me closely and to drop my dosage as you see fit. I'm ready for this."

He knew, as he said those words, that the stakes on his new life had just been raised.

CHAPTER THIRTY-TWO

A S THE MONTHS progressed, the psychiatrist reduced the dosage of Epilim as Rick went about monitoring his lifestyle and stress levels with ever more vigilance. He focused more than ever on meditation, yoga, walking, diet and the most important factor of all: his mind.

The mind, in Rick's view, was the key to wellness. He likened it to re-learning how to drive a car, as if a lifetime of habits needed to be examined, evaluated, and often changed. He investigated his attitudes toward his life, he reflected on himself, and he rebuilt the way he viewed himself and the world. It was similar to having suffered a stroke: on a mental and emotional level, something had malfunctioned and needed to be examined.

Rick was surprised to find that, as doctors had warned him, his ability to handle stress since his breakdown had indeed decreased. It became clear to him that those who had experienced a breakdown, or were in danger of one, needed to acknowledge the fact that their tolerance for stress would be much lower than it was preceding their breakdown or illness. Stress was, for the most part, an ever-present reality in daily life to some degree, and part of rebuilding oneself was understanding how to gradually become reacquainted with the stresses of normal life. It was a process, and those who rushed the return to their previous way of life did so at their own peril. In his experience with others who had suffered from conditions of the mind, the most common obstacle to a true recovery was the reluctance to make substantial changes in one's life.

Although he had the opportunity to include a thorough overall approach to physical wellness to assist in his recovery, he began to notice, the more he spoke with people on such topics, that many felt unable to make similar commitments to optimum physical health. Whether it was a lack of time, financial pressures, or family demands, people often found justifications for not tending to their physical wellbeing. What Rick noticed in his research, though, was examples of people in tight situations who, nonetheless, managed to turn their health around by making it a priority.

Rick came to believe that, in the absence of a full physical health routine, there could at least be several priorities that could be followed by all who were committed. Eating fresh fruits and vegetables; working toward eliminating processed and artificial foods; and avoiding alcohol and other harsh toxins would, alone, generate huge benefits for most people. Rick developed a simple exercise routine that could be practiced in a hotel room, a bedroom or a living room, and didn't require any equipment or expense, and he considered it proof that anyone can make regular exercise a part of their life, even in the face of time and money restraints. The final component of a simple and effective approach to physical wellness was daily time alone. It didn't have to be for long, but it was important for a person to have at least some time without distraction, company, or work.

When these three components became true priorities, which would sometimes require letting go of other time commitments in one's life, there was no reason for basic physical wellbeing to remain out of reach. There was no substitute for attention to the mind, however, and it was imperative that anyone who experienced a nervous breakdown, or was heading to the edge, made examining their mind a top priority. In its simplest form, it consisted of asking three simple questions on a regular basis: Am I angry? Am I sad? On a scale of one to ten, how do I feel? Investigating the answers was the beginning of changing one's experience, and of eventually attaining peace of mind.

Rick was confident that he was making progress in his own path to wellbeing. Yet he couldn't help but feel nervous, and sought the doctor's confirmation every week that his behavior was stable. Rick was worried that he wouldn't, himself, possess the objectivity to adequately assess his condition on his own. He asked his friends and family whether they had noticed any worrying changes in his outlook. It was a strange place to be in, he thought: to constantly seek an outside opinion on whether or not he appeared sane. But it was a necessary precaution. He could not trust his own judgment – at least, not yet.

Not all were supportive of his new approach to health. Maria and other family members and friends were concerned that Rick had lost too much weight and was looking gaunt, prompting him to pay a visit to his physician, Wayne, whom he had been with for fourteen years. In carrying out Rick's request for a full physical examination, Wayne was stunned to find that his body was in peak condition. The doctor reached for his medical books, remarking to Rick that his cholesterol, blood pressure, pulse, height to weight ratio and body fat were all at their optimal level as described in his medical texts. The transition from such an unhealthy state to an optimal state was something the physician had never seen in his own experience.

"Well, I can't fault it, Rick, you seem to have done it in a very natural way, without overextending your body. I would venture that you are an example of the body's ideal condition before diet and lifestyle became what they are today. That may be why people are having a go at you for being too thin – possibly you look a bit better than they're comfortable with – their wives must be noticing."

The doctor's affirmation that he was heading in the right direction, coupled with his psychiatrist's satisfaction with his progress, was the first time for many months that his outer world had granted him any extra room to breathe. It had been an uphill journey all the way, and the greatest surprise of it all to Rick was that he had managed to survive. His new direction *was*, in fact working, despite his fears to the contrary. It only saddened Rick deeply that he had never made the transformation earlier in his life. He knew there had been no space for it; the challenges had been too overwhelming, and from too many directions. But he couldn't help but wonder, with a heavy heart, if such foresight and resolve to make his inner and outer health his priority might have saved his marriage, or averted his breakdown. He would never know.

His disillusionment over Rosa continued to grow with each passing month. He was still unable to work her out. He recalled her words to him that day in the office: "Any problem that's ever come between us has been Kate's doing, not yours. You're my brother."

But everything Rick saw was in direct contradiction to her argument. Where his sister's support had previously been unreliable, it was now entirely absent. She had blamed Kate for being the source of friction in the family but now, with Rick on his own, the friction was the worst it had ever been.

It was never about Kate. It was always about me.

He had always hidden it from himself, even after so much had been revealed. Even in the face of the glaringly obvious pattern. But only now was he willing to admit it to himself. Only now, when the severity of the past year stripped the layers one by one from everything in his life that was a lie, was he beginning to see the emptiness of his own ideals.

For so long his hopes had blinded him, his ideals steering his action at the expense of hearing his own heart and his own wisdom, those ideals that he had held above all else: family, loyalty, unity. He remembered his father's words to him, in those final days of his life: 'Look after your sister. Look after the family. Keep the family together.' He had promised his father he would, and it had not been a difficult promise to make: nothing could be more important.

But time had proven those hopes to be nothing more than illusions. The more he saw, the more it made sense. The competition had been there ever since childhood. She was the one always in the spotlight: the best grades, unrivaled popularity, and the apple of her father's eye. She knew how to get what she wanted. But it was never enough. Rosa was uncomfortable with any hint of success on Rick's part. Any of her friends that showed a liking toward him would quickly be swayed or replaced. Was it any different now?

She was so good at it. He recalled Maria's prolonged delay in revealing to Rick the real reason for his grandparents' sudden cancellation on

Christmas Day, shortly before their deaths the following year. Rosa and Rick had always alternated hosting the extended family on Christmas Day. Rick hosted the gathering that year, but when Maria arrived and informed him of his grandparents' last-minute cancellation, he was not ready to accept the mystery without a reason. In the following weeks he asked his mother, more than once, as to the reason for their absence, but was met with the same equivocal reply.

It was only some months later that Rick was able to uncover the truth from his mother when she passed on an apology from his grandparents for their absence. When pressed for the reason as to the apology, she conceded that they had been told stories about Rick by Rosa that had convinced them to avoid the family gathering. They later found the stories to be untrue and apologized. Rick found the episode too hurtful to raise again with his mother, his sister or even his wife. His grandparents died not long after.

Andrew, once his dearest friend, was firmly under her spell. He had become nothing more than an extension of Rosa herself, though lacking her viciousness: a mouse without the courage to pull the trigger himself but, nonetheless, one who helps place the bullet in the chamber. Like most weak people, he enjoyed the benefits of Rosa's malice but was not prepared to admit his own part in it, not even to himself. Rick tried to convince himself that it was just Rosa and that Andrew was still his friend. But he knew that he would once again be deceiving himself.

He almost wanted to believe his sister – that the intensity of his breakdown was more Kate's fault than Rosa's: at least he could understand how Kate's exhaustion with the situation might have caused her to lose sympathy for her husband. At least, if he believed Rosa, the beautiful illusion of family unity and the infallible solidarity of family could be sustained – his promise to his dying father would not be in vain. But he knew he would only be fooling himself. The truth was staring him right in the face. He recalled Rosa's instructions to her friends as a child: that anyone who was friends with Rick, was no longer allowed to be her friend. He remembered the day that he arrived home, as a young boy, to find his piggy bank smashed into pieces, lying on the ground. Each of them were gifted a porcelain piggy bank, and Rick's had grown heavier than Rosa's as he worked his odd jobs and did his best to save the money. No one ever offered an explanation for how Rick's was smashed, or why the money lying on the ground was less than what he recalled placing into the bank, but there was little doubt in his mind as to the perpetrator. The sibling rivalry that had begun with her persistent claim of being the older twin, had grown into a monster that had torn the family apart. Only now, did he see it.

Yet in the face of it all, he felt somehow freer than he had for years. Still, he found it hard to believe that his plan to rebuild his life was actually working under such trying circumstances.

His separation from Kate, the greatest tragedy of his life and one through which he desperately yearned for comfort and support from those he loved, had only exacerbated the problems between him and Rosa. It was one more opportunity for her to isolate him, another chance to exploit a weak position.

He felt that life was throwing every challenge it could muster at him, as if to test his commitment to this new life that he had chosen. And every time, he rose from the ashes stronger than before, more committed than ever to his truth. Now, at long last, with Wayne's and Dr. Korovin's independent assessments of him, there was outward confirmation of what he felt deep within: that he was living his new life exactly as he should be, in spite of the challenges that refused to subside.

CHAPTER THIRTY-THREE

I T FELT LIKE an old, haunted manor from a horror movie. The home of his dreams, built for the family of his dreams, opened its doors to Rick to reveal a hollow interior, devoid of the warmth that once dwelled in every room. It was just a memory now. This house was empty.

It should have been a moment of triumph. Here he was, two years after fleeing the house amid turmoil in every facet of his life, scaling its gates with his enraged wife in hot pursuit, now returning to that same spot having overcome the apparently insurmountable obstacles that had littered his path.

He was off the drugs.

'*Off the drugs. I'm off the damn drugs!*' he would spontaneously burst out on his own when the joy of it was too much to contain. He wanted to jump up and touch the stars, shout it out to the world that he had made it. He was free. Even he found it hard to believe; it was almost too good to be true.

Rick had been surprised by the lack of drama as Dr. Korovin steadily decreased the dosage. He braced himself for a fall; it seemed to be running too smoothly, but none came. His focus on wellbeing was such that everything else seemed to pass by in a flash until, during one of his appointments with his psychiatrist, it dawned on Rick that the moment he had been waiting for, the moment his sights had been trained on ever since those first days in the Jennings Clinic, had finally arrived. He was free of medication. He was Rick.

He was liberated. Stunned, too, that such a task had been achieved without a further crisis. At the same time, it brought with it a nervous sense of freedom, that perpetual fear of his ever lurking in the background of his mind: *Am I going to flip out?* He couldn't shake the memory of the last time he had stopped his medication: those four figures walking menacingly down his driveway to take him away in a straight-jacket, and his family protecting him from such a fate.

Turning his back on his medication the last time had precipitated the breakdown that stripped him of his rights and freedoms, kept him prisoner in his own home and then saw him confined to a mental institution to rebuild himself from the ground up. But this time, it felt different. This time, he had won, and he knew it.

He and Kate had even become close friends. She had been offered the house in the divorce settlement but, for reasons Rick could understand all too well, she declined, instead renovating a home she found on Auckland's waterfront. It was a fresh start. But with the completion of Kate's home came time for Rick to make a decision on Waterford. He couldn't sell it yet – the sentimental value was too great; it just felt wrong. And to leave it vacant felt equally wrong.

Rick, his mother by his side, stepped through the front door for the first time in almost two years.

He took in the foyer, the piano, the pool table where he played with his sons. Slowly, he approached the stairs in front of him that would lead up to the master bedroom. He inched his way closer, as if in a dream. He climbed the first stair, then turned around to look back through the open door at the fountain. It had been turned off in the absence of an occupant. He would have to turn it on again when he remembered. He walked up to the second stair.

That's it — that's what's missing. Flowers.

Kate had always arranged a vibrant bouquet on the antique console in the foyer to greet visitors. Now the black and white marble floor looked just that; colorless. Lifeless.

He remembered teasing her about the cost of the floral displays they enjoyed. The florist had visited weekly and Rick had joked to Kate that they would surely be better off with imitation or dry arrangements. But, underneath it, he had loved the color, the fragrance and the life it added to the home.

He stood for a moment, as if in a daze, on the stairs, turning slowly on the spot to absorb his surroundings.

It's gone. It's really over. . .

Maria could see that her son was in his own world, and when he began walking again she followed quietly at a distance, so as not to distract him, as he tried to make sense of what he was feeling. He walked back through the foyer and hallway, and then down a separate flight of stairs to the first level, and stopped by the bar and games room, leading to the outdoor pool. Many times, he remembered, it had seemed so natural to walk by the room and hear the sound of children's excited voices, or his sons' pool parties. Not far away was the movie theater, which became so popular, with each member of the family wanting to enjoy it with friends, that there developed a kind of informal booking routine, and later, a second home theater system was introduced to ensure that no passing whim would go unmet.

James had often recruited his father for his seemingly interminable games of hide and seek, as Rick scoured the whole house, with its generous number of viable hiding places, in search of his younger son and his friends.

He thought of the many airsoft BB gun wars that he had participated in with the boys, the outdoor grounds that completely encircled the house providing the perfect environment for the skirmishes. What he wouldn't now give to have those days return; to be able to enjoy the company of his sons freely at home, without planning and without thought of their imminent departure. He would happily be stung by those plastic pellets again and again – they could shoot him all they wanted – if it meant he could just see them, and hear their voices filling the home that he built for his family, and for it to again be *their* home.

He took another step, but found himself unable to continue. It was his wallet. The wallet that he had last seen on the day of his breakdown sat, solitary, on the empty table before him. He didn't know what to say.

"They told me this would be waiting for you, Rick. The plumber found it wedged between the sink pipes in your old bedroom. Probably it would never have been found if there hadn't been a drain blockage."

Rick approached the table and as he reached out for the wallet, an eerie feeling overtook him. Knowing where he had hid it made no difference to his complete absence of recollection of the event: it didn't ring the faintest bell. They had searched the entire house for it one day, some months after the breakdown, but never found it. Rick had absolutely no memory of where he had concealed it in his paranoia.

He opened it and found it almost empty. Certainly, there was no cash left in there; he had given it all away at the gas station that day. His credit cards had all long since been canceled. And then there was his drivers license. He pulled it from its place and examined it. The ID photo of the old Rick – the one who never imagined the impending breakdown of his mind, and the breakup of his family – stared back at him. That man was gone. His dreams had crumbled.

The emptiness of the vacant house seemed to pull him down to the ground. Slowly, Rick gently lowered himself to the cushion on the floor by where he was standing. It was too much. His head fell into his hands and emotion overtook him.

I'm alone. There's no denying it: I'm alone.

If he had hoped for comfort from this building, his hopes were bitterly disappointed. It seemed now only to echo his profound loneliness. It amplified every yearning he had experienced during those past two years: for family; for belonging. The bizarre pairing of the many rooms of this grand home with this one, solitary man, served only to reveal in sharper light the deep chasm that had opened between the reality of Rick's life, and where he longed to be.

He felt a caring hand placed on his back and an arm tenderly wrap around his shoulders. He continued to sit quietly with his sadness, coming to terms with the reality of the past two years and the pain that, alongside his instinctive drive to rebuild, had contended for his attention.

"Rick, I want you to go and see your psychiatrist." It was his mother's voice. It was the same, sweet voice that would ask him what he would like her to cook when he would visit for dinner. But the words and the voice seemed to be at odds.

"What?" Rick asked, lifting his moistened eyes.

"You're not well, Rick," she said, the concern evident in her voice. "Look at you – you're crying. Please phone your psychiatrist now – I can drive you over there."

"Mum... wait. What are you talking about? This is the first time I've been in the house without Kate and the boys. How would you react?"

Maria spoke softly, not wanting to see her son in any more pain. "Please, Rick, you have to see him immediately. I'm worried. I can see that you're not well."

He didn't have the resolve to convince his mother otherwise. After a few minutes seated on the unassuming cushion, he walked to his car and drove to Dr. Korovin, who confirmed Rick's reaction as a normal emotional response to the situation.

He phoned his mother on the way home and asked if she would allow him some time in the house alone before the two of them made it ready to live in once again. There were boxes to unpack and groceries to buy, but Rick could not bear to think of either task. He would go hungry and sleep on a bare mattress if need be. What he wanted was time alone.

Rick returned to an empty, silent house. As he had more than two years ago when he returned from Topeka, he walked the grounds of the house. He walked inside and out, just as he had those many months ago in what seemed like a different world. He felt so much older now. His body would have taken exception to the thought, but there was something about calmly walking the hallways and grounds of the home that spoke of acceptance; the acceptance of change.

So this is what freedom feels like, is it?

He turned in a circle and lay down in the middle of the lawn, gazing up at the palm trees above.

Free of medication. A healthy body. A healthy mind. Free to live how I want to live.

He took a deep breath and sighed.

It rings empty.

For the rest of the afternoon he surveyed the grounds, walked the hallways and sat in the rooms that had once nurtured a family.

Why don't I feel like I'm at home?

I feel like a visitor. A guest. A passing tourist. On a journey... but where to? Where is my home? This is not it, anymore.

He had spent two years searching for his new home, but what he had suspected during that time was now confirmed: it was not here in Auckland. His birthplace, his sole residence for his forty-eight year life, could no longer provide what he needed.

He was free. But free of what? Certainly not of loneliness. Nor of his search. Or his need to find whatever it was he was bent on discovering.

Already, he had searched the globe for his soulmate, with no luck. But he would not give up. He would not rest until he had found what he was looking for. His pilgrimage to the heart of life, to the woman who would understand him, to his new home, wherever they may be, could end in only two ways: with his arrival, or with his death.

⌒

CHAPTER THIRTY-FOUR

T HE CHURCH BELLS contended with the crowd's excited chatter and the organist's rendition of Elton John's *Your Song*. Row upon row of family and friends poured out of the richly decorated chapel, all beaming, some with damp eyes glistening in the summer sun. The photographer's appeal for the guests to gather around the bridal party to capture the wedding's entire attendance initially fell on deaf ears, until Rick himself gestured for those around him to huddle into place so that the photographer, elevated on a platform aimed at the entrance to the chapel, could fit the crowd into his frame. The photo shoot would last for another hour, as every combination of the couple's close relatives and friends was captured by the chapel. Never did the man behind the camera need to ask for a smile from his subjects. Their smiles were permanent, and none more so than Rick's: it was one of the happiest days of his life.

The bridal party began making their way to the reception. It was to be held on a nearby privately-owned island, and as the cars made their way through the entrance to the driveway, one felt as if the threshold to a new world had been crossed. *How appropriate for the day*, Rick mused.

The sub-tropical flora that lined the long, winding driveway wrapped the guests in a welcoming embrace. On arriving at the estate's venerable house, which would form part of the reception area, the cars circled the fountain, and the bridal party, giddy with excitement, made its way to the upstairs section of the house.

The guests flowed through the reception area, making their way past the fountain, through the grand foyer and onto the terrace, from which the full expanse of the area was visible. The wide, stone stair-case led down to the main marquee that had been erected to facilitate the three-hundred wedding guests, where they were greeted by a string quartet. Rick and the rest of the bridal party watched from their upstairs van-tage point as the guests chatted over Veuve Clicquot and hors d'oeuvres, eventually finding their places at the dining tables. Soon, the guests were seated, and the time came for celebration. It was difficult to believe that the day had actually arrived. Rick pinched himself.

Yes, he thought, *it has arrived. This is it.*

They walked down the terrace stairs, slowly, the bride and groom, hand in hand. Rick was having trouble containing his emotion, an inde-finable concoction of joy and tenderness, as he trained his eyes on the path in front of him, though still catching a glimpse of the stunning woman at his side from time to time.

Was it just him, or was it the room that seemed to bore a hole in his chest and suck the breath out of him? Wherever he looked, all he saw was overflowing smiles and a feast of color: the purity of the white table-tops and ceiling turrets that seemed to reach into the sky, and the pastel deco-rations that were so vividly contrasted by the lush, brighter-than-the-sun floral displays on each of the circular, ten-seater dining tables, and then the earthy, polished hard-wood floors. It was a fairytale wedding, and a delight to behold.

They arrived at their seats at the head table; the music stopped. And then, all together, the bridal party and the guests sat, and almost imme-diately the wait-staff circulated with the night's dinner menu.

Wasting no time, Rick thought. *Just as planned — there's sure as hell enough to get through tonight — and they've all told me not to draw my speech out too long. But how can I not? How can I truncate the song in my heart on a day like this?! On this day, of all days, I can't help but —*

"God, I can barely breathe," came the voice from beside him. That familiar voice. That beautiful woman. And today, looking every bit as dazzling as she ever had.

"Tell me about it," Rick replied to Kate.

They each glanced over their menus, doing their best to settle their nerves as an endless stream of eager guests approached them with their excited congratulations. It wouldn't matter what Kate ordered, reflected Rick; her appetite vanishes the moment her nerves arrive.

It was beautifully done, Rick had to admit. Despite his rampant perfectionist streak, he couldn't argue that every detail hadn't been attended to. And all had gone smoothly, so far.

The crayfish appetizer arrived: the moment he had been waiting for all day, he joked to himself.

Then the speeches. First, the father of the bride. And then, the mother of the bride. When Rick's turn came, he had to swallow hard before beginning.

"This is one of the most beautiful moments of my life," he started, very slowly, doing his best to convey in words what was welling up inside of him. He turned to his son. "Michael, I'm as proud of you as a father could be. Amid the vast sea of sand, you have found that sparkling diamond. You have found your true love."

Yes, true love, he mused to himself. *That sense of contentment that just feels effortless; the joy of simply co-existing. How beautiful it is to love and be loved. How any challenge is manageable with love in your life.*

He could understand why his son admired her, and he understood his love for her. They were a wonderful match. It made him happy to watch one of his own family discover one of life's most precious gifts.

But Rick couldn't deny that he, himself, was yet to find that sparkling diamond. Not that it was for any lack of opportunity – it had been years.

Neither had Kate. He wished she had – he wished she had found someone special to be in her life. Rick remembered phoning the country's leading match-maker to enlist her services: she was surprised to discover, after introductions, that the subject of the matchmaking would not be Rick, but his former wife. But Kate didn't want any part of such a process. Who would have thought that both would still be alone, after all this time?

He still couldn't quite put his finger on what went wrong in the relationship. Maybe the foundations of the marriage crumbled long before it hit a brick wall that March day of Rick's breakdown. Maybe it could all be traced back to her feeling that she came third in his life; her impatience with his appeasement within his family, his peacemaking, his apologies – or was it because he tried to treat her like a princess? Was it reality's ruthless entry into a dream-life created by Rick?

Quite probably, he would never really know the answer. One of Kate's comments often returned to him whenever he asked the question: 'You find it easy to express what's in your heart, Rick. I just don't.' Strange that they should become such close friends after such a heart-rending separation. But, Rick knew, it would never again be anything more than friendship. They were different; they were no longer a match for each other. He wished that Kate would find someone special, and he wished the same for himself; but he knew they would not find it in each other.

He had tried. He dated women of a variety of nationalities, ages and situations, and found each one fascinating and beautiful in her own way. It disappointed him immensely that he had found it difficult to fall in love over the years. Was it that he hadn't met the right person? Or was it something inside of him that, for whatever reason, was preventing him from what he so desperately wanted?

We're all the same, he concluded after considering the different people he had met in his search for a meaningful relationship. *We all want to feel free, respected, and loved. We might give reasons as to why we're not with someone — but a lot of us live alone. Relationships are not simple.*

Maybe it will never happen to me again — maybe I'll never find another love. One thing's for sure — I'm done with the search. I can't push love: the harder I try, the less it works.

He paused as he came to the end of his speech, and looked to the guests one last time, and then to his son, knowing that the occasion was once-in-a-lifetime. There was more he could have said – he could have talked all night.

"Anita, I welcome you into the family – I've always wanted a daughter. And now that wish has come true."

His speech went over the suggested limit, but so did everyone's. How could it be any other way?

Kate made hers, followed by the bride, the groom and the best man.

And then the busy, joy-and-alcohol-fueled conversation resumed. From the elevated table at the front of the room, Rick could see every guest at the wedding. He scanned the floor; so many happy faces. But some, he knew, didn't wish him well. Two, in particular.

He sighed, returning his attention to the delicately arranged food in front of him.

"I know what you're thinking about," said Kate. "Don't let it get to you tonight — you've allowed it to taint far too many occasions in the past. I think it's time you let it go — especially tonight."

He nodded slowly. "You're right." He was happy that the two had become close friends over the eight years since their separation and then divorce. He was sure they always would be. The shape of his family had warped and shifted beyond recognition. But it was reassuring to know, that beneath the changes, a current of love still flowed, despite the very different appearance it took. Here he was, eight years after separation, celebrating his son's wedding with his former wife, a true friend, at his side. Maybe his most important hope of his adult life — for his family to be happy — had, in fact, materialized, just not in the form he had expected.

There was a contentment about the family; a relaxation. There was nothing wrong here, and nothing lacking, in spite of Rick's years of concern that he had broken a family that *should* have remained together.

For a moment, he glimpsed the perfection of it all.

CHAPTER THIRTY-FIVE

THE PLANT-LIFE THAT surrounded him had an immediately soothing effect, as if he could finally take a long-awaited breath from the wedding's constant activity. Rick stood for a moment and allowed his mind to relax amid the stillness of the estate's gardens. They reminded him somewhat of the lush foliage of Waterford.

He noticed a dark, red-brown tinge creeping across the full moon as the day's lunar eclipse began. It was something he had never seen before, and was glad to be able to witness the first moments of it. The sky was clear and the full moon had so far been shining down on the party. To be able to watch the silent dimming of that light to darkness, eventually lifting an hour or so later to reveal again the full moon in its wake, fascinated Rick.

The night continued to blossom and nothing more could be asked of such a perfect occasion. It was a magical night, with the traditional Croatian band's music reminding him of his childhood, and the times that he would dance the kolo, alternating with the rock band to please both young and old alike. The idyllic setting of individual cabanas nestled amongst the gardens enhanced the evening's splendor as he made his way along the path.

Yet, there was still something; something lurking in the background

— a reminder just waiting to be noticed by Rick's attention. He had done almost all the dancing he could for one night, but it wasn't physical exertion that motivated his stroll through the gardens. It was that vague unease that had stalked him all day.

He somehow didn't fit in. That was it.

It was his own son's wedding; almost every face at the reception was a familiar one. Yet, he knew he didn't belong.

His friends were there; but instead of bringing him joy, they only reflected back what had been lost. The times shared together seemed a lifetime ago, and he was aware of his failure to stay in contact with them as much as he would have liked during his travels, and through the mesmerizing activity of the recent years.

Rick noticed he couldn't help but be drawn to the bride's family's side of the reception during his speech; there was something uncomfortable about seeing his own family right there in front of him. Rosa and Andrew — the mere thought of them generated a flurry of discomfort in his solar plexus. Whenever he thought it couldn't get any worse between them, the situation deteriorated even further.

He wondered what it was that motivated them to push so strongly for control of the firm, only to let it die. The numerous heated debates over the direction of the firm, over Rick's view that it was being neglected in favor of individuals, had brought him no closer to a clear answer from his sister. Rick brought all his investments to the family as a whole, as he had always done since the very beginning. But it seemed that, for all his effort, his sister and brother-in-law preferred to siphon off whatever worthwhile ventures they discovered — ventures that often came to them in their capacity as members of the family firm — to their own individual interests.

Rick had conducted his own chairmanship of the family firm with a serious sense of responsibility. Although the repercussions had sometimes angered and disappointed Kate, he had always believed that unbiased leadership was a requirement of the holder of that position, and that he or she was to act in the interests of the group as a whole, without partiality toward any faction or segment of the family. It meant that he had never hesitated in bringing opportunities to the firm, and gladly handing them to Andrew's children, when his own children lacked the experience or interest in such opportunities. Furthermore, shareholders in the family firm – namely, the family members themselves – were always beneficiaries of the firm's profits, regardless of who was running the projects within the firm structure.

Now, all that had changed. Without their need for Rick, every effort was made to plunder the assets of the firm and the infrastructure for individual interests. Andrew, his erstwhile best friend, was now a shadow of who he used to be. The darkness that had latched onto his soul, facilitated with such enthusiasm by Rosa, and that had slowly ensnared him, feeding on his weakness, had now grown to a point where its hold over him was unequivocal. The light that once shone from his eyes was now but a dim remnant of its former self; an expired star vaguely hinting at its former glory.

What was worse, getting a straight answer out of his sister for the downward-spiraling family situation had proven impossible.

One answer still stood out: "Plenty of families don't get along," she had responded. He still had trouble believing his own sister had said such a thing. He knew all too well that many families were not close, but it had always been his strong belief that *his* family was different. All his life, he had held the family above all else. But time had confirmed that his ideals had betrayed him.

The damaging neglect of the family firm was one thing, but the demise of the family itself was quite another. At least, now, he was free of the anguish that his involvement with the family firm had entailed.

⌣

'BUY ME OUT.' Two weeks earlier, Rick had spoken the words with more conviction than anything he could remember in his years of disagreement with his sister. He was simply giving them a direction, and it wasn't open to discussion. Rosa and Andrew looked at him disbelievingly and with dry-mouthed nervousness.

'What are you talking about. Take your pills and stop acting like a madman.' Rosa knew he had been off the medication for years, and her words were deliberate barbs to make him bleed a little. In the past it would have worked. He would have been hurt and wondered how he had upset her. He would have tried to make it up to her, just to keep the peace. Now, however, she no longer held the same power over him, and that was an exhilarating feeling for him after all the years of failed peace-making.

Rick refused to take the bait. 'I want out.' Andrew could tell by the tone of Rick's voice that this wasn't something they could argue about.

'When?' he asked quietly. Rick actually felt sorry for the man.

Rosa looked aghast. 'You can't do this. We're in the middle of several substantial acquisitions. You can't leave now.'

Rick gave a sardonic laugh. 'You're in the middle of them Rosa, and you are using the company's capital. How much say did I have? None. And that's fine, despite the fact that we founded the company together. I don't want to be involved; you've built a new structure that excludes me, and I don't agree with the investments you're making. I've had the papers drawn up, and I'm sure we all want this to be as painless as possible.' Rick paused, nervous to voice his next wish for fear of a backlash from his sister. 'Perhaps then we can get back to being just family again.'

'We can get back to being a family as soon as you pull yourself together and start contributing to this business once again, Rick!' she yelled. 'You can't just walk out on a multi-million dollar firm!'

'Well which way do you want it, Rosa?' he shot back. 'It seems to me that you want complete control of the firm, with me out of the picture, *except* when you've screwed things up and need some help. The Dellich name was a highly respected seal of approval. You two knew how to use that brand, and the infrastructure we had built over thirty years, for your own benefit. You seized power and took it over, using it for your own ends, penalizing the rest of the family. And it became cloaked in secrecy, even from me.' Rick was angry, but he spoke calmly, knowing that his decision was final, but welcoming his one, final chance to express his deep sadness at the firm's dissolution. 'What was once for the good of the family became a tool for your own ambitions. What was built on the wisdom of All for One and One for All, was plundered for the benefit of the few. From what I have been able to see, the standards on which our business was built – standards of performance and professionalism – have deteriorated. I've already asked you to rebuild the family firm, and you've demonstrated many times that you would prefer to let it die and be forgotten. I have no choice but to ask you to buy me out.'

He handed the papers to his seething sister, her eyes betraying a fury that searched for words, but knew it was no longer of any use. She snatched the papers out of his hands and quickly read them.

'Is this all you want?' she said sneeringly. 'You truly are mad.'

'It's what I had twenty years ago – before Best. I'll leave with as much as I put in.'

He had let himself be sidelined when he needed his energy to salvage his marriage and failed; he had let himself be over-ridden in important decisions and witnessed the waning of the company's strength. He had endured the malice of his sister for too long. Now, it seemed even to be corrupting the next generation of the family. Andrew's son, who had become involved in the family firm's business ventures, acted with unjustified aggression toward any suggestion or decision of Rick's. The only way it could be explained, was by a lifetime's exposure to the animosity of his parents, Rosa and Andrew. Indeed, Andrew appeared to relish the friction between the two in the boardroom, and refused to mediate the exchanges between them. He found himself between a rock and a hard place: on the one hand, he had always led any business with an intention for consensus amongst its executives, knowing that either they would make it to the other side of the stream united, or they would drown. On the other hand, the opposition he came up against was so unreasonable as to require Rick to fold on every important point if they were to reach a consensus.

He couldn't help but be reminded of the many people he had met who gave everything to their loved ones, only to find that they were ushered out of their homes later in life to vacate lucrative property for their offspring's benefit. Or forced into rest homes by their children, hoping to speed death's arrival, as they impatiently awaited their passing and the ensuing payoffs.

How vulnerable we are as we enter this world, Rick reflected, *and at the end of our lives, too. So strongly are we motivated toward individualistic goals in our society, that it breeds an 'out of sight, out of mind' mentality.*

Now it was time. Rick's departure from the firm was over within just a matter of hours, and he felt for the first time that his quest for freedom had come full circle. Rosa glared at him as she slowly told him the truth, savoring the moment.

'You were always Dad's favorite. You thought you were special and you wanted everyone to love you. Well, I don't. And I never have.'

Rick shuddered inside, making no attempt to conceal the hurt that was written all over his face. 'Thank you,' was all he could answer. At least, for once, he had the truth.

RICK FOUND A seat and sat amongst the trees, gazing up at the night sky, and the dark, silhouetted moon.

There were many at the wedding who knew him, he reflected; but none, he feared, who understood him. He was alone. Alone in a sea of people. He sensed the openness of those closest to him – their willingness to extend their hand, their eagerness to convince him that all was well – but it was not something he could hear right now. There was so much hurt; so much to let go of. So much had been strived for – indeed, it had actually come to be: and now it all seemed to burst as unassumingly as a soap bubble in a breeze. His marriage; his family.

And, his grandiose dreams of a new life in the United States. He remembered its inception, nurtured by hope, and full of promise. It was to have been the beginning of a new life for Rick. He had been eager for his next adventure, one that would take him out of his comfort zone, in a new country in which he knew no one and that he had always thought of fondly since first visiting on his honeymoon. No longer could he keep playing the same game of business that he already knew how to win: it was time to explore a new world. It was with such ambitions that he had begun his two years at his new home in Los Angeles.

Had it delivered on its promise? Had it provided the long-awaited answer to his search for fulfillment? Not at first glance. His soulmate, his purpose – they had remained elusive. But, concealed within the shadows of his failures at home and abroad, something more was starting to reveal itself. He was beginning to glimpse a treasure that was most unexpected in the midst of his frustrated search.

A SURGE OF noise from the distant party brought Rick back to the gardens, and the occasion of the day. He felt that he still had some dancing left in him yet, and rose from the bench to make his way back to the dance floor, before the night was over – maybe the band was getting ready to finish for the night.

But it couldn't be that late already. . .

It's after 1 a.m., he remarked, glancing at his watch. And there was the date staring back at him: '18', it said.

The eighteenth. I almost forgot.

Nine years. To the day — exactly nine years, he repeated, scarcely believing that it had been that long since the day of his breakdown. It spooked him for a moment when he first heard the date they had chosen for the wedding. He never spoke of the coincidence, and did his best to push it out of his mind.

What an unspeakably rich ten years it had been. What was left of that man that he once knew as Rick all that time ago? So much had changed. His elder son was married. The boy who had once asked Rick to teach him how to ride a bike, now had a wife.

Life had rushed by. How old was he, now? Would he soon be a grandfather?

Hell, it's happening too fast, he smiled to himself.

It was grand. It was all such a game, this life, in all its drama, he thought. It was moments like these that put it all into perspective.

He stood and made his way along the winding garden path to rejoin the activity of the party.

So that's about seven and a half years since I last took any medication, he reflected. *They told me I wouldn't last seven years even if I took the medication, let alone without it. But I haven't touched any of it — not a* dose of Epilim; not a sleeping tablet; not even a session with a psychiatrist or therapist. The symptoms that plagued me — the dullness in my stomach, the depression, the euphoria, the mood swings — none of it's ever returned. And even with everything that's collapsed around me, I feel stronger than ever.

Even I'm surprised.

CHAPTER THIRTY-SIX

M Y SON'S MARRIED. Isn't that incredible? Three nights ago – a day to remember, that's for sure. You know how much it means to me. You know that family is everything to me..." Rick's voice trailed off into the silence of the early morning, his lips hinting at only the faintest smile, and his gaze settling on the distant horizon of Auckland Harbour.

"I still can't quite grasp what's happening. I can't quite get my head around the fact that what was most important to me – what I dedicated my life to, what I gave everything I had for – has fallen apart. It's as if it's all a dream and I'm about to wake up.

"I feel it even took *you* a while to understand me. For you to realize that I was doing everything in my power – giving everything I could – for this family. Do you remember how many times you asked me to take care of the family? How you charged me with the responsibility of 'keeping the family together'?" The frustration was creeping into Rick's voice. He was still standing. He couldn't sit yet – it wouldn't have felt right. He was standing to be accountable; and to request accountability.

"You told me to look after the whole family. And I did – heaven knows, I did everything in my power toward that end. It became my purpose in life. They wanted to be involved in my first businesses, so I welcomed them on equal terms.

"We founded Naturally Best as a family, and it wasn't long before Andrew was unhappy in his position. I found that he was closing in on my own role, and so I made allowances and welcomed him closer to my own position, hoping he would be happier.

"Rosa would complain about Kate — I would apologize over nothing to keep the peace. Rosa would destroy friendships, spread lies, grab for more and more control and attention — and for some reason, somehow, I think I even apologized for that.

"But even with all that, they still appeared to be unhappy. Is that what you had in mind?" Rick demanded of his father.

He sighed. "After a lifetime of work for the sole purpose of the greater good of my family — those that I love — this is where I find myself? *Family was my higher purpose.* It was all that mattered.

"And it was an illusion," he spoke to himself, struggling to accept the truth of it.

It was 5:30 a.m.. The late-summer sun was showing the first signs of life behind the hills to the east. In front of him, to the north, lay the volcanic island of Rangitoto in the Waitemata Harbour. And, to his left, Rick could see the high-rises of downtown Auckland. The cemetery was silent but for the singing of birds.

"I remember what happened to your family — how you and your sister stopped speaking, even until you passed away. Over the owner-ship of a single building; over the betrayal of loyalty you felt. Well, we're not talking about a building, here — we're talking about a whole life's work. I finally had to walk away from it all. Just two weeks ago I left the firm. I gave everything I had to build this family's strength, and now it's come to this.

"Maybe it's my fault. Maybe I refused to believe what was right before my eyes all my life. As Mum used to say to me, as Kate used to say to me — Rosa has never liked me, she's never been comfortable with me. They would tell me she saw me as nothing more than a rival. But I never believed it. I was blinded by my hope, by my ideals. I didn't want to believe it… family was everything to me. I didn't want to believe that it might not be real…"

A cat approached Rick. It was a housecat, with an unusual coloring.

Rick was surprised to notice that, after the many cats he must have seen in his life, he had never seen one like this. The two locked eyes. It seemed an eternity that they looked at one another. Rick was reminded of the movie that had stuck in his memory since childhood: *High Noon*.

"It's the biggest failure of my life, Dad. The biggest disappointment; the deepest hurt. I'm having difficulty coming to terms with it. But there's no escaping the truth: the family I believed in, the family that I lived my life for, doesn't exist."

Although it was still summer, Rick noticed that his feet were wet from the early-morning dew on the grass. It had seeped through his shoes. The first hint of the approaching autumn. The blemish made Rick smile ever so slightly – a reminder of the ever-changing seasons of life, not for a moment stationary – always changing, always moving.

He decided to sit on the bench by his father's grave. From the seat, he could still see Rangitoto, downtown, and the awakening sun. But he could also see a bird – a fantail – nestled in a pohutukawa tree. The housecat was approaching stealthily, the bird oblivious to its muted movements.

"Do you remember what I asked you in Topeka, during my first night at the Jennings Clinic? 'What would you think of me now?' That's what I said. It was almost nine years ago now – it was nine years on Sunday since my breakdown. I look back on those nine years, and I can't help but ask you the same question today. What *would* you think of where I am today?

"It seems that so much that was important to me has collapsed. I left the Jennings Clinic with such hopes, such dreams of the life I would rebuild. But almost everything I've touched has turned to dust."

Light was now creeping over the hills, ever so slowly. Rick had watched the cat make a leap for the fantail as it flitted within reach, but the bird managed to dart aside in time. He doubted the cat was hungry – clearly, it was a housecat. But hunting for the sport of it, he supposed, was in its nature.

"I've learned a lot about mental illness. Dealing with a nervous breakdown has been an enormous challenge. So many people know someone who's affected by it, but so many are intolerant of it. They're scared of it, but only because they don't understand it. And they don't want to understand it, because it scares them. All that's required is for us to recognize unhealthy tendencies within ourselves – that's where imbalance comes from. It's not something families should be afraid of. We should be eager to increase our awareness of the issues, so that we can help those who are close to us, instead of being afraid of it. It's too widespread, and too serious. We need to help one another.

"Many times I paid a price for refusing to accept the golden rule. I found myself the target of attempted blackmail in L.A. on a number of occasions. You know I never bought into the golden rule at the Jennings Clinic – 'don't tell anyone, under any circumstances, about your experience with mental illness.' You know I took it seriously, but that I made the decision to leave myself open to attack whenever I saw someone whom I could help. Prevention is the key to solving the mental health crisis that is upon us – and if that means exposing my own experience, it's a price I'll willingly pay."

He paused again, considering the disappointments he had experienced.

"No matter how much I want to make a difference, I seem to have failed many times. A good friend of mine, Sally – you'll remember her – who's been with me since I first started in business, tried to tell me I'm only focusing on the downside of the situation. She said it's insubstantial compared with the difference that I have made.

"But I'm moving on. I'm letting go of the past. I have no regrets in trying to make a difference the way I did, with the people I cared for and others I met, because how else could I really be sure that I had done everything I could to make a difference, without experimenting in a lifetime's work the way I did? I had to try, and I gave it my best."

The fantail had returned to its original position on the pohutukawa tree. The cat resumed its stalking. Rick watched, perplexed by the bird's innocence. Conflict, it seemed, was everywhere – inescapable in some form, whether it be mild or severe. Even intelligence appeared powerless to thwart it. He recalled driving through the streets of the Balkans, a region scarred by centuries of sporadic warfare. He was amazed by how even in the modern world, where many were well-educated, seemingly arbitrary and simplistic divisions still gave rise to an apparently unending cycle of violence.

"Such a strange feeling, after the wedding, catching a taxi back to my mother's house. Never, in my wildest dreams, did I think I would be staying at my mother's home while in Auckland. Only a two-minute drive from Waterford, but there I was, staying with my mother in my home-city.

"I still can't really understand it, Dad. Sometimes it seems that the more I've given in life, the less I've gotten back." A quiet laugh escaped him, as he bent forward and ran his hand through the grass, feeling its texture. "I know what it is, though it pains me to say it. It pains me to say it because it means that all my effort, in the end, wasn't as necessary as I thought it was. Maybe all my efforts have, almost, been a complete waste."

Rick sighed. He couldn't help but notice the appropriateness of reporting to his father at a graveyard at a time when it seemed that he, himself, had lost everything of meaning in his life. He felt he was in the midst of a death of his own, and not a quick one.

"But here it is: I've been trying too hard." He could feel his smile widen as he said it, as it sank in. "For as long as I can remember, I've done everything I could to find a solution for every problem I encountered; to make things how I thought they should be; to get somewhere... though I can't really say where it was I was trying to get to.

"I've spent my whole life trying to live the life I thought I wanted, the life that I thought I *should* be living. But for what? What have I been chasing? Some secure, stable life, with all the bells and whistles to go along with it – some illusory image of perfection? Well, I don't want that anymore. I would trade it all for this. For who I am now.

"And I believe that's not what you would want for me, either. I know there's a rawness in you that would recognize the truth in me. So be proud of me now, Dad. This is the real me. This is the real Rick." He felt the tears welling in his eyes. "It's been a struggle for me. I don't always know the right way, I only hear what my heart is telling me. And I've found that sometimes following my heart means that I hurt the people I love the most.

"I still don't see it all clearly — why I went where I did, why I got bipolar, why I had a breakdown. All I can say is, I know I wasn't being true to myself. I may have made it in society's eyes, but when I look back on my life now, I see that there was little left of the real me. It had all but died.

"Maybe I'm the only person who sees it that way. Maybe people pity me, seeing what I had, and what I lost. But not me. I am more myself than I've ever been, and that's more meaningful and brave than the life I had built for myself. I've taken responsibility for my own life." Rick could feel a sense of strength permeating his being.

He chuckled softly under his breath.

"I just wonder why it took me so damn long to realize that everything I was holding onto wasn't as real as I thought it was.

"Maybe it's just like these flowers that they plant here at the cemetery, or like the gardens that grew at our old home. In time, they grow. But it can't happen all at once. Give them too much water, and they'll die. You can't force them to grow. Nature has its own rhythm — its own mystery. Maybe these nine years are the time I needed to learn — I wish I could have learned faster; made each mistake only once. Yes… maybe it's the time I needed to accept that there are some things that are out of my control."

Already Rick could sense a light breeze and noticed the cloud formations shifting. "Everything I strived for — marriage, family, my business success, someone to share my life with — it can all evaporate in the blink of an eye. All my hopes for a new life in California, as much as I loved it there… it's as if I was searching for answers, for belonging. Searching for permission to simply be myself. I don't quite know, it's still not completely clear to me. But I feel that I was searching for something that was here all along, if I only stopped to see it."

Rick stood, scanned the horizon, and took a full breath. He opened his hand, and glanced at the small object there.

"So much of what I had, I've lost.

"Everything I've searched for has eluded me.

"But, as strange as it sounds, I've never felt more alive. I've never felt more at peace. I've never felt more 'me' before.

"I'm a better man than I've ever been, Dad, and I'm grateful to have been blessed with a wealth of amazing experiences in my life. I'm a stronger man than I've ever been. I feel lucky to have my health – after all that I've been through, I can't believe how I've seemed to grow stronger with each challenge. And how, at times when others – and I, I might add – have wondered if my circumstances might be pushing me to the edge again, I'm actually fine. I've handled it all.

"I hear my own voice clearer now than I ever did, and I know I've been true to myself. And I have my two wonderful sons. Nothing is more important to me." He had to fight back the excitement that was ready to burst out of his mouth. "I have to tell you, there is another adventure I'm excited about. There is something that's come to me, something I want to do... but I can't share it with you just yet. Although I want to, it's not quite time... but you'll be the first to know. I feel that I've been wandering in the wilderness for some time now, but I'm sensing a new purpose, a new direction. I know this new purpose will require all my courage – I don't know if I will succeed, but the courage is in trying, and to me, it's all or nothing: I'll give it everything I have."

He crouched beside the gravestone and placed the rock, that had been sitting in his hand, by the small arrangement of flowers on the ground.

He stared for a while, laughing to himself as he recalled the first moment that he held the rock, and thought that maybe he had within him the strength to turn it to dust.

"I wanted to leave this with you, Dad. It's my rock from Medjugorje." The jagged stone from Bosnia had accompanied Rick across continents and through the years. He gazed at it one more time before slowly standing.

"I carried it for almost eight years to remind me of the new life that I asked for, and the new life that was given to me. It was more challenging than I expected it to be; and it taught me more than I expected to learn. But, if nothing else... well, it's been a journey, that's for sure.

"But it doesn't feel right to carry it any longer. I feel I've learned what this chapter had to teach me, and I'm entering another. I thought maybe you could take care of it – my little memento – for as long as it remains here with you."

He touched the rock one last time, then brushed the earth from his hands and looked up to the sky. "Well, I suppose that's it for this visit, then. I don't know when I'll next be in town — I'm leaving tonight. I've become something of a gypsy, you know, with my two suitcases — one for summer, one for winter. But, as I always say, a lot of the people I saw on Santa Monica beach only had one suitcase — not including their sleeping bag or blanket, that is — so I consider myself very lucky! Who would have thought that, after building a home for those that I love most with fourteen bathrooms, I now find myself unable to call even one bathroom my own. But I'm more at peace than I've ever been.

"I thought of traveling to Africa — wouldn't that be an experience? And then I considered the Middle East — or India. And then I almost decided to visit Argentina and learn some Latin dancing. But maybe I'll leave that for another time.

"Something tells me that I would be best to take Steve up on his offer and stay with him in Sydney. Who knows what will come of it." The sound of birds was now supported by the occasional distant car, and a light rustling of leaves in the morning breeze.

"So, there it is: my good health, my two suitcases, my two boys, and my heart speaking softly to me."

He took one last look at his father's final resting place. Never could he have imagined the tumultuous years that awaited him following that day when his world caved in and all sense of certainty and stability vanished, that day when he became a prisoner in his own home. Never could he have imagined, all those years ago, the life that he now lived, with all that he once valued apparently absent. Yet, never would he have anticipated the hidden treasures that it would reveal.

He turned and walked to his car, stealing one last glance at the bench where he met with his father, his rock, and the gravestone.

"I miss you, Dad."

END OF PART TWO

PART THREE

For Love and Freedom

CHAPTER ONE

H IS HEAD WAS locked, unable to move. His eyes refused to obey the natural impulse to blink as their gaze seemed to burn through the words staring back at him. For what seemed like an interminable moment, he was frozen solid, the force of the memories evoked by the headline ambushing his usually casual glance over the front page headlines.

Luke Powers could not believe it.

But not just because of what he was reading. *Anna Chen, global business leader, dies,* stated the headline.

Miss Anna's death was an event of sufficient magnitude to warrant shock for Luke. But what he was feeling was more than mere shock. It was a veritable assault of emotions, so overwhelming as to leave him in a state of temporary paralysis.

His breath once again began to move and he slowly shook himself out of his otherworldly state.

"Charlotte," he softly spoke into the phone in front of him. "Coffee, please."

"Right away," came the reply.

He sat back in his chair and looked out over Central Park and at the skyscrapers lining the South end of it, reflecting the morning's spring sunlight.

"Miss Anna…" he whispered to himself, shaking his head. "Why? I'll never understand it. Why did you do it?"

The door opened, and in walked his personal assistant holding a small china tray.

"Charlotte, why did no one tell me about this?" Luke asked, holding the front page toward the neatly dressed woman.

"It only came through a few hours ago – I assumed you knew."

"No, not until now."

"Oh, I'm sorry, Luke. I'm so used to leaving the news for your morning briefing with Maurice – he didn't mention it?" she asked, perplexed.

Luke nodded. "I missed his call on the way in. He'll probably phone through here soon. Don't worry about it," he waved a hand dismissively. "Just give me a few minutes on my own, if you don't mind."

"Of course." She closed the door behind her.

He turned his attention back to the news of Miss Anna's death. It was as if it had opened a dormant wound. But he was sure he had left it all behind.

It was over thirty years ago! he thought.

But he couldn't deny the devastating pain that it had caused him, all that time ago.

"Jade," he whispered, almost inaudibly. "Jade…"

For years, her memory had stalked him. Not once had the two spoken, nor had an exchange of any kind, since that sickening phone call in Hong Kong, and her final words: 'Forgive me someday.'

For a while, he had held true to his promise to himself: to never love like that again. His relationships were little more than fleeting, thrilling encounters, offering little more than an escape from the day-to-day isolation he felt.

Yet his defiance of his own deepest yearning for belonging in this world did not last. *Be careful what you wish for,* he sometimes found himself pondering. His promise to himself, as much as he determined to relinquish it, eventually became a curse.

He searched and searched for a love that would match what he had felt first for Kiri, and then, in all its perfection, for Jade.

His talent for business never failed him: he bounced back from Wong

Peng's initial setback. He returned to the United States, the country of his childhood, hoping for a sense of stability that had eluded him in New Zealand and Hong Kong. Maybe it was part of who he was, or maybe it was an underlying refusal to back down from a confrontation, but he chose to make his mark in media. It would transpire to be the same area of Wong Peng's expanding influence in Eastern Star.

Luke was at a loss to understand the man. He was a walking contradiction: a high-profile benefactor to charitable causes, and, on the surface, widely respected as a business-world role model. But those who had dealings with him knew better. The man's aggression knew no bounds, and Luke often found himself walking away from business deals that Wong Peng insisted on derailing the moment he caught wind of them, it seemed for no other reason than to spite Luke. From what Luke had seen, nothing was more important to this man than saving face, and the possession of absolute control.

He wondered, was Jade happy? Was she satisfied with her decision to marry Wong Peng? How much was she respected by her husband? Luke wondered if the beauty of her spirit had been allowed to flourish, or if it had been stifled. He knew, by virtue of her family's prominence and visibility in the public eye, that she had given birth to two sons, many years apart, the older of whom had since been killed. He recalled their own marriage plans, their excitement at the prospect of a large family of their own, and their dreams of having six or more children together. It was what she had wanted for her life. But not anymore, he could only assume.

He had done his best to distance himself from that period of his life. He knew that there was nothing there but pain; nothing but agonizing disappointment. It had been a painful decision, but when it became glaringly evident that Jade was lost to him forever, he resolved to move on. Luke ultimately resolved to find the love he had been looking for, and to build his business to be the most magnificent creation he could imagine.

His success in the latter, and utter lack of it in the former, reinforced his growing superstition that he was cursed in love. The more he searched, the more discouraged he became. And all the while, Powers Media expanded beyond recognition. He enjoyed every minute of it. Even if the responsibility he felt for the world at large and for those in his immediate sphere of influence sometimes weighed heavily on him, as a business leader in an age when the pen was indeed mightier than the sword, he felt satisfied with his conduct. Luke was proud to have pursued his dream with what he felt was a measure of wisdom and a desire for the betterment of humankind.

How ridiculous, he had sometimes lamented. *How absurd that I could find true love as a teenager. That I could find true love again in my twenties. And now, with everything I need at my fingertips, I can't find a thing.*

Two tantalizing tastes of what it was to be deeply, wholly in love. Both to end in disaster. And, for almost thirty years, finding nothing that would measure up to what had been experienced earlier in life. He was almost tempted to write the experiences off as nothing more than young, idealistic romances. But he knew that was not the truth. He knew that what he had experienced was real.

And he had almost resigned himself to a life of loneliness.

Until he found her.

"Luke," came Charlotte's voice.

"Yeah," he replied, wearily.

"I thought you would probably want to take this call."

"Who is it?" he asked.

"It's Emerald."

P ATIENCE," CAME THE voice from across the table. "We will do our job, Mr. Peng, you can be assured of that."

Wong Peng recalled his first encounter with the Society's liaison. It was exhilarating to discover the existence of such an organization: one that had managed, despite his own breathtaking power, despite his every effort to forge connections to those who wielded power, to evade his own attention. How could a body of such profound influence remain undetected? He gleaned a clue from Robertson's remark on the art of manipulating political power: 'The belief of the masses that they are in control of their own government is our greatest ally. We wholeheartedly support the façade of democracy, in order to shape the reality of it.'

It was tantalizing. Control. Power. Surrendered willingly; voluntarily; without struggle. The thrill even at the mere thought of it – the idea that he would be in proximity to such a thing – sent adrenaline rushing through Wong Peng's body. And he wanted more. He wanted to be done with Robertson; he wanted to go deeper. He wanted to meet the real puppeteers. His impatience for the day when he was admitted to a higher tier of the organization had gripped him since the day of his discovery. The mystery that enshrouded the Society's workings only intrigued him further, only made him hungry for more. He was like a boy on the verge of uncovering a female's body for the first time, face to face with the possibility that his wildest dreams may materialize right before his eyes.

"Mr. Robertson," he began slowly. "You know how important this is to me. I don't need to tell you that I cannot tolerate failure."

"Mr. Peng, you forget yourself. Let me remind you that it was you who came to us. We are the experts. We've taken out one target, successfully, without anyone so much as raising an eyebrow."

"I could have had that done myself," Peng replied dismissively.

"But you didn't, did you?" Silence. "Anna Chen's job was executed flawlessly, a hallmark of our work. Why else would you have come to us? Why else did you so willingly pay our entry fee?"

Robertson had never revealed to Wong Peng the contradiction that the Society faced in Peng's approach. On the one hand, he was a liability; a loose cannon; overrun by his passions, his lust for control, his flamboyant, boyish imagination that ran rampant through his secretive dealings.

But even the custodians of the Society could see value in him. It was clear that he would never reach the inner circle, but with the apparently unstoppable growth in his sphere of influence, they could hardly refuse him. The world was changing, and none knew that more than the Society. The APEC convention in Sydney, during which Presidents Bush and Putin paid visits to China's Hu Jintao at the Wentworth Sofitel hotel, rather than the reverse, painted a clear picture for all to see of the shift away from a primarily Western power base. For the first time in the Society's more than two-hundred year history, they were facing the prospect of a dramatic shift in the way their strategy was administered. Not that it would pose a problem. Already, their integration of the East's and West's power structures was taking form. Wong Peng was merely another step in the process.

Indeed, their own plans toward securing Peng's cooperation and allegiance had preceded his own approach. With his own links to organized crime, they were surprised to receive such a request. His infatuation with control, they had anticipated; but not this. It was in the peculiarities surrounding his request that his motivation was revealed.

"Mr. Peng," Robertson continued, "In light of your visible impatience, allow me to ease your mind by explaining, once again, the complications and the resulting degree of difficulty surrounding your request. I trust that this will satisfy any anxieties that you may be experiencing at this time."

Peng nodded reluctantly.

"Your request is most unusual. What you are asking for, as you are well aware, could never be achieved even by those whom a man of your means would ordinarily enlist for this line of work. Even with the vast resources at your disposal, you know that this is not attainable by ordinary methods.

"But there is nothing ordinary about us, Mr. Peng. We do not meddle in the affairs of the mundane world. We govern the balance of power. And whatever task is accepted by us, will be completed. Of that, there is no question.

"What you must understand is the degree of precision with which this task needs to be executed to ensure success. Legal experts; profilers; psychiatric teams must all be brought into the planning phase. The police department; the first-responders at the scene; outside experts consulted by both the victim's team and by law enforcement – we must maintain a presence in all of these, and this presence must remain undetectable. Security cameras; witnesses; and the king of them all – forensics – need to be tightly controlled and accounted for down to the most minute detail."

Robertson watched Wong Peng's attitude shift from impatience to a wide-eyed excitement. It irritated him to be pandering to a man of such whim.

"We must anticipate and neutralize the target's every viable response," Robertson went on. "And, as you can well imagine, the force with which this target will respond to the situation will be considerable. Every avenue of recourse will be attempted, and therefore countered by us.

"It is possible that, even of those who have been deliberately brought into the loop by us, some will have to be silenced to avoid leaving any loose ends.

"Add to this the element of unpredictability, with which every aspect of our dealings is inextricably bound. This elaborate network of personnel and situations can only be triggered under the correct conditions, some of which depend solely on the target's behavior, and are therefore out of control. Understand, Mr. Peng, that this trap may need to be masterminded and set not just once, but two, maybe three times, before it has a chance to be sprung. We will proceed only under the right conditions.

"So, I say to you again, deadlines are irrelevant. Yours is a request demanding the most careful attention to detail possible."

Wong Peng only tightened his lips, impatient for the day, yet relishing the anticipation of it.

"But I assure you, Mr. Peng," Robertson concluded, "It will be done."

Peng stood, and nodded sharply. "I will be waiting," he said, and made his way out of the unassuming office and past Robertson's assistant.

Robertson turned in his chair to the globe sitting beside his desk as he heard the door close. *Oh for the simplicity of the good old days,* he lamented.

The thought of the Society's inception never failed to strike a romantic note in him. Emerging in the wake of Napoleon's spread of civil liberties, and the threat to the rule of Europe's establishment, it rapidly became the instrument through which the European monarchies could maintain their control. At first little more than a clandestine collection of mercenaries, it soon morphed into a sophisticated network of those who sought to manage power. Its reach extended across nations – both at war and at peace – and united those who held the reins of influence.

No longer was conflict a haphazard drama of reactions and nationalistic interests. War became a tool with which to divert wealth to the chosen few, at the expense of many. Stealth being its most effective weapon, the Society operated outside the awareness of even those who considered themselves the decision-makers in matters of great consequence. Its influence was maintained at a level sufficient to guide nations and industry to the desired ends, but never so much that its presence would be detected. Governments came and went; appearances changed; but all the while, those who held true power, retained their power. Indeed, it grew.

If there were ever a silver lining to a cloud, it was surely the American Revolution. At first, it threatened to snuff out the fledgling Society. The power bases, in disarray, sought to quash any opposition to their absolute rule. But their world was changing. Try as they might, they could not stop the wave of progress of the masses from a state of ignorance, to a state of relative awareness.

The days of explicit control were numbered. But the Society saw an opening. Rather than oppose the shouts of freedom from the masses, they would embrace them. They would give the people exactly what they wanted, and in doing so, conceal their own presence still further. The strategy's success exceeded even their wildest projections.

No longer were people forced to generate wealth for their masters; they now became willing, even enthusiastic, participants. With the guidance of the Society, new players emerged. The established elite welcomed the expansion of their sphere of influence by creating industry giants in the emerging hubs of wealth. Only those who were believed to be receptive to the centralization of power were permitted the success that created true power.

With the advent of industrialization, the power bases throughout the globe solidified, and what would eventually become the ruling class began to take shape. No longer were the ruling families exposed for all to see, as was the case in the monarchical system. Now they were veiled: evidently successful capitalists, those who had accumulated great wealth, became the new monarchies in all but name. Power was passed from father to son; alliances were forged; dissenters were usurped. And the beauty of it all was that operations were sanctioned by law, and by the very people who had become the unsuspecting victims of the tightening grip of the few who held power.

By the twentieth century, the structures of power that determined the planet's course were well in place. Democracy became the Society's greatest asset, allowing the people the ability to determine their government, and putting to rest any suspicions that all was not as it seemed. Governments appeared, made decisions, and were replaced. What did not change was those who controlled the flow of information; those who controlled the options presented to the elected representatives; those who molded government departments, the legal system, and the appearance of democracy to suit their own ends.

When those elected were connected – albeit never more than on a rudimentary level, and never aware of how far the reach extended – to the Society itself, its job was easier, and nations were manipulated in such a way that those in power gained ever more power. Those with wealth multiplied their wealth through legitimate means, and through a legal and financial system that, on the surface, appeared to create a level playing field, but which in reality bound entire populations to a form of slavery that even the slaves themselves wholeheartedly believed in. No more were the owners of assets required to motivate serfs and peasants to generate wealth for their masters; the masses now enjoyed a sense of independence, control and progress, and happily served the system that had bound them since the opening of those narrow windows of opportunity known as revolutions.

When those elected were expected to offer little cooperation, the Society's charge increased in difficulty. Greater control of information was necessary; farsightedness in strategy became all the more important; and the skill with which personal attacks and smear-campaigns were implemented often rose to a whole new level. By the end of their terms in office, the custodians of governmental power were often left wondering what went wrong. As were the people who elected them. It seemed that, no matter who was elected, war was an inevitability, as was the gradual erosion of civil and property rights, as these rights became vested no longer in the individual, but in the corporation – a vehicle which allowed for the accumulation of the rights of many to be concentrated in the hands of a few. All within the law. All in accordance with people's best intentions, intentions that time and again revealed a string of unintended consequences as they were hijacked by those who saw the big picture.

From the reality of democracy had emerged the illusion of democracy which, along with the impression of self-determination and economic freedom, had created the most effective means of control yet seen: one in which the victims were willing participants. Even those who believed that they knew the deeper nature of things had no idea how far the Society's reach extended. The secret of its reach was that the vast majority of those who were involved in its operations were unaware of its true nature, and generally unaware of the involvement of others.

Robertson wondered how much even he knew; certainly, he could not be sure of the identities of those above him in the order of command. Still, he knew enough to be apprehensive about the level of complexity that the modern world was demanding. Murder was never a first option. It was a messy affair, especially given the level of forensic investigation that had become possible. It was not that the Society didn't have the ability to manipulate the situation to suit their ends; they absolutely did. But the potential for error had escalated, and it was Robertson's responsibility to ensure that every loose end was tied.

Still, he reflected, technology was a double-edged sword. Although the dramatic liberalization of information across the globe had presented a new challenge for the Society, it was also strongly believed within the organization that an opportunity was opening. On the one hand, the availability and freedom of information, and the speed with which it could spread, left the workings of the Society more vulnerable to exposure than ever before. To contain every credible hypothesis, every shred of evidence that emerged, was becoming increasingly difficult, and their tactics to counter challenges to the established power base were evolving out of necessity.

But on the other hand, technological advancements were concentrated, for the most part, in the hands of those aligned with the Society. Governments and corporations over which the Society exerted its influence to the desired degree were the proprietors of astounding new technologies — those that, soon enough, would be used to interfere with, monitor and account for every individual on the planet. It offered a new level of control, if only it could be harnessed. Not a corner of the globe would any longer be out of its reach. Not a single individual's activity could remain concealed. It would not be long before technological might, centralized in the world's hubs of power, all united by unseen forces, became so overwhelming as to undermine any efforts to oppose it.

Again, the genius of this next step in the evolution of the ruling class would be that the victims would be the strongest advocates. In their fear and panic at the ever-increasing unpredictability of the world, they would be the very people demanding a new level of control by their governments, all with the intention of tempering a dangerous and hostile reality.

It's for their own good, Robertson reflected. *Without our guidance, this world would be out of control.*

Still, there were those within the Society who worried about the imminent showdown between fear and freedom. It was clear that the growing momentum of those who questioned the nature of the world could not be stopped; but, as before, it was possible that it could be harnessed. Indeed, some even worried that a second window of opportunity for the masses might open, during which the control exerted by the established power-bases could come under threat.

Robertson recalled a theory circulating through the inner circles of the Society: that an organization such as theirs was inevitable in some shape or form. The brand of control they exercised was no simple matter to exterminate: it was a virus. The Society was its current host. But if the Society were to ever become a target itself, the virus would simply migrate to another host. It was insidious.

The only true hope the people had of destroying such a system was to shift their focus away from what they perceived to be the enemy, in this case, the current incarnation of Society, and instead to recognize the root of the problem, one which extended through all humankind: the desire to control. This, he suspected, would never happen. People defined themselves by their enemies. They were dependent on them. It was one of the major tools at the Society's disposal.

Robertson turned his attention back to Wong Peng and his woefully personal demands for the job. It was wrong that the Society should be accommodating the requests of such a volatile individual, he thought. Peng was being given too much leeway, and the need-to-know basis of information flow being what it was, Robertson was in the dark as to why such concessions were being made. He could only surmise that Peng was of considerable importance.

He resented the predicament that the Society found itself in: the need to welcome new members, even if on a superficial level. He resented the change that the world insisted on. And he wondered what it was about the world that ensured it always hovered just out of reach of total control. Why couldn't it just be stable; simple; predictable?

He handled the list of names in front of him, anxious to comb through the details of the plan one more time, though he knew it would make no difference. The strategy was in place, and the only unknown element was that of chance.

Robertson nervously squeezed his pen in his left hand as he reached for the phone. It was time to set the first phase in motion.

CHAPTER THREE

WONG PENG GRINNED as he surveyed the ship slowly pulling into dock. It was the shipment he had been awaiting. As much as he enjoyed the thrill of being a global industry leader, it was not what he loved most about being a businessman. His passion for business had found a new focus, and the beaten-up, unassuming cargo ship appearing in the satellite feed on the screen in front of him was the most recent import of raw materials.

He had to laugh to himself whenever he picked up a copy of Forbes or Fortune claiming to list the one hundred wealthiest individuals in the world or, more amusing still, the world's most powerful individuals. It was well that it should be so, he admitted. Were people to know his true wealth — and that of others like him — their dealings in illicit industries would surely come under greater scrutiny, as would their attempts to mask the assets under their control.

Besides, he thought to himself as he saw several figures disembarking the ship, what fun would his newest passion be were it legal? He so loved the game that the worldwide legal framework and network of law enforcement agencies had created, that he regretted not a single cent that he had donated to those charities and awareness groups who sought nothing but the demise of men such as himself.

If only they knew, he relished.

He thought back to his earlier forays into the less visible industries constituting his empire. Surprisingly, he had his wife to thank for his major turning point. It was on his wedding night that he discovered the intoxicating allure of pushing sexual highs to the limits. He had left his bloodied wife on his bed as he stormed from room to room in his house, fumbling through bottles of alcohol, his stash of drugs and his collection of firearms in search of something that could satisfy his uncontrollable rage. Eventually, an aide came to his rescue, and Peng eventually found himself descending into the basement of an unassuming warehouse near the city's periphery. What a bittersweet night it would prove to be.

Never had he imagined something as overwhelming as the thrill – the sheer ecstasy – of raping a woman, bound by her wrists, her ankles, until she could no longer move. Inflicting pain, and watching the pain morph into what it could not be denied was a sublime level of pleasure. Ravaging her; wounding her; watching her squirm, until, finally, she was taken by death.

What began as a release from the rage at his wife's promiscuity on his wedding night, grew into his most beloved pastime. It seemed there was no end to the pursuit's potential. It wasn't long before he secured an endless stream of entertainment through the use of video cameras. Soon enough, what had begun as a hobby expanded into a new business venture.

The satellite feed showed one of the figures reaching his team's position in the parking lot. The phone rang.

"Sir, I have our man here."

"Put him on," Peng responded.

"Mr. Boss, I just arrive," came a new voice.

"How many?" Wong Peng asked.

"None."

"What?"

"Zero," the man confirmed.

Wong Peng's surprise gave way to a wide grin.

"You have done well." The absence of casualties was a rarity. The transportation itself usually cost lives, so anytime that a shipment arrived fully intact was a bonus in Peng's eyes. He only wished he could be there in person, like in the old days, when his identity was less of a liability.

He often marveled at the wonder of it all; at the scale of the grand enterprise he had built. His operation was administered by the local organized crime syndicates in each territory, yet it was Peng who had devised the plan, and streamlined it for profitability. The setup, in addition to his bureaucratic connections, insulated him and his assets from legal probes. It cost him a sizeable chunk of the profits, but as he well knew, there was more than enough to go around.

Human trafficking ranked as the second-largest criminal industry globally, equal with trade in illegal weapons, and surpassed only by narcotics. The CIA estimated that between fifty thousand and one hundred thousand girls, boys and women were trafficked into the United States, alone, every year to be sold as slaves, usually for forced sex. With his expanding presence in the pharmaceutical industry, he had found a further use for those that came into his possession, often via the Chinese government's disposal of political prisoners: he now had human guinea pigs on which to experiment with new pharmaceutical developments, not to mention continuing his profitable operations in the human organ trade.

The beauty of it all was that slavery was believed to have long since been eliminated when, in actuality, it had only become more widespread.

"Did you take good care of her?" Peng continued to the man on the other end of the phone.

"She's in good condition. She be ready for you soon."

"Good," Peng nodded. "I've waited too long for this. I just hope the world's not running out of prime candidates such as herself. Call me when it is time," he said, ending the call.

The thrill of raping nameless, faceless whores to their death had soon worn off for Peng. Besides, he detested the necessity of condoms to protect himself from his victims' filth, so unnatural did he find it.

Yet, as he had discovered, boredom with one level of the game only opened the door to the next level: virgins. Pure, young, scared — no, terrified — virgins. Not only could he look deep into their eyes and feel the palpable terror residing there as he penetrated them; and not only could his deflowering of them purify and rejuvenate his own being; but, best of all, he could send them to their death with the ultimate experience of being transformed from a girl into a woman.

And what when the euphoria of even a game as delightful as this had worn off? The answer was lurking there in his imagination all along. In his many years of martial arts training, he often drifted into fantasy, his subconscious creating a skilled female opponent against whom he could test his skill. He prided himself on his proficiency in unarmed combat – Kung Fu being his primary modality – as well as on his swordsmanship. Here, he had found his latest treat.

His main interest in his most recent shipment was not the many whom he would sell into slavery and prostitution. It was the one that had be found to fulfill the role as his next personal victim. That his men were able to secure an American pleased him greatly. Her growing prominence as an athlete to watch in years to come first caught Peng's attention in a martial arts magazine feature on the young fighter. She had made her mark firstly in Judo, and more recently in Shotokan Karate. Her family, who kept close watch over her training and progress, had high hopes for her, as did her community. So did Wong Peng. In the time that she had been missing, the U.S. law enforcement agencies scrambled to pick up the trail, which nearly immediately went cold. She now belonged to him.

How would he savor the gift? Certainly, he knew how it would end: the girl, bound and immobilized, would scream out in pain as he ravaged her repeatedly. He would feed off the horror that lived in her eyes. When the virgin had become a woman, he would release her, knowing that the rage that welled up within the spirited teenager would propel her to use all her skill and fury against her perpetrator. The two would fight, and it would be a fight to the death.

But how would it begin? How long would he enjoy the anticipation of its climax? As he drove back to his house, his mind conjured images and possibilities that whet his appetite. Confronted with the pleasurable tension of the wait, he even considered the possibility of seeking release in his wife's body that night, though the seriousness of her last threat lingered in the back of his mind.

Long ago he had tired of Jade and her timidity. She had borne him two sons, and that, it appeared, was the limit of her usefulness. That, and providing the gateway to Anna Chen's empire that he had effortlessly passed through. Jade's fragility had disappointed him. It took only two years of his spirited approach to their marriage for her child-bearing capacities to be all but spent, before the surprise of their second son, many years later. Peng resented the fact that she was unable to cope with his beatings; with his toying with her; with her fateful tumbling down the staircase. He, himself, had survived worse than her in his time, and he was still quite capable of producing children, he was sure of it.

He cared not in the slightest for her. If her presence validated the merging of two dynasties; if she managed to bear two sons, despite one of them having already died; and if she obeyed his every command and bent to his control, then she had done her job. Indeed, as far as Wong Peng could see, her role had come to an end.

CHAPTER FOUR

J ADE'S THOUGHTS SWIRLED uncontrollably. She lay in bed, fidgeting, restless. The image of his face, fresh from but a few hours ago, plagued her mind wherever she attempted to turn her attention. Not that she would have had it any other way: Luke's fleeting presence had been a torturously brief encounter with another reality, one in which she was no longer confined to the prison cell of her current existence.

She was still experiencing the aftershocks of her reaction to Luke's sole sentence to her that night, 'I was sorry to hear about your Aunt.' Although she fumbled to politely accept the commiseration, everything inside her screamed out in anger at the mention of Miss Anna. Lying in bed, she began to understand that the anger was not so much directed at Miss Anna, as at Jade herself, for the decision to surrender her life to the traditions of her family.

Tears welled in her eyes as she contended with the tidal wave of emotion that the chance meeting had triggered. So long had she denied her own deepest yearnings that they had all but been extinguished, pushed out of her sphere of awareness. The mere sight of Luke had unleashed a torrent of pain, loneliness and regret that had been suppressed in the name of family for thirty years.

The moment they had locked eyes, she was touched by a force that only existed in the deepest recesses of her memory. Images of walking freely, hand-in-hand in Singapore, surfaced once again, along with the distant memory of what it felt like to be touched with gentleness; with care; with love. It was so foreign to her that it felt like it had all happened to someone else, not her. The only touch she had known since her wedding day was the unpredictable, animalistic roughness of her husband, that sought nothing but its own gratification.

Despite the scars left by his tyranny in their married life, it was his tyranny in the larger world that repulsed her most. It was the falseness that enabled him to deliver a keynote speech at the United Nations function that night, supposedly promoting awareness of human trafficking, while that very day he was no doubt jeering at the authorities' apparent blindness to his own dealings. She sensed the depth of evil that dwelled below the surface in this man, though even Jade was unaware of the extent of its malice in his victims' final hours.

How she yearned for the touch that she remembered, but had all but forgotten until her and Luke's eyes met hours earlier. From that moment on, she was thrust into a world of memory and regret so overpowering that she simply lay wide awake in bed, muffling her sobs to avoid waking Wong Peng, tears streaming down her face. The truth that she had been avoiding for so long was now staring squarely at her: hers had been a wasted life.

Jade had never guessed that Luke would still hold such a place in her heart after so many years. But to see him for the first time, unexpectedly, in the flesh, awakened ancient feelings.

The urge to be touched, to be heard, to be held, overtook her and the tingling sensation through her body intensified. She remembered the caress of his hands on her skin, and the openness with which she had so eagerly received him, and she instinctively moved her own hands across her chest. Then down, her nails scraping her abdomen and digging into her hips and upper thighs. The fingers of her right hand were drawn to the front of the opening between her legs and she pressed against it firmly.

It was a visitation to a long-forgotten world. The ease with which her body had once opened to Luke's returned to her. Her breath seemed to move through her entire body, sending it into uncontrollable spasms of heightened desire as she rubbed herself, the charged movement of her pelvis falling into rhythm with her hand.

She longed for all else in the room to disappear, and for Luke to appear and take her in his arms like he so many times had done before. To feel his breath against her skin, his weight pressing down on her body, and the comfort with her own self, and with life itself, that she once knew. For the first time in many years, she sensed the freedom of release she once knew in Luke's arms. She rubbed herself faster and harder, her body writhing uncontrollably as she gripped her skin in her left hand, screaming out within herself for it to be true, for it to be real, if only for a second.

A wave of ecstasy enveloped her and poured through her body as she came to a climax and had to muster all of her will to suppress the moans of joy demanding voice. She felt alive.

The faint smell of cognac leeching from the man asleep in the other room repelled her to the edge of the bed. It had required all of her discipline to weather the marriage to which Miss Anna had bound her. The sole gift of the marriage to her, and part of the reason why she felt impossibly bound to it, were her two sons, one of whom had already died. She didn't know how her difficulty in conceiving, after the birth of her first son, had begun. Was it the psychological barrier of knowing that any offspring would be born to a demonic father? Or was it the physical damage she had sustained from Peng's beatings, the beatings that had caused her final miscarriage, before the arrival, many years later, of her only living child?

Her last visit to Jade Dragon Snow Mountain, in China's Yunnan Province, came to mind. The backdrop of misty peaks; the abundance of wildlife and rare flora; the outlook of spectacular valleys, craggy slopes, and the drop-off where lovers would end their lives in each others' arms.

The mountain had once been a last haven for lovers doomed to separation. With the enforcement of pre-arranged marriages, many couples chose to die rather than live without the freedom of choosing their own spouse. Couples eloped to the mountain meadow for a few days of shared bliss before killing themselves.

Jade often marveled at the near-inability of mountain climbers to conquer the highest peak of the majestic mountain: only one climbing team had ever done so. She had made the journey to Jade Dragon Snow Mountain on three occasions, each time to reflect on her own personal tragedy, her own personal mountain to conquer. Each time, she arrived carrying the very real possibility of suicide as an option.

Her betrothal to Wong Peng had inflicted more misery upon her than she could have expected. Had she known what awaited in her married life, would she have still obeyed her Aunt's commands? In the fullness of her adulthood, the answer she had found herself giving, was an absolute 'No'. Her regret haunted her and nearly drove her to ending her life on each of those three occasions.

But never was she able to abandon her son. It was on her third trip to the mountain that she was finally able to look clearly at her situation: there was no escape. The thought of suicide could no longer offer her any solace, for she could no longer believe it was possible: she would never leave Zhu. And she also knew that she could never leave Peng without fearing for her own life, or hoping to still be a part of her son's life. Either way, Zhu would be alone with a father who both terrified and confused him.

Jade had long since resigned herself to the reality that she would have only one child, and maybe, she thought, that was better. Why bring another baby into a world ruled by a madman? Such was her justification for her inability to produce more children after the final miscarriage. The tumble down the staircase in the midst of Peng's fit of rage was surely what left her barren for all those years.

She still recalled the night when she would finally be spurred to reclaim a portion of her dignity. It was the last time Peng would demonstrate his power over her in the arena of sexuality, and it was also the night that she would, to the surprise of them both, fall pregnant with their second son.

With a glowing pride, she remembered the following night: her slumbering husband waking with a start to find a blade pressed firmly against his throat, and his wife's other hand gripping his testicles. 'Do that again, and I'll kill you,' she had whispered piercingly. It was not the first time he had heard threats from his wife's mouth, and usually he responded with vicious punishment. But it was the first time he believed her.

Peng would never rape Jade again. From that night on, they would sleep in separate rooms. But his abuse persisted on multiple levels.

She had given freely of herself, and from her had been taken all that she offered, until there was little left of whom she once knew herself to be. With Zhu's sudden death years after the birth of her second son, her life's sole purpose seemed to be to protect her remaining child from the madness of his father. She despised the sense of worthlessness that had slowly filled her during her marriage, permeating her life, for she knew there was no truth to it, other than what Wong Peng's abuse would have her believe. Even so, it stalked her, as did the suffocating numbness of a life lived by default.

She knew what she must do. It would no doubt be her only chance, given the rarity of her joining Wong Peng during his travel to New York. If it was the last thing she did, she must let Luke know how she felt. She could not lie to herself: she had missed an opportunity in life to be true to herself; maybe it had arrived too early for her to appreciate its importance. But she would not miss another. Regardless of the risk involved, she would ensure that Luke would know her truth. It was too late to resurrect the life that once beckoned to her, but she owed it to Luke, and she owed it to herself, to honor what it was they once had, and to acknowledge her failure: Luke deserved that much.

More importantly, she felt more strongly than ever that she owed it to herself to honor that long-suppressed part of who she was, even if it were thirty years too late. At least she could live in the knowledge that, when her second chance presented itself, she had found the courage to be true to herself once again. At least she would know that, despite having missed her chance at a charmed life, she had reclaimed her adulthood, her freedom of choice, and her all-but-extinguished spirit.

CHAPTER FIVE

"Hi, it's me," came the voice over the phone.

"I wasn't expecting a call from you until tonight," Emerald replied, surprised. "Don't you have your board meeting in...," she checked her watch, "well, now?"

"I know, I know," Luke hurried, the anxiety audible in his voice. "I just had to speak to you."

"About what?"

"Not about anything — I just wish you were here," he mumbled. "No, I wish I were there with you, in London — everything feels wrong right now without you." Being in the same room as Wong Peng was always enough to make him uncomfortable in its ability to awaken unsavory memories. Though this night had been different, he knew, and he was still having trouble believing the affect Jade was having on him — the aftershocks of the brief encounter were still bouncing around his head. In earlier years he had spent much time drifting through an imagined reunion with Jade, wondering what such a meeting would look like. Now, after that moment's final arrival, all he felt was confusion.

Emerald sighed, her eyes resting on the unconscious figure lying in the hospital bed, unmoving. "I wish you were here, too. But I need to be here with Alexis, and you need to be there today." She said it regretfully, wishing that her stay in London had not been extended, both for Alexis's sake, and for her own.

"It's just that, after the eight months that we've been together, I can't believe that we had to be separated right now, on this day," came the voice from New York.

"Why, your meeting? Is it going to be that bad?"

"No, not the meeting – the function last night. It was bizarre – it's thrown me right off. I just don't feel myself, and now today..." he trailed off, not wanting to open the discussion over the phone, preferring to share it when they were once again in the same city.

"What was it?" she questioned, confused.

"I'll tell you when you get back. It's nothing I guess, just phased me a little."

"Unusual for you," she smiled, hoping to bolster his spirits. "Is there anything I can do to help?"

"No, I have to go, the meeting's about to get underway. Just take care of yourself."

"Luke, I'll leave my phone on through the night – phone me whenever you want to. And whatever it is, don't be hard on yourself."

"Thanks. I'll speak to you again soon. I love you," he said.

The line went dead. Luke's apprehension was unmistakable, but she was bewildered as to its cause. Emerald only hoped that she would hear from him again soon.

It was strange indeed that her dear friend should fall victim to a hit-and-run, right before Emerald's eyes, on one of the few occasions that the two were in the same city. If it meant that Emerald was unable to show her personal support for a cause that was close to her heart, and for which she had campaigned, then that was a price she was willing to pay in the name of friendship. Her service to Alexis came before her altruistic commitments. But it pained her that it should mean she would fail to be at Luke's side when he needed her.

What could have happened, she questioned, that Luke would suddenly phone her in a near-panic? She shook her head, knowing there was nothing she could do, other than await his next call.

A smile escaped her lips for a moment. How she would have loved to have been there, she thought, if only to relive part of the excitement of their first encounter. Emerald recalled the Human Trafficking Awareness fundraising event during which she first laid eyes on the renowned Mr. Powers. Already the two had come close to crossing paths at the time of her appearance on one of Powers Media's networks. Still smarting from Luke's last-minute cancellation of their scheduled meeting months earlier, Emerald decided to make the most of her position in the auction after noticing Luke's presence in the room.

'$240,000, going once, going twice…'

'Oh, well there's Mr. Powers himself,' Emerald innocently spoke into her microphone, interrupting the closing of the bidding, with a smile in Luke's direction. 'Mr. Powers, it's the final item for the night, are you sure you don't want to make a contribution to our fundraising efforts? We can't say how grateful we are to have had your support from the beginning.'

All eyes turned to Luke. With little hesitation he responded, 'Well of course, I've been waiting all this time for my invitation. I'll pledge half a million dollars.'

Pleasantly surprised, though also feeling as though she had been out-maneuvered, Emerald approached him before the night was over. 'Well, I suppose I should say I'm honored to finally meet you, Mr. Powers, given how difficult it seems to be to pin you down to a meeting.'

'I sincerely apologize for that, Ms. Steel. With the crisis I was facing that day, I really had no other option but to reschedule our meeting, though my office seemed unable to arrange another time with you.'

Though it was the first time the two had met, each had developed a deeply-entrenched opinion, far from positive, of the other before a word had been spoken. Stories of the hotshot media mogul had found their way to Emerald, and impressions of the tough-talking, blond, former supermodel with the striking green eyes had left their mark with Luke. It was an encounter that, while each possessed a certain curiosity about an in-person exchange, neither would ever have considered as having the potential to affect their life in the slightest.

Emerald smiled to herself again, her gratitude for that night, that first inkling of a profound connection, welling up inside of her.

She took Alexis's limp hand in her own, and closed her eyes, willing her best friend to recovery.

"Alexis," she whispered. "My dear, dear friend. I hope you can hear me. I trust that you can," she spoke softly.

"I know you're hurt. I fear that you feel I've abandoned you. But nothing could be further from the truth. That's why I'm here. Because I love you. Because I love you as my closest friend."

Something in Emerald told her that Alexis wasn't fighting hard enough to live. She could lose her friend forever. And Emerald suspected that she, herself, wouldn't be entirely blameless in such a fate.

"It's true, I love Luke as I've never loved anyone before. And it's true that my life has changed because of it. But I need you, Alexis. I need your friendship. You are close to my heart, please know that."

She paused for a moment, thinking back to the beginning of their friendship and their first forays into the upper echelons of the modeling industry. Meeting for the first time in Milan as rivals, it did not take long for their friendship to take hold and for their notoriety as a pair of rising stars to spread. Their careers moved almost in tandem, and as they neared the top of their game, their duo grew into a trio.

"Iara," Emerald whispered her name. "We lost Iara. Please, don't make me have to live without you, too."

The Brazilian was a natural fit for Emerald and Alexis: each exemplified glamour in her own way and was riding a wave of fame and success. The apparent inseparability of the three goddesses only added to the mystique of the supermodel lifestyle, and served to reinforce their growing celebrity profile.

Emerald was grateful that Alexis was spared from the first-hand horror of the night that Iara was seen for the last time. It was a night that continued to haunt her: the sound of Iara's nails screeching along the air vent as her kidnappers dragged her by her ankles; her screams as she knew that her only chance for both of them was to get herself to safety.

It was only due to the stimulants that she already taken earlier in the night, the doctors suspected, that Emerald woke from the drug-induced sleep earlier than her captors would have expected. She managed to shake Iara awake, and though still dazed, Emerald forced herself into the holding room's air vent, with Iara hoisting herself up by her grip on Emerald's ankles, her legs scurrying below for a foothold.

In that moment, Iara's fate was sealed, and Emerald made the split-second decision that would ensure her eventual safety as she emerged into the crowded Istanbul streets.

Emerald had been devastated to find that the Turkish authorities were powerless to recover Iara, telling her the chances of ever finding the woman were close to zero. How could a face familiar to so many evade recognition, she questioned. The search lasted months, but revealed nothing. It was not until she began her own research into human trafficking, as part of dealing with the tragedy, that Emerald understood that predators were never far from the circles she moved in. It was not an anomaly for models to be targeted; to some buyers, the higher the risk, the better. Like purchasers of priceless works of art on the black market, there were men who would pay top dollar for a prize that they would only enjoy personally, without ever revealing their possession to others. Like a masterpiece locked in a hidden room, Iara's identity would remain buried deep enough to effectively end her existence.

Emerald came to accept that it was a man such as these that had bought her friend, and would do with her what he pleased for as long as he cared. Then her life would end.

It would mark the beginning of Emerald's life as an activist, and the beginning of the end for her frustrating attempts to escape the pain of her earlier years. The three had again become two, and Alexis and Emerald would discover a new closeness in each other's arms.

"Alexis, won't you please come back." She squeezed her friend's hand tenderly. The waiting continued.

CHAPTER SIX

H ER BODY LAY motionless, comatose, but there was a part of Alexis that was awake. Part of her was aware of the room; of her lifeless body; and of the decision that rested with her: to continue, or not.

It was otherworldly, the awareness she was experiencing. Like nothing she had known during her life, but still, not unfamiliar. And yet, she knew that she was only touching the periphery; that a more drastic change awaited, if she chose it, though her will was still uncertain. She tried to grab onto her wakefulness, to fully emerge from the dreamy state in which she found herself, but it persisted. She was not fully asleep, yet not fully awake.

She knew that her own hand was in Emerald's, not by sensation in her body, but by a knowing that preceded it. But even if she could feel Emerald's hand, would it have felt the same as it once did? Would it have held her with all the intensity, the longing, the unbridled sensuality, that it once did?

Theirs had been a deep connection. It was a connection that Alexis had only ever experienced with another woman, and only with Emerald. In all her many interactions with men of all kinds, none had ever touched the power she had experienced in Emerald's arms. She wondered if what Emerald had with Luke rivaled what the two women had shared together. She wondered if Emerald had ever told Luke of their secret.

Its beginnings could not have been more beautiful: two women, each yearning to be loved, and finding it together. Alexis recalled Emerald's fragility in those earlier times, fresh from the heartache of witnessing Jimmy's death, unable to find solace in the profusion of men falling at her feet. She remembered their first interactions as competitors in the modeling industry, and then the youthfulness of their early friendship: the fun, the drugs, the experimentation. And the surprising deepening of a bond they had previously thought would be limited to friendship; the belonging that the two experienced in each other's arms.

But it had vanished. It had been over a year since the two had made love, and Alexis sensed a coolness from her friend, and the clear intent to let go of the love that the two formerly had. It was as if Emerald had now relegated Alexis to the secretive, all-but-forgotten, areas of her past. Emerald wished to move on from her wilder years, to pretend they never happened. Had Alexis, too, been placed in that category? Was the love they shared simply a shameful burden to Emerald?

Again, she became aware of the decision before her.

CHAPTER SEVEN

L UKE'S HAND FIDGETED in his pocket. The cell phone offered his last bastion of comfort before entering the hotel, and the ambivalence that had plagued him since Jade's morning phone call became all the more palpable as he paced by the hotel entrance. It propelled him past the Peninsula Hotel's doormen as he kept walking on Fifth Avenue, unable to bring himself to enter.

The name itself evoked memories of his first encounter with Jade in Hong Kong's own Peninsula, a hotel that he had vehemently avoided in his few necessary visits to the island since. Was he re-opening a chapter of the past that was best left undisturbed? He stopped at the corner of the block and removed the phone from his pocket, pressing Emerald's speed-dial. Immediately he shut the phone in frustration; it would do no good to involve Emerald at this stage. The decision to proceed with the meeting rested solely in his hands.

But as much as he had labored and analyzed the decision, he couldn't shake two unmistakable feelings that percolated up through the cloud of confusion: firstly, that he was entering dangerous territory; and secondly, that his curiosity would get the better of him, regardless of his sense that he would do well to never set foot in the hotel.

'I'm in town for one more day – my husband got an urgent call and left early this morning. Luke, I want to see you before I leave,' he recalled from Jade's phone call. From the beginning, his instincts had quietly urged, 'Bad idea'. And he knew it. Even still, he found himself turning back toward the hotel entrance.

He assured himself that he had no interest in anything more than a resolution with Jade; a chance to put to rest hurt that had lingered far too long. The timeliness of the meeting, he had to admit, was a true blessing: poised to embark on his new life with Emerald, he was being presented with an opportunity to finally say goodbye, once and for all, to the hurt that had never fully healed, despite his best efforts to be free of it. It was something he had to do. He had to see Jade one more time. He had to hear what it was she wanted to say.

He stepped over the threshold of the Peninsula's entrance and his heart began racing as he walked down memory lane, the anticipation of her presence playing on his nerves. He again questioned his ability to handle a meeting, alone, with Jade, given the strength of his reaction to the mere sight of her the previous night. It was the first time that the two had set eyes on each other for more than thirty years. Never before, in the years that the two men had crossed paths in New York, had Luke seen Wong Peng accompanied by his wife. His first surprise glance of Jade knocked the wind out of him. He stood there, staring intently at her from a distance, adorned in her Valentino evening gown, the epitome of elegance, disbelieving his eyes. For a moment, lost in a dream, he forgot himself. Everything he knew about who he was seemed to vanish into thin air.

He snapped himself out of it and made his way to his table, wishing that his fiancée, Emerald, was accompanying him to the U.N. function, and not on the other side of the Atlantic. Luke wasn't sure when Jade had first sighted him, but it was clear that she was as shaken as he was by it. The two did their best to conceal their involuntary glances through the night. A verbal exchange was unavoidable, but consisted only of two awkward sentences: 'I was sorry to hear about your aunt, Jade.'

'Thank you,' she had replied politely.

Luke thought that was the end of it — a freak encounter with his long lost love, never to be repeated. Until her phone call.

He fidgeted in his pocket as he watched the numbers in the elevator display climbing. The doors opened in front of him. Hesitantly, he made his way to Jade's suite. They had decided that, given Luke's profile in the city, and Jade's need to keep the meeting private, the only sensible location was a private one.

His hand rose to the doorbell, leaving the phone in his pocket, and once again, he felt certain that he was playing with fire. But he had to know her motivation for requesting the meeting. It was a chance for closure to an enduringly traumatic episode of his life; he could not refuse it.

Luke pressed the doorbell.

The peephole went dim momentarily before the door swung open, revealing a warmly-smiling Jade. He sank deeply into her welcoming eyes, finding a momentary place of calm in her gaze, before being drawn to a solitary object resting on her chest. A translucent green pendant hung from a simple gold chain. In an instant, he recognized it: the stone was imperial jade, and it was carved in the shape of a heart.

"I gave that to you," he said softly, half to himself.

"I've kept it close to me ever since," Jade replied. "Though, it's rare that I have a chance to wear it."

He tried to wrap his mind around the distance that now separated them from their former life, shared in Hong Kong, and their paradoxical proximity to it in the pendant's reappearance.

"Come in," she said.

He walked into the suite, and into one of the most awkward situations he had encountered. Unsure of himself, he wandered to the end of the room and stared out the window at Fifth Avenue – anywhere to avoid setting his eyes on Jade.

He heard her approaching to his side. "Thank you for coming, Luke," came the voice.

To hear his name spoken by her, to be in the same room as her, conjured an eerie and vivid recollection of their past. It was as if he had been transported to an earlier time in his life: the innocence, the hope, and the dreams of that fantasyland were tangible. The scent of the perfume that she had once worn rose up through his memory as strongly as if she had been wearing it that very night. The sounds of Singapore, the very feeling of that island, the sensation of being in her apartment, all came back to him. And with it was triggered the long-dormant memory of Jade's touch; her lips; her body.

Luke turned to face Jade. The lady before him was no longer the youthful, exuberant girl of decades ago. No, the lady in front of him, while still possessing an air of elegance, while still without a doubt exuding a sense of beauty, was older. It was an age that was obvious to Luke not so much in her physical features, as in her demeanor. She had experienced more of the world. And what the world was capable of.

But even if time had passed, and the two young lovers had aged, Jade had not lost that which had always made her beautiful in Luke's eyes. Whatever may have happened to her since they parted, she had not forsaken her openness, nor her tenderness. In her eyes, he sensed a willingness to receive life in its fullness; to receive each moment as a gift. It warmed his heart to see that, in the many years since their parting, she had not lost her underlying innocence. To be sure, a woman married to a man such as Wong Peng could stand no chance of protecting the innocence of youth; but this woman's innocence was more than that. It was the innocence of maturity; the innocence that was not separate from the knowledge of all the great and terrible deeds of which the world was capable. It was the innocence of choice: the choice to receive life, in spite of the risk involved. Luke smiled to himself.

"I could hardly believe it was really you last night. When I saw you – " she trailed off, looking downward. "Luke, it means a lot to me that you've come here," Jade spoke softly, placing her hand on his. The touch of his skin immediately sent a shiver up her spine, and her whole body seemed to awaken in a way that she could barely recall. She felt within her an uncontrollable urge to be near the man that stood in front of her, as the memory of the previous night's fantasy returned and she began to moisten.

The force of the pull toward Jade that Luke was experiencing scared him, and after a long, involuntary pause of allowing his hand to be held in Jade's, he withdrew it.

Jade spoke again. "I had to contact you. With so much changing – so much uncertainty now with my aunt gone – I couldn't let the chance to see you slip through my fingers. I would have never forgiven myself."

"I'm sorry about Miss Anna. I know how much she meant to you," Luke offered for the second time.

She couldn't be sure of the intent of his last statement, or if he meant more than he was letting on by it. "Yes, well, thank you," she said, unable to meet his gaze for a moment. "Since her death, I've watched everything she worked for fall under my husband's control. And that is as she wished. But I ask myself, why? What for? Is family loyalty so blind that it rewards one such as my husband simply because of his matrimonial connections to my aunt?"

"I would have thought that would make you happy," Luke retorted, feigning innocence. "He is your husband, after all – you chose him, right?"

Jade now looked up to Luke. Her eyes softened, betraying her hurt at Luke's words. Not knowing how to respond, she rested her eyes once again on the table in front of her. "You know my husband, Luke. Please don't pretend otherwise."

Luke let out a long sigh. "I've thought about you often, Jade. Many times, I wondered if you're still the person I once knew. If you're happy. If you've found what it was you wanted. And I hoped with all my heart that you had."

"I know you have," she said in a fragile voice. "I know you have," she repeated. "Because I have felt the same for you."

The two sat quietly for a moment.

"Well, have you?" Luke found himself asking.

"Do you really need to ask?" she said, the tenderness in her eyes telling him everything he needed to know. He turned his head away, not wanting to leave himself open to her; not wanting to be touched by her words.

Then she smiled; a warm smile, but saturated with sadness. "But I think you have," she said.

He nodded.

"Congratulations, Luke. You deserve it."

He felt the softness of her eyes on him, and despite his best efforts to shield himself from her presence, he was unable to ignore the subtle pull of her perfume.

"Jade, I shouldn't be here – please, just tell me why you asked me here," he said, turning away from her. "Tell me why it was that this meeting was so important to you."

She nodded. "Would you like to sit?"

"I'd rather not – I hope you don't mind."

"No, of course, not. I understand." She looked away, paused, and then turned back to meet Luke's eyes. "I asked you here because I wanted to tell you that I'm sorry.

"I'm sorry for what I did to you, Luke," she said, looking directly into his eyes. "You deserved better. Not a day goes by that I don't regret that decision. That I don't wish that I had stopped the family madness that was in my power to stop. Not a day that I don't wish I had chosen a lifetime with you." Her welling eyes began to tear over. "I failed. I failed myself. And I failed you, Luke. And I could not go on living with the possibility that our lives might end without ever telling you this, Luke: that I'm sorry."

Luke felt her words pulling at his insides. In spite of all his effort, he was powerless to stop the flow of energy that coursed through him, rising up in his throat.

"Luke," she continued, her voice little more than a whisper, "You don't have to say anything. Just please know that I understand the pain that I put you through – the same pain that I have carried ever since. And I am truly sorry. I was wrong. And I had to say it to you. I've been wanting to say it since the day we parted."

Luke's hands were shaking. His chest and belly felt as if they were on fire as the tidal wave of emotion he was experiencing threatened to overwhelm him.

"Now?" he said indignantly. "You want to tell me that you're sorry, now, after all these years?"

She didn't move, but only looked at him softly.

"Why not thirty years ago? Why not even five years ago? Why now? When I've finally found someone – when I've finally found what I've been looking for? I don't want to lose that again. Not this time," he shook his head. "You could have phoned me anytime – but I never heard a single word from you. Until now. Until I walked through that door," he pointed, "and saw that pendant around your neck – that damn pendant, reminding me that I was some kind of fool to want to give up everything for you."

"Luke – " she began.

"Yes," he cut her off, in a coarse, yet quiet, voice. "You were wrong." He was looking directly at her. "And you damn well knew you were wrong!" he let out, raising his voice. "Why?"

She said nothing.

He began to pace the large lounge area, unable to stand still, unsure of what to do with the huge amounts of pent up energy shooting through his body and making it tremble. It was as though he was in quicksand, sinking fast, any attempt to stay above the perilous depths dragging him down being instantly revealed as futile. "Of course you can't answer, because there is no answer," he snapped. "No answer other than your stupid, foolish, childish obedience to that stubborn old aunt of yours and your psychopathic husband!" he shouted.

"And you abandoned me for that!" he yelled, his arms, the tension his hands, emphasizing every word. "You sat there and promised me that we would be together, and then you broke that promise. Without so much as a word! So, yes, you were wrong! And you – you – " he no longer knew what he wanted to say. He sat down and hung his head in his shaking hands.

"I don't know how you ever did it, Jade," he said softly, his speech muffled and shaken. "I could never have done it to you. I loved you more than anything. I wanted nothing but you."

He felt Jade's face, wet with tears, touch the backs of his hands. Her arms wrapped around his shoulders as she knelt in front of him.

"Luke, I'm sorry," she whispered. "I'm sorry," she said again, in between her teary gasps for air. "I wanted only you. Mine has been a wasted life. I threw it away. I threw it all away. If only I could tell that young girl, that stupid girl, to be strong – if only I could tell her to be true to herself – I would. I would take it all back, Luke. Just look at us – no more are our futures wide open. I'm no longer a girl. I threw it all away. A wasted life. And I have only myself to blame."

He wanted to stay angry with her. He wanted to yell at her all night. But the anger was dissipating with her touch, and in its place, a new sensation emerged.

She pressed her face tightly against Luke's hand. "Luke. I don't want anything from you. I don't want you to forgive me — God knows, I will never forgive myself, and I certainly don't expect you to. But I want you to know that I loved you. As weak as I was — as wrong as I was — I need you to know that I love you. And that I can never not love you."

Luke had never before felt what he was feeling in that moment. It was a freedom that he had never known. Years of burden melted away from his being. He felt as if he were about to be pushed out of his body for all the warmth flowing through it.

He dropped his hands and pressed his face against Jade's, their tears meeting, and each finding release in the other's touch. They stayed there, embraced in the purity of the exchange, almost overwhelmed by the liberation of their years of hurt.

Luke's lips found Jade's. He kissed her softly. He breathed deeply, his nostrils drawing in her scent and screaming out to be flooded in it. And then he kissed her with all the pain and longing that welled up inside him. They were incapable of stopping it. It was as nothing they had experienced.

CHAPTER EIGHT

L UKE STOOD, SILENT, wanting to speak, but knowing that words were no use.

"That's it? You're just going to stand there? Why won't you answer me!" The horror of the last three days' happenings and the consequential near-absence of sleep had left Emerald's voice hoarse.

He went to speak, but stopped before a word could escape. What could he possibly say to justify the disaster in which he had found himself? 'Why did you do it?' she had demanded. But an explanation was far from within his grasp. His only understanding of the night was that he had been carried away by something more powerful than he was able to control; locked into a roller-coaster, not knowing what to expect. Indeed, that was his only recollection of the night. Whatever happened after sleep overtook Luke was a mystery. That was what scared him the most.

Smack! The sound of an open-palmed hand fueled by the full force of a woman betrayed connecting with Luke's cheek echoed through the room. Still, he couldn't answer her. His gaze fell onto the exquisite, fifteen-carat, emerald-cut, flawless diamond engagement ring that she had thrown onto the table. She had wasted no time in making her anger known to her fiancé. It was the first opportunity the two had been afforded a meeting in private; Luke had been taken into custody before

Emerald had touched down from London. By the time she arrived at the jail on Riker's Island, Luke was dressed in orange overalls, his eyes red and his face unshaven and haunted. The panic following the arrest had allowed no time for the two to talk, until now, when Luke's rapidly-growing legal team had secured an hour of private time for the couple. The guards hovered outside the meeting room, and Luke's wrists and ankles remained manacled.

"Luke," she said one more time, exasperated, "I don't understand it. I just don't understand it." She began crying wearily, overcome with desperation. The shock of the past three days – the relentless public outrage over Luke being found covered in another woman's blood, let alone the personal trauma of coming to terms with the catastrophe – subsided for a moment. They were finally alone once again, temporarily shielded from the constant turmoil.

Her panicked breathing became uncontrollable.

Luke struggled with the chains to bring his hands toward hers. Still unable to summon words that would be meaningful under the circumstances, he awkwardly held her hand between both of his, and leaned in close to Emerald's neck.

"I want to tell you how sorry I am," he whispered, "but I know that 'sorry' is meaningless right now. And it doesn't come close to describing how I feel. Just as the word 'love' doesn't come close to capturing what I feel for you." Every noise she made, every cry, tore at his heart.

"You finally found," she began, interrupted by her erratic breathing, "what you wanted in life – we found each other – and then you went to see this woman, Jade. And you had sex with her. Or did you make love to her? Or what the hell was it all about anyway?" she shouted, her fists clenched in anger.

"After we had found each other," she continued. "What does that mean? What am I supposed to think?"

He was silent.

She recalled seeing the news footage of Luke, handcuffed and dazed, as though he didn't believe what was happening to him, being led from the Peninsula Hotel by the police. It had been on the plane that she had first seen it, feeling a stab of pain through her heart as silent tears started to fall. But she didn't know if the pain was for him or for herself, or for the love they shared which he had seemingly thrown away. She could believe that he wasn't a murderer, but he hadn't denied sleeping with the woman in his brief phone call to Emerald, as she boarded the flight, and so she knew she would be a fool to hope that it wasn't true. He had willingly slept with her; that much was clear.

"Was it worth it?" she asked, never looking at him, too involved in the tears pouring from her eyes. "Was it worth destroying our lives for? Did she mean that much to you?"

Again, there was no answer.

"And now, they're saying you're a murderer. They're saying you *killed* her!" She raised her wavering voice. "And you can't even deny it!

"I just don't understand it, Luke. I don't understand why."

He wished there were words for the remorse he was experiencing, but if there were, he didn't know them.

"I want to hate you, Luke. I want to stay mad with you for a long, long time. I want to be furious with you. You don't hurt someone you love like this. I could never do this to you." She turned to her side, staring into space, the hurt written all over her face. "I wish there were some way that you could explain this, but I know there's not. Maybe I should thank you for your honesty in not even trying. At least you can't bring yourself to lie to my face."

He stood there without a word, his head hanging, his body slumping; demoralized, beaten, exhausted. Only listening. What had happened? What was this world he had found himself in? He knew that, whatever she said, it could never be as damning as how he felt toward himself.

"And, my god, how I wish, how I *wish*, I had more time than this. More time than this to scream at you, for you to know how you have hurt me. But I don't. There is no time, Luke."

She wiped the makeup from her eyes and suppressed her crying.

"I hate myself for it, but I can't help it. I still love you. Even after this, I still love you."

She took his face in her hands, searching his eyes.

"Even if you can't be sure that you're not a murderer, I am sure, Luke. I know you're not capable of that. You are not capable of such a thing. You could not have killed a defenseless woman."

Emerald gripped his face tighter in her hands, her anger and love flowing in equal amounts.

"If I'm not going to leave you — and part of me wishes that I damn well would — then I had better get busy helping you. And if you're going to get out of this goddamn mess, you're going to need my help."

She turned her back on him, walking a few steps. Then she returned to the table and took a moment, simply looking at the ring that lay there, considering what it meant to her. The hand-crafted, gold ring on her right hand, for a moment, caught her attention, the two green stones seemingly looking back up at her. Damn him for letting her down all those years ago, she fumed inside. And damn Luke for doing the same. Were both of the two most important rings in her life destined to bring her as much pain as joy?

Taking a deep breath, and not without a substantial amount of resentment, she took her damaged pride, her anger, and her humiliation, and set it free. There was no room for it where she was going. If this was what love required of her, then it was a price she was willing to pay.

Emerald reached for the ring.

CHAPTER NINE

L UKE, YOU MUST consider it. You must take this possibility seriously. The trial is looming, and this is our last chance."

He regarded Rachel Wallace, the head of his legal team, with the look of a man who was not quite sure if he was really awake, or if he had tumbled into some alternate reality.

"Luke," the smartly-dressed attorney, her white cuffs contrasting sharply with her coffee-colored skin, walked around to her client's seat and placed a hand on the table in the Riker's Island meeting room. "I know this isn't the news you were hoping for, but a psychiatric defense might be our best shot at ensuring you get to spend some of your remaining days outside of a prison cell."

"Are you kidding me?" he burst out, and stood to his feet. "Who's side are you on here?"

She took a moment before responding. "I'm sorry, I didn't mean it like that." Rachel Wallace let out a sigh. "I only mean to underscore the seriousness of your predicament. It's not looking good."

"As if I don't already know?" he retorted. "As if everyone out there except for my fiancée doesn't already think I'm a murderer? And even she can't get a moment's peace, with those goddamn magazines and their surveys saying she should leave me! She barely has a friend she can talk to without the conversation turning into a well-intentioned argument on why she should jump ship. And all the while, I'm stuck in this god-damn prison for who knows how many months, awaiting this apparently doomed trial!

"I came to you, Rachel, because you have fought your way to the top, and because you are supposed to be the best. Are you telling me that you want to throw the towel in this soon? Are you telling me that you, that *you*, of all people, cannot keep an innocent man out of prison, an innocent man who, furthermore, is willing to spend a veritable fortune proving it!"

"But that is the problem, Luke," Hughie, his wheelchair adjacent to Luke's seat, answered his friend. He had traveled to New York to support Luke, his legal experience enabling him to sit in on the proceedings. "It's been seven months, and not one shred of evidence has been uncovered in your favor. Every single piece of evidence points to you as the murderer. And that's only thus far. That's not taking into account our own experts, whom we've pushed to go even further and faster than the prosecution's. And what they've told us, is the further they dig, the darker this tunnel gets. There's no light waiting at the end of it. Not any sign of it yet.

"As if that's not enough, you, yourself, can't even deny it."

"Well, of course I can't, I can't remember a thing," he dismissed.

"And you're not willing to say you do, either," Wallace interrupted.

"I'm not gonna lie, Rachel," he looked at her.

"Exactly. So where does that leave us?" she responded.

"There's the sign. The 'Please make up room' sign. Why would I leave it on the door if I had murdered Jade? It's an open invitation for the housekeeper to walk into the room. Why would I have stayed there. Why wouldn't I have gotten out as fast as I could?"

"We know about the sign, Luke," she said with a hint of frustration. "It's been noted. And it's almost been forgotten. It's nowhere near enough to sow seeds of doubt in the jurors' minds."

Luke sat back down, staring out the window, while Hughie laid a hand on his shoulder for a brief moment.

Rachel Wallace, leaning against the table, spoke in a softer tone.

"I wish I had better news. I wish I could say that you were in for the celebrity treatment here, but it's not looking that way. It looks like it's even working against you – we're going to have trouble finding an impartial jury. Everyone's already aware of the case. They've already heard you labeled a murderer.

"I think you're innocent. I'm not just saying it. I believe you did not do this. But even with all the cases I've seen – cases where I've succeeded, in the absence of the defendant's innocence – something tells me I'm going into this trial knowing that I can't win. Something's not right about it – I can't find any angle to work."

Luke interrupted. "But something *could* turn up."

"Who knows what miraculous piece of evidence might fall into our lap? But do you want to gamble with that, Luke? Is 'could' worth risking everything for?" she responded. "If, on the other hand, we give notice of a psychiatric defense – we say you were of unsound mind and lapsed in normal intent to commit murder – I think that we can get you facing manslaughter instead of first degree murder. Then I can guarantee you a much lighter sentence. If we don't, the prosecution is going to push for life without parole. The evidence supports our defense: you blacked out, with no recollection of the event. Your history allows room for it: childhood trauma, psychiatric care, a traumatic history with the victim."

"You both make it sound so hopeless, like we shouldn't even try," he said, his sense of justice outraged.

Hughie leaned forward in his wheelchair, his voice betraying the urgency of his entreaty. "Luke, I've seen you since the first year we've been friends – I've seen you on your birthday. You lose it! You completely lose control."

Luke shook his head in annoyance.

"Luke, you've had a problem, I know it, you know it," Hughie continued. "You've taken the polygraph – you know you don't remember anything of that night. All the evidence points to you; you've had no response to your offering a $25 million reward; you own some of the press, but sure as hell not all of it, and they have it in for you Luke!"

"I'm not doing it," Luke said, staring at the table in front of him. "What you're proposing would be tantamount to admitting guilt in Jade's death!"

"Damn it, Luke!" Hughie thumped the table. "I don't want to see you behind bars for the rest of your life!" He sat back in his wheelchair. "We simply do what makes sense — what's best for you, and what is also our best honest explanation for what happened that night. We say that you cracked, that you blacked out, that you have a psychiatric history. We have two highly respected psychiatrists who are prepared to evaluate you. You're not asking to do anything differently from other defendants over time. Take the opportunity."

"But it's not me, Hughie," he shook his head, "That's *not* me. That's *not* what happened."

"Of course it's not you, Luke," Rachel Wallace retorted. "You weren't 'you'. You weren't yourself. You weren't of sound mind. You're an over-achiever — you've burnt yourself out — you snapped. You can't even remember. You can say that, with the full force of your honesty, because you have absolutely no recollection. It's a no-brainer."

"But that means accepting that I killed Jade! I can't do that! I don't believe it!"

"Believe me, Luke," Wallace said with renewed urgency, "When this goes to trial, and the evidence — a great, big, heap of undeniable evidence — is paraded in front of that jury, you will not stand a chance. This is your chance."

"No." He sat motionless. "No," he repeated. "I will not do it. I will not confess to something I believe I have not done."

Hughie was silent, despairing for his friend's life and pained by his stance. Rachel Wallace nodded to herself. Then, quietly, "Very well, Luke. I understand. And I will do everything I can."

She picked up her phone. "It's settled then. We're going to trial."

CHAPTER TEN

R OBERTSON SAT BACK into his chair, allowing himself a moment of
satisfaction as the journalist reported on the grim circumstances
surrounding the trial of Luke Powers. The TV flashed back to the news
room, the anchor summing up the opening statement of the defendant's
counsel.

"See," he swung his chair around to face the other two men in the
room. "Not a chance. They're grasping at straws, and it's only the first
week." He took a sip from his glass. "Not a goddamn chance," he repeated,
more to himself than to the others.

"OK, I realize I'm hopelessly advertising my inferior security-level
clearance here," the younger of the two seated across from Robertson
spoke up, "but I still just don't get it. How the hell can you pull something like this off?" The professional demeanor he had worn with the
familiarity of an industry veteran for the previous months was finally cast
aside. "I mean, seriously, you gotta throw me a bone here. The strategy
I get. Eliminating some of the players, yes, I get it, because of course
Powers is going to offer an absurd reward. But from a purely practical
point of view, how do you contain the non-personnel related loose ends?
The hotel security cameras; the forensic evidence. I mean, I just find it
hard to accept that you could contain every potential leak."

"Because we don't," Robertson responded. "It's the art of deception. You've seen a magic show before, no?"

He nodded.

"And you've had the experience of the workings of the trick revealed to you, after you had already swallowed it whole and thrown your hands up in bewilderment?"

"Yeah, sure."

"It's the same principle," Robertson said. "Every magician knows how to create an illusion, the true workings of which are so unapparent to the observer, that the observer doesn't know where to start looking. There's just no initial trail to pick up on. What we do is infinitely more complicated, because we deal in minute detail, and the extent of our network would shock even you. But it's not the detail that is our focus. It's the same principle as the illusionist."

"But the evidence — "

He was cut short by the abrupt raising of Robertson's hand. "Kohl, you don't have that clearance. Maybe one day you will. But that's why people will pay us what we demand. That's why we are effective. Secrecy is our greatest ally. There are levels of information that even I don't have access to. And try as I might," again, a part of him drifted back into his own world, "my superiors will ignore my advice when they choose to."

"Peng should be pleased," Kohl remarked.

Robertson merely winced at the thought of the man, and took another sip of his single-malt.

"He's not going to be happy about the sign left on the door," remarked the third man.

Robertson sat forward in his chair, returning his glass to the desk, taking his time. "That's because he has not the least understanding of what we do. He appreciates neither the precision required to pull this off, nor the perfection with which it has been executed. I care not what Wong Peng thinks. I believe my superiors have made a mistake in bending to his every whim, but they believe his allegiance is sufficiently important in the grand scheme of things. Peng can whine and complain all he likes," the calmly-spoken man continued, "but I don't work for him, and neither do you. We work for something bigger than all of us. There are times when we have served individuals of far greater merit than Wong Peng," he writhed. "But even then, we have never served a man. We have never served a group of men." He looked each of the men in the eye, in turn. "We serve a cause."

He turned his attention back to the TV screen, as did the other two. "The sign was a necessity. Without it, the discovery of the crime's timing was no longer under our complete control. I couldn't let that happen. Control is primary."

He again leant back into his leather chair. "It's meaningless. You'll see."

CHAPTER ELEVEN

I S THAT ALL *you've got!* Jiwun watched the newscast in horror. It was true. His worst fears had been confirmed: Luke Powers had nothing. No defense. No evidence. This far into the trial, and still, nothing.

He glanced around the room, considering his options. But they were unthinkable. He quickly pushed them out of his mind, and returned to the earlier avenue that had offered solace when the catastrophe first hit: *Luke will prove his innocence. New evidence will come to light. He will prove his innocence, and the whole thing will go away. It will remain a mystery. As it should.*

Jiwun slammed his fist onto the desk. And again. He hung his head in his hands and wept.

Again, he asked, he begged, for Luke Powers to be found not guilty. For the nightmare to end.

For him, it wasn't an impossibility. Surely a man of Luke's means, of his influence, would find a way. How could he not, Jiwun demanded, when he was innocent?

CHAPTER TWELVE

I ASK YOU TO put aside the technicalities of the circumstances for just a moment, and examine the situation for yourselves. I ask you to investigate for yourselves the plausibility of the prosecution's case." Rachel Wallace's practiced voice carried through the room with confidence, with certainty, betraying none of the despair that had enveloped her for months.

"The case that they have put forward is as follows," she continued. "One of the country's most successful individuals, a man who is respected as an industry leader of the utmost ethical standards, and who takes an active interest in a number of charitable causes worldwide, was invited to the hotel suite of an old friend, a girlfriend from his twenties." She tried to ignore the fact that it was her closing statement in what had become the most dismal case of her career; the pressure was distracting enough as it was.

"The two had consensual sex — the prosecution has suggested otherwise, but Luke Powers has been adamant about this portion of the night — after which Mr. Powers proceeded to indulge in a cocktail of alcohol and drugs — entirely out of character for him, by all accounts. It was during this time that Mr. Powers was suddenly overcome by a fit of rage, causing him to rape and murder his friend, strangling her with his bare hands, rupturing her trachea, and cutting off her air supply until she was dead. He then fell asleep, somehow placing a sign on the exterior of the suite door, inviting the maid service to enter. The only other explanation is that it was already in place, which, given the nature of Mrs. Peng's intention for the meeting, as apparent in Mr. Powers' recollection, is highly unlikely."

In that moment, Wallace had almost convinced herself of the case for Luke's innocence. It was tantalizingly persuasive. But then the devastating impression of the prosecution's mountain of evidence, debunking any notion that Luke was not the perpetrator of the crime, briefly surfaced in her awareness. The security cameras showing Luke's entry to the room, with no activity until the maid's entry the following morning; the psychiatrists' reports; the toxicology reports; the forensic reports. All were ironclad support of their case. And yet, there was something obvious, to Rachel Wallace's honed legal instincts, about Luke's innocence. If only she, or one of Luke's detectives, had uncovered something more than their feelings, to suggest it.

She continued with her argument. Her final, feeble attempt to save Luke Powers.

CHAPTER THIRTEEN

V AGUELY AWARE OF the sound of Rachel Wallace's voice, Luke's thoughts sifted through that night, trying to separate his own memories from those that had developed during the trial. Trying to at least retain his integrity in the knowledge that he, himself, had no recollection of anything sinister in his intent with Jade that night. It had all become a blur, with the prosecution's accusations now firmly implanted in his mind.

He sensed, not far behind him, the support of his friend, Hughie. While the urge to turn in his seat, to look over his shoulder at Emerald, continued to arise as it had throughout the trial, he resisted it. He knew she was there, watching him, living it with him. But he had to bear it on his own, as much as possible. She had already borne too much, both in public and in private. Every time he looked into her eyes, his heart fell to the floor with the weight of the humbling it felt in this woman's willingness to give it all up for him. And he knew he deserved none of it.

He no longer felt afraid of the verdict; his fear was drowned out by his bewilderment. It made no sense. He was incapable of understanding the situation in which he found himself. And beneath his bewilderment, there lurked an aching regret; an acknowledgement that none of this was possible without his participation.

Luke noticed Wallace returning to her seat. It was over. The trial was over. He glanced at the twelve individuals, expressionless and bereft of any visible emotion, seated to the side of the courtroom. His fate now rested in their hands. How long would it take for them to decide, he wondered. What were they thinking? Did they see the absurdity of it? Did they know he was incapable of such a deed?

He would find out soon enough.

CHAPTER FOURTEEN

SYDNEY

"SHIT..." THE WORD came slowly, under his breath, almost imperceptibly. He froze in the middle of his dinner preparations, the kitchen knife falling into the sink. He glared at the TV screen:

Luke Powers found guilty. The story was being broadcast across the globe.

Rick stood silently, dumbstruck. How could it be? He was immediately overtaken by a deep sense of sadness for both Luke and Emerald.

Would he phone her? Or should he leave her in peace?

Steve quietly walked into the room, Rick's face staying glued to the screen.

"I don't know what to say," said Rick's friend.

"Neither do I."

MOSCOW

SHOULD SHE BE ashamed of her reaction, she asked herself. Certainly, she was not proud of it. Still, it was something she could not deny: it was a simple reflection of her truest feelings, beneath all the layers of explanation and justification that she enlisted to buttress her favorable image of herself.

Alexis admitted it to herself; amid the fear for Emerald and Luke's wellbeing, she felt a definite rush of delight on hearing the verdict. Was that why, on some of those occasions during the trial, while she supported Emerald, her closest friend and former lover, she couldn't help but have a dig at Emerald's fiancé? Was that why her thoughts, and her words to Emerald, had a way of coming around to directing blame at Luke?

It was true. A part of her was happy to see her love's partner confined, punished, and out of reach. She had done her best to stand by Emerald through her immense challenges with only her friend's wellbeing in mind, as Emerald had done for her, despite sensing Emerald's continued attempts to keep her out of her inner circle. Now, revealed in the shock of her own reaction to Luke's conviction, Alexis came face to face with the horror of her own deepest motivation. She didn't simply want what was best for Emerald; she wanted Emerald for herself.

NEW YORK

"I DON'T KNOW what to think," one of them let out. The disbelieving handful of executives, their eyes drawn to the plasma screen in front of them in the Powers Media building, grappled with the verdict. The potential for it had existed for some time, but the reality of the situation had never been within grasp.

"I'll tell you what it means," another volunteered. "It means a new boss. It means Luke's personal finances, and by implication, the company's ownership, picked over and rearranged in light of his new criminal status. It means a restructuring of our company. People being axed. It's the beginning of the end for our empire's power as we know it."

HONG KONG

AT THAT MOMENT, two men's lives in Hong Kong could never be the same.

Wong Peng, overcome with jubilation, had succeeded in crippling his

arch-rival, to an extent more satisfying than a mere death. It was confirmation of his dream becoming reality: no man, no matter how powerful, could stand in his way. No man, regardless of his position, or his
character, could insult Wong Peng and escape the consequences. And no
man could covet property of Peng's — his wife, his business, or otherwise
— without answering for his arrogance. Wong Peng had become a force
that could not be withstood. His power was unrivaled; his control was
total.

The other, his hope finally slamming into the wall of reality which
it had done everything to avoid, fell to the floor in desperation. Jiwun's
hope was unsalvageable. There was no denying the situation: Luke would
spend the rest of his life in prison, with Peng laughing all the way. Jiwun
could no longer run from the truth: it was he who had allowed it to
happen.

CHAPTER FIFTEEN

WHAT DID THE old place by Taupo look like now, after all this time, he wondered. Many years had passed since Luke last laid eyes on the closest thing to a childhood home he had ever experienced. Was the old house still standing, witnessing the slow passing of the seasons just as the great Lake Taupo watched the passing of the centuries, or had it gone the way of its inhabitants?

Luke stared at the empty, lifeless wall of his meaningless prison cell. Five months had passed since his sentencing, but it might as well have been five years. Each day was the same. The only difference was the new depths of depression that seemed to be revealed as time drew on, sinking a little lower each slow, gray day.

Thoughts of his grandparents floated through his mind, invoking an otherworldly presence, taking him back to the peace of New Zealand and away from the jeering reality in which he was enclosed.

His last encounters with Sandy had not been a tidy bookend to a well-lived life, but rather a gradual fading of what was once strong and certain. Though even the slow diminishment of his grandfather's character, as Alzheimer's consumed his mind, in itself spoke of a beauty that defied description. Beneath the deterioration of everything he had grown close to in this man, he glimpsed a fragility — the same fragility, the transient nature of life, that imbued meaning to its passing forms of expression.

It was with a profound sadness, the sadness of realizing that he was, once again, alone in the world, without a family, that he received the news of Gwen's death four years later. But all that was a distant memory now, and made to feel all the more distant by his sterile surroundings.

What of Hughie? What was he doing this very moment? Luke smiled widely at the thought of his good friend. Perhaps he was singing his youngest son one of Granny Moana's old songs. It warmed Luke inside to know that his dear friend was immersed in the love of his family, his years of struggle having eventually blossomed into a tender embrace of life. Who would have thought, Luke reflected, that his once-defeated friend would once again bask in the warmth of fortune's smile? He deserved it, Luke grinned to himself, his eyes welling up with joy for his high-school companion.

He had stayed for four weeks after the verdict, before returning to his family, who had patiently waited out the trial. He thought of the last time he saw his friend. It was awful. Humiliating. Empty. The thought of it was enough to make him gag. Hughie wore a brave face, trying to appear upbeat about the appeal process, but both men knew there was no return. That much was clear.

Would he ever see Hughie again, he asked himself. He could not see how it was possible — at least, not in the environment in which he desired to see him — amongst the unadorned beauty and rustic simplicity of the lakeside. No, he would not see it again.

And Kiri, did she still remember Luke and their fairytale summer in Taupo? Was the heartache of their separation still accessible in her memory, as it was in his? The same dullness in his abdomen, the anguish of being torn away from a loved one, returned to him now more strongly than he could recall. But it was merely a trigger for the despair of knowing he would never again see Emerald outside of the prison walls.

Emerald, he whispered. *How could it have come to this?* The memory of that first trauma, of Kiri, held a strange desirability; there was an innocence to it. It came with a second chance.

What a wonderful thing — hope. Hope! How I long for hope! Anything can be borne when there is hope! Abandon me a hundred times, I beg you, abandon me a hundred times — just don't let it end!

The disillusionments of his lifetime, from his changing families to the loves of his life, had culminated in one final realization, staring him in the face: this was the end. He would die in this prison.

Never again would he truly hold Emerald. Never again would they dream of sharing a life together. And never again would they talk of children, of family, of their gratitude to life for bringing them together.

He could read it in her eyes — the many times she had visited him, he could see the toll that it was taking on this beautiful person. It tormented her. It affected her every bit as much as it affected him. He had aged these past few months; he felt it. And he saw the same in her.

Was it worth it? He remembered her question, spoken in times of anger.

What was he to her now? He was a shadow of who he used to be. He couldn't love her. He couldn't offer her any sort of life outside of the confines of visits to one of these depressing buildings. Even his personal fortune was in jeopardy. Not that it mattered now — he would walk away from it all in a second for the chance to be with Emerald. But he didn't have the luxury of any say in his future. What more could he be to Emerald than a dead weight around her ankle? He could see the agony written all over her face every time she visited. His own misery only grew every day, and she saw it, she felt it, which only made it all the more unbearable; his misery was stifling the light within her. The court had sentenced Luke Powers to life, and he, in turn, had sentenced Emerald to the same. Maybe he did kill Jade, he sometimes found himself musing bitterly. If this was the fate that life was delivering to him, then maybe he had done something to deserve it. How would he know for sure?

Why was I spared? Why was I not killed with my family? I should have been! He pounded the bed with his fist. *I should have died long ago!*

Luke stared pleadingly at the wall. *What do I have to show for it? What can I show for it, dammit!*

His heart sank to the ground with the weight of the pain and isolation that he had run from all his life. There was nowhere left to run. It was the end.

CHAPTER SIXTEEN

T IME'S UP," CAME the guard's voice.

Emerald placed her hand to the dividing screen with more desperation than usual. Luke had barely looked her in the eye for the entire visit, and the brief glimpses she gleaned had revealed a distant, hardened man. His demeanor panicked Emerald; never before had she seen him like this.

"Luke!" she yelled, flustered. Her hand awaited his on the other side of the screen. "What are you doing?" She screamed it, distraught.

Slowly, he brought his hand to hers, and looked at her directly for the first time that day. During the visit, he had not allowed himself to truly see her, or to truly hear her, until that moment; he knew that he would be incapable of withholding his emotions. But for those few seconds, as their eyes met, the veil was lifted for Emerald to see, one last time, into the soul of the man who loved her.

His face was a battleground of his will's savage attempt to silence despair. His muscles quivered, his entire face contorted, as he ruthlessly slaughtered whatever softness was left within his soul. It required all of his strength to make the decision, and the casualty of his sacrifice would be the glimmer of light that had remained within him, and that was now extinguished before Emerald's eyes. Killing his own heart was the cost of setting hers free.

The guard placed an envelope in front of Emerald. She vaguely heard him mention something about granting the prisoner an unofficial request. And with that, Luke turned and walked determinedly to the nearest guard, and then through the doorway, out of Emerald's sight.

Her breath, thus far suspended as she watched, immobile, returned with a jolt. Her chest heaved and she let out a cry akin to that of a wounded animal, slamming her fists against the divider and screaming at the top of her voice. She spent the rest of the day futilely demanding to see Luke. She couldn't bring herself to open the letter while still in the prison grounds, as she knew what it would say.

Luke's final, tortured expression would haunt her forever; he was saying goodbye to her for the last time.

CHAPTER SEVENTEEN

I T WAS CREATED with two in mind, not one, and it felt empty without him. It seemed that no sooner had they moved into their new home together, than their lives were turned upside down. The night was deathly quiet, except for the occasional distant sound of a car horn. Emerald, unable to rest, gazed out the window and surveyed the sleeping city, considering its abundance of people and their stories: their successes, their failures, their comings and goings.

Hers was a story of the darkest disappointment. But did it matter, in a city such as this, where hearts were broken every day? Did anyone care? She was alone in a sea of people, of friends, of well-meaning colleagues. Alone without Luke. Separated from him forever.

It pained her to think of him, confined to his cell. Every visit she had made was followed by a period of deep, unrelenting despair. The scene was sickening: it was like witnessing a lion, king of the jungle, cruelly stripped of his nature, and caged in an alien environment. It was to witness in his eyes the beginning of a slow death, as he began to give up on life.

Three months had passed since she last beheld the love of her life. His words in the letter, the final communication she had ever received from him, had pierced her heart through. They had been clear: Emerald was to begin a new life, without Luke, and the two were never to speak again. She knew he had made the ultimate sacrifice, and it was only a mark of his love for her that he did. But how she yearned to reach him, to have him know her love for him. No agony matched that, it seemed, of the strength of one's love being unheard, of it never finding its home. Would she never again express her love to Luke? Would he never again receive it? It would be as if it didn't exist.

For the weeks following their final exchange, Emerald would appear at the prison on every visiting day, requesting Luke's presence. Every time, it was refused by the prisoner. The closest contact she was permitted was the secondhand exchange from the prison officer, 'Sorry ma'am, prisoner refuses to see you.' The same response every time. Her attempted visits had now dropped to one each week. She still held hope that, one day, she would again lay eyes upon Luke. But his letter's final words forever gnawed at what little hope she retained: *In the name of the love we have shared, do this one last thing for me. Forget me and find a new life.*

She took a sip from her glass of wine and sat in the darkness of the night, the lights of the city skyline dimming with the passing of the hours. As was the case with every night she spent in the lifeless apartment, Emerald's melancholy was only accentuated by being in the home that was meant for them both. It had all happened so quickly: their first meeting and the endless hours they began spending together; the recognition of her heart's longing to be with this man; the clarity with which they knew they would be married within months; and the excitement of dreaming up their own space together, here, in this tall building, on these three upper stories and amongst these half-finished walls of art and photos.

Less than a month was spent in their home before Emerald departed for London. She would return to a shattered dream. Since his incarceration, she had not had one night of sleep in the home. Each night she spent there was a wakeful, torturous one, and she had taken to spending most of her time at her prior residence, from time to time still wandering back to her would-be love-nest in anguish, in search of something that had been lost. Back and forth, she wandered between the two dwellings, feeling at home in neither, feeling at rest nowhere.

She wanted to be angry with Luke, but had found herself incapable of it. Any anger that surfaced was drowned out by the sadness, and her need for him in spite of his unforgivable betrayal.

Yes, she had been betrayed, she accepted long ago, not without difficulty. And more than anything, it scared her. It unsettled her. She doubted herself, and questioned the premise of their relationship.

How could a man so in love with her commit such an unthinkable act of disloyalty? Jade clearly wielded a power over Luke. There was a past there that was possibly more potent than Emerald cared to imagine. And he had never once mentioned her. She shuddered as the name, Jade, pestered her mind. She was a phantom, an unseen threat, whose place in Luke's heart would now never be known. She would forever be a presence lurking in the background of their relationship, Emerald thought. But it was hardly relevant anymore.

Would it have been different, had they come clean about their pasts? She, for one, had to admit that there was much in her life that had remained beyond Luke's awareness. Not by design on her part, but not unconsciously, either. But was it relevant? It was the past. Her heart hadn't deceived her in her love for Luke, and she was certain that neither had his. It was their love for each other that trumped anything else that words could communicate, and that rendered any discussion of the past insignificant.

But why did neither of them ever broach the topic of the past? Was she afraid to confess the strength of her love for Jimmy, the love that possibly still lingered? Could she be certain of her own closure of feelings for Jimmy if, as had been the case with Jade, he had miraculously appeared again out of nowhere? Was it possible that she could betray Luke, had Jimmy reappeared from the world of the dead?

The memory of Jimmy was strong in her in that moment. He, too, had betrayed her by his untimely death. Indeed, life had betrayed her, she saw clearly: twice it had offered a taste of heaven, only to callously snatch it away, without warning.

She stared at the glass in her hand. And at the sleeping tablets. How long could it continue like this, she asked herself. How much longer could she stay in this surreal state of nothing, this limbo in which she had found herself, unwilling to move on in her life, and unable to reclaim what was lost?

Emerald placed the glass on the table and stood to walk the room. Seeking solace in substances was not a place that she wished to explore again, she thought as the pain of Jimmy's death surfaced in her mind. It was a slippery slope that she knew led nowhere good.

Her patience having reached its limit, she removed the engagement ring on her left hand, and the gold ring on her right, tossing them irreverently onto the table. It only angered her at this point to be in constant contact with the reminders of the failure of her love.

The ring from her right hand insisted on her attention, landing with the two small emerald stones staring back up at her.

"What?" she demanded. "What do you want from me?"

Was it herself that she was seeing in those two, glistening, emeralds, the very stones that had inspired her name when she chose it those many years ago? Or was it the ring's maker, Jimmy, staring back at her, disappointed in what she had become after his death, and in where she could feel herself slipping back to even now?

Of all the rings she had owned throughout her life, this one was unique. He had crafted it out of his love for her, and he was her first love – her one true love, until Luke. Given form by his dying, cancer-ravaged body, the ring became a distraction for him from his own predicament in those final months: that he would die and would no longer hold Emerald in his arms. Creativity running strong in his nature, and architecture being his natural outlet for it, he took quickly to shaping the ring himself, at first working with a goldsmith, and soon working the piece of jewelry himself with a care that only the solemn purpose of the project – his last project – could inspire.

She stared at those two stones, the stones that Jimmy had selected himself, in reference to his own observation of her eyes resembling emeralds. It was not an expensive ring. But it was priceless.

As was the diamond engagement ring next to it. Where were the givers of those symbols of love now?

Emerald hung her head in her hands, trying to find a way out of the situation, but to no avail. Her mind searched in the future and found nothing. It searched for an easier time in the past, but found only pain and emptiness, episodes she would rather not recall, and then everything culminating in this.

Her hand shot out with a scream as she swiped at the wine glass, knocking it to the floor.

But how much longer could she fool herself? Luke was gone. Was she refusing to accept reality? Maybe, she thought, even as she entered her late thirties, she was being a naïve girl, like she had been all those years ago with Jimmy. The opening she had experienced with Jimmy was rewarded with betrayal and pain. She had learned from it never to open herself again to that degree, and had stayed true to that strategy until meeting Luke, and she had once again begun to open.

It won't happen a third time.

Emerald took the diamond engagement ring from the table, and hastily made her way to the bedroom, opening the bottom drawer of the dresser and burying the ring underneath Luke's folded t-shirts, the ones he used to wear only around home. She slammed the drawer shut and there, collapsed on the floor, she buried her head in the foot of the bed. Her panicked cries eventually died down into slow, pained murmurs.

After some time passed, she rose, drearily regarding the dresser, staring at the bottom drawer that housed her engagement ring and handling her now empty finger. She kicked at the drawer with frustration and with bitter resignation.

Shit, I'm exhausted, she mumbled as she fell onto the bed. *Why can't I just sleep?*

She was tired of listening, of searching for a resolution or a way to cope. She was tired of her friends' persistent encouragement to find another man. She was tired of people telling her to give up on Luke. She was tired of her doctor's warnings to pull herself together before her life spiraled out of control. There was no one else for her. No one else could suffice. She wanted only Luke.

She lay for a while, her eyes closed, and her mind racing.

Dammit. Her eyes opened wide. *Dammit, why can't I just sleep!*

She turned her head to look at the clock: 3am.

I have to get out of here.

I have to get out of this city.

I can't do this anymore. I can't stay here, alone, doing nothing!

She closed her eyes again.

Alexis? she wondered. She had recovered and returned to Moscow. Could she escape to the security of that comfortable relationship, to the nurture and love of her friend?

It was after the verdict that Alexis's warmth had hardened. Throughout the trial, her support had helped Emerald stay afloat, traveling back and forth between Moscow and New York. Maybe she had still held hopes for the rekindling of their relationship in the event that Luke was imprisoned for the rest of his life, Emerald reasoned, as it was only after Luke's sentencing that Alexis was able to accept the truth of Emerald's feelings for her: that she was a dear friend, but would never be anything more.

Emerald could sense it was a huge blow to the woman. She tried hard to be what Emerald needed as a friend, but she would always want more.

No, I can't. It wouldn't be right. It would be unfair to Alexis.

Jobs were still being offered, though she had only ever given them a cursory glance, not wanting to put more distance between her and Luke. A true modeling or screen job was out of the question; she was in no state to engage a camera and voluntarily re-enter the public eye. She doubted she ever would. Even before Luke's trial, her most frequent work was in an on-shoot consulting capacity. It so far had never occurred to her to begin working again, especially if it required her to leave New York. Though, maybe a job of some sort was what was needed. Maybe distance, a break from her overwhelming reality, would provide the clarity she needed.

She remembered her agent mentioning a consulting job in Antigua, and one in Sydney. They both sounded appealing: warm beaches, far from New York. Maybe they were just what she needed. But which one?

Rick. The name popped into her head out of nowhere, and she felt a hint of something that she had not felt in some time: happiness.

Yes, there's a friend away from all of this. Someone who doesn't want anything from me. Someone who made me laugh.

Yes, I would have a friend, away from this place. She smiled at the thought of it, and her happiness at the prospect of a temporary respite from her world shocked her.

She made her way to the study and fired-up her computer, finding the email from her agent about the job. She checked the time in Sydney: it was the afternoon. She smiled at her unwillingness to trust her own time zone calculations: the two had been talking frequently for eight months now. What had begun as a desperate attempt to connect with a friend who was removed from the drama in her life, during the first week that Luke spent in prison after his sentencing, had developed into a profound friendship. Emerald felt in her conversations with Rick an ease within herself, and an acceptance for who she was. He was sufficiently disconnected from her everyday drama that she could be herself without fear of judgment, sensing that Rick had no personal investment in her situation.

She dialed the number and was greeted by Rick's strong New Zealand accent.

"Rick, it's Emerald."

"Hi, how have you been?"

"Well, not much changes here these days. But I might be visiting your neck of the woods for the first week of next month, so I wanted to see if you'll be in town – maybe we could try some more New Zealand wine?" She did her best to sound casual, masking her desperation for a friend outside of her stagnant life.

"Damn – I wish I were going to be here! But I'll actually be in your country – looks like we're swapping places, ha?"

Her heart sank, and despite her efforts, it was reflected in her voice. "Hmm," she tried to laugh, "Well, I thought it was worth a try. Maybe another time."

Rick pressed his palm to his forehead, silently cursing his stupidity at turning away a friend whose world had collapsed. He knew what it was like. "No – that's silly of me. Of course I can just change my trip – it's not important. I would much rather catch up with you.

"Tell me the dates," he said, "I'll be here."

CHAPTER EIGHTEEN

F OR THE FIRST time since Rick had picked her up from Sydney airport, he noticed the sparkle returning to Emerald's eyes. He had
concealed his shock a few days earlier on greeting her at the terminal:
the woman standing in front of him bore little resemblance to the radi-
ant being he had met almost two years ago at David Jones, shortly after
Michael's wedding. A stunning woman, still, that was undeniable – but
what had stood out to him on their first meeting was her magnetism,
her charisma, and these seemed to have evaporated on her recent arrival
into Sydney. Rick had known, from their frequent phone conversations,
that she was in a starkly different place in her self than she had been on
their first meeting. Regardless of his adjusted expectations, he still was
not prepared for the fragility and lifelessness of the Emerald that arrived
that day.

He remembered worrying to himself about her state of mind, and how
much more stress his friend could handle. Rick did not want to see her
where he had been; she was treading the edge, he sensed, and it scared
him.

As the waiter took their orders and collected their menus, Rick
realized that the time for immediate concern had passed. Emerald had

regained some of her spark. She looked alive, once more. He hoped her return to well-being would continue.

"I don't know what to say," Emerald let her eyes rest on Sydney Harbour, taking a small sip from her glass of wine before continuing the conversation. "I still feel as if I stumbled into a nightmare that morning that I haven't woken from since. But," she shook her head slowly, letting out a breath, "I had honestly begun to think that all I would feel for the rest of my life was misery. It seemed like there was no other way."

"Not anymore?" Rick questioned as the waiter cleared their plates.

"These two weeks are the first time I've felt that I could breathe once again. It's been a true blessing. I don't know what will happen when I return to New York, but at least I know I have some measure of choice," she said, a quiet laugh escaping her. It was the end of the final day of her consulting assignment, and the last day of her stay in Sydney.

Then her face took on a pained expression as she remembered her situation: Luke, her rock, was disintegrating, and she knew of nothing she could do to prevent it. Her right hand automatically found her left ring finger, feeling the absence of the engagement ring. "But I feel awful. I feel guilty. How can I allow myself to even smile when the man I love is in a prison cell? When I'll never hold him again, or touch him, or cook with him? Or even have a conversation with him?" She quickly caught a tear with her hand before it rolled down her cheek. "He can tell me to go and find a life. But I had a life, Rick, and that life was with him."

"I know," Rick responded. "I know."

"I'm trying. I even thought about putting the apartment up for sale and not going back to New York, ever. But the truth is, I can't stand being without him. And this utter loneliness – my heart feels as if it's broken in two, with half of it residing in a prison cell. I don't want to go back to drinking and drugs and all the other escapes I've tried – I said goodbye to it all, but now it's just getting so much – I'm a poster-girl now for people who have moved past that. If I lose it again, I'll be letting them all down."

Rick placed his hand lightly on her wrist. "Emerald, I've been worried about you. I don't want to see this all get too much for you."

She sighed, shaking her head. "I never thought love could be so magical.

I would do anything to just be able to sit with him for hours, talking endlessly, just spending time together. But he's taken away my hope. It feels like a cruel thing for him to do, but I know he's doing it for me."

They sat quietly for a moment. There were no words that could console her – she was right; she would forever be separated from Luke.

"Are you still enjoying your work?" Rick inquired. "Do you have space for it in your life right now, or is it just adding to the pressure?"

"Well, last week was my first foray into the world of modeling for over a year – I wouldn't say it was inspiring, but it kept me busy, and my mind off everything else for part of the day."

"But what about your real work – what you've told me is your purpose. Human trafficking, slavery – raising awareness. It's amazing work that you do," he said with genuine admiration for the woman before him.

"I want to continue. I can't see myself ever stopping. It's bigger than any one of us – it's about the global community," she replied.

"It's such a powerful difference you're making in the world. I was surprised when you told me that human trafficking is one of the three largest illicit industries in the world. It seems that it doesn't do much good to abolish slavery if people are still being bought and sold."

"Yeah, you're right. In fact, slavery is more prevalent than ever – people think it's a thing of the past, but it's more alive now than it was two hundred years ago."

Rick stared pensively at his glass. "At least there are countries in which that is not true."

"Such as?"

"Well, your country, to begin with – the land of the free."

"If only it were true," she started. "I once visited a brothel not too far from Las Vegas, comprised exclusively of trailers in the middle of the desert. The perimeter was lined with tall, barbed-wire fences; the closest town was fifty miles away. They call them ranches, and it's no different from being in prison. The only food they're allowed is the instant noodles that the owners buy from Costco. I talked to one of the local landowners who had befriended some of the girls – her property bordered that of the ranch. She tried to offer the girls more food that she had purchased herself, but they refused it, saying that they would be found out and punished. The only way she could help was to buy the same packets of instant noodles they were already eating, and smuggle them through the fence."

Rick didn't speak immediately. "There's no way for these girls to leave?"

"It's complicated," she said. "First of all, there's no means for them to leave. They have zero financial independence; none of them have vehicles; they are completely dependent on the owners. But more important, these women feel worthless. The only reason they found themselves in such a situation to begin with is because of their total absence of self-worth. I spoke to one woman there who told me that almost every one of the other girls she knows at the ranch, was at one stage a victim of sexual abuse before gravitating toward prostitution.

"So there you have it. No escape; no financial independence; substandard living conditions; required to provide labor – in this case, sex – without sufficient compensation; and it all happens within the law. Slavery."

"But why isn't it stopped?" Rick protested. "Isn't that what you were trying to do by being there? Why doesn't it work?"

"Because it's a symptom of the society we live in. Domestic violence, abuse – it's rampant. One in four women in the U.S. will be violently abused, raped, or molested in their life. There's an undercurrent of fear amongst women, and there always has been. The only way to change it is to change people's attitudes, especially men's attitudes toward women."

"You're blaming men?" Rick asked, somewhat defensively.

"The only customers at the brothel are men. They're the one's paying, keeping places such as these in business. It's simply about the rights of women being valued by men." Anticipating Rick's next question, she quickly added, "Think about it, if men did value us, why don't they do something about it?"

Rick pondered the account for a moment, not certain what to make of it, before Emerald launched into the line of thought that had roused her curiosity more and more as her time in Sydney progressed.

"I'm surprised I don't know more about purposes close to your heart," she remarked inquisitively. "You've told me some of your past, and how you've been to the edge, but I don't think I know what it is that you're most passionate about in your life. Irrefutable evidence that I spend way too much time talking about myself!" she laughed.

Rick laughed too. "No, I think it's more that my ideas are still forming, and I don't have anything concrete at this moment."

"Rick, surely a person like you has interests greater than your solitary walks along the beach and investing — come to think of, I don't even know what you've been investing in."

"Well, it feels like a period of transition for me. One thing I believed in was organic foods, and I was involved in it globally. It was an amazing journey, that dream of feeding the body. And since then, I've felt that my purpose has been to fulfill the second half of my dream; to feed the soul. To be honest, the purpose that's closest to my heart right now is helping people who are heading for the painful, dead-end road that I've been down. I've always spent a lot of time advising people and friends in their business ventures and in achieving their dreams, but this feels more important to me."

"What does?"

"Confiding in them how I went to the edge; how I lost it; and how it's the worst thing that you can do to yourself."

"It sounds like a dangerous level of exposure. Is it wise?"

"Probably not," he said. "But whatever ridicule or blackmail I fall victim to — and believe me, I've had plenty already — it's worth it, if I can prevent people from going to the edge."

"They're lucky they have someone who can warn them — who can help them."

Rick took another sip of his wine. "It's sad, but I've found it rarely makes any difference. Often, people will phone me later, when they've already had a breakdown and tell me how sorry they are that they didn't listen to the warnings earlier… which is exactly the mistake that I made, myself. They went where I went, and they find it very difficult to come back. Many never come back, and their addictions and medication remain. I've discovered that telling someone of the danger doesn't mean that you'll have an impact on that person's life."

Their conversation continued, and in an attempt by both to balance the heaviness of the earlier topics, avoided anything remotely related to Emerald's personal life.

She regarded the man in front of her, wondering why she had found such comfort in his presence during the past two weeks. It was the best she had felt in a very long time. There was a warmth, an openness to him, and a friendly smile that naturally engendered a level of trust in his sincerity. Despite their often light-hearted discussions, she sensed that this man of slight but athletic build was one to be reckoned with, one capable of a fearlessness in meeting life's challenges.

Her first nights in the city offered little respite from the problems which she had hoped to escape. Frequently waking in the unfamiliar, sterile surroundings of the hotel suite, she contended with her scattered sleep and nightmares for rest. It stalked her like a shadow: she would not spend her life with the man she loved so deeply. It would not happen. The inevitability of it seemed to pound at her brain day and night, yet it was something she could not accept. She wanted to feel loved again; she wanted to feel Luke's love for her; to be touched by him.

She had begun to question her decision to spend time away from New York. Not only had it failed to offer the rest she had desired, but she worried about burdening her friend, Rick, who was making every effort to ease her mind. The confusion was overwhelming her, she felt herself breaking down, and she wondered what drove her to attempt a job in such poor condition. She regretted ever committing to it.

Then a strange thing happened on the second day of her job, when she realized that the week was nearly over, and she would soon return to New York: it scared her. She wasn't ready to return home. And she was surprised to notice that she wanted to stay in Sydney.

From that moment on, she wondered if it was possible, in this foreign land, away from constant reminders of her former life, to leave her baggage behind for a few days. As an experiment, as an exploration into whether or not the remainder of her life needed to be dominated by despair, she wondered if it were possible to enjoy herself, despite her loss. She extended her stay by a week.

Emerald found herself in the perfect environment for such an experiment: Rick was the ideal friend. They took a day trip to the Hunter

Valley; to Bondi and Coogee; the ferry to Manly; a visit to the zoo; an impromptu picnic, reminiscent of their first encounter; and outings to the city's finest restaurants. A part of her questioned the appropriateness of such a friendship, and part of her felt a terrible guilt at enjoying herself while Luke was confined to constant misery and loneliness. The pain never abated. But she found relief in Rick's carefree company.

"Well, as always, you've managed to make me laugh, Rick," she remarked as the waiter cleared their dessert plates. "And, to my great surprise after eating with you daily for over a week now, you still haven't lost your appetite."

"What do you mean?" he smiled innocently.

"I mean that I remember my shock at your insatiable appetite from the first day we met, in David Jones, and I imagined that spending time with you would eventually reveal the secret to your eating habits! I am in awe of your metabolism – that you can devour huge meals on a regular basis, and still look like you live off salads and carefully-controlled portions like every model I know. I was certain that I would find you skipping meals, or at least compensating somewhere else."

Rick sat back in his chair and opened his palms, adopting a mock-serious expression, "I enjoy all of life. Especially my food."

"Yes, I noticed that when I was sitting at the seafood bar and some guy from New Zealand sat next to me and ordered three appetizers and a salad for lunch."

"Well, there was a time when I was very strict about what I ate. I noticed that I was addicted in some ways to eating – it was my comfort. It wasn't unusual for me to mindlessly devour a whole box of chocolate cookies at night, or a whole tub of popcorn," he chuckled. "But once I broke myself of those habits, then I could choose if I wanted to eat more than I needed, on occasion, just because I appreciate the food." He shrugged. "What do you expect me to do? Our Sydney rock oysters are some of the best in the world, as are our scallops and prawns – I had to have them all. If I had known who you were, I would have copied you and ordered champagne," Rick laughed.

"I know," she rolled her eyes jokingly, "You didn't even *recognize* me. So offended." She grinned. "But I got the benefit of some expert advice on

Sydney's seafood delights, followed by a bottle of – what was it – Cloudy Bay?"

"Correct," Rick nodded.

They reminisced a little longer over their first meeting in Sydney, almost two years earlier and in less complicated times, recalling Emerald's disbelief at Rick's comment that he knew her fiancé once it had become clear that it was Emerald Steel he was talking to.

⁓

'I RACED AGAINST him in athletics when I was sixteen. The 100 meters hurdles. He won, of course,' Rick smiled. 'In a way, we actually became friends – we were meant to stay in touch, but we never did.'

'Is he still athletic?' Rick wondered aloud to Emerald, and then they both burst into laughter as she confirmed that, indeed, he was.

It was as the two were in conversation that Emerald's phone rang; Luke was calling to say goodnight from New York, wishing that he had been able to escape the demands of Powers Media to make the trip along with her. Emerald's excitement at having met one of Luke's teenage friends was audible as she told Luke of Rick, while the New Zealander awaited Luke's response with great curiosity.

When eventually Luke's memory clicked, his affection for Rick poured out naturally: 'Oh, he's a good guy, he got me out of a real tight spot. I was in a lot of trouble – I can tell you that. If it's the Rick that I know, I'm sure you can trust him.'

To both of the men's surprise, within minutes they were talking to one another from opposite sides of the globe. It was clear to both that the sincerity with which they had originally struck up their friendship remained alive and well in both men, and the short phone call was punctuated with much laughter at each end. 'Look after Emerald for me while she's there, will you, Rick? I wanted to make it down to Australia – hopefully show her around NZ too – but it doesn't look like it's going to work out this time.' Little did the two men know, it would be the last time the three would share a conversation together.

Feeling a responsibility toward Emerald and her experience of the city, the two had bought dessert and took it to Hyde Park, a short walk from David Jones.

THEY WERE STILL laughing, recalling that day when bird droppings had landed on Emerald as they enjoyed their dessert underneath a tree, as they left the restaurant and made their way through the fresh, coastal air to the city waterfront. It was a relief for them both to reminisce about simpler times, and neither was in a hurry to return to the heavy conversation of Luke's incarceration, human trafficking, and mental illness, as they left dinner.

"Such a beautiful city," Emerald remarked as they turned the corner onto the boardwalk. The soft breeze played delicately on the calm water, the moored boats bobbing up and down, framed by the Opera House and the Harbour Bridge. "The two most-photographed objects in the Southern Hemisphere," she said smugly, looking to Rick to see if he had noticed her recollection of his trivia.

"Yes, they are," he smiled.

"Do you still walk the route you had on the day you met me?"

"Most days – usually right along here," he replied, but then was silent.

They said little, both of them thinking that the tranquility of the night was better left unspoiled by conversation. But Emerald felt as if there were an energy between the two that was growing; something powerful, as if their aura's were melting together to become one. For a moment, it both exhilarated and unsettled her, and she instinctively fumbled for her ring finger with her right hand. For a moment she was taken with a sense of panic as she found the finger empty, but was immediately reminded that her fiancé had pushed her away, hoping she would find a new life.

"Do you ever walk up that way?" she said, more quietly now, as if the excitement of the earlier part of the evening had given way to a calm.

"Usually I do," he said of the botanical gardens, "but they may not be open this late. We can try?"

"Let's."

They made their way up the gentle hill and toward the garden, cloaked in darkness.

Emerald began to feel a sense of euphoria rising up through her body as they walked, alone, under the majestic trees of the garden's surroundings. They both sensed that they were coming into a space of knowingness where everything else was becoming a blur. Emerald, wondering if she was feeling light-headed, turned around to examine her surroundings, and was confronted with a picturesque view of Sydney Harbour, the flickering boat lights dancing like fairies on the water.

She instinctively moved toward Rick, turning to face him. She felt his arms wrap around her back and, without warning, they were embracing, their lips touching. The kiss lingered before they each drew back, and Emerald gazed deep into Rick's eyes. It had taken them both by surprise, and she felt a certain shyness at what had happened. But at the same time, she could sense an openness from Rick: it had surprised him, too, but he wasn't retreating from it. The two stood for a moment, looking intently at the other, neither one succumbing to the pressure to say something, or to do something, but both enjoying the mystery of what had occurred.

Her heart sank with guilt. She had enjoyed the moment, though she shouldn't have. It should never have happened.

What more is there to lose? she asked herself. *It doesn't make sense to me. But how can this be wrong, when it feels so true?*

Then they walked, ever so slowly, continuing up the hill, and Rick took Emerald's hand in his. They were silent, only walking, listening, and watching.

As they drew nearer to the garden, they could see that the towering, iron gates of the gardens were closed. But they walked on, hoping to find an opening somewhere, and, nonetheless, enjoying the prospect of a journey into unknown territory.

They walked the boundary of the garden, occasionally glancing through at the gated beauty of Australia's flora, and came upon a majestic fig tree. It drew them to it. They gravitated to the trunk of it and there, upon a bed of leaves, shielded by the tree's lush canopy, they sat. For a moment they admired their view: a lush lawn, falling away down the hill to a view of the Harbor Bridge and the activity of people at the waterfront. But where they were, nestled against the tree trunk, side by side, they felt secluded, as if they were spectators of the night's display of beauty that had been conceived just for them.

Emerald, her hand still in Rick's, pressed her back against the tree. There was something about it, some presence in it, that comforted her. It was as if magical forces were coming alive in the spot that they had chosen to sit.

They kissed again, and this time with more intensity. Her body was held by the curvature of the tree as she felt the strength of Rick's body pressing into hers. Before she knew what was happening, they were lying on the ground, in a bed of leaves, making love. Emerald was overwhelmed by the sense of well-being that rose up through her body, and she smiled, resting her face on Rick's neck, as she reveled in the intensity of his passion for her. He was opening all of himself to her, without any of it being withheld, and she knew it.

They were oblivious to all else that was taking place in their surroundings, and any peripheral awareness of the danger of being caught in an uncompromising situation, only heightened the excitement of the exchange. Emerald, cradled by the tree, stared through the branches and up at the moon, suspended high above, and at once felt that she had merged not only with Rick, but also with the magic of the night.

Emerald's eyes opened with a start. "How long did I drift off for?" she said, her eyes darting around her surroundings.

"Only a minute or two," he answered.

She breathed a sigh of relief, and slowly moved to sitting position. "We had better get moving – I must be crazy to have done that here – anyone could have seen me!" She laughed nervously as she kissed Rick on the lips, hurriedly pulling her clothes toward her, and both feeling like teenagers making out behind the school bicycle shed.

An awful feeling came over her as she glimpsed her empty ring-finger. She froze, staring at it, her face contorted. She wanted to burst into tears, but knew she couldn't; she had to be strong, she had to see if she could take control of her life once again.

As was her habit, Emerald's left hand searched for the ring that lived on her right ring finger, the ring that for years had been a source of comfort. To her horror, it was missing.

"My ring!" she gasped.

"I know, I'm sorry," Rick replied, assuming she was lamenting her separation from Luke.

"No, my other ring – it's gone!"

Rick turned on the spot, staring down at the bed of leaves. And then, in a wider diameter, taking in the area in which they had made love.

"You mean it's somewhere in there?" he said, the tone of his voice reflecting the sheer magnitude of a search effort.

"It has to be," she replied, still panicked.

"Don't worry," he reassured her, "We'll find it."

Rick dropped to his hands and knees, as did Emerald. He began to examine closely the area by the tree trunk, being careful in his movements not to disturb the leaves, lest he concealed the ring even further. The hopelessness of the task soon dawned on him: not only had they lain together in multiple locations under the tree, but the floor was well-masked by the darkness of the night, with the street-lighting some way off.

They searched in vain until it became clear that it was no use.

"Emerald, please don't worry – I'm going to return as soon as the sun begins to rise and find the ring in the daylight."

She forced a smile, "Thank you, Rick. That ring means everything to me." He suddenly felt an enormous sense of pressure: it would be a horrible memory to be associated with, the loss of so precious an item. An omen. The sudden transformation of their relationship that night had taken him by surprise, and he knew immediately that this woman was unlike any other he had met: he was connected to her in a way he had not experienced before. He didn't want to lose her.

Rick walked Emerald to her hotel, the two kissing goodnight before he turned and headed back toward Steve's house. His thoughts dwelled entirely on Emerald's feelings, their night together, and what on earth she was thinking now. Was she regretting it? Would she leave the city that day, hoping to forget everything that had happened? He couldn't read her during their walk. She was withdrawn, pensive. Though whether it was because of the ring, or because of what their night together could mean, he knew not. One thing was for sure: he had to recover the ring.

His pocket began vibrating. He reached in and retrieved his phone, noticing the same phone number that Emerald had phoned from during her stay.

"Emerald?"

"Rick," she began, unsure of herself. "I don't know what to think about what happened tonight — it's taken me by surprise, but I had to phone you."

"I know, I never expected it either," he replied.

"Rick — I feel strange, I feel alone. Would you mind staying with me for a while longer? Losing the ring made me realize how short life is. I don't want to hold off spending more time with you — being with you is wonderful."

Rick felt a sigh of relief. Maybe she felt the same way he did. "I'll be right there."

He woke to the sound of his alarm at 5 a.m. the next morning, and as much as he wanted to remain right where he was, he hauled himself out of bed and ensured that Emerald had fallen back to sleep before slipping out of her room.

HE FOUND THE tree and planned in his head the most effective way to search the area. Visually, he divided the area into individual one foot by one foot squares, knowing that any larger an area would be too challenging, given the density of the leaves. Then, he reached into his bag and pulled out nails and string, arranging them in such a way that the squares were clearly marked out.

Rick began to work the grid, thoroughly searching each square, first carefully, and then scouring over the leaves. After three hours, he approached the final square. The sun had arched over the east side of the gardens, its light now beaming through the branches and onto a frustrated Rick; the morning joggers and walkers stared curiously at this man and his grid. Once again, squatting at first and peering into the area like an eagle high above the ground, searching for its prey, he saw nothing but leaves and dirt. Then, moving to his hands and knees, he carefully lifted and brushed aside each leaf, being careful not to displace the ring in the process. And then, he rummaged through the earth, but to no avail.

He sighed, resting his eyes by taking in his beautiful surroundings. He leaned back against the tree trunk, as Emerald had, and thought back to their almost otherworldly experience. It still seemed as if he were in a dream, as if he hadn't quite been himself, but had fallen into something magical.

A memory flickered across his mind. *Someone was there. . .*

"Yes," he let out, audibly. So enraptured had he been, that the thought hadn't fully registered at the time.

Yes — I know I felt someone else there. In the distance. Someone knew we were there.

He turned his head, taking in the area. *But they weren't close enough to see — at least not while we lay. But maybe they could see us looking for the ring. . .*

Rick hadn't allowed himself to notice the presence while in Emerald's embrace. But he knew they were not entirely alone. Besides, there was nothing sinister in it, he sensed.

He stood, searching with his eyes. And he saw a slumped figure, in the distance. He approached, and as he drew nearer, could see that the homeless man was comfortably leaning against his rolled up sleeping bag, pressed against the wall of the gardens. He hadn't a care in the world, seemingly watching the passers-by and wearing a hint of a smile.

"Excuse me, I hope you don't mind my asking you a question?" Rick ventured.

The man's head moved ever so slightly to look at Rick. He didn't speak immediately. "I don't mind," he said.

"Well thank you," Rick said, squatting to the ground so that their eyes could meet more easily. "My girlfriend and I were over there last night," he pointed, unsure of how to describe the situation, "And she lost a ring of hers. It's not a fancy ring or anything — but it holds huge sentimental value for her. We searched for it under the tree last night, and I've spent hours searching this morning, and still I can't find it. But I would do anything to get it back for her. I'm just wondering if you might have seen anything, or have any ideas — I would gladly give a reward if you could help me find it."

There was silence. Rick couldn't be sure that the man had even heard him.

"You're not an Aussie, are ya? You're a Kiwi, aren't ya?"

"Yes, I am," Rick said.

"So am I. I came over here years ago." He looked toward the harbour and smiled. "I like it here," he nodded. "I'll tell ya what, mate, maybe I can come over and have a look, too."

"Oh," Rick said, grateful but impatient at the prospect of searching the same area once again. "Thank you very much. I don't know if it will help us though, I've already searched for hours."

"Yeah, but you've been looking too hard — I saw ya! People call me crazy, but I think you're the crazy one today. Ya never find anything when ya look that hard for it, mate."

They made their way back to the tree, the man leaving his bags by the wall. Rick took another long look at the grid, taking it all in. He walked the grid, slowly, carefully, spending a moment in each square and taking in all the earth beneath him. He peered deeply at each square. Then, he squatted again, moving from square to square, concentrating all of his focus on the ground in front of him.

"Well, look what I found! Ha!"

Rick snapped his head around to the direction of the old man's voice. The man was looking at him, standing, holding a ring in his right hand.

"I don't believe it," Rick laughed, walking toward the man. It was the same ring he had noticed on Emerald's finger during their time together. The man handed the ring to Rick.

Rick almost said what was on his mind; that this homeless man must have found the ring after the two of them had left the previous night. He probably had a flashlight, and they hadn't. But he thought better of it.

"I can't believe you found it," Rick said again. "Thank you," he said with all his gratitude.

The old man just smiled mysteriously, enjoying the exchange.

"Here," Rick said, pulling his wallet from his jeans, "Let me give you something." He handed the man three hundred dollars, all the cash that he was carrying, but was refused.

"No, no, no," the man said, holding his palms up toward Rick.

"Please, it's for you, please take it," Rick tried, handing the money over again.

"Hey, hey, what are mates for?"

Rick, humbled and feeling guilty for taking back the piece of jewelry, tried again. "Then let me buy you some beers — how about some Steinlager, ha?" he grinned. "Or are you on to the Fosters, now?"

The man laughed. "Nah mate, I'm alright. It's all good." He walked back to his pile of belongings by the garden wall, Rick watching him, not knowing what to do. He opened his hand and looked at the ring.

Shit, am I lucky!

CHAPTER NINETEEN

H ER NECK LEANED effortlessly into his hand; their lips touched; her expression was one with which he was familiar. She looked open. She looked happy. She even looked like she could be in love.

Luke sat there, motionless, observing the complete absence of his breath. Time seemed to stand still. And he would be glad if the next breath never entered his lungs.

He stared at the photos in his hands. Though it appeared that the shots had been taken from outside the room, looking in through the window, there was no doubt: it was Emerald. Could it have been doctored? he asked himself. No. There were too many shots. Too many perfectly natural exchanges between the two individuals — the lighting, the settings, the expressions, the interaction.

It was what Luke had wanted for Emerald; he had cut himself off from her. But nothing could prepare him for the moment of recognizing that it was done, that it had worked, and that she was gone.

He turned the final photo. There was a single piece of paper, with four words. "Kiss it all goodbye."

He clenched his jaw, attempting to unleash his fury, but to whom? It was useless. There was no one to hear. There was no one who cared. He was confined to a cell, and would never be afforded the opportunity to confront them.

"Fuck you!" he threw the package at the wall, the photos flying about in the air and scattering on the ground, some face-up and staring right back at him. He kicked at them. He tore them with his hands, and threw himself onto his narrow bed, defeated, helpless.

For a few minutes he simply lay there, fuming, breathing. His long unspoken suspicions were confirmed: he was the victim of foul play.

It was the missing piece of the puzzle. Everything made sense, once seen in that light. It pained him to see how right he had been in his instinct that he had not killed Jade, yet how cornered he was in his complete inability to defend himself.

He did not for a second question who was behind the conspiracy. His business interests were being sold off in pieces, asset by asset, with Wong Peng prominent among the bidding parties. Wong Peng had won. Maybe the success of his ploy even exceeded his expectations.

The photos were Luke's hemlock; the final decision by his peers that he must die. He wondered, had he ever been lower than this before? Was it the same when he was branded, at the age of eleven, by the burns that covered his arms? Watching his family's death. Losing all connection to his known life.

Only to finally discover the courage and means to build another life, and then to have it, too, crumble before his eyes. What was the point in it? Was nothing in this life capable of lasting, at least for him?

Who am I now?

He still lay there, unwilling to move, staring at the ceiling.

Who am I now, without family, without a place in this world, without Emerald? What have I left?

It was as if he had entered a state of shock, and felt nothing but emptiness. The despair surrounded and permeated his every cell. But he didn't move. There was nowhere to move to. There was no hope that he could look to. This was reality. He had nothing left.

CHAPTER TWENTY

'THERE'S NO PAIN while you're asleep.' She remembered Rick's words as she handled the bottle of sleeping tablets. It was true, Emerald reflected, that she had abused such medications in the past, and probably more than ever in the past twelve months, as the other alternatives became less and less appealing. But this was no ordinary night, she reasoned, as she swallowed the two small pills with the remaining mouthful from her wine glass.

"Another glass, Ms. Steel?" the air stewardess asked.

"No, thank you," she responded, gazing out of the window of the first class cabin at the Pacific Ocean below.

The flight to Los Angeles would take over fourteen hours, and the connecting leg to New York another five.

Plenty of time to try and make sense of my life, she lamented, knowing that there was no easy answer to the problems that confronted her.

Emerald would touch down in New York, and the following day, attempt once more to visit Luke. The two had not spoken in seven months; the day that she would return to the prison would be one year since the beginning of his sentence. She hoped he would deem it long enough to grant her a visit, despite his strict instructions. She considered the seemingly interminable time that the two had spent apart, and the melancholy so familiar to her returned, reminding her of the indefinite separation from the one she loved.

The time spent with Rick had brought her back to life. It amazed and surprised her. Her feelings for him were strong, and the abrupt separation of boarding the flight, after spending every minute of the day together, had left her feeling suddenly vulnerable. He had offered to take the flight with her, and she had wanted him to. But she knew it was something she must do alone.

She longed to lay her eyes upon Luke again, to simply sit there and stare into his soul. Yet, the thought of seeing him again made her want to throw up. What had she done? Supposing he were to see her this time, she knew she couldn't lie to him, and she would never want to. But what an agonizing ordeal it would be, she imagined, to come to Luke with such news. Would it be the final blow to him? The final disillusionment?

She shuddered at the thought, shifting in her seat.

The night that Rick and Emerald first embraced had taken them both by surprise. They decided together that, instead of Emerald returning to another job, she would extend her stay, at Rick's insistence that she take the opportunity for some space to herself, and allow him to show her some of the wonders of Australia and New Zealand. Until Emerald's arrival in Sydney, Rick had been working diligently on his new awareness project for the wellness of the mind while living with his friend, Steve. He decided that it was time for him to finally see some of the local spots he had always been curious about, but had never experienced because of his past international travel, which was less common these days.

Their first adventure was through the Australian Outback as they made their way to Uluru, the large sandstone rock protruding out of the center region of the Australian continent. Sacred to the Aboriginies, and a World Heritage Site, the two had watched the rock glow a deep red as the sun set on the scorching, summer day.

The initial powerful connection between the two deepened as their explorations continued, snorkeling in the Coral Sea's three thousand-kilometer-long Great Barrier Reef, and then flying to Auckland. Emerald's state oscillated between the extremes of guilt and joy while in New Zealand: Luke had often talked of showing her the country of his youth And there she was, falling in love with someone else. She decided that it would be too painful to visit Taupo and Rotorua, and was happy to hear that Rick's plan had been instead to spend a week on his friend's boat in the Waitemata Harbour and the Bay of Islands, Rick introducing her to fresh pacific oysters that the couple pried off the rocks of Waiheke Island in between their long walks around different parts of the island. There, too, they sampled some of the country's finest pinot noirs, and Rick managed to find some Bluff oysters, the pride of New Zealand seafood lovers, which they enjoyed in a variety of preparations: in a light-tempura style; dusted with flour and pan-fried; and natural. They spent their offshore time listening to music on the fifty-five foot motor boat, dancing, and talking late into the night. It seemed that both discovered reservoirs of boundless energy, and the long hours of the day spent together never seemed to be enough time, each of them always wanting more of the other.

Rick's contentment and simple enjoyment of life rubbed off on her. Exploring the numerous bays and coves of the Bay of Islands with him was one of the most magical experiences she could recall. It began with a rush of adrenaline as Rick steered the boat, much to Emerald's panic, through the Hole in the Rock at the entry to the Bay. As soon as his daredevil intent became evident, she vigorously protested, pleading with Rick to bypass the surging water flowing through the small passageway housed by Piercy Island. 'Trust me,' he had replied, as they cruised through, with little space between their craft and the jagged interior of the rock, and out the other side. 'You can't forgo the grand entrance to the Bay of Islands,' Rick had smiled as they emerged. One afternoon, as the two were fishing for snapper, he pointed to two islands – one near and one in the distance – and shared a story from his teenaged years, when a five-dollar bet with his father led to his swimming the distance between the two islands, his uncle close behind in a row boat in case he didn't make it. She noticed that she laughed easily in his presence; indeed, she felt an ease within herself just being in his company.

She had felt herself beginning to heal some of the hurt of the past two years, and she had hoped that the time would grant her greater clarity. Confusion, it seemed however, would be her truest companion for now. What scared her most was that she had fallen deeply in love with Rick, and had now shared her life with him for four months. It was half the amount of time she had lived with Luke, before he was taken into remand. But she didn't want to run anymore. She had left New York in pain, running from the agony of her life, and then finding herself in love with Rick. It couldn't go on that way. She had to make peace with the fading hopes for her life with Luke.

Jimmy. Luke. Both of them snatched away from me as soon as they had my heart. Would it be the same with Rick anyway? Is fate determined to shit on me regardless of where I find love?

She was proud that she was a strong woman, that she had not gone the way of her mother. The memories of her and her siblings hiding in bed before their father returned home for the night, not knowing whether his mood would be amiable or overflowing with rage, still haunted her: her mother's screams, as they tried to block their ears and fall to sleep, the utter worthlessness that her dear mother felt after years of abuse, still echoed in Emerald's mind. She was proud that she had taken hold of her destiny with her own two hands, changed her name, and found respect and success in her field. But there were some things, she admitted, that were still out of her control.

Emerald pulled the blanket closer and closed her eyes. She was still at the mercy of love, and there was nothing she could do about it.

CHAPTER TWENTY-ONE

J IWUN SWALLOWED THE whiskey as best a seventeen-year-old could. It burnt his throat and was certainly stronger than the drinks he was accustomed to. But he had seen it used a hundred times to escape demons, and he hoped it would offer him the same.

It hadn't yet. He was incapable of learning at school anymore; his focus slipped too frequently. His sleep was plagued by the distress of knowing what he knew, and failing to act. And more than anything, his soul was being overthrown by the hate running through his veins.

It was a hate that only he could know, for to disclose it was to disclose his darkest secret. What scared him most was that the more he hated his enemy, the more he discovered he hated himself. He could feel the irony of his turning to alcohol choking at his throat: he was emulating Wong Peng in the very act. Despite his hatred for the man, he was becoming like him.

"I hate you!" he whispered, with all the venom he could muster, at the photo of the two of them that sat on the corner table in his room. The only reason it remained there was the same reason he was forced to hide his knowledge: to risk being seen as knowing anything of Wong Peng's dealings, was to risk his very life.

"Why?" he whispered, through painful tears. "Why are you my

father? Why you? Why?" He never realized he could hate someone so much.

He shook his head, sobbing, remembering his mother; her love for him; her painful death; her painful life.

She had given him strength. She was there for him. He remembered the afternoons they would spend together with their violins, Jiwun learning the instrument from his mother. And the numerous times his father would come home drunk, both Zhu and Jiwun knowing they were in for a beating. Jiwun would hide; Zhu would try to stand up to his father. But it was always Jade who would step in and take the blows, protecting them both. The boys feared their father.

"It can't go on," he whispered to himself. "He can't get away with this."

If only his brother were still alive, he thought, this would never have happened. Zhu would have stopped it; he would have known what to do. If ever he felt a fatherly presence during his childhood, it was from Zhu, sixteen years his senior. Would things be different, had he never learnt to pilot the helicopter that took him to his fiery death?

Jiwun recognized that he held his family's destiny in his hands, and that he had a choice. But neither option seemed acceptable. His choice was between a lifetime of shame, and on the other hand the collapse of his family, his tradition, and the generations of investment that had been made in building his family's dynasty. He could bring the entire structure crumbling down, at the risk of his own life. Or he could live the rest of his life in a secret, cancerous, world of shame.

It was time for him to make his decision. It was a decision that was first postponed in the expectation of a successful defense by Luke Powers; and then excused in the hope that evidence would come to light and the conviction overturned. He convinced himself that such a false conviction could not endure; he justified it by reassuring himself that he really was doing the right thing, and that if Luke was still in prison after a year, he would make his move at that time, never really expecting that day to arrive. But it had.

Jiwun replaced the lid of the whiskey bottle, and picked up his mother's photo, sitting by his bed. He held it, gazing into her eyes, wishing that all the hurt could be erased; wishing that she had never married his father; wishing that he had never been born to such a family. But knowing that he was.

CHAPTER TWENTY-TWO

H AVE YOU BEEN seeing anyone?" Luke would never have thought
he would be able to talk to her about it, face to face. The days
following his receipt of the package, he wrestled with his response to
the knowledge. Indeed, he thought that maybe he would never find the
strength to see her again, and that had always been his plan: push her
away, as painful as it would be for both of them, in the hope that one of
them might have a real life. Or should he seize the opportunity to pick a
fight in the hope that he could drive her away from him more effectively,
tainting their history together, absolving her of guilt?

But he had changed since then. He felt it. It had been seven months
since they last saw one another. And she had returned like an unchanged
childhood home which, nonetheless, can never be seen in the same light,
because the child himself had changed. He saw the surprise on her face
on entering the visiting room. Clearly, she had not truly expected to be
permitted a visit. But Luke knew there was no longer any danger in it,
there was no longer any reason to hide from her; he was changed. This
would only make it easier for her to live her life.

Emerald was taken aback by the question. She had resolved to tell
Luke about Rick, should he agree to see her, but he had taken her by
surprise by beating her to the topic. She hesitated for a long while, and

knew that her hesitation in itself was confirmation. But she couldn't bring herself to crush Luke's spirit, whatever meager amount was left of it, with the final blow. He had to know, above all else, that he was loved by her. That she was incapable of not loving him. He had to know that.

"Emerald, it's okay," he nodded. "I understand. I asked you to move on. That's what I wanted."

"But Luke," she started, her throat catching. She took a moment before speaking again. "I only wanted you – it's you I love. It was only you that I needed. I didn't want it to happen like this." She hated the situation into which she had been forced. She hated the hurt she still felt at Luke's infidelity. She hated the soulless, inhuman prison, that was now her fiancé's life, and she longed to somehow break him free of it, and reclaim the life they had lost.

"Are you in love with him?"

"That's just a word – a word that can mean a thousand different things," she searched his eyes, yearning for him to recognize what she felt for him.

"Then tell me what it means to you."

"It's not a word that comes close to capturing what I feel for you, Luke – how can it? What we have can't be captured. *We* can't capture *it*; *It* has captured *us*."

"Then imagine, for a moment, that there's nothing between us – that you never met me; that there's no comparison to what we have, because it never existed." He saw the pain contorting her face, though it wasn't his intention. He looked at her reassuringly, with the slightest hint of a smile. "Just try it, Emerald. Please. And tell me, without any thought of you and me – do you love this man?"

She sighed. And took another, slow breath, and sighed again. "Yes." It tore through her heart like a knife. "Since I've been seeing him," she continued, struggling to voice the words, "I've felt... I don't know... some part of me has felt at peace again." If only she had words to express what she felt for Luke. If only she had access to true touch, to his body and hers, meeting, to express what could not be defined by words to him. But the touch she longed for was prohibited. Restricted by this building, by these guards, by courts, lawyers, twelve strangers, and by a whole country and system that would forever prevent her from it. The entire world, it seemed, was against her.

And yet, she was surprised by his reaction. She had expected him to break down. Or to witness the dying breath of hope in her husband-to-be's eyes. She had feared watching helplessly, through the glass barrier, as he doubled over in defeat. What had he left? Nothing but his orange suit and the cold numbness of the prison. He had spoken to her of the constant, biting chill in the air, that he attributed to either an attempt to minimize bacteria, or more likely, a strategy of dehumanizing the occupants. Before, she had watched the pain and agony in his eyes compound with each visit she made as the life visibly drained from his being. But this was a different man.

He sensed her hurt. He saw the awful confusion. "It's okay," he said, without any sign in his voice that he was lying.

"But Luke, how can it be okay? I wanted to be strong for you. But I've lost all hope!" the sentence found its way out through tearful gasps.

He longed to hold her. "So have I, Emerald. So have I."

She looked at him quizzically through teary eyes.

"But not without a fight," he said. "I did everything in my power to avoid this. I did whatever I could to keep my hope alive, to battle this incarceration, this separation from you, this loss of everything I had built. I was sure that I could somehow escape it. Why wouldn't I be able to? I am innocent, I know that much. Surely, then, I would make it out of this place.

"And every week, every month that I spent here, I felt myself dying a little more. The anger, the hate, the despair – it consumed me. But always, always somewhere deep down, there was hope. I could feel it. And I knew I would never give up while it didn't give up on me.

"My hope and my despair waged war on each other, and it seemed it would never end. My body, my mind, my spirit, were the victims, and they were slain without mercy while these two adversaries tore at each other on the battleground of my being. It surely would have ended only by the dissolution of the battleground; whether it was the collapse of my body, or the failure of my mind, it would have continued until then.

"Never would my hope abandon me – I knew that much. Always

it denied that my life was doomed to this cell. And it defended itself valiantly from whatever my despair could muster.

"But it was naïve. As was I. It failed to anticipate the obvious, the inevitable. It failed to recognize that the last remnant of what I called 'me', of what I knew to be my life, would be stripped from me as had everything before it.

"I discovered that you had been seeing someone."

She went to speak.

"It doesn't matter how," he held up his hand. "But it wasn't deliberate on my part. I thought it was what I wanted, though I found that to be a lie. It was the last straw, and it was a battle that my hope was destined to lose.

"I writhed in pain. I did everything I could to grasp at some shred of hope that I might reclaim my life. But it was useless. No longer could I convince myself that it was anything other than it was. There was no denying it any longer: I had lost all that I had valued. Everything that was once important to me had slipped from my grip. There was nothing left to hold onto. Nothing. What I thought was my freedom – gone. What I thought was my love – gone. All gone.

"There was nowhere left to run – no future to look to, no alternative to turn to, no hope to cling to."

They sat for a moment, looking into each other's eyes. She couldn't read his expression. His eyes no longer seemed dead, as they long had. But the excitement, the energy that she knew as Luke, also seemed absent.

"My hope was slain, and my despair overthrew me in victory. I didn't fight it. There was nothing left to fight for. I let it take me. There was no struggle: everything I thought I was and that I hoped I was, was crushed, destroyed – it all went up in a puff of smoke.

"And a strange thing happened." His eyes now left hers, as if he was searching for words.

"The pain ripped me apart. Whatever was left of me was annihilated. All that time – trying to pretend that one day I would get out of here, one day I would hold you – it all seemed so ridiculous. It was so obviously a denial of my worst fears. I saw that. And I saw that what I had held onto as my idea of freedom, was not freedom itself – but the fear of not being free. It was what had separated me from freedom. And I saw that what I had held onto in you was not the love between us, but the fear of not having you. And I saw revealed what it was to know love, without need.

"The pain became something else. Gone was my hope. And gone was my despair. And I don't know what's left in its place, but it's not empty, though maybe it would look empty if emptiness could be seen.

"All I know is that I'm no longer the person I was. That I no longer wish things were different. That I love you more than I ever knew was possible. And that you have to live your life, without waiting for me."

CHAPTER TWENTY-THREE

T HE FLIGHT TO New York was maddening. He couldn't sleep for more than a couple minutes at a time, though that was nothing new to him. For all the hundreds of miles he would be covering, Jiwun was effectively confined to one place for sixteen hours: if anyone had become suspicious over his activities, they had sixteen hours to plan for his certain arrival at JFK.

Would his father's men be waiting for him? If so, would they snatch him at the airport, with such skill that they evaded the attention of airport security? Or would they remain concealed, tailing him until a more opportune moment arose? He had hours to contemplate it, but a complete dearth of alternatives. It felt almost as if it were his final day on death row, with no option available but to walk right into the execution chamber.

His alibi, if all went according to plan, would hold for at least another twenty-four hours. Ordinarily, none of them would raise an eyebrow at a weekend trip to Macau. But his father had a nose for things that were out of place. Despite his care in maintaining the appearance of normalcy, Jiwun feared that the tyrant would sense something amiss. All it would take, then, would be two phone calls to confirm that Jiwun's story was a fake; and then a handful more to ascertain his true destination. The discovery that it was, in fact, New York, would surely be enough to spring him into the most immediate and severe action.

But what if it didn't even require his spotting a fake story? By tomorrow night, he thought, Peng's network in Macau would likely make contact with him, revealing that the son he had advised them to keep an eye out for had not once been seen. *No, I'm being paranoid. He knows Macau's safe for me. He won't be checking in that much.*

But the room — God, he's gonna notice the room. . .

Though how could he, Jiwun answered himself, when every detail had been attended to? Not one paper clip left out of place. The only way he would notice would be if he were so obsessive that he actually drooled over the evidence every day, noticing its partial absence today. But that was ridiculous: it had been over two years since that night; Luke Powers had been serving his sentence for more than a year, and would be indefinitely; his empire had been partitioned and subsumed; and his engagement to Emerald Steel had reportedly fallen through months ago. Wong Peng couldn't still be so engrossed in his own victory over Luke, his obsession with his own genius deception, that he reveled in reviewing the photographs and planning, in all their gruesome detail, day after day. *It wouldn't surprise me, that sick bastard. . .*

Cameras! But were there cameras in that seedy cavern of a room? Did he monitor every entry and exit? Or was he so certain of its secrecy that he thought it unnecessary?

Stop thinking about it, stop thinking about it! There's nothing you can do about that now. Besides, he's gone for the night — he won't be back till the afternoon. Just wait. Just save your energy for New York. Sleep, dammit, sleep.

He stared out the window, way down at the ocean below, into the deep blue of the Pacific. It drew him deeper and deeper into its vastness, and staring into the endless waters, sleep overtook him.

THE CUSTOMS OFFICER, he thought as he handed over his passport after retrieving his suitcase, was his last bastion of safety. Once he walked down the hallway and turned that corner, there was no more protection. He was out in the open. An easy target until he could secure police protection.

He bit his lip, knowing, from the evidence he had seen, that his hope for police protection was a misguided one. *What if the lawyer's even in on it? What if she hands me right over to one of his hitmen?*

It was the chance he had to take. There was no mention of her in the documents. He had researched her earlier cases. Rachel Wallace was his best bet. If she were in on it, then the whole world might as well be in on it. And then where was he? What, indeed, would he be fighting for? It wouldn't be a world worth living in, he thought to himself.

The officer took his customs form, handed back his passport, and gestured for him to move on. He walked past the baggage transfer station, and to the end of the hallway. Then he turned the corner, and into the crowd of relatives and drivers that awaited. Men in suits — men in suits everywhere.

Which of them worked for his father?

Which of them set up Luke Powers?

Which of them choked his mother to death?

"I NEED TO see her right away," he urged. "Believe me, she'll understand."

"I will bring it to her attention that you're in the waiting room when she is finished with her client, Mr. Jiwun."

He considered removing a sealed envelope from his tightly-gripped backpack and telling her to deliver it to Rachel Wallace immediately. But even if Wallace wasn't in on it, could the receptionist be? She had asked for his surname, but he had refused, willing to reveal information only to Wallace, privately. What about the other lawyers? Surely, they had someone in the firm they could rely on.

Jiwun sat, nervously awaiting his presumed savior.

Will she actually be able to do anything? Will they even be able to protect me? Or is Robertson gonna get me either way, even if my dad doesn't?

Robertson... The name sent shivers down his spine. Who was he? From what he had seen, he was untouchable, an agent of this 'Society', with the power to erase lives. But who would Robertson kill first — Jiwun, or his father? Jiwun could glean from his father's treasures only enough about the Society to be petrified of it. But maybe his father should be even more scared after compiling his own file, through his own people, on the job; on the grand scheme; on the magnificence of it all. But, then, would such an organization risk confirming its existence by eliminating one who had conspicuously spoken of them? *No — maybe they wouldn't. . . their best play is to stop it before it happens.*

He held the bag close. Waiting. Waiting. Eyes darting between the front door, the receptionist, and the hallway leading to her office, he assumed. Each coming and going rattled him, his hands beginning to shake as he imagined his impending death.

"Mr. Jiwun."

He looked to the desk.

"Ms. Wallace will be right out. But she will not be meeting with you privately until she knows why you're here."

He sighed, and nodded.

She appeared with all the understated self-assurance of one who had won her own place in the world. She was definitely the woman whom he had seen in photos during his research. This was her.

He withdrew a sealed envelope from his bag and handed it to her, without a word.

Wallace flipped it twice, examining its outer appearance, feeling inside for any irregularities in the package from the well-dressed, exhausted-looking teenager. She opened it and, without any visible reaction, examined the contents; a single sheet of paper, and a photograph. Jiwun, his heart racing, noticed the receptionist's curiosity.

"You can come with me," Wallace said, turning on the spot and walking back to where she came. She nodded to the receptionist.

Jiwun followed her.

They entered her office, closing the door behind them.

At first, she just stared at him.

"Who are you?" she demanded.

"Is this room safe — I mean," he paced, "is it absolutely private? Can anyone hear us?"

"No. It's safe."

"But could it be bugged? Can you be absolutely sure that it's not bugged?"

She opened a drawer and withdrew a handheld device. She began to move around the office slowly, waving the device. It took several minutes, Jiwun's gaze moving nervously between the door and Wallace.

"I can be now," she eventually said, placing the device back into her drawer.

"I'll tell you who I am once you can guarantee that I'll be safe."

"Jiwun — is it?" He nodded. "You have to understand — I've had my suspicions about the Powers case from the start. Something in it doesn't add up, and believe me, I've pursued *every* possible lead to find an answer. I believe Mr. Powers was set up. I don't know how you got your hands on a photo from the crime scene, but if I've ever seen a cursed case, it's this one. It's going to take much more than an accusation and a photo to have this case re-opened."

He had left Hong Kong with three large envelopes in his backpack, never leaving his sight. Two he had dispatched en route to the legal firm. He withdrew the remaining one, solidly packed with documents and photographs. He placed it on the desk.

Rachel gasped. "You cannot be serious," she said, the eagerness in her eyes spoiling her controlled composure.

"Evidence is making its way to media outlets as we speak," he said plainly. "I don't know if that's a good thing or a bad thing, but I had to hedge my bets as best I could. If you're who I hope you are, you had better think fast: within an hour, the people who put Luke Powers behind bars are going to be hell-bent on finding me."

CHAPTER TWENTY-FOUR

L UKE WANTED TO pour out his gratitude. He was overflowing with it. He was overwhelmed by it. Alone, silent in his cell, he basked in the humbling gift that life had presented him.

The phone call had been brief, and it was well that it was: he was lost for words. He could only listen to Rachel's voice. 'The District Attorney has said he won't be taking a position in the appeal. We're speaking with the Governor's office now — he's considering a pardon, which could be quicker,' her voice trembling as she shared the news. 'I'll be there soon. I wanted you to hear it from me — we'll get you out as soon as we can. It's just a matter of time now — you're going to be free.'

A month had passed since new evidence came to light. The initial euphoria with which Rachel Wallace had first greeted it quickly faded as it became clear that the evidence that Wong Peng's son had managed to secure amounted to less than undeniable proof of Peng's guilt.

As all were preparing for a re-opening of the case, and a second long, drawn-out hearing, they were surprised by the sudden involvement of the Chinese legal authorities. What they uncovered in their swoop on Peng's premises was ample to ensure his imprisonment for the remainder of his life, the image burnt into most news-watchers' minds being that of the cremation chamber. Concealed within the network of tunnels and rooms, it appeared to have been utilized by Peng to dispose of the bodies of those who had outlived their usefulness in his pursuit of pleasure.

Privately, Wallace questioned the story that had been presented to the people, primarily because of Peng's apparent awareness that the swoop was imminent. He had been prepared for it, having fled into hiding, the authorities supposedly unable to track him. Was the sudden revelation of Peng's guilt the Society's way of keeping the story out of the courts and the public eye? To kill him would have only added to the intrigue; it now seemed that Peng would take the fall personally, keep his life, and ensure that the Society's part remained undetected. The details were still shrouded in mystery, and Wallace wondered if any of it would ever be clear. Even the speed with which the Governor's office was willing to discuss the possibility of a pardon aroused her suspicions. But it wasn't a perspective she had yet been willing to share with Luke. He was being released. That was all that mattered, and it was what he deserved.

Luke recalled again Rachel's last words, 'You're going to be free.'

It had been all over the news for weeks, and whatever the latest development was, Luke thought, he was sure it would be blaring over the common room's TV set at that very moment. The details, he did not yet know, and he was glad for it; he was having enough trouble comprehending the immensity of what would be returned to him: his freedom.

Freedom, he whispered. But it wasn't the freedom that abided. It was a freedom that could be snatched from him at any moment. It was the freedom to move within the limits of the everyday world; it was necessarily a freedom with restrictions. And it was fickle.

He would enjoy it. He would cherish it. For as long as it was his, he would be thankful for it. And he would remember, he promised himself, that it was not guaranteed; that it could be rescinded as quickly as it was given.

'Free,' she had said. But free to do what? Free to walk in his city once again? Yes. Free to lay eyes and hands on one he loved? Yes. But still, he persisted in his reflection, it was a conditional freedom. He hadn't always been as free in his life to walk his city, to enjoy the simple things, as he would have liked; nor would he be free to walk his city anymore if he were ever to suffer a similar fate to Hughie. And he knew all too well the precarious nature of loved ones: they could vanish in an instant.

But free to love? Free to be Luke? Yes, he would have these. But he already did. They had never abandoned him.

And still, the unexpected gift of life opening to him once again, the potential of the days that still remained before him, brought him to tears of joy. He would embrace every moment, knowing that it could be his last; he would revel in his newfound freedom, knowing that it wasn't this world of possibilities that allowed him to be free, though enjoying it all the same.

What a gift, he remarked. *To release life, only to find it waiting for me.*

What now? he questioned. So unexpected was it, that he had no idea what he would now choose to make of this new life. Would he reclaim Powers Media? His rightful place in industry? He didn't know. It felt so remote.

Emerald. The name itself, whenever he now heard its music in his mind, filled him with an unbearable euphoria. *I can touch her again. . .*

It was almost too much to fathom.

Yes, he thought. *If I could have but one taste of anything in this world again — if my freedom lasts for only a day — I would spend every second of it with her.*

He pondered it for a long while, using the last of his solitude, the last minutes and hours of it, to prepare for the shock of his return to the world.

Can she forgive me? Can she forgive me now — now that I'm no longer a victim? Now that I'm released, with no common enemy to fight, will she forgive me?

She stood by me all this time. She endured the humiliation, the pain. All that mattered was the love between us.

But things have changed.

I've changed.

I'm not the person I was.

Is she?

He stared into space for a moment.

No. No, she's not. It changed her.

Was this what he wanted? Did he want to return to the world of choices, of preferences, and decisions, and consequences?

To re-enter that world was to risk pain. To seek happiness was to risk the bitter disappointment of not finding it. And to seek a reuniting of his love with Emerald's was to risk the heartache of it being denied.

It didn't scare him. If this was the world that was once again opening to him, then he was ready to open to it.

"Inmate Powers," the guard's familiar voice pulled Luke out of his contemplation. He looked to him, still unable, or unwilling, to break the surreal space he had entered with words. He wanted to savor the day's magic for as long as it was prepared to remain.

"You're being allowed to take an unscheduled call. Come with me."

The guard escorted Luke to the phone bank. It would be his last such phone call.

"Hello," he said, hoping the other voice would be the one he wanted to hear most.

"Luke... Luke..." She couldn't say anymore, between the sobs of joy.

"I know," he smiled, "I know. Rachel's coming now."

He only heard her crying, her breathing.

"I'm coming as soon as I can, Luke – the next flight is this afternoon. I'm already booked."

"From Sydney?"

"Yes. I'll be there late tomorrow night."

He nodded, his throat tightening too much to speak. "Thank you."

❦

CHAPTER TWENTY-FIVE

T HE TOP DECK of the ferry offered a perspective on the city that was only available when one stepped outside of it. All morning, she had strolled through the neighborhood where Luke and she had planned to begin their life together, on the edge of Central Park. Then through the park, and down, past the offices of Powers Media, and toward the areas she had frequented when she first arrived in the city.

It was a long walk to Battery Park, but she had the time. She needed the time.

The Staten Island-bound ferry pulled out from the dock, and she felt the late-spring breeze against her face. It had been over two years, she thought to herself, since the feeling of the New York air, and the presence of her own city, had last evoked a sense of home, rather than acting as a trigger for her lurking grief. She breathed in deeply.

As the ferry moved farther from the city, the Financial District and Downtown condensed into a manageable frame. Emerald recalled her first years in the city, how the Twin Towers rose high above their sur-roundings, and how a twist of fate could change the course of the world. A single day was all it took.

A single night was all it took for her. *There are some things that are out of our control,* she thought. *Many things. Life is capricious. Or perhaps just mysterious.*

How did my life come to this?

How did I end up in love with two men?

For all their sakes, it couldn't continue any longer.

But how could love be weighed, and then chosen between? Indeed, what was it that she felt for each of these men? Each of them, she had known only briefly, on the scale of one's life. Though, they had both drawn her in; there was a closeness that existed with each man that had nothing to do with the length of time they had known each other.

She looked to the empty ring finger on her left hand, and then she reached into her pocket and took out the diamond engagement ring that she had retrieved from the bottom drawer that morning. It stared back at her, reminding her of the moment she received it, at the time not for a second doubting that the giver would be her husband.

And the simplicity of the emerald ring on her right hand, crafted with love, struck her with the memory of the second time it was handed to her, by Rick.

But even more potent than that, was the memory of Jimmy, the first man who presented her with the ring; who still held a place in her heart; who still held sway over it. Why?

Surely, it was their agonizing separation, she answered herself. She recalled the last times that they had made love, nearing Jimmy's death. It had become a rarity at that stage: the cancer ravaged his body, and the drugs consumed his mind and energy. It all came back to her: the constant crying; the tears that flowed and then hid under a brave face whenever she entered the bedroom; the inadequacy of bringing herself to orgasm in the bath, yearning for her beloved's touch.

On those rare occasions when he found himself with more than minimal energy, they would make love, candles and incense adorning the room, Emerald doing all the work as Jimmy lay there, gazing longingly into her eyes. The guilt she felt at depleting his energy contended with the anxiety of knowing that one of the episodes would become their last. The more she felt him slipping away, the more she wanted him. The more she saw the wonder of his being dimming – his imagination, his joy, his strength — the more she cherished that which had always warmed her heart.

His death, soon after her eighteenth birthday, marked the solidification of a personality that had been developing since her earliest years. She recalled her oldest memories: her mother, sobbing, apologizing with all the shame she could muster, while her drunk father punished her. 'Sorry for what?' she would ask herself. 'What did she do?' she would inquire, until she understood that such a question would be met with the same punishment. She loved her mother, but what began as pity grew into anger as she witnessed, again and again, her unwillingness to stand up to abuse, and her attempts to become a better wife for one who was never satisfied, and often drunk.

On one hand, she had understood her mother's predicament, and her responsibility to Emerald's four older brothers and her. The more it was hammered into the woman, the more she no doubt believed it: the worthlessness; the threat of being alone should she ever leave; the terror of her husband's fury.

But it was also something for which she could never forgive her mother. The first glimpse of an opportunity she encountered to escape her miserable home, she seized. And then she was alone, but no longer captive.

It was Jimmy's passion that initially attracted her to him. His dreams of architecture, of creating living works of art that enhanced lives, soon came to include the dream of building a home in which the two would share their love.

Her life had been marked by hurt, but in Jimmy she had chosen differently. She had begun to forge her own life; her own dream. He was the antithesis of everything she had known in her father.

Yet time betrayed her; she was robbed of him.

He had likened her eyes to emeralds, and she adopted it as her name.

Her heart, broken as it was, was now hers and hers alone, and she determined to never allow it to break as such again. It would be as hard as steel, and perhaps as cold. Emerald Steel was born.

FROM THAT POINT on, the ring never left her finger, a reminder of the life she had chosen, a testament to the birth of Emerald Steel. With her new identity came an invigorated drive for success, one that was realized and reveled in.

The ferry slowed as it approached Staten Island, some of the passengers making their way to the lower deck. Emerald's gaze remained fixed on her home island of Manhattan across the water, the culmination of her ambitions. And yet, had it delivered on its promises?

She had seen it all, and tasted it all. Every thrill she fancied was available. Hurt became a thing of the past. She was in control of her own life. But her search was never-ending, fulfillment always lurking just around the corner, and pain never far behind, it seemed. It had become a hollow life, and one from which she was still recovering when she found Luke.

Her eyes moistened as she recalled the day she was struck, taken completely by surprise, by the realization that she had started to return home to her heart in Luke's presence. Something had begun to open, a vulnerability that had been lost, though she couldn't say why. She felt within herself a subtle transformation, and a deep desire to continue it with this man. It was a flowering that didn't cease as time drew on, but only became more pronounced.

But he had betrayed her. Once again, her trust in love had been rewarded with pain. Was it worth it? Did she want to continue to trust; to continue to expose herself to such pain?

Fate intervened. With Rick's appearance, she found herself confounded by the continuance of her heart's opening. It was not dependent on Luke. Was it even dependent on anyone other than herself? She couldn't say.

'Go to New York,' Rick had said, more as a command than a request. 'Be with Luke. Be true to your heart. Whatever comes of this, I will understand.'

How can I weigh love against love? She asked herself again the impossible question that had been wearing her down, ever since she fell once again into Luke's embrace on his release from prison.

She could not answer, and thought perhaps that she never would. There was no answer. No answer other than what she felt in her heart.

It spoke to her, and it scared her. She wanted to ignore it, for if heeding its call had already led her to betrayal twice, would it not do so again? There was nothing safe about hearing its voice; no guarantees; no control. The less she resisted, the clearer its sound, and the greater her vulnerability.

It's time.

Time to move forward.

Time to let go of what I'm holding onto.

Downtown came closer into view, the distant perspective of Manhattan dispersing into the myriad windows, rooms and lives that were revealed as the ferry drew near. She gazed down into the Hudson River, the water forever moving, never stationery as it lapped against the hull, and she removed Jimmy's ring from her finger.

She cradled it in her hands, taking one last look, saying goodbye to all that had defined Emerald Steel. Saying goodbye to all that no longer served her. She drew her arm back above her shoulder and looked deep into the water below.

Emerald launched the ring over the side of the ferry with all the force of her joy and pain of the past. Propelled by the weight of her childhood hurt; of her love and her heartache for Jimmy; of her reaction to it and her denial of love; the two emeralds, spiraling through the air, fell to the Hudson River below and disappeared from sight. She squeezed the diamond ring tight in her left hand.

The ferry pulled into the dock. Emerald was home. She knew what she had to do.

END OF PART THREE

EPILOGUE

F IVE MONTHS OF single-minded focus. Of the pursuit of a phantom. Of patience; perseverance; orchestration. And he had succeeded. The headline was the final confirmation:

'*Wong Peng dead. Body recovered from hideaway. Murder suspected.*'

The U.S.'s outrage at the Chinese government's reluctance to enforce Peng's extradition did little to change the situation. Without opposition, it seemed, he had slipped away into hiding and was rumored to relocate with regularity. Those few with awareness of Peng's ties to the Society knew only too well what he was up against: the excessive measures and reported paranoia to which he had resorted were understandable.

Yet it would not be the Society that would end his life. Indeed, their strength, as always, was in the belief that they did not exist. Precious few details of their involvement, all too vague to present a threat to their stealth, had come to light during the re-opening of the case. It remained that way, with the only surviving evidence of their involvement being the Jiwun Peng files, which were damning in their details of Wong Peng, but scant on those of the perpetrators' identities. Little could be concluded regarding the identities of those involved, other than Peng.

The assassin sipped his tea. He was satisfied with his work; his final job for one whom he had served with all his heart, though it was a satisfaction colored with deep sadness.

His eyes moved down the newspaper, settling on the phrases that caught his attention.

'... *victim of poisoning... police report that assistance from within Peng's own ranks is suspected... The man responsible for the deaths of Jade Peng and Anna Chen meets his own demise.*'

"Anna," he said under his breath. "What we could have had together. What a waste. If only..."

Thomas Ho cut himself short. There was nothing to be gained by dreaming now. What was done, was done. The tragedy of Anna's and Jade's deaths and, Thomas reflected, their lives, should not be allowed to mar the beauty of them. It all came back to him – the first time he cradled newborn Jade in his arms; the delightful surprise of his and Anna's first kiss; watching Jade's eyes light up when Luke walked into the room; the secretive touches and glances that Anna would make, and the discipline he would exercise to suppress his smiles in the company of others. It floated in his consciousness, he himself floating in a dreamlike state.

He folded the newspaper and placed it on the table, taking his final sip of tea.

"Such beauty," he whispered. "What a gift to have loved you both."

"Luke, you stay here, I'll go and you can come tomorrow – you can't leave on such short notice," Emerald pointed out.

"I know, I know," he smiled. "I just don't like letting you out of my sight anymore," he said with a laugh. "I've been spoilt – I'm too used to having you near to me."

"I'm always near," she placed her hand on his chest, "no matter where in the world I may be." She accepted the last-minute trip to Paris knowing that Luke would be able to join her the following day. "And," she said, taking his hand in hers, "I have news."

"News? Hmmm... I feel like I've had enough news to last me the rest of my life, and beyond..."

"Well, I hope you have room for this headline, because you're going to want to hear it. You, my love, are going to be a father."